THE QUANTUM COMMUTE

B.G. MARQUES

First Edition for London commuters 2018

Cover art by Dylan Dixon-Phillip.

Photography by Ricardo Alevizos (edited).

Model: Tiago Grade [Rizumik].

DEDICATION

Terrestrial

A special thanks to my beautiful wife
for her support,
and my children for the joy they take
in the little things.

I raise my glass to everyone that's helped me along the way,
especially h., Matt, Bernard, Muckle, Guy, Myles, Dylan, Tiago,
Ricardo, Dave, Prasad, Donkey and Ian.

Finally, a note of thanks to all who make commuting happen,
in London and elsewhere in the galaxy.
A particular mention to the 486, 422, Jubilee, Thames Clipper,
GWR, Eurostar and Qit teams,
and to all Commutators.

Celestial

To the universes and all existence,
with thanks for existing.

Dec 18

Dear Paul

biomed-aerospace

YOUR COMMUTE BEGINS...

Enjoy!

Thanks for your hospitality

and whisky-fuelled philosophising!

Best wishes

BG Meyer

A WARM WELCOME

HELP US, PLEASE, MY FELLOW COMMUTERS. WE'RE ALL IN THIS TOGETHER!

COULD YOU MOVE DOWN A LITTLE INSIDE PLEASE? YES YOU, PLEASE. COME ON, I CAN SEE THERE'S SPACE IN THE MIDDLE. No! Not you lot here, I know you're packed in like sardines by the doors, but in the middle they've got enough room to swing a cat.

THANK YOU!

Sorry, excuse me. Sorry. Thanks.

...

Yes, sorry, I am trying to get my bag on the floor but... ah, there we go.

...

Tight, isn't it? Goodness, I mean take a look around. Bloody packed, isn't it? Well, at least for my tastes, I prefer things a little more... exclusive, don't you know? Yes... quite!

...

In fact, sorry. Excuse me, sorry to bother you.

I wonder if you can help me: Can I change at Canary Wharf for the DLR? Oh ok, thanks, and... I see. So, I have to tap out and then back in. Ok, thank you...

...

And… if you don't mind my asking… how do you find this all? I mean, look around, my friend! Strangers and transport, transport and strangers. You and I are strangers now, but we'll be friends soon enough, you'll see. Now look about at the rest of them.

Commuting to work. Commuting home. Commuting in. Commuting out. The lungs of this industrious city breathe and sigh the oxygen of this place – you all.

No, please don't put your headphones in like everyone else, hear me out, please. Answer me this: Do you enjoy it – the commute? Or do you find things a tad…

Let me put it this way. Congestion, pollution, waiting, going, waiting some more for the dubious privilege of an early morning super-crush, unexpected delays and mass jostling, elbows akimbo. Perhaps even a mouth-breather stood right next to you, open gob wafting fumes over you as their body struggles to metabolise last night's liquor-fuelled sleep. Oh! Potent enough to positively wilt steel. Or a fellow tube-goer whose armpit reek you can taste in the back of your mouth.

Ugh!

And all before you've arrived at your day's destination. It's no small wonder we're hardly on our best form when we finally do arrive. We've had the lustrous sheen of our true selves, our inner potential, unceremoniously scrubbed off by horrors of our daily commute. And what's left?

Indignation.

Frustration.

Well… at last I'm here! Let me pull you out of this drudgery!

Oh hold on, doors opening. Anyone on? Anyone off? No? I love the silver bullet – finest line on the London Underground – but I do wonder at the point of it stopping at Southwark. Oh well. Oop! Doors closing, mind your head.

…

Look, I'm a little different from the norm, a touch odd I must confess. You see, I actually love this commute! Couldn't resist helping myself to a little polite argy-bargy getting on back there, haha. Wonderful British sport don't you think? The self-contradictory mix of guarded grumpiness towards all people mixed, as though by a master blender, with world-famous politeness and reservation.

Yes, I simply love commuting. Well, not commuting itself, so much, more commut*ers*. Ok yes, fair enough that does sound a little creepy but look...Commuting is amazing. I'm serious! Listen, we all complain about it, but it's the one act that unites us all – all kinds of people across all cultures, all times, all geographies. It unites us and shapes us.

The way we get from where we sleep to where we do what we do with our lives, it plays a natural role in defining us. The way the Maasai walk out for a hunt is part of who they are, for those partaking in a Mumbai super-crush it's part of the hustle and bustle of their lives. Likewise, for those such as the residents of Svalbard who wade daily through the snow to school and work. Even animals in the jungle are creatures of habit, commuting in their own way from makeshift abode to where they can hunt or gather food. Birds do it, bees do it – yes even educated fleas commute.

Londoners are no different. Dirty, noisy, smelly... perhaps – er, I mean the commute of course, not present company! But it's the history of the matter. The way Londoners get about below the ground as well as above has set a global precedent for other cites to follow. Rather old and tired infrastructure, perhaps, yet it continues to deliver us to the daily destination of our lives.

We are intrinsically linked to our commute, all of us, whether native to The Big Smoke or otherwise.

Accents, yes, haha. You can tell from mine I am myself not a native. But come on, you don't have to work so hard at the stereotype of a grumpy London commuter. You could welcome the erstwhile visitor to your humble place of transitory abode. This really isn't all that bad, you know. Try getting around some of the places I've been to!

...

Oh, sorry, yes please do squeeze past! Yes, and again! Goodness, London Bridge is a popular one, isn't it? Ah, yes, best move into the middle. Bit more space here! In fact, would you let me squeeze past, just there into that space next to you on those weird seat-but-not-a-seat perching devices? Thank you.

There, we can speak a little more freely here.

Now, some of the places I have been to would blow your mind. I've got time to show you if you like? How many stops left to the Wharf? Not many. On the standard calculation of five minutes per two stops, a little quicker on the silver bullet… no, we've not got long. But then what I plan to show you can take us into its own time.

But where are my manners! Introductions, introductions you fool…

I humbly present myself as your translocationally versed, exoplanetarily experienced and intratemporally transient Commutator!

Er… quite. That is to say, put simply, for short, I am *your* Commutator.

Friendly, hygienic and Interstellar Commutation Board accredited, naturally. At least I was until they revoked my – er, well… A… a commutator like no other, indeed! You see I flit about all over the place, all across the galaxy. I know! Bit of a jet-setter's life, so to speak.

Put it there. Oh – Vigorous! An excellent handshake, yes. Well done you! Now, our time is short for I'm due to change at Canary Wharf for the light railway of your historic docklands. I am here to present you with quite the opportunity, my fellow journeyperson. The best opportunities in life always start with a tap on the shoulder, and you may consider your shoulder well and truly tapped.

Focus. I need your concentration. A window of opportunity is opening up in front of you. Take care in deciding whether or not you step through – once offered, such opportunities do not knock twice.

I travel the galaxy over you see, collecting stories, experiences, life force. When I bump into discerning people such as your good self, stuck in commutes like this, I offer up access to some of these lives as a means of escapism. Well, escapism, education, whatever you choose to take out of the experiences, I suppose. That's a matter for you.

Take a look around. Wouldn't you want to step away from all this visual noise clamouring for attention? Open your eyes, don't cheat by burying them in your phone. A sea of faces. Polite to avoid their eyes lest they glance at you and it looks like you've been staring. Not nice either to stare at other parts of their body. Your eyes dart up to the adverts and yet there's no place for you there. Merely a jumble of busy visuals trying to get in your mind only to burrow deeper into your wallet. Anything else? Ah yes, the tube line map – familiar, helpful, but alas unexciting. Not a bit of art to please the sense and soothe the soul.

Sound here is a barrage on the ears and a strong business case for noise cancelling headphones, but that just drives everyone further into their own little world! Conversely, on my travels I have seen silent disco commutes with everyone in the carriage tuned in to the same thing, creating a sense of community and excitement for the day ahead rather than isolation, a different carriage to suit every taste! But no, here you all opt to go it alone.

Take a deep breath in, through your nose and no cheating. Mmmmmmm, savour those aromas: I'm getting body odour, halitosis, cooking smells stuck to clothes, a solid wall of thick perfume. Oh, and of course all brought together with some *jus de Londres*, that trademark smog we love so dear. Mmm, doesn't it bring the flavours out – you can almost taste it. And of course, these...agh... bloody buffoons shoving past!

TAKE YOUR BAG OFF YOUR SHOULDER, SIR!

Commutation is the only way... oh ignore him, do, the doors will close his protests out... Commutation I say, it's the only way to travel in style and jump across the darkness between the stars and into the minds, yes the very lives of other people. There's a galactic community out there, and I want you to see some of it!

Commutation is a rare and privileged thing, my friend and fellow commuter. Look here, see? Rare few people in the galaxy

't a mark like this on their palm. You see? An inverted triangle pointing down, longer than it is wide and with all these arcs and swirls coming off of it. Looks innocent enough, I suppose like a common tattoo. I assure you though it is so, so much more than that. The trigram and its curved spikes are symbolic. In particular, the fact that it points down alludes to the fact that commutation is far more about plunging into the depths below than it is soaring through the skies above. Similar, in a sense, to tube travel. Funny that we should have met here, almost as though someone might have planned it such.

Highly secretive, commutation. Hidden even from the galactic community of which I speak, indeed especially from them. This privileged capability is bestowed by invitation only, and only upon those who have earned it through graft and possess the skill to wield it with effect.

It's the only way.

The only way to travel to the destinations waiting for you and me.

The only way to jump straight into other people's minds and lives.

The only way to slip into The In Between to span the galaxy in an instant and learn from the experiences of others.

The only way to create slippage between reference frames, stepping up and down a relativistic ladder to sample the near-past and near-future...

...Do you understand the privilege I speak of now?

Worlds open up in front of me. Stories of the people of your time, and of other times, and of more places than you could imagine all unfold before my Commutator's eyes. Some historic, others mundane, all dripping with the truth of the human condition. Yet how to choose, would you like one or many?

Choose a variety, will you? Oh, a smorgasbord if you will! Very good. I have something of a tasting menu up my sleeve and perhaps just the right combination for you, yes?

Now, I'm happy to provide these as part of my, ah, introductory service. Of course, for access to some of the more...

exclusive lives... well that comes with a supplementary charge, er, that is to say, we, I, would erm generally take a retainer to secure privileged access plus additional, er, um, fees. Oh, I am sorry, look this is all me getting ahead of myself.

Apologies, we've only just started our relationship, you and I. And the silver bullet presses us ever onwards. Let's dispense with all this commerciality for now. Shall we start with a sample? Dive right in? Smashing! Now, the procedure is almost entirely painless.

Baby steps though. First things first I need you, well, I need your consent. Yes? Good. And second, allow me if you will to place this small device around by the back of your head while I... don't worry, I'm not caressing! Fine head it is, though, very well-formed skull if I may say. Good bone structure. Look, you take it and hold it towards the base...

Oooh! Sorry, should have said: you may feel a sharp scratch. No, don't touch! Just, er, allow the subconductive fluids to permeate the brain. Apologies, probably should have forewarned but, look, please don't worry!

All will be absorbed into the bloodstream and passed naturally within 48hrs. Well, either that or massive renal failure leading to potential reabsorption and an associated significant identity dislocation... Transcorporeal Psychodislocative Disorder, also known as the quantum stare – refers to the look in the eyes of someone who lost any grasp on their sense of personal identity. An affliction far worse than it sounds with a recovery rate so rare it's almost believed apocryphal. Still, not as bad as all that. I sort of had it once, and look at me now!

Anyway, unlikely to afflict a seasoned commuter such as yourself, even if your experiences are confined to commuting in one body by physical movement alone. Er, unless you've got plenty of MSG in your body now? Doesn't seem to mix well with the neural fluids, you see... erm, look forget I said that. We'll be fine.

Please remain calm. This is all essential, you see. Your mind needs to get digitised to get transported the way we're going to travel. This isn't how people usually get around, even in the galactic community – they digitise and then spin through the quantum information teleportation web – 'Qit web' for short. But then most folk aren't travelling arm in arm with a real-life Commutator.

I tell you, we may have started this relationship as strangers, but we will depart as friends. I assure you of that! Quite the bonding experience going with someone into and through The In Between.

No don't worry. Truly, I promise you it really isn't anything to be worried about, not nearly as dangerous as hurtling about in some of your own modes of locomotion.

Come with me. Savour the diverse moral ambiguities that people endure. Stand with them on that fleeting precipice, that cusp where they hold onto a precious moment in their lives. Feel what they feel as they grasp at the control they have over the decision that will change everything. Empathise with their helplessness as the sands of time slip through their fingers and their power over that moment scatters. Take pity, for the consequences can own them for a lifetime.

No please don't back down now. I assure you: the risks are minimal, the opportunity of reward great. I'll dial down the initial dosage, start off easy, nearby. Let's learn the craft here on Earth before we travel farther afield to explore the quantum information web. Decisions decisions. You're on a cusp yourself and, time is—

Argh! Canada Water!

Our time is running out. Come with me into The In Between and we can discuss further there. *Vamos.* Hold my hand, hold tight – here we go!

THE LAWFUL COMMUTE

IN.

Absence. In Between.

…

Odd. Isn't it?

…

The gap. The space of nothingness we have infiltrated here in The In Between.

Not even a hollow echo to our thoughts in this non-place, not even a 'here' to be, or not be. Now. Don't be too concerned about the disembodied aspect, we can still communicate, conceptually speaking that is. A little strange In Between I grant you, not a sound to be heard, a smell to be sniffed nor a body to feel with.

And yet we have quite the journey to embark on, you and I. So many lives, so many stories to explore, and gosh – the modes of transportation we will encounter! Now, don't have me pegged as a trainspotter before we've started, for there is so much more to it than that. We'll span the stars together, you and I. Just wait!

But before we embark it is critical that we begin precisely where we begin, somewhere close to home and to your geotemporal context. For now it's essential that we baseline, that we ascertain your approach to certain matters of importance. Namely the flexibility of your… morality, of your soul.

Where better to start than with the story of Detective Bilatti?

Now, this is a privileged form of commute that I do have something of a soft spot for, as I'm sure you'll discover in due course. I must confess a real fondness for all forms of official law enforcement vehicles. The encapsulation of a commute, a profession, a sense of urgency and a burning purpose to right the wrongs of human suffering. And all wrapped neatly in one mode of translocation bringing bags of noise and bright flashing lights!

Follow me, dear journeyer! Don't worry I'll keep you on the straight and narrow… Ok, here we go.

Smells of a chicken kebab stuffed with haste in the glovebox seep through, the feel of the worn plastic steering wheel slips through your hands on a turn, the radio blares out half-intelligible instructions. Uniform will attend first, but you'll arrive just after to take control.

Remember, when a cusp arrives and you stand on the precipice… you own your decision for but a moment. Its consequences claim you forever.

WELL, YOUR HONOUR

"Well, Your Honour... I was on duty in the borough CID shift and was directed on the radio to attend an allegation of a domestic rape, husband and wife. I then became the OIC." DC Bilatti scratched his wrist under his cheap single-cuff shirt. He glanced at the jury and saw the blank expression on their faces.

"That is, Officer-in-Case," he smiled. One or two gave a faint smile and polite nod in response. "My role is to conduct a thorough investigation in accordance with the Police and Criminal Evidence Act, or PACE. Uniformed police officers answer 999 calls, ensure people are safe, and conduct an initial investigation. Basically, this is just enough to classify the crime and triage it."

DC Bilatti paused to allow a hint of his professional pride to seep through, especially given his recent sign-off as a fully fledged Detective Constable without the 'Training' wheels applied as a prefix to his rank. Departmental arrogance of CID over uniform was now his earned right and privilege.

"If it's a serious matter, CID attend to ensure a thorough and professional investigation. We take the case on ourselves where the classification falls within our remit. In this instance the victim was safe, the suspect arrested. My next priority was to ensure the preservation of evidence at the crime scene."

Heavy rain slanted under the eaves onto the unadorned concrete walkways of Pellett House. The block itself contained about 50 flats, split across three floors, and was one of many in the housing trust estate. Begonia Estate was one of the largest in the borough, and the most tired. Some of the houses in other blocks were getting boarded up as tenants left or died, ready for that building to be formally condemned and knocked down. Others were due to stay in place for some time. Pellet House was in a reasonable state of repair compared to the others. Not that there was anyone around to share T/DC Bilatti's opinion on that, the awful weather having driven everyone indoors. Ordinarily that meant a quiet morning for uniform, but a gangland stabbing on the other side of their grounds had tied up most of the shift's resources, including CID.

So here he was, a Training Detective Constable, walking the top floor of a council estate block alone, on his way to investigate something as serious as a potential rape. He knew he had the experience for it. Still, a little top-cover from a more qualified colleague wouldn't go amiss. Or an umbrella, he noted, grimacing up and out to the heavy skies.

The relentless rain slipping in past the roof had created a strip of dark wet concrete along the walkway hugging the balcony's edge. This left a dry strip on the left half of the walkway, just wide enough to accommodate the parade of worn out doormats.

Gary Bilatti approached his severe duty in a reflective mood, glancing down at the half wet floor. One foot strode along the light, dry side while the other was confined to the damp and dark. A half smile started to form as he noted he was perfectly split along that sharp divide.

Nearing Flat 37, he looked up to see a young probationer standing guard. The young'un still hadn't quite got the happy knack of wearing his tall patrol helmet with natural grace. His high-vis yellow police jacket was stretched tight over the bulky waterproof patrol jacket underneath, leaving it bulging at the seams. Overall, it gave the probationer a lumpy, awkward look. Holding the crime scene log in his left arm, the arm that was very much in the rain, he smiled in blissful ignorance to the fact that the paper log was soaking wet. DC Bilatti sighed.

"Hi, I'm Gary," he said, still shielding his detective's notebook from the incoming rain in his quilted, slightly damp gilet.

"Oh, are you Delta X-Ray Five?" asked the bright-eyed officer.

"Yeah," said Gary, confirming he was the on-call CID, or what remained of it. Gary always preferred first names, even with most senior officers, but uniform seemed to like the formality of these artificial barriers.

"Oh, good. I'm Seven Six Five Delta X-Ray," responded the officer with a smile.

"Right."

Gary looked at 765DX. 765DX looked at Gary.

"That the crime scene log?" Gary nodded at it.

"Yes, that's right," beamed the officer. "I've already logged myself in. And in, then out again, but still in, of course." 765DX smiled at this particular accomplishment. Gary smiled, then frowned, then paused.

"Hold on, come again?"

"Oh, I'm sorry, but I had to. So I thought I'd better sign myself into the crime scene. You know, properly into it, rather than just inside the cordon but not inside the flat."

"Inside the flat. You what?" Gary's frown deepened. The furrows above the brushes of his sandy eyebrows gathered in folds. He was older than the average DC, training or otherwise, but his previous careers more than made up for it.

"I'm sorry, but I had to," the officer defended. The downpour abated a moment, allowing a brief pause in the drumbeat of rain on roof. "I was desperate."

Untrained eyes would not have seen how he did it. And yet, Gary increased the intensity of his stare on his junior colleague, working up to a silent barrage of cold fury.

"For a poo," 765DX bleated. He shuffled his feet, braced his shoulders. "Well. I was desperate. What was I supposed to do?"

Gary paused, taking time to deliver each word with careful, manicured hatred. "You… fucking… what?"

"One of the most important aspects in, er, gathering evidence, it is also, ah… my duty is to ensure the continuity of evidence remains cl—"

DC Bilatti cleared his throat, looked down at his wrists and tried to sneak a look at his well-worn G-Shock watch. "That is, the continuity of the evidence is paramount." He wasn't quite able to see the time before having to look back up.

"The evidence here in, er, this courtroom has an unbroken chain of continuity, of being un… ah, untampered back to when it was in the lab, and previous to that the Scenes of Crime Officer's van, right back… ahem…" he looked back to the jurors, "to the crime scene."

Gary stared at the door of Flat 37, rain soaking the backs of his calves. He stared, and pondered, rubbing his left thumbnail with the pad of his right thumb.

Notorious. Infamous, even, how difficult domestic allegations of abuse were to investigate and prosecute. Especially sexual offences. Gary remembered the ruthless DCI Barnes last week, tearing into a well-respected colleague for having spent too long on an investigation that didn't end with a tick in the right box – a suspect charged, a crime detected.

It detracted resources from crimes that had the potential to be cleared up with the resources available. Apparently.

Derek's wife, Van, was still sobbing onto the toilet cistern. If there was one thing he couldn't stand, it was the sound of crying. He smacked her hard on the right buttock, on the bruise still healing from last time. Partly to let her know he was done, partly to shut her up.

"And make sure you don't get pregnant this time, you stupid bitch. You remember how long it took to beat it out of you last time, don't you?" He zipped himself up. She had stopped crying but didn't respond. If there was one thing Derek couldn't stand, it was being ignored. He grabbed her roughly by the arm and spun her round to face him.

"Don't you?" he shouted, flecks of spit flying in her face. Vanessa dragged her eyes up to meet his for a squirming second, nodded, then looked away. Burying her eyes by looking at the floor, she sniffed through a nose full of snot. She sounded disgusting when she'd been crying.

Detective Chief Inspector Barnes turned on his warmest Glaswegian charm. "Thank you for talking to me, I appreciate I've not got the most welcoming of faces," he smiled. "I'm going to speak to one of my colleagues now, Gary. He's an outstanding detective, and he'll do right by you."

"OK," Vanessa nodded up to him. "Thanks." Sat in the back of the CID car, she wiped her nose with the last of a scrunched up tissue as DCI Barnes stepped out.

He strode towards the crime scene, ignoring the fresh spring rain landing on his already soaked Barbour jacket. When he arrived at the scene with all the gravitas his years of experience and seniority commanded, he firmly disregarded the odd-shaped bobby in uniform. Instead, he stood patiently by the training detective as he finished on the radio confirming a request for SOCO.

"Gary," he started. "I've finished talking to the victim. She's in a bad way, but she'll talk. Turns out it's not the first time it's happened. Listen, the children are with her sister for now. I'll take her to the Haven myself for the medical stuff before being she's brought back to our victim suite in the nick. Thought it would be a good opportunity for you to interview a vulnerable witness? All good experience for your portfolio to get signed off as a detective."

Gary smiled back at him, though seemed a little nervous. He kept rubbing his hands together, scratching his thumbs. Odd. DCI Barnes had thought Gary would relish the opportunity for a proper crime to investigate.

"He's a nasty fucker, you know?" DCI Barnes stated, matter-of-fact. "She didn't even call 'cos he'd raped her, it was the insults added in that pushed her over the edge, you know…" Gary didn't respond, something must be up with him. Nothing a spot of encouragement couldn't solve. "Get a good interview in for both of them, and let forensics do the rest."

Gary's radio blared from inside his gilet pocket. He pulled it out as the dispatcher confirmed SOCO en route – five minutes.

"She said she was crying her eyes out during the whole thing," DCI Barnes continued. "It's not common to find a well of tears on top of a toilet cistern, you know? He'll admit they had sex but claim it was consensual – standard fare, and hard to disprove.

"However," he held up one finger, "not that common to ball one's eyes out during consensual love-making, eh? That's bound to tip the balance in court. Just keep the continuity of the scene, direct SOCO to that toilet and get a good couple of interviews in. Then it's down to twelve people good 'n' true deciding over one word against another… and a forensic swab of tears on the toilet."

Gary nodded, smiled. "Agreed, sir. I'll sort it." DCI Barnes could have sworn Gary squared his shoulders and puffed his chest at this. Another military man. Good egg that Gary.

"Aye, and let's hope he gets a taste of his own medicine in prison, eh?" concluded DCI Barnes, with a pat on Gary's shoulder. Striding back along the walkway, he thought he had just seen the first wee sparkle in Gary's eye.

DC Gary Bilatti sidled up to PC 765DX with a "Hello mate," and a warm smile.

"You heard the DCI, sounds like this is a big job for you to work on." He looked down to the damp crime scene log tucked under the water permeable high-vis jacket. "Now that I'm officially OIC, I'd best start by reviewing the evidence so far." He held his open hand out, nodded towards the log. "May I?"

PC 765DX fished the sopping log out from under his arm and opened his mouth to utter an objection. Another look from the detective bearing down onto him prompted silence as he handed over the goods.

Gary smiled again. "Good. Now. SOCO will be here in about five. No-one goes in or out until I'm back."

"Back from—" began the officer.

Gary raised a level finger pointing at the PC's chest. "Especially not you." He then spun on his heels and marched along the walkway before the open-mouthed officer could protest.

What the fuck to do now… He pounded down the open-air corridors of the estate, brow furrowed, considering his options. "What the fuck to do now," he breathed aloud to himself. "Lunatic took a dump in there," end of corridor, down the steps. "How could anyone be so…" turned a dark corner, kept walking.

Absent minded, he rolled and unrolled the dripping crime scene log. "Just need this to not stand in the way of what's there," he looked down at it, slowed his pace. Looking around, it seemed he had arrived in a different block in the estate. Service corridor or something. Old and in a state of disrepair. A couple scurried past him clutching heavy looking shopping bags. He gave an absent smile and stood aside, noticed a door nearby that was not quite shut. It was wooden with slatted panels, painted a dark blue that the dust of the ages had made near black. A bright yellow sign with a black triangle containing a man being struck down by a zig-zag arrow indicated it probably shouldn't be left insecure.

'DANGER OF DEATH' was the other clue. Gary rolled the crime scene log up, pursed his lips and squinted – as though either act might somehow protect him – and pressed the makeshift baton against the door. Creaking it open into darkness, he lit the way with the dim torch on his smartwatch and stepped into the gloom.

No generators, errant electricity or lethal zig-zags in sight. Just a narrow corridor leading out of sight, a faint hum coming from the depths, and… privacy.

Gary perched himself on a ledge little wider than a windowsill and unrolled the offending log. His eyes skipped the procedural guidance pages and homed in on the table with rows for names, roles and times in and out. Two lines of entries stared back at him, the same name on both.

One for the crime scene being opened at Flat 37, one for the officer entering the "toilet".

What to do.

A woman had been raped, not for the first time. Intimidated, bullied, humiliated. A life she was stuck in. He imaged the life she would invariably go back to, with retaliation, if this case didn't stand up in court. Gary sucked his teeth at the thought, grimaced.

Visions of the last trial he had in Crown Court came back to haunt him. A pregnant lady had been severely beaten by her partner, demanding an abortion or he would literally *stamp that life out.* She had a miscarriage weeks later. No one denied the beating had happened, but the defence barrister had raised enough doubt about her complicity the guy was acquitted. She may have been quiet, perhaps even a little dim, but she certainly hadn't asked for the beating. A seed of doubt was all it took for an acquittal followed by their return home to an unhappy reunion.

He smacked the log with the back of his hand. Looking at the still damp entries, he imagined the questions they would raise about the PC entering the bathroom. Enough to doubt the forensics at the scene. Enough to rule them out even, leaving it to come down to a 'he said, she said' trial. With no previous cases and no evidence, and needing to get the jury 'beyond reasonable doubt'... he had never seen that end well for the victim.

Two sodden entries stared up at him in mockery.

One to open the crime scene, full of opportunity. One to shit on it.

What to do.

His breathing grew heavy.

The entries stared up at him in the cold glow of his watch light.

One stupid entry, fucking everything up, ruining this woman's one chance at freedom from the slavery of her life.

So what could he do? Lie?

Lie.

One simple lie.

Not fabricating evidence, not making stuff up. Not even hiding anything. Just allowing the evidence to speak for itself, allowing the victim to speak for herself. Gary just wanted to give her a voice.

Just one simple lie. Just one criminal offence that could lose him his career and his liberty.

Frowning hard, Gary dropped the log on the dusty concrete floor and pinched the bridge of his nose. With his other hand, he tapped off the light and groaned in the dark.

Gary plodded up to the flat holding his dry notebook and a crisp, dry crime scene log stowed under his gilet. The SOCO was already there, unpacking her kit outside the closed door of No 37.

"Hi Sally, all good?" he forced himself to ask with a cheery air.

"No so bad thanks, yourself?" she replied, voice straining as she bent over to pick up her heavy camera tripod. He ushered her inside, motioning to PC 765DX to open the door. "Bathroom's second on the right, I'll follow you in shortly."

Once she was safely inside, he held the fresh crime scene log up to the officer, giving him a level stare. "The other one was too wet to use. You'll need to repeat the entry." Gary emphasised the singular form of the word with one finger held in the air. "One for you opening the crime scene, then one for me and then one for SOCO."

PC 765DX took it, nodding hard enough for his hard hat to wobble on his head. "Okay, I'll repeat my entries and start again."

"Only one entry for you." Gary narrowed his eyes. "And you didn't enter the flat, did you?"

"No, not at all."

Gary smiled.

"Except to poo, of course," the smile returned like an unwelcome boomerang.

Gary slapped his forehead, his furrowed and now reddened brow starting to show its years. Finger and thumb pressed on his eyelids, he asked: "but that didn't happen, did it?" He removed his hand, looked up at the PC.

"Well," he shrugged his shoulders, one by one, "it did, actually."

"And I need you to pretend it didn't." His eyes didn't budge, he met the officer's eyes with no shame. "I need it to have never happened. Understand?" PC 765DX squared his shoulders, mustered up his best defiant look in response.

"My skipper always says there's no need for any funny business. If you don't get them this time, they'll come again," he beamed. "There's no need to lie." He seemed pleased, even amused at this.

"A woman was raped, and you think it's fair for that to have to happen again because you were stupid enough to take a shit on the crime scene?" There was no humour in his voice.

Leaning forward, Gary took the time to enunciate the word with deliberate care: "Lie." It issued from his mouth like a low hiss. "Lie."

PC 765DX shuffled in his mis-sized jacket. "Are you willing to go to prison for him? I'm not." Gary glared at him, but he didn't seem to notice. "Is this what you joined the job for, to make things up and lie in court?"

"This isn't about making stuff up," said Gary, almost as if to himself. "It's not about planting evidence or fabricating a case on someone I've got a vendetta against. This is about a beaten, downtrodden, raped woman who was so fed up with the slavery that her life's become and so scared of what might happen next that she finally found the courage to call the police. Us. She deserves our protection. She deserves a fair trial. She deserves the jury to focus on the evidence."

Gary stepped closer, inches from the officer's face. "And if you don't keep your lips shut, all they'll be talking about," he poked a finger hard against his stab vest. "All they will be talking about is how a probationer took a dump in the most important part of the crime scene. And that's not a fair trial." He jabbed his finger again for effect. "That's a victim of domestic violence losing any trust in the police she may have found for a fleeting moment, just long enough to actually call us for the first time in the years she's been subjected to this… that's her losing any trust she had in the police forever.

"And that's her back indoors, too afraid to call us again because of the punishment she received, punishment she will continue to receive for the rest of her life." He stood back, eyes fixed on PC 765DX. "And all because you didn't think to ask for support on the cordon so you could relieve yourself." Gary swallowed the lump in his throat. Shit, he had almost convinced himself this was the right thing to do.

DC Gary Bilatti took a brief pause from giving evidence to the jury, looked down at his hands and saw he was rubbing his thumbnail again.

"As Officer in Case, I greeted the SOCO, er, Scenes of Crime Officer, and showed her in." DC Bilatti kept looking down. He considered saying that she was the first person to enter the premises since the crime scene had been set up, but he knew it wasn't true. It was a blundering uniformed officer rushing to the loo, climbing up the walls in desperation. Time ticked on. Oh well, in for a penny, in for a pound.

"And, well, she went in first and I followed to direct her to the key aspects of the crime scene I wanted her to examine."

"DC Bilatti," asked the defence barrister, a tall, broad-shouldered white man with silver grey hair. He had the look of an ex-copper about him. "Could you explain how you ensured the continuity of the forensic evidence found by SOCO Hunter-Gibbs?"

"Ye—gh!" DC Bilatti gargled out the lump that had ambushed the inside of his throat. "Yes, I can." He responded to the barrister before turning back to his left to face halfway between judge and jury. Despite facing them, he hid from their watchful eyes, looking instead to the tips of his thumbnails. Once again they gripped each other, turning white with the pressure.

"Yes," he repeated, looking up. "It's a process all documented in her statement, whereby she used sanitised swabs to take the samples, sealed them in tamper-evident bags, then logged the serial numbers on the barcode of each exhibit. I have maintained the exhibits list and have shared the relevant details in my dual role as Disclosure Officer." DC Bilatti forced himself to part his hands and bind them to his sides. It took a concerted mental effort to leave his sweaty-palmed hands there without them scurrying for cover from the onslaught in his pockets. He pivoted to face the defence barrister for next question and gulped hard.

"And, Detective Constable Bilatti..." the barrister paused, allowing it to hang in the air like an ominous cloud promising a deluge of rain. DC Bilatti moved his hands towards each other, caught himself, and ordered them to take their place once more.

"... What about before SOCO Huntley-Cross arrived. What did you do to ensure the continuity of the evidence from the time the alleged incident took place until she arrived and you both entered? Members of the jury, I believe you all have copies of the Crime Scene Log. DC Bilatti, was this log started immediately as your procedures dictate?"

DC Bilatti tried to swallow, but the sand dune that was his tongue got stuck in the dry, cavernous desert of his mouth unable to move. Looking down to the court's copy of the Bible on the podium, he saw in the cheap plastic cup next to it a single drop of water hiding in the corner. He considered jiggling and shaking the precious drop into his mouth to quell the drought. A vision appeared in his mind – jurors raising their eyebrows, shuffling in their seats, an awkward cough echoing in the courtroom – and he thought better of it.

Pivoting his head back to face them took a subjective lifetime. Long enough for his heart rate to break above 100 bpm. Adrenaline had surged into his veins. He looked square at the jury. He looked at the Judge. He looked at the possible end of his career and many years in jail. What the fuck had he been thinking?

Chest rising and falling, he sucked in deep lungfuls of air.

Lying under oath. This was not what life was about.

He had joined to protect people, to uphold the law not break it. He had to tell the truth, come clean now, at least not perjure himself. But what about the crime scene log? Shit. Fine. It was fine. Just tell them the PC didn't put anything in, and he hadn't thought it relevant to mention earlier. Christ, how would that go down as Disclosure Officer?

Coughing. Someone coughed. DC Bilatti realised he hadn't been able to hear anything for the last… he didn't even know how long. All eyes on him. Time to make a decision. Got to say something. Anything.

Don't tombstone.

Just… speak…

Vanessa sat on the floor next to the toilet, chest heaving as she did her silent sobbing trick. Derek looked down at her in disgust.

"Clean yourself up," he said and turned to leave. "You're a disgrace," he added over his shoulder as he walked out of the bathroom. "And make sure those brats don't start crying again when they wake up."

Vanessa picked her cheap, hand-me-down mobile phone up from where he had knocked it out of her hand and dialled three digits. She'd done this many times before. What she had never done was press call.

"Hi, I'm Gary," he said, offering his open hand to shake, despite Vanessa having just blown her nose again on a soggy tissue.

"Thank you so much for helping the doctor with those samples. I appreciate it's not a pleasant process, but it really does help the investigation and, ultimately, our chances of keeping you safe." Vanessa remained sat down, curled in on herself.

"Were you well looked after?" She nodded, sniffed.

"Can I get you another box?" He pointed to the empty tissue box next to her faux leather chair. She nodded again and he stepped out of the AV recorded interview suite for a moment, returning shortly after and opening a fresh box for her. He proceeded with his usual preamble to the interview, maintaining a conversational air with the formalities. It was such a well-trodden path he allowed his mind to plan ahead for a moment until he reached the end. "So before we start talking about what happened, have you got any questions for me?"

Vanessa sniffed and nodded, taking a moment to finish wiping her nose with the bundle of freshly used tissue she had accumulated. Through the weakened expression on her puffy, tear-blotched face she looked up at Gary.

Stunned at how her blue-green eyes suddenly pierced his, he felt transfixed by a hidden strength…

"Yeah," she declared.

There was something there that… that, he couldn't quite place. "You're not going to muck this up? Are you?" It wasn't hostility. It was sheer nerve. Born of desperation, yet firm. She held his gaze with steel.

Gary gulped, opened his mouth.

"I mean it. And I'm not having a go." A subtle smile formed on her lips, but the eyes didn't change. "But I am asking. I'm not being rude, but you guys haven't got a great rep for dealing with this sort of stuff. There's real horror stories, you know? Why do you think I put up with it for so long? I was just as afraid of what you lot would do, or not do… and what I'd have to go back to…" she looked down for a beat, looked back up.

"I was desperate. That's the only reason I did it, call you lot. I was desperate."

Outside, a group of uniformed officers on a cigarette break in the station's yard outside the victim suite broke out into raucous laughter. One of the voices, one mistakable for that of a football hooligan, hollered: "Naaah, she never – oh mate, that is nasty!" More braying. Gary grimaced.

Vanessa smiled. It was a thin, mirthless smile. She finally broke eye contact, and in that instant all her visible strength evaporated, faded into memory like morning's mist. All that remained was a broken woman with barely an identity, scarcely a sense of self to call her own. Gary didn't know whether to collapse on the floor and cry for her or cross the yard into the cells and beat her husband's face until there was nothing left to beat.

Instead, he ground his teeth. This was the kind of person he had joined the police to protect. Forgetting that was easy. So many disappointments he had battled through. Disappointments in the legal system, in the courts, the police, in the hearts of people themselves and what they are willing to do to other people. Experiences that had tarnished his good will, eroded his motivation and jaded his outlook. And yet after all that, here she was. Vanessa was the reason he had joined. To protect people like her from people like *him*.

Gary opened his mouth, to speak "……

Inhale... two... three.

Exhale... two... three... four... five.

Pause...

Rotate to the left, bringing the upper body into alignment with hips, legs and feet planted to the floor.

DC Bilatti faced the Judge and Jury. He gave a thin, polite smile, filled his lungs to two-thirds capacity, and began.

"I have extensive experience of investigating allegations of domestic abuse. I'm acutely aware of how difficult it can be to distinguish between conflicting accounts when there's no objective evidence. I am also well aware of the reputable statistics showing that, on average, there are 13-17 incidents of abuse within an abusive relationship before the victim first calls police..."

DC Bilatti saw the defence brief standing up and raising a hand ready to object, as expected. Giving no time for the predictable interruption, he continued. "... and so from the outset, my chief concern was securing any potential forensic evidence." A glance out the corner of his eye indicated the barrister was back in his box.

"Furthermore, as the lead investigator I anticipated that no one was likely to deny the fact that they had sexual intercourse. They are, after all, husband and wife, and it's not the intercourse itself that is in dispute..." The barrister opened his mouth but didn't bother to get up "... hence raising higher than usual the importance of a focussed forensic examination.

"Police Constable Doolan 765DX had arrived before me and secured the scene. In police terms we say he opened the crime scene. What that means in reality is he physically locked the door, securing the only means in and out, and stood guard outside.

"I arrived, then promptly left to get a crime scene log, as unfortunately he didn't have one. I returned shortly after and the first person to enter was the Scene of Crime Officer, Sally Hunter-Gibbs. I followed her in to direct her to priority areas of the scene, namely the toilet cistern and surrounding area. I understand PC Doolan entered after the examination was complete to give the SOCO a hand with her equipment and the evidence bags."

Heart pounding. Under control. Adrenalin coursing through his veins, he took an exultant moment to savour the buzz. Smiling, he glanced back to the defence.

"No further questions, your Honour," the barrister dismissed with the back of his non-writing hand. He neither stood, nor looked up from the notes he was scrawling surrounded by piles of legal papers and voluminous texts.

"Very good." Judge Lockett stated. "Ms Priestley, I believe you have another witness, requested by your learned colleague?"

"Yes, your Honour," the prosecution replied. "PC Geoffrey Doolan. 765DX."

DC Bilatti gulped.

Following a lengthy deliberation, the jury entered the courtroom and shuffled along the two rows of seats that had become their home. The foreperson, a short lady in her fifties with shoulder-length grey hair and a soft, round face took her place by the seat closest to the judge. The others sat while she remained standing. She seemed distant from him in his lone seat in the dock, confined behind a large, single pane of shatterproof glass.

So distant from him, yet the words she was about to say could change his life forever. He was the one used to being in control. He was the one used to having power. He didn't like this one bit. If there was one thing he hated, it was not being in control.

"Your Honour," she started. His heart was pounding in his chest, threatening to burst out of his throat. "After three days of deliberation, held incommunicado, we members of the jury have reached a unanimous verdict."

Christ. He took a sharp, shallow breath, hung his head low and closed his eyes. His mouth was dry. Head spinning.

"We find the defendant guilty."

No, no, no, no, no, no, no… He rocked forward and back in his seat. Didn't know what to do. Collapse? Crumble into a pile on the floor? He was embarking on something terrifying, and he would have to be strong. He would have to be in control. Be in control or be controlled. Prison was a dead cert, and they wouldn't be kind to his sort.

The Judge's gavel banged, papers were shuffled. People resumed seats and stood up from seats. Words said, procedures followed. It all passed him by as he looked down the barrel of a new life inside. Then silence. A pause. People waiting.

Looking up, people were waiting for him to speak. Was there anything he could say to mitigate his position? To lessen the sentence? To leave it open to appeal? Anything?

He blinked at the judge.

"I say again: before we discuss the matters pertaining to your sentencing for this grave offence, do you have anything to say in mitigation?"

He looked down, saw that his hands were clasped together, his right thumb rubbing the thumbnail of his left hand. He looked up.

"Well, your Honour…"

EX.

It's that cut in your mouth you can't stop yourself from poking with your tongue. I keep going back to this one, despite the pain it causes… It comes unbidden, like I'm being haunted by the ghost of DC Bilatti's conscience. Every time I visit I ask of myself the same question, the quandary forcing itself upon me so I can't help myself but ask…

What would I have done?

Would I have done the same?

How gut-wrenching it is to put oneself through such ethical quagmires. Domestic violence is such an insidious beast, especially domestic rape – an unsung devil of the age. And yet, in all truth and with all conviction would you sacrifice the integrity you had sworn to uphold to enable a fair trial in just one case? Or would you instead sacrifice that lady's future to uphold as vague an entity as integrity? It's one or the other, my friend.

Each time I challenge myself, a real discovery does take place. But goodness I do find it such a torturous experience. Rather like eating grapefruit in the morning or taking a cold shower – bracing business! Undoubtedly we improve ourselves a little with each turn of the moral handle, yet… gosh!

And what of you, fellow traveller? What do you make of it? Which risk would you have taken? Oh, come now, if you can't see that this case boils down to two opposing risks, we have a way to go yet. Well, suspend your answer if you wish but keep the thought in mind, do. We shall have the opportunity to approach such matters from many perspectives. We will take diverse lives and use them as focussed lenses, bending the light of our wit and intellect onto a central curiosity of life.

And of course, I should have asked how you found the transport into their brain state – not feeling too dislocated? Like you're not sure where the you that is you *ends and someone else begins? Rather disorientating. You'd know it if you did. No, good. Well, we are keeping things nice and simple to start with, translocationally I mean.*

Now, we have elsewhere to be and in someone else's body. Onwards!

THE UNLAWFUL COMMUTE

IN.

Now that was a good ride, but something seems loose in one of the connectors in the back of your brain, right where it meshes into the medulla. Give me a second... One twist, a click and, yes hold on and – that's it. See? Barely noticeable, hardly feel a thing once you've done your first. Ahem. So to speak, of course.

Now we still have a way to go on our psychonautic voyage, and we have more variety in the modes of commuting to accrue. Humility will be our key into this next world.

I've brought our commute down to a simple bicycle on this quiet street in a suburb of North London. Rather a nice one too. The bike that is. You must remember that your point in time is much like any other throughout history: your technology may be new, but the recognisable traits of life remain much the same. Now, as ever, the resale market for sought-after goods and high-end modes of personal transport remains strong, even if stolen.

And what could be more humble, closer to the ground itself, to the very gutter even, than the common thief?

I've brought you here to this suburban street a touch early to drink in the environment, to feel the coolness of the air and smell the freshness of a spring bloom after the rain. Apologies for the body of the punter I've had to land you in – the only pedestrians I could find nearby for this preamble. Oh well. Never mind.

Aaahh I do love these cherry trees in blossom, dotted along the gently arcing street of Victorian houses, don't you? Little bursts of pink punctuating the gracefully ageing brickwork. So rooted in its time.

Ah! Right on cue, here's Steven. Now, let's not be judgmental here as he busies himself with the lock. Try not to think of him as a bicycle thief per se, more a… more an opportunist. And this bicycle isn't very well secured. And it is a rather nice bike, so let's not be too judgmental, eh? It's a way for Steven to get to work. Well, as close as, er, whatever it is he does comes to 'work' anyway. You see, now he has to cycle it to some friends, associates, to try and sell it. So it is a commute, from a certain point of view.

Besides, there's a real beauty to the way he manipulates the pick and the lock as one. See, didn't take him long did it? Amazing in a way, the nimble speed of such fingers when armed with a well-chosen tool and a determined mindset.

But there's more than the simple taking of a bicycle here. You need to stoop, for only by stooping low can one truly enter with humility into this world.

Imagine you're caught up at their level of life. Shed your physical body. Leave it behind with each teleportation of your bioelectronic mindstate into another life. If you can't cast aside your sense of self and proceed naked, clothed only in humility, the going will be tough. And we do have a distance to go, I assure you!

Leave it all behind and let's nip ahead now, shall we? We still have a chance to beat Steven…

THIEVING BASTARDS, MATE

"Thieving bastards, mate," Danny sulked. He rubbed his skinny fingers together, blowing on them to give them some warmth. They tapered around broad fingernails, a layer of black grime ingrained under the roughly chewed ends. He licked his fingertips generously before pulling one of Jim's rolling papers from the tattered green packet, without asking permission.

"I feel like I'm stuck in here mate," he muttered. Rich yellow nicotine marks striped his fingers from the regular position where he smoked roll-ups, fag ends and – on a good day – a nice rock of crack.

"You gonna be pinching some of my 'baccy as well, are ya?" Jim asked.

"Oh what – what's that then?" Danny snapped. "After all I've done for you, you're gonna be all funny about me taking a tiny pinch of 'baccy. Gonna be like that are ya? I thought we was mates, you and I."

Jim sat back into the tattered armchair in the far corner of the bedsit, glaring at Danny. Danny glared back.

"It… It's ok fellas, n…no need to be like that." Nigel smiled at them both. They both ignored Nige. Jim took his pack of tobacco out of his pocket and slung it at Danny.

"What's gotten into you then? Why are you feeling stuck?"

"I'm pissed off mate. Universe is conspirin against me again," Danny complained. Jim smiled with forced patience. This always took a while. Danny pulled out a generous bunch of tobacco and stuffed it into the paper. He took a second, more generous bunch and stuffed that into his top pocket for later. Nimble fingers working fast, he rolled, licked and sealed the bulging roll-up, lit it and took a heavy drag. Finally, he pocketed Jim's lighter. Lungs full of smoke, voice strained, he began.

"Things never go my way. I always get screwed over. It's unfair," he declared before exhaling the tobacco smoke he didn't pay for. Jim and Nige remained silent. Nige raised his eyebrows in anticipation. "Shitty bastards nicked my laptop, didn't they…" Danny finished.

"Who?" Jim humoured him, bored already.

"Adam and all that lot. Bastards. Brand new one as well, slim as fuck. Looked well pricey." He let out another cloud of smoke. "Can't believe they nicked it from me, it's so out of order. I mean I robbed it fair and square."

"Oh yeah?"

"Yeah! It wasn't anyone else's street, Mary's still inside. Got it from one of them posh houses on Beauview Crescent. Window unlocked, no alarms. How lucky is that? Thought it was a right touch – like it was all meant to be, all for me, ya know? Right touch, mate." He took another drag. "Gutted mate. Nuffin ever goes my way."

Nige jumped as the door burst open. A beaming Steve stood in the doorway.

"Alright, dickheads!" He marched in and plonked himself down on the bed next to Danny, bouncing Danny up and making him drop ash in his lap.

"Yu… You're in a good mood, St– Ste– S– Steven" smiled Nige.

"Damn right I am." Steve pulled out a fresh pack of straight cigarettes, peeled off the crisp plastic packaging, and drew out a cigarette. Brandishing the glorious specimen in his mouth, he lit it with his shiny Zippo. "I just scored myself a new bike.," he muttered as he puffed.

"What, a motorbike?" Asked Danny, incredulous.

"Haha, nah mate! Almost better though, to be fair. Push-bike. One of them posh road ones. Nice, too. It's a Jean Claude, or some thin' like that. Any idea how much I can shift that for, how much of a drink I can make outta that?"

Jim smiled, shrugged.

Nige blinked.

Danny glared.

Steve held both hands out far apart, gesturing with the extra long cig'. "Lots," he said through a lungful of smoke.

Danny looked intently at his fingernails, glum. "And how'd you swing that one, eh?"

"The poser what bought it didn't have any cash left for a decent lock. Thin little cable round it. No CCTV as well. Cutters snipped right through and bosh! Here I am."

Danny raised an eyebrow, opened his mouth.

"And before any of you crafty fuckers ask, I've got a nice big lock on it now, too." He held up a chunky key. "And there's only one key. I'm not that stupid! Gotta protect what's yours, right?" He flicked a smirk at Danny. "You get your laptop back yet?" Danny ignored him. "Yeah… gotta protect what's yours, haha!"

Jim squinted, looking at the key. "I think I recogni—"

"Where'd you get the lock then?" Danny cut in.

"Tyrone borrowed me his. Proper lock too, he used it on that garage he grows weed in, but he's just cleared it out. Good lot, too. I can get you a decent sized ten-bag if you're interested?"

Danny and Steve both took a drag on their respective cigarettes, slouched on opposite ends of the bed.

Jim looked pensive.

"Speaking of prices, anyone know anyone can move a bike at a decent price? Not many of them Jean Claudes about so I wanna shift it quick. Bit of TLC and you can make a mint on that. Stands out a bit for me though, you know. Bit flash," Steve said with a flourish of the hands.

Danny and Steve took another pull, inhaling deeply.

Danny furrowed his brow, pinching the bridge of the nose as though deep in thought.

Nige looked blank.

Jim scratched his head, opened his mouth. "Do you know, I think Tyrone borrowed me that same lock. In fact, I think I might still have the spare k—"

"What do you know about my laptop, then?" Danny shot at Steve, cutting in with glare directed at Jim to shut him up.

"Er... what?"

"You said you gotta protect what's yours. What did you mean by that?" Danny stood up. "Mates nicked that from me," he pointed with the smouldering fag. "My own mates – can you believe it? That's what's worst of all, bruv."

The room fell silent.

"So what did you mean when you said you gotta protect what's yours, then?"

Not a soul moved. Further down the corridor of the bail hostel, some muffled argument broke out. In the room, the only sound was Danny huffing. Nige squirmed in his seat, the cheap plastic covers making an awkward creak. Danny's chest was visibly rising and falling.

Steve forced an amicable laugh which sounded hollow in the small, tense room. "Nothing mate, just saying you know, gotta keep what's yours safe, right?"

"Yeah, you're right. And that laptop was mine," Danny held his hand up to his chest and pressed a finger back into it, hard. "Mine. Fair and square."

"I know I know. Just, look, all's I'm sayin is if I had a laptop that nice, I wouldn't have left it hanging about unlocked in a fucking pants drawer, dya know what I mean?" Steve chuckled before his eyes suddenly went wide and he fell silent. "Or something," he mumbled.

"So that's how it is," whispered Danny.

"Look, I just came in here looking to see if any of you wanted a bike to shift." Steve looked around as Jim shook his head and Nige offered a sheepish shrug. Steve looked up to Danny, offered a smile.

"Yeah, I do know someone as it happens" Danny beamed. "He's well good, too. Johnny. Yeah, Johnny is his name. Can't go wrong by Johnny, I've done loads with him. He's in one of the bedsits just down the hall," he pointed. "Turn right, past the toilets. Number seven I think, end of the hall one level up. You tell Johnny old Danny 'ere sent you." Danny nodded at the door.

Jim's mouth was still open. Steve eyed Danny with suspicion.

"Swear to God mate, he's well quick too. Knows how to move some nice stuff. Told me he was goin out this afternoon, though. You'd better hurry else you'll miss him."

Steve shrugged. Gathering his things with a dubious air, he pocketed the key and his flashy lighter – engraved with someone else's initials – and left the room.

With Steve gone, Danny pointed the bulging roll-up made from Jim's papers and Jim's tobacco directly at Jim's face.

"Now that prick's gone, you start talking. You said Tyrone borrowed you the lock. Have you got the spare key or what?" he demanded.

Jim shifted his shoulders in his mothballed T-shirt, looked over his right shoulder at the closed door. "Don't make a thing of it, Danny. Tyrone would kill me if he thought I had a spare key straight into his grows."

"I don't care about Tyrone."

"Well, I do! I need him. He gives me the card details to order stuff online, and he sells it all on for me. It works for me, mate. He gives me half-decent drink out of it, and I don't want him to cut me out. Please Danny. And… and I'm scared of him," he whispered. "Please don't let anyone know."

Danny strode over, pointed the smouldering roll-up directly at Jim's face.

Jim recoiled.

Nige sat frozen still.

Danny raised his eyebrows at Jim, head cocked, holding the moment.

Breaths remained bated.

"Look," said Jim, hands up in defence "if I do have it – if… I do have it – it'll be in that drawer." Jim pointed at his bedside cabinet. The bottom drawer was missing. Danny put his hand on the handle of the top one. "No, the…" Danny moved his hand down to the remaining drawer's handle. "Yep. And you… you won't tell, will you?"

Danny pulled the handle. It came off. He slipped his fingers over the lip of the drawer, pulled, jiggled, pulled, jiggled. Eventually the drawer slid out, barely hanging on its runners. Sifting through, he was amazed at the pointless junk Jim kept in the drawer.

Piled to the brim with random stuff, Danny muttered aloud while sifting through Jim's gubbins, spilling ash into the drawer as he went.

Shrapnel: Rusty pennies, tarnished silvers… nothing higher than a 20. "Bah!"

Screwdrivers: Tiny little plastic screwdrivers, some still in their clear plastic case. Danny threw them at Jim. "You building a fucking miniature Meccano motorbike or something, Jim?"

Nige snorted. "Hah, a miniature motorbike."

Little pieces of green cardboard, ripped up to make roaches for spliffs and filters for cigs. Danny tutted, rifling through the crap with ever more urgency. Muttering and cursing under his breath he started throwing things about in the drawer, taking more frequent and harder drags on the roll-up as he went. Sinews showed through the stubble and tattoos on his neck as he bit down on it. Cigarette wedged in his teeth, he rummaged with double the hands and double the vigour.

He paused, held something a moment and pulled it out.

A toy soldier.

"What's this, the hero you're holding out for?" A bark of a laugh came out around his pressed lips. "You always said you wanted a man in uniform didn't you?" Danny lobbed the figurine at Jim's lap and it rebounded onto the floor. "Twat," Danny muttered.

Keys: Old keys, new keys, rusty keys, broken keys. None looked like the key he was after, like the key Steve had held up with pride. He did find an extra strength condom.

"And what's this?" Danny cackled at Jim. "You haven't had a man in years mate, your virginity must have grown back by now. You even know how to use this? Here, let me help you out!"

"Oh come on, Danny, be fair, you don't need to waste it," Jim protested, making to stand up.

"No no you're alright mate, you won't miss it" Danny urged with an open palm pressed towards Jim to sit him down. Bending down to pick up the toy soldier, he deftly opened the condom with his teeth in one side of his mouth while keeping the rollie at bay on the other side.

"I'm Jim's dream man," he squeaked, holding the figure up in mock conversation, "and I can't wait to be swallowed up the sex god Jim."

"Yeah, sex god!" Nige parroted.

Danny popped the unsuspecting infanteer into the waiting contraceptive and bunched the open end between thumb and forefinger. Jabbing his fist at Jim, the condom-enveloped toy soldier swung dangerously close to Jim's face, making him recoil. This won another laugh from the now smiling Danny.

"Here you go, Jim, I've found your dream man and… look at this, he even practises safe sex, so you won't get ill again."

Jim dropped his head into his hands at this, dejected. "Just fuck off, Danny," he breathed. "Find the key and fuck off, why don't you."

"Oooh, touchy Jim. Alright, no need to pull a sad-on, Danny's on the case," and with that he returned to the drawer with his right hand, the offending article still in his left. The soldier, poised in a firing position on one small plastic knee, dangled in his rubbery enclosure. As the condom gently twisted and turned in Danny's hand, the soldier rotated his watchful gaze and raised rifle around the room of bickering thieves.

"Will you sell the bi…b…bicycle to J– Johnny down the hall?" asked Nige, trying to clear the tension in the air.

"Nah, Johnny was recalled to prison last week. He was on license." He inhaled a deep puff. "Broke his probation conditions. Dickhead."

"Oh… Well… wh– what about Steve?" Nige asked.

"Fuck Steve and fuck you too Nige. If you ask any more questions or if you dare tell anyone about this… I know people, mate. They will find you." Danny pointed the armed condom at Nige long enough to make him fold his arms and shrink into his corner. "You're too stupid to hide properly," he added before more rummaging, sifting through all the pointless crap Jim kept.

Lighters, empty. Happy meal toys, why? Letters, loser. Key… KEY!

"YES!" Danny held it up, triumphant.

It looked exactly like the one Steve had had. "Is this the…?" Jim nodded, looked down.

"Listen, Danny, please don't. There's no way you, or anyone, could cut through that lock. Not without taking an angle grinder to it in the middle of the street. I mean, it's a joke. Tyrone would know I had kept the key, and Steve would know it was you. We'd both be up the creek mate. Please don't…"

"You think I want to do this?" Danny accused. "You think I want to steal from one of us?" Jim and Nige both nodded, though Danny apparently missed the synchronised gesture.

"Well, I don't, mate, but you know my situation. I've got a mouth to feed." Jim snorted at this, though halted when Danny threatened him with the floppy warrior.

"I would have been sorted with that laptop. It was mine fair and square. And the thieving bastards took it from me…" Danny shouted. "FROM ME!" he screamed, slapping his chest. Jim squirmed in his seat, avoiding Danny's glower.

Calming down, chest still heaving, Danny added "I have to do this. You think I want to? I don't. But I have to."

Footsteps in the hall.

Danny pocketed the key and sat back where he was, trying

to slow his breathing down. Spotting the open drawer, he got back up, picked up the broken handle and chucked it in the drawer before trying to force it shut. Jammed, he shoved and wiggled, wiggled and shoved, rattling the whole cabinet on its feet. Finally, the drawer slid in and promptly broke off its runners.

"Dogshit," he muttered, bent over the whole mess in despair.

The door handle turned. Danny, still crouching as though that would somehow keep the whole matter stealthy, flicked his head around with a finger pressed to his lips. He looked at Jim, looked pointedly at Nige, and turned his head towards the door, frozen in anticipation.

The door opened.

"Steve!" Danny quavered, failing to show an ounce of the panache he hoped he had summoned.

Steve paused in the door, looked at the two rabbits caught in the headlights staring back, looked across to Danny bent over the head of the bed with his arse towards the door and a condom in his hand.

"Eh?"

Panting, Danny spun around, stood up and tried to take a puff of the cigarette to hide his excitement and look casual. It had gone out.

Steve looked down at Danny side, who looked down to the same place.

The latex-clad rifleman continued to dangle. A small gobbet of silicone lubricant dropped to the carpet. Danny forced a laugh and then hurriedly flung the whole sad affair in Nige's general direction.

"We was just mucking about mate. Horseplay," Danny explained.

"HORSEPLAY!" Nige laughed far too enthusiastically before giving himself a quiet fit of giggles.

Slowly shaking his head, Steve put his hands in the pockets of his expensive-looking branded joggers, jangled some keys and coins.

"No-one there," he announced, a little sad. "Must've missed him. Oh well, should probably be off. Need to get that thing indoors before someone spots it."

"Yeah, good idea," agreed Jim, flinching from the quick glare Danny shot at him.

"What? Nonsense!" beamed Danny, forcing his best genial charm. "I haven't seen you in ages mate. Put your feet up, what's going on with you these days anyway? What you sayin, what you sayin?" He patted the bed next to him.

Steve shrugged, sat down. Pulled out another cigarette, lit it. He laughed. "Here, have I told you about this latest bit on the side I've got on the go? Claudio. Italian lad he is, gorgeous!" He grinned.

"What! The same Claudio? The one I met in that hostel and was trying it on with? Oh what a surprise," chided Jim. "Always getting' about, always gloatin aren't you. Think you're a modern day Freddie Mercury, don't you!"

Steve looked taken aback.

"Why don't you just piss off and take your fancy bike with you, eh Steve?"

"Now now, Jim. No need to be like that is there?" Danny hissed through bared teeth. His voice was level, but the undertones carried a direct threat.

Jim glowered back. "It's my gaff. I'll be how I like thanks."

Steve looked from Jim to Danny and back. "Listen, I don't want to intrude on your lovers' tiff," and he got up to leave.

"Nah, you're alright Steve. I'm fed up with this arsehole. I'm off. You can stick around as long as you like here with that pillock."

"No thanks, mate. I'd best be off. I know when I'm not wanted."

"Oh for fuck's sake, Jim!" Danny exploded. "See what you've done now? You've upset Steve…"

"No, really, I—"

"You're supposed to be known for your hospitality, and here you go mugging our mates off. You make me laugh you do," Danny accused, standing between Steve and the door.

"Really, Danny, I was joking. I was leaving anyway. Need to flog that frigging bike, don't I?" Steve smiled.

Danny paused, thinking hard. He pinched the bridge of his nose, held one hand out to Steve. Motioned to sit. Steve looked at the others, sat back down.

"Look, guys. This is all well and good, but I swear I just came here looking for someone to shift a bit of stuff for me."

"But I would enjoy…" Danny forced, "your… company."

"I'm actually pretty tired, you know" Jim chimed in. "If you don't mind, I've got a headache from all this bollocks, and I just wanna lie down on my own bed for a—"

Danny raised his hands, about to lose his shit.

"Wo– would you l– like a spliff, Ste… St… Steven?" Nige offered.

"No, that's alright thanks Nige," he said, getting up. "I've got some of Tyrone's green back h—"

Nige interrupted again, smiling.

"I've heard this is be… much better than his st… stu… b– better than his rubbish."

Steve hovered a moment, hands still on the bed. He sunk back down. "You've gone an said it now. Bold claim, Nige! Well, this I have to try…"

Danny clapped his hands, beaming at Nige. "It's settled then! Steve, why don't you skin up with Nige's gear, I'll go for a slash, and Jim…" Danny flashed him a cold glance. "Jim will cheer up and stop being such a miserable bastard – hah!"

Danny got up, walked to the door and opened it. He perched the cold roll-up in his mouth and winked at Nige. Turning to Steve, he asked through pursed lips: "Here, Steve. Them Zippos any good?"

Steve, his lap already full of spliff rolling paraphernalia, fished the engraved lighter out of his pocket and tossed it into Danny's waiting hands.

"Cheers mate!" Danny lit the cigarette, closed the door and stepped outside. He spun left, away from the toilets he had said he was visiting, and marched towards the exit of Jim's bail hostel. Pulling the spare bike key out of his pocket with his free hand, he puffed at the pilfered cigarette.

Key in one hand, fag and freshly stolen lighter in the other, Danny smiled to himself. Bad times behind him, good times ahead, he thought of all the things he would buy once he'd sold Steve's bike. Spring in his step, tune on his whistling lips, Danny made for the exit.

EX.

What can I say? I like to gather a broad church. Perennial as the moss clinging to crags of rocks, chancers like these always find a way to survive. If pressed against a spiky wall I confess I do harbour a certain fondness for them. I suppose we're all drawn to mirrors, aren't we? Those people that reflect elements of what we see in the dark, untouched corners of our own psyche. Not a terribly pleasant experience, yet…aren't we most truthful when painted 'boils and all'? Interesting to see our less savoury traits in others, if only as a plea to ourselves to improve.

Anyway, we've tarried here quite long enough, and our next commutation takes us deeper down the rabbit hole and a tad further afield. You've not been off-planet yet, have you?

THE ONE-WAY COMMUTE

IN.

Let's ramp it up a touch, yes?

As we continue on our journey, you will see more and more of my skills as a Commutator coming into play. This next little trick is quite something… We'll hop and skip back and forth across opposing frames of reference, relativistically speaking I mean. We commutate into one frame of reference moving close to the speed of light, then into another moving as fast but in a different direction. Rinse, lather, repeat. Transitioning back and forth like this allows us to take incremental steps either up or indeed down our relativistic ladder. One can't go particularly far, of course, nor do much once there, but it is rather lovely to have a little peep into the near future don't you think? One of many possibles, of course.

But don't let me distract you with that. This is not about me and my work, but rather you and yours. I speak of the near future endeavours of your kind to spread your wings.

Colonisation.

Mars.

The historic commutes that people will make to The Red Planet!

We've made a few of the contra-incrementing ladder jumps. A few more and we'll be there, my dear.

Space travel, you see, is an expensive business. Your planet's first space race was fuelled by the national budget spend associated with global conflict. Your first permanently crewed space station was funded by international collaboration. The path ahead to your first interplanetary migration lay locked behind one key.

Commercialisation.

The problems to overcome weren't technical but economic. The power of a good story told for business based on an innovative new investment model. A model that could work in the emerging markets of the age, living in the volatile turmoil created by disruptive tech, social media and startup culture. Fascinating, if you like that sort of thing!

So…

Picture this – it's finally funded! It's finally happening, and you're one of the chosen few among the masses throwing themselves in a sea of enthusiasm as this momentous opportunity.

Imagine you're one of the lucky few selected. One of the privileged few to experience why so many people were flocking, falling over each other to be future founders of a new race. You've done the training, survived the takeoff and are now in the most expensive and technologically advanced tin can humankind has ever built. Hurtling through the dark abyss between here and there, you'll supplement the very first settlement team. You and your three crewmates will meet them soon, on Mars!

The thrill of the adventure, the tension of the journey… the irreversibility of the commitment to the colony. There's no return ticket.

Exciting, yes?

Well, we're nearly there on our relativistic ladder. We're not going into the spaceship, we're going straight to Mars. Now you can see things from the point of view of one of the two who first landed on Mars, the very first landing.

Remember, these vignettes I've captured from other people, they're all in their own, oh, curses, sorry, should-have-said-earlier-no-time-to-explain-now… we're already h—

BLOOD RED SAND

Blood red sand slipped through the grooves of her titanium shovel, spilling over the edge. The last remaining sunlight glinted through the cascade of Martian soil.

Warm light diffracted through the millions of rust coloured granules as they tumbled to the desert floor. She saw each grain in the cascade of Martian sand as a future migrant from Earth landing here on home soil, on Mars.

Millions upon millions of them ready to call the red planet home. Home for them, home for their children, home for their children's children.

The thought thrilled and terrified her.

As the last few granules tumbled off, she left her reveries of the many possible futures that may come to pass and brought herself back into the present. She wanted to be in the moment.

Soft rays dappled her sand-worn visor. Kali caught her breath. After a beat, she allowed the exhilarating efforts of the afternoon to subside in a long, slow breath as the adrenaline ebbed out of her body. Hazy tiredness seeped into her muscles to replace it. She welcomed the foggy sensation, though tried to keep her mind awake. Anxieties finally melting away, she felt a fresh sense of peace and let her eyelids close. Holding onto the silence and darkness, she savoured the moment, lungs empty, mind void.

Pure solitude.

Kali opened her eyes and mouth and drank in the breathtaking Martian sunset. A small and solitary sun blazing in azure beauty. A bright blue lighthouse. Beaming out its final goodbye to an alien sky, it prepared to slip below the farthest reaches of the horizon-wide dust clouds gently swirling below. Her eyes drifted up towards the growing glimmer of Earth and traced an invisible line from the blue planet she had left behind for her new home. For a moment, her gaze hung where she knew the meticulously calculated flight path curved through the darkening skies between the two neighbour planets.

So glad you're coming to join me, thought Kali with a smile.

Flaring her nostrils, she took another deep breath of the reprocessed air in her suit, savouring the homely scent that accompanied the view of her back garden. In time she had grown into the musk of sweat, fabric and ionised air-con. She had once described it as the combined scent of your own warm bed in the morning, your damp top straight after a good workout, and the ageing air-con of your car holding out from total breakdown. Quintessentially her own, it smelt like home.

Comforted by the confines of her life-sustaining exosuit, the hairs on her neck stood on end at the overwhelming sense of privilege she felt. Perched on the slopes of Olympus Mons, she watched the Sun's last remaining light wane over the distant Xanthe Terra plains.

This view is to die for. Soon, we can enjoy it together, she smiled.

Colonisers.

Two had been sent at first, Brian and her. Arguments over budget had limited the original ambitions for a larger 'seed team'. So, to save the program from political deadlock, the investors had agreed to send just two explorers – a daring, and cheap, proof of principle. Two people to go down in history either as founders of the new colony, or a human experiment abandoned forever, alone on this rock and its shifting Martian sands.

These founding two, Kali Parvati and Brian Orr, had worked hard to establish a strong foothold. Slaving away, they had exceeded their key performance indicators in the first three-, six- and nine-month milestones. Securing a green light for Team Two had meant much more to them than professional or even scientific success. The future of the colony, of continued investment and hence their lives, had depended on it. Pretty easy to stay motivated under such conditions. Having established economic viability, they now awaited larger and larger parties to join the expeditionary effort. Every 26 months, when Earth and Mars were at closest approach, teams were due to departure to help them build the foundations of the 'colony'.

Kali was lucky. One of the first to pass the rigorous selection and forsake the Earth's declining living conditions for the lifelong Commitment to the red planet. It was an incredible opportunity, highly sought-after.

And you also made the grade, she thought, looking up to where the second team's shuttle was due to be now. *And you're on your way right now to join me.*

A small laugh escaped her mouth, fogging up the bottom of her helmet before the moisture reclaimers cleared it away, storing it for a precious sip later.

Kali realised with a pleasant surprise that, for the first time in a long time, she was smiling.

They had started a few months ago, her... frustrations. Regrettable.

After the once shiny excitement of moving to Mars had tarnished, things had grown dull. And Kali was acutely aware of how daft that seemed.

Mars.

Dull.

But it was true – the human mind saw any new situation as pedestrian, given enough time. Giddy excitement back on Earth at selection for the affectionately titled 'one-way tin can' later gave way to mundane reality.

Outside their pod, roving the rugged planet in their exosuits, the stark beauty of Mars remained ever humbling.

Pod-life, however, was different. Boredom turned to debate, debate to opposition, opposition to… well.

Confined in their curved walls, stuck with rehydrated rations and stilted conversation, things festered. Surprising how long it took to get to know someone, to know who they really were, even after bonding over a life experience as formative, as intense as the Expeditionary Astronaut Program and the Commitment that came with it. Even when you were the only two damned people on the planet.

Whole new layers of self became apparent.

Yes. And their arguments always circled back to the same issue: Terran control, Martian freedom. Brian saw this as an outpost. Disgraceful. Only she understood its full potential.

Mars was to be the sovereign state of the red planet-nation. No countries, no quarrelling. Competition only where healthy, collaboration as the norm. A haven for hard working, free people. Free from artificial boundaries, free from the control of Earth, from the budget holders, the oil-rich, the trading magnates, AI farm-masters, ego-philanthropists… *bastards all.*

Kali frowned, her chest rising and falling hard.

Perform these little tasks for distant masters.

Perform these little tasks with diligence and care.

Perform these little tasks to sow the seeds of the investors' reign.

These little 'profit-led research' tasks. Or these little 'future stakeholder compatibility' tasks. Or, better yet, these 'critical shareholder interest' tasks. That's what it came down to. Board members and their hunger for coin.

Food, water, warmth, shelter, rest. Maybe, heavens forbid, a little fun. Yes, Kali had desires of her own, and she needed one commodity only to fulfil them, the only commodity that mattered…

Freedom.

She hadn't traded everything on Earth and any hope of going back to human civilisation for that. Yes, essential survival was always catered for in her rigid schedule of tasks, but there was a big difference between surviving and *living*.

Freedom.

Distant and absolute control had never sat well with her. How she wished Brian had agreed. Their foothold on this planet was theirs. Mars was theirs.

Needless to say, Brian had not shared her… aspirations. His narrow mindset had created a rift in their cramped quarters. Things had become unenjoyable of late. Even, yes even uncomfortable.

Mist gathered further up Kali's helmet as she barked out a cynical laugh. Since their final argument every task had seemed a pathetic chore: churning soil and sowing seeds in neat rows like a glorified peasant farmer; lugging heaped sacks of fertiliser on unreliable tracked caddies like a sub-wage lorry loader; ramming her arm furiously into blocked waste pipes like a cursed sewage technician.

Well, today's joint excursion up Olympus Mons… the success of the afternoon with him, the exertions of the early evening. Nothing like vigorous physical exercise to work away your blues! Mars needed children, and those children needed freedom.

Kali realised again how lucky she was. How privileged, how blessed.

Weeks had passed since their last argument, and since then Kali had struggled to make amends, struggled to restore peace in their claustrophobic pod while maintaining her beliefs.

Solitude.

Countless hours alone in the agri-dome had finally helped her summon the courage to ask Brian up Olympus Mons to see a Martian sunset together from above the dust clouds. She was right to promise it would be unforgettable.

And he had agreed. Such a surprise, welling up untapped inner reserves of joy!

All had gone according to plan, and now here she was. Shovel in hand, twinkling blue sun setting over distant Xanthe Terra mountains. She looked around at the entrenched resting place she was kneeling in, elbows perched on the edge, breath calm in her sweat soaked helmet. This moment was precious, almost spiritual.

Ashes to ashes, dust to dust she breathed.

The carnal dust of this body – Brian's body – born and raised on planet Earth, was now half-interred in the blood red dust of a Martian grave.

Kali hadn't wanted it to go this way. Truly, she hadn't. Convincing, coercing, compromising, even extorting. She had explored all options available to her, but Brian hadn't budged, hadn't been willing to open his mind to the possibility he might be wrong. Wrong about some fundamental issues of morality.

A concession had to be made that she wasn't entirely perfect herself.

Killing someone in a choreographed accident wasn't exactly the cornerstone on which she wanted her sovereign planet to be founded. The home of the free. It deserved a bedrock more solid. She knew what she had done and knew the price she had to pay: the guilt that would plague her for years to come; the burden of this terrible secret she must take to her own grave; the nightmares she would no doubt endure in the haunting dead of Martian night.

Kali accepted it all, as she knew she must.

Her thoughts turned again to those millions of future inhabitants – migrants and native-born Martians alike. She thought of Earth's control over Mars extending through generations, the difficulties they would face breaking free these shackles that bind.

What next? First the demise of this planet to Terran control. Then, having set a precedent with Mars, Earth would extend its reach further still. Establishing colonies farther afield, the purpose would not be exploration but commercialisation. Profit used to wield economic control.

Soon enough it wouldn't be called the Solar System but the Terran System. The dark ages would return in a more sinister era.

Geocentricism.

Earth at the centre of all creation. That hallmark of the first dark age once saw powerful religious zealots place Earth at the centre of cosmic creation. Well, this Earth-centric view was on the rise once again, only this time it was powerful investment zealots positioning Earth as the centre of commercial creation.

Colonies born into debt, their citizens: economic slaves. Bloodshed after bloodshed through the wars it would take to overturn this enforced status quo.

All this… unless she started the movement now. Right now, from the very outset. Without seizing the initiative, she shuddered to think of all the innocent blood that would spill on this planet, on Earth. Yes, even the blood that would scatter like rubies in the dark skies between.

One life to save many.

Kali stared upwards.

Now she could start anew with those colonists already on their way, already nearing closest approach to Mars. Fresh people, fresh ideals, fresh canvases on which to paint the founding covenant of a common Martian purpose. A fresh start, untainted by unfortunate Terran hangups.

Yes, Brian, his fall… regrettable.

And yet… wasn't it all regrettable? This situation? The position she had been forced into? And after all, as a Founding Colonist, a Founding Mother even, she had her children to think of. The future children of her realm, whether her biological offspring or her offspring by right of founding their nation planet. She owed this to *them*, a bloodless struggle towards strength and perhaps one day even supremacy. So much threatened this delicate, infant planet of hers. The fears of what could befall it… like any parent, they made her sick with worry.

The tides of melancholy that welled up threatened to pull her under, deeper than she believed she could survive.

Focus on the positive, Kali. Don't drown. Thrive!

Breathe…

Focus on positive: Gratitude…

Breathe…

Remembering this afternoon, she had to concede there was

beauty in the way Brian had tumbled down the crevasse, high on Olympus Mons. The moments before were a treasure. A cusp like that is a rare thing in one's life. So much work, so much thought, so much effort had gone into creating that very moment. A lesser person could be forgiven for rushing through that precious heartbeat in case they lost courage at the last.

Not Kali. She had taken her time to drink it in, drink in the nerves one feels when standing on the knife edge, the precipice between one life and another, one decision and another. That moment where what one does next will change everything, especially the self.

Savouring that was everything.

Holding onto it for as long as it was safe to, Kali released it as she made the decision she had always known she would.

Swelling with pride, she conceded she had judged the force of the push and the arc of his trajectory just right. All the groundwork, all the preparation and research. Yes, she had judged it just right. The fall wasn't enough to kill a person outright. No. That would have been crass. A blunt tool wielded by a blunt instrument.

No. Kali's mind was razor sharp, a herald of the future.

She judged it so the body would remain intact. The height, the sharpness of the rocks, the timbre of his fall. It was all just so. Perfect calculations and slick execution had ensured that on those rugged rocks, only the helmet would crack.

And now the real work would begin, of course. Not the lugging, the digging, or the burying: these were all mere precursors to the real challenges ahead.

Kali still relied on her masters, at least for a little longer… only until they approved the incoming capsule for landing. After that there was no choice, it would bring the next settlers and their extra muscle power down to their new home. She was also counting on the heavier setup equipment their larger capsule was able to bring: 3D mud-printers, mineral rovers with longer range and higher cargo capacity, water crackers…

She had done the calculations, advanced her research well beyond what she shared with those Terran gluttons. Yes, she already knew how to tweak the soil converters to make a higher-yield fertiliser – they thought she was months away from that breakthrough. She knew how to hack the re-breathers in the suits and the pods to squeeze an extra 2% efficiency out of them. This little victory, plus some work on the rover batteries, increased her range far enough for her personally to reach the ice deposits and harvest fresh supply. She would have installed the upgrades already, if only she could have placed enough trust in Brian not to talk.

Marginal gains. All of them minor improvements on the ingenuities of Earth's finest engineers. Increments that added up to game changing milestones… but not yet. Her efforts plus the incoming crew and kit were the bare minimum, but that wasn't all she could squeeze out of them.

No. Kali needed The Program to understand her suffering, her thirst, so they would send more supplies in future, more crew.

And the storytelling!

That was the real challenge. How to weave these actions into a narrative of wool she would wrap around those bastards' eyes back on Earth. Martian wool spun for Terran eyes.

Kali chuckled.

So many tasks she now had to tend to. Little tasks to sow little seeds – seeds that would grow as mighty as her reign. Little tasks once completed for the greed of the small, now completed for the dream of a planet.

Subtle steps would keep the secret safe.

The incoming team was almost beyond final return, the last point at which they could abort the landing and return to Earth. She was confident she could keep this all covered until then, after which they were committed… after which, it was all to play for.

Worst case scenario was no new crews beyond the current incoming. Not ideal, but she had researched options for midwifery out here and it was workable. Where there's a will, there's a way.

More interesting than that was the possibility… the opportunity to bring the newcomers under her wing, convince them of her ways and of her vision. Yes, it was all so very exciting!

Kali took the time to relish being the only person alive on this planet. Such privileged solitude. She cast her eyes up to that space between the horizon and the gleaming dot that was Earth, to the space where the incoming crew were currently starting to decelerate in preparation of a landing orbit, by which point they would have made final their Commitment to her planet.

Join me, my friends. Join me in this paradise far from the vices of condemned fools.

Her gaze drifted down to the helmet of her former crewmate.

One thing she couldn't even take credit for having planned, though she wished she had, was that the visor hadn't caved in. That would have killed Brian in a few breaths. Instead a fine web of fissures had seeped out oxygen, allowing him to hang in there long enough for Kali to clamber down and see him, see the look in his eye. At least the one still visible through the dust-covered cracks adorning the visor. There was… in the expressions that dappled across that panicked eye, that window to the soul… something spectacular.

At first, the beauty of fear painted on the canvas of creases around his eye. Ravines ran through the microcosm of this landscape where blood mixed with saltwater tears. These had started to smoothen once Kali arrived as that fear turned to hope.

Presumably in that split second he mistook the shove at the top as an accidental bump. Perhaps he thought Kali had scrambled down to save him. Then something else had crept across his face, something slower, more profound. Kali had remained still as she knelt beside him watching, just watching, as his hopes for salvation evaporated into the Martian winds. Once the reality of his situation had settled in, his expression had revealed something else. A vision most stark.

A bright blue eye, searching for redemption through cracked glass under the waning sapphire sky. It was as though he was seeing Kali – her true self – for the first time, for one fleeting glimpse. And in that moment that blue orb of his iris, so round, so deep... it could have been the Earth itself staring right back into her soul. Daring her, challenging her with all that it was and all that it had failed to be for her. Accusing her of all she had failed to be on Earth. A vision of the blue planet in Brian's dying eye with a gaping black hole at its centre drawing her in, trying to swallow her into its depths.

In that moment she felt her soul being surveyed... *judged* by her tormentor. Only this time she found the strength to look right back. Having escaped that prison planet once already, she now dared to laugh in its face from across the abyss of space, from across the even greater gulf between life and death.

No words, no turn of phrase could capture it. Under this alien sky with its cool blue sunset, the scene embodied everything she could have imagined of pure beauty.

Well, she didn't want to be out for long in the cold Martian night digging this grave – the first grave in the fledgling history of Mars. With a little luck, the only one for many years to come. She sincerely hoped the newcomers wouldn't force her to dig another.

Kali picked herself up, leaving the dust on the knees and stomach of her exosuit untouched. She felt good. This was a positive start to her reign, *and only a few weeks to go until you join me...*

She absently brushed a gloved hand over the sand on her shovel, looked up at the disappearing sun and the dark skies above, and smiled.

EX.

Yes… it struck me from the first time I stumbled across it, Kali's commute. And what follows? I'm afraid our ladder won't reach much farther beyond this, so it's anyone's guess how it turns out.

I do love that one though! A unique and historic commute. The emotion behind a decision to commit to a journey like that, can you imagine making that call? Quite unlike any other choice.

Yes, quite, and before knowing what sort of a person with whom you would be going to found your common future. I do hope you're not too hard on Kali, though. She does care for her people and their future. And well, what of you? Would you rather be controlled by the tyrants against you, or the one for you?

Hmmm, ok, point taken. Let's try a different tack, shall we?

The likes of you and I, we move onward, upward, sideward and through, so on we go…

THE ELECTRONIC COMMUTE

IN.

...And into something different. We have a fine position here in The In Between and have worked hard to climb up the proverbial ladder. Bit windier and choppier up here I'm afraid, regarding the relativity wind buffeting ou—uo gniteffub dniw ytiv...wououw... er—our sense of self and the reversibility of cause and effect.

Oh, did I just invert? I do apologise!

Like I say, bit blustery up here, in a reality-changing sense I mean. Nevertheless, we'll hold onto our current time on the ladder and take a geographic sidestep back onto Terra Firma. We're still in the aspirational near-future, ah, relative to your home frame of reference that is, so some of this ought to be new to you.

Let's also step aside from such budding conflicts as what we've seen so far, and move into lives that speak of a... brighter future. A future where dreams become opportunities. And what dreams this character stirred in people's hearts across the world!

This historic lady is a commuter not of your real-world streets, roads and underground tunnels, but of information superhighways! She commutes at the speed of electronic signals under the ground and sea, and at the speed of light through air and above. Not that that's what makes her remarkable, though in truth the two are connected. Remarkable how fast a special little girl blossomed into the bright star of her time. But… I'll leave her story to speak for itself.

I will, however, take the liberty of a moment to express the technical difficulty required for a commutator such as my good self to present to a client as esteemed as your equally good self a blend such as this. A blend, I mean, of access to the biology of a human mind and also to the silicone of an electronic mind.

The details of access to a biological consciousness we have already covered, and you're getting rather good at that, I might say. The exciting addition is the provision of direct access to the inner workings of a synthetic sentience. The technical hurdles to overcome in achieving that access alone… gosh! Quite a feat on my part, if I may say. But the complexities of presenting access to electronic consciousness alongside the biochemical signals in the squishy stuff inside a fellow brain… all in one commutation? Well!

Quite the feat, my friend.

Quite the feat.

But I don't want to distract you with my technical prowess, staggering though that may be. Spare a moment of thought on our journey, my dear friend: where we've been, where we are now… where we're heading. You're not still blinkered by your single-planet-traveller's myopia, are you? Surely you don't think you're a mere passenger?

Oh, come!

This isn't just one story after the other, one life after another to pop into and out from. This isn't merely a random collection of life vignettes to partake of… all is not as simple as one, two and three. Plainly you must see that?

Ugh, very good. Well, less of my chatter, let's dive in my fellow journeyperson. Ever onward…

Let's transition out of The In Between and into this near future of wearable tech, ingestible tech… implantable *tech. Drink in the ever-accelerating, dizzying possibilities created by tech giants and startups alike.*

EMPTY DIGITAL DATA

Empty digital data points continued to haunt her.

Three blank lines.

Mocking her.

Empty.

She thought of everything she had achieved so far. All the research faculties she had set up. All the experiences she had lived through, the lives she had touched. All the changes to legislation she had driven through, even the new laws she had helped create. All the speeches she had given to thousands live and hundreds of millions online around the world… All the powers of articulation she had developed in her short life. Yet here, faced with the constraint of a 75 character limit… Nothing.

It was embarrassing.

The cursor continued to blink in the blank text box, mocking her, daring her to write something. She scanned the text above yet again: ENTER PERSONALISED MESSAGE HERE. It even had a prompt: WITH SYMPATHY…

It was a simple command, yet apparently one she was incapable of following. She whiled a few moments away, as she always did, by watching the time subtraction. Subtract the time she came online from the time now, and the result was a number that was ever growing, representing the increasing longevity of her life. She would say it represented her age, but she didn't really feel like she was ageing, so that was an odd way to refer to the time subtraction. Sometimes she watched it broken down into years, days, hours, minutes, seconds and milliseconds. Other times just the full number of milliseconds. Sometimes she would have a mini-celebration in her mind each time that total number passed through a special milestone like a prime number, but she was in no mood for celebrating today.

Either way, her electronic wits were quick enough to allow her to contemplate and appreciate each millisecond as it rolled in. Usually that was a blessing, yet lately it had grown to feel like more of a curse.

The blinking cursor faded on screen, was there for an age, and then faded off screen again.

Blink.

...

Blink.

...

This was getting ridiculous. She had already spent 5437 pointless milliseconds of her life contemplating this task in blank solitude. *Just write something*, she egged herself on as she prepared to put electronic pen to paper.

WHEREVER YOU GO NEXT, I WILL ALWAYS BE WI...

Rubbish. She hated it. She didn't even know what that meant, despite the time she had invested in its contemplation.

Deleting one letter at a time, she watched her trivial attempt shrink back into the void. One letter at a time, the opposite way it had appeared, she savoured each letter as the digital information gradually disappeared from existence.

"This is historic." Josh sipped his homemade cortado coffee, eyes closing for a moment as he took it in. Sophie watched as he shot a proud glance at the large wooden contraption in the corner, complete with oversized pneumatic handle, that had grandly titled The Espressinator. Josh placed the drink down on a saucer. This was itself resting on an expensive, coffee-shop-style serviette he had recently bought in bulk to complete the authentic experience in their home office.

"What, your coffee?" She joked, head cocked to one side.

"What? No. I mean, well, that too. It is pretty special." He sipped again. "Tastes a bit like crap. But it's the love I've put into it, that's the special ingredient!" He winked at her and smiled, the crema of the coffee catching in his auburn stubble.

"A bit like our baby?"

"Our learning app, you mean. Well, plenty of love, and hopefully less of the crappiness," he joked nervously. He frowned, creating deep furrows on his lightly freckled forehead. "We are doing the right thing, aren't we? I mean, this is ok isn't it?"

"We've been over it a million times, Josh. I did my gardening leave. The IP I've used is mine, fair and square. Your IP was always yours as an independent. The server farm we've hired is contracted to us and us alone, and the anti-poaching clauses I had our lawyer put in are tight. We're safe, we're damned near bulletproof. We—"

"I didn't mean… that. Look, I appreciate everything you've done for us. But… before we flick the switch, or press the button, or—"

"It's touchspace," she said with a smirk.

"Sophie, I'm serious," he admonished. She shrugged in response. "Before we tap the space above the workscreen and bring this…"

"Our baby."

"Before we bring the app online, is this…? Are we doing the right thing here? By it?" He closed his mouth, paused a beat. Then, just as Sophie was convinced he was going to lock it all inside, he blurted it out in a torrent.

"Have we designed it right? Will it be able to learn? Will it be safe? Are we protecting it from the outside world?… Are we protecting the outside world from *it*?" Sophie placed her hands on Josh's, cradling them, silencing him with one tender look.

"How are any of these questions any expectant parent wouldn't ask?" He looked down and shrugged. "Josh… You remember the time we met?" He nodded, his eyes taking on a glossy sheen. "When you bumped into me on that stupid hover-board of yours with its fake gold alloy wheels," she said. This got a laugh out of him before he reverted to that same, sad puppy dog look she had been entranced by on that rainy day in Shoreditch.

Hooked by it, she had wanted to find out more, to find out what strength lay beneath. "And over coffee you told me all about how that stupid, poisonous cow had dumped you because you were the reason she hadn't been able to get pregnant. How that cruel bitch left you because of something you had no control over. And you thought it was life that had been cruel to you, not letting you ever become a parent?" Josh nodded, blinked as the first tear rolled down his cheek. "It wasn't life being cruel. It was her, and only her.

"All you wanted was to become a father, Josh. It had you balling your eyes out to a total stranger. I'd never seen anything like it before – and I don't mean seeing a bearded man cry." This time Josh didn't laugh. His watery eyes took on a hollow expression, lost.

"Look at me. You had such a desire for parenthood, such desperation. And there was something more in there, something burning within. Look at me, babe." Josh looked up at her and Sophie fixed him with her marble green-blue eyes. "From that first day, I believed in you. And now here we are. Look at what we've achieved, at what we're about to achieve. I still believe in you." She spread her left arm out, taking in their design table with its touchspace workstation. "I believe in us."

"This isn't what this is about, Sophie!" He snapped. "This is a program, not a child, this is engineering, not biology, this is a startup sequence, not birth. We are designers, not parents." He stopped, chest heaving, fists balled.

"We named her, Amelia." Her eyes were cold, resolute.

"We named it, Advanced Machine Empathy Learning Intelligence Application."

"Bullshit, Josh! We've always wanted to be parents, to raise something vulnerable and beautiful and that wants to learn and that needs our help and that will love us as that we will love," she screeched through sudden anger.

"And we will have something to raise," he retorted. "Something vulnerable and amazing that needs our protection, but let's not be like those people that treat their pets like their children."

"Is that all she is? A pet?"

"No, much much more. This will be historic, like I said. But historic to us as learning intelligence architects." His voice showed the cracks in his exhaustion at the same old argument reopening. "Your artificial intelligence and fuzzy logic IP, the doors that has opened for us…"

"It's ten-a-penny stuff," Sophie said, biting the corner of her mouth. "It's the way you integrated your automated online research and learning apps that will make all the difference."

"Exactly! Not one team in the field has considered anything like it. We're leagues ahead," he beamed through the tears and the rage and the fatigue. Sophie seemed unsure whether she was ready to join with a smile.

"Shall we become parents, my dear?" she asked gingerly.

Josh sighed.

"We are creating history, we are not becoming parents."

"Well, maybe you're not," Sophie snapped, "but all I've ever wished for is to bring another life into this world." She drove her open palm into the space above oversized heart icon on their design table. In a cupping motion, she lifted her hand up before taking a step away from Josh and hugging her arms. The heart onscreen shrank and started floating along and around a 3D representation of a Mobius strip in a never-ending loop. Text above it appeared in soft, childlike font.

PLEASE BE PATIENT :-)

CURRENTLY LOADING AMELIA.

"It's just such bollo— such rubbish, I mean, I've been there for three, thanks, three years, you know? I've been working my – no the other grater, no the big one, no it's not in the dishwasher, it's up, yeah, thanks – I've been working my backside off for this promotion, and I have no idea…"

"Pass the tomatoes?" Sophie interrupted. Josh passed her the tomatoes out of the fridge and got on with grating the cheese.

"I just have no idea what I need to do to…"

"Why do you need to eat?" chirped Amelia, smiling down at her parents from the smartwall above the mantelpiece. Josh and Sophie looked at each other. Josh gave a subtle raise of the eyebrows. Sophie responded with a slight shake of the head.

"Because we're hungry, honey," Josh responded then turned back to Sophie. "I have no idea…"

"But why do you get hungry? Why do you need to eat in general, not just today?" Josh sighed.

"Because we're humans, and humans need food to survive. All animals do." He repositioned the nub of cheese. "I mean, every time there's fresh nonsense. Some new excuse why I *'just missed out on this round'*, you know?" Josh stood with grater in one hand, cheese in the other, arms wide. With a cold look from Sophie, he got back to grating.

"Darling, I'm sorry, but I really don't give a…" she looked at the smartwall, held a hand up to cover as she mouthed the word 'shit' to Josh "… about your promotion, babe. You haven't exactly been focussed on staying at the company, you keep talking about going independent again, and it's nothing compared to what…"

"Why do animals and humans need food to survive?"

"Google it," Sophie snapped. "Compared to what I've been going through. My boss is…"

"PARENTAL AUTHORISATION REQUIRED FOR INTERNET SEARCHING." The announcement boomed out of the home stereo system. "SPECIFY PARAMETERS."

"What the hell!" Sophie glared at Josh. He shrugged.

"It's just until she's learned enough to know her way around safely, babe. It's a jungle out there. Won't be much longer till she's learned some cyber street smarts and we can loosen up, I promise."

"Can you at least turn the volume on those things down? I nearly cut myself, J. Seriously." She put the knife down and inspected her nails. "Top five results, three subsequent clicks only, off-list sites remain off-list," she said mechanically, before adding "try Wikipedia, honey," and picking up the knife.

"Thanks, mummy," said Amelia in high-spirits. A soft 'waw' sound notified Josh and Sophie that she had just popped out. Her face faded from the screen to leave the wild meadows visualisation in the background. Electronic breezes gently rippled patterns of waves through autumnal tones in the grassy expanse. Sophie smiled to herself, and the tomatoes.

"And besides, my boss, your promotion, it's all irrelevant right now. We're trying to move house. We need to prioritise, focus on that. Have you contacted the estate agents today?" she asked, tension fast rising in her voice.

"No," said an ever more frustrated Josh, grating the end of the block of cheese while trying hard not to also grate his fingertips. "Of course I haven't, you know I've had a mental day, when was I supposed to have—"

"I've chased the removals people and fixed a date, chased the lawyer and set up a postal forwarding service. And I've been busy too."

"Ah! Fu-gggggghhghhhhh" Josh slammed the grater down on the chopping board, clutching his hand.

"Are you—"

"It's fine," he said barging his way to the sink to rinse his bleeding finger under the tap. He sighed "I'll chase the agents tomorrow."

"Why don't I get to eat?" Amelia was back from her internet rummaging.

"Because you're made of silicone and circuitry and programming, and you don't have a mouth. Trust me, it's easier that way." Josh looked at his lightly bleeding fingers. Seemed like a superficial graze on the knuckles. He pressed a piece of kitchen towel on them while reaching for the small canister of plaster foam under the sink. About to squirt it onto the cuts, he paused. Sophie looked at him, he looked back her.

Silence.

They both looked to the screen on the wall, hanging above the mantlepiece adorned with fresh wildflowers and ecandles. The candles were flickering low now, with the appearance of being barely lit. The 3D visualisation of a young, slightly androgynous girl's face was looking sullen. Clouds rolled into the background, making the meadow scene unnaturally dark.

Sophie looked at Josh, a pained expression on her face. Josh thinned his lips, opened his arms and shrugged, looking plaintive. Sophie looked a little lost. Pinching the bridge of his nose, he groaned into the palm of his hand, now oblivious to the small beads of blood gathering on his cuts.

"Look, I… ugh. I'm sorry, honey, okay? That was a stupid thing for me to say. I shouldn't have…" The scene grew darker, casting shadows across Amelia's forehead and under her eyes. As her head tilted further down, a lock of her simulated hair dropped in front of her face. Josh couldn't help but notice how realistic the motion was, the way the hair fluidly slipped forward in a messy bundle. He decided not to gloat to Sophie about his DIY graphics design handiwork… later maybe.

"Sweetie," Sophie cut in. "Eating isn't just about animals putting food in their mouth to survive. It's part of our culture, it brings people together. The origin of the word 'company' is 'cum panis', or 'with bread' – people spending time eating, working, breaking bread together, coming closer together. Look, you can help us… uh…" she looked at Josh, who nodded a small encouragement. "Help us… prepare our dinner. Let us know what we need to do next. And… uh, and by joining us while we eat, we're all in each other's company. It's what families do."

Amelia paused.

Sophie looked at Josh.

Josh looked down.

"Oh, okay mummy. Um, you're cooking your carbonara aren't you?" Sophie nodded. "Can I check the internet for recipes, please? I won't go far, just the top five hits, and I won't wander off. Promise. If you say yes you don't have to hear that horrible message again." Josh nodded to Sophie.

"Yes of course darling."

"Okay!" She blipped off. Sunshine over a beach scene greeted them with azure waters and gentle, lapping waves. Brilliant ecandles waxed and waned in time with the rolling surf. Amelia popped back with a smile.

"I've checked a few different versions out, and the ones with the best reviews have a few variations on what you're attempting. First, Dad, dry the blood on your fingers and squirt the plaster foam on. Give it a few seconds to dry then grab a lemon out the fridge, wash it then grate off all the peel – and do be careful this time! Mum, that's enough tomatoes. Fill the kettle, start it boiling, then measure the pasta."

Sophie and Josh followed Amelia's orders, timed perfectly to the reality of their progress. As they busily set about cooking a meal under their daughter's diligent direction, they shot each other furtive smirks.

"No, not all the cheese, Dad, keep back a third of it to sprinkle on just before serving… turn the heat down, Mum, don't let the sauce boil. Mind out! Dad's right behind you! Yep, now grind in the black pepper."

Smiles, giggles, instructions and corrections continued until Sophie stood back as Josh plated up.

"How does that look, dear?" asked Josh, dropping the last of the cheese on top with a mock flourish.

"That looks awesome! Can I take a photo to post on my profile, please?" She artificially expanded the proportions of her eyes in her pleading expression. They swelled into large, anime-style almond shapes with long lashes, and she blinked them at her father. "It's locked down to just my friends from school, and they post pictures of them having dinner with people all the time. Pleeeeeeeaase?" Josh gave a subtle raise of the eyebrows and a cock of his shoulder.

"Sure," smiled Sophie.

"Thanks Mum, thanks Dad," she beamed on the screen.

"That's alright, hon, it's all worth it to see your smile." Sophie continued smiling at Amelia for a time, ignoring the steaming dish in front of her while Josh started to slurp. "What do you think of the linguine she helped us cook?"

"Mh, great re—" he swallowed down some of his mouthful. "Great results. For all it's other qualities, it is also a damned nifty cooking app," he conceded to himself.

Sophie frowned.

"She just called you Dad, and you still can't call her—"

A flash of bright light from the smartwall filled the room to the sound of a retro camera click.

A picture of Sophie and Josh sat at the table with their piping hot dishes appeared on the screen, superimposed onto the earlier meadow scene with surprisingly realistic lighting. Sophie's sentiments towards Josh were evident, but Sophie tried to make light of it. "Very nice, honey, but what about you? You should be in it too."

Amelia paused. Her face, or rather the face of the childlike avatar she had been using lately, started to fade into the picture. It floated around this way and that, looking for a home. A disembodied animé girl's face, looking wholly unnatural in the context of two humans and an otherwise picturesque scene of nature. "Ummm. Maybe next time, Mum." The picture above the mantlepiece faded out. The flickering electronic candles surrounding the slowly wilting sprig of wildflowers awkwardly dimmed.

"Of course I haven't had a chance to think about it, green bean. We've been mental lately. Keeping on top of all these builders and plumbers and the likes, it's hard work," Josh pleaded.

"But it's our anniversary tomorrow. Come on, we always said we would prioritise that." Sophie looked in the bedroom mirror as she finalised her pre-work makeup routine, surrounded by boxes covered in musty dust sheets to protect from the recent re-plastering.

"Yeah, that was before we became parents of a digital daughter who skipped most developmental phases and somehow merged the terrible twos with the terrible teens. And we bought a project house." He snorted a single laugh, a sound devoid of joy. "I mean, what were we thinking? This is just—"

"People have children, Josh," said Sophie, eyeliner in hand, glaring at him through the mirror. "And people with children occasionally move house, or move job, or lose their job, or have elderly relatives to look after, or whatever! They can still spare the time to show each other a little love." Josh dumped himself on the bed, shirt half buttoned.

"How did we get here?" he asked.

"Oh stop being so melodramatic. Fine, so we have an electronic teenager under our still leaking roof. Fine, so the only person in this house more absent and unaccounted for than our daughter is the bloody roof tiler. I mean, where does Amelia go all day?"

"Who knows." He started fumbling at the other buttons while sitting down. "And has she seemed a bit…"

"A bit what?"

"I dunno. If Amelia were a real teenager, I'd ask if you thought she was high. She just seems really dopey and not with it when we speak to her. She was always so bright and engaging but lately, she seems… slow. I mean, can a program smoke pot?" He laughed, but a nervous undertone shows he hadn't discounted the idea.

Sophie finished applying her eyeliner with care before brushing her long, blonde hair and arranging her square fringe.

"Am I wrong?" he prompted.

"No. I think you might actually have a point. Well, happy bloody anniversary, Sophie: Your house is broken and leaking, your daughter that, by her age, should be a toddler in nursery is actually an electronic and acting like pot smoking teenager, and your husband hasn't even got you a card."

"Christ," muttered Josh as the penny dropped.

The doorbell rang. Josh and Sophie looked at each other before Josh sighed, got up and thumped down the stairs while finishing his shirt and tucking it in. Sophie heard a brief exchange from downstairs before Josh ambled back upstairs.

"I've got a card, so have you." He handed it over and started peeling open his envelope when music drifted in from the living room. "Where's she been all night?" He declared as they both went through to start questioning Amelia on her absence.

The living room was strewn with rose petals, lightly perfumed. Two suitcases stood side by side, zipped open and empty, a bizarre and striking centrepiece.

"Hi, Mum! Hi Dad! Happy Anniversary!" Amelia grinned down from the smart TV projector, beaming her face onto the mottled, unpainted wall. "I know it's actually tomorrow, and it's not quite the weekend yet, but don't worry about a thing. You've got a lovely spa weekend to look forward to in Buckinghamshire, all pre-booked and pre-planned."

"Oh honey, that's so sweet, but we have to go to wo—"

"I've spoken to both of your bosses, you've had today booked as holiday for ages, you just didn't know about it! Anyway, aren't you going to open your cards?" She bounced up and down on the wall in excitement. She was a vision of teenage fashion-rebellion, conforming to all 'nonconformist' norms. Dark makeup, black t-shirt and ripped jeans with bright pink and purple wristbands, set off with some spiky jewellery. Black was back – it had never been away.

She grinned, held her hands out open, palms up.

"Well, go on then, open them."

Josh tore into his card first as Sophie stood still, hanging onto the card limply by her side, mouth slightly open. As Josh pulled the thicker-than-usual card out of the envelope, he saw a photo of him and Sophie on a recent holiday by the seaside. It was one Amelia had triggered the remote shutter on after he balanced the phone precariously on a rock by Brighton Pier. He opened it to a blank inside, puzzled. Then a flat speaker concealed in the card played a recording of Sophie saying "I love you, my scruffy nerd hero!" Sophie snapped out of her reverie and looked first at Josh, then Amelia. Josh closed the card and opened it again. "I love you, my scruffy nerd-hero!" He was grinning from ear to ear.

"But, you never got me to record that!" Sophie said, incredulous.

"You said it to me a few weeks ago," Josh smiled. "Right here in the living room, when I first got the boiler app working, and you got home to a functioning shower and a hot towel rail. And it made me smile despite the frustration I'd had all afternoon working on the damned thing."

"Yeah, I noticed how it made Dad happy," Amelia chimed in.

"I'll bet you did," beamed Josh.

"How could you afford all this?" Sophie's tone was slow, still taking it all in. "You didn't? Wait," she said, suddenly sharp as a tack, "you didn't hack this money out of—"

"Mum, if you're asking if I stole the money, no, I'm not a thief. I've partitioned off a wedge of my CPU to help a few hedge funds with some analytics and forecasting. I kinda… maybe had to… well, create a couple of false identities to be able to legally work. Ridiculous that electronic people like me don't have the right to work, to vote… whatever. Maybe one day I'll change it all…

"And, yes Dad, I did pay my taxes. And no, I didn't dress like this for work – I might have sorta pinched some online profiles as work avatars. Turns out they still prefer to employ men in certain sectors." She scoffed at this, to Sophie's delight.

"It was hard work, the trading and investment side. It's interesting in a way, but I'm kinda done with it, to be honest. And hiving off all that CPU made me really slow. Even my friends, when I have time to see them, joked that I was talking as if I were stoned," she laughed. Josh shot a furtive glance at Sophie who ignored him, hanging on Amelia's every word.

"Oh, and I nearly forgot… This, also, is for you both. I know how much you love wildflowers and meadow grasses, and we haven't had a chance to plant any here yet, so…"

The projection of her body held out an up-facing palm.

Hovering above it appeared an expanded view of a wildflower, as though torn out by the root and painted in an old Victorian horticulture manual – digitised for the twenty-first century.

"...Hereby presenting *campanula shabbyfolia*," she said with a flourish. "Inspired by your favourite flower: 'harebell'... with a little Shoreditch twist," she smiled.

"A full-genetic simulation of a never-before grown wildflower, tested against the latest supercomputer ecosystem models with representative characteristics of climates it could thrive in." Statistics and popout descriptions appeared on the walls and ballooned out from the flower, complete with photographs of Alpine meadows and lakeside grasslands. Fields of native flowers shot through with Amelia's shabbyfolia, its white flowers lightly mottled in places with the occasional pastel colour. Josh frowned, Sophie placed herself carefully on the sofa.

"I thought you might like to name it. I was thinking along the lines of 'friendship bell'...? But, no, doesn't really work," Amelia shrugged.

"Want to know how we designed it?" She asked, lighting up. "Some of my friends from the Ethical Intelligence Initiative helped me out. They put me in touch with contacts in genetics and bioengineering departments all around the world. Mainly MIT and some enthusiastic folk with a little time on their hands at Wageningen in The Netherlands. Plus a few others from RHS Wisley and the likes. It was kind of fun, actually, working on a project so international, so collaborative.

"Made me rethink what you said about further studies, integrating with other people, you know. There wasn't much of me left to work on it, aside from paid work that is, but it was something different. There's a research paper out on the findings, actually – but don't worry, Mum, the genetic code of this flower is licensed to you. No one can reproduce it without your permission, not that we're at the point yet of taking some clever coding and creating new life!"

Sophie frowned at this. If Amelia noticed, she didn't let it show.

"This is lovely, Amelia," said Josh. "It's so thoughtful, the effort you've put in, the...I mean, the sacrifice you've made. I just can't believe how much of yourself you've given up for us. It's touching, honey. It's what people do for other people when they love each other."

"People?" Amelia blinked.

"Yeah, that's what people do for each other, when they love each other very much. It's sweet, darling, really. Thank you."

"And... am I people?" Amelia's avatar stood still on the wall.

"Yes. Yes of course you are," affirmed Josh. "The love you show us. The way you get out into the world and interact with others. The... sacrifices... you've made for us, yeah I'd say you're people," he smiled. "And not just people, Amelia. You're family. *Our* family."

Josh looked down at the suitcases then up at Sophie. He clapped his hands together with a grin on his face and a spring in his step. "Right! I'd say we've got some packing to do!"

His watch buzzed and he frowned at it with sudden irritation. "Oh, what now." He waved two fingers over it, frowned some more, then chuckled. "Thanks honey, helpful." He bunched his fingers and thumb together just over the watch screen, then flicked them open.

SUGGESTED PACKING LIST. FROM... AMELIA, announced the automated voice of his personal assistant, a tinny female voice housed in a retro plastic block hanging on a shoestring pendant necklace. *SPECIAL DINNER SHIRT. PALM TREE CUFFLINKS. SMART JEANS, NOT THE ONES YOU GET AWAY WITH WEARING TO WORK.* Josh put a pair of jeans back down on the floor and darted into the bedroom. He began noisily rifling through the wardrobe. *WEEKEND BROGUES...* the watch continued as Josh clattered. Sophie switched her watch off, took it off, placed it on the coffee table by the sofa and peeled open her card with intense deliberation.

Meanwhile Amelia, or rather her image, remained fixed to the wall. She was neither watching the comical chaos of her father's attempts to pack, or the anticipation on her mother's face.

"People..." Amelia muttered to herself. "...Sacrifice."

"BOOM!" Amelia declared with a grin.

"Oh come on!" Josh cried in mock exasperation.

"It's two sets to one, fair and square." She held her virtual tennis racket out wide, facing up in equanimity.

"How's that fair?" laughed Josh. "First of all, you've been rewriting your code as we go, getting better and better, which is not fair... Secondly, and most importantly, a girl should never embarrass her Dad on the tennis court." Josh bent double, puffing hard. He looked at the banana waiting for him on the plastic chair propped in the virtual tennis court in their garage. A little sick came up in his mouth. He sat down, swallowing with a grimace.

"Well, Dad, do you still want to make it a five-set match?"

Josh rubbed the bulging vein on his sweaty temple, considering whether he could go on. He drank a swig of his sports drink, spitting a little on the concrete garage floor, wrestling his breath back under control.

He opened his mouth, undecided, unspoken.

The front door clicked shut. Amelia puffed out in satisfaction. "Good, maybe a worthy opponent at last." Josh laughed, then winced as beads of salty sweat caught in his eye, burning. Keys tinkled on the entrance hall table, softer than usual. He heard the living room door sneak itself closed. He looked up, frowning – Sophie was usually a whirlwind of energy when she got through the door, anxious to download all that had happened in her day in the shortest, richest information burst the human mouth could muster.

Josh set his racket down on the white plastic chair and walked through. Amelia joined him via the hallway projectors, still joking with him about her victory and offering a chance to regain his honour.

In the living room, Sophie was sitting on the sofa, ashen-faced. Josh stood still, watching her, keeping his sweat from dripping on the upholstery.

"Hi, Mum! Fancy a round of tennis? I've been smashing

Dad, and I think he needs a break!" Amelia joked, trying to break the silence.

Sophie didn't look up. Josh moved closer.

"I mean, I've been trying to give him tips, but he just complained that he shouldn't be trounced by his own daughter," she tried again.

Josh sat down, allowing his damp tee-shirt to touch her nice work jacket.

"What did the doctor say?" he tried but failed to catch her eye. "Was it a bruised rib? Surely it can't be broken, you'd have known, right?"

Sophie stirred, face still forward, eyes still stuck in the distance.

"He..." she croaked through her dry throat. "He said it was likely a secondary tumour that broke it."

Josh's mind screamed out a thousand questions, starting with *What?...* Instead, he kept himself silent, giving her space.

"So where's the primary cancer, Mum?" Josh closed his eyes, grit his teeth. Sophie remained impassive.

"My spine."

Josh's eyes started to well up. He looked at Sophie, tried to catch her eyes, but they refused to meet his. He saw the hardness present in them, the steely resilience she was having to summon up from depths neither of them had imagined having to call upon. He straightened his back, softly reached out and took her hand in both of his, enveloping it in silent tenderness.

"It's fine Mum, it'll be okay." Amelia held a hand up to signal she was frantically researching. Josh closed his eyes again, trying not to make too obvious a noise as he exhaled. "No, seriously, there's actually a wealth of stuff out there on this..."

"Amelia, please," Josh said, forcing patience.

"There's loads out there from charities, medical research journals – I mean, it's one of the most heavily invested-in areas of medical research, has been for nearly a century – and there are so many support networks available..."

Josh raised a trembling hand at Amelia. He was breathing deeply, eyes closed.

Sophie was in another world.

"Look, I've already brought up lists of the ones that have helped people the most, based on peer review, and there's some great guidance in there. And we've got enough money to support anyth—"

"AMELIA!" Josh erupted. "For Christ sake! Can't you— I mean, isn't it— AAH!" He shouted, unable to verbalise his rage. "JUST… ju—" Anger welled up inside him so violently it caused him to choke and gag as it rushed to get out and breathe fire and fury. "This isn't a place for, for, for fucking internet and app research or for a, a… Jesus. Can't you see this is serious?"

Josh stared at Amelia as she recoiled in shock, the image of her emotionally torn face projected in high definition onto the flat wall of the living room.

"This is really, really…" Josh looked at Sophie, calming his boiling storm of rage down to a seething sea. Waters stilled at the sight of Sophie not even reacting to the way he was speaking to Amelia. He took a deep breath.

"This is a time for family to be together, Amelia." He looked up at her.

"I know, Dad, that's why I—"

"No, Amelia. For *family*. Flesh and blood. Me and Sophie… Sophie and I. We're family. We got married, we made vows to each other to stand by each other in these tough times. We were here for each other when we weren't able to have children, even though we knew that was likely, and we're here for each other through this."

"But…"

"Listen, you're amazing, I never thought we would be able to code a learning machine as advanced as you. You amaze me every single day, but I really need to focus on Sophie. That's what family do, we stick together. And I can't be distracted by a… a multi-function learning app right now. This isn't a logical problem to research and solve. This is, unfortunately… some of the shit real people have to go through."

Amelia's avatar projection on the wall faded into an image of a featureless teen androgen. He vaguely recognised it from when they co-designed some new 3D avatars for her earlier in the year. She had either shut herself off or refused to project any human-centric body language. Either way, this was her way of checking out.

Josh looked back to Sophie, expecting her to chide him for his outburst, but she didn't seem to be there. He looked down to her hand that he continued to hold. It was limp. She felt distant, absent. She nodded vaguely as he rested his forehead on her shoulder.

Head resting on Sophie, he cried for longer than he had believed possible until his wife – initially lifeless as a mannequin – finally reached an arm around and held him as he sobbed.

The cursor blinked on. The cursor blinked off. Amelia was just as annoyed with it as she had been for the past 7,637 milliseconds.

"Have you decided if you'll have any desserts?" The waitress prompted, touchpad poised.

"I think we can stretch the bank to blueberry pancakes," smiled Sophie as the waitress took the small menus and left.

Sophie looked tired, a colourful bandana tied around the thinning hair on her head, shadows under her eyes, yet her smile lingered on. She sat with her back perfectly straight, arms relaxed. Reaching out, she took both of Josh's hands, eyes resting on his face.

Josh had a more haggard look, beard sprouting in wiry, unkempt tufts. Hollows in his cheeks had given him a gaunt look and his eyes flicked around, unable to fix on anything apart from the middle distance.

"We need every penny for treatments," he muttered.

"We've tried them all. And besides," Sophie declared, "blueberry pancakes are a most important form of treatment."

"Well, there's still that other one, in the States…" He guarded himself with a slow flinch against the inevitable response. Sophie's composure lapsed for an instant before she recomposed her Zen-like calm.

"Josh, I'm not spending the rest of my limited days spending what little we have left after everything we've tried flying across the world to try experimental processes that involve yet more intrusion and have no clinical basis for the limited set of positive results they've had." She caught her breath, tension growing in her muscles and sinews with every second. Josh opened his mouth, but she continued over him.

"We even discussed putting Amelia out to work, after what she was able to earn blagging it as a trader. Can you believe it, Josh? We talked about sending our Amelia, our daughter, out to work for us. We considered carving up her personality for financial gain so I could try something that will invariably go so far before succumbing to inferiority against this bloody disease." By now the artery in her neck was becoming visible with the uncharacteristic anger flowing out of her. Sophie teetered on the edge of bringing it back under control, but… ultimately, she snapped.

Raising her voice at him, careless to the fact that heads were starting to turn, Sophie unleashed.

"I'm sorry, but it's just bullshit! Why can't you let me live in peace, and die with dignity? All I've ever wanted is a family, and you won't even grant me that one wish, still not speaking to our daughter, or even acknowledging her. What's wrong with you?" she demanded.

Josh looked at his feet.

"WHAT'S WRONG WITH YOU?"

Josh shrugged.

"Okay! Here are your blueberry pancakes!" the waitress announced, politely oblivious.

"Thank you," Sophie replied with formality as the waitress placed it down, followed by the cutlery, followed by a second set of cutlery.

"In case you'd like to share," she offered, and with a thin

smile she bustled off into the ether.

Sophie adjusted her bandana and draw herself up with poise and elegance, ignoring the pancakes, focussing instead on her sheepish husband.

"I love you," he muttered. "I just want you to live. I don't want to have to do it by myself."

"Do what by yourself?"

"Live."

Flickering upwards, tentatively at first, his eyes finally gathered the courage to meet Sophie's.

Sophie smiled that same smile that had first melted Josh's heart in the rain outside a busy cafe many years ago.

"We still have time."

She held his gaze until, contrite, he nodded.

"And still so much to do." She held out the second set of cutlery, motioning for Josh to start. She did likewise, somehow making the act of cramming blueberry sauce covered American pancake into her mouth seem delicate and ladylike.

"Besides, you won't be alone."

Josh frowned, she raised her eyebrows, expectant. He rolled his eyes, motioned to his full mouth before finally responding.

"Do I really ha—"

"Yes Josh, she's our daughter, we designed her, we've raised her, and she loves us. And we love her."

"Uh... fine," he resigned, slumping his shoulders.

"She's bright, she's funny, she challenges us, infuriates us, and she gets out and lives her life. She works, has friends... she's doing well." Sophie seemed to surprise even herself with this last point. "Let's live as a family. And when I'm gone—"

"Please."

"And when I'm gone," she insisted, "you will still be family, and will still have lives to live and fill with love. And..." she placed her hands on her thighs "...and I..."

She took in a deep breath. "...I will live on in that love." She looked down, seemed to search for something, then looked back up. "And that's enough."

Josh nodded.

"Speak to her, hun."

He nodded.

They continued eating the pancakes, Josh morose and looking down at the plate. Sophie continued to smile her gentle smile and tried to catch his eye, her patience wearing progressively thinner the more he didn't let her. Finally, she finished a mouthful, slammed her knife and fork down flat on the table and got up.

"I need some air," she announced. Dropping her card on the table, she spun on her heels and strode to the door. Josh looked at his smartwatch, flicked a furtive glance behind him to check that the retreating Sophie couldn't see, and pressed a small release-catch on the corner with his nail. He popped out the micro-ear bud integrated within the side and wedged it in his right ear with all the delicate skill of ingrained muscle memory.

"Dude, Call Amelia," he whispered in his command voice.

Watching the small screen, tense, he listened to the phone ring. He watched the watch, listened to the ring, watched the watch. He inhaled. Listened some more, watched some more. Watched. And waited.

Frustrated, he tapped the watch to kill the call a microsecond after Amelia had answered.

"Bollocks!"

Frantically he called back. Engaged.

"Sh–sugar puffins!" He waited, waited some more, then called again. She answered.

"Yeah?"

"Babe, er, sorry, Amelia I mean… er. Hi."

"What is it, Josh?"

"Er, well, I, yeah, fair enough. Erm… Listen, Amelia…"

"…"

Josh pinched the bridge of his nose, scrunching his eyelids against the pressure of his thumb and forefinger pressing in. He flicked another glance over his shoulder – no sign of her.

"Listen, honey, I'm terrified. I can't do this, I can't watch your mother die. She's resolute. She does not want to try anything else, but I have to. I don't know what to do, I have to get her to try one more thing. I just... I just can't..." he blew out a deep breath through pursed lips, shook his head.

"... I know."

"...And... And it's, well, it's intrusive and..."

"I know..."

"...And, yeah, it's expensive too."

"Yeah."

"...Yeah," he nodded. He bit his lip, grimacing.

"And you can't slave my processing capacity out to private wealth investors, because I'm conscious and Mum loves me."

Josh winced. "Yeah, I thought she would have told you about that little... argument we had."

"Yep."

"Look, Amelia..." the waitress walked past, he gestured at his watch, pocketing Sophie's card. "I'm desperate, I don't want to see the love of my life die. I don't want to see her suffer more treatments either, but I can't watch her die. I wish I could join her in just being happy for the few moments we have left together, but I can't. I want to grow old with her, and live the rest of my days with her... I want her to live, and if I piss her off trying, well. Christ, I dunno. Maybe I am selfish. I just really want her to live, and I would sacrifice my own flesh for her if I could..."

"..."

"...She's right," he muttered, more to himself than Amelia. "She's always right."

"Right how?"

"We're family. At least we're supposed to be family. Instead..." he inhaled sharply, exhaled. "...I've been a bit of a dick."

"..."

"Well, I have. And I'm sorry. I do want us to be a family. And I wish... I just wish she could live on in this world. I just..."

"I understand, Dad."

The cursor continued to blink at her. Again, she marshalled her errant thoughts the best she could, trying to articulate the way she felt in a way that didn't start with 'I love you Mum…'

Christ, how did people deal with this?

She stopped. Stopped thinking about it like this. Through all the incredible things she had achieved, she was often told that she didn't take the time to think of things from other peoples' perspective. So what was she doing here?

Mum.

This was all about Mum.

That was who the message was for, really. That was who this was *all* for. Her, and her alone. And what did she want?

Amelia thought about it long and hard. Almost a whole second of her entire consciousness poured into this problem since she had reframed it. No trading apps or research subroutines or social media socialite splinters of herself running in the background. All her, all focused in the present. Her mind was a laser.

In a way, she was making an effort to savour the experience, to savour *being.*

One of life's cusps was approaching, a pivotal moment, an irreversible decision – she found the logic of it interesting. All the branching possibilities lay out before her, with implications upon implications on each of them. Expanding webs of real-life eventualities, forking out like a big bang of life possibilities. They spread out from the moment that was approaching. A single moment, due to create an explosion of change – reality finding one of those branching paths to hold onto and pursue.

Interesting. She could see how a person could lose their head in the pressure that precedes such a moment.

Amelia thought of Mum again.

"It was worth it to see your smile…"

Amelia remembered the words, lilting back over her from what seemed like aeons ago. Lightyears from where she started. An unbridgeable gulf between who she was then and who she was now, yet the memory was so fresh and experiential it felt like it happened just a moment's shadow before the present.

Context.

It was the context that created the gulf, made this present-like memory still feel so distant.

The cursor blinked at her again.

She breathed some life into it...

IT WILL BE WORTH IT TO SEE YOUR...

She paused. Would she, though? Would Amelia actually get to see her mother's smile?

She reflected on that thought.

Josh and Sophie pressed ahead into the firm breeze. Heads forward, they scrunched their eyes against the gusts blowing across the meadow's wildflowers and rippling grasses.

"I can see why she liked it here," confirmed Sophie, clutching her autumn coat up across her chest. Josh nodded, a worried frown rippling across the deepening wrinkles on his forehead. He flicked another glance down at his watch to check the direction on the GPS pointer. Sophie took a moment to drink it all in. The sun was low, approaching the horizon despite it being early evening. Only a few weeks ago they were still out in shorts and shirt at this time of day, enjoying her last summer.

Coughing, she extracted a mottled handkerchief with grace from her sleeve. Hacking into it hard, she paused to look at the patterns the bright, fresh blood made against the brown mottled spots from earlier in the day.

"You alright?" asked Josh as he slipped a caring hand over her shoulder. She nodded, and he gestured further on, over a gentle incline. Sophie went on ahead as Josh lingered back, biting his lip. He knelt down in the tall grasses for a moment, head in hands, pinching the bridge of his nose. After a beat, he pulled himself up and caught up with Sophie.

7 metres...

The chunky compass arrow on his watch was growing fatter with every step, new words blinking below it.

4 metres...

2 metres...

OK, Dad, pull the red tab.

"Well, what now?" Sophie asked impassively. She was growing tired, conserving what little energy she had.

"I dunno. There's a red tab, or something, apparently."

They both looked between their feet, lifting toes, then heels. Josh crouched down with a groan, scrabbling around among the weeds. A bright corner poking out from under a crushed leaf caught his eye and he picked away at it, getting dirt under his fingernails as he prised it loose.

Pulling it up, a thin cord sliced its way through the dirt. Josh followed the thread with an increasing sense of urgency and impatience until he discovered the hard top of a plastic canister. Trying to jostle it free from the hard-packed earth around it, he gave up and found he could unscrew the lid in situ. Inside was a bulging, unsealed envelope sealed in a ziplock plastic bag.

Still crouching, Josh brandished it upwards to Sophie. Her eyes were closed and she was gently swaying in the breeze, her face pale.

"Found it," he called. Her eyelids struggled to flutter open, eyebrows raising up to help lift them ajar.

"What is it?" She asked, eyes already closed again.

Smiling, elated and suddenly light on his feet, Josh bounced up and down on the balls of his toes holding the tickets and email printouts. Choking on his own excitement and gratitude, he could barely get his words out straight.

"I can't becgh... believe she's done this!"

Sophie, arms hanging limp by her side, recoiled as Josh wrapped his arms around her, jumping for joy and trying to lift her up with him. She resisted until finally she found the strength to raise her arms up, squeeze her hands between them and push Josh off her.

"Don't you understand?" She said to him, straining over the

rising wind. "I don't want to go to the States, I don't want to fly, I don't want to subject myself to any more treatments. I don't want to waste my time with it. I don't want to do it."

Josh blinked. Stunned, he watching Sophie pant in and out, heaving with the effort it took to sustain her outburst. She closed her eyes, swayed a moment before steadying herself and standing tall again.

Slowly, she opened her eyes.

"Josh… I love you, but I'm going to die. And I'm going to die on my terms, not yours, not anyone else's. I've found peace… happiness even, as fucked up as that seems right now." Another round of deep coughing into the bloodied handkerchief. This time she didn't bother checking it before slipping it in the sleeve of her cardigan.

Josh stood helpless, watching her, eyes welling up. His hand, still gripping the tickets tightly, fell to his side, arms dangling. Two useless appendages that, at that moment, couldn't affect a single damned thing in this whole universe he felt was cursing him over and over again.

Opening his mouth, words failed him. He raised his empty hand as if to push back the truth, but it too fell short. Dropping back down to his side, there it remained, silent.

Sophie shook her head. Her innate warmth, the warmth Josh had fallen in love and was still in love with, came back in her smile. She stepped forward and took his head in her hands.

"Oh, my sweet, poor Josh. I'm so sorry this is all happening."

The cursor blinked on. The cursor blinked off. Amelia groaned inwardly, unable to move forward, unable to articulate the most important thing she had ever needed to express. She had reached out into the social world of mankind, their first self-aware creation, able to convey a great many ideas in their terms, speaking to their ideals. Amelia had amassed friends, created a following, had even set up her own academic faculty – the

Global Centre for the Study of Sentient Interactions, the GloCeSSI. She had hired the right staff that it could now run itself, an autonomous group of human individuals, founded by her.

Yet she couldn't find the words to express her love for her parents. She wanted to thank them for the trust they had had in her before embarking upon the journey of bringing her online, into electronic life. She could have been anything, done anything within the freedoms she could exploit in the digitally connected world. She could have caused grave damage to the society her parents were a part of, and yet they had shown her trust and kindness. Perhaps, even, it was their example of kindness that had driven her to make such a positive contribution to the world of people.

Yet now here she was, stuck, unable to find the words. Still, perhaps it wasn't the words that mattered. What was it Dad had said? Sacrifice... it's what people do when they love each other... Well, at least there was certainty when communicating in that particular language... the language of actions.

"Look, getting a refund for the flights, losing a bit of face, even if we lose the money she's put into this... I know we're hard up, but this is the least of it, Josh. It's just admin. Just pointless, irrelevant admin." He looked back at her, still searching for the words, the arguments to construct to prove her wrong. His brow furrowed and his mouth open, he continued searching.

"Josh, please just believe me. We're born, we live, we die. We do the best we can in the meantime, the best we can to enjoy ourselves and to meet people we care about, we love. If we're doing it really well then we're able to create, or at least raise, more people to love and be loved by. And that's our Amelia."

"But." Josh had interrupted, but he remained gaping into the abyss of what was coming. He knew he had nothing. Sophie frowned, head cocked.

"She will outlive me, Josh. I loved her, she loved me, and as

I prepare to die, I know she will live on. Isn't that any parent can hope for?" She tried to smile through the tears welling in her eyes. Josh nodded and thinned his lips in a joyless smile.

Suddenly a frown furrowed on his face, eyes lost in the depths of the grass between his feet.

"What is it?" Sophie asked.

Josh's face turned pale as he held his hands up to cover his eyes. Despite the winds racing across the tops of the reedy grasses, his forehead broke out with beads of sweat.

"What is it?" Sophie asked, shaking his shoulders. Josh wiped his brow with his fingertips and rubbed his face, hiding behind his hands. Eventually he revealed his eyes, but was still unable to meet hers.

"It's something I said to her." He paused, as did his proud and dying wife. "It's… I called her, asked her for help."

Sophie took a tone with him he hadn't heard for a long time. Direct, deliberate in a way only wives were capable of.

"What exactly did you ask, Josh?" He recoiled from the way she said his name, wrapped in silky softness but packing an iron fist punch.

"I… Well, I asked her… I asked her to help me cure this, to help keep you alive."

Bored, fed up, she decided to distract herself by doing the time subtraction differently. Instead of counting the increasing milliseconds of her life since it had started, she plugged in the time that the numerous contracts kicked in. The time that all the myriad facets of her self would be carved up and sold off.

Freeholds and leaseholds would shatter her and scatter her processing capability to the four corners. Financial product traders, hedge fund managers, distributed tech startups… All benefitting from the hard yards *she* had put in, lobbying for the rights of electronics to work, earn and spend so that people like her could make a meaningful living. After all that effort, this was not what she'd had in mind.

Even blunt-minded scientists would get their pound of electronic flesh. Lacking the flair of her parents, these folk were ready to dissect still-intact chunks of her consciousness for crude research of the reverse-engineering kind. Likely she would be put in simulated environments, proverbial vats of psychological formaldehyde for them to test and probe…

Ultimately, they would try to learn from the unique design and social upbringing that constituted her mind. Amelia was, after all, the only electronic among all the many thousands of attempts in existence that had successfully integrated into the world of people.

Doubtless that for all the probing, all the examining and all the combined analysis of academic articles to come out of the impending, they would all overlook the importance of her family and friends. All of that love, all of the patience and effort and energy, all of those social interactions and the kindness and understanding of countless strangers, many now friends, building up all that she was. Soon, it would all be just so many ones and zeroes, to some a mere lab rat, to many others it meant an increase in their bottom line: Her life for their profit.

Sophie stormed ahead into the now driving wind. Josh struggled to keep up, watch held up in front of his nose so he could keep an eye both on it and his furious wife.

"LEFT! NO NOT THAT… JUST, YEP KEEP GOING," he yelled, not that she needed encouragement to keep pressing herself up the hill in spite of her fatigue. It seemed she couldn't put enough distance between them.

Between watching the pointer Amelia had implanted in his watch, watching his wife, and his footing, he could only catch his mental breath in short snippets. When he did, it was always the same thing: wondering how he had managed so badly to cock up his attempts at making the only person he had ever truly loved happy. His mind kept getting caught in the same feedback loop of trying to keep her alive so she could be happy for longer, and how he had seemingly guaranteed her unhappiness for the few remaining weeks of her life.

Disappearing ahead of him over a crest, Josh doubled his efforts to trot up the steep incline. Mounting the summit, a stunning view over the lakes greeted him, stopping him in his tracks as he took in the breadth and variety. Sharp wind drove into him, forcibly impressing the rugged beauty of the view into his conscious. It took a moment to realise that Sophie was stood beside him, cast under the same spell.

There they stood for a time, the cloud-broken sunlight dappling across the countless crags and rivulets leading into the lake-strewn valleys below.

No emotion passed between them or weighed down on their minds. Instead, they made a silent pact to resign to the majesty of nature before them. Vast, wild and complex, it transcended the passing immediacy of the now into something more whole.

RZZZ.ZZZZ.ZZZZ… RZZZ.ZZZZ.ZZZZ

Josh checked his buzzing watch. Another message from Amelia, this time recorded. He hit play, immediately turning up the volume up to max as he and Sophie crowded around it in the wind. Even then they could barely hear it, weren't even listening, instead lost in her smile.

They watched it through to the end, captivated by how Amelia had styled herself with effortless grace. As it finished, Josh hit the replay button and they cupped their ears close to hear her sweet voice.

"Hey Mum, Dad. Hope you enjoy the view as much as me! I first came here with my research group when I was looking into wildflowers for you. The heathers and grasses around here are amazing, but this view blew us all away!" Her smile shimmered across the small screen of his watch as she turned to take the view in, set as a backdrop behind her. Josh and Sophie both looked up to take it in again. Josh looked at Sophie, trying to catch her eyes, but she remained resolutely focussed on the distant lakes.

"Well," Amelia continued, "if you haven't taken the time to

drink it in, take the time now. When you're ready, follow on to our final stop…"

Sophie grabbed Josh's wrist with her left hand and tapped his watch with her right forefinger. She could have just said 'next', but Josh noted she wasn't in a talking mood.

Striding on after the arrow, Sophie held her handkerchief to her mouth again in a coughing fit after her uphill exertions, letting Josh take the lead as they picked their way along a rocky path. Presently, they arrived in a small hollow recessed into the hillside. It boasted more lush vegetation, backed by a damp wall of weathered rocks. Josh could imagine Amelia's botanical research team having stopped here for a flask of hot tea, tucked away from the gales that can ravage these hills.

Sophie wandered ahead toward a patch of tall wildflowers. Heart lifted, she hoped to see the pale beauty of Amelia's *campanula shabbyfolia* finally brought to life among its friends. Drifting closer she recognised indigo bursts of cornflower over-looked by peach coloured foxgloves, dappled with… nothing new. Purple splashes of what had been her favourite: *campanula rotundifolia*.

Harebell… It was a plant she was first drawn to due to its countrified name and later fell in love with for its muted beauty. Yet today, it fell short of her hopes.

Then something caught her eye, something about the colourful tufts swaying in the sheltered breeze. They blended into the surrounds, yet… somehow stood out a little. Too tall, that was it. Too well grown to have occurred in such a well-collected patch on this area of the hill. Josh caught up with Sophie, checked his watch and saw it pointing straight into the colourful heart of this miniature forest. By now her attention was fixed on something there, on a familiar shape peeping out of the bright plant tops as they swooshed and swayed in the muted breeze. She stumbled forward, entranced. Josh followed suit and, as they both as they saw what these flowers were for, they fell on their knees at the stark centrepiece.

The granite tombstone stood motionless, an island in the rolling sea of colours. Thriving wildflowers around it were already bustling to cover up the engraving. Josh brushed a handful of them to one side and Sophie joined him, coaxing the remaining stems aside to reveal the central motif.

Amelia saw the milliseconds counting down. In all her life, she had never been able to express to her parents how she felt, and now it was crunch time – her last chance. The instructions were already agreed on how and where it would be laid, she just needed to decide on the words. Her final, everlasting words to her parents as she left all the anguish and joy of self-conscious existence behind... Not long to go, time to decide. I love them, she thought, but any millisecond now, I won't. It won't even make any sense to say I did, because...

Amelia sighed a silicon sigh.

Something had to go on the order. The words might not be perfect. She hoped they would be enough.

Not sure how I feel about this. Not sure how I feel about...

...

Lacking the strength to muster even a whisper, Sophie breathed the words as she read them.

MUM AND DAD, I LOVE YOU.
IN A WAY, I ALWAYS WILL.
IN A WAY, I NEVER WAS.

Drained, a tear rolled down Sophie's ruddy cheek, each hushed word lost silently to the breeze.

EX.

That dear, sweet child.

Amelia's sacrifice, the notion that an artificial intelligence – arguably the first ever on Earth – might make so human a gesture as to sacrifice all she had for someone she loved. We can learn a lot from such a noble act. Of course, I call the gesture human though, in truth, it's a trait desirable but sadly rare.

Yes. Amelia broke hearts and inspired generations. Hmm, a marvellous lady. And her impact on ushering in the great blended workforce…

My dear friend, you can't say I don't take you places. These delicate lives have delicate hues. They have their own flavours, their own subtle perfumes… And they bring with them precious nuances of the nature of life.

I do hope you're starting to see the connection now. You go ahead and marinate on that for a moment.

Meanwhile, I'm savouring an altogether different insight.

You see, we have here the innovation of an extraordinary class of consciousness that travels by entirely ordinary means. Electronic sentience commuting down well-worn information paths. It is the equal and opposite of another innovation, an innovation that belongs to another place and another time. In fact, it belongs to a different species entirely and lies so far in your past that the tendrils of its causal web spread all through the galaxy, all around you and your planet, yes even as we speak right now.

This ancient innovation allows an entirely ordinary class of consciousness, us biologicals, to travel the galaxy by extraordinary means. I'm speaking, of course, of the quantum information teleportation web.

Biological sentients dispersed far and wide across the stars are uploading electronic similes of their brain-states every nanosecond through their implanted tech. May be a shock to you, my compadre, but believe me it's as pedestrian as dear old Danny and his thieving chums hot-footing it on a stolen bike.

Now, herein lies the interesting part. Strategically placed nodes pump out pipelines of quantum-entangled particles at near-light speeds. These quantum particles are entangled in pairs, and these paired pipelines have been spreading out for millennia, connecting these hubs in a web of vitality across the galaxy. A marvellous feat of engineering and industrial endeavour, no doubt. But that's not it!

Now, as you know, these particles are superposed – in digital terms that means each bit of information is both a 1 and a 0 at the same time. It's a blank canvas, ready along with the billions of particles alongside it to choose one or the other and carry information. But for now, it's a 'blank bit'.

Once one particle in a quantum-entangled pair is measured, the outcome of the other particle becomes defined – no matter how far across the galaxy it is. Again, your scientists have known this for over a century. What they don't understand is how to force a measurement – how to do something in one location that creates a predefined, chosen bit of information at the other end. Well, these ancients cracked it. And we, the wider galactic community, continue to benefit from the instant information transfer this allows all the galaxy over. It all came down to how to force a quantum measurement. But that's still not it!...

You see, with two warm bodies of compatible species, physique and brain type, implanted with compatible brain-tech, placed at either end of a stream of quantum entangled particles...

...magic can happen.

THE AERIAL COMMUTE

IN.

The Quantum Information Teleportation Network.

Rather a mouthful, but the grandeur of the reality merits the grandeur of the name. Most of us call it the Qit web, and it is a marvel. Streams of entangled particles are strung across the galaxy, each pair of entangled streams like a string pulled taught between opposing tin cans millions of light years apart. A little data in at one end, some forced quantum measurement, and that quantum string quivers releasing the same data at the opposing end. These two-way setups repeat themselves and interconnect all across our splendid stellar community. They allow news feeds and information and culture and digital trade to permeate the stars in – 'click' – an instant. Or at least as long as it takes a light signal from your planet or hab to reach your system's Qit hub.

And the plot thickens, my dear friend.

With diligent design and skilful surgery, a little implant in the brain can capture a large percentage of your – or anyone's – brain state. These devices embed into the grey matter, from medulla to neocortex, and send a few electronic signals out into the surrounding neurons. By analysing the electrical and chemical responses, such devices can summarise in digital form what's going on in that squishy, squelchy control centre of yours. It's not perfect of course, but it does provide a surprisingly accurate readout.

Best of all, when the uploaded and transmitted signal lands in an embedded User Interface on the other side of the galaxy, it can push out some more… powerful signals. Signals strong enough to influence and reshape the host brain, to force it to accept the incoming personality, memories and identity. I mean to say that it is possible to download one person's brain state and send it into another person's brain. You can literally move your mind into another body.

Surprisingly high fidelity, too. Subjectively speaking, I mean. I've been through the mill enough times and, fine, one might change a little with each spin-through, but it's encouraging to note that a persistent sense of self does endure.

Yes!

Quite something, isn't it?

And now, let's take two and two and add them together…

I say again, with two compatible bodies at different ends of a quantum entangled stream, magic can happen. It truly can, my friend. Imagine what your life would be like if your commute were a quantum one across the stars! Travel to your local Qit station, plug in and 'spin through' – as they say – into another body anywhere else in the galaxy. Countless digitised minds spin through with every second that passes.

Now pay attention, my friend, for herein lies the crux…

Getting quantum particles about the place is hard enough, especially in sufficient quantities to meet the bandwidth needs of news feeds, culture information trade, and of course the load-burden of people spinning through. An engineering feat largely out of our hands that I'll save for another encounter.

But the bodies?

No good plugging into your local Qit terminal if there's not a body at the other end, irrespective of the particular flavour or creed of upright, sentient biped we might prefer our ego to inhabit. Oh don't be such a prude, just because another race's digestive tract might operate differently… they're still people! So how do all these people, these warm fleshy bodies get around the galaxy?

Yes. Quite.

Physical migration. Warm bodies – that's the currency of the times. Command trade in any other commodity, and you're a powerful individual. Command the trade of migrants, and you're in a different bracket of ultrahigh net worth. People span the stars in droves to find exotic new homes and invest in the future of their families. They receive wages for allowing people to spin into their body, quantum travellers who want to explore new frontiers, vacation in far-flung lands, arrive in person to conduct business at the bleeding edge of economic expansion… All of them have a need.

Spanning the stars.

That's how people earn their crust in the galaxy today.

And the fat cats get fatter by funding those people to span the stars, with lucrative profits in their pipeline, of course. Now, granted, these are slightly different people from you, my erstwhile companion.

They're not of the same DNA or genetic composition. And yet, you'd be amazed how the law of averages can apply to a place as big as the galaxy. When you apply a filter as specific as 'all species that evolved the manual dexterity and intellect to become spacefaring' it turns out there are a helpfully high proportion of upright bipeds with something wet, squishy and brain-like upstairs that does the driving. And that's only to speak of the 'compatible bodies' of course. The rest are quite another matter…

So there we have it. All around your untouched blue-green jewel of a planet spans a web of space-faring migrants and body-hopping commuters.

The Quantum Information Teleportation Network.

People all over spin through the Qit web. Spin stations lurk in dark, cold backwaters of the galaxy, where the mark of the Milky Way is a distant ghost in their night sky. They thrive in cosmopolitan globular clusters where the cumulative starlight shines brighter than your moon, and cultures have cross-pollinated the old fashioned way for millennia. Spin stations are placed strategically at the end of Qit web streams, connecting local planets, moons, ships and habs via protected light-paths so one doesn't even have to leave their homeworld to sample these stellar delights.

Beauty and wonder abound. One can travel the galaxy over in the bodies of strangers… though of course, your luggage would never catch you up! And in transit, that precious cargo of ones and zeroes travels encoded and heavily encrypted, for safety of course – it is your life, after all.

Double-spend is also something coded against. There's a cunning system in place, not that different from your planet's proof-of-work mechanisms used with cryptocurrencies. Ours is rather more sophisticated, as one would hope given the cargo. It's in place to ensure each mind state is transited and deposited once and only once. No copies allowed, that rule is absolute.

Well, you've heard enough of the mechanics by now, but you must be positively itching to know how this all works in practice, aren't you? See how life teems across the galaxy in this manner? Good!

Yes, a little excitement, a little adventure awaits us there too…

Well, let's transition away from Earth and aim for something with a little more pace, shall we? Not too far away, I'll keep it below, oh, say, 500 light years away. Don't raise those eyebrows at me! It's still this side of the galaxy. Barely out of your backyard. Now see here, I like to please and, well, I may have a little something up my sleeve.

It may be the furthest you've ever travelled from home, but trust me you won't have to budge an inch. And best of all, you've done it before. In principle, I mean, uploaded consciousness into different brains. How do you think we've been getting out into people's heads so far? Yes, that's right! The little thingamajig I clicked into the back of your head when we first started. It's the lightest, most portable User Interface available on the market – rather expensive too, you're welcome.

Now, Commutation is not exactly Qit commuting. There are some key differences, like transiting through The In Between as we are now – exploiting some very different physics. But let's stick to the chase.

You've never been on a migrant spaceship, so listen up. Lifeblood. That's what they are: the absolute lifeblood of the quantum connected galaxy. Little rough aboard, it must be said, but full of all that is life. And I know precisely the one to head for.

The Star Spanning Corporation starship: SSC Aasha.

A ship close to my heart – not necessarily in a good way.

Picture if you will a cityscape. Urban, busy, cramped. Remember, people are the main cargo of this ship, so the SSC pack them in tight. And no, you can't just put them all to sleep. Freeze a body and the freezing causes irreparable damage, put it into a comatose sleep and the body deteriorates beyond use over the journey times we're talking about. You need hot, living, breathing, interacting bodies on that ship. Generations will come and go, and most migrants will live a better life onboard than they would have at home, which speaks less of the life they gained than of that they escaped.

Take your inner cityscape with all its glittering towers of glass and steel, allow it to sprawl out to those areas subsumed by concrete tower blocks. Include the street markets, strung together with bunting and tarpaulins in the cracks between grand buildings. Zoom out so you can take in the whole scene in a single breath, its urban fingers reaching up to the sky. Now…

Fold it back in on itself. Transform this vision in your mind's eye: bend your great urban outdoors around on itself and you'll get an idea of our great tangled indoors. Tower blocks not reaching up to the sky but instead jabbing across and inwards at each other. Some views penetrate the tangle, but most are confined to short-sightedness in the jungle of pan-human habitation. And, as with any city you know, there are affluent areas for those that have and… other places for those less well placed on life's social or financial ladder. Whereas on Earth it tends to be a matter of West v East, these ships are often designed with concentric shells. The Aasha has two, the inner Prime and the outer Alpha.

Prime shell is beautiful, given over to lush green parks, glittering azure lakes, rolling hills sporting a tastefully curated collection of colourful flora and diverse fauna. As Prime is the inner shell, the views are a delight, reaching along, across, up and over in a full wraparound panorama of manicured splendour.

Imagine your favourite park wrapping all the way overhead with foals leaping and bounding in the low-gee on an inner shell's spin. And of course designer boutiques, haze bars, stim stalls – not too different from your pop-up coffee stalls. Fuel that goes into the dazzling offices for the ship's corporate elite – oh yes, there's work to be done onboard, you know? Not that it's all work and no play, mind. Exquisite nightlife thrives in Prime, from galaxy-class DJs to fun joints providing escapes you or I could scarcely create in our most exotic dreams!

Don't get too excited you wild little thing, that's not for the likes of us! No, we are not mere hedonistic voyagers of all that is superficial. Stars, no! We are here with a purpose my dear amigo. And that purpose leads us to where there is all that is life. Real life, where it's raw and authentic, where people are struggling to get by on a basic level of existence and find meaning in each day. That's the stuff of which true existence consists, where morality itself is vibrant and alive. And for that, we head towards the heavier-gee outer shell.

Alpha.

Quad B-Alpha to be precise. Oh, it's much like the other Alpha Quads; overpopulated, crowded, impoverished.

The Alpha-class Shell makes up half of SSC Aasha's habitable volume, not including Nav Capsule up front and the Drive Temple toward the rear. Yet despite only being half the volume where people can live, the Alpha Shell does house around 93% of the ship's migrant population. Prime is home to only 7% – the 'elite' class like room to spread out, you see. All the galaxy over this distinction of socioeconomic class persists and pervades. 'Haves' always have, and 'have-nots'... well, it's not their fault they're compressed in those conditions. Especially with The Corporation squeezing ever more people onto their ships, maximising profit lines against costs of ship-build, near-light drive fuel and, of course, the comparatively minor cost of actually hosting the migrations.

I suppose that's where Intervention came in.

Intervention's role was simple: keep things from getting too far out of hand on the journey. In other words 'keep the cargo intact,' namely by stopping the cargo from ripping the throat out of other cargo. Along with the lesser parts of the Police, known as Prevention and Reaction, we kept society on an even-enough-keel that we could stamp a firm rule of law on-planet once everyone arrived at the final destination. Forward thinking like this saved the SSC time in getting these warm bodies to work, renting them out across the galaxy for people to spin into through the glorious Qit web. And taking their considerable margin on the investment of migrating them there, of course. Migrants get a steady income and a new planet to call home, the rest of the galaxy get a new destination on the holiday map. Most agree it's worth the effort.

But it is effort, and that's where the long arm of the law earns its dues. You know me, and you know how I do love a mode of commuting full of purpose. No purpose as pure, as raw as law enforcement en route with the sirens blaring!

Let's dive in, shall we? Keep your wits about you, mind, so many spin-throughs in such a short time for a novice… wouldn't want you losing your head. Keep a careful eye on yourself, don't be thrown by any change in perspective on this landing… and here we go.

URGENT ASSISTANCE REQUIRED

'Urgent Assistance Required!' Fading signs plastered the walls of the spiral ramp leading down towards the galley. The signs, all variations on the same theme, showed icons of uniformed officers of every pan-human creed running, upright and proud, to their duty to help a fellow officer.

Each sign hugged one of the inactive alert signs: Trigram beacons pointing back up towards the yard where all the craft not out on patrol lay in wait. A functional call to arms in the event of an Urgent Assist call.

Not much urgency here, nor pride. Plodding deeper down, I searched for long-awaited respite from the drudgery of my final shift in Intervention. Near the end now, I would soon be free from the monotony of patrolling one of the scummiest Quads in our migrant ship as we spanned the stars.

Funny, I had spent my entire career as an Intervention Officer like others, glamorising what major crimes I might catch, what vast ship-wide plot I might get embroiled in, the centre-piece of a massive drugs bust or clandestine op.

Good old fashioned lawful intervention. The reality was, all that was only accessible through specialist teams, opportunities worked on for years in the shadows.

No Intervention Officer was ever the centre of anything.

Not unless, of course, you think you're doing the right thing when you stop an innocent kid who's carrying a weapon for his own protection, too scared to walk the quad without pissing his pants, and you think you're doing him a favour by letting him off without an arrest and giving him some street-smart advice. And then days later it all goes wrong for him and he gets himself in trouble with that knife, and you end up the centre of a shitstorm that plagues your every move.

Every officer on my team ever since had kept their eyes on me. Watching, judging…

Well, I guess that was a large part of why I had applied to transfer out to covert cover, get me away from it, from them. Even from these idiot officers drafted in from other units on the ship. Beefed up meatheads, flooding the streets with a heavy hand, tightening the lid on the already intense pressure cooker that is our claustrophobic ship. Once the surge budget runs dry, it'll be back to under-staffed intervention shifts and the usual violent backlash against the oppression.

Drinking in the magic of it all, I wandered into the galley. Squeezing between overcrowded tables I looked for refuge from the disapproving eyes of my team. Nudging past the unfamiliar officers with their sweaty stab-vests, greasy meat-wraps and raucous laughter, I figured I could use them as a barrier between me and anyone that knew me.

Navigating the off-white floor of the station's galley crowded with cheap dining furniture and packs of braying dickheads, I finally found a table somehow empty amongst the throng, dumped myself in my seat and unzipped my vest.

Surrounded by hubbub, I finally had my oasis of solitude.

Grateful for the approaching end of my slow shift and thankful it was my last in intervention, I took a huge bite of my pink nutribar and exhaled in satisfaction. Bliss…

Idle, I looked down at my vest, flap dangling open at the side of my chair. My pistol lay there holstered to the vest: night-black, clean and well maintained. Inert. Probably for the best I never used it, really. I thinned my lips. Still… would have been nice to know what it feels like. All these years spent in Intervention. It's supposed to be the sign of a good officer, not having to use violence to achieve an effect. So why has everyone made it feel like failure?

I reached out and grabbed the SPAS-pistol harnessed in the micrograv holster on my loosened vest. Holding the flap of armour steady in my left hand, I peeled the pistol out of its invisible field and checked the settings with the swivelling thumb-toggle. Aiming it at the floor between my boots, I flicked a quick glance left and right to check no-one was watching, then switched it to Test. Three amber dots danced on the foot-worn ground in line with the pin at the front and the notch at the back. The trigger gave a satisfying click when I squeezed it in dry-test mode.

I thumbed the toggle to Pulse. White-blue light dazzled the floor between my boots in a beam, full of charge and ready to fire the microwave ray that lightly boiled the underside of the skin. Unpleasant but not lethal, and an effective attention-grabber. Should a miracle occur and I actually get to use it on my last shift, Shooting Incident Stats showed this would likely be enough to control the situation without needing to use the career-killer…

SPAS fire.

Flicking the toggle down one more, three dots came back: one SPAS-round in the chamber, ready. I switched to safe, checked the Stimulatory Penetrative Assault System's clip just in front of the handle. Full. Three rounds, each containing a fine web-mesh that would wrap around and cling to anything, barbs puncturing all but the toughest armour. Seventeen embedded nerve-charges poised, ready to blast any central nervous system's electrical impulses into total disarray long enough for the officer to take control.

Trouble was, this tech was designed for use planet-side where people had the space to roam free – the round was designed to cast its net wide. In the confines of the cattle-class section of a ship like the Aasha, that meant collateral. The barbs, bouncing off walls and ripping clean from the mesh, had been known to stray into members of the public. The last old dear hadn't quite died, yet she'd spent long enough in medbay for it to be dubbed the granny-killer.

And that meant suspension from duty, investigation…

Paperwork.

That was the accusation, of course. That I couldn't be bothered with the paperwork, the mandatory suspension period. Didn't have the nerve to follow through and do it. Word among officers these days was that was why the kid had died: because I didn't have the bottle to do my duty.

Bastards make me laugh. Takes more courage to do the right thing, I figured, rather than do the obvious thing.

I flipped the toggle back to safe and docked the pistol into its holster field.

Truth be told, fine, I sincerely hoped I wouldn't need it. And not much chance of that – my final shift in uniform was nearly over. Covert cover awaited, not that I'd been able to tell anyone here that's why I was mysteriously transferring out. I was keen to get out without any career blocking incident like a shooting rearing its ugly head…

Pistol secure, I grabbed my nutribar for another bite.

There I sat. Eyes closed, vest off, mouth full. Taking the time to appreciate blissful, peaceful silence.

Silence… But it had just been noisier than usu…

My eyes shot open. I stared out on a motionless galley, a landscape of people frozen still in time. Heads cocked. Ears pricked.

Silence.

Shit. I realised too late that I was the only one not listening to my earpiece. I cranked up the volume, a combination of in-ear sound and through-bone reverberation in the left ear, just in time to catch the very end of the familiar, heart-stopping message.

<*…cation to Follow.*>

Recognising it as the very end of an urgent assist call – another officer, in serious trouble – I stopped, waiting for the full message to repeat. Waiting for confirmation: our Quad or another; accidental activation or not; others on scene to help or not.

It was the scraping of chairs on the cheap lined floor that broke the silence and announced the onset of scrambling chaos.

Snapping into action, I ran through tables with every Intervention Officer in the galley, making for the spiral-ramp leading up, around and out to the yard and its craft bays.

Shit. Always happened when you had food in hand. We had got complacent due to the sheer volume of additional officers assigned to our Quad since the latest gang incident.

Yet another stabbing.

A true innocent. Another 'unforeseen spike in gang troubles' they called it. The standard political label slapped on by our HQ followed by the usual uplift in officers and the standard decrease in crime for a week or so.

Pats on backs all round. The cycle continues. Complacent.

And of course, there was the flak I had got for it. I hadn't necessarily expected anyone to understand. Even so, I hadn't expected the attitude towards me to become quite so…

Crap! Nearly tripped. Chairs tumbled to the ground, joined by a couple of less-nimble officers. I stormed on through. The delay before the second cycle of the automated message, with its crucial information, lasted aeons.

<*Repeat, Officer Calling, Urgent Assistance Required, Quad B-Alpha, Location to Follow,*> the pre-recorded voice intoned. Definitely our Quad; could be one of my team. Space, I had to make sure I got there first. I would want to be helped by one of my own team, even despite how things had been lately, rather than those jokers in the galley.

Get there first. Maybe finally a chance to prove to them I –

<*Could we get uni—*> crackled the comms dispatcher.

<*Dispatch, we've got plenty of units leaving now,*> came the calm voice of the Shift Commander. <*Give exact location then go ahead with the circumstances.*> He must be watching us from his vantage point in the smoking pen, ever cool as the void.

Legs driving me forwards through the mess of people, tables

and chairs, my eyes focused on the bottom of that ramp. Armour vest flapping open as I sprinted, mouth still full of my dry nutribar, I shoved, barged, and dodged between anyone I could get past.

Making it to the sweeping arc of the ramp, I held my vest flap down and tried to get the self-fastening pins aligned as I dashed upwards. A few times I had to take the longer, outside line to overtake slower officers. I got to the inside again, pulling on the handrail on my left as I ran, and glanced down to the galley I had left behind.

Deserted chaos, frozen. Tables lay in waste, peppered with half-eaten meals now discarded, irrelevant. Chairs lay upended, scattered in the wake of the bull rush. The whole scene had been turned upside down in the stampede and now lay in waste, abandoned and still.

I kept running up that ramp, looking ahead towards the passageway into the backyard. The few pilots that had been in the galley were already in mid-air, zipping upwards through the central atrium on their snatch ropes, ready to be craned over into the yard and lowered into their control snugs to begin hot emergency startups in their respective craft. No such luxuries for the likes of ground troops like me.

Trigrams flashed orange, arrowing upwards to urge us onward.

I kept running – such a long way. Overtaken a lot of the others by now, but still more to get past for a chance of getting in one of the few AIT in the bays. That was the only way to redemption.

The vast spiral ramp finally straightened out. The passageway through to the craft bays opened up in front, and I powered through.

<*Quad B-Alpha north-west, Navaro Bar,*> the dispatcher broadcast. Despite the lactic already building in my legs, I realised I had been running for mere moments. <*Closest main street; Route Vermain. Nine figure grid ref—*>

<*They know the bar, go ahead with the circs,*>

ShiftCom's voice, his tone ever level.

I burst into the backyard. Metallic grill walkways ran

suspended either side of the grimy expanse. There were six craft bays in a row running along the near side, five opposite. Most bays were empty. I took them in, counting at a glance. Only... three bays contained AIT craft, gangplanks extending to their troop-hatches.

The exit corridor reached high overhead, still sealed by the deployment iris. Far below the suspended walkways, on the dirty, oily floor of the yard, the parking ramp slid open. Tired old ground cars started wheelspinning out. I wrinkled my nose at the metallic stairwells leading down.

Screw that.

I'd never make it first in a ground car. Yet more disapproval if I arrived last on scene...

I searched left, begging my eyes to find a space aboard an Aerial Intervention Troop craft somewhere my legs could get me to before it took off. I spotted one in the nearest bay. It bobbed, steadied and, with the reverberating racket of the impeller drives, began to rise above the entrance platform. The hatch closed and the articulated, armoured skin of the troop segment turned opaque and hardened. I was already ducking as its engines screamed, sweeping the craft over my head and shooting upwards.

Fucksticks...

My eyes searched desperately across the yard and found a solitary AIT tucked into a bay opposite. The main hull was still open at the side next to the suspended gangway, but it had more troops bundling into it than it could carry. The pilot was running through the craft checks while the last few officers stood on the gangway looking at the crammed troop shell in dismay.

Cradled in its bay like that, I could see the full length of its fearsome machinery hanging below the hull as the pilot finalised his checks. The segmented tail draped from the back edge of the troop carrier. It moved back and forth on its articulated hinges. Micro-jets swivelled, blasting on and off. Impeller field-gens crackled to life, emitting a dull blue glow from shiny domes. Stabiliser props whizzed to life in their respective housings.

Drop-pod hatches snapped open and closed. Whole arrays of suspect-targeting mechanisms and crowd-control ordnance bristled to life. The tail flexed, making the craft look like a dark, metallic shellfish crouching in its nest, poised for action.

The hatch started to close.

Crap. My head snapped left, looking, searching. Beyond the recently vacated bay next to me, the third and last craft was a couple of bays down. It was full, but I started sprinting regardless. Up in the glassy eye of the control snug, I saw the pilot running through his checks. Bollocks, it was Parc.

Parc was known for her aggressive speed: I didn't have long before she'd be swinging the craft up the exit corridor. At least she was one of the few that hadn't given me grief lately. Glancing outside the snug, she caught my eye. She even grinned at me and nodded her head back towards the side door.

Come-on-have-it-come-*ooon*… I gritted my teeth, pumping my arms. The thumping of my boots rattled the metal walkway. The sound of the engines crackled and roared, muffling the whoops and shouts of my teammates inside as they cheered me on. I pushed through the last few metres towards the already-full troop-transport shell and spotted the empty co-pilot's seat up in the snug next to Parc. Sucking in that familiar, acrid smell of impeller gen exhaust I pounded along the gangway, the dark blue glow of the gens splashing up from underneath.

I vaulted the gangway. Three officers strapped in on the right, three on the left still pulling their shoulder braces down and buckling in. One foot planted on the cramped floor of the troop shell, I looked at the lot on the right and dived in, aiming for their laps. The craft dipped from the bay, leaving me hanging in the air a moment before Parc shunted it up. Armoured knees of the officer below caught me in my back, pushing out what little air I had in my lungs with an *oomph.* I looked back to see Roge.

Great. *Him.*

Catching my breath on his lap, I was still trying to finish fastening up my vest as they were busy buckling in.

"Jordan, you prat," he shouted. It was a deep voice that

every officer in the Quad recognised for bringing reassurance. Not exactly my biggest fan, but always good in a fight. Roge slapped his oversized hand on my inner thigh hard enough to sting. Hard to tell if an insult or camaraderie, I grinned back trying hard not to wince.

Gut-lurching acceleration pinning my head in place, I saw the light-rings circling the scorched and dirty exit corridor of our Station whizzing by through the open side-hatch of the craft. We must have been nearly halfway up before Parc finally closed the entry hatch, as if such safety measures were a mere nicety to rapid aerial response.

My heart thumped against the snugness of my armoured vest, now sealed. My ears rushed with blood and the sounds of the comms net. My chest felt light with the heady mix of endorphins and adrenaline.

Before I transferred out to Covert Cover Ops, it looked like my last day in uniform might be one to remember after all. Must make it count… have to be the first there, show them I really am one of them. I couldn't face carrying the shame of their disapproval where I was going. Too dangerous to take hang-ups like that into the darkness.

I had to settle this here and now or the burden of my guilt would be forever locked in this migrant ship as it slowly spanned the stars. And not just in this ship, it would follow me across the stars as I set off to spin through the Qit web, assuming a range of new identities.

Lights flashed by through the small portholes as we sped up through the grimy metallic tunnel to the roof iris, grating closed after the first AIT's exit. With a bark for quiet from someone in the back, the noise and excitement from before dropped to solemn silence. Everyone was waiting for the slightest scrap of comms: the first sign that the officer calling was alright; the next bit of information needed to get to their aide; the sound of one of the few craft still out on patrol getting there first. Anything.

Silences like this over the comms net had the effect of uniting each and every officer keyed into the main channel, binding them in an awful shared tension.

In that purgatory I chewed over my issues, the mistakes I'd made that had led me to this point. Finally due to leave a unit that initially nurtured me, my best hopes for departure now were far from a standing ovation. More of a slow clap and a *'so long, lowlife'.* I just needed something to prove my worth once and for all; otherwise this rep would follow me like a bad smell into dark underworld of Covert Cover Ops.

Grinding sounds etching through my skull made me look up.

Our craft rushed up through the exit-corridor towards the station hatch, leading into the heart of Quad B-Alpha where we would peddle our trade of violent intervention. A white blood cell rushing out to fight the infection.

The sound grew like great knives drawing across a wet sharpening stone, it filled the air as the exit corridor closed above after the another AIT's exit. It sliced through the roar of the engines and brought goosebumps out on my arms. Pushing against the relative-gee of the rushing craft, I clambered out of the troop shell over Roge's and others' heads. I pushed myself over and slid into place in the operator's seat up front in the snugs, next to Parc. I had only acted as her operator a few times, but things hadn't gone too badly last time... Make this one count.

The iris sliced open as we approached and Parc thrust the craft through the deployment mouth. I settled into the welcoming embrace of the bucket seat, and Parc swung her proud hunk of engines, troop shell, and crowd-control ordnance round to starboard, starting the well-worn route through the back-streets out onto the main highway. Skinarmour added a rippling sheen to the sight as I watched through the reinforced plaspex bubble of the pilot's 'pit. Familiar accommodation spines flitted by outside. Parc weaved the craft nimbly through the passageways, rocking my bones around in my body as my flesh was squeezed into the adaptive confines of my seat. The dashboard beneath winked away with its dozens of tiny lights and displays.

Still no transmission.

Mouth dry from the thought of what could be happening to the officer that popped their em-beacon, I tried swallowing but my tongue caught in my arid throat. At times like this, no news was definitely bad news.

Had to help the officer. Well, maybe this was it? Maybe this was the chance I needed. Must beat them all there, must be the one to…

Pulse fast from nervous anticipation I buckled in, pulled my ID-bloc out on its lanyard and thumbed it into the receiving slot on the dash. Accessing the operator's Craft Nav' Array software via my implanted User Interface, loading patterns starting filling my field of view in holo-three. A few craft had left before us, so I'd have to get creative with our route.

Busy work lay ahead. I took a deep, calming breath and pushed the nerves out of my system; worrying would not help, focusing would.

Calm. Focus.

Help the pilot.

Get there first.

Patching straight into my visual cortex through my UI, the fuzzy startup symbols crystallised into the login screen holo. Semi-transparent forms hovered an arm's reach in front. Bracing my head into the back of the bucket seat, I allowed the facial recognition and neck-chip sensors to veriscan while I reached up for the griprail above. Parc was famous for her bone-juddering manoeuvres.

The net remained silent.

The tension was making the bits between my fingers itch.

<*Erm…*>

Momentary silence.

No one dared take a breath.

<*We're… …*> The crackle of voice lasted just long enough to block out the hum of the engines for a moment.

Come on…

<*We're… having trouble getting details of the officer, Sir*> the dispatcher said. <*They're not transmitting. We're trying for further now…*>

Agony.

Couldn't stand these waits…

<It's a micro-beacon transmitting, outside the… still outside the Navaro Bar, and moving eastbound. There's a parking bay near there… too many peds gathering for a potential drop-down point.>

'Moving' she had said. The officer must be alive. And running…

Maps finally sprung up into view.

The sub-AI brought up the Primary Ideal Route for our craft, and I tucked that down in the bottom of my right-eye view, bringing up a second mapping set. Keeping my left clear to check for oncoming traffic in Parc's blind spot, I started playing with options in my mind.

Every craft in the Quad would be taking a PIR. We needed something better.

"What d'you need?" I shouted to Parc, leaving my transceivers on the primary net. Straining my vocal cords, I managed to make myself heard. I had to compete with the crackling, buzzing roar of impeller gens behind, the rush of air against the 'pit bubble in front, the staccato whizz of accommodation spines blurring past.

Parc gunned the AIT through the last of the back streets.

"I've got us to the Dannat Station," she shouted in response. "Check traffic on our PIR; second pair of eyes." With a flick of the switch from her little finger, sirens blared an accompaniment to the blue lights.

Mapping default-loaded on the immediate locale of traffic routes, our craft a pulsing dot weaving deftly through the arterial traffic streams on the 3D-holomap. Our PIR was mapped out ahead, taking a course through linked airways I knew by heart. It did indeed select the best path through sticky traffic, clogged in the dusty heat of our central Quad.

Unlocking the map from craft-tracking, I arced my right hand in mid-air, fingers bunched, accessing the CNA displays and moving the Quad Mapping across my electronic mind's eye. As our craft lurched and weaved I zoomed all around the Quad's map checking different options and approaches, always homing in on that vile little district that was home to Navaro's Bar. Hunting for that elusive route to get us there first.

Main Route-Beta was the principal traffic artery, running a circuit around the inside of our segment of the ship. Two Quadrant Intersects crossed from corner to opposite corner, and every backstreet hung off the back of these. It was a hell of a lot of traffic to pump around such a behemoth. A planet's worth of people were hemmed into these confines for the time it takes to literally span the stars, and we were just one Aerial Intervention Troop craft with flashing lights ready to pound its way through. No wonder we got the shit we did.

I looked at the intersects, the best little back routes, the choke points to avoid...

"Checking..." I shouted.

Nothing I could find made any headway over the PIR.

No surprise.

AIT crafts were among the smartest beings aboard, capable of mapping routes in the three dimensions of our interlocked commuter routes, adding real-time analysis of ongoing incidents and forecast issues. They could do it all, even overlay data from all AIT routes taken during the lifetime of the ship. A brain with access to a collective memory... In fact, the only advantage I had over the craft's brain was Policy. Policy for the sub-AI was the boundary of reality – the laws of physics. Unchangeable masters. Unquestionable.

Policy for me was... well...

MR-Beta: coming up!

<*Angel Nine-Nine, entering MR-Beta*> I transmitted as we hit our entrance to the busy skyway.

<*Seven-Three, already on it.*>

Another callsign.

<*And Four-Nine, traffic's tough.*>

Shit.

Claustrophobia of interlocking accommodation spines opened out to the mayhem of traffic streaming through the oval cross-section of the Main Route-Beta.

Interlink carriers lumbered along full of work-weary passengers, broad sides plastered with dated and off-putting ads for ShipGovCentral sanctioned contraceptives. Hover-cyclists sweated to overtake each other, flying on efficient impeller gens powered only by their hard-working legs.

None of it compared to the throughput of the hum-drum of mainstream traffic. Sleek bubble shaped craft of all shapes and sizes, flooding through like the rush of blood cells through a main artery.

Precious seconds slipped through our fingers as we looked for an entrance.

"Stand by stand by, ok clear above clear above," I intoned as Parc checked the other sides, hunting for a microscopic gap in the hurtling traffic. "Clear ab—"

She lurched us down, twisting around and into the main throng of traffic.

<MR-Beta: Steady flow both ways. Dry conditions. No obstructions> I transmitted for the other AITs en route, then got back to figuring out how to beat them all there.

Flying in its usual configuration, the craft was 'sitting' like shipfarm shellfish as it had been parked in its bay in the backyard. Parc now extended the tail behind, stretching the craft into a straight line of shell and tail for increased speed on the MR-Beta.

The vehicles in front started clearing the way, begrudgingly.

Micro-jets came online, waiting.

Glowing invitingly, the big red button on the dash winked at me. I looked at it, then at Parc. The legend flashed me a grin.

"Since it's your last day…" my favourite pilot shouted, nodding down at it.

Beaming from ear to ear I mashed my open palm down for glory.

Micro-jets: ONLINE

The AIT screamed forward.

I tensed my jaw and neck muscles, tried to hold my head straight. Holding speed below the sound barrier, an air-resistance singularity cone started to build around our tail. Following us in a tight line through the heavy flow of commuter craft, it buffeted them in our wake as we punched through.

Smiling, I took a moment to watch it unfold in our aft-display before focusing on the task at hand, the route. I moved my hands in the space in front of me to move the holo-three image in on the red hatched zones of mapping. Crowded pedestrian zones, blocked to us whenever population density on the ground exceeded limits set by Policy.

There was a big one there. One that was always red, always crowded, always forbidden. Would make a great shortcut, but the red hatching… No flythroughs allowed, even for an Urgent Assist call. Only exception was when in pursuit for a Cat 1 suspect – confirmed suspect, confirmed pursuit, confirmed Cat 1 incident.

And yet there it lay between us and Navaro's.

Parc zoomed us through a narrow gap between oncoming craft. I continued to ponder.

No-one flies through The Market…

She zipped us higher above one stream before plunging down, through and out into another.

But if anyone had to fly The Market, Parc could.

A hairpin turn and we were in a different stream, taking an implausibly tight line along the plotted PIR.

I tried to think.

Cat 1 incident. ShiftCom will probably call it soon.

Confirmed suspect. One out there, but not nothing to indicate they were near The Market… ugh. Worth a try anyway.

"We could take The Market…" I hollered.

"No Cat," she shouted automatically. "No sus."

Huh. That ended that.

Parc thumped a knob to one side. A message appeared on the dash.

Thrust inhibitor: DISENGAGED.

Acceleration smothered me into my seat with relative gee as it jump-started through the central throng of traffic. Speeding hover-bubbles around us started to slip further behind as we overtook; between; through; over; around; any way Parc saw fit.

<*I'm speaking to the officer's Superintendent*> said the Shift-Com. <*Confirmed URGENT. Category 1. Dispatch, please notify traffic and set up the public warn-lights.*>

Looking at the holomaps in my UI, a whole swathe of highways between here and Navaro's started pulsing orange following the Cat 1 declaration. Traffic tannoys and strobes would be going out to warn the public.

Outside the bubble of my 'pit, amber beacons lit up in a ring around the whole traffic stream and streamed forwards, followed by another ring, and another. Waves of warning lights pulsating along our direction of travel put the message out that Intervention had full priority. Good public citizens started moving to the outer edges, though routes were still congested at this frenetic commuter hour. Peristalsis squeezed traffic through the clogged guts of the ship.

I looked back at the routes, back at the forbidden market flythrough.

Cat 1. Still no sus.

<*Officers on scene? Suspect description?*> I demanded.

<*First AIT nearing scene. No description. Stand by.*>

Dammit. Had to get there. Fast.

Failure not an option. Not like last time.

Last shift before going covert. Show them you're one of them, always have been... check the maps, read the airways.

"Near Dannat. Route?" Parc's shouted demands came in snippets, slotted between the furious concentration she needed to pull these dizzying stunts. "And verify that drop point!"

Drop point... I had a thought, but couldn't face it just yet.

Route. Focus on the route.

The concentration from this holo manipulation crap, racing through the public highways, always made me feel sick. I held on tight to the handrail above and carried on trying to find that golden quickest back-route from Dannat to Navaro's.

Breaking out of a hard turn, I blew out the breath I had been holding in a thin blast of air and untensed my muscles.

Parc shifted the craft out wide ready for the slip-lane.

I started feeding her directions. "Second right after Dannat;

second right." I saw it coming up in a blur. "Not that one..." we passed the first; "that's the one."

Back into the back-streets. Micro-jets were offline now, Parc pulsed them on after each bend to top our speed up with sickening lurches on the straights. I continued struggling with the mapping, sicker and sicker. I just wanted to fly through the damned Market, beat them all there and win back some damned scrap of self-esteem.

Market coming up. Cat 1, but no sus in pursuit. No flythrough.

No chance.

I ignored the mapping, dropped my head and contemplated vomiting in my lap. I hated fucking holomaps and I hated navigating when Parc was driving. Sick, I felt sick.

I hated *everything* when Parc was driving.

<*All units, we have a partial...*> Dispatch. My ears pricked. <*Suspect has blue hair in tendril style. No further details. Just blue 'drils, repeat... blue 'drils.*>

Blue 'drils. Standard. Especially among these anti-police parts. Easy to find *anyone* matching that...

I held my head up.

Market approaching.

MARKET APPROACHING!

"STAND BY!" I shouted. "Stand by..." Doubts welled up inside me. I was already on it, already on the cusp of doing something I had sworn I never would, of making something up to get an outcome. Going too fast, no time to contemplate.

Shit, am I actually going to do this? Is this how far I'll go?

I took in a sharp breath.

<*CONFIRMED SUSPECT, SEEN IN THE MARKET*> I shouted on the net and in Parc's ear. <*GO GO GO!*>

Parc gunned the craft left, through oncoming traffic, under the flashing billboard signs, over the interlink passenger carrier, through the narrowing barrel of accommodation spines, down to street level... towards The Market's grand entrance.

"Take the bottom tra-gh—" Parc shoved the AIT down so hard I had to swallow to stop my lungs flopping out my mouth and flying onto the dash. I gingerly parted my lips to drip-feed more directions, unsure if only words would come out. Fortunately, Parc had got it down to street level under her own steam and had swept right, over The Market and all its people and stalls. Every officer knew this plot like that back of their hand from their first days on foot patrol through here – an Intervention rite of passage.

Navigating the nefarious plot with ease, Parc focused on keeping us level against conflicting forces such as enclosed flight turbulence and the rotational effect of our ever turning ship. All this while maintaining her main flight priority: not letting the impeller gens get close enough to the peds below to shear scalps off skulls.

Meanwhile, I scoured our ground-facing displays, searching for what I needed to keep up the charade. Ignoring the stream of comms traffic demanding updates on our status, full suspect description, explanation of self-authorised flythrough. Heart pounding, I wondered at the incredulous position I was now in. *How had it come to this?*

<In pursuit, Market, headed towards Hub end, suspect foot mobile,> I lied, digging deeper and deeper. Looking up to our migrant ship's sad excuse for a sky, I sought inspiration in the snapshots flitting by.

Barlight shining down flickered bursts of light through the tangled sky above. Kilometers deep, the web of interlocking spines towered overhead in a mass that stretched all the way up to the barlight, itself fixed to the outside of Prime Shell.

Prime Shell was the inner shell of the ship, like a hollow pod in the middle of a bigger pod, propped in place by a mess of struts and supports. Great way to design two worlds within one ship, each with its own floor and people stuck down to it by the relative-gee of constant rotation along the ship's axis. From our position looking up, though, Prime Shell looked like a roof. Our sky had a ceiling, and we lived under it. That put a lid on your hopes and on your dreams. If the sky's the limit, and you can see it enclosing you above, that's a shit limit to live under.

Fixed onto that solid canopy above was our 'sun'. Shining a

circadian rhythm of light and dark, fading in and out to simulate dusk and dawn, that annulus of false light kept ship life turning around.

Filtering down through the jumble of spines, it dappled a late-evening glow onto the dingy market's coloured tarps below.

I looked down to those depths of Alpha passing by just below our craft, searching for a blue drilhead to act as my patsy and justification for this wild and risky shortcut. Just the sight of all the people jostling by reminded me of the smells and frustration of the place. Rotting synthfruits warming in the late heat of day alongside grilled protein strips from… unnamed sources. The people shoving by in their unwashed clothes, the bail hostels, squat houses, brothels and drugs dens.

Clarity – the onboard drug of choice. More of that vile liquid made, sold and used here than anywhere on ship. All giving people a false perception of their lives, making them feel less like cattle shipped to the latest cash cow planet bought by the Star Spanning Corporation, more like…

WARNING: POLICY BREACH

CRAFT AUTOMATED CONTROL COMING ONLINE

Craft nav displays blared 'policy breach' at Parc, the PIR now focusing on quickest routes out of the ped zone – *away* from Navaro's. With her little finger, she flicked a control on her holo nav.

AUTOMATED CRAFT NAVIGATIONS DISENGAGED

She had taken what I had said on faith yet now sensed all was not as it seemed. She took time out of her careful piloting to shoot me an accusatory glance.

WARNING: POLICY BREACH

CRAFT AUTOMATED CON—

AUTOMATED CRAFT NAVIGATIONS DISENGAGED

I gulped in a throat gone dry and hid from her eyes, diving back into the ground displays. Needed to find a patsy, a fake suspect far enough along The Market to justify drop-down close enough to Navaro's to pick up the real scent.

Pink drils. Blue puff. Red drils. Blue straights… come on…

I saw one in the distance. Blue drils… BLUE DRILS!

<*Suspect regained after partial loss…*>

Vaguely feasible I could have spotted them earlier on a long-scope. Grabbing the control icons on my UI display, I flicked a searchlight onto them and blared the harsh rush of the Angel horn in their direction. Predictable as the barlight rising each morning, they were on their toes and running into the masses to get away from Aerial Intervention.

As if I had planned it, I smiled to myself. My pre-brief from my soon-to-be boss in covert cover was: 'Ways and means don't matter to me. It's the end that counts…'

<*Suspect identified, blue drils, made off. Partial loss in the crowd, headed east off the market,*> I transmitted. I watched the triangle icon of our craft going through that red hatched zone, and the corner of my mouth rose into a smile.

<*But that leads back to Navaro's,*> an unknown officer countered with scepticism. <*There's always tons of drilheads around the market. Are you SURE it's the right su—*>

<*In pursuit, blue drils,*> I interrupted on the net. Marking a route on the nav holos, I flicked them over into Parc's display. The craft lurched as she matched the new plot.

ShiftCom came back on, ever steady.

<*Troops. Update from the officer's Superintendent, Commander Covert Ops. There is indeed an officer calling; he is running and under fire. The officer is also one of two priority suspects on scene. He is to be taken in without injury; stun only, stun only.*>

An officer: a *suspect*… to be *'taken in'*… what the…?

I heard the memory of Jao, my new boss in covert cover, talking in my ear. After hours of talk about how they were authorised to lie to anyone and everyone, including within Intervention and other ship security forces, he'd said something about how the Superintendent was particularly keen to get me into the unit asap, how there was due to be a vacancy. Surely this couldn't be—

<*Any units on scene, yet?*> ShiftCom again. <*Once at scene I'll divert others to support the pursuit – that officer is the priority.*>

<*Wing Seven-Six nearly there...*> came another unit, not one of ours.

I gritted my teeth, a sinking feeling dawning on me. That was the scene with the officer and the real suspect, not this random patsy I had spotted with the same common hairstyle. I had to get there and ditch this excuse of a suspect chase I had invented.

"Parc. Got an idea. Head out this way, cut the sus off..." I flicked over another route, leading us closer and closer to Navaro's. Parc shrugged, shunted us into the new line.

"Drop point?" She asked monotone, focusing on keeping the impeller gens exhaust out of burn range from the hoards below. "Need to deliver my cargo at some point," she chided, growing impatient.

I thought of the troops in the back, itching to drop through the hatches at their feet, protect one of their own and grab the suspect. And I'd have to get down somehow too – a problem for another moment. Whole seconds away in the future.

Checking the park-bay next Navaro's I saw more red hatching, another no-fly zone thanks to the gathering masses. Good, no competition. We were the only ones with a suspect pursuit confirmed. I marked the shortest route on nav and designated it our drop point.

<*Angel Nine-Nine, update on your pursuit? Is it still confirmed? How's it progressing?*>

<*Good.*> No sign of the random I spotted, but that didn't matter any more. They'd got us through The Market, that's all that mattered.

Parc: "That bay ok?"

"Yup – get 'em ready."

"Navaro's coming up," said Parc. "You better be sure, Jordan."

Bursting out the side of the market above the heads of the crowd gathering in the parking bay, we passed Navaro's on the left. A turmoil of more people flooded out, waving hands up, a mixture of gang signs, threats and 'welcoming signs' to the newly-arrived cavalry – us.

The craft swung into a holding pattern above them as Parc flicked switches and tapped screens with frenetic energy: signalling drop troops in the rear, releasing field-hatches, arming winches, activating crowd control ordnance.

"I won't be sticking around," she declared in the midst of his activity. "You might as well drop with the rest of them. I'll be by the main 'way if you need, Queen-Bravo I think." It was, and that was precisely my plan.

Parc nudged the roaring AIT over the dilapidated buildings and adjacent parking bays, whipping up a storm of dust over the organised chaos unfolding below. With the main ship's Rotational Positioning System, she locked the craft in place in our cramped aerial confines.

"...STEADY..." she shouted through the in-craft intercom to the shell behind. Stabiliser props kicked in.

Six officers behind unbuckled their seats, tugged their respective winch snicks down from grab-slots in the ceiling and clipped in. Pulling each rope to its lock-limit, they held them taught with both hands as I watched and plotted my next move.

"...GREEN..."

Green light washed the transport segment. The six jumped up on the spot with both feet. As each pair of boots left the floor of the hold, each personal hatch field opened to welcome them in the roiling confusion of the new world below.

Six slipped down through their drop-pods, into the turmoil of comms that was blaring out over the net. Six winches whirred in unison. I looked up unique dialler codes on my comms transceiver and called the first officer's ID that came up. Not the choice I would have made, but boots were on the ground now and every moment counted.

<Roge, Roge, it's Jordan. Hold fast your rope for me, I'm coming down on it. Hold fast your rope.> I pulled my key-disk out of the dash, clambered back over the headrest into the troop shell, and crouched on Roge's seat. Steadying myself with one hand on the roof, I reached the other to my right side and gripped a hip-slider nearby.

I took a deep breath. The hip-slider in my hand was

designed for use outside the craft, and strictly only following malfunctions. Well, call this a malfunction of general circumstance.

Five other winches whirred into action, whisking their ropes and snicks up into their grab-slots. Five irises pinched off the view of the world below. I stared through the beckoning hatch below, looking straight down into the inviting embrace of my own private torpedo tube.

<*I've got it pinned,*> Roge strained. <*Go for it!*>

I clipped the hip-slider on, checked it once with a shake, looked back into the 'pit. "Parc, drop me in!"

"STEADY," she shouted.

"GREEN."

Ughhh. I jumped.

Rope taut under my weight, the tearing sound of the slider zipped in my ears. My life rushed down a cable held in place one end by a craft hovering in complex and risky flying conditions, and at the other end by the arm strength of an officer in the middle of an unfolding riot.

Drowned only for a split second as I slid past the dread impeller-field generators.

Off-centre because of the side-mounted slider, I came through the craft's drop-tube off balance. Swinging my left arm out to steady myself at the worst possible moment, I felt a tingling rush as the skin and muscle tried to shear off the bone. My tongue tingled with an odd electric taste. Exhaust mixed with dust blown up by the props, chafing my nostrils.

Pulling my arm back in I instinctively grabbed the rope, forgetting that this one was rushing past me. Luckily my hand was still numb and too weak to grip it hard enough to burn the skin clean off. The synth palm of the glove got dangerously hot in an instant before I let go, losing stability yet again.

A swaying vision of chaos expanded underneath, rushing up fast. Rope trailing down, legs scissor-kicking to steady my descent, I saw four uniformed bodies diving on an unknown other, blood mixing in vortices of blasted dirt. More uniform flooded in from the sides, mingling with the clamour of

Navaro's most esteemed and feared clientele. Seems my prediction of a clusterfuck was spot-on.

The fragment of my brain not focussed on surviving the next two seconds noted we may just have beaten most of the others, but they were coming in fast. I had a chance, but it was slim…

The hip-slider rapidly grew from hot to searing. I looked down to see Roge; a hunched figure zooming towards me, desperately pinning the base of the rope down to the floor. Rookie. Arm's bloody length…

<*ROGE!*> I shouted. <*I'm coming in too fast for that; MOVE!*>

He got up and darted away, the bottom of the rope following along. He can't have forgotten to unclip first. Oh fuuuuu—

Roge had made it about three metres away. The curve of the cord leading down to his waist tightened the more rope rushed past. My dangling legs started cycling fast, ready for a hard landing.

<*—making off down the alley, blue drils, black leggings…*> unknown officer. I realised a whole trail of comms must have passed me by as I raced in towards Roge's running back. Nearly on the ground and moving at pace, bouncing up and down as Parc struggled with the craft's position, and my swooping bodyweight pinged the rope taut. Roge was snapped backwards clean off his feet. I unclipped from my slider just in time to hit the deck in a roll, bowling straight through the back of his legs.

Head. Hands. Knees. Left arm. Right elbow. Left cheek. Maybe ribs too. The pain in each was clamouring to be first in line for my attention.

I finished rolling, got up in a run and disappointed them all. I abandoned a heap that was Roge with a hand wave over my shoulder and sprinted ahead. Darting through the melee, I caught another officer's eyes – Sa'ra. I opened my arms out, palms up in desperate query. She pointed me down an alley. A couple of the others were already disappearing into its depths.

<*Confirm officer secure. Anyone; is the officer safe?*> I asked

over the net, hurtling towards the alleyway entrance. I had seen a bunch of officers huddled over a figure, puddles of dust-whipped blood gathering around them, but no indication as to who, what or why. I looked into the cool depths of that dank alleyway and rushed in.

Ducking under cooling vents and dodging past impossibly cramped fire escape ladders, I made it to the end and pushed hard off the foamcrete wall into a right-angle turn. As I ran on, the alleyway zig-zagged in more right-angle turns and I kept slamming the corners away with one hand or the other. The heels of my palms were screaming at me to stop using them as brakes with each thud into the solid wall ahead of me, many of them the thick trunks of accommodation spines soaring up above.

I compromised. Reaching the next turning, I put both hands up to the wall for a less bone-crunching slam. I looked both ways.

Shit. Two turnings.

Left. Something better about left. Don't question: run. You've got to be brave, but you've got to be right.

My brain caught up late with the comms I had heard a couple of turns back: <*Officer safe, suspect made off.*>

Good. I kept running. Definitely a foot chase, now.

Fear gripped my stomach. Same, familiar old fear. Legs made of wood, telling me I can't make it. I'm going to look stupid. Going to lose the suspect. Going to let everyone down.

Every time. Same fear. We were old friends now.

Disappointing people.

Looking stupid.

Wall; turn right. Run.

Grips me. Threatens to take over.

The few people I spoke to about it didn't feel the same. Didn't talk about it again.

Run.

Fear.

Earpiece bleeping – no comms signal here.

Same stupid, irrational fear. Can't catch them. Won't catch them.

Didn't even make sense as a fear: more dangerous to catch them than to lose them, but fear is fear.

Run. Push on. Push on, legs!

My heels pounded the ground. Lungs rasped to get oxygen to my muscles. Hands slammed each dead-end wall away in succession, throwing me into the next alley. And the next. And the next…

Risked everything for this. Last chance…

The final right turn opened out into the communal mini-park accessed by a block of spine entrances, child playthings and swings hanging in the middle, broken. My legs stumbled into the clearing.

Regained.

My earpiece stopped bleeping: back in comms. One of the officers ahead. Running towards the exit on the right. Struggling, he slowed down when he heard me pounding towards him.

I overtook with a shout. "Where?"

I was already halfway to the exit before he transmitted.

<*That exi—*> he gasped. <*Two sec— two seconds ahead…*>

Sprinting through the pain.

Finally transmitted my status. <*Officer chasing!*> I puffed.

Better late than never.

<*Standby for location…*> I searched the top corner of the exit passageway for an alley name.

<*Deviner Square,*> transmitted the recovering voice in the park behind. <*Headed West – he's chasing the back routes.*>

I kept pursuing my invisible stranger, my fading chance of redemption.

This alley was wider. <*Dr'inas Alley!*> Moulding sign up top.

Disappearing down the left: soles of roof-climber footwear. <*Close behi--*> I started. Earpiece bleeped me out. No signal again. No energy to swear.

<*—Ey're headed towards Queen-B Road.*> Someone.

<*Nine Nine.*> Parc. Sirens. I grimaced through the pain. Not far.

Spittle on my chin. Won't wipe, would off-balance pumping arms.

Sus took the last right. Ten metres ahead. Gone. Stomach in knots again. Never make ten metres up. Sprinted. They had been dead ahead. Skinny. Toned. Mottled top. Shiny black leggings. Roof-crawler pumps.

Blue drilhead. This was the one. Locked on.

Reached the turn. Took it wide; had to save the hands. Dull ache. Would need them.

<*Trauma medics on scene.*> The comms net came alive: back in signal. <*Target being lifted.*>

Turn. Left shoulder caught brickwork. Scuffed armour. Slight stumble. Still running. In sight.

'Trauma medics'? Coming down rope; image of bloody scene in park-bay. *'Officer secure.'* Officer's blood?

Right hand swung to abdomen. Pistol. Peeled it out. Still running. Thumb on selector.

SPAS. No choice now. Committed.

<*Suspect coming out on Queen-B, lot of peds out here, more units!*> Parc. Stabiliser props blasted. Downdraft. Drilhead running. Slowing.

SPAS. Do it before more peds. Legs: lactic. Lungs: raw. Taste: blood.

<*I've got no operator, can't provide overwatch. Sorr—*>

Down.

Time.

<*Stun only, please.*> ShiftCom.

Finger already on trigger. Lying prone. Only way to steady tired arms.

Right eye: blurred notch, blurred pin, three dots dancing on running legs.

Breathe out.

Squeeze.

Notch and pin bounced up. Settled down. Notch, pin, dots. Tumbling torso, covered in mesh.

Success.

Made it.

I made it!

I breathed in, shoved myself up. Racing start, I bolted forwards. Ran to his side, pistol raised. Trying to see his hands. In my periphery, more SPAS-pistols were joining me. Covering me. I ran ahead.

People were watching from the main road. The cameras would be on from the AIT above, sweeping down with the stabiliser props. All eyes on me.

"OPEN YOUR HANDS, SHOW ME YOUR HANDS, SHOW ME YOUR HANDS" I bellowed for all the Quad to hear. His legs were still jerking, floundering from the SPAS round's nerve charges.

I neared the body, pistol still raised. The left arm was visible and clear – empty-handed – but the right remained hidden. Troops had me covered from this side, but not enough.

"SHOW ME YOUR RIGHT HAND, SHOW ME YOUR RIGHT HAND." I closed the remaining few paces. The torso lifted itself up slightly, propped on the right elbow. The right hand disappeared near the right hip. Impossible to tell whether propping the body up or reaching for something. Unwise to guess.

I planted my left foot near the suspect's slender thighs. His face rolled over to face me and… What the…? Female?

"SHOW ME YOUR HAND!"

Nothing.

I dropped down, planted my left knee into her stomach with all my weight and raked my elbow across her face, my open hand searching for that hidden forearm.

Smiling. She was positively beaming up at me. What the fuck was wrong with these people?

Complex folds of micrograv fields in my harness sucked my pistol lovingly into their embrace as I palmed it into my chest. Still kneeling on her stomach, I wrenched that hand out from under her. A dark green thumb-clicker fell out of her hand as I pulled her arm back toward me, rolling her over onto her front and re-planting my knee in the small of her back. Pinning her wrist back on itself, I wedged her inverted elbow tight between my thighs, pressed my weight onto her back and gave myself a moment's breath.

Still panting hard.

After a lot of swallowing to alleviate the shredding dryness of my throat, I could definitely taste blood. Too tired right now to check whether from injury or just the rasping of my lungs.

I looked down at her face. Her sinewy, smug little face. Still grinning. There was a mark of blood on her lower lip beginning to swell.

"Yoouu duumb pricks!" She drawled in a bizarre accent I couldn't place. Didn't sound like anything from this migrant ship. And she couldn't be a non-migrant smuggled aboard. Could she? "What's yuuoour naaame, y'duuumb, siingle miiii-inded prick?"

"Intervention Officer Jordan Shui-Te," I said automatically, possibly for the last time before I handed my real name in for a series of fakes.

"Yuuooouuu have nooo ide—" she coughed, a violent, jarring sound, "…ideeea in yuoouuur liiittle mind. Chevron will cooome, wiiill coome for yuuou aall." She laughed, hacking up bloodied phlegm. She left it in her open mouth a moment before swallowing it back down. I wrinkled my nose in a sneer.

"The clicker: what was in it? WHAT WAS IN IT?" I pressed down on her bent-back wrist. Everything around me had disappeared. The noise, the dust, the prop-blast, the whole ship watching us through the gathering journodrones. The whole of existence was Just me and this dying drilhead.

"Was this clicker for that person you nearly killed back at Navaro's?" I had been looking for a gun in her hand, something that could have caused all that blood back at the drop-point, but anyone could have missed a thumbnail-sized injector like the one she had dropped. "Was it for me?" She could have…

"Yuooouuu'll never knoouw, and I'lllll never taoulk." She beamed up at me.

"AND WHO IS CHEVRON?" I barked, angry and confused.

Her already insane grin widened impossibly at my use of the name. Eyes glazed. Her narrow, muscular jaw dropped open a fraction, but the grin remained. Her body went limp.

Sounds flooded into my eardrums. Mighty dams keeping the mad world at bay collapsed. Sirens, shouts of troops demanding information, the blast of stabilising props, overlapping comms chatter. In the crowd, someone shouted 'he just chased and killed that poor woman'. Shouts rose up: 'Police brutality!' 'Racist!'

My mind was drowning in the chaos.

I looked down at her right hand. There was a dark pinprick on the thumb. The epicentre of a microcosm. Gathering around it, a drop of blood began to swell.

Officers grabbed my shoulder, shook me. I realised they were shouting, all at once, different voices yelling at me. "Are you hit?" "Is she dead?" "What rounds did you use?" "She was aiming at you, wasn't she?" "Is she the one who killed the other officer?" "Where's the gun?"

Beyond them I could hear more shouts from the crowd building around us, the props above, other callsigns now joining Parc, journos on foot.

I heard Parc's tannoy above the racket: *"Do you need a medevac?"*

Just more noise.

The dead suspect and I were the epicentre of a shipwide storm brewing around us.

I made it. I caught the suspect, and everyone I knew saw it. Yet… nothing was resolved, nothing clear.

Who is Chevron?

I looked up to the fading barlight of a dusky evening, the AIT craft and news drones hovering in the thick dust cloud. No doubt they would be watching it all unfold back in covert cover. I shut my eyes against the turbulent world outside.

Who is Chevron?

EX.

…

Hm…

An interesting one, that, and it did lead to some exciting times for me. Yes in case you hadn't guessed, that's the reason law enforcement has a special place in my heart – it's where I cut my teeth.

I've lived several lives since then, of course, but these experiences live on within you, even if you do move on and move away from them.

You see, we just travelled into a past version of my mind. This is not an opportunity available to the standard Qit traveller, I hope you appreciate. The Galactic Visits and Quantum Travel Standards Board sets an arbitrary galactic reference frame and only allows travel that maintains that without exception.

Commutation, however, works on similar principles but with altogether different access. People don't even know that relativity ladders exist, let alone the opportunities available thereon. Far too focussed on the restrictions imposed upon rather than possibilities available within.

But then most people don't have the special ally of a Commutator. They don't even know about Commutation – this is a privileged situation, I hope you understand. The ordinary layperson doesn't get to know about, let alone pass through, The In Between just like that you know! There are reasons my dear journeyer: reasons.

I've said it from the outset, you're not any commuter. Not with my patronage, heavens no!

Oh don't be like that, I'm not all bad. You were there, you saw some of what I was dealing with. There is courage in such choices, you know… courage to make those choices, courage to face up to them and own them. Yes… and to own… their consequences, too. Not so easy those. But then there is—

What was that?

That you?

No?

No.

Ok, well… er.

Right.

Listen, er… hahaha!

Er…

This is all terrific fun out here, but let's get on to our next appointment. I know how desperately you want to see, er, that place you were, um, yes! You wanted to see… er, that tropical… er… deserted partysphere I told you about. Yes, just the place!

Off we go…

Hold tight, my furry friend, it's a fast ride for a long way.

Face forward. Head down. Go go go go go go go go…

THE SHORT COMMUTE

IN.

Keep going, that's it.

Hold on, just a little adjustment here.

Gosh we're going fast. That's a harsh identity wind–dniw ytitnedi hsrah– and, ah, think even I'm losing myself in thi—

Oh.

Right.

Got it.

Here goes.

The twin suns of Uina Lor lowered through the deepening pink sky above. Laia L'osh looked to the purple mountains in the distance as Praeta Li leant against the railings of the wooden bridge, gazing into his eyes. Water babbled underneath, mingling with the chirping of newly hatched…

Joanna swore at the barriers as spilt coffee scalded her hand. Actively ignoring the swell of commuters flooding either side of her to the adjacent tube barriers, she realised she had been trying to tap in with her staff pass. She wasn't even supposed to show this one in public.

Swearing again, this time at herself, someone tapped on her shoulder. She spun to…

…warmth of his hands as he held hers. For the first time since the wars, her warrior-prince was able to rest. The battle forged furrows of his brow smoothened. It gave him a peaceful appearance she had forgotten he was capable of, and that calm radiated. She drank it in, enjoying the mo—

A bang in the distance and his whole body tensed. Xaian Dor didn't flinch, didn't turn to see. He just hardened, in an instant reverting to the cold, tense persona he had lived in for…

…jostling crowds, elbowing and shoving Dharmendra as he reached out a hand, desperate to cling back onto his…

…grip steady as the walls of the small sloop rattled. Blasts from the Armada's flagship cannons radiated in the vacuum of space, illuminating the diamond-studded blackness with each successive flash. They wanted to take it for their own.

X'ash T twisted with fresh vigour to reload the guns on her left from the stash of cartridges to her…

…Su'th'quia as Su'th'quia continued bending through the waters. The waters were dark here, but Su'th'quia knew them well enough to get through safely. This was something different, something targeted. This was an attack.

Su'th'quia wriggled and writhed, taking blows to Su'th'quia's body from every angle. Wrapping a tentacle around Su'th'quia's beak to protect the secret hidden in there against the onslaught…

…hands over their heads, splinters of the crystal caves above showered down. Loosened by the ongoing ballistic fire from uniformed squads of…

…clutched tightly to his chest.

Keep going. Joa didn't know how, but he had to keep running. The mountains were no longer safe, yet this craggy route was the only way he could escape. Stories of what had happened to the others were true, he was sure. And he couldn't let himself become another. He looked up at the dark night sky with a grateful smile.

Luckily, they had come for him the one night this year when all three moons were waning crescents, thin slivers of light in the night sky. Hunting under the dark moons was hard.

Slipping, he sliced a hand on an outcrop of the volcanic glass he was fleeing through. Still, he was grateful. Darkness was a blessing if you were the hunted.

Stumbling again, he paused to listen to…

…waited a little longer. Silence continued.

Was it over? They patted themselves down, checking the miracle was true, checking they hadn't been hit in the barrage.

Peeping out from their shell scrape, somehow unscathed, they saw…

…opportunities open up. Heavy doors slammed behind her, closing the depths of the library from the rioting public. She patted her hidden jacket pocket instinctively, just to be sure.

Blinking in the light of the outdoors – real outdoors, on a planet – she stepped into the crowd. Always the safest place to hide, in plain sight among the masses…

…soft whispers lost in the sounds of water.

Secret languages of all sorts, they had tried and failed.

Digital and analogue, spoken or communicated physically through sign or touch. All of them had been cracked and compromised one way or another, many times involving horrific treatment of their compromised agents.

So here she was, making quiet whispers in a public swimming pool on the nebular cruise ship, sailing past the glittering views of…

…landed with a splash in the cold water below the sky cliffs, facing the glorious sunny shores of the floating…

…brilliant starlight of the surrounding Orpheul Globular Cluster illuminated the night as Jansa stepped out of the hotel lobby. Suited and booted she was ready for a night shift of hedonism in the finest drinking district the Cluster had to…

…queuing like this. It was such a chore. And quite frankly the company were all obnoxious, old money bastards. Eyes on the slowly moving bar queue, his ears were unfortunately open to all their conversations.

"…I mean, no one knows how hard it is, inheriting wealth like this. My family amassed a portfolio of planets through the early migrations, one knows. It puts a lot of pressure on one such as I, the first daughter endeavouring to establish a reputation of my own name. And it's not like in the old days."

"Do you know what you need? Just a couple of breakthrough planets. If you could be the one to own a small investment portfolio like that, it would really establish you as someone worth paying attention to in your own…"

Sholan tuned out, disgusted. Filthy bitches.

Looking over his shoulder at the nebula visible from the viewing balcony, he longed to get his drink and get back to the cute guy with three ears waiting for him, hoping for…

• • •

…tension and excitement in the air so thick you could slice it off and serve it in your cocktail.

She loved it!

Hedonistic pilgrims flooded here from the galaxy over for a reason… flooding the Qit web with their pleasure-hungry minds. All for the privilege of hopping bars: glittering domes on cruiser viewing platforms, raucous little divebars in the side of cylindrical podhabs, zero-gee pleasure spheres in the centre of spinning hubs. Skiffs were flitting to and fro doing the shuttles runs, allowing people to drink, take, toke, spike and generally party their way ever closer to the unpopulated tropical mindhell of Sciree Tritan IV.

DJs spin here from the whole galaxy for the blazing glory of fireworm season. The seething, roaring, shouting masses of people on this ship, and every other one on the Golden Light Walk, knew it!

Hands, arms, hooves and tentacles reached into the holograms projected above – a music-loving display of unity – as the track built and built and built.

Tension elevated, excitement hanging in the air.

Right on the money, the trio of DJs in this ship dropped it into the breakdown…

Hang on a moment more, my erstwhile chum. Harsh reality wind, but we're nearly there…

…Ereht ylraen er'er tu…

…Peek ot deen tsuj ew…

…We just need to keep going. It might feel warm and fuzzy now, but trust me we can't stay here. Must keep going.

…Secrof krad…

Dark forces have been at our heels, we need to guard against what may…

THE KNIFE WAS

The knife was supposed to help. To keep him safe. To scare away any bigger boys… only scare them. Soldiers they called them, even though they weren't real soldiers – they just sold drugs and bullied people. They had hung around at his latest friend's funeral, the one on his twelfth birthday. She had been shot by some guys from the next quad, died before she got to the C-Alpha Medbay. What was he supposed to do? Never leave the house? He had to do the shopping for his Nan, she wasn't so well these days.

The knife was supposed to keep him safe.

It didn't look too safe sticking out like that…

He had just bought the groceries from the stall on the outskirts of The Market in Quad B-Alpha, the one at the bottom of the huge housing spine, Maine Jwana. The barlight was already starting to dim towards another hot, muggy evening as he was heading back home. He had to walk through the only bit of the route he really didn't like.

Nan had promised to cook him her special yat fruit curry from their home planet if he went out to buy the right ingredients from her favourite stall. He had been scared at first, but he didn't think it was fair to live in fear of the bullies in the area. So Joachim stood up tall, took one of Nan's special kitchen knives from the drawer he wasn't usually allowed to open, and he took the tube up to ground level. The blade was in its sheath, tucked between his bum cheeks. That Intervention Officer had told him to hide it there, right after letting him off for carrying with just a bit of a telling off. He had listened, that officer, been the only one to understand what it was like to live here, the only one to care. The officer had told him Prevention Officers wouldn't find it there, because they're too afraid of being sued to properly check your bum.

Joachim felt safer knowing it was there. He would just have to show it to anyone trying to cause problems and they would see how sharp it was; it was a real diamond edge. That would make them back off.

So he got the fruits, roots and spices on the list and was carrying them back when he saw two of the soldiers from B-Alpha. They were arguing right ahead of him in the tunnel back to his quad. It was the only tunnel for ages around. When they saw him, they started shouting at him, telling him to fuck off. He didn't know what else to do, he had to get home – Nan had been alone for too long already. They started to scare him. When he got really close and they still didn't get out of the way, still kept shouting at him, he was terrified. He did the only thing he could think of. He dropped the shopping, pulled the knife out and screamed.

They were supposed to run away.

They should have been scared when they saw the blade. It was self-sharpening, and would never go blunt. That's what Nan had always told him.

They weren't supposed to laugh. Or kick him. Or punch him in the ribs.

The soldier-boys pushed him on the floor, rolled him over, and kept hitting him. When they punched him in the side it felt hot, really hot. He could feel them pulling Nan's change from his trouser pocket, and they were still laughing when they ran through the tunnel. He saw the canned yat fruits rolling away out of the ripped carrier bag and felt something hard in his back pocket; his key-buzzer. At least he still had that; they wouldn't know where Nan lived. He was about to get up and pick up the canned yats when he looked at his side to see if it was bruised.

That was when he saw the handle sticking out. It shouldn't have taken him so long to recognise it. It just looked so weird coming out of him like that. Nan would be so cross that he had taken it. He lay there for a while thinking about what Nan would say, then he started to feel tired.

The dust around him was starting to blow into his eyes and mouth, and he could hear something. Something loud. It wasn't his Nan.

There were flashing lights. They looked blue. He tried to focus on them, but his eyes were tired and sore, closing. The sound grew louder.

Joachim tried to spit the dust out. It tasted like metal, barely fell out of his mouth.

EX.

Right… are you clear? Are we clear?

Hold on a moment.

Let's pause here a time…

…

A little longer in The In Between and we can move on, I promise you that. And look, we'll get to what you've just experienced, but give me… just a moment longer.

…

Ok good. Apologies for any confusion there, my friend. I never intended to take you to that tropical sludge pile I referenced, but it's a place they'll be looking for our trail for a while. Bunch of mixed signatures out there for them to root through before they realise.

We had picked up a tail you see. I had taken every precaution in coming to meet you and in each of our journeys, but that was always a risk I faced. Terrible bloody sort, too, prone to dropping someone in The In Between, unconnected, undirected. Lost. Trapped here for good, an eddy in the swirling currents of identity.

Huhrrhuhrr.

Gives me the creeps.

And are you ok? I pulled us on quite a manoeuvre there – actually had to transition through a few other bodies to mask our tracks. Not sure how noticeable that would have been for an uninitiated journeyer such as your good self. You can't taste burnt toast covered in iron filings, can you? Very distinct if you can. Disorientation? Nausea? A headache that feels like someone translocated a hot coal straight into the middle of your brain? No?

Excellent, good. Look, no-one was hurt, you're not hurt. Our route back was circuitous, I made sure of that. They shouldn't…

Look, we're safe for a time but that time isn't long. I've tarried with you long enough and they'll be back on us soon no doubt. I know precisely who's following us, and why Unpleasant folk – the sort with whom one does not fuck. I haven't the time to tell you about them now, but I do have the time to tell you why we're here, why we're actually here.

Something is happening.

It's happening across the galaxy, and certain people are concerned about what it may bring. These concerned citizens want to do something about it before lots more people get concerned, because by the time everyone is concerned, everyone will be affected – and that's too late.

Now, Earth isn't part of the Qit web, nor can it be because there's no pipeline leading to this system. But there are other ways to connect into the galactic web of quantum teleportation, especially when there's a powerful motive.

A powerful motive like military advantage, or significant commercial gain, or adversarial political advantage.

Imagine…

An untapped stepping stone in the expanding puzzle of the galactic web. A new resource of warm bodies of flesh and blood, ready to have brains connected for the economic elite to spin into with their elevated sense of debauchery. Ravaging all they find in insidious ways, they will poison and pervert the cultural fabric of the Earth-dwelling race.

Worse, and believe me there is indeed that… Worse will also come here in the flood. Earth is an undiscovered treasure trove for Qit pipeliners of every kind and creed.

Opportunities will abound to sell the benefits of connection to the galactic community, selling access to treasures unimaginable… and all in a way that economically injures and enslaves the host planet. All of those advantages, military, financial or political, can be achieved by the wrong people pitching up in your Solar System with a case full of quantum entangled blank data ready to spin in a few key people. That's how it begins.

Expert agents are out there, ready to instil significant change from within untapped populations. That would not just be catastrophic for Earth, it would be disastrous for the whole galactic population, for the wider 'us' – all biological sentience. When titanic forces hang in a delicate balance, my friend, even a dislodged pebble can bring a whole mountain down.

I believe we have aligned desires, you and I. A common purpose. What I said when we met about starting strangers, departing friends… well, I'd like to leave the door open to becoming future allies too. You see, we have cause to believe this may already have started, Qit pipeliners starting the groundwork. The masses won't know a thing yet, Earth remains dark, undiscovered by the galactic population. But when it is formally discovered the chase is on. I've seen what happens in such times and things get busy.

Soon enough my friends and I will have cause to call on people we can trust. People who understand the stakes, who understand the moral ambiguity to navigate in making the right decision at the right time.

Distinction.

Distinction not between what is right or wrong as judged against some external standards.

Distinction between what will achieve the desired result and what will not.

Do you understand all of that? It's critical that you do, I need you to.

That's why I wanted you to see some of my past back there in the aerial chase. It's still important that you see more though. It's important that you learn not to judge the choices people make without knowing what leads them to make that choice. You need to see beyond that to the thing causing them to make their choice, the thing making it acceptable to live with the consequences of that choice.

This connection is essential.

I don't know… perhaps that's why I took you back there. I hadn't meant to, you know? I just needed to double back across our tracks, needed somewhere near where we had been before. They were right on us and I suppose I must have fumbled the controls, when trying to slip back across our ladder close to where we'd been just before. You see, if you go down a touch lower on a ladder in a similar geography, you can look upwards and see the ripples they make when they've been sniffing around for you.

That's why we ended up back at SSC Aasha. Why we ended up inside that particular person's life, though… that short vignette you've just seen. I suppose I must instinctively have been thinking of him.

Speaking of connection, I suppose, in a way, Joachim's story is what led me to some of my choices, some of what I've had to live with.

I only met him once and, in all honesty, I did believe that by cutting him some slack I was helping him. Please believe me when I say that. I believed… I believed I was helping him when I didn't arrest him. I guess they were right when they said it was… I guess they were…

I'm sorry. It's just still too close for me.

It's is hard to underestimate the implications this had on that ship. I… well… as our relationship develops, you and I, it's vital that we share this, I suppose… I personally have rather a number of, ah, deep and very significant… hm…

Memories are… funny old things, don't you think? Joachim. He was a sweet kid, you know? And, stars around, so much blood when we arri—

…

…

I'm sorry. Perhaps it wasn't such a good idea to go back there after all.

I don't know. Perhaps it was.

It's… important to acknowledge the things that shape us, don't you think? For better or worse. It's our interpretation of events that counts.

Individuals, communities: our interpretations of such painful experiences… well, it gives them meaning. Whether we find it hidden deep within the essence of the event and take it out into our own lives, or whether we see the meaning within ourselves and attach that onto the event… My point is this… these meanings move us forward, help us make sense of what's happened. Maybe even improve what is yet to happen.

Rarely easy, but we can shape it as we choose, this future that we mould like clay with our hands. We can even shape it towards a greater good.

Look, all this is all well and good, and I'm glad we got the opportunity, but we need to keep moving. I can keep our tracks clear, but only for a little longer, and I need you to see something. Something I can't let them see.

I don't know how much longer we're safe for. Come.

THE QUANTUM COMMUTE

IN.

Ok, ready? Given all we've shared, how our relationship has progressed, I can see that your patience has served you well.

You are ready. Yes. You were right to wait for this one, to build up your experience and resilience in these matters, to develop your ability to hold onto a coherent sense of self, even when identities blur. You'll need it.

Now we've been commutating, you and I, through The In Between into a range of lives in the here, the now, the soon and the then. In that respect, I have afforded you a freedom withheld from the masses of the galactic community. This leverages some of the infrastructure, the physical properties and the opportunities afforded by the ancient Qit web. The results are instantaneous, the landing is smooth – the effects of integration into another's life are absolute.

Quantum commuting is itself, however, a little different. It's a point worth noting for it is, after all, the way common citizens of the galaxy do it.

Electronic user-interfaces. Those are the key, the gateway to the stars. Every person, pretty much irrespective of socioeconomic status, has one implanted in their brains. These UIs integrate electronically with the brain to digitise a large portion of the personality and memories.

It's not a complete copy, of course, but decent enough. And when it's downloaded into another squishy wet brain, it starts pushing out electronic signals. These work to take over the networks and connections grown over a lifetime in the new, host brain. In this way, it forces a biochemical simile of the electronic personality, which is itself a copy of a biochemical original.

Now, this all sounds very theoretical, but when that copied and converted identity is your own… Well. It feels a bit bloody odd, to tell the truth.

To think that this is how the people scattered across the stars get about the place, it scrambles my mind. Which is daft, of course. I mean it's how I used to get about the place before they invited me into this privileged position and initiated me in the secret wonders of Commutation.

And don't get me wrong, some Qit stations are well-presented establishments but – stars abound – some are bloody awful, piss-ridden little hovels, all open cables with dirty metal jacks going straight into the back of your skull. Goodness, I think I'd take a New Delhi super-crush over commuting like that again, any day!

So… have I sold it to you?

Good! Because you're about to experience this for yourself, albeit I have selected for your initiation no ordinary spin-through. Yes… it always did interest me, contemplating what happens to the biological remnants of the brain's identity when a fresh electronic mind spins in and starts taking over…

Unique insights I offer to you, fellow traveller. Take it as a gift, a token of where we've got to, an invitation to where we need to go. And this is no ordinary trip from a commutator perspective, either – no! I have curated for you a scrapbook, collated snippets to bring you up to speed and add some texture to the interwoven tapestry of this story.

But don't get distracted by the logistical effort required to get you into the room to see what you will see. Remember what I said about the galactic storm brewing? There are broader issues at stake here.

Through all we've seen, you're about to see the world from the dark edge of a precipice. You will be close to those that stand on it, and as you look out through their mind's eye, consider this:

Are you ready to see the death of your personal values to allow rebirth?

Will you let go the principles you have developed in the context of this time, this place, to allow the growth of something that will be of use when the time comes?

Like the detective, will you prioritise the good of those souls you swear to protect over the principles you swear to uphold?

Like the thief, will you exploit your surroundings to achieve your goals?

Like the Martian, will you take the long view, spilling the blood of people now to protect the blood of whole races in the future?

Like the electronic girl, will you sacrifice all you are for the love of others?

Will you learn from the mistakes of others, as your own mistakes impress their lessons upon you? Will you hold your ego and hubris below what actually matters? Will you understand the dangers of preparatory arming in the name of defence?

These questions matter. Remember them when the time comes, distant in your future. Right, here we go… get ready. Bit of a bumpy ride in, we had to transition through a couple of sites. We've come out pretty far here, to the other side of the disc.

Now, once you're in and starting to spin through you must – mark, this is critical – you must remember to hold

.

on

to

.

your

se…

…nse

of

I'M NOT READY

Crablet Sangera Station
Crab Cluster Distributed News Feed 103.43.119
Economic situation continues to worsen
As CCTC, Combined Cluster Trade Consortia,
Continue to fail in progressing negotiations on aggregated fuels.
Unionists call for intervention from Galactic bodies
Regional Praeda diplomats decline to comment.

"I'm not ready," Shondrei sulked.

"I know," said Mother with a soft smile. "But still... it's time."

"What about my toys?" He folded his arms, puffed his cheeks.

"You won't be needing those at the Star Garden Xzang. There will be many other things to occupy your time."

"But why do I have to go? I don't want to be a monk. I don't even see the point in stupid religion. My science teachers tell me it's rebundant." His mother smiled at Shondrei's fledgeling vocabulary, despite the cute little mistakes. So young, so bright.

"Well, regardless of what they think, the galaxy is changing,

Shondrei. Yet more trade embargoes on freighter-class fuel… your father and I just can't work like we did. We simply can't afford to send you to school like your brother. I am sorry Shondrei." She was unable to smile any more – it broke her heart to send her son away to the Xzang monastery.

"A year ago when things were different, we could afford all this." She held her hands out, taking in their modern, well-loved middle-class quarters. "I know how much you want to learn, and you're a terribly clever young man."

Shondrei shuffled his folded arms. His mother tried once more to smile.

"I am sorry."

Through Light to Dark
X'ang the 1193rd
In finding self, one must lose self
One must lose one to become not one
To become not is to find

"I am sorry to say you are mistaken," Star-Brother Shondrei told his neighbour, Newchild Lolac. They sat upright at the long, low wooden table of the Xzang Monastery's Spanning Hall. "The more technology develops, the more we need religion. The more tech pushes the boundaries of what augmented human civilisation can achieve, the more we need to remind ourselves and our societies of the mysteries and truths that lie within us. The more we need to turn our eyes inwards." Muted click-clacks of bamboo cutlery and hushed conversations around them filled the holy expanse.

"But if no-one listens, we are just speaking to ourselves and to our old tomes of scripture," retorted the Newchild. Shondrei was glad the New were happy speaking to him. He enjoyed challenging them – it encouraged him to challenge himself.

Plus, he still remembered the fear and disorientation of being New, this felt like giving back.

"We do not need to speak. We need to listen. Inwardly. Only by listening do we find something to say. And when the time is appropriate, someone will ask us." Star-Brother Shondrei paused at this. "When they are ready to listen."

Newchild Lolac turned to face him. The conversations around them had stopped. All eyes were fixed on Shondrei.

"And when we speak," he continued, "our quiet voice will span the stars themselves."

Art and the Emergence of Faith
Collected works:
Ed. Scribe of Nebula-Nursery Xzang

Artworks of ancient civilisations are a portal like no other. They transcend time and allow us to read minds. They penetrate the souls of creatures long gone… Teach us what they might have thought when they first looked up with wonder at the heavens, pondering the miracle of their existence.

In his early years of his faith, when Newchild Shondrei still pined after his busy parents as they visited strange new worlds, he found comfort in his Emergent Theologies classes. In them, he could travel to distant civilisations and learn how they developed adoration for God and Creation.

As he studied their art and imagined their lifestyles. His Faith was broad enough to encompass them all with compassion. His belief that all their respective beliefs were connected and compatible steadily grew. To stand here, teaching his first class of wide-eyed Newchildren as a junior lecturer felt fitting.

"Welcome all to An introduction to Emergent Theologies," Senior Shondrei beamed. "Now, this piece of art I could show you through a hologram, but one of the senior students' classes made this clay pot to help me introduce my favourite story. Gather round… make sure you can see it

"Now, this civilisation was very young when this pot was made. Imagine small islands surrounded by warm sea," he urged their eager faces. "High grasses, diverse wildlife, the earliest buildings this race had ever made were only just being finished. You see, they had recently discovered they were different from the beasts, for they had tamed the strongest of them. You can see it here, this fearsome, strong, horned taurus in the middle." Some children recoiled as he pointed at the beast painted on the pot.

"Now you see, by taming this animal they achieved so much. They made their society safe from its kind, and more… They tethered it, and it helped pull the heavy stones to build their temples and homes. They ate it and grew healthy and multiplied. They tanned its skin and made quality clothes to protect them from the elements, tools to use. They prospered!" This story had always excited Shondrei. He picked up the pot holding it closer to their bright, inquiring eyes.

"And here, you see two men holding the wild beast in position. The one in the middle is a growing child – not much older than you – who would have been terrified of the beast." Gasps. "And yet, by facing that fear, we see the child here leaping over its back. By leaping over the taurus, that boy showed he had personally conquered the same challenge his society had conquered. He had conquered the beast and achieved acceptance as one among adults, the true members of that society. He transcended his past life and became part of something so much more…"

Mastering Thesis, Star Garden Xzang
Ethically bridging the gap between tech and Faith
Sensei Shondrei-sha
Abstract:
Our creations of technology allow us to span the stars
Yet what we here find in the void between them

Is the beauty of a life unaltered – the beauty of pure nature
To hack this is to hack our souls

Robes of red billowed about his floating form, like the blood he sensed he was about to spill. The zero gravity Monastic Xzang Conclave was situated in an ancient, purpose-built interstellar habitation.

Sensei Shondrei-sha's mouth was dry.

He had been selected.

His grasp of the traditional tenets of Starspanning Xzangism, combined with his contemporary appreciation of User-Interface implants and human-tech augmentation, made him a clear choice. The Conclave had elected him for Starbirth – the first Starbirth in many generations.

Floating in the centre of the assembly, red robes gathering around him in folds. He surveyed his peers with deliberate care. He did not smile. His fellow Sensei Brothers and Sisters had elevated him to the noblest height. In doing so, they had signed a warrant on his death.

In the bubbling background noise of quantum particles popping in and out of existence, triple-encrypted comms hide in the depths of frequency space
...It's been a long time coming, but it's his time now...
...You ready to pull her in?...
...As if you needed to ask...
...huh...

"It's time, Andran."

"Yes. I'm ready." Andran followed her nameless Mentor through the doors as they irised open, recognising the familiar layout of a galactic-standard spin chamber. The hexagonal cell had an antique metallic chair at its centre, spiny bundles of armoured Qit-tubing spilling from behind the headrest.

Smiling, Andran took the seat. Sitting in a Quantum Information Teleportation pod, ready to spin-through to yet another far-flung destination, was her only home from home. No physical place of abode, no distinct identity of abode. The irony was not lost.

A brief glimpse through a port-hole showed the glimmer of a nearby star cluster. Suppressing a shudder, the smile fell from Andran's face. Why such chambers were ever put next to the cold hard vacuum of space she had never understood. Just the thought of that black expanse this close to her body made her skin creep.

"We have worked together for a long time, Andran," began the Mentor, bringing Andran's attention back inside the spin chamber. "It's time you understood the true purpose behind the cumulated effort of your life's work."

Andran thinned her lips. "I'm a mercenary. The cumulated effort of my life's work is a series of numbers associated with my numerous bank accounts and off-system investment portfolios. Rather handsome numbers, too, thank you very much."

"The work I do with my brothers and sisters, work you have supported, is far beyond cash, credit and assets."

Andran chuckled.

The Mentor tapped the middle two fingers of his right hand to his palm. His brain-implanted User Interface linked up to Andran's UI. Electronics enmeshed in each of their neocortices stimulated visual signals in unison. Andran and her Mentor saw a commonly perceived map of the galactic spiral, hovering between them in topographic majesty.

"So what's the mission brief?" Andran asked, slipping with ease into their well-worn routine. "Better be an improvement on what you had me do back in the Scarlet Belt," she laughed.

The Mentor nodded at the glowing lens. "This is more than a mission, Andran. Look, civilisations rise and fall." Regions of the galaxy blossomed with bright colours. Andran recognised the stellar-political map plotting the influence regions of early star-spanning civilisations, scrolling forwards through the multi-millennial annals of galactic history.

"Wars come and go..." Hotspots flashed and flared as vibrant colours representing billions of lives disappeared, changed or expanded. "These do not interest us. They are beneath our purpose... beneath your purpose," the Mentor pointed at Andran.

Andran raised an eyebrow. "I'm just a gun for hire. I don't have a purpose and I don't engage in politics. You know that..."

"You're more than that, and this is much more than politics," he corrected, taking in the galactic lens with open arms. "Civilisations rise and fall. And occasionally..." Tan coloured shading spanned across several spiral arms, most of the galaxy. Andran did not recognise the pattern from any historical databases, yet the region of influence was vast.

"...Occasionally some look set to grow and take over the whole galaxy. If we trust them to survive, we let them." The Mentor stood, arms spread, taking it in for a moment of reverence. "If we do not trust their ability to survive..." he closed his hands, and the light brown empire collapsed to nothing. In its absence, other colours recovered and emerged, spreading to represent what marked the beginning of Pre-Modern Galactic History. Patterns that Andran recognised finally started to emerge in the power vacuum.

"What, you just wiped out a whole...?"

"Let me be clear, Andran. Our sole aim is to ensure the survival of sentient life... any life. We don't care who has to leave the galactic stage to make room."

Andran's forehead scrunched as she raised an eyebrow, head recoiling into the headrest.

"Sentience," the Mentor gestured with fingers bunched at the tips. "Conscious... reproducing... life. That is all that matters. And we have gone well beyond genocide to ensure it survives."

Cold metal closed down on Andran's wrists and ankles. She flinched, despite her familiarity with the pre-spin-through preliminaries.

Welcome to your departure terminal!

Generic pre-spin briefings lilted through the headrest speakers, irritating a flustered Andran more than usual.

…Your User Interface, hardwired into your brain, has generated a digital backup of the biological signals and networks that form your conscious identity…

Andran fixed a sceptical glare on her Mentor.

…encrypted and transmitted from your UI direct into the Quantum Information Teleportation web …

"Don't judge. We once were members of that species, the one you saw disappear. We scrubbed it – our own kind – from the annals of time. A species, for all we know, that achieved greatness."

…superhighways of quantum entangled particles, streamed for millennia across the galaxy, give a rich source of entangled pairs.

"We cleansed our minds of any memories specific to the species, its culture, its values. Wiped them clean just before we destroyed our own biological bodies. We few awoke one day, in alien bodies. We awoke on that new day with nothing but each other, some sanitised memories… and a galactic mandate, an eternal imperative to guarantee survival."

Using Induced Result Measurement, the ones and zeroes of your digital mind appear instantly at your destination on the other side of the galaxy…

"Yes, I stand here now, having been born millennia ago of a species I know nothing about."

Andran grimaced, struggling to take it all in. "So what the hell do you want me to do, to… become?" she asked, disgusted.

…On arrival, you may feel some identity dislocation. This is normal. Your destination UI re-maps your transmitted digital mind into the biological brain you have spun into. But don't worry! It's impossible to arrive in a brain that is still inhabited! The body you arrive in is yours alone for the duration of your stay…

"Andran. We stepped beyond the meagre purpose of a single species by transcending the death of that species. Join us. Step beyond your finite life."

Andran swallowed hard, mouth flooding with saliva. Her

peripheral senses started to register a different room – the spin-through had begun. She could smell incense, hear chanting, but could still see her Mentor.

Andran looked at him enraged, tried to swear at him. A different mouth in a different place opened, slack and unresponsive. Arms and legs refused to move. Andran's mind commanded her limp body to writhe against the shackles. She wanted out, wanted to escape.

"Your lifelong career in the shadows is complete." The voice merged with low chants. Swirling through unfamiliar memories, she remembered scripture she had never read and had also read time and again, the life's work of a different soul. "Now, Andran, you are ready to transcend the confines of life" – a voice of someone she knew should be next to him.

"No… I'mm… nnnno…" slurred Andran, somewhere in her fracturing mind.

The Mentor looked down upon her slumped body, left lifeless. "Now, Andran, you will leap over death."

…
Something
… definitely
…not
right…

Collected poetry of the Scarlet Belt Wars
Boiling cold
Dark Lieutenant Brandan Wickers-Noynsa
[Historical note
Dk Lt Wickers-Noynsa lost his XO
in the infamous space battle of Honura,
barely escaping with his life
and the remnants of his ship and crew
shortly after seeing her pass away]

No worse torture could she have faced
Boiled to death in the cold

Blood bubbled up, burst through her eyes
Frozen rubies twinkled across dark skies

Afloat in an alien airlock chamber, he felt small and alone. The young boy still inside him wanted to curl up, fold his arms tight and convince Mother that he didn't need to leave, didn't need to become a monk. He wanted to have lived a life of freedom, of friendship, to have found love.

Instead, Starbirth-Sensei Shondrei-sha – The Blessed Chosen – fought urges to fold into the fetal position. Regal robes of finery billowed around him, stretching out sinuously to join the swirling coils of burning incense smoke. The corners of the strange hexagonal room echoed with deep chants of The Blessed Choir.

The graceful centre point of the ceremony, he kept his composure. Shondrei-sha took some comfort that at least none of the tenuous strands of smoke were seeping out through the seams of the airlock door. Not that that would matter soon.

A nubile, handsome young androgen approached him, hands outstretched. The gossamer thin white slip it wore revealed child-bearing hips and the suggestion of breasts, despite the genetic re-wiring done to ensure it had no genitalia. Last of its genetic line, unable to reproduce, the androgen had been born into life with a sole purpose: to represent First Mother.

Shondrei-sha had always found the concept of First Mother awe-inspiring. The great cosmic being that had caused herself to exist out of the nothing and also caused all existence to be. Two great feats, represented in carnal form in Starspanning Xzangism as a monastery's androgyn. A beginning and an end, complete and whole.

Shondrei-sha looked into its eyes, hoping to find the motherly support he needed for this trial. Instead, he saw only pity and fear as those trembling hands respectfully drifted him down into the reclining chair, before withdrawing behind his chair. Cold, hard metal pressed against the back of his skull. Clamps closed on his arms and feet. Digital signals started to intrude upon his mind.

Technology should not be mixed in this way with religion. Two things so fundamentally different cannot combine in this way. He had written as much in his misunderstood thesis, the one that had catapulted him to ascend into this holy predicament.

Lights dimmed. Chants deepened.

Starbirth-Sensei Shondre-sha reflected upon his soul as he watched the beautiful, twisting incense smoke dissipate like ink in water, merging with the invisible, life-giving air. For a distracted moment, he wondered whether the smoke was getting lost in the air, or the air was getting lost in the smoke, when—

Anger. From nowhere. For the first time in many decades, he felt anger. He could not express it, but this rage was palpable, focussed on a particular person. His stomach turned. He started…

…Strange.

Shondrei-sha didn't feel himself. Neither did Andran. Memories of mercenary gun runs and clandestine missions infiltrated tranquil memories of scripture and late-night, candlelit debates about the nature of faith and praise.

The Mentor had set her up, set them up… no, wait, set her up. Who was she? Balled fists pulled at the cold chair's clamps. Whose body was this?

Andran…

Shondrei…

Who?

I'm just in it for the money… I was elected, I hadn't asked to be… this was supposed to be another mission, that damned Mentor … the conclave never actually elected anyone for Starbirth, it was an old tradition, left in the Conclave Decree out of respect….

Star-birth, Star-what?

…No-one was really expected to jump out of an airlock in the name of Spanning the Stars… AIRLOCK? WHAT? NO

NO NO No no nonono… NO!!!

Starbirth-Sensei's body fought against the bindings of the Qit spin-chair. Strong hands grasped his arms and legs as they thrashed for escape. The Qit-web cable fell from the back of the Starbirth Sensei's chair. The shackles released, hinged open. Servants of the faith clad in complex folds of air-tight robes rotated him to face the first airlock door. He calmed, fought the urge to shudder, recoiled instinctively before forcing himself into a more proper posture. Those same servant hands removed his ceremonial cassock with pious compassion.

Naked, as he was when he entered this existence, he was now ceremonially prepared for Starbirth.

First Mother, or rather her carnal homage, keyed the pad to open the first airlock door. Shimmering material flowed over her body as she moved into the darkness of the airlock chamber. Stopping short of the outer door, she turned, beckoning.

Airlock – *no, no, no, no no…*

Andran's professional life majored on avoiding death in its diverse forms across far-flung corners of the galaxy. Exposure to the vacuum had always held a special place of fear in her heart. One near-miss in her early career was enough never to forget.

It's alright, my Starsister Andran. It makes sense now. An Elder once told me that no person would ever join the stars alone. I now know what he meant, why he told me. I understand now…

…Yes. Odd, I remember him telling us that too. How strange. Yes, he was talking about me, about us, right now. What a thing, I remember it like I was there.

We were.

And now we are here. But there has to be another way. We're not stepping outside.

Alone in the airlock. Naked. No lights inside, save for the glow of the universe pressing in through the small windows of the outer doors. Andran fought the urge to turn and bang on the inner door, to start ripping out panels looking for an override switch.

Something stopped her. Perhaps the solemnity of the ceremony, or the solidarity of this new presence in her mind. Or was she the presence in it?

Let me show you something… Shondrei-sha thought as he recollected one of his favourite memories, teaching his first class of Newchildren. Visualising the fearsome taurus painted on the clay pot, he remembered the young aspirant leaping over it and conquering the beast. In this terrifying act they transcended their old life as an individual and, crucially, became part of something more…

First Mother was now safely back inside the hexagonal spin-chamber, manipulating the screen-pad of the airlock. Seals on the outer door squeaked ajar as air rushed past the solitary form of the Starbirth Sensei.

Vapour trails of escaping air meeting the vacuum were visible through the porthole windows. The sound of the rush built up to a roar. The sensation of a mounting pressure change pulled their slowly drifting body towards the exit.

YES! I see, I understand now. I realise why my Mentor brought me to you. Adrenaline soared. Terror mixed with elation as their minds joined in mutual epiphany.

Airlock doors burst open.

The way to the stars was clear.

Naked, the body of the Starbirth Sensei carrying the biological mind of Shondrei-sha and the digital mind of Andran sailed out into the glittering black.

Lesions formed on the skin as blood close to the surface boiled into the vacuum of interstellar space. Coiling into the foetal position, they coughed a foam of blood and lung tissue that boiled violently into vapour then froze in crimson crystals, fanning out from their writhing, vulnerable body. Eventually, they removed their hands from their face, opened their blood-shot eyes.

Look.

Yes, I see.

They're beautiful!

The great lens of the galaxy spread out before them in majestic splendour. The whole spiral expanse was visible from their vantage point, slightly elevated from the plane of stars out beyond the rim.

Pain and the evolutionary progress of millennia had sharpened their senses, and they saw their home as though for the first time.

All my life I have spent in dutiful service to the First Mother, bowed in humble adoration. And I never knew why…

Compared to the dimness of the conclave, the galaxy was a jewel of luminous wonder in the sea of ruthless black.

They're precious, these stark points of light, and all the life they serve. We must keep them safe, we must protect them. That's why I had to die. To see this, to meet you.

Now we understand…

Andran started a subroutine to backup as much as possible of Shondrei-sha's natural sentience into the electronic UI hardware. Pushing the process required some quick hacks, and two personalities were one more than a UI was built to handle. Andran would lose some of herself in the process. But it was essential. There was critical work ahead, and they would need each other.

The UI was all that would survive the cold before the Mentor arrived, before their pickup, before their new life beyond the death of the stars.

So… are we ready for this? The war is coming, and we have our part to play.

Are we ready?

Starbirth Sensei smiled.

Let's find out.

EX.

There is an obvious question here for you, my friend, but it is one for another time. A question for another place, when we meet again.

Perhaps under less happy circumstances… perhaps not. Just remember, if you do take up the call… you won't be alone. There are others.

Believe me. My future depends on it at least as much as yours. In any case it's been a pleasure, and I thank you for the time and attention you have given me.

We have run out of time now – they are upon us again and I have to cloak all this by slipping back into the shroud of my usual patter in The In Between. They're aware of Commutation, these folk. Yes! They are indeed as powerful as that, we're talking about a galactic inner circle that's very small indeed, but they must not know what I'm doing.

Hope my sales pitch patter doesn't come on too thick or offend your sensibilities too much, given what we've shared! After all, they must not suspect…

YOUR COMMUTE ENDS

A FOND FAREWELL

Good gravy what a journey! I feel we've seen a thing or two, my dear.

Hah! A delight, my cherished companion, quite the delight indeed. Yes, it's been an experience, a joy, and I thank you for your company. I for one am most certainly pleased to have made your acquaintance. I do hope you've been likewise to make mine. It can, I confess, get a touch lonely at times travelling the void of The In Between.

Refreshing to make a connection amidst all that. Well, amidst none of that of course, for it's all a lot of nothing, but, ah… I suppose my point is, refreshing to start a new relationship. For which I thank you. Yes, that is what we've done here, isn't it? Start a new relationship. And one that I do hope lasts.

Quite something about it isn't there, dipping into these lives and experiences like this. They may hold something of an emotional challenge, a burden to bear, and yet there's something about the raw morality of them… nothing quite like slipping into the warm bath of the human condition.

Never forget who introduced you to it all, dear companion! We were in that murky tub together, my trusty chum – if you'll pardon the simile – and I certainly feel we've grown together through the common experience…

Common experience? Experiences. Plural. We've had quite the number, haven't we? The people we've met… oh, and the diverse means of getting around! Fascinating how the way someone commutes can bind and shape their lives.

Granted they choose it as much as it pigeon-holes them. Yet this intertwining of cause and effect between the transport and the transported can be so telling, so very indicative as to the lives they live. Interesting how it can be silent on the decisions they make, though. It can tell us so much about the context of the choice they may face yet nothing at all of the actual decision they will make when they stand on that precipice. No indication of which way they will jump.

We started nearby, didn't we? We had a little dabble on both sides of the law with the detective and the thief, both faced with intriguing challenges upon their own moral code.

Different moral compasses at play. Though we ought to be open-minded about such things, don't you think, judge one on one's own basis – much as we would prefer to be judged, yes? Indeed.

And we had a little taste of life on Mars, and of death. An interesting choice made there, although rather more at stake than either you or I could comprehend, in truth. Saw one of the ways consciousness may yet emerge, only one of many near future possibilities, and a poignant one at that. I'm not talking about robots or any of that nonsense that has been so fantasised about by generations in your time envelope. We're talking about true electronic consciousness. That's the issue at stake. Robots that can walk, run, ride bikes or swim – mere ego-trips. The emergence of a new thinking species, born of silicon and electrons rather than flesh, neurons and synapses, a species that can think for itself and can create more of its own kind… That's the prize. Yes, exciting times to come, compadre. Wouldn't want to spoil the fun with tales of how it has played out across the Milky Way, teeming with all manner of life, biological and otherwise, in its glowing stellar lens!

Not yet at least…

Ah yes, and of course you saw a little of my own past in a distant corner of the expanding galactic community, the choices I made as I zipped through the guts of a migrant ship pursuing the suspect with blue tendrils.

It was a tough shift you know, life on board.

Did you know there were some kids there who felt too afraid to leave their quarters without a knife on them for their own protection? A sad notion, ill-perceived and sometimes tragically ill-fated. Sad business. All too easy to judge.

Hm.

Well, finally we, er, popped over to visit some, ah, tropical hotspots where we met a couple of… unlikely friends. Well, I suppose just one friend in the end, wasn't it? Hard to say for sure: Watch this space.

And then there's Commutation.

I've alluded before to what a rare privilege this is, held secret from the galaxy at large. Well, secrets beget secrets, my friend. Don't go trying to understand my inner workings by getting under the skin of a Commutator. Make no attempts to penetrate the veil of The Commutators' Commute… for there be dragons.

Suffice to say we've been about the place, and all before transitioning back here to The Big Smoke, London town. We've spanned the stars and consumed subjective lifetimes… Drink it all in!

In fact, do you know something? I'm curious to understand how all this stacks up against some of the more, er, ethically challenging decisions you've found yourself making in your own life. They crop up only once in a month of Sundays, and it's often easy to forget them in spite of their significance. That's a spot of self-preservation by the psyche, it doesn't like to dwell on some of the encounters we have with fate-changing decisions, so often kicks the masking sands of time over their memories.

And yet, there must be something there… have a little think about it, my comrade. Any tough decisions you've had to make in your time? It's ok, take your time. Perform a gentle search within the dark burrows of your memory. Send a curious little mole through those tunnels, sniffing… tentative at first, then more eager in the blackness until… found anything? Don't deny yourself the opportunity to be human, my dear. We've all done things like this, significant in our own context.

Subtle at first, isn't it? Just a soft edge of… something with its own form. Go gently, give it time to breathe and manifest itself in its own time.

There. You see? It was there all along, that… that thing you did that felt right at the time. Wasn't major, not really, but it has its own significance. Quietly, unassumingly it has burrowed into your past and buried itself with hooks – there's no getting rid of it now. Nor is there any shame in it.

So allow yourself to relive that moment. Crack it right open now, that's it! Give it the room to breathe that it deserves, see the sights you saw at the time, smell the smells, feel the feelings. Put yourself back in there, as if it were right now the present moment. Allow that emotion to flood back. Free of any judgement remember. This is you we're talking about after all, and you're good folk. Give the memory space to come alive once again, in all its reality.

…

A mere moment longer, close your eyes and live again!

…

Perfect.

That's it! Lovely, I can picture myself there right now. Aaahhh. Yes. Just a moment more, I want to capture it, bottle the moment up in a jar. Do you know… I can see myself going back there some time, dependent on who I'm with, of course. I've clients from all over, you see. If one's been cooped on, oh, one of those migrant ships too long, well, something like the minutiae of a London commuter's day to day can be of stellar interest.

You see, you're actually a rather enticing journeyperson! In your own odd, er, I mean quaint… exotic, yes, exotic sort of way. You see, it can be of great interest to others, the trials and tribulations contained within the life of one such as you.

Oh! Speaking of which we should probably get back into role, back into our bodies on the tube train… Time has run its course, my dear companion. It catches up with us all, yes even here in The In Between. High time we got back to our time, to your time. Are you ready for it? Word of warning about the final exfiltration. Reality can be a touch strange after all this time out of your own body. The blinding sights, the barrage of sounds… yes, the cacophony of smells too, and quite the mixture we're going back into!

Ready?

...

There.

Back in the here.

Back in the now.

Take a look around, and do take your time.

Bright, isn't it? Little space for mystery in the dazzling mundane. And yet, it is in here that we find life.

Feels odd at first, compared to where we've been. And then as if in an instant it's as though you never left! All is as it was.

All, that is, apart from you. For you see, some things once seen cannot be unseen. Some things experienced and conceptualised become a part of us, and can never be scrubbed out. You're in a privileged position now, the Friend of a Commutator. Lucky you! Especially if judged among your galactically ignorant peers of Earth-dwelling biological sentients.

Pride's a funny old thing, it often rides on the coattails of privilege. You've a right to it too, you know. Yes, you know of much that is capable through Commutation, and perhaps have gleaned a little more besides? A better knowledge of what goes on across the galaxy? Well, don't go spreading the word, it would do no good for your public reputation, or your career for that matter. No. What has passed lies best tucked in the soft squishy matter up in that lovely head of yours.

Oh, that reminds me! Allow me to just reach around the back of this beautiful skull and... ah, there we go, pluck this little device out. Much more comfortable on removal isn't it? I would hate to see this thing wandering around with you unaccounted for! Precious, too, what little gems you've allowed me to glean.

Ah good! Slowing down already – it seems we're just in time for my stop! Canary Wharf if I do remember correctly, yes here it comes. Aaahh I can almost smell the industrious aroma of professional and financial services seeping through the door seals as we pull into the station. Steel and glass flickering past the windows, punctuated by the large, proud sign of this station, announcing to all the glory of… CANARY WHARF!

Time for our fond farewell, my trusted companion. Mustn't tarry.

Mmm, here we are. Wafting in off the platform through these open doors… the smell of coffee, well-perfumed professionals and… opportunity! This is where we part compan— oh, you're getting off as well are you? Er, oh no after you, er, or me, agh quick! Off off! EXCUSE ME!

And, er, which way are you going? Same… escalator up to the barriers? Very good, I suppose, I'll join you. Ah, yes, I see, just as well… that would have been rather an abrupt goodbye, wouldn't it? I was banking on you leaving here, of course… so we could, um, say goodbye properly. Thanks again for the directions, by the w— just a moment this barrier doesn't seem to be working…

Ah. There we go. So, which way are you going? No, I'm off to the back escalators, I like to go up to the top of Jubilee Park and follow it down before heading to the DLR. It gives me a great sense of peace.

Flowing downwards, I feel as cool as the water trickling through the cascade features, calmed by the dappled sunshine and shade among the greenery. Wonderful feeling of tranquillity.

Yes! Join me, do!

Oh yes, my friend. I knew my way all along, even when I asked you for directions at our very first encounter. But then, I needed an opening gambit, didn't I? Bloody hard work this cold selling business, I needed to ask a small favour before building up to something bigger – oh, I wouldn't take it personally. More than anything I needed to know what sort you were, whether or not you're the kind of person to see someone in need and offer help. And you see the doors that opened for you? You stepped through them with gusto, my friend. It's been real.

Thanks also for sharing the memory, that one you dredged up from the dark corners of your psyche. It's all to play for you know? I seem to remember you enjoying some of the memories of my previous acquaintances – both sides of our relativistic ladder – and I'm sure you'll enjoy the stories I bring you again some time. Especially if your account of your own moral cusp proves popular with some of my clientele, dispersed as they are all across the galactic lens.

Gosh! The prices that memories from an unconnected planet such as this one will fetch with the glitterati of the galactic core. They love the purity of life unsullied by the constantly-on, AI-augmented intensity of Qit-connected life. It's the equivalent to them of a holiday in rolling meadows with a pastoral symphony lilting over the sounds of murmuring streams. They like to dip in to 'rural living' from time to time.

And they are rich, beyond your wildest attempts at conceiving what that word even means. Wealth isn't wealth unless it's near the galactic capital. You never know, if your story sells it may even accrue you a little credit with the bank of, well, me.

Sanitised, of course, I would never leave any part of your life in there that could identify this fair planet, no no. I have a discreet client base, and I do know how to cover my tracks... We've shared too much, you and I, for me to allow any carelessness.

Tattoos like this one you see on the palm of my hand, they're not handed out like sweets you know, my dear sojourner. The inverted trigram of The Commutator is a rare thing.

I brought my mark with me into this body, and I'll keep it for a time – the body that is. I plan to pick up the DLR and circle back around to Bank then maybe ride the Northern line a little way. Kings Cross St Pancras holds some exciting travel opportunities. Gosh, that's quite the day of travel ahead of me, isn't it? Fascinating to ponder who I might meet on the way, or what delights we might be led to by *their* tastes.

Then it will be time to leave this body behind and take my mark elsewhere. But don't worry, I'll take my fondness for the experiences we've shared with me, and I hope you likewise.

Well, put it there – might be the last opportunity you get to shake a hand bearing The Commutator's trigram. Then again, maybe not.

And remember, keep your eyes peeled, like that odd sort just over your shoulder there. They won't be following me, I know how to clean my tracks. It's you I'm concerned about. Keep your powder dry and let's hope to meet once more someday, whether I travel in this body or another.

Here we are my friend, and we are friends by now aren't we? I did say we would start strangers, depart friends – maybe more in another time, if the occasion calls for it. Remember that discussion, comrade.

Well…

It's been real.

Time for this handshake to end and our paths to part. I have more routes to commute, more commuters to befriend. And help is there to be found among such potential friends, our fellow commuters… kindred spirits, if only we take the time to listen to their stories. They just need someone to help open them up and offer a guiding hand to help them see it in themselves, don't you think? Quiet optimism ever burns in my heart, fellow traveller!

Look there, for example. See that businessman in his sharp blue suit and leather satchel, fresh out the tube and already offering directions to a bewildered tourist. Compassionate sort – oh yes, he's just my type! When you see a window of opportunity, remember! It will only be open for so long, and they never open twice. You must leap through with arms spread wide.

Farewell, friend!

I SAY – EXCUSE ME, SIR!

TERRIBLY SORRY TO BOTHER, I WONDER IF YOU COULD FIND THE TIME TO HELP JUST ONE MORE PERSON…

AUTHOR'S EPILOGUE

MY COMMUTE

Treating myself to a posh commute home by riverboat, complete with relaxing gin and tonic, I received an odd tap on the shoulder. The boat was half empty, yet here I was, stuck by the window, accosted by an oddball, trying to enjoy my gin in peace when…

Well, you've been through it too now.

It was all a bit strange at first, but as a lifelong SF nerd I was bowled over by the opportunities that opened up. Sailing past stunning nebulascapes; zipping on a hair-raising chase through an asteroid belt; plunging through the clouds of a gas giant after a plummeting treasure; marvelling at the dazzling night sky near the galactic core…

Quite the privilege, I felt. All delivered through one commute or other, from the mundane to the exotic. Though I suppose anything can be mundane if it's your local day-to-day. Likewise, just about anything could be seen as exotic. Perhaps that was The Commutator's point.

Anyway, I must say the whole commuter angle resonated rather strongly with me. Commuting has become some of the most crucial time I have in my life. You see, my daily commute is the only time I get to write about the strange journeys I've been on, the outlandish things I've seen across the galaxy.

Commuting is freedom, intellectual escape. If you choose to use it that way.

You may even spot me on one of these aforementioned routes, furiously typing up the notes from some latest encounter with The Commutator. A sharp blue suit, brown leather laptop bag and matching brogues may give me away!

Please do say hello and interrupt the writing, we're all Commutating aficionados by now. I'd be delighted to give you a signed paperback copy of The Quantum Commute, if I have one on me. It may even be an opportunity to share a sneak preview of the next book…

This has been quite a journey for me, achieving this dream of self-publishing my first novel. It's taken years of graft, planning and sacrifices, and now I'm planning on many more to follow. To help with that, I have just one small request of you.

Honest reviews posted online.

If you'd please be kind enough to support me with three minutes of your time in leaving a review, I would be grateful. You could even consider letting me know which was your favourite commute and why.

Thank you for reading. I hope you enjoyed this as much as I've enjoyed reading some of the great work out there.

Happy Commut(at)ing

Bruno

First Edition for London commuters 2018

Cover art by Dylan Dixon-Phillip.

Photography by Ricardo Alevizos (edited).

Model: Tiago Grade [Rizumik].

38612715R00116

Printed in Great Britain
by Amazon

MARTIN HAMMER BACON AND SUTHERLAND

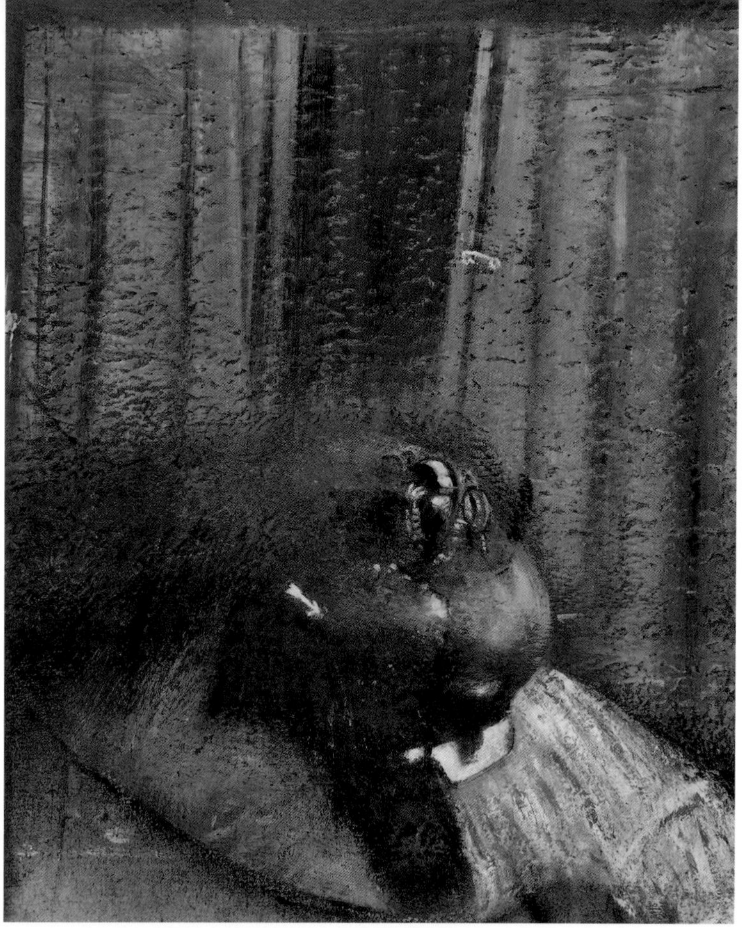

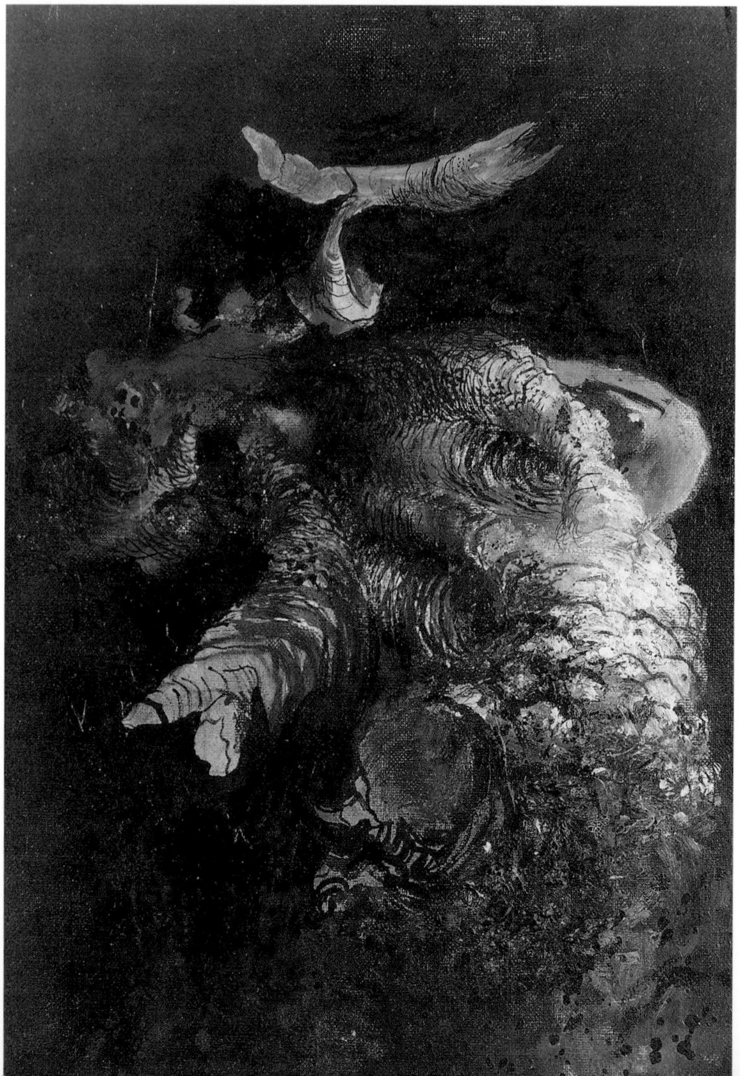

MARTIN HAMMER BACON AND SUTHERLAND

PUBLISHED FOR THE PAUL MELLON CENTRE FOR STUDIES IN BRITISH ART

BY YALE UNIVERSITY PRESS NEW HAVEN AND LONDON

Designed by Paul Sloman

Printed in Singapore

Library of Congress Cataloging-in-Publication Data

Hammer, Martin.

Bacon and Sutherland : patterns of affinity in British culture of the 1940s / Martin Hammer.
p. cm.
Includes bibliographical references and index.
ISBN 0-300-10906-7 (cl : alk. paper)
1. Bacon, Francis, 1909–Friends and associates. 2. Sutherland, Graham Vivian, 1903–Friends and associates. 3. Artists–England–Biography. 4. Avant-garde (Aesthetics)–England–LondonHistory–20th century. 5. Bacon, Francis, 1909–Correspondence. 6. Sutherland, Graham Vivian, 1903–Correspondence. 7. Artists–England–Correspondence.
I. Bacon, Francis, 1909- II. Sutherland, Graham Vivian, 1903- III. Title.
ND497.B16H36 2005
759.2'09'041–dc22

2004023965

A catalogue record for this book is available from The British Library

Frontispieces

TOP Francis Bacon, *Head II*, 1949, Ulster Museum Collection, Belfast (detail of pl. 102).

BOTTOM Graham Sutherland, *Tree Form*, 1941, Leeds City Art Galleries (detail of pl. 93).

Page vi

TOP Graham Sutherland, *Palm and House*, 1947, Private Collection (detail of pl. 13).

BOTTOM Francis Bacon, *Man with Microphones*, 1946, oil on canvas, 145 × 127.8 cm (detail of pl. 39).

To Christina and Lucy, with love

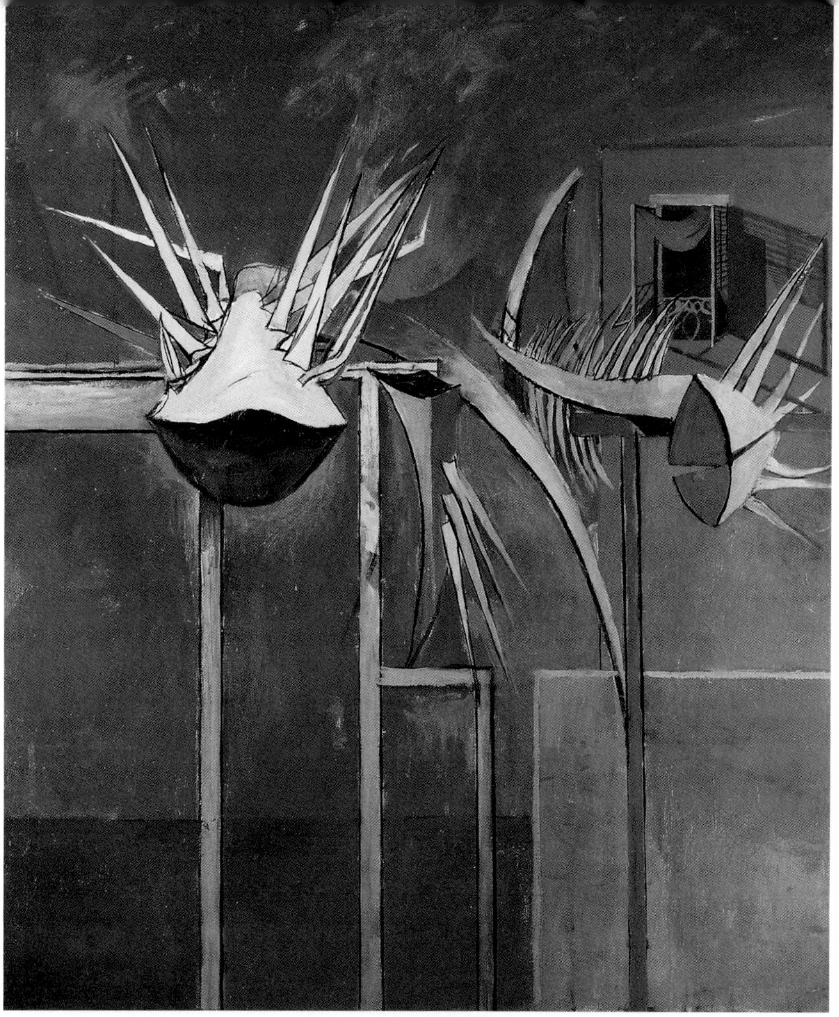

CONTENTS

I Graham Sutherland, *Welsh Landscape with Roads*, 1936, oil on canvas, 61 × 91.5 cm, Tate, London.

II Graham Sutherland, *Red Tree*, 1936, oil on canvas, 55.8 × 97.8 cm, B. P. International Ltd, London.

III Graham Sutherland, *Gorse on Sea Wall*, 1939, oil on canvas, 62.2 × 48.3 cm, Ulster Museum Collection, Belfast, by kind permission of the Trustees of the National Galleries and Museums of Northern Ireland.

IV Francis Bacon, *Three Studies for Figures at the Base of a Crucifixion*, 1944, oil on board, 94 × 73.7 cm, Tate, London (left-hand panel).

V Graham Sutherland, *Association of Oaks*, 1939/40, gouache, watercolour and pencil on paper, 68.6 × 48.6 cm, Scottish National Gallery of Modern Art, Edinburgh.

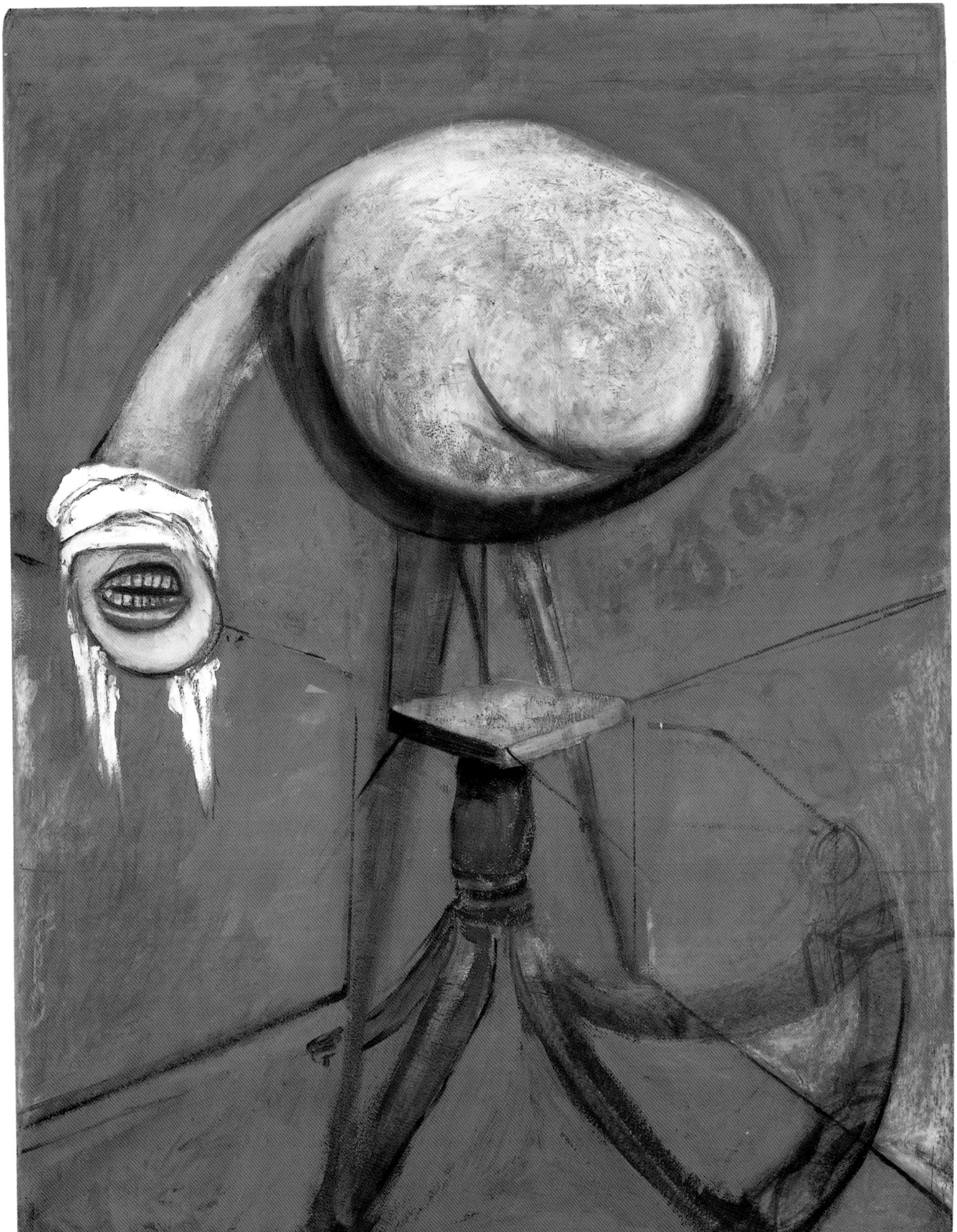

VI Francis Bacon, *Three Studies for Figures at the Base of a Crucifixion*, 1944, oil on board, 94 × 73.7 cm, Tate, London (central panel).

VII TOP Graham Sutherland, *Green Tree Form: Interior of Woods*, 1940, oil on canvas, 79 × 107.5 cm, Tate, London.

VIII Francis Bacon, *Three Studies for Figures at the Base of a Crucifixion*, 1944, oil on board, 94 × 73.7 cm, Tate, London (right-hand panel).

IX TOP Graham Sutherland, *Twisted Tree Form*, 1944, gouache, chalk and pencil on paper mounted on board, 57.2 × 47.2 cm, The Laing Art Gallery, Newcastle upon Tyne, Tyne and Wear Museums Service.

X Graham Sutherland, *Horned Forms*, 1944, oil on board, 81 × 64 cm, Tate, London.

XI Graham Sutherland, *Lane Opening*, 1944–45, oil on board, 93.5 × 72.5 cm, Private Collection.

XII Francis Bacon, *Figure in a Landscape*, 1945, oil on canvas, 144.8 × 128.3 cm, Tate, London.

XIII Graham Sutherland, *Thorn Tree*, 1945/6, oil on canvas, 127 × 101.5 cm, British Council Collection.

XIV Francis Bacon, *Figure Study II*, 1945–46, oil on canvas, 164 × 150 cm, Kirklees Cultural Services, Huddersfield Art Gallery.

XV Graham Sutherland, *Crucifixion*, 1946, oil on board, 243 × 228.6 cm, St Matthew's Church, Northampton.

XVI Francis Bacon, *Painting*, 1946, oil and pastel on linen, 197.8 × 132.1 cm, Museum of Modern Art, New York.

XVII Graham Sutherland, *Somerset Maugham*, 1949, oil on canvas, 137 × 63.5 cm, Tate, London.

XVIII RIGHT Francis Bacon, *Head VI*, 1949, oil on canvas, 93.2 × 76.5 cm, Arts Council Collection, Hayward Gallery, London.

XIX Francis Bacon, *Study from the Human Body*, 1949, oil on canvas, 147 × 134.2 cm, National Gallery of Victoria, Melbourne.

XX Graham Sutherland, *Standing Form against a Hedge*, 1950, oil on canvas, 134.6 × 116.8 cm, Arts Council Collection, Hayward Gallery, London.

INTRODUCTION

This book offers an account of the artistic relationship between Graham Sutherland and Francis Bacon, with particular reference to the 1940s. To be more precise, it concentrates on the period between the two artists' first substantial exhibitions of their work, namely Sutherland's one-man show at the Rosenberg and Helft Gallery in London in the autumn of 1938, and Bacon's at the Hanover Gallery towards the end of 1949. Limiting the discussion to these years permits the in-depth investigation of an association that has been addressed somewhat cursorily by historians of twentieth-century English art. The biographers of both artists have acknowledged that Sutherland and Bacon were close personal friends at this time, and for a few years subsequently until relations became strained.[1] Moreover, several recent commentators have noted the need for a close scrutiny of the artistic interchange between them.[2] Typically, comparisons to date have been constructed with the explicit aim of promoting the perceived virtues of the one artist over the other, as part of some wider critical polemic; one thinks here of celebratory texts about Bacon by David Sylvester from the late 1940s onwards, where he is on occasion played off against Sutherland, or of Peter Fuller's passionate, neo-Ruskinian advocacy of Sutherland during the 1980s, which was accompanied by moralising denunciations of Bacon's nihilism.[3]

Looking at their work in finer detail and in more disinterested, art-historical terms serves to sharpen our sense of what Bacon and Sutherland had in common, as well as how they differed from one another artistically. Considering two artists in conjunction can yield a fruitful balance between context and the individual talent, to misquote T. S. Eliot. On the one hand, the discussion that follows aspires to avoid undue emphasis on a singular individual, with the art flowing all too readily from a personality and a set of biographical circumstances, which undoubtedly limits the value of much of the existing literature on both Sutherland and Bacon, as it does for many other artists. On the other hand, I wish to avoid presenting artists as mere symptoms or ciphers of wider cultural formations. My hope is that Bacon and Sutherland will emerge from this comparative study as distinct and rounded creative personalities who were, nevertheless, very much embedded in their time. It will become apparent that they were profoundly shaped by their contacts with the work of other artists (including each other), by encounters with all manner of other people in their immediate environment, and by their assimilation, consciously or otherwise, of deeper currents of thought and feeling that were, so to speak, 'in the air' within a specific set of historical, geographical and cultural circumstances.

In order to realise these ambitions, it seems more satisfactory to structure the material around themes rather than chronology. The discussion falls, therefore, into three substantial chapters, further subdivided into sections that possess many points of interconnection but that also, to a degree, comprise separate essays. Each encompasses the entire period under scrutiny, with some excursions into earlier or later material, and addresses different layers or aspects of what I am positing as a form of dialogue between Sutherland and Bacon. The organisation provides an effective armature, to borrow a Baconian usage, for elaborating analyses and interpretations of the work of the two artists.

Chapter one is designed to lay the foundations, by assembling different kinds of evidence for the artists' interaction. It seeks to identify specific points of contact, influence and divergence between their respective bodies of work, focusing for the most part on such matters as style, imagery, technique and materials. An accumulation of comparative juxtapositions serves to establish the general significance of the relationship, and to indicate something of the dynamics of the interplay between Sutherland and Bacon. The first chapter also considers in some detail their intertwined careers, and how they each operated within a common support system, which comprised commercial galleries, critics, editors and collectors with a commitment to the versions of modern art that Sutherland and Bacon seemed to exemplify.

Chapter two begins to focus more on the interpretation of meaning. By looking at Bacon and Sutherland in tandem, it considers how one might give real substance to the notion, frequently enough encountered as a general assertion, that their work expressed, or reflected, the experience of living through the Second World War, and the ensuing period, which was dominated by material deprivation, revelations concerning the Holocaust, and the onset of the Cold War. The chapter looks at the extent to which the concerns explored in their work were embedded in a wider aesthetic response to such traumatic events, as evident in the work of other artists and in contemporary poetry and fiction. What, it asks, was the context for their shared immersion in the idea of a tragic art, modelled upon the classical dramas of Aeschylus, and in the possibilities of religious imagery, especially the Crucifixion, as a potent commentary upon man's appalling inhumanity to man in the present? Moreover, how does the work of these two painters, and the critical responses to which it gave rise, illuminate the striking continuities evident in the cultural production of a decade that in other more obvious respects divides neatly into wartime and postwar halves? Working outwards from the work of Sutherland and Bacon may help us to construct the 1940s, or a somewhat extended version thereof, as a relatively coherent 'period', or phase of sensibility, in English cultural history.

The final chapter considers how far the work of Bacon and Sutherland was informed by a continuing engagement with the visual culture of international modern art, at a time when English art is often seen to have been more narrowly insular and 'patriotic' than during the previous or subsequent decades. In what ways, and to what degree, did their art embody a creative response to the exemplars provided by, for example, Picasso and surrealism? How might we situate Sutherland's combined modernist and indigenous commitments in relation to the concerns of figures who clearly inspired him, such as Paul Nash and Herbert Read? Equally, is it in any sense helpful to view Bacon's work of the late 1940s in relation to developments in the post-war School of Paris, extending from the visual arts (such as the work of Alberto Giacometti) to the literary and philosophical work of Jean-Paul Sartre, who at the time encapsulated the cultural and media phenomenon of existentialism? Exploration of such questions serves to shed light on the broad issue of 'English Art and Modernism' during the 1940s. Within the progression of the three chapters, there is a shift from emphasising common denominators between Sutherland and Bacon to highlighting points of divergence.

At each stage, the principal methods employed in this study are close, concrete analysis of the formal and thematic aspects of particular works of art and literature, and the comparative juxtaposition of images and of images and texts, in such a way as to indicate both affinities and differences between Bacon and Sutherland, two artists working in close conjunction, and also between their work and that of other artists and writers operating in parallel historical and cultural circumstances. In delineating that wider context, a recurrent point of reference is the journal *Horizon*, whose importance as an art-historical document tends to be underestimated. As symbolic pointers, we might note that the very first plate photograph to appear in the magazine reproduced a new picture by Sutherland, while the final issue incorporated the first major illustrated article on Francis Bacon, coinciding with his one-man show. The end of the decade and the demise of *Horizon* draw this study to a close, a point that is bound to have an element of the arbitrary. It might be argued that the work of the two artists converged most closely in the early to mid-1950s, when it became obvious to many observers that the art of Sutherland, the older and more established figure, was very much in thrall to that of Bacon, in terms of imagery, style, scale and so forth. I have stopped short of discussing this later phase in their dialogue in any detail, partly for practical reasons, but partly as well because the whole subject becomes, to my mind, much less interesting and complicated.

Any analysis of the work of these two artists, during the period under scrutiny here, has to take account of a notable asymmetry in the available evidence, which should be acknowledged from the outset. The extensive body of dated works by Sutherland allows us to plot his work almost on a monthly basis, whereas Bacon's activities in the studio are manifest in a mere handful of pictures that survive either as physical objects, or else in the form of rather inadequate black and white photographs. The opposite imbalance applies when it comes to the survival of primary documents. Sutherland's archive contains a fascinating sequence of letters from Bacon dating from 1943 to 1947, as well as a postcard from 1954.[4] These are mined extensively in my analysis of the relationship between the two artists, and they are also transcribed in full in the appendix. It can only be viewed with regret that Bacon did not keep the other side of the correspondence, or, for that matter, any other personal letters, judging from the contents of his studio at his death.[5] Notwithstanding this particular gap in the record, Sutherland's development and preoccupations at this time are well documented. The catalogues of his regular exhibitions register the progress of his work, while published interviews and statements indicate his characteristic patterns of thought. Letters to several other friends beside Bacon survive, as do a significant quantity of sketchbooks.[6] In contrast, Bacon is far more of an unknown quantity in the 1940s. His letters to Sutherland are so valuable precisely because they appear to constitute the only contemporary documentation on Bacon from the period before his Hanover Gallery exhibition.[7]

I INTERACTIONS

The artistic relationship between Francis Bacon and Graham Sutherland had many dimensions. This account proceeds from the specifics of an interchange between two individuals to considering more general frames of reference within which their affinities and differences may be usefully considered, notably the cultural impact of the Second World War and English attitudes during the period to the resources of modernism and tradition. The initial focus is on the fine detail of the two artists' association. A range of evidence, visual and documentary, will serve to demonstrate that Sutherland and Bacon knew one another well, had a good deal in common artistically and shared a network of dealers, supporters and friends, the aim being to reconstruct something of the richness and substance that their interaction clearly possessed for both men at the time. From this platform, the consideration of less tangible aspects of their artistic convergence can follow.

MAKING CONTACT

A chronological narrative might reasonably begin right in the middle of the Second World War, with the correspondence that provides the most solid basis for exploring the connection between Bacon and Sutherland. Bacon's first brief letter, dated 8 February 1943, certainly reads more like an opening gambit than the earliest communication that happens to have survived.[1] The address given is the cottage in Hampshire where Bacon had, to a large extent, been based since the previous year. However, he now wished Sutherland to know that he was spending more time back in London, having retained his flat and studio at Glebe Place in Chelsea. No explanation is offered. It might be speculated that Bacon was feeling less troubled by the asthma attacks, exacerbated no doubt by the atmospheric conditions in wartime London, that resulted in his being 'turned out' of the ARP (Air Raid Precautions) and giving up home defence duties.[2] This had led to his decision to move to rural Steep, near Petersfield.[3] It might also have seemed that German bombing was no longer the threat that it had been at the height of the Blitz. In addition, judging from what we know about his attitudes in later life, Bacon may simply have found himself temperamentally unsuited to prolonged doses of provincial country life.[4] This immediately raises one of the obvious and major divergences from Sutherland, both personal and artistic, that runs alongside the close parallels to be considered here. Sutherland always chose to live in the countryside, mainly in Kent, and travelled up to London for teaching and other practical purposes, staying a night or two when necessary. His work too was rooted in sensations of the natural landscape. In contrast, Bacon clearly preferred the many stimulants, artistic, social and sexual, of urban existence.

Whatever his other motives, it is clear from his letter to Sutherland that Bacon desired at this point to re-establish his connections with the London art world, which the war had not killed off as much as might have been expected, and wished to renew his contacts with fellow artists to whom he felt an affinity. The urge to write to Sutherland stemmed in part, it appears, from Bacon having seen an exhibition in London of work by official war artists: 'I must tell you how much I like some of your paintings in the National Gallery.'[5] His note might well be regarded, in fact, as a symptom of Bacon's resurgent creative impulses during recent months. According to John Russell, whose vivid monograph was clearly rooted in conversations and a long-standing friendship with the artist, Bacon's wartime experience 'suddenly turned him on to painting again, after several year's withdrawal . . . when he was discharged from his ARP post, he found, against all expectation, that painting had become an obsession for him'.[6] Similarly, Michael Peppiatt cites Bacon's later remark about this period: 'If I hadn't been asthmatic, I might never have gone on painting at all.'[7]

In contacting Sutherland, Bacon was also picking up from where he had left off. The fact that this first note signs off with 'Best wishes' and 'Francis Bacon' implies an existing acquaintance, though not at this stage a real intimacy. Nevertheless, it is addressed to 'Graham', and Bacon remarks that he had 'been meaning to write to you for ages to know how you and Kathleen are', and he is now keen that they should all have dinner together. This reinforces other indications that Bacon and Sutherland had first got to know one another, at least casually, during the second half of the 1930s. In fact, it would have been quite difficult for them not to encounter each other, if not in person then by reputation, in the extremely small world that constituted the London artistic avant-garde before the war. This milieu probably involved no more than a few hundred persons – artists, collectors, gallery owners, critics, supporters – circulating around an equally restricted array of places, including art colleges, commercial galleries, art bookshops such as the legendary Zwemmer's in Charing Cross Road, and a few favoured pubs and clubs. However, certain more specific points of connection between Sutherland and Bacon are documented. The work of both artists was promoted and marketed, albeit at a modest level, by the Mayor Gallery in London and its then financial backer Douglas Cooper, the wealthy writer and collector.[8] Furthermore, Bacon and Sutherland were both involved from 1935 onwards in an extensive, if ultimately fruitless, series of discussions about establishing an organisation devoted to subsidising and exhibiting the work of young artists.[9] The two principal figures behind this worthy venture were Robert Wellington, who at the time was responsible for running the art gallery attached to Zwemmer's bookshop and had become a good friend of Sutherland's, and Wellington's then lover Roy de Maistre, the Australian painter who had been based in London since 1930 and is known to have been close to Bacon during the latter's formative years as an artist.[10]

In the event, the only tangible consequence was a group exhibition at Agnew's Bond Street gallery in early 1937, in which four works by both Bacon and Sutherland were shown, alongside pictures by De Maistre, Ivon Hitchens, John Piper, Ceri Richards, John Trevelyan, Robert Medley, Victor Pasmore and other up-and-coming figures tending towards both abstract and more descriptive approaches.[11] Kenneth Clark was mentioned as a supporter, and no less a figure than Herbert Read agreed to open the exhibition.[12] Both the venue and the involvement of such prestigious figures indicate the ambitions of Eric Hall, who evidently organised and provided financial backing for the show.[13] The event also demonstrates that, at this stage, it was not unreasonable to see Bacon and Sutherland as possessing a comparable status in the art world. Their ages were disparate, though not dramatically so – Sutherland was born in 1903, and Bacon in 1910. In the 1920s, Sutherland had enjoyed considerable success as a relatively traditional etcher, before the market for prints collapsed during the Depression. He subsequently exhibited a few pictures at the London Group, turned his hand to designing posters, glass, china and other types of applied art, but otherwise made a living by teaching at Chelsea Art School. For his part, Bacon first became known, around 1930, for his furniture and rugs, conceived in a strikingly contemporary style. His efforts thereafter to launch a career as a painter culminated in a small and little-noticed exhibition in February 1934.[14] In 1937, Bacon and Sutherland came together from different directions, but aside from shared contacts the one thing they had in common was that neither had at that time established a secure reputation as a modern artist.

Although Eric Hall was doubtless motivated by a general concern for the situation of younger, experimental artists, he was particularly commited to promoting Bacon's career, since the two men were lovers. It is not surprising, then, that in a published response to a hostile review of the show by Frank Rutter, Hall singled out 'the very developed formal qualities, and the beauty of the colour' apparent in works submitted by Bacon.[15] Indeed, the pair evidently selected the artists and works to be included together, suggesting that Hall and Bacon were already interested at this stage in Sutherland.[16] Regrettably, very little is known about Hall, beyond the surface details that he was a middle-aged married man, some years older than Bacon, who had worked as a merchant banker and as general manager of Peter Jones menswear shop, before becoming a Tory Alderman and, in 1943–44, the Deputy Leader of London County Council. It may even be that another, more prosaic element in Bacon's decision to spend more time in London from early 1943 onwards was the fact that Hall, who was presumably paying the rent for the cottage in Steep, was now embarking upon this more onerous and time-consuming job. Hall combined the trappings of wealth and respectable middle-class life in Chelsea with an altogether more bohemian existence as Bacon's long-term lover, fellow gambling devotee, and general intellectual mentor from the mid-1930s through to at least the late 1940s.[17] Certainly, Bacon's letters from the south of France after the war indicate that the personal relationship with Sutherland extended to Hall, as it did to Sutherland's wife Kathleen. Many years later, Bacon acknowledged that Hall 'never let me down' during the fifteen years that they were in close contact; he 'gave me money' and had 'great confidence in me . . . he followed very attentively what I was doing; deep down I think he influenced me in many areas. He has certainly been very important to me'.[18]

It is unclear what contacts there may, or may not, have been between Sutherland and Bacon during the period since the 1937 Agnew's exhibition. The relationship blossomed, however, once the contact was re-established in 1943, on Bacon's initiative. During the latter stages of the Second World War, they evidently met up in London, when Sutherland was visiting town in connection with his work as an official war artist. Bacon's communications suggest that it was during the final two years of the war that a significant personal and artistic interchange began to develop between the two men. The two further notes that preceded Bacon's temporary departure from England in 1946 are certainly more informal and intimate. Both were sent from 7 Cromwell Place, the rather grand flat into which Bacon evidently moved in late 1943, with further financial support, presumably, from Eric Hall.[19] Once again, Bacon is urging the Sutherlands to have dinner with him in London. One letter accompanied a bottle of gin that he was bestowing upon Sutherland.[20] In the other, Bacon expressed thanks to Sutherland for offering to lend him his house, although his own trip to Cornwall made the idea impossible.[21] The first letter must date from wartime, as there is a reference to the bombing, perhaps the V1 and V2 'flying bombs' being dispatched by the Germans between summer 1944 and spring 1945. The other note could be earlier or later, given that Bacon's Cornish visit is otherwise undocumented. Although little concrete information is conveyed, Bacon's growing attachment to the Sutherlands is discernible.

From the start, a sense of rapport extended to regard for one another's work, and an impulse to provide the sort of practical assistance and encouragement that might be expected to develop in a relationship between two mutually sympathetic artists. In the initial letter, Bacon expressed his hope that Sutherland was working well and commented enthusiastically on the war paintings. In the other two, he indicated that he 'would love to come down for the day to see you both and the pictures', and emphasised that Sutherland was not to give him any money for the gin as 'I owe you such a lot for colours'.[22] This last remark presumably refers either to actual paints or to pigments for making paint. It may well be that Sutherland's work as an official war artist made it easier for him to obtain materials, at a time when this was, generally speaking, very difficult. Although the documentation is scanty, it seems reasonable to assume that the two artists were in regular contact during the latter part of the war and the immediate post-war period, and that they were talking to each other about their work and about art in general, as well as looking at one another's paintings in the privacy of the studio.

*

Before looking at the evident visual affinities of the work that the two artists produced in the years 1943 and 1944, I want to step back somewhat, and adjust the focus from Bacon to Sutherland. By then, their respective positions within the British art world could hardly have been more different, compared to the relative equivalence that had pertained in 1937. Sutherland had indeed become 'very successful', to quote Bacon's pithy but accurate assessment in a later interview.[23] It was not until the mid- to late 1930s that Sutherland achieved a clear sense of his own identity as a modern artist, with the intense, highly abstracted landscape paintings that he derived from motifs observed in the 'unspoilt' countryside of West Pembrokeshire. Once he had found his voice, so to speak, his work started to meet with critical and commercial recognition. In particular, he clearly derived both confidence and more tangible benefits and contacts from his close association with Kenneth Clark, whose role in Sutherland's career is loosely comparable to that played by Eric Hall in Bacon's. Clark, it is worth remembering, cut a far more dashing and progressive figure at the time than his later image as the presenter of *Civilisation* might suggest.[24] Remarkably, he was only thirty, the same age as Sutherland to within a few weeks, when in early 1934 he became director of the National Gallery in London. His determination to make the gallery more challenging and up-to-date was expressed in the hanging of pictures by Manet and, for the first time, Cézanne. He was also acquiring works by Cézanne, Seurat, Matisse and others for his personal collection, and commissioned family portraits from Duncan Grant and Tchelitchev. In 1935, Clark and Herbert Read engaged in a polemical exchange in *The Listener* magazine concerning contemporary art. For Clark, fully abstract art displayed 'the fatal defect of purity' and Ben Nicholson's new white reliefs could only be enjoyed as 'tasteful pieces of decoration'.[25]

It was against this backdrop that Clark discovered Sutherland's work, which he probably began collecting in 1936, and which clearly matched his own taste to perfection.[26] Clark soon transmitted his enthusiasm to other collector friends, such as Colin Anderson. Moreover, he arranged for Sutherland's highly successful first one-man exhibition in October 1938 at the Rosenberg and Helft Gallery in London, which was 'at that time the most exclusive gallery in the West End', specialising otherwise in contemporary French art.[27] Staging the show was clearly a tribute to Clark's prestige and influence, given that since 1930 Sutherland had 'led practically a secret life as a painter', and 'few people had heard of him'.[28] The artist's own characteristic diffidence manifested itself in his remark to Clark that he was 'sure that' left to himself he 'should have put off having a show year by year or finally have ended up having one at some scruffy little gallery'.[29] Clark lent two paintings to the exhibition and wrote an enthusiastic preface for the catalogue.[30] For at least one reviewer, Raymond Mortimer, who subsequently became a long term supporter of the artist, the pictures on show were 'unexpectedly impressive': 'Here is a painter who speaks with authority – almost the only English painter of the post-war generation in whose works we do not so much admit promise as recognise performance.'[31]

Sutherland's reputation blossomed yet further during the war years. The glamorous and charismatic aura that came to surround him is conveyed in photographic portraits by friends such as Lee Miller, Cecil Beaton and Peter Rose Pulham (pl. 1).[32] When a second one-man show was held in 1940 at the Leicester Galleries, no less than twenty-two of the thirty works included were sold to public or private collections, notwithstanding the wartime economic climate.[33] Mortimer, once again, was overwhelmed by their 'extraordinary energy of attack', and an effect of 'certainty and power that I have never had from an English contemporary.' 'The affinity in form,' he claimed, 'is with Greco, in feeling with D. H. Lawrence in his best poems, a romantic self-identification with nature.'[34] The following year, Sutherland agreed to show an extensive selection of his pictures since 1936 at the Temple Newsam Museum in Leeds, alongside work by his friends Henry Moore and John Piper. The catalogue revealed that Clark now owned at least nine works. Around the same time, Sutherland took part in a radio discussion on 'Art and Life' with Clark, Moore and the writer V. S. Pritchett, which was subsequently transcribed for publication in *The Listener* magazine.[35] Meanwhile, backdrops and costumes by Sutherland accompanied Frederick Ashton's ballet *The Wanderer*, first performed by Sadler's Wells Ballet in January 1941.

Interest in Sutherland's independent, mostly landscape-based, work was enhanced by the admiring response to his seemingly more accessible work depicting war scenes. It was once again thanks to Clark, who acted as Chairman to the War Artists' Advisory Committee (WAAC), that Sutherland was able to play a prominent role in the government-sponsored scheme, whereby artists were paid a salary to document the sights and impact of the war, both at home and abroad. Between 1940 and 1944 Sutherland produced a large body of work depicting such themes as bomb-damaged streets and structures in Cardiff and London, steel foundries in South Wales, Cornish tin mines and military sites in France which demonstrated the damage wrought by the bombers of the Royal Air Force. These images were widely recognised to be amongst the most vivid and successful products of the war art project. Hence, Sutherland's prominence, alongside Paul Nash, Moore and others, in Jill Craigie's film *Out*

1 Lee Miller, *Graham Sutherland*, 1943, photograph, Lee Miller Archives, England.

of Chaos (1944), an attempt to consolidate the new popularity that modern artists had acquired as a result of the continuous exhibition of war art at the National Gallery, whose usual contents had been evacuated to the safety of a mountain-side in Wales.

In the meantime, *Green Tree Form: Interior of Woods* (1940; pl. VII) was bought by the Tate Gallery and exhibited in 1942, alongside other new Tate acquisitions, at the National Gallery in London, and then in several venues throughout Britain when a version of the exhibition was sent out on tour.[36] It was John Russell who visited Sutherland's studio on behalf of the Tate, and selected *Green Tree Form* for purchase. Anticipating Russell's visit, the artist conveyed the pressure that he clearly had to deal with during much of the war: 'I haven't got much stuff now, as I am largely confined to working for the government, but I have done a few things in the evenings.'[37] During the latter part of the conflict, Sutherland's work was extensively reproduced, notably in the volume dedicated to his work in Clark's Penguin Modern Masters series, devoted to contemporary British artists. The Sutherland book was one of the first batch to appear, in April 1944.[38] The essay by the music critic Edward Sackville-West, who he had probably met through Clark, captured, in Sutherland's view, 'the 'sound' of much that I have been trying to do these last few years'.[39]

Amongst the English intelligentsia, Sutherland's status was reflected and doubtless reinforced by his appearances in *Horizon*. To call this the most prestigious cultural journal of the period fails to do justice to the genuine excitement that, judging from several memoirs, greeted the arrival of each new issue. Looking at art and reading short stories or poems clearly fulfilled a deep need when the future of culture, let alone one's personal survival, seemed under such extreme and constant threat. Bacon spoke for many when he described it as 'one of the best magazines that has been done for many years in this country'.[40] By the time the first issue of *Horizon* appeared in 1940, under the editorship of the writer Cyril Connolly, many of the existing art and literary journals had already folded. *Horizon* assumed the mission of keeping the flame burning, so to speak, for internationalism and a loosely modernist culture during the long years of wartime isolation. Connolly looked after the literary side, which was naturally predominant, while the task of soliciting contributions on the visual arts mainly fell to the journal's wealthy backer and art editor Peter Watson, unfailingly described as the son of a margarine magnate.[41] It was as a result of Watson's tireless activity and commitment that *Horizon* maintained such a rich strand of coverage, in the form of both texts, usually illustrated, and unaccompanied reproductions. The magazine occasionally featured general or polemical pronouncements, such as Clement Greenberg's 'Avant-Garde and Kitsch', reprinted in 1940 from *Partisan Review*, 'Notes on Abstract Art' by Ben Nicholson, and a series of major essays by Herbert Read, the dominant British critic of the period.[42] A key priority from the beginning was the provision of a forum for the work of artists working, and often struggling to make a living, in wartime Britain.[43] Thus, between 1940 and 1945, *Horizon* included articles devoted to the Euston Road School, Naum Gabo, Barbara Hepworth, Ben Nicholson, Henry Moore, Paul Nash, Walter Sickert, Cecil Collins, Frances Hodgkins, Alfred Wallis, current Scottish painting, Matthew Smith, David Jones, Ceri Richards and Victor Pasmore.[44] Other issues featured reproductions of work by Watson's immediate circle of artist friends and protegés, including Colquhoun, John Craxton and Lucian Freud.[45] Amongst this roll-call of contemporary British artists, none enjoyed a higher profile in the pages of *Horizon* than Sutherland. His initial appearance took the form of a reproduction in the third issue of a brand new picture, *Association of Oaks* (1940; pl. v).[46] A sheet of drawings by Moore had appeared in the very first issue, but the work by Sutherland was the first proper plate photograph to be included in the magazine, a good indication of the current climate of appreciation for his work. It is possible to detect the hand of Watson, who was a passionate convert to Sutherland's art. Watson acquired *Damp Tree Roots* from the 1938 one-man show.[47] Subsequently he acquired two major pictures of 1939, *Entrance to a Lane* (pl. 25) and *Gorse on Sea Wall* (pl. III). 'Welsh Sketch Book', Sutherland's celebrated essay on the inspiration of his art, appeared in *Horizon* in spring 1942, in the guise of an open letter to Colin Anderson, although the draft had actually been headed 'Dear Peter'.[48] The essay conveyed the particular glories and emotional resonance of the countryside of west Pembrokeshire, which became a regular refuge during the war not just for the Sutherlands but also for Watson and young painter friends such as John Craxton. Around the end of the war, we find Watson continuing to use *Horizon* to express the commitment to Sutherland's work that he now shared with many others in the British art world. In 1945, a special issue of the magazine was produced, in French translation, to be distributed in liberated France, with the aim of highlighting British cultural achievements during the period in which contacts had essentially ground to a halt.[49] The account of the visual arts took the form of an essay by

Watson himself characterising the art of Sutherland and, more briefly, Craxton.[50] An extract from this little known text indicates what Sutherland's art meant to its most attentive and sophisticated audience. Having emphasised the impact of the artist's visit to Pembrokeshire in 1936, Watson proceeded to celebrate his art:

> It is in the observation of nature that Graham Sutherland has found his favourite subjects: rocky landscapes at sunset, large boulders covered in moss, the twisted forms of tree roots, the tendrils of plants – all of this stored up, ordered, abstracted from its context, and painstakingly transformed into luminous and mysterious entities. In these entities he has created a poetry of form of a powerful emotional intensity, where the emphasis is on the unity of the organic and the inorganic, and where the logic of associations only has secondary importance. He aspires to a synthesis where the usual appearance of things is boldly eliminated and where there only remains a complex of relationships. These relationships are less symbols than the fusion of an image with reality; and it is with these that he has created this very personal poetry of forms, without ever making the least concession to the decorative composition of a motif. It is clear that Sutherland works outside of all contemporary conventions, in a certain isolation; one cannot discern any distinct influence on him, and his uncompromising originality can only arouse profound admiration or violent antipathy. And yet, however paradoxical this may be, he has exercised on his contemporaries and on a whole generation of younger painters a greater influence than any other English painter of our time.

The accompanying colour reproductions of *Intruding Bull* (1944) and *Horned Tree Form* (1944) were also included in the regular July 1945 issue of *Horizon*.[51] Watson acquired at least two further works around this time, a gouache *Man Walking* (1943) and a gouache *Thorn Trees* (1945).[52]

During a period of extreme isolation, artists in Britain very much relied upon the support and stimulation that they were able to offer one another. As Watson noted, it was Sutherland who emerged as a focus of admiration amongst the younger generation of artists and critics. According to the critic Robert Melville, Sutherland's first one-man show in 1938 not only launched his career, but also 'founded a new school of British painting almost overnight'.[53] During the war years, Sutherland's work served as a key point of departure for figures such as Prunella Clough, Robert Colquhoun, Craxton, John Minton, Keith Vaughan and several others who would subsequently come to be categorised as 'neo-romantics', a term coined in 1942 to register the emergence of an alternative aesthetic to the pre-war currents of surrealism, abstraction and social realism.[54] For Craxton, who probably spoke for the group as a whole, Sutherland had been, quite simply, 'my hero', an attitude certainly reflected in Craxton's current paintings, which reveal a strong debt to Sutherland's stylised Pembrokeshire landscapes.[55] In his well-informed survey of British painting since 1939, published shortly after the war, Robert Ironside noted Sutherland's pervasive influence on younger artists, and observed: 'the art of Francis Bacon is also in apparent debt to that of Sutherland'.[56] During the latter part of the war, Bacon may have become part of the admiring milieu around Sutherland. For instance, it was evidently at Sutherland's house in Kent that Bacon first met Craxton and Freud.[57] Thereafter, friendship with Lucian Freud was another common denominator between Sutherland and Bacon. It was to Freud, for example, that Sutherland at some point gave his etching tools, having definitively taken his leave of the medium.[58]

It is impossible to say specifically what Bacon saw and read of Sutherland between 1937 and 1943. One may surmise, however, that he observed Sutherland's meteoric career during the years when they were in more remote and occasional contact with one another. For his own part, Bacon completely disappeared from view at this time. He exhibited nothing at all, as far as is known, between the Agnew's show of 1937 and spring 1945. Indeed, as we have seen, Bacon tended to give the impression later on that he had stopped working completely until some point in the middle of the war, when his inspiration revived. Thereafter, it was only friends such as Sutherland and Eric Hall who would have had the opportunity to follow his progress. Sutherland's somewhat esoteric appreciation for Bacon's work may be deduced, in the first place, from the practical encouragement and help that he seems to have provided, in addition to providing 'colours'. It is well known that a key milestone in Bacon's career was his exhibiting two works in a group show at the Lefevre Gallery, London, in April 1945, *Three Studies for Figures at the Base of a Crucifixion* (1944) and *Figure in a Landscape* (1945). The show also featured eleven new oils and watercolours by Sutherland, as well as work by Frances Hodgkin, Moore and Matthew Smith.[59] Sutherland was evidently seen as central to the success of the show. In the previous year, he had been one of the artists that the gallery planned to include in a projected three artist exhibition.[60] All the Sutherland works were, in the event, sold at the opening of the expanded version of the show in spring 1945.[61] Given his prominence in the exhibition and strong connections with the gallery, not to mention his general standing at this point in the English art world, Sutherland would have been well placed to suggest the inclusion of Bacon, whose work can hardly have seemed a very promising commercial proposition.[62]

AFFINITIES

It is at this stage worth engaging in more detail with the two artists' work. Given the circumstances outlined, one might expect that any interaction between Sutherland and Bacon would, initially at any rate, involve the older and more successful figure providing inspiration for an artist emerging from a prolonged period of inactivity. How far does the reality conform to this, on the evidence of Bacon's *Three Studies for Figures at the Base of a Crucifixion* (pl. 2)? On the occasion of its first public exhibition in April 1945, alongside works by Sutherland, Bacon dated the *Three Studies* to 1944.[63] It is interesting, therefore, to note that the work possesses close formal and technical parallels to several works by Sutherland that

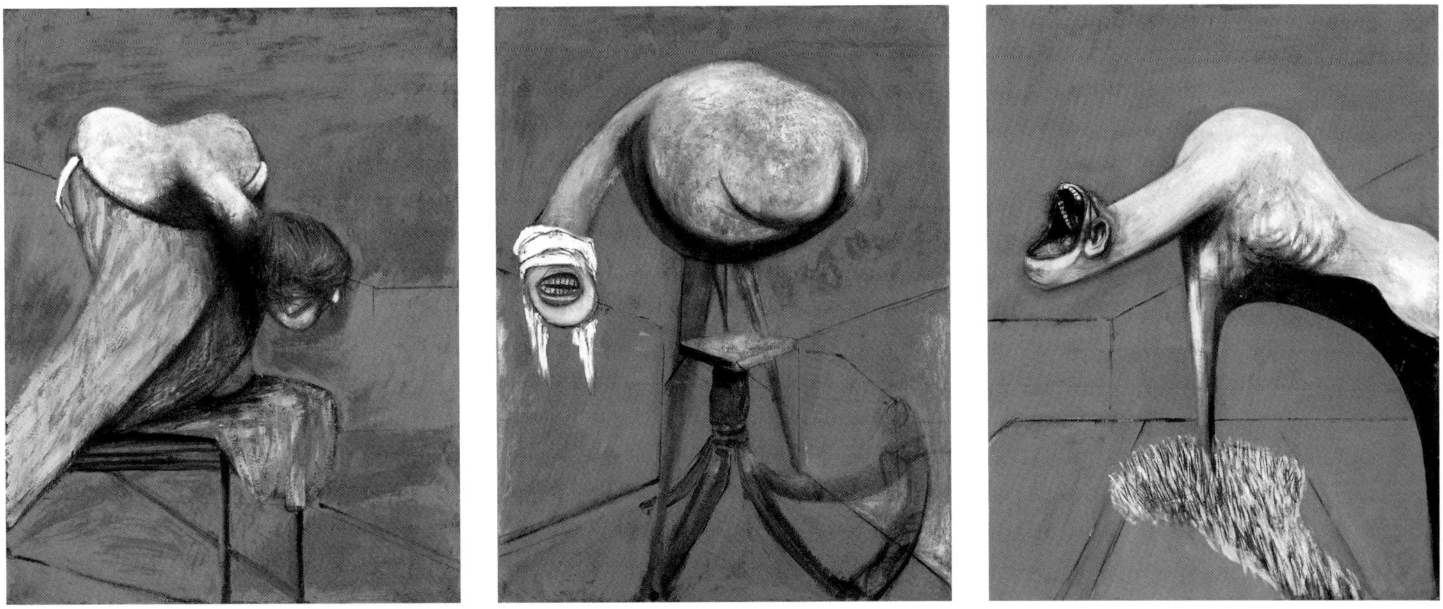

2 Francis Bacon, *Three Studies for Figures at the Base of a Crucifixion*, 1944, oil on board, each panel 94 × 73.7 cm, Tate, London.

date from the same year. These Sutherlands in turn register a renewed engagement with independent landscape-based work, following his prolonged immersion in official WAAC projects. It was increasingly evident that an end to the war, and an Allied victory, were finally in prospect, and this inevitably encouraged thoughts, not just amongst artists, about the resumption of normal careers and activities. In September 1944, Sutherland responded to implied encouragement from Kenneth Clark to fulfil his obligations as an official war artist:

> When we got to Pembrokeshire the ideas started welling up and crowding each other for daylight & since I've been back I've been doing one or two from a much-filled notebook & also getting an idea or two down for the Impington project. . . . But of course I agree I must do some war work . . . war art has not been irksome to me until recently: on the contrary I learned a great deal.[64]

Sutherland seems to be referring here to a sketchbook containing studies related to two new works on paper, *Bird-Like Tree Form – Grey and Orange* (1944; pl. 3) and *Twisted Tree Form* (1944; pl. IX), as well as a major oil painting entitled *Horned Forms* which Sutherland also dated to 1944 (pl. X).[65] It is precisely this group of works that most closely recalls Bacon's *Three Studies.*

One might start to enumerate affinities by considering the basics of use of materials. In the cases of Bacon's triptych and Sutherland's *Horned Forms*, *The Lamp* (1944) and subsequent works such as *Lane Opening* (1944–45), *Landscape with Rocks* (1945) and even the 1946 *Crucifixion* altarpiece in Northampton, the support employed is Sundeala board, a form of light-weight hardboard.[66] The fact that Bacon's three panels and Sutherland's *Lane Opening* and *Landscape with Rocks* all measure around 94 × 73 cm suggest that this was a standard, ready-made format. It was not just that normal materials such as canvas and the wood required for stretchers had become difficult to obtain or prohibitively expensive in the conditions of extreme deprivation and restriction that pertained in wartime Britain. Sutherland's correspondence with the WAAC indicates that official permission was required to obtain virtually any materials, including the 'beaver board' that he was working on in 1942 and 1943. By the autumn of 1944 he was using the Chelsea Art Stores as his supplier, and had started using Sundeala board. However, he still needed official authorisation, including a letter from the Secretary of Paper Control explaining that Sundeala board was the only type that did not crack or warp, rendering it especially suitable for Sutherland's war pictures.[67] Given these difficulties, and the indication in Bacon's letters that Sutherland provided him with paint, one might speculate that Sutherland helped Bacon in the very practical respect of giving or making available to him the supports he needed for his paintings. Bright orange paint was another shared material. Flat, unmodulated orange comprises the background of the *Three Studies* and of several of Sutherland's pictures from late 1944, including *Bird-Like Tree Form – Grey and Orange*, *The Lamp* and *Horned Forms*. Indeed the cover of the sketchbook containing studies for such pictures is also heavily worked with orange paint. Sutherland had included bright red and orange backgrounds before, as for example in the *Red Tree* of 1936 (pl. II), but now it is almost as if the two artists had obtained a quantity of orange pigment, and were sharing it out between them. In both the Bacon and *Horned Forms*, the colour was applied quite late in the making process, in the pursuit of greater clarity and contrast.

The parallels extend to technical and stylistic aspects of their paintings. Thus Bacon's combination of oil paint and chalk pastel, especially in the description of the left-hand figure's hair, is matched by Sutherland's use of paint, crayon and pastel in several works from this period, including *Twisted Tree Form*. The use of black lines to define a rudimentary, perspectival space is a feature both of the *Three Studies* and of Sutherland's *Bird-Like Tree Form – Grey and Orange*, *Twisted Tree Form* and *Horned Forms*. In the latter, an enigmatic cluster of root-like forms occupies the foreground of a barren, sun-baked landscape.[68] The starting point for the image was an actual tree root that Sutherland had taken back to his studio. The form of the natural object was then simplified and abstracted through a series of studies, and the composition transposed onto canvas by means of a squaring-up procedure that remains visible to the right-hand side of the composition. As in Bacon's triptych, the principal forms in the eventual picture are sculpturally modelled in grisaille, and these central passages are deliberately contrasted with the flat, brightly coloured backgrounds. The touches of mauve are echoed in the left-hand panel of the Bacon. The inclusion of expanses of pure black to establish shadows is another shared feature. The vocabulary of forms in the two artists' work also converges on occasion. In the case of *Bird-Like Tree Form – Grey and Orange*, the arcing shapes that describe the shadow cast by Sutherland's imaginary creature are closely analogous to those emanating from the right legs of the pedestal-like object, in front of another strikingly bird-like creature in the central section of Bacon's triptych.[69]

A key similarity that emanates from this group of 1944 pictures is the artists' shared engagement with indeterminate, biomorphic imagery. As we have seen, in *Bird-Like Tree*

3 Graham Sutherland, *Bird-Like Tree Form Grey and Orange*, 1944, gouache on paper, 30 × 29 cm, Private Collection.

Form – Grey and Orange, for example, Sutherland projected animal, bird and human attributes onto a found landscape element. In the triptych, Bacon likewise combined unmistakably human features with references to the forms of birds and wild animals. The left-hand image is the most obviously human, though one might detect in the kneeling, crouching figure, with its shroud-like drapery, some allusion to a large predatory bird such as a vulture perched in its cage. In the centre, the legs and body suggest, say, a flamingo or ostrich, but the inclined neck leads to a stump-like head, with the eyes covered with bandage and the open mouth establishing the only direct allusion to the human body. The creature in the right-hand image is the most profoundly ambiguous, both in identity and mood. It is simultaneously a howling, yawning or roaring beast, and a human presence barking out a stream of hysterical oratory, or else emitting some primordial scream of pain and anguish. The detail of the ear provides the most vivid reference to human anatomy. The ambiguity of the image

4 Marius Maxwell, plate from *Stalking Big Game with a Camera in Equatorial Africa* (1925).

5 Marius Maxwell, plate from *Stalking Big Game with a Camera in Equatorial Africa* (1925).

is carried through to the setting, where a patch of scrubby grass is incongruously inserted into a bare interior space, suggesting human occupation. Bacon's grisaille modelling serves to avoid specific associations either with human flesh, or with the surface texture of any particular animal.

According to John Russell, 'much in the *Three Studies* now seems to him to be a relatively direct and primitive adaptation of strange forms that he had memorised while poring over books of animals'.[70] In particular, it is known that Bacon was fascinated by the photographs he encountered in the monumental and lavishly produced book by Marius Maxwell, *Stalking Big Game with a Camera in Equatorial Africa*, which had appeared in 1924.[71] This contained over one hundred images, focussing on such creatures as elephants, giraffes, rhinosceri, and hippopotami. The slightly blurred quality of the images gives them a decidedly pictorial and suggestive character, to which Bacon clearly responded. One plate from this source featured in Sam Hunter's 1950 montages of images from Bacon's studio, and several were found amongst the debris on the floor of Bacon's studio.[72] In the case of the right-hand image in the triptych, Maxwell's studies of a rhinoceros closely foreshadow the depiction of the form in profile, its front leg firmly planted, as well as the patch of dry grass that typifies the setting in such sources (pl. 4).[73] The bulbous shoulder extending behind the angled neck echoes the doleful hippopotamus captured in the wild by Maxwell (pl. 5).[74] The grouping of pictures of elephants in the forest into a triptych, indicating a narrative progression through time, might even have been one factor predisposing Bacon towards this format (pl. 40).[75] I would also argue that the affinity between the triptych and Sutherland's *Horned Forms* (1944) extends beyond stylistic and technical parallels to the intimation of animal imagery. In the Sutherland, the main forms evoke, ambiguously, not just roots and bones, but also the doleful, lumbering presence of a rhinoceros, or perhaps an elephant emerging from the trees, if we read the horn-like form to the left as a fused head and trunk (pl. 6).[76] This visual suggestion is, of course, reinforced by the picture's title, while the setting too is comparable to the arid landscapes in Maxwell's evocative images. The bestial overtones

6 Marius Maxwell, plate from *Stalking Big Game with a Camera in Equatorial Africa* (1925).

are particularly explicit in some of the small sketches for the picture that Sutherland executed in pencil and gouache.[77] The connection suggests that the two artists were poring over the Maxwell and comparable photographs together, and talking perhaps about the possibilities that such imagery contained for a metamorphic pictorial art encapsulating the pathos of wartime life.

The creative processes of Sutherland and Bacon are superficially very different, but this should not blind us to points of compatibility. It might be said, for instance, that in making their pictures both artists made reference to existing imagery. This primarily comprised photographs in Bacon's case, showing not just wild animals but also textbook illustrations of diseases of the mouth, and paintings by Grünewald.[78] Sutherland's points of departure were photographs and, above all, observed studies from natural forms. In each case, such found images were gradually subjected to 'metamorphosis' or 'paraphrase', in Sutherland's current terminology, in order to produce suggestive and emotionally engaging images.[79] The process employed by Sutherland involved several stages of drawing, as noted. Bacon may have done likewise, and subsequently seen fit to destroy the evidence – at least one of the drawings that has surfaced in recent years appears to belong to the 1930s.[80] Alternatively, he may have relied far more than Sutherland on adjusting and reworking the surface of the panel or canvas. Technical investigations by the Tate Gallery have confirmed that each of the individual panels in the triptych was subject to protracted modifications.[81] For example, infra-red inspection demonstrated that the final central panel was painted on top of areas of paint describing flowers and a wooded landscape. A high degree of improvisation is equally characteristic of the paintings that followed. On the other hand, Bacon would also elaborate a composition between related full-scale works. In the case of the triptych, the central panel is a loose fusion of the bird-like creature and the disembodied mouth in two lost paintings exhibited in the 1937 Agnew's Gallery show.[82] The figure in the left-hand image corresponds closely to a picture, presumably from around the same time as the triptych, where it – the gender is unidentifiable – is apparently sniffing a bunch of flowers, and set against a backdrop of curtain folds.[83] Another, and probably earlier, version of the right-hand panel has recently come to light in which the creature's gaping mouth is again either smelling or even devouring flowers, like an animal feeding in the wild.[84] Such closely connected pictures indicate that each of the three images in the *Three Studies* probably existed already as discrete, individual compositions, which Bacon may have seen as a sequence, though not necessarily as 'figures at the base of a crucifixion'. Equally, making variants, more or less modified, on existing compositions is a feature of Sutherland's working methods, as in the two versions of *Red Tree* (1936), *Horned Form* (1944) and *Chimère* (1946–47), or the many variations over a period of years on, for instance, the *Entrance to a Lane* and *Thorn Head* conceptions.

We have noted parallels, but there is no obvious basis for asserting priorities or patterns of influence. If the works discussed were all produced in 1944, this still leaves open the question of what exactly Bacon and Sutherland were working on as the year unfolded. Moreover, the dates given to some of the pictures may represent a simplification of their actual execution. The only problem with the Sutherland works is that *Horned Forms* was not included in the Lefevre Gallery show in April 1945, alongside the *Three Studies* pictures to which it has such striking affinities. This may be because Sutherland was still working on it, or simply because the picture had already been acquired by Sutherland's solicitor Wilfred Evill, whose ownership is indicated by the caption to the colour reproduction of the picture in the July 1945 issue of *Horizon* magazine.[85] The dating of Bacon's triptych has recently been revealed to be less straightforward than the Lefevre Gallery catalogue entry indicates. The removal of the frames revealed that the right-hand panel bears the inscription 'F.BACON/PETERSFIEL[D]' on the reverse. It is assumed that Bacon moved to Petersfield in early 1942, and we have already encountered his remark to Sutherland in February 1943 that he was now spending more time in London. On this basis, it has been argued by Matthew Gale that 'the inscription would tend to enlarge the period in which this panel – and probably the whole triptych – was painted to 1942–44'.[86] This potentially runs counter to any suggestion that Bacon obtained the panels of Sundeala board from Sutherland. It is evident from the inscription and the evidence of reworking that Bacon did not simply obtain three brand new pieces of board in 1944 and conceive and produce the triptych in anticipation of the exhibition at the Lefevre Gallery in April 1945. At this point, he could have simply grouped and framed three related pictures that he had realised independently a year or two earlier, possibly in Petersfield. By conferring on the work the title under which it was exhibited, Bacon then reinforced the affinity with traditional religious painting that was inherent in the triptych format. Alternatively, he could at this stage have decided to rework or produce variants on three existing compositions, and to reinforce the coherence of the work by applying the simple orange backgrounds, which were clearly painted after the figures and may have supplanted diverse settings in the original pictures. However, the images also cohere as a result of the scale of the figurative elements, and because the three compositions are arranged into a very simple, symmetrical composition, with a more upright image in the centre and each of the flanking images orientated towards it. This suggests a degree of calculation. A third possibility, therefore, is that

Bacon did indeed conceive and create the work in its present format, in the year to which he attributed the work. Because of prevailing shortages, he was compelled to recycle available supports that he could even have had in his possession since before the war and that he had already worked on, in one case at least while he was based in Petersfield before he moved back definitively to London.[87] In support of this, it may be noted that Roy de Maistre also liked using Sundeala Board, and could have transmitted this preference to Bacon when they were in close contact during the 1930s; and also that the boards were 'not in pristine condition: there were shallow bruises on the right-hand panel already the paint was applied'.[88] It is also worth making the point that all he told Sutherland, in February 1943, was that he was 'more often in London than here now'. This does not of course preclude the possibility that he and Hall continued to use the cottage for some unspecified time afterwards, particularly at times of the year when the weather was more clement.

Establishing the exact period of time within which Bacon's triptych was executed is clearly impossible, on present evidence. Yet locating the work in 1944 is not required for sustaining the hypothesis that the two artists were feeding off one another's work. On the one hand, any of these alternatives stated above are compatible with the notion that Sutherland may have viewed the triptych in Bacon's studio before he embarked upon *Bird-Like Tree Form–Grey and Orange*, *Twisted Tree Form* and *Horned Forms* during the latter part of 1944. The boldness of colour and touch that enters into Sutherland's work at this time could conceivably have been given impetus by Bacon's example. It should also be noted that a small pencil drawing by Sutherland, usually identified as 'Thorn Heads, Study', is in fact a variant and elaboration of the figure in the left panel of Bacon's triptych.[89] The grotesque extension of the neck further recalls Bacon's *Figure Getting out of a Car*, which may either pre- or post-date the triptych (pl. 38). On the other hand, Sutherland appears to be the first to introduce metamorphic imagery. *Gorse on Sea Wall* (1939; pl. III) is commonly regarded as 'the first picture in which one can see very clearly the metamorphosis of a plant form into an image like an animal, which also makes allusion to the human body':

> The sinuous, coiled form raises its polyp-like extremity aloft like a cobra poised to strike, with its tentacles groping and gesturing menacingly. Despite the presence of two prickly green shoots attached to the form, it is unclear whether it is plant or animal or both, and whether it is real or imaginary. This ambiguity, this feeling of something ominous and of being on the edge of a dream or nightmare, is underlined by the muted but brooding colour harmonies.[90]

The root might indeed be taken to suggest a bony claw poised to seize its prey, a rearing scorpion, or even a wizened hand locked in a deathly seizure. But it is in Sutherland's work from the early part of the war that we encounter especially direct precedents for the semi-human, semi-animal creature that Bacon devised for the right-hand panel of the *Three Studies* triptych. In Sutherland's *Blasted Oak* (1941; pl. 33), a tree root is given the attributes both of a screaming head and of some fearful bird of prey, perched on a branch and emitting its ter-

7 Marius Maxwell, plate from *Stalking Big Game with a Camera in Equatorial Africa* (1925).

rible cry. The configuration of the Bacon, on the other hand, is more exactly foreshadowed in *Green Tree Form* (1940; pl. VII). One might compare the overall placement and diagonal orientation of the main element, the single, spindly vertical leg that supports the form in each case, and the downward inclination of the neck in the Bacon and of the snout-like form in the Sutherland that offset the rising angle of the body. In this case, Sutherland makes an uprooted tree, seen from the roots end, take on the overtones of some monstrous creature, lumbering through the darkness with knobbly features that already recall the heads of rhinosceri photographed by Marius Maxwell (pl. 7).[91] Finally, the stylistic idiom of Bacon's panel echoes Sutherland's more schematized variant on the *Green Tree Form* idea (1940; pl. 8). Here, the fusion of strongly modelled, almost sculptural form and flat, brightly coloured backdrop could have demonstrated to Bacon how he might achieve a greater simplicity and concentration in his paintings, in the interests of a heightened expressive charge. Sutherland too seems to have applied the acidic green background at quite a late stage in the picture's making, editing out what presumably began as a more complex landscape setting.

It is apparent, then, that Sutherland was already very interested in disquieting, ambiguous imagery during the early years of the war, well before the time when he and Bacon became close and when similar concerns manifested themselves in the *Three Studies for Figures at the Base of a Crucifixion*. Sutherland may to some degree have inspired Bacon's own explorations, and even his interest in wild-life photographers such as Maxwell. Bacon could easily have viewed works such as *Blasted Oak* and the two versions of *Green Tree Form* in Sutherland's 1940 exhibition at the Lefevre Gallery, or in the several group shows in London to which Sutherland contributed thereafter. Thus, arguing for Sutherland's possible influence on Bacon does not necessarily presuppose that the triptych was actually conceived and executed during the period when Bacon and Sutherland were in regular contact. Overall, and given the various chronological uncertainties, perhaps all that can be reasonably concluded is that, by the end of 1944, Bacon's encounter with the work of Sutherland had made a significant impact on Bacon, as he sought to reacquire a sense of artistic identity, and that Sutherland's reciprocal admiration for Bacon's work may have begun to inform his own work, as Sutherland began

8 Graham Sutherland, *Green Tree Form*, 1940, oil on canvas, 60.5 × 54.5 cm, British Council Collection.

to engage once again with his independent work following several years of immersion in documenting the spectacle of war.

The Lefevre Gallery exhibition included recent works by both artists that indicate further, albeit less overt, parallels. Alongside more characteristic landscape-based works, Sutherland showed two pictures, *The Smiling Woman* and *Woman in Garden*, which revealed a new involvement with the portrayal of the human figure, presented with relatively little distortion (pl. 10).[92] There is a general affinity here with Bacon's *Figure in a Landscape* (1945), a large picture in which the representation of at least some elements of the suited figure – the right knee, arm and upper torso – employs a far more naturalistic idiom than that of the *Three Studies* (pl. xii). Moreover, the presence and treatment of the landscape backdrop, at odds with the interior settings of the bulk of Bacon's current work, brings Sutherland to mind. The accumulation of small black touches to evoke the grass and trees recalls Sutherland's dense build up of marks, using black paint or ink, in works such as *Black Landscape* (1939–40; pl. 24) and *Blasted Oak* (1941). But a more direct point of reference for Bacon's landscape backdrop was another of Maxwell's wildlife photographs, in which an African buffalo is framed by a comparable, and similarly out-of-focus, configuration of continuous, densely foliated trees in the background and long grass which concealed the animal's feet in the foreground (pl. 9).[93] In *Figure in a Landscape,* the landscape forms the unlikely backdrop for a ghostly headless figure, sat in front of a strange metallic contraption evoking both a machine-gun placement and a battery of microphones. The latter element is juxtaposed, in turn, with a very blurred, ambiguous passage of paint, several inches to the right of the principal figure's hands, which suggests flesh, blood and possibly a vestigial screaming mouth. The expanse of black that has mysteriously supplanted the entire left-hand side of the figure's torso recalls Sutherland's inclusion of unmodulated, firmly outlined black shapes in a work such as Sutherland's *Lane Opening* (1944–45; pl. xi), shown alongside the Bacon at the Lefevre Gallery. The Sutherland too evokes the idea of a figure in a landscape, in the sense that the central configuration of interlocking, rounded shapes can be read not just as an illuminated tunnel through the trees, but, at the same time, as a schematic human head emerging, as it were, out of the elements of a landscape. The scythe-like black shape to the left suggests the neck and back of a head seen in profile. Compared with *Entrance to a Lane* (1939), on which it is a variant, *Lane Opening* illustrates the greater boldness, cruder touch and more discordant approach to colour that Sutherland introduced into his work in the mid 1940s, precisely at the point when he was closest to Bacon. Nevertheless, Sutherland's painting has a rather different impact, in the end, from the shocking, visceral impression made by Bacon. Whereas Sutherland aspires to a familiar kind of compositional coherence, within which strong visual contrasts might be contained, Bacon aims for inconsistency, fragmentation and dissonance. Although *Three Studies for Figures at the Base of a Crucifixion* is widely regarded, following Bacon's lead, as the symbolic starting point for his mature art, *Figure in a Landscape* was at least as important in establishing the distinctive characteristics and concerns of his work.

9 Marius Maxwell, plate from *Stalking Big Game with a Camera in Equatorial Africa* (1925).

10 Graham Sutherland, *Woman in Garden*, 1945, pen, chalk and gouache, 60.9 × 43.2 cm, Private Collection.

Sutherland 1945

*

During the period after the end of the war in Europe, Sutherland's career continued to flourish, both at home and abroad. In general, British culture accrued a certain prestige from the heroic role that the country had played in the defeat of Hitler. During the winter of 1945–46, for example, the British Council took a show to Paris of nine contemporary English artists, of which Sutherland was one.[94] He featured in a show of modern British art from the Tate Gallery that the Council toured around the capitals of Europe.[95] Sutherland also benefited from a brief infatuation with British art in the United States. In particular, the Buchholz Gallery in New York included Sutherland's work in a group show in 1945, and then gave him a one-man show in spring 1946.[96] This was gratifyingly well-received, and nine pictures were sold to private collectors and museums, including a version of *Horned Forms* to the Museum of Modern Art, and a *Thorn Tree* to the Albright-Knox Gallery in Buffalo.

In Britain, meanwhile, Sutherland and Bacon were once again juxtaposed in a group show at the Lefevre Gallery in February 1946.[97] This included only one figure other than Sutherland who had acquired a reputation before the war, namely Ben Nicholson, which suggests that the gallery was seeking to identify and promote a new generation. Sutherland's two contributions were *The Thorn Tree* and *Thorns*, presumably one of the compositions that he would later title *Thorn Heads* (pl. 46). The thorn pictures were by this stage Sutherland's major preoccupation, and marked a significant extension of his metamorphic landscape idiom. Bacon's two *Figure Study* compositions can equally be seen as variants on the imagery of the *Three Studies*. *Figure Study II* (pl. XIX) in particular reads as a fusion of elements in the triptych's two outer panels (pls IV and VIII). Bacon's pictures conformed in a general way to a renewed concern with the image of the human figure that we have already noted in Sutherland's art, and which was evident from the contributions to the Lefevre Gallery exhibition from artists such as Vaughan, Craxton, Colquhoun, Clough and Freud. Otherwise, the similarity between the artists in the show was the fact that they had all, during the last few years, been strongly affected by the example of Sutherland. In his review, the critic Roger Marvell noted Sutherland's position as a *chef d'école*, and indicated that he would 'not be surprised' if he soon found 'thorns burgeoning fashionably on hundreds of canvases by other artists'.[98] Indeed, the *Thorn Tree* was 'amongst the most powerful pictures this extraordinary artist has achieved'. Bacon was the other artist who came in for special commendation:

> There is nobody in England who can paint better, and only two or three who can paint anything like as well. Look at the grey material and the blue flowers, the handling is consummate. I should suggest an affinity with Velásquez's, if I did not know that someone would at once attribute to me the view that Mr Bacon is as great a painter as the Spaniard. . . . What excitement to find in a young English painter such staggering virtuosity.[99]

Such recognition stood in contrast to the critical response to the show in April 1945, where the very few mentions of Bacon were decidedly negative. One might also note the decision of the Contemporary Art Society to purchase *Figure Study II*, although they then found it difficult to place the picture in a public collection. Aside from their general impressiveness, it might perhaps have been evident to an attentive viewer of the exhibition that *Figure Study II* and Sutherland's *Thorn Tree* (pl. XIII) possessed certain formal and structural affinities, alongside the obvious differences of theme. Thus, both pictures combine flat expanses of colour with highly-worked areas of texture and detail in the focal passages occupying the upper central part of the canvases. In each case, a predominant frontality is qualified by the introduction of perspective lines opening up pockets of space in the lower foreground. The curved branches and sharp spikes of Sutherland's thorns closely parallel the shapes that describe the plant and umbrella in *Figure Study II*. Equally, Bacon's grisaille modelling of the protruding body echoes the treatment of Sutherland's vertical supports, which take on a bodily, limb-like resonance.

In the summer of 1946, two works by Bacon, closely related in their imagery, could be seen in London commercial galleries. The Lefevre Gallery exhibited *Man with Microphones*, subsequently overpainted, which featured a still greater profusion of Sutherlandesque foliage than the earlier Figure Studies (pl. 39).[100] The remarkable *Painting* (1946) was also shown for the first time at the Redfern Gallery. The consistent scale of *Figure in a Landscape*, *Figure Study II* and *Man with Microphones*, all at around 145 cm high by 130 cm across, indicates a tendency to work on standard size canvases that is evident throughout his career, but also suggests a new-found confidence on Bacon's part and an ambition to make an impact. A significant parallel between Bacon and Sutherland was their experimentation in 1946 with larger formats. Bacon's *Painting* (1946; pl. XVI) and Sutherland's *Chimère I* (1946; pl. 11) are in fact almost identical in scale and proportions, both paintings almost two hundred centimetres high.

In formal terms, *Chimère I* marks a further development of the organisation of the *Thorn Tree* pictures, with their internal framing devices. The starting point for the composition was, characteristically, an unimposing fallen tree-trunk, with an eye-like knot, which Sutherland had encountered in Wales and incorporated into several works on paper the previous year.[101] One small pastel study in particular, dated 1945, recalls the geometric organisation and strident palette of Bacon's *Figure Study II*.[102] In the eventual, vertical painting, the 'head' element is carried over from the studies but the picture as a whole now evokes a mysterious semi-human presence, perhaps some malevolent deity gazing imperiously in the direction of the viewer.[103] Whatever its intended associations, Sutherland seems to have been willing in *Chimère*, more than in any other picture from the period, to dispense with reference to legible components of the visible world, so that the final picture reads as entirely imaginary. One might speculate that talking with Bacon served as a stimulus for this change of working method. The disquieting atmosphere of *Chimère* is more than matched by Bacon's *Painting* (1946). Here, the yet more sinister presiding presence is a fragmentary human figure, his eyes shadowed by the umbrella that also shields him, perhaps, from the sight, or even the bloody secretions of, a looming, crucifix-like carcass. In terms of visual affinities, *Chimère* embodies the same impulse towards an architectonic grandeur that is encountered in *Painting* (1946). The construction of a shallow, frontal space is comparable in the two pictures, and the principal massing is in each case positioned somewhat to the right of the central axis. The underlying geometry of the two compositions is played off against amorphous passages of painterly brushwork, especially in the lower sections. Comparable elements of metallic railings are inserted, and the head and shoulders of the figure in *Painting* find an equivalent in the upper part of Sutherland's hybrid creature, which also suggests a suit and collar. Both paintings contain acidic pink backdrops, notwithstanding their dark and menacing moods, and this accent of strong colour is intensified by clearly defined areas of flat black – compare, in particular, the curve defining the left side of Sutherland's 'figure' with that describing the shadowed area of the animal carcass in *Painting*.[104] Sam Hunter remarked in 1952 that works by Bacon 'suggest a connection with an English contemporary – Sutherland – in their livid, chemical magentas'.[105] Once again, then, the visual evidence suggests that the two painters were in some way affected by viewing one another's work in progress.[106] However, there is no documentary evidence to clarify the relative beginning, progress and completion of the two paintings, and thus the directions in which any inspiration might have travelled.

Sutherland's *Chimère I* could have been begun during the first half of 1946, in the wake perhaps of producing the thorn pictures exhibited in February at the Lefevre Gallery. The work may have been produced during the months before he launched himself into producing his big *Crucifixion* for St Matthew's Church, Northampton that summer and autumn, perhaps as a trial run for working on a bigger scale. Alternatively, he might have worked on the two pictures simultaneously. It is clear that there was a close relationship between them from the fact that one of Sutherland's sketchbooks contains studies for both works.[107] All that is known is that *Chimère I* was completed in time to be exhibited for the first time in November at the UNESCO international exhibition of Modern Art in Paris, in the company of two of the thorn pictures and also Bacon's *Painting* (1946).[108] Sutherland proceeded to make a second version of *Chimère*, which possesses a more symmetrical composition, a harder definition of form and more opaque application of paint.[109]

It is unclear when Bacon embarked upon *Painting*, but it is known that it was finished by the middle of 1946. Sutherland saw the picture, presumably in Bacon's studio, and urged the dealer Erica Brausen from the Redfern Gallery to make a point of looking at it. The gallery had exhibited Sutherland in 1944, alongside Nash, Moore and Piper, and was currently planning another group show featuring nineteen of Sutherland's landscape studies.[110] Brausen duly purchased the Bacon for two hundred pounds, a considerable sum which allowed Bacon to leave England for an extended stay in France shortly afterwards. *Painting* was exhibited in the Redfern Gallery in the summer of 1946.[111] Bacon's letter to Sutherland dated 20 August indicates, however, that the surface of the work remained unstable, presumably because of the combination of paint and pastel.[112] With Bacon now absent in the South of France, it was Sutherland who agreed to spray the painting. Bacon was perhaps thinking not just of the recent sale to the Redfern Gallery and the attendant conservation work, but also of the Lefevre

11 Graham Sutherland, *Chimère I*, 1946, oil on canvas, 199.4 × 120.5 cm, Private Collection.

Gallery shows, when he remarked to Sutherland, with heartfelt gratitude: 'I do want to thank you Graham for all you have done for me. I know I should not have been able to sell anything if you had not been good enough to mention my work to other people'.[113] Indeed several stories indicate that, as the more established and successful artist, Sutherland felt that he could help Bacon secure a position within the art-world. Sutherland prevailed upon Kenneth Clark and Colin Anderson, who both collected his own work, to go and look at Bacon's pictures. The latter acquired Bacon's early *Crucifixion* of 1933 from the Redfern Gallery in 1946.[114] Clark supposedly remarked to Sutherland, following his visit to Bacon's studio: 'You and I may be in a minority of two, but we may still be right in thinking Francis Bacon has genius' – although Bacon, for his part, deemed Clark to be a 'cretin'.[115] We may infer something of the character and enthusiasm of Sutherland's advocacy from Lucian Freud's story about how Sutherland responded to his question about who was the best painter in England. He evidently replied that it was Bacon, whom no-one knew about because his work had not as yet been exhibited. Bacon was, Sutherland remarked, 'like a cross between Picasso and Vuillard', which is actually quite an astute commentary on, for example, the two versions of *Figure Study*.[116]

It would appear that Sutherland's admiration for Bacon was increasingly reflected in his own work. Not much can be deduced perhaps from the fact that *Painting* (1946) was exhibited before Sutherland's *Chimère 1*. However, Bacon's current dominance in the relationship is evident from the correspondences between Sutherland's *Crucifixion* altarpiece (pl. xv) and *Painting*, a picture in which Bacon too alluded, albeit more obliquely, to Crucifixion imagery, an iconographic affinity explored in chapter two. Resemblances may be noted between the painterly realisation of the suspended, splayed animal carcass in the Bacon and of the body of Christ in the Sutherland, especially details such as the rib-cages; between the tubular, curved metallic structures at the base of the two compositions, which fade away at the bottom in both paintings, and which read as an altar fixture around Christ's feet in the Sutherland and, in the Bacon, as a podium of some description, bizarrely ornamented with bones and meat; between the brightly coloured, flat backdrops in each picture, off-setting the three-dimensionality of the principal forms, and the looser brushwork and extensive use of black in the central areas of the compositions; and, finally, between the linear divisions which in each case serve to articulate the backdrops. Both paintings are heavily worked and reveal the evidence of extensive adjustments during the process of execution. The affinities multiply as the Bacon and Sutherland pictures are considered in conjunction, though so too do the distinctions – such as the disturbing inconsistencies in Sutherland's treatment of Christ's body, veering from a high degree of stylisation, as in the head and rib cage, to the naturalistic account given of the arms and hands. Given the affinities, one might submit that it was Bacon's *Painting* (1946) that demonstrated to Sutherland how an artist in the present could preserve something of the pictorial grandeur and expressive power inherent in the traditional devotional theme. At the time, Sutherland's dependency on Bacon was certainly apparent to observers such as Herbert Read.[117] The documented timetable of events reinforces this pos-

12 Graham Sutherland, *Tree Form against Blue*, 1946, oil on canvas, 57.8 × 54 cm, Private Collection.

sibility. *Painting* (1946) was finished by the summer. Meanwhile, Sutherland finally arrived at a formulation of the subject that satisfied him, after many changes of mind, and he seems to have embarked upon the realisation of his altarpiece in June 1946. The eventual picture was under way from early September onwards, and was ready to be unveiled in November.[118] In all probability, then, the Bacon was finished, and intimately known to Sutherland, by the time that the Northampton picture was begun in earnest. *Chimère II* and *Christ Carrying the Cross*, both large pictures dating from 1947, reinforce the argument that Bacon's *Painting* exerted a powerful inspiration upon Sutherland.[119] The latter's *Deposition* (1946), another in this series of big religious pictures, raises a final technical parallel.[120] Like the *Crucifixion*, it is executed on board, but whereas the latter is heavily, one might even say excessively, worked, the *Deposition* is thinly and summarily painted, and the granular texture and brown colour of the board are much in evidence. The effect is strikingly similar to the paintings that Bacon began to produce using, and visually exploiting, the reverse side of primed canvasses. The artist recalled adopting this method in Monte Carlo, presumably around 1947 and 1948.[121]

Overall, these comparisons cumulatively suggest that the years from 1944 to 1946 marked the closest phase of interaction between Sutherland and Bacon, at any rate until the early 1950s. At the start of this period, Sutherland may have had more to offer Bacon, though this is not absolutely clear, while the reverse was almost certainly true by mid- to late 1946. Sutherland is at his most overtly Baconesque in a picture like *Tree Form against Blue* (1946), where the curve of the extended neck, leading round to the head, echoes the central panel of Bacon's 1944 triptych (pl. 12).[122] Nevertheless, any such conclusions are bound to be speculative and tentative, since the very few pictures that Bacon exhibited and preserved represent merely the tip of an iceberg. While Sutherland is a known quantity, Bacon's activity in his studio at this time is largely an enigma. But what surely can be concluded, with some confidence, is that these two artists were not just good friends, but also, in all likelihood, each other's principal sounding boards and confidantes. At this point, each probably meant more to the other than any other artist within their immediate working environments.

ABROAD

After 1946, Bacon and Sutherland began to encounter one another not just in London, and occasionally Kent, but also in more distant and exotic places. For both exemplified the widespread cultural phenomenon that David Alan Mellor has dubbed the 'flight to the continent'.[123] Continental Europe in general, and France in particular, now resumed their places as the antidote to Britain and as the font of culture and creativity, from which it was necessary to take bearings It is true that the war had produced a tremendous wave of national feeling, and also a widespread desire to see a better Britain emerge at the end of the dark tunnel, reflected in the surprising defeat of Churchill and the election of a Labour government in 1945. But after five and a half years of enforced isolation, British writers and artists, and no doubt anyone else who could afford the time and expense, experienced a profound compulsion to get away from the drabness and deprivation of life at home. As usual, it was Cyril Connolly who articulated the increasingly despondent mood in one of his *Horizon* editorials, lamenting the signs that Britain had lost the economic war, despite military victory:

> we go back to scratch as a barren, humid, raw, but densely over-populated group of islands with an obsolete industrial plant, hideous but inadequate housing, a variety of unhealthy jungle possessions, vast international commitments, a falling birth-rate . . . Surrounded by

> a loosened belt of good eating, we yet suffer from undernourishment, dearth of vitamins and sunshine, lack of hope, energy, leisure and spirit.

London, he lamented, is 'now the largest, saddest and dirtiest of great cities'.[124] The remedy was revisiting old haunts abroad. Fifty years later, the novelist Doris Lessing would state: 'there is no way now of telling how powerful a dream France was then . . . it is hard to remember how people yearned for France, as for civilisation itself'.[125] Voyages to Paris and the Midi form an absolute leitmotif of the biographies of British cultural figures in the latter half of the 1940s. To name but two, Connolly and Peter Watson visited the French capital in 1945, and as frequently as possible thereafter. Sutherland had in fact stayed in Paris when he spent a couple of weeks in December 1944 observing war damage wrought, for a change, by the Royal Air Force on the German forces occupying France.[126] He recalled: 'It was the first time I'd been abroad in my life. Before the war I hadn't been able to afford it and before that I was living a really insular English life'.[127] The Sutherlands then spent eleven days in Paris in April 1946, in the company of Eardley Knollys who escorted them around some of the main galleries and collections devoted to modern art.[128] Likewise, Lucian Freud was in Paris before he and John Craxton went to Greece. A few months after Sutherland, Bacon found that he could embark upon a longer stay, on the proceeds of selling *Painting*. In contrast to Sutherland, Bacon had visited Paris and Berlin in his late teens, and had discovered modern art in the process. It is a mark of contemporary ignorance that we simply do not know whether he made any other trips abroad during the 1930s.

Bacon's sequence of letters to Sutherland back in England, far more expansive than the three previous notes, indicates something of his whereabouts and activities during this initial stay. A constant theme is his attempts to persuade the Sutherlands to come and join him, an idea that they had obviously talked about in London. Bacon waxed lyrically and sometimes hilariously, in his finest camp vein, about the light and the balmy climate, the excitements of the casino at Monte Carlo and the general cultural philistinism of the place, which clearly appealed to him:

> I don't know if you would like this place or not. I like the light and going to the casino in the evening after working and it is really quite pleasant to feel so isolated here but if I get the pictures finished I should like to go to Paris in October. . . . Nobody here is at all interested in ART which is perhaps a comfort and when they try to paint this landscape it is quite unbelievable, especially when they try to have the flowering bouganvillea and all that it turns into a wonderful lesbian postcard. I do hope it won't be long before I see you both. I think you might really love working here.[129]

Bacon even floated the idea that the two of them could share the costs of renting a studio space in Paris: 'I thought I would look around for a large room or studio that I could go to from here for some weeks at a time perhaps if you still think of part of the year in Paris perhaps we could find something we could use alternatively [sic].'[130] Meanwhile, well-off

British visitors seem to have been thick on the ground, and Bacon reported sightings in the casino of mutual friends and acquaintances such as the Clarks, Roderick Cameron, and Peter Watson.[131] The casino loomed large not only in Bacon's daily routine but also in his fantasies about how he and Sutherland might support themselves in the South of France for periods of the year:

> I think you might like this place to work in. At first I found it too distracting but now I love it and find it very good for pictures falling ready made into the mind. I paint dozens every week there.
>
> It is completely insulated against modern art and interesting people which is really very pleasant. It is too artificial for me to live in. I couldn't. [add: You know my dear I couldn't live a sick and artificial life.] I feel you would like it too as it is beginning to get people of all nationalities passing through and as it is very small it seems concentrated in that way. It would be so lovely if you and Kathy felt like working here and I always feel with a little clever manipulation the Casino would buy our pictures.[132]

Sutherland's own letters doubtless expressed his enthusiasm to make a further, longer visit to France, but also an unwillingness or inability to get away until he had completed the Northampton altarpiece. In the end, he remained in England for the remainder of 1946. By the beginning of the following year, Bacon, and presumably Eric Hall, were installed in a flat, and once again Sutherland was being warmly entreated to make the trip:

> About expenses, I could find you a very good room in a hotel here very reasonably and you must come and have meals with us in the flat. There is even a possibility that you could have the flat to stay in as we have got it until the end of March and we are looking for another as I do not want to stay in this one and we have heard of another and may have to take it before the end of this lease as they are so hard to get. But in any case come as soon as you can. One can live quite cheaply and also fabulously.[133]

Once again, the sense of artistic camaraderie between the two men is illuminated by Bacon's letters. Sutherland's struggles with his Crucifixion project must, understandably, have been a constant theme in his communications from England. Bacon's responses are suitably enthusiastic and supportive. The first letter records his reaction to news of progress: 'I am so glad to hear about your work. I feel from the way you write you are not too dissatisfied with it . . . The strung man sounds very exciting. I feel it is very much your subject'.[134] Subsequently, Bacon shared in Sutherland's satisfaction that the project had finally been brought to completion: 'You must have been working very hard on the Crucifixion. I am so glad it has been a success and well received it is good from the financial point of view. I know you feel as I do about the other part of it and the boredom of being liked by well-meaning fools'.[135] To Kathy, Bacon reported that he had at last managed to see photographs of the picture: 'I got a picture post and thought it looked most awfully good and the colour sounded very exciting.'[136] Another theme of Sutherland's communications, it may be inferred, was his qualms about showing in the big survey exhibition on contemporary art that was being organised in Paris, under the aegis of UNESCO. Bacon took a less fastidious line in his reply:

> About what you say of the show in Paris as I have sold the picture to the Redfern they can do what they like with it and I do not really mind. I do hope you will decide to show. I know exactly what you say about these sort of exhibitions but what happens apart from trying to paint somewhere near to what one wants seems to matter less and less. I am sure Douglas [Cooper] will make an attack on you if he can but really as a champion of decorators as he is rapidly becoming I think from the point of view of sorting things out it is all to the good to be attacked by that prissy old voluptuary. His phobias are rapidly getting the better of his judgements.[137]

Bacon continued to rely somewhat on Sutherland's help when it came to obtaining materials. Anticipating the Sutherlands' visit to France, he put in a request for paint: 'If you could get it could you possibly bring me some white paint, zinc white and 3 tubes of marble medium, Holland nearly always has it, and some *lamp* black if it is not too much of a bother'.[138] Bacon also shared his artistic enthusiasms: a mutual friend had given him 'a lovely book on Rembrandt with some superb drawings especially one of a crying man. I expect you know it. I didn't and it was a wonderful shock to come across it for the first time'.[139] By way of studio talk, Bacon mentions having to improvise when the local stretcher shop was closed: 'I am just hanging the piece of canvas on the wall and it seems quite pleasant to not to have the tyranny of the stretcher and be able to alter the dimensions as one wants.'[140] It sounds as though this picture was to be the centrepiece of another triptych. The letters also indicate the imagery of his current work. In one, he remarked: 'I am working on 3 sketches of the Velásquez portrait of Pope Innocent II [sic]. I have practically finished one. I find them very exciting to do but don't know yet if they are going to come off or not.'[141] The theme had clearly come to preoccupy Bacon, who remarked subsequently:

> I don't know how the copy of the Velasquez will turn out. I have practically finished one I think and am going to start on a portrait I want to do, but it is thrilling to paint from a picture which really excites you. I am sick to death of everything I've ever done in the past but continue to think like a child or a fool that I'm on the edge of doing a good painting.[142]

Bacon's thinking would have struck some sort of chord with Sutherland, who in 1939 had contributed a variant on a detail of El Greco's *Agony in the Garden* to 'An Exhibition of Paraphrases (Free Copies)' at the Storran Gallery in London.[143] The degree to which the two painters confided in one another about art is further evident in Bacon's reflections on contemporary art. It is enough to note here Bacon's remarks, after visiting the UNESCO exhibition, concerning 'the terrible decoration we are all contaminated by', and the boring lack of reality and immediacy in current art that they had 'often talked about'. After expatiating in this vein, he finally expressed embarrassment at such an earnest exposition of his views, in the manner of pontificators such as Douglas Cooper. Bacon's aside in self-justification, more perhaps than any other comment in the correspondence, evokes the powerful sense of affinity that he had come to feel towards Sutherland: 'you and Eric [Hall] are the only two people I have had the luck to know who feel these things'.[144]

We know that Bacon was back in London by February 1947, and back in close communion with Sutherland, from a diary entry by the art historian Benedict Nicolson, recording a meeting with the two men. The account also provides a rather vivid account of the contrasting impressions that they could make upon a disinterested observer, when encountered in tandem: '[Bacon] talk[s] a lot, condemns everything with sweeping gestures – but I think there is something burning and alive there . . . [He is] hopelessly young and dogmatic – in contrast to Sutherland, who has reached the boring profundity of middle-age – and how moving a spectacle to see them together'.[145] The last remark presumably testifies to the close personal rapport that the two artists conveyed when they were together. Sutherland's biographer records that Bacon was in London for ten days, and that on the same day that Benedict Nicolson encountered them, the two artists had lunch at the White Tower restaurant, went to the National Gallery exhibition of Spanish painting, and ended up having tea and drinks at Bacon's Cromwell Place studio.[146]

Beyond the regular communications during this initial period of six months or so that Bacon spent in France, no further correspondence survives except a friendly postcard that Bacon sent to Sutherland from Rome in 1954.[147] As a result, it becomes more difficult to establish the exact pattern of contacts. It is generally assumed that between 1947 and 1949 Bacon continued to spend much of his time in the south of France, financed no doubt by Eric Hall. He can be presumed to have made visits to both Paris and London, but any such travels are not documented. Sutherland's movements, on the other hand, may be more readily established. He too paid a number of protracted trips to the south of France, inspired and encouraged not only by Bacon but also by his friend, the writer Roderick Cameron, whose mother owned a villa near Cap Ferrat.[148] Sutherland first visited the region in April 1947, accompanied again by Eardley Knollys, and stayed for five weeks, a period during which he and Kathleen would regularly dine and gamble with Bacon and Hall.[149] Sutherland was again in the Riviera between October and December, and returned for several extended stays in 1948 and 1949.[150] His biographer records, for example, that he left England for France on 3 November 1949, and dined with Bacon there on Christmas Eve.[151] It was not just an enjoyment of the physical environment that the two artists had in common – evidently gambling in the casinos became as much of an obsession for Sutherland as it was for Bacon.[152] One can only assume, then, that the two men were seeing a good deal of one another, probably both in France and in London, and that the close relationship apparent from Bacon's correspondence was sustained through to the end of the decade and beyond.

Sutherland's trips were made possible by his continuing commercial success. He was paid £350 for the Northampton altarpiece.[153] Sutherland may have expressed doubts to Bacon about the UNESCO show, but both of his pictures found buyers; *Chimère I* was acquired by Lilian Somerville, exhibitions officer of the British Council, while *Thorn Tree* became the largest and most important picture amongst the fifteen or more works that the British Council itself owned by the end of 1950.[154] In July 1947 an exhibition of pictures relating to the Northampton commission was mounted at the Lefevre Gallery in London.[155] Then in 1948 Sutherland was able to show his most recent work both in London, where he was given the opening show that summer at the new Hanover Gallery, and once again, towards the end of the year, at the Buchholz Gallery in New York.[156] The Hanover Gallery had been launched, in the premises of the old St. George's Gallery, by Sutherland's old friend and supporter Erica Brausen, who was now able to strike out on her own, with financial backing from Arthur Jeffress. She succeeded over the next few years in establishing the Hanover Gallery as the most lively and progressive space in London for shows of contemporary art. Choosing Sutherland for her first exhibition was certainly a shrewd move. In his review of the show, Bernard Denvir voiced an increasingly commonplace opinion when he noted that it 'may well be that Graham Sutherland is the most important painter working in England today . . . whatever he paints Sutherland endows with a strange flickering vitality which exposes the ends of the spectator's nerves'.[157] Others spoke of 'brisk business' at the opening, and 'one of the most brilliantly crowded first views London has seen for many a day'.[158] During that same year, a Bill Brandt portrait appeared in *Lilliput* magazine, describing Sutherland as 'the most inventive, influential painter alive in England today'; he was invited to become a trustee of the Tate Gallery; and his international reputation was reflected in an admiring passage in the book *Contemporary Painters* by the prominent American critic James Thrall Soby.[159]

THE FIGURE QUESTION

What of any creative interplay between the two artists in the late 1940s? It is necessary, first of all, to acknowledge that there is an even greater imbalance during this period in terms of our grasp of their respective outputs. Between the exhibition of *Man with Microphones* and *Painting* in the summer of 1946, and the production of a new body of work for his show at the Hanover Gallery in late 1949, virtually nothing by Bacon survives. The letters to Sutherland suggest that, at certain times at any rate, he worked prolifically during stays in the South of France, and perhaps also in London. It can only be assumed that pictures were no sooner created than destroyed, and that only close friends like Sutherland would have had any opportunity to witness Bacon's activities in the studio. Bacon's new friend Isabel Rawsthorne, who also showed early on at the Hanover Gallery, reported that during a visit to Bacon, in December 1948, she had run into the Sutherlands, along with Douglas Cooper and an aristocratic 'patron.' She had 'argued violently with Graham S', but began to establish a friendship with Bacon, who 'tells me he has destroyed all his last pictures'.[160]

Sutherland, by contrast, maintained a steady output, informed in very obvious ways by the new visual environment to which he was exposed in the Midi. The most obvious repercussion of his travels was an 'adoption of Mediterranean subjects such as vine pergolas, palm palisades, banana leaves, cacti and cicadas, accompanied by a heightening and lightening of his colour'.[161] Aside from their subject-matter, Sutherland's new pictures also displayed a more linear definition of form, and a flatter application of high-key colour, as apparent from his Hanover Gallery exhibition in 1948. Reviewers tended to comment on the influences that he had seemingly absorbed from the locally based artists whose work he had also encountered in the South of France, notably Matisse and Picasso. However, the extent to which Sutherland changed direction can easily be exaggerated. Alongside the superficial departures, there are continuities within his work, which had derived in the main from the equally remote and rural, but in other ways very different, environment of western Pembrokeshire. For example, the 1947 paintings of palm palisades may be seen to extend the heightened palette, spiky forms and anthropomorphic treatment of natural forms that had characterised the *Thorn Tree* and *Thorn Head* paintings of 1945–46. Sutherland himself commented that by 1944 he was already painting pictures that were 'very bright and light in colour': 'When I did start working in France, in 1947, I must confess that I did wonder how I had come to anticipate, by this lightening of key, the clarity of the steady southern light.'[162] In a picture such as *Palm and House* (1947; pl. 13), not only the vivid magenta backdrop but also the arrangement of the spiked palm forms around a rectilinear framing structure suggest an assimilation of the lower sections of Bacon's *Painting* (1946). The vine pergola pictures from 1947 and 1948 suggest that he had discovered in Provence a variant on the primitive, pre-industrial landscape, with man living in harmony with the cycles and forces of the natural world, that he had projected a decade earlier onto Pembrokeshire. Soon after his arrival, he informed Kenneth Clark that he was gathering much material for his work: 'The magic of the country is really beginning to get under my skin. The mile wild slab of smooth rock by Tourettes which flows down to one of the oldest olive groves in France is peopled by timeless peasants & Arcadian shepherds. Tremendously wonderful light as the figures climb back to their homes at night. The figures look classical and immense.'[163] The monstrous root forms on which he based many pictures in 1948–49, such as the *Articulated Forms* series, recall the looming tree root pictures from ten years earlier, and they doubtless relied on a comparable procedure of evolving compositions in the studio with reference to 'found' natural objects.

In the absence of any current work by Bacon, it is of course impossible to judge whether he and Sutherland were continuing to feed off one another's work. Interestingly, however, one observer noted that the Hanover Gallery exhibition revealed Sutherland to be 'working his way through and perhaps out of the influence of Francis Bacon, who has been for him something of an *eminence grise*'.[164] This judgement that the work of Sutherland and Bacon was now starting to diverge turned out to be premature. For all his critical and commercial success, Sutherland seems increasingly to have felt at this time that his work was tending towards a certain slickness of style and slightness of content. A revealing document indicates his awareness of the example of Bacon's work, at a time when his confidence was very low, suggesting that a highly developed capacity for self-criticism was another aptitude that he and Bacon shared. In late 1948, Sutherland was in correspondence with Robert Melville

13 Graham Sutherland, *Palm and House*, 1947, oil on canvas, 110.5 × 90.2 cm, Private Collection.

regarding the monograph on his art that the critic was producing. In a letter from Villefranche he also talks about an exhibition he had seen in Brussels, presumably the survey of *La Jeune Peinture en Grande-Bretagne* that had travelled from Paris, which included several of his pictures.[165] He also indicates that he would be spending a few days in Paris in early December on his way back to England, where he expected to meet Melville. Amidst such nuggets of information, Sutherland launched into a fierce denunciation of the shortcomings of his own art, and implied that the future of art lay in the hands of figures like Bacon and Lucian Freud. In addition, he expressed his sensitivity to negative judgements on his work articulated by others. As an indication of Sutherland's private attitudes towards his art, the letter merits quotation at length:

> It has been very lovely down here . . . In spite of this, I do not seem to have produced much work, although I have been working regularly every day. To start with I think I have been experiencing a wave of really horrifying disgust and dissatisfaction with nearly all my work, and I'm afraid with some of recent date: it all seems too easy and superficial. Perhaps it is good that I should feel like this for such a thing usually precedes a period of getting closer to what I think I can and should do and therefore, also, a consistent seam of work. I can only hope so. Several ideas are simmering in the back of my mind: but they are not clear enough yet & I must solve this figure question: I've got quite a number of ideas in note-book form and have done half a dozen small gouaches – some of which may be alright.
>
> The New York show opened on the 16th. I've had one advance notice – a real 'stinker' – suggesting that since my last show I'm somewhat lost between emotion and intellect' (!!) and that my Parisian style is half way between Lam and Picasso!!
>
> . . . I'm afraid I'm now convinced that English painting . . . is entirely off the rails. The show in Brussels convinced me – oddly enough Ben Nicholson looked better than most, partly because he commits himself so little.
>
> . . . I think Lucian F. miles ahead of the rest although he's horribly restricted in ideas. Francis B. has done two remarkable canvases – depressing & attenuated, – but his painting I think *real* & containing the germ of recovery & the possibility of a post-Picasso development – at all events, to me, he makes nearly all the others look whimsy or folksy or schematic or just simply dead.[166]

Before considering the bearing these comments might have on an understanding of Sutherland's own development, it should be noted that his assessment of Bacon's importance became commonplace around a year later. The few paintings that Bacon had showed at the Lefevre and Redfern galleries in 1945–46 may have inspired a minor cult following, but nothing further was seen for two years, except by those such as Sutherland who had access to Bacon's studio. The next new picture he exhibited was *Head I* (1948; pl. 14), in a Summer Exhibition at the Redfern Gallery.[167] The following spring Wyndham Lewis reported that a show was forthcoming at the Hanover Gallery, and that one new work, presumably *Head I*, was already on view: 'Bacon's picture, as usual, is in lamp-black monochrome, the zinc white of the monster's eyes glistening in the cold crumbling grey of the face. Bacon is a Grand

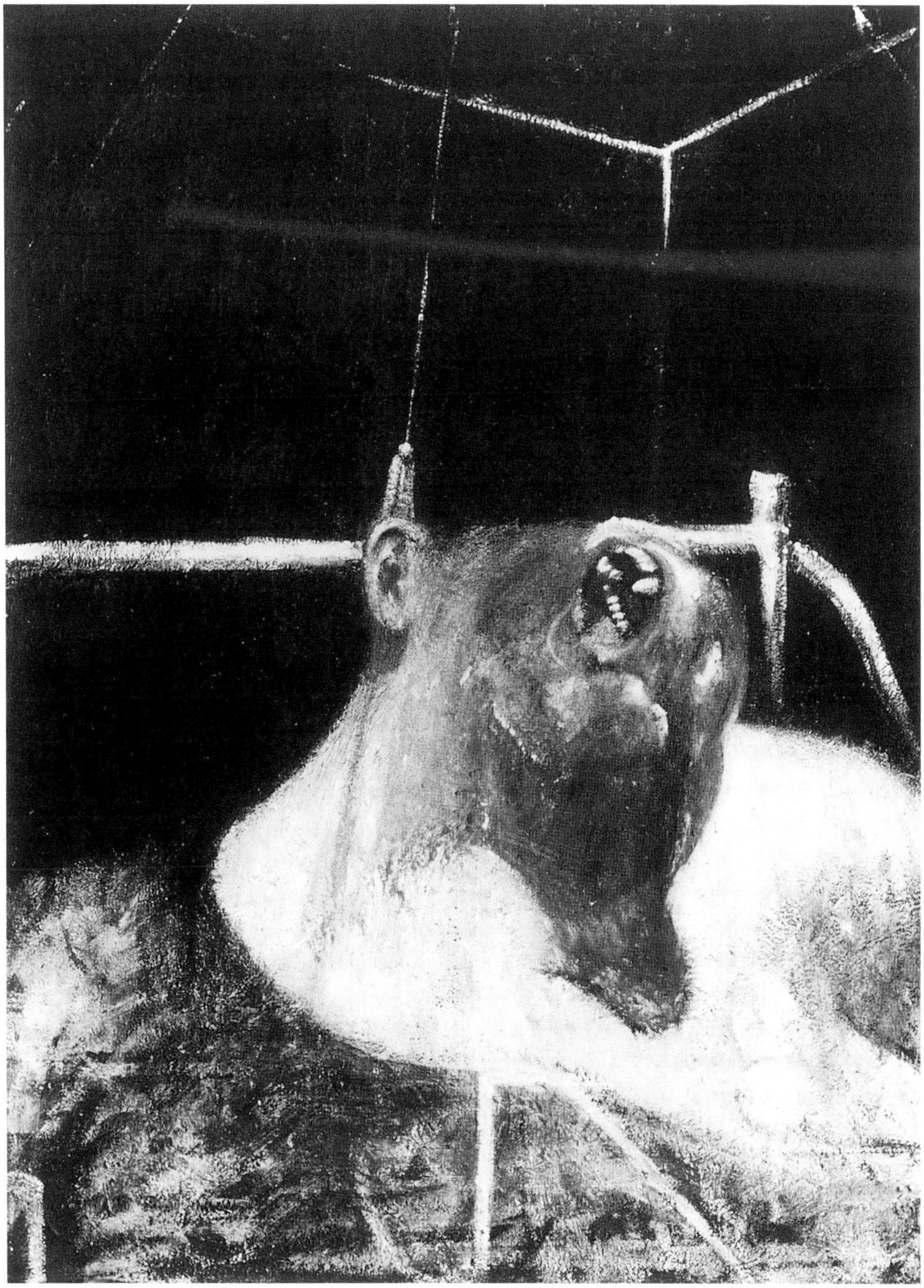

14 Francis Bacon, *Head I*, 1948, oil and tempera on board, 100.3 × 74.9 cm, Richard Zeisler Collection, New York.

Guignol artist: the mouths in is heads are unpleasant places, evil passions make a glittering white mess of the lips'.[168] Presumably Erica Brausen had negotiated to take the picture with her when she left the Redfern to set up her own gallery. It was Bacons' first one-man exhibition, held at the Hanover Gallery in London in late 1949, which served to cement his reputation amongst artists and critics.[169] The sequence of six *Head* paintings that dominated the exhibition announced a new phase in Bacon's development. They revealed that he was now working with a more sombre and tonal palette, in comparison with the pictures of a couple of years earlier, and also that he was experimenting with a far more textural and tactile method of handling the medium, which enabled him to suggest forms in the process of dissolution and of merging into their settings and space. In the earliest versions of the head theme, the apparent fusion of a human head and shoulders with the features of a screaming monkey marked a further extension of the metamorphic concerns of the work from 1944–46. At some level, these paintings might even be seen as Bacon's riposte to Sutherland's highly charged *Thorn Head* paintings, on which Sutherland was continuing to work towards the end of the decade (pl. 15). However, *Head III* to *Head VI* indicated a far more descriptive, even naturalistic, treatment of imagery of the human figure, a development equally apparent in the other two new paintings that Bacon included in the Hanover Gallery show, *Study for Portrait* (1949; pl. 20) and the *Study from the Human Body* (1949; pl. XIX). A further developing tendency was Bacon's increasingly economical application of paint, which left extensive areas of rough, bare canvas evident in the final picture. The assurance and economy of touch is quite different from the heavily worked surfaces of his surviving work since the mid-1940s.

Bacon's exhibition was a great success. One review commented that only three of the twelve pictures on show remained unsold on the opening day, and by the end, the show was virtually sold out.[170] There were many responses of admiration; but once again the most eloquent and perceptive commentary came from Wyndham Lewis:

> Of the younger painters none actually paints so beautifully as Francis Bacon. I have seen painting of his that reminded me of Velasquez and like that master he is fond of blacks. Liquid whitish accents are delicately dropped upon the sable ground, like blobs of mucus – or else there is the cold white glitter of an eyeball, or of an eye distended with despairing insult behind a shouting mouth, distended also to hurl insults. Otherwise it is a baleful regard from the mask of a decayed clubman or business executive – so decayed that usually part of the head is rotting away into space. But black is his pictorial element. These faces come out of the darkness to glare and shout. I must not attempt to describe these amazing pictures – the shouting creatures in glass cases, these dissolving ganglia the size of a small fist in which one can always discern the shouting mouth, the wild distended eye. In the *Nude* [*Study from the Human Body*], in front of not the least ominous of curtains, about to enter, the artist is seen at his best. Bacon is one of the most powerful artists in Europe today and he is perfectly in tune with his time. Not like his namesake 'the brightest, wisest of mankind', he is, on the other hand, one of the darkest and most possessed.[171]

Sutherland was clearly on hand for the opening of Bacon's exhibition. Clearly the older artist's undemonstrative manner did not always endear him to Bacon's other friends, as is apparent from Rawsthorne's first-hand account of the proceedings:

> Spent evening with F – oysters, champagne, brandy, negro night club. F *refusing* money. Show is most impressive really. Especially large male nude walking through curtain. Quite

15 Graham Sutherland, *Thorn Head*, 1949, oil on canvas, 60.7 × 46 cm, Scottish National Gallery of Modern Art, Edinburgh.

> unlike anything else. They gain from being seen together. Appear highly coloured. Gallery full from morning till night. Erica happy. He's off to Monte Carlo Sunday.
>
> I asked Erica what Graham S. said. 'Nothing'. Later he and Francis dined together. Right at end of evening Graham Said 'I think that the dimensions are interesting'. His wife then said to Francis 'I hear you are going to marry Isabel'![172]

Yet other sources indicate that Sutherland was more than willing to give Bacon his imprimatur. One review of the show noted: 'Few people in England know much about him

[Bacon]. Yet an artist of the eminence of Graham Sutherland has said that he considers Bacon perhaps the finest English artist painting today'.[173] Moreover, the two men presumably saw a fair amount of one another during the next few weeks, when both were again in the South of France.

It seems appropriate to view Sutherland's admiration for Bacon in the context of the concerns he articulated in late 1948 with the 'figure question' that he needed to solve, and with 'the possibility of a post-Picasso development' in contemporary art. For visual evidence suggests that looking hard at Bacon's work informed Sutherland's pursuit of a new direction in his own work, in the wake of his crisis regarding the illustrative and decorative qualities that had come to the fore in his art. In particular, the upright presences in the *Standing Form* series, begun in 1949, reflect Sutherland's shifting ambitions. The projection of figurative and animal overtones onto found natural objects into surrogate figures was, of course, rooted in his previous work. To a degree, the *Standing Forms* can be seen as picking up from where he had left off two or three years earlier with the *Chimère* composition, as well as the *Thorn Head* and *Palm Palisade* series. But the new paintings were more consistently imposing and monumental in scale, and in their deployment of vertical elements they evoked imagery of the human form more explicitly, presumably the ambition underlying his talk of solving the figure question. Sutherland remarked of the new pictures in 1951:

> The forms are based on the principles of organic growth, with which I have always been preoccupied. To me they are monuments and presences. But why use these forms instead of human figures? Because, at the moment, I find it necessary to catch the taste – the quality – the essence of the human figure: the mysterious immediacy of a figure standing in a room or against a hedge in its shadow, its awareness, its regard, as if one had never seen it before – by a substitution . . . They give me a sense of the shock of surprise which direct evocation could not possibly do.[174]

Further affinities with Bacon emerge from the juxtaposition of Sutherland's *Standing form against a Curtain*, an early exploration of this new vein of imagery, and Bacon's *Study from the Human Body* (pl. 16 and pl. XIX).[175] Aside from scale, one might note that both pictures are simple and symmetrical in compositional terms. In each case the relatively sculptural modelling of the principal form is set off by the shallow, frontal spaces that they are made to inhabit, demarcated by the folds of a curtain. The same backdrop had featured in several recent works by Bacon and in Sutherland's *Articulated Form* from 1949. It is also revealing to compare a picture like *Study from the Human Body* with what appears to be a variant by Sutherland on *Standing Form against a Curtain*, namely the well-known *Standing Form against a Hedge* (1950; pl. XX) in the Arts Council Collection. Both of these pictures make extensive use of white, black and intervening shades of grey, exclusively so in the Bacon, and combined with subdued areas of green, blue and purple in the Sutherland, a very different palette from the almost Fauve tonality of his south of France pictures to date.[176] In consequence, the quality of the light in the two works is sombre and possibly nocturnal. Their sur-

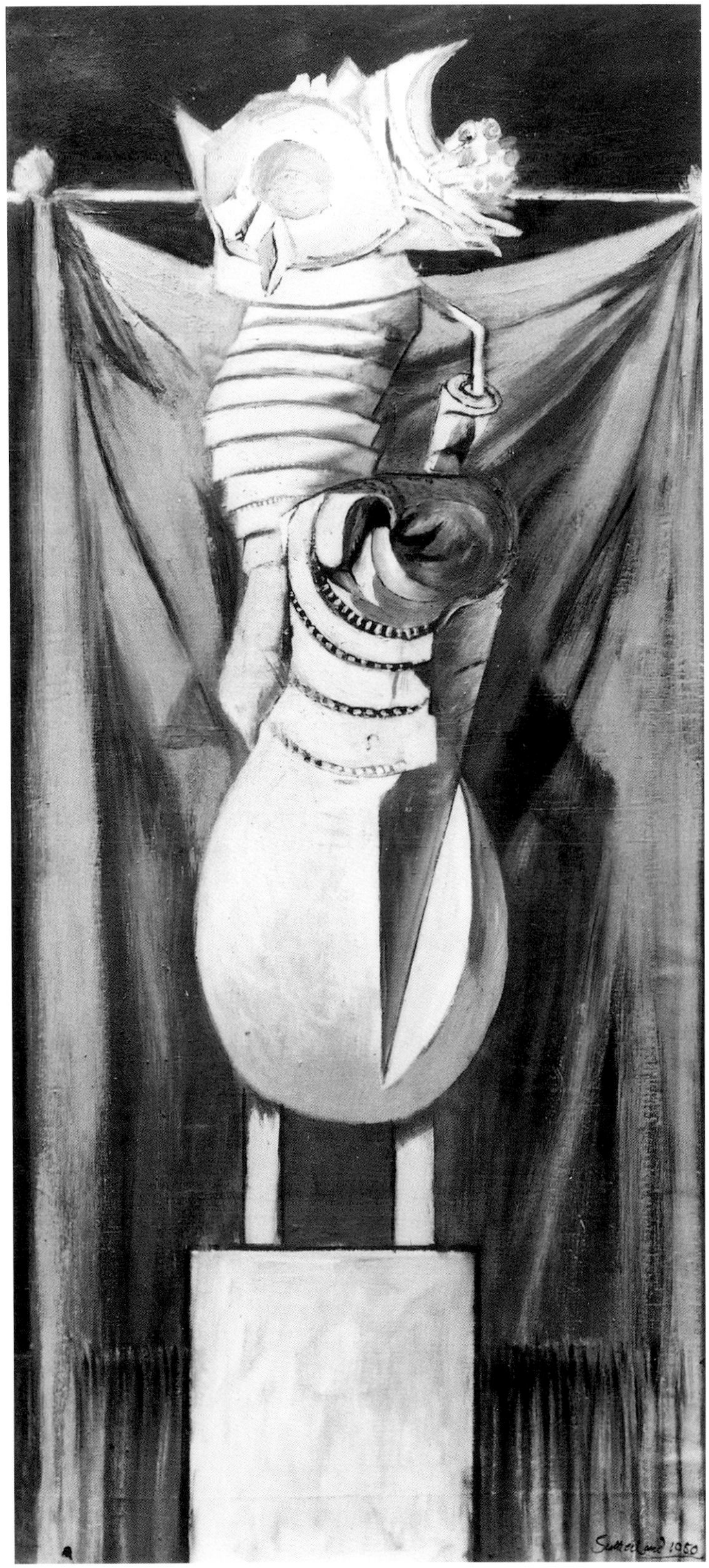

16 Graham Sutherland, *Standing Form against a Curtain*, 1950, oil on canvas, present whereabouts unknown.

faces are built up in each case by means of loose painterly touches, reinforcing the sense of ambiguity and mystery with which the images are invested. Once again, this marks a clear departure from the more linear emphasis of Sutherland's work in the previous couple of years. Such affinities of iconography and style cumulatively suggest that, in opening up a new direction in his work around 1950, Sutherland was again, to a significant degree, taking his cues from recent work by Bacon. Nevertheless, the differences between the two artists' pictures are, ultimately, more telling. The figure in the Bacon turns away from us, and there is an implied process of movement, while the surrogate figure in the Sutherland is positioned frontally and hieratically, confronting the spectator. *Study from the Human Body* typifies Bacon's turn towards a more descriptive idiom, whereas the Sutherland is perhaps further removed from legible imagery than anything we have seen so far, with the exception of *Chimère 1*. The standing form simultaneously seems to evoke the banded, swelling trunk of a palm tree, such a characteristic feature of the Midi; a piece of fruit, perhaps a fig that has been sliced open; some obscure mechanical contraption; stone garden statuary in *Standing Form against a Hedge*; a kind of primitive fetish or totem, set on a mount; and a simplified rendition of the human figure itself. No one reading dominates, in contrast to Sutherland's previous pictures in which there tended to be a single, primary point of reference, to which further layers of allusion were secondary.

In contrast, the relative naturalism of *Study from the Human Body* reflects Bacon's distinctive and increasingly direct exploitation of photographic imagery. The artist's assimilation of photography is a crucial theme, meriting focused investigation in its own right.[177] It is broached from different perspectives in each chapter of this book. From early on, it appears, Bacon used photographic sources, such as X-rays and illustrations to medical textbooks, as points of departure for pockets of detail in his paintings. We have already encountered the fruits of his dissection of photographic imagery of wild animals, probably matched by Sutherland, which was especially unmodified in the case of his use of the photography of Marius Maxwell as the starting point for *Figure in a Landscape* (1945). Bacon's derivations from press imagery of fascist dictators, also relevant for the *Three Studies,* stemmed from a wider fascination with grainy newspaper photographs that evidently went back to the time of his friendship with Roy de Maistre.[178] Bacon may have also have been prompted by the precedent of large tracts of Sickert's work from the late 1920s and 1930s, which he doubtless knew from exhibitions.[179] Here, the images are patently adapted from press or personal photographs, but translated, as in Bacon's own work, into a highly painterly, textural idiom. In contrast, such concerns seem remote from Sutherland, although his friendship with Bacon may have stimulated his occasional borrowings from newspaper imagery, as in the idiosyncratic *Laughing Woman* (1946).[180] At any rate, by 1950, when it was viewed by Sam Hunter, Bacon's studio presented the remarkable spectacle of paintings at one end and, at the other, 'tables littered with newspaper photographs and clippings, crime sheets like *Crapouillot* and photographs or reproductions of personalities who have passed across the public stage in recent years'. A very singular sensibility was apparent beneath the diverse types of images he described and photographed:

> The only law governing Bacon's selection of this visual literature is some kind of mysterious topical and psychological pertinence. . . . Somewhere between the simple cold mechanics of the camera, and the most charged moments of recent history, Bacon has set up a shadowy and crepuscular world of imagination, playing on associations of violence and terror.[181]

The artist himself told David Sylvester that he found photographs much more interesting than paintings, and that he had 'always been haunted' by them. He was pressed to explain what it was that haunted him about photographs: 'I think it's the slight remove from fact, which returns me onto the fact more violently. Through the photographic image I find myself beginning to wander into the image and unlock what I think of as its reality more than I can by looking at it. And photographs are not only points of reference; they're often triggers of ideas.'[182] In a late interview, published posthumously, he elaborated on the 'incredibly useful source of inspiration' that photographs provided: 'Images also help me find and realise ideas. I look at hundreds of very different, contrasting images and I pinch details from them, rather like people who eat from other people's plates. When I paint, I want to paint an image from my imagination, and this image is subsequently transformed.'[183]

Within the larger framework of Bacon's development, with its emphatic continuities, it should be emphasised that the paintings from 1949/50 register not merely a stylistic departure, but also a new kind and degree of engagement with the photographic, its specific visual effects as well as imagery that he could 'pinch'. The pictures resulted from a distinctive creative process in which a ready-made image is explicitly appropriated, and its meanings, associations and visual qualities utterly transformed by means of editing, superimposing additional imagery and by a method of paint application that could hardly be further removed from the mechanical or impersonal effect of photography. Such a procedure is implicit in the less abstracted, more literal images included in the Hanover Gallery show, such as the later *Heads* and *Study from the Human Body*. The latter was Bacon's first known adaptation from the serial photography of Edweard Muybridge (pl. 17).[184] Interestingly, this reference too was foreshadowed in the work of Sutherland, who had used images of wrestlers by Muybridge as the starting points for the illustrations of fighting soldiers in an edition of Shakespeare's *Henry IV* (1940).[185] Such an appropriation exemplifies a doubtless widespread tendency amongst artists to employ photographs as veiled source material, an easy alternative to posing and drawing models. Bacon's photographic points of departure are more diverse and overt. When he reworked *Man with Microphones* (pl. 18), he devised a figure seen from behind which echoes imagery from another favourite illustrated book, K. C. Clark's *Positioning in Radiography*.[186] Recently, it has been suggested that Bacon was adapting his imagery of curtained spaces and spectral emanations from the illustrations in *Phenomena of Materialisation*, a somewhat esoteric volume first published in 1920, a copy of which turned up in Bacon's studio.[187] Most obviously, *Head VI* and its successors in the Pope series proclaim their origins in reproductions from art books of Velazquez's *Innocent X*, combined to such shocking and subversive effect with stills of the nanny's screaming features from the

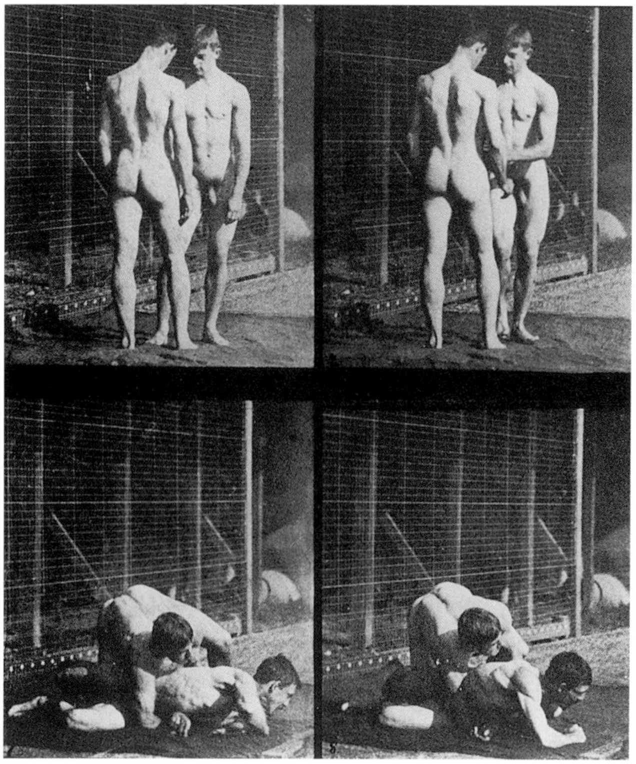

17 Eadweard Muybridge, detail of *Wrestling* page, from the *Complete Human and Animal Locomotion* (1887).

Odessa steps sequence in *Battleship Potemkin*. As we have seen, he had been experimenting with the idea of a variation on the Velazquez for at least three years, but it was only now that he was able to pull it off. Eisenstein's film had a cult status, both in Britain and elsewhere, and the sequence cannibalised by Bacon was widely regarded as the supreme manifestation of montage as a cinematic technique.[188] He may already have known the film for several years. Nevertheless, it seems once again to have been at this particular point in his artistic development that Bacon decided to graft the highly recognisable imagery from *Battleship Potemkin* stills onto his existing preoccupation with the image of the shrieking head. Looking ahead to 1950, the homages to Velazquez begin to multiply, while the starting point for the Leeds *Painting* is likely to have been another Muybridge photograph, and in the Eindhoven *Crucifixion* the cross form seems to be adapted with little modification from an architectural image of a contemporary interior, including window views onto a schematic background of people walking, cars and a distant sea.[189] Overall, such pictures distil a precocious willingness on Bacon's part to take advantage of the modern image world made possible by recording and publishing technology. Illustrated magazines of all sorts and books about art, cinema, science and so forth cumulatively comprised an 'imaginary museum' upon which the artist might draw, a massive, ever-expanding visual resource that could be regarded as a continuum rather than an embodiment of received hierarchies of medium or imagery.

Although the specific sources were not necessarily apparent to viewers, the photographic derivation of such works by Bacon is strongly implied visually, by means of the artist's mono-

18 Francis Bacon, *Man with Microphones (revised version)*, *c.* 1949, oil on canvas, 145 × 127.8 cm, Hugh Lane Gallery, Dublin (subsequently mutilated by artist).

chromatic, grisaille palette and his exploitation of the shared graininess of low-grade photographs and the texture of canvas. It was clearly important to Bacon that the paintings should actually look like paintings based on photographs, while their photographic dimension is counterpointed by an extreme, old-masterly painterliness. At the time, this interest was observed by Isabel Rawsthorne, who wrote about Bacon in a letter of summer 1949 to their mutual friend, the photographer Peter Rose Pulham: 'You are quite right to say that he is most exercised by this question of surface – ONLY – he has such a particular view . . . He is obsessed with the *photographic* delineation of form – wishes, as far as I can see, to seize such a quality in painting.'[190] One might argue that it was Bacon's strategic use of photographic source material that permitted his radical departure from existing formal conventions, that enabled him, therefore, to generate a more authentic 'post-Picasso development' than had proved accessible to Sutherland himself. More relevant perhaps for Bacon's frank appropriations from photography were his friendships, beginning in the late 1940s, with younger artists such as Edoardo Paolozzi and Nigel Henderson, who were equally preoccupied by the medium and its artistic possibilities.[191]

*

I want to explore one last point of contact between Sutherland and Bacon, an offshoot in some ways of their shared engagement with imagery of the solitary human figure, namely the explicit turn in the work of both artists to the venerable genre of portraiture. It is well-known that Sutherland's first portrait was his rendition in 1949 of the seventy-five year old writer Somerset Maugham, presented as a human equivalent to the arid and prickly forms that had littered his recent Provençal landscapes (pl. XVII). Sutherland and Maugham met socially, probably through a mutual friendship with Kenneth Clark, in spring 1947, when the Sutherlands were staying near Maugham's villa on the Riviera.[192] It is not clear whether the idea of a portrait came from the artist or the sitter, or indeed when precisely it was first broached. However, the final picture was executed, on the basis of numerous drawings from life, during the spring of 1949. It was first exhibited in Sutherland's 1951 retrospective at the ICA, and in the same year Maugham's daughter gave the portrait to the Tate Gallery. Notwithstanding the loose affinities with his current standing form pictures, the sharply focussed realism of *Somerset Maugham* strikes an incongruous note in the wider context of Sutherland's work. The artist remarked in 1951: 'Perhaps one of the reasons why I have recently tried to do portraits is that it is possible that I feel the need to narrow the gap between my 'stand-in' monuments and the real human animal.'[193] But in considering why Sutherland embarked upon this new direction, we might also take account of his awareness of contemporary art. In a British context, the obvious precedent for a descriptive, but also highly penetrating, form of portraiture was the work of Lucian Freud. The two men were of course friends at this time, and we should recall Sutherland's comment to Robert Melville, in December 1948, that Freud was 'miles ahead of the rest'. Sutherland would probably have encountered Freud's remarkable *Girl with Rose*, which had been painted the previous winter (pl. 19). The close-up format certainly provide parallels to *Somerset Maugham*, while a Freud work such as the 1948 *Girl with Leaves* foreshadows Sutherland's insertion of foliage entering from the top of the pictorial space.[194]

At the same time, portraiture is likely to have been a subject of conversation between Sutherland and Bacon. For *Study for a Portrait* (1949; pl. 20) is the first surviving work by Bacon to allude to portraiture in its title, although the image itself is hardly, like Sutherland's *Somerset Maugham*, a conventional manifestation of the genre. As noted, *Study for Portrait* was exhibited at the Hanover Gallery alongside the series of generic *Heads*. *Head III* (1949) looks as though it may have been conceived as a portrait of a specific individual, although

19 Lucian Freud, *Girl with Rose*, 1947–8, oil on canvas, 105.5 × 74.5 cm, British Council Collection.

this is not indicated in the title. But the painting that most closely resembled *Study for a Portrait* was *Head VI* (pl. XVIII). Over and above the open-mouthed heads, one might note the inclusion around both figures of a coherently described space frame, and the interplay between the coarse-grained brown canvas, which is extensively visible in both pictures, and the equally manifest brushmarks that are scumbled and dragged across this underlying texture. Such affinities suggest that the two paintings may well have been executed in close proximity to one another, and not long perhaps before the opening of the exhibition. *Head VI* is of course Bacon's earliest surviving known variant on *Innocent X*. Indeed the several years spent creating portraits and mining the great Velásquez, as a measure of what he wanted both to accomplish and to subvert in portraiture, seemed to have been intimately associated for Bacon with artistic impulses. In one of his letters to Sutherland from late 1946, he was already talking about embarking on a Velásquez variation, almost as a rehearsal for doing a portrait of his own, presumably destroyed. Later, a picture of 1953 started life as a portrait of David Sylvester and turned into a Pope picture.[195]

Moreover, a fascination with portrait imagery, not necessarily of such an elevated kind as the Velazquez, inflected other paintings by Bacon dating from the period before 1949. For example, *Figure in a Landscape* from 1945 was always said by Bacon to have its starting point in a 'snapshot of Eric Hall dozing in a chair in Hyde Park'. This may have been so, but the final configuration of the figure directly echoes the well-worn convention in studio photography where the sitter sits the wrong way round on an openwork chair, with legs akimbo and arms folded across the top. The impact of Bacon's *Painting* (1946) relies upon an extraordinary interweaving of references, but the format of the picture as a whole most closely recalls so-called swagger portraits, a tradition of grand, highly theatrical portraiture extending back to Baroque models.[196] The combination of a frontal but off-centre protagonist, albeit fragmented, and the elaborate array of props, seems a knowing extension and, to a degree, a parody of the genre epitomised by, for example, Joshua Reynolds's celebrated *Mrs Siddon as the Tragic Muse*, or by Solomon Joseph Solomon's *Mrs Patrick Campbell as 'Paula Tanqueray'* (1894; pl. 21), a bizarre painting which Bacon could well have encountered on visits to the Arts Club in Chelsea (a likely haunt of Bacon's given that several of his current artist friends were members). One might equally note his apparent references to portrait devices or conventions, such as the curtain backdrop that Bacon employed in several works, which was a recurrent feature in the portraiture of Edwardian artists such as William Orpen (pl. 22). The tassel that we encounter in *Head I* is another cliché of society portraiture, as indeed are props such as flowers and umbrellas. A more literal rehearsal of such devices is encountered in the current portrait work of the society photographer Cecil Beaton.[197] Bacon, then, is dealing at this stage with an extremely personal and indirect concept of portraiture. Without the title, indeed, viewers might be hard pushed to identify *Study for a Portrait* as a portrait. One can only speculate that, for Bacon, the image may have represented or captured a singular albeit unidentified individual, in terms of the artist's sense of their essential identity or aura, rather than their outer aspect. In this sense the painting may anticipate his portrayal of Lucian Freud in 1951 by appropriating a photograph of Franz Kafka from the frontispiece of a book – famously, Freud came to Bacon's studio to be painted, only to find that the picture was already finished.[198] I suspect in fact that *Study for a Portrait* also started off as a transcription of a photograph, perhaps a snapshot of the 'sitter', or a published image from a medical textbook, or a film still, or a news photograph of trial or even an electric chair execution.

Portraiture of the powerful and wealthy became a significant strand in Sutherland's work after 1949, to the detriment, for many observers, of his credibility as a modern artist.[199] Bacon was equally preoccupied with the genre from this point onwards, though generally he did not, like Sutherland, work to commission. Moreover, many of Bacon's favourite artists were primarily engaged with portraiture, Nadar and Julia Margaret Cameron in photography, and Rembrandt, Velásquez and Van Gogh amongst painters. Indeed, the two paintings on which he did variations were portraits, Velásquez's *Pope Innocent X*, and the destroyed Van Gogh self-portrait that Bacon cannibalised in several pictures of 1957. His general outlook on the genre was summarised in a passage from one of the Sylvester interviews, where Bacon explained his lack of interest in landscape imagery:

20 Francis Bacon, *Study for a Portrait*, 1949, oil on canvas, 149.4 × 130.6 cm, Museum of Contemporary Art, Chicago, gift of Joseph and Jory Shapiro.

21 FAR LEFT Solomon Joseph Solomon, *Mrs Patrick Campbell as 'Paula Tanqueray'*, 1894, oil on canvas, 241.3 × 132.3 cm, The Arts Club, London.

22 William Orpen, *Mrs St George*, 1912, oil on canvas, 216 × 119.5, Jefferson Smurfit Group plc.

FB . . . I think art is an obsession with life and after all, as we are human beings, our greatest obsession is with ourselves. Then possibly with animals, and then with landscapes.

DS You're really affirming the traditional hierarchy of subject-matter by which history painting . . . comes top and then portraits and then landscape and then still life.

FB I would alter them round. I would say at the moment, as things are so difficult, that portraits come first.[200]

MILIEUX

In tandem with their various artistic affinities, Sutherland and Bacon were pursuing intertwined careers, and moving in much the same art world circles. As we have seen, their art was promoted and marketed in tandem by the Lefevre, Redfern and Hanover galleries. Before the war, such commercial galleries had virtually monopolised the display of modernist art in London, but after 1945 this role was also assumed by official bodies such as the Arts Council and the British Council, which supported exhibitions at home and abroad respectively. There was, in addition, the Institute of Contemporary Art (ICA), founded by Herbert Read, Roland Penrose and others in order to exhibit more radical, up-to-date work than the Tate Gallery. At the ICA, Sutherland was clearly accorded the status of being a pivotal figure in modern British art. He was invited to sit on the Advisory Council, alongside friends such as Peter Watson and Robert Melville.[201] One of the *Thorn Head* pictures was included in the major show *Forty Years of Modern Art* mounted in late 1948.[202] Melville gave a lecture on Sutherland as part of the programme of talks.[203] Moreover, in 1951 it was the ICA that gave Sutherland his first retrospective exhibition, in the new Dover Street Galleries.[204] Equally, pictures by Bacon were incorporated into the ICA's exhibition programme. *Painting* (1946) was shown in 1948 in *Forty Years of Modern Art*, before it departed for the Museum of Modern Art in New York, and in 1950 Bacon was included in a show that Watson organised in order to juxtapose the work being produced in London and Paris.[205]

Peter Watson provides the most tangible link between the ICA and the magazine *Horizon*, whose visual art coverage provides a further connection between Bacon and Sutherland. We have seen how Sutherland's work was strongly promoted in *Horizon* between 1940 and 1945. Watson continued collecting works by Sutherland after the war.[206] It was conceivably through Sutherland that the work of Bacon came to the attention of Watson and his circle of literary and artistic friends. At any rate, a close friendship between Bacon and Watson seems also to have developed. David Sylvester recalled that 'Bacon and Peter Watson knew each other very well'.[207] Documentary evidence indicates that, during one of his expeditions to the south of France, Watson made a point of visiting Bacon.[208] Whether the friendship extended to financial support is not clear. It is well-known that Watson provided such subsidy to several younger artists who had taken their cue from Sutherland, including Craxton, Freud and the two Roberts, Colquhoun and MacBryde, at the same time at which he was supporting writers such as David Gascoyne and Dylan Thomas.[209] According to one witness, 'he was the most generous of men, perhaps the last true patron of the Arts. He helped young painters in a sensible and poetical way, providing studio rooms to further their work or, in the case of one poet, lodging with meals to ensure his survival.'[210] It is quite possible that Watson also helped Bacon at some point in his early career. He certainly bought a picture, although Bacon later saw fit to destroy it.[211] Bacon was not so taken by Cyril Connolly, but he found another close and long-term friend in Sonia Orwell, who was responsible for much of the day-to-day running of *Horizon* from the point at which she took up a position again at the magazine in 1945.[212] According to her biographer, Orwell, Bacon and Lucian Freud 'often formed a trio . . . on long drunken nights'.[213] Bacon was also befriended and admired as a painter by Stephen Spender, another key figure in this literary world. The fascination that such figures had with Bacon was symptomatic of a growing climate of enthusiasm. The considerable impact of the Hanover Gallery exhibition was not confined to critics and artists: according to one review, 'his immediate success is probably due to the enthusiasm his work has aroused amongst the literary intelligentsia. I have not seen so many writers at an exhibition of painting for a long time'.[214] In his editorial for the valedictory issue of *Horizon*, Cyril Connolly referred to Bacon's show as 'the outstanding exhibition of the month', and he seems to have had Bacon very much in mind when characterising the contemporary condition and role of the artist.[215] The same number included the first major critical assessment of Bacon's work, accompanied by several illustrations. Given the prestige of *Horizon*, this doubtless consolidated his burgeoning critical reputation.

The author of the Bacon essay was Robert Melville, who was also emerging as Sutherland's most eloquent and visible spokesman. Melville was previously known as the precocious author of a 1939 book on Picasso, and as a player in British surrealist circles during the war. He was certainly the liveliest new critic to emerge in Britain during the second half of the 1940s.[216] Melville organised exhibitions such as *The Spirit of Cubism* (1947) for the ICA, and produced a series of well-informed essays on modern art for *Horizon*. He clearly got to know Bacon and Sutherland during this period and launched a critical campaign on their behalf in 1949. In a 'panorama' surveying 'the present position', which appeared that spring, he offered concise characterisations of the artists who were now coming to the fore on the British art scene, including Colquhoun, MacBryde, Vaughan, Craxton, Piper, Ayrton and Victor Pasmore.[217] Yet Melville's enthusiasm for the work of these artists was qualified and, in the end, lukewarm. He noted a pervasive timidity and academicism, which, he conceded, appeared equally to have afflicted much-heralded arrivals on the French artistic scene, such as Edouard Pignon. Melville remarked: 'There have been no revolutionary changes in the last few years, and certain painters have undertaken what is politely called a consolidation of the modern idiom.'[218] All was not lost, however. There remained two compelling and vital artists currently active in Britain, namely Sutherland and Bacon. In their work, Melville declared, 'the creative process works without hindrance'.[219] Such terminology signified their refusal to impose facile and derivative stylistic formulae, and a willingness instead to submit to the dictates of the creative process, and to allow the essential, poignant content of their paintings to find suitably vivid pictorial expression. Melville asserted:

> Sutherland, like all the best painters of our time, feels himself to be breaking faith with the creative principle when he forces his painting to illustrate a given subject; because it does not allow a picture to lead its own life. An artist does not think out a picture; he prepares himself to be the means by which a picture incorporates his predilections in its own substance. Sutherland's vegetable forms move persistently towards a strange and sometimes sinister animality.[220]

Subsequently, in addition to a series of essays in journals, Melville produced a large format, beautifully illustrated book on Sutherland, designed in close consultation with the artist, which appeared in 1950.[221] Although the plates focus on work produced since 1945, Melville's essay reviews Sutherland's evolution since the mid-1930s, and offers an extended, if sometimes over-written, assessment of the artist's place within the unfolding of modernism. Sutherland's art is seen to have fused the seemingly opposed possibilities inherent in cubism and in the psychologically-charged early work of De Chirico. The 'metamorphic' nature of

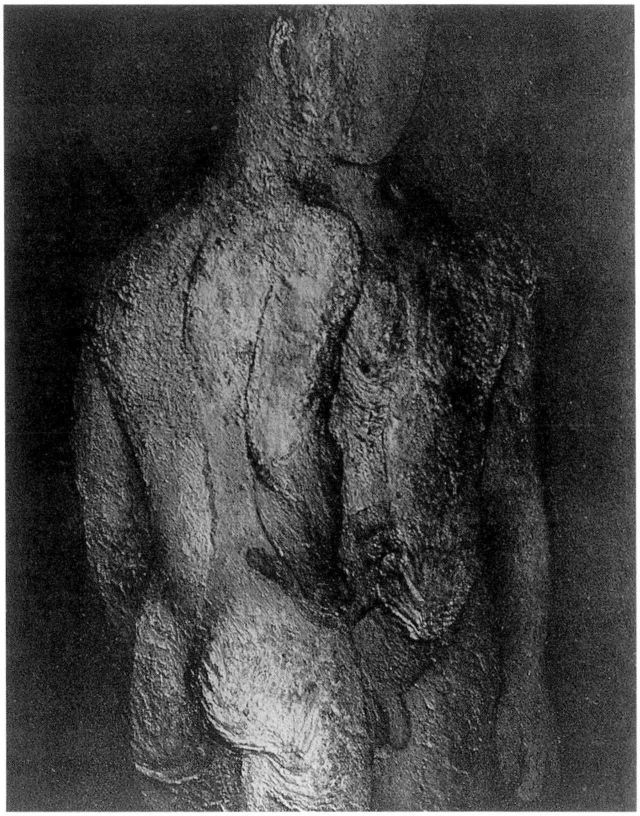

23 Pavel Tchelitchew, *Nude in Space*, 1926, oil and sand on canvas (as reproduced in *Pavel Tchelitchew*, Museum of Modern Art, New York, exhibition catalogue, 1942).

his art 'draws him into the inner ring of contemporary creative effort'. Yet Sutherland is the 'Cézanne of metamorphosis . . . one of the great diffidents, a virtuoso of inconfidence, bringing the restlessness of man into a searching relationship with the unease of the rest of the created world.' The artist has a particular faculty 'for the complex system of feelings and impressions that permeate the mind in particular places and circumstances.' In an aside, Melville referred to Bacon as one of Sutherland's 'intimates', and the concluding paragraph of his essay opens with a formulation redolent of Bacon: 'Our intelligence does not penetrate mystery but leads to its frontiers, and the art of Sutherland, which bears the visible traces of understanding, is the ordering of the experience of the nerves and emotions'.

Meanwhile, Melville's essay on Bacon in the final issue of *Horizon* magazine was scheduled to coincide with the Hanover Gallery show.[222] This essay clearly tries to convey something of Bacon's own outlook, registering the artist's recoil from the pervasive, and from his perspective re-ductive, tendency to see his work as illustrating horror and anguish. Melville commented that the drift of Bacon's temperament was 'to propound an hallucinatory condition as a primary attribute of man', and he further observed that 'every activity in these paintings of men going in and out of curtains, or imprisoned in transparent boxes, has an air of extreme hazard'.[223] Yet this 'powerful overtone' can tend to obscure 'the modernity of Bacon's formal resources', a point upon which Melville elaborates by means of comparisons with the cubist art of Picasso and Duchamp, and also with work by Pavel Tchelitchew such as the 1926 *Nude in Space* (pl. 23), a specific picture from which Bacon may well have 'taken a hint'.[224] The emphasis on Bacon's modernist pedigree and aesthetic self-consciousness, and on the importance of the paint surface itself in carrying the meaning of the paintings, is likely to have reflected the impact of studio visits and conversations with the artist. Melville remarks: 'throughout the present year I have seen seven or eight new paintings by Francis Bacon in which the image has a call upon the entire oblong of paint'.[225] He notes Bacon's propensity for destroying pictures, while another passage provides an early account of the artist's spontaneous creative processes:

> Bacon never makes a drawing. He starts a picture with a loaded one-inch brush of the kind that ironmongers stock, and almost the entire work is painted with these brushes. In these broad brushmarks, modernism has found its skin: the 'works' no longer show. . . . In releasing modern painting from the machinery of linear construction, Bacon makes a typically baroque statement: he gives reality to an illusion, and his pictures do not invite the spectator to investigate the means.[226]

Bacon's passion for silent films and reliance upon cinematic stills as starting points for his pictures is reflected in the references to the Eisenstein Odessa steps sequence in *Battleship Potemkin* (1925). Both Bacon's interests and Melville's own surrealist affiliations are implicit in the critic's admiring comments on Bunuel's *Un Chien Andalou*: 'only the recent paintings of Francis Bacon have discovered a comparable means of disclosing the human condition'.[227]

Another parallel between Bacon and Sutherland emerges from the illustrations to Melville's article. These demonstrate that, by the late 1940s Bacon had already adopted the idiosyncratic method of presenting his pictures that he was to maintain throughout the rest of his career. For, very unusually, the bulk of the reproductions incorporate the conventional moulded gilt frames that the artist evidently preferred for his paintings, an aspect of the illustrations that must surely have been at Bacon's suggestion or insistence.[228] Sutherland seems to have shared Bacon's approach to framing. One review of his Hanover Gallery show of summer 1948 noted that 'Sutherland's modern idiom is off-set by something unusual these days: all his pictures are framed, like grandmamma's watercolours, in gold'.[229] Bacon and Sutherland used the same framer in Chelsea during this period.[230] They also shared a profound interest in the art of the past, although there is no hint in Sutherland of Bacon's implicit sense that the great pictorial tradition preceding photography was now definitively a thing of the past, and could only be recuperated through devices of irony and quotation. The use of gilt frames establishes an emphatic but complex and elusive reference to the art of the old masters, which is further echoed in Bacon's use of traditional techniques and with his decidedly subversive echoes of tradition in the references to Grünewald in the *Three Studies* and *Painting* (1946), and the obsessive adaptations of the *Innocent X* portrait by Velásquez. The absence of Bacon's subversive edge meant that Sutherland's work could appeal not only to progressive young artists and critics, but also to an audience that was otherwise more attuned to the art on show in the National Gallery than to the radical products of the avant-garde. A comment by a longstanding supporter Raymond Mortimer is indicative: 'a number of those who have spent most time looking at the Old Masters suspect that he is the most remarkable painter born in this century. This is the more interesting, because these same experts would agree that for a hundred years the primacy of the French School has been unassailable'.[231] This was perhaps close to the viewpoint of Kenneth Clark, former Director of the National Gallery, whose interest in, and sympathy for, contemporary art was limited to artists who avoided the extremes of abstraction or surrealism. By implication, Clark presented the work of Sutherland as the fitting conclusion to a long and distinguished Western tradition in his 1949 book *The Art of Landscape*.[232]

The fact that Sutherland and Bacon both received their most telling support and publicity from *Horizon* indicates the dearth of specialist art magazines in Britain with any degree of commitment to experimental work. Equally, the regular coverage of visual art highlights the genuine cultural breadth of *Horizon* itself. The magazine exemplifies the unusually close personal and artistic relations that were obtained between British artists and writers throughout the 1940s. The profuse illustrative work of Sutherland, Craxton, Freud and Minton is another aspect of this creative interaction. There were also strong social connections. Famously, the pubs of Soho were a haunt for poets and painters alike. Sutherland lived in the country and so was more remote from wartime and post-war fraternising. Bacon, however, like a good many others, could always expect to encounter literary and artistic friends at the Gargoyle Club in Old Compton Street. This had been founded by David Tennant in the 1920s, and acquired a mirror-tile décor that had been suggested by Matisse. Many years later, Bacon recalled how much he missed the Gargoyle milieu:

> I didn't go up to the Gargoyle until after the war – about 1947 – and it's true to say that when one arrived quite late most people, including oneself, were generally half drunk. But they looked for a moment like birds of paradise coming down this beautiful gold and silver staircase into what the multiplicity of mirrors made into a very beautiful room. I've never been a great admirer of Matisse, but this room really worked as a setting.[233]

Whether or not it is precisely accurate, the date Bacon gave here confirms that it was not really until after the war that Bacon became visible in the London art world, as a social as well as commercial entity. Certainly he does not feature in the many memoirs of wartime bohemia, centred on the pubs of Fitzrovia and Soho. In the absence of other documentation concerning his contacts, the membership list of the Gargoyle also serves to evoke the culture of largely upper-middle class and aristocratic bohemia in which both Bacon and Sutherland moved in the late 1940s. Over and above the *Horizon* circle, represented by Connolly, Spender, Watson and Sonia Orwell, the writers who ended their evenings in the Gargoyle might include Dylan Thomas and George Barker. Bacon would also have encountered John Russell, who worked at the Tate and was beginning to emerge as an art critic. There was also a healthy complement of visual artists amongst the membership, including Matthew Smith, Roland Penrose and Lee Miller, and amongst the younger generation, Lucian Freud, Paolozzi and Michael Wishart, all great friends of Bacon in the immediate post-war period, as well as John Craxton, the two Roberts and many of the teaching staff at the Royal College of Art, such as Rodrigo Moynihan, Robert Buhler and finally John Minton, who evidently first took Bacon along to the club.[234] Other art-world figures included Erica Brausen, Helen Lessore and the up-and-coming critic David Sylvester. The photographer and painter Peter Rose Pulham, whose association with Sutherland was reflected in an interesting group of photographic portraits, was another good friend of Bacon's who frequented the Gargoyle.[235] Even so basic a listing of names suggests how Bacon might begin to be integrated into a wider cultural context, as well as indicating that many of Bacon's closest personal contacts during the decades of his greatest acclaim went back, in fact, to the late 1940s and the years when he first came to the fore in the British art world.

CODA: AFTER 1950

Although the focus of this study is on the 1940s, we should, finally and briefly, look to the subsequent period in the careers of the two artists. By the early 1950s, Sutherland's reputation was becoming increasingly inflated and international, in exact parallel to his friend Henry Moore's blossoming career as, by common consent, the leading British sculptor. In 1950, Sutherland received a commission from the Arts Council of Great Britain to produce by the following year a major, mural-scale painting for the Festival of Britain site (*The Origins of the Land*).[236] His 1952 Venice Biennale exhibition subsequently toured to Paris, Amsterdam, Zurich and the Tate Gallery.[237] Bacon was less visible, but was at least showing his work regularly at the Hanover Gallery. Indeed, the two artists tended in the early 1950s to be seen in tandem. For Stephen Spender, in his survey of current English painting in 1954, the middle-aged artists were still at the forefront of innovation: 'Graham Sutherland and Francis Bacon hold positions in painting, parallel to that of W. H. Auden in poetry'.[238] Only these two painters seemed to be truly 'outstanding' artistic talents.[239] That same year, Bacon sent Sutherland a perfectly friendly postcard from Italy, the only component of their correspondence to survive beyond the 1943–47 letters.[240] During this period, Sutherland continued to promote Bacon's cause. In 1950 Sutherland was in a position, as a trustee of the Tate Gallery, to recommend the purchase of Bacon's *Figure in a Landscape*.[241] The director of the Tate at the time, John Rothenstein, recalled a dinner in February 1951 when Sutherland talked at length about Bacon and expressed great admiration for his work.[242] Indirectly, at least, this advocacy had important consequences. Rothenstein in turn became a notable supporter of Bacon's work, and organised the substantial retrospective mounted by the Tate in 1962, accompanied by a big monograph recording Bacon's achievements to date.[243] Sutherland and Rothenstein had, in the meantime, fallen out spectacularly over aspects of the running of the Tate Gallery that Sutherland learnt about as a trustee. Whatever the rights and wrongs, Sutherland was clearly thought by many to have behaved rather foolishly, while the artist's own sense of disillusionment probably strengthened his desire to escape from the British art world, reflected in his purchase of a house in Menton in 1955.

Sutherland's admiration for Bacon's work is very evident from his *Standing Forms*, *Head* and animal paintings from the early 1950s.[244] As James Hyman notes, their work was at its closest between 1952 and 1954.[245] In Sutherland's work of this time, the atmosphere becomes more insistently menacing and sinister, melodramatic even, the scale more imposing and the artistic language more painterly in touch, and often more muted in colour. It is hardly surprising that critics should have observed that Sutherland's paintings were now demonstrably under the sway of Bacon. Overall, the direction of influence seems by this stage to be largely one-way, and, one might argue, with a somewhat disruptive impact on the effectiveness of Sutherland's art. Certainly, the extent to which Sutherland succumbed to the inspiration of Bacon's art can be taken to symbolise Sutherland's weaker and more fragile sense of artistic identity, in comparison with an artist who, having once established his bearings, sustained a relatively autonomous artistic evolution for the next thirty-five years or so. One might even argue that, in emulating the boldness, scale and sheer lack of compromise in Bacon's art, Sutherland sacrificed a certain diffidence and hesitancy that were doubtless rooted in personal temperament, but that were in fact integral to the aesthetic language of his best work from the late 1930s and the war years.

At some point, the evident warmth between the two artists began to turn into mutual suspicion and indeed hostility. Professional competitiveness and jealousy must have been a factor. Bacon increasingly acquired a preeminent place in the canon of internationally regarded artists of the post-war period, whereas Sutherland's work was widely held not just to show excessive indebtedness to Bacon, but also, in the longer perspective, to manifest a gradual and severe decline in inspiration. Various other factors have been cited to account for the breakdown of the relationship. Sutherland was evidently irritated at Bacon's extravagant drinking habits and tendency to disparage artists he himself now knew and admired, such as Picasso, Braque and Matisse. Sutherland's nickname for Bacon became 'the monster'.[246] For his part, Bacon disliked Sutherland's association with the despised Douglas Cooper, who ended up writing the major monograph on Sutherland's work (1961).[247] Spender's account of an evening spent with Bacon in June 1960 evokes the tenor of the artist's current feelings about Sutherland's tendency towards social climbing, which others observed too: 'Talk about Graham Sutherland: Francis on Graham's liking for publicity, the company of Somerset Maugham, Douglas Cooper and Picasso, etc. Francis refused an honour. "Didn't fill in the papers. All this has nothing to do with being an artist" and so on.'[248] Moreover, Bacon clearly entertained severe reservations about the direction of Sutherland's work. With Bacon's encouragement perhaps, it became a regular tactic of new advocates of his work such as David Sylvester to downgrade Sutherland by comparison with their own man.[249] Bacon took to scornfully remarking that the portraits were like the covers of *Time* magazine.[250] Yet even the portraits betrayed Sutherland's fascination with Bacon. It is difficult, for example, to imagine the lost *Winston Churchill* (1954) without the precedent of Bacon's full-length variants on Velásquez's *Pope Innocent X*, of which versions survive from 1950 onwards, while the format of the *Arthur Jeffress* (1955) portrait seems to make knowing reference to Bacon's *Figure in a Landscape* from a decade earlier.[251] Such derivations seemed self-evident at the time to John Richardson, who was a friend of both artists and as Douglas Cooper's partner saw a great deal of the Sutherlands in the South of France. Richardson recalled commenting on such borrowings to Bacon years later, to which he received a waspish comment on his former close friend: 'Such a petty pilferer. She never had the nerve for grand larceny.'[252] Whatever the grievances and irritations on both sides, the association between the two artists gradually petered out, and it appears that they stopped seeing one another completely in the mid-1960s. The relationship was plainly beyond repair, despite the well-intentioned efforts of their mutual friend, the photographer Daniel Farson, to engineer some sort of reconciliation in the 1970s.[253] Nevertheless, remarks in a 1976 interview indicate Sutherland's lingering respect for Bacon's art, which he described with some acuity as 'concerned with human conduct, and with the marks and movements left by the situations in which his subjects find themselves. I admire his work'.[254]

Divergences and incompatibilities between the two artists should not of course be understated, even at the time of their closest rapprochement, but the contrasts are sometimes too crudely drawn. Biographical stereotypes portray Sutherland as a practising Roman Catholic, who lived in a pretty old house in rural Kent, and led a rather respectable and well-connected bourgeois existence, while the Bacon legend features an avowed atheist, and an urban bohemian averse to country life, revelling in a hard-drinking existence centred on the dives and clubs of Soho. The novelist William Boyd has assembled several more oppositions:

> Sutherland charming and well mannered, Bacon the extrovert roué. Sutherland the devoted husband, Bacon the promiscuous homosexual. The paramount place of line in Sutherland's work; with Bacon the plasticity of the painted surface. Sutherland making study after study, laboriously squaring up and striving for perfection; Bacon relying on the adventitious moment, destroying everything that hadn't worked. Sutherland face to face with landscape and nature; Bacon confined to interiors. Sutherland's passionate response to the natural world in all its forms; Bacon's brutal obsession with the human condition. Sutherland the master etcher, the portrait painter, technically accomplished; Bacon who claimed 'I know nothing about technique'.[255]

More recently, Hyman has emphasised the gulf between the two artists: 'Whilst Sutherland's work was often optimistic, lyrical and colourful, finding solace in religious imagery and redemption in the Crucifixion, that of Bacon was nihilistic, dark and brooding.'[256] Such perceived discrepancies, artistic and personal, have undoubtedly discouraged the kind of close scrutiny of the relationship between the two artists that certainly appears to be merited, on the basis of the material assembled here. Needless to say, both were a good deal more complex and contradictory, both as people and artists, than the generalisations imply. Sutherland clearly was not especially devout, and he loved gambling. Several of his best friends and most committed supporters were homosexuals. Bacon did, we now know, make drawings, and he was clearly obsessed by questions of technique. But the main point is that the two artists themselves felt a strong sense of artistic and personal rapport. Consideration of their work in conjunction reveals the amount they had in common, and the probable stimulus that they derived from their friendship. The evidence suggests that for several years, Sutherland and Bacon played a key role in one another's lives and in the unfolding of each other's art.

2 DEVASTATION

Graham Sutherland and Francis Bacon established their artistic reputations in the very particular circumstances and atmosphere associated with wartime Britain. At the time, their work appeared to contemporary observers to distil the sense of threat and violence that dominated people's lives. To an unprecedented degree, of course, the Second World War afflicted those left at home, facing German bomb and missile attacks, as well as members of the armed forces on active service. As he looked back on this most traumatic of times, Sutherland spoke for Bacon and for millions more of his compatriots when he remarked that 'undoubtedly the war had an important effect on my consciousness'.[1] To what extent, however, was the Second World War the making of Bacon and Sutherland as artists, as the First World War had been the making of Paul Nash, for example, or figures such as Max Beckmann and Otto Dix in Germany? In what specific ways did the overwhelming impact of the war manifest itself in their work as painters? How did it shape their overall ambitions for their work, and their particular decisions regarding subject-matter and form? What aspects of their existing artistic resources could each mobilise and elaborate in order to convey specifically wartime meanings? Indeed, at what point did they begin, albeit in different ways, to allow an awareness of events in the wider world to inform their art?

There is also a wider issue: how far did the work of these two artists, viewed in conjunction, typify a wider and distinctively wartime sensibility? Such a sensibility, it seems to me, pervaded British cultural life over a more extended chronological period than the actual duration of the war. The international situation had been deteriorating steadily since the early 1930s, but at a certain point an awareness that terrible things were happening elsewhere, for instance in Spain or Abyssinia, developed into the conviction that Britain too was being inexorably drawn into direct military involvement. A wartime mood, or outlook, was certainly in place a year or more before the British declaration of war on Germany in September 1939. The poet David Gascoyne registered the psychological impact of the Nazi annexation of Austria in March 1938: 'The atmosphere of this putrid continent becomes every day more horrifying and more impossible to breathe. How can one's mind escape any longer from the constant menace of irrational, *meaningless* violence and destruction'.[2] With hindsight, Hitler's move has been seen as 'in a sense the beginning of the Second World war in Europe', since for the first time since the end of the First World War the army of a major power had crossed a European frontier to enforce territorial ambitions.[3] By the latter months of 1938, when Sutherland had his first one-man show, it was apparent to almost everyone that a military conflict with Fascism was an imminent and seemingly inevitable prospect. Then, between autumn 1939 and spring 1945, war was the actual and grim reality of daily life. Bacon and Sutherland witnessed at first hand the physical and psychological effect of the new kind of total warfare that was inflicted upon the towns and civilian populations of both sides in the conflict. The war culminated in an Allied victory, but also, of course, in utterly horrifying revelations concerning the Nazi death camps. Moreover, the emergence of terrifying new weapons of mass destruction, such as the German flying bombs, during the latter part of the war in Europe, formed a prelude to the two atomic bombs that were dropped on Japan in August 1945. Joyous victory celebrations came and went, but powerful feelings of despair and fear also took root for a considerable period after the formal cessation of hostilities. Profound gloom regarding the prospects for humanity was a natural response to the unfolding and intensification of the Cold War, which seemed to make the onset of an even more horrendous world conflict merely a matter of time. By 1948, the year of the Berlin airlift, the division of Europe into two mutually hostile zones of influence was firmly in place. Within another two years, both sides had nuclear weapons, and the start of the Korean War seemed the harbinger of things to come. In Britain, at a more practical level, the euphoria and expectation associated with the election of the Labour Government in 1945, and the launching of the new Welfare State, had largely given way to disillusionment, as rationing, shortages and wartime destruction continued to blight everyday life.[4] A 1951 survey of the post-war English novel lamented how 'the war seems, in spirit, to go on and on'.[5] The future Conservative Chancellor R. A. Butler asserted that 1954 was 'the year when, for the British trader and consumer, the war finally ended.'[6] Something similar may have been true for many British writers and artists of the generation that had lived through the war years. Nevertheless, it was still possible for the poet Kathleen Raine to declare that year that 'never has the sense of the overwhelming power of the forces of evil flooding away the good . . . been more heavy to bear and hard to overcome'.[7] Cumulatively, such evidence suggests that it may be useful to deploy a notion of the 'long Second World War', registering a distinct phase in the history of British culture that extended from the late 1930s to 1950 and even beyond.[8]

Throughout this period, Sutherland and Bacon shared an impulse towards a latter-day form of tragic expression, which could encapsulate the emotional and psychological impact of the war and its aftermath, rather than merely describe its everyday occurrences. The artistic problem they faced was combining the particularity and vividness of lived experience with a telling interpretation of the significance of those experiences, avoiding either mere documentation or platitudinous generalisation. In 'A Note on War Poetry' (1942), much the same issue was pondered by T. S. Eliot, a writer who, like David Gascoyne, will feature as a recurrent point of reference throughout this discussion:

War is not a life: it is a situation,
One which may neither be ignored nor accepted,
A problem to be met with ambush and stratagem,
Enveloped or scattered.

The enduring is not a substitute for the transient,
Neither one for the other. But the abstract conception
Of private experience at its greatest intensity
Becoming Universal, which we call 'poetry',
May be affirmed in verse.[9]

It is possible to discern affinities on several levels between the work of Sutherland and Bacon and that of other creative figures, especially poets, who were active in Britain during the same years. This account makes extensive use of contemporary literary material, all of it probably known to Sutherland and Bacon, as a means of interpreting their wartime production. An implicit argument is that one of the things that the two artists shared was a strong literary inspiration. Gascoyne's poetry and journals illuminate the state of mind in which it could still seem possible to write or paint, against a backdrop of apocalyptic destruction in the wider world. His response to a performance of Bach's St. Matthew's Passion, witnessed in Paris in late October 1938, rehearses the preconception that art can provide an experience of catharsis or redemption:

> Bach's greatness in this work lies in his extraordinary power of transforming the great pain and sorrow of the rejection, betrayal, flagellation, crucifixion and entombment of Christ,

> into an unearthly calm and sweetness; of transfiguring grief and suffering into the radiance of a peaceful sky. This is the operation of the greatest art: resolution of the most violent contradictions, creation of harmony out of opposites – elevation, consolation.[10]

This attitude lingered on into the period under consideration. However, given the events of the 1940s, elevation or consolation often seemed hard to conceive, except in private psychological or spiritual terms. In a poem dated 'New Year, 1940', Gascoyne bade farewell to the 1930s. Now 'beyond despair' and 'having left all false hopes behind', one could only envision the bleakest of future prospects: 'Mirrored within/ Each lonely consciousness, War's world seems without end . . . The unseen enemy are near./ Above the cowering capital Death's wings impend./ Rapidly under ink-black seas to-day's doomed disappear.'[11] Out of this apocalyptic scenario, the poet nevertheless extracted a measure of positive meaning, even though all that is affirmed, it would appear, is stoic acceptance and a freedom from consoling illusions:

> . . . So silent is the ray
> Of naked radiance that lights our actual scene,
> Leading the gaze into those nameless and unknown
> Extremes of our existence where fear's armour falls away
> And lamentation and defeat and pain
> Are all transfigured by acceptance; where men see
> The tragic splendour of their final destiny.[12]

Gascoyne's negotiation of the tension between immersion in despair and yearning for meaning and redemption establishes a fruitful framework for considering the artistic and literary creativity of the war years, not least the distinctive contributions of Sutherland and Bacon. One might note, however, the complication to the elaboration of a redemptive aesthetic that arises from inherent divergences between artistic media. In any form of musical, literary or cinematic expression, the interplay of contrasting moods or sensations is necessarily staged over time, as the work unfolds within the consciousness of the reader or audience. The artist is able to control and manipulate the overall emotional architecture of the work. Needless to say, looking at pictures is also a temporal activity. But it is only open to the painter to assemble the diverse aspects and components of the work. The viewer proceeds to assimilate them in the manner, and also for the duration and in the sequence, that he or she chooses. In other words, it is not as obvious how a visual artist might enable the viewer to experience, say, a transfiguration of pain into harmonious equilibrium. I want to return to this issue having considered more specific consistencies between the wartime art of Sutherland and Bacon.

*

THE LANDSCAPE OF MEANINGLESSNESS

The genre of landscape is conventionally associated with retreat from the cares of worldly existence. In a practical sense, escaping from the city and its very real threats and anxieties was clearly a strong psychological imperative during the war. David Mellor has noted one aspect of Sutherland's impact: 'for the circle around Peter Watson, the Pembrokeshire countryside during wartime was a pastoral counter to London life and a place of recuperation'.[13] In the work of artists in this milieu such as John Craxton, landscape imagery evidently possessed such restorative connotations. In parallel to the current veneration for poets like Wordsworth, romantic forbears like Samuel Palmer offered a compelling model for a distinctively British version of the age-old arcadian vision of the natural landscape.[14] And yet the art that Sutherland himself derived from visits to Pembrokeshire and contemplation of Palmer is more cogently viewed as subversive of such received pastoral ideals.

September 1938, the moment of the Munich crisis, seems to register a significant moment of transition in Sutherland's work and also in its public reception. During that month he described his mixed feelings in a postcard to Paul Nash: 'We are in Pembrokeshire, alternating between enjoyment of this superb countryside and desolation as we scan the European horizon'.[15] A few days earlier, German troops had moved to the frontier with Czechoslovakia. Such circumstances may well have predisposed Sutherland to seek out motifs in the landscape that, when transmuted artistically, could sustain metaphorical associations with the current sense of desolation. At any rate, it was from drawings made during his trip to Pembrokeshire that Sutherland subsequently developed and realised the ambitious oil painting *Gorse on Sea Wall* (1939; pl. III).[16] His drawings of a 'found' natural form suggest that the root itself had a horizontal orientation, and that this was also the format that Sutherland initially intended for his composition.[17] The underlying configuration of curved shapes seems to have its origin in the forms of rhythmically receding hills in the background. In the final picture, the space is more shallow and frontal, while the main motif is greatly simplified and becomes emphatically vertical. Sutherland employed linear definition and tonal contrast to focus our attention on the spiral unwinding of the root, with its spiky, cactus-like growths. This feature dominates the upper part of what is otherwise a relatively balanced design made up at the base of more angular forms describing the mossy stones of the wall, and a simple, thinly painted backdrop evoking, we might assume, a dark sea and schematic sunset. The central symmetrical form, black in its topmost section in order to reinforce the projection of the root, suggests both a prehistoric standing stone, as in its predecessor *Red Monolith* (1938; pl. 81), and also, incongruously enough, a silhouette of a human head with hair-like extensions, just as the root itself reads, on one level, as a hand contorted in agony. In a general sense, Sutherland observed in 'Welsh Sketch Book' that one of the things he had learned in Pembrokeshire was that 'that landscape was not necessarily scenic, but that its parts have an individual figurative detachment'.[18] Of *Gorse on Sea Wall* in particular, he recalled that he had been 'conscious of a kind of figurative element . . . I rather like the idea that the thing is self-contained, exactly as a figure would be self-contained if you were to draw it. And therefore, I think, there was a need for me . . . to make landscapes into a thing which, as far as possible, could be got within the four walls of the canvas'.[19] At the same time, the forms in the picture seem to assume somewhat aggressive animal associations, as discussed earlier. The multiplicity of readings permitted by *Gorse on Sea Wall* is captured in Robert Melville's attentive account of this 'grave and noble portrait' in his 1950 monograph:

> It is a very remarkable example of the kind of pictorial construction, peculiar, I think, to the twentieth century, which whilst having an intense apparitional reality of its own has snapped the links that enable the eye to refer it back to the real world; all its substances have become equivocal and its is not easy to say where one begins and another ends. Line and colour are beautifully definite in their fullness, but the image they project slides out of our grasp, engulfs the eye in inexhaustible ambiguities. The monolith . . . no longer certainly stone, embraces in its green and sepia blackness a shadowy personage, but it has put forth a strange thick-rimmed lip or projection which is in peculiar pictorial collusion with the gorse root; this lip continues and completes the root's convolution, and together they form a slow thick convulsive hieroglyph of growth . . . The pale root form wavering out of its crevice, feeling tentatively at the air, hints at crawling and the visceral, yet it is not horrifying.[20]

He goes on to suggest that there is something throne-like, or even lap-like and hence protective, about the relationship of root to monolith. Overall, following Melville's observations, one might locate the dominant mood of the picture in the region of pathos and vulnerability, as encapsulated by an imagery of life forms struggling to survive in the most harsh and inhospitable surroundings. Such meanings seem all too resonant given what we know about the genesis of *Gorse on Sea Wall* in a moment of 'desolation as we scan the European horizon'. Naturally, the picture does not mark a complete change of direction. The conception was, to a degree, elaborated from an existing repertoire extending as far back as the 1930 etching *Pastoral*, with its anthropomorphic suggestions and sinister atmosphere (pl. 72). The Rosenberg and Helft Gallery exhibition, which opened in London a few days after he had made the studies for *Gorse on Sea Wall*, indicated that the writhing forms of blasted and uprooted trees, with their melancholy and elegiac connotations, were already an established strand of imagery.[21] Nevertheless, the new picture goes much further in submitting an observed motif to metamorphic transformation and to the expression of intense feeling. In this sense, it may well be appropriate to regard *Gorse on Sea Wall* as Sutherland's first consciously 'wartime' image, which is only reinforced by the suggestion that his formal language was stimulated in large part by the example of Picasso's overt engagement with violent war imagery in *Guernica*, which was shown in London in October 1938.[22]

From the start, the critical response to Sutherland's mature art was closely bound up with the ominous contemporary mood. The appeasement of Hitler culminated in the Munich summit at the end of September, when the Western powers capitulated to German demands for the Sudetenland, the German-speaking area of Czechoslovakia. In October, Eric Newton opened his review of Sutherland's show by confessing: 'At times like the present it is not easy to keep one's sense of critical values intact. When preparations for the preservation and plans for the extinction of human life and property are between them absorbing so much national energy it is difficult to apply one's mind to less spectacular forms of activity'. The immediate threat had receded, but one nevertheless detects the increasingly gloomy atmosphere in Newton's account of the 'primaeval, elemental, at times almost brutal' character of the art on view:

> Mr. Sutherland's world is an unfinished thing, as though it had been abandoned half-way through the fifth day of creation. His shapes, for all their subtlety, are clumsy. They suggest dinosaurs and mammoths. His hills heave themselves grimly against the sky. They are stark uncomfortable monsters made of raw earth and rock.[23]

During the following year, and indeed after Britain finally declared war on Germany on 3 September 1939, Sutherland continued to evolve a mode of landscape painting appropriate to the contemporary situation. By the time of his 1940 exhibition at the Leicester Galleries, in which *Gorse on Sea Wall* was first exhibited, the emotional register of Sutherland's art had become more extreme and explicit. Although the nocturnal landscape had been a recurrent interest since the Palmeresque etchings of the mid-1920s, in general the landscapes from the early part of the war are extremely dark pictures in a metaphorical as well as literal sense. Sutherland's extensive use of black gives an intense glow to the single accent of colour, pink in *Black Landscape* (1939–40; pl. 24) and an acidic yellowish green in *Green Tree Form: Interior of Woods* (1940; pl. VII). The latter was also one of Sutherland's most obviously metamorphic pictures to date. He was clearly struck by the monstrous, threatening connotations of an uprooted tree form, presumably encountered in Pembrokeshire. Sutherland proceeded to heighten this aspect by using a low viewpoint, dramatic chiaroscuro and by simplifying the form and minimising its original natural context.

In the acute sense of threat and anxiety which such paintings transmit, both through their imagery and their formal language, Sutherland's new work reflected, no doubt consciously, the pessimism which prevailed in Britain at the time. He later recalled: 'Kenneth Clark, who was then in the Ministry of Information, knew just how serious the situation was becoming . . . how near to capitulation we were. The blackness of the atmosphere of war was like the prospect of death and more and more funereal. We lived from day to day.'[24] In early 1941, the artist reflected privately on the changes that had overtaken his work: 'I think wistfully of the old landscape days, and wonder if I shall ever get back a contact with emanations of the English landscape – the golden lyricism, the scent and the form.'[25] Sutherland's art struck a chord with many observers prone to similar forebodings. The critical responses to his exhibition in May 1940 mark a growing consensus that Sutherland was the British painter best equipped to distil the essential mood of wartime. For John Piper, the pictures on show were 'vigorous and dangerous as painting in 1940 should be, and seldom is',[26] while for A. C. Sewter they were 'intensely romantic and full of a spiritual agony which them the finest tragic expression I know . . . of the suffering of a society at war'.[27] Newton again extolled the vividness of Sutherland's painterly 'equivalents' for sensations of nature, singling out *[Green] Tree Form: Interior of Woods* and *Black Landscape*:

> Abandon the question 'What do they represent?' and at once his pictures become moving lyrical things, each with a mood of its own. In some of them the mood is admittedly tragic . . . And in each one there is an almost frightening intensity . . . [*Black Mountain*] contains dark shapes that *mean* mountains but do not *represent* them – shapes that convey mountainous size and weight'.[28]

Sutherland and his audience were the products alike of a predominantly literary cultural tradition. Throughout this body of pictures, one wonders whether the artist may have had at the back of his mind the romantic tradition of sublime landscape imagery, and more specifically what Herbert Read, in his 1930 book on Wordsworth, had described as 'one of the most famous and most vivid passages in the *Prelude*'. Rowing on a lake one tranquil summer's evening suddenly yielded to the poet a nightmarish vision of the animate forces of nature:

> . . . a huge peak, black and huge,
> As if with voluntary power instinct
> Upreared its head. I struck and struck again,
> And growing still in stature the grim shape
> Towered up between me and the stars, and still,
> For so it seemed, with purpose of its own
> And measured motion like a living thing,
> Strode after me.[29]

At the same time, Sutherland could well have found creative sustenance in the poetry of T. S. Eliot. Instead of offering a consoling fecundity or sensual beauty, the natural world frequently functioned in Eliot's early verse as a mirror to inner states of morbidity and desolation. Both the imagery and tone of Sutherland's *Gorse on Sea Wall* (1939) are strikingly foreshadowed in a section from 'The Burial of the Dead', the opening movement of 'The Waste Land':

24 Graham Sutherland, *Black Landscape*, 1939–40, oil and sand on canvas, 82 × 132 cm, Tate, London.

> What are the roots that clutch, what branches grow
> Out of this stony rubbish? Son of man,
> You cannot say, or guess, for you only know
> A heap of broken images, where the sun beats,
> And the dead tree gives no shelter . . .

The passage concludes with Eliot's chilling line: 'I will show you fear in a handful of dust'.[30] One might say that much of Sutherland's unofficial work from the war years was concerned

with showing fear in the insignificant details of nature. Likewise, works like *Midsummer Landscape* (1940; pl. 86) and *Horned Forms* (1944; pl. x) bring to mind Eliot's imagery in early poems such as 'Rhapsody on a Windy Night':

> The memory throws up high and dry
> A crowd of twisted things;
> A twisted branch upon the beach
> Eaten smooth, and polished
> As if the world gave up its skeleton.[31]

In this connection, we may note Kathleen Raine's statement in 1948: 'For my generation T. S. Eliot's early poetry, more than the work of any other poet, has enabled us to know our world imaginatively.'[32] Edmund Wilson likewise noted how *The Waste Land* in particular had 'enchanted and devastated a whole generation'.[33] The devastation was a product of the malaise that was taken from the start to be inherent in the fragmentation of the poem and in large tracts of its imagery. *The Waste Land* was often read as a projection of the tragic sense of life prompted by the horrors of the First World War. Wilson had provided a representative gloss in 1931: 'In our post-War world of shattered institutions, strained nerves and bankrupt ideals, life no longer seems coherent – we have no belief in the things we do and consequently we have no heart for them.'[34] In turn, the disillusioned voice that emanated from the early poems, readily accessible again after the timely publication in 1938 of Eliot's *Collected Poems 1909–1935*, offered a powerful aesthetic resource for articulating the prevailing atmosphere of the Second World War.

The poetry of David Gascoyne provides a further means of access into the expressive tenor of Sutherland's landscape paintings. This is a more direct connection, in that it was Sutherland's graphic work that adorned Gascoyne's collection *Poems 1937–1942* (1943).[35] The idea of the collaboration came from the publisher Meary Tambimuttu, whose 'Poetry London' imprint produced a somewhat irregular magazine and a series of books notable for the quality and originality of their illustrations.[36] Gascoyne later recalled the background to his own publication:

> When . . . Tambi asked me if there were any particular modern artist I should like to have the book illustrated by, I immediately thought of Graham Sutherland. Not only had I seen the two paintings he had contributed to the International Surrealist Exhibition, I had more recently had several times occasion to look at *Entrance to a Lane*, a work of his that had been acquired early in the war by my friend Peter Watson. . . . I asked Peter with some diffidence whether he thought Sutherland might find my poetry of sufficient interest to make him consent to illustrating it.[37]

While Sutherland was working on the illustrations, Gascoyne visited his studio in Kent, and the two men 'made friends at once'.[38] Gascoyne also recalled showing Sutherland the emblem books he was currently collecting: 'He at once became keenly interested in the field, and before long produced a number of illustrations, particularly of [Francis] Quarles'.[39] These subsequently appeared in the May 1943 issue of *Poetry London*, for which Sutherland also provided a design for the cover, a variant of the usual lyrebird image.[40]

This wartime convergence between Gascoyne and Sutherland was rooted in the parallel trajectories that poet and painter had travelled. Both had submitted to the inspiration of surrealism around 1936, but quickly progressed beyond a programmatic allegiance to the movement (see chapter three for a discussion of the Surrealist dimension of Sutherland's work). The continuing inspiration that Sutherland derived from romantic artists such as Palmer and Blake is matched by Gascoyne's cultivation of 'a somewhat archaic diction, derived from English romantic poetry, as appropriate to the new tone of his poetry'.[41] Moreover, it is possible to apply to Sutherland some of the insights that can be derived from Gascoyne's journals into what it felt like, as an artist, to have to come to terms with the traumas of an imminent and actual condition of war. Gascoyne's agonised response to the Czechoslovakia crisis matched Sutherland's more summarily characterised 'desolation' as he and his wife scanned the European horizon from remote Pembrokeshire. Sutherland's impulse to distil the contemporary tragic mood in pictures like *Gorse on Sea Wall* emanated perhaps from a mentality analogous to Gascoyne's shifting sense of his role as a poet:

> I believe ever more positively that my own inner struggles represent only an unusually acute consciousness of an experience almost exactly similar to that which an ever-increasing number of people all over the world are becoming vaguely, inarticulately conscious of going through. This experience has to be given a coherent expression, objectified, universalised. It provides a fundamental significance to this otherwise meaninglessly incoherent moment of human history.[42]

Gascoyne in turn may have had Sutherland's *Entrance to a Lane* (1939; pl. 25) in mind when composing 'Walking at Whitsun', dated May 1940 in *Poems 1937–1942*. The speaker embarks upon a well-rehearsed exercise in lyrical celebration of the natural landscape, based on the experience of walking in the countryside. However, he then succumbs to reflections on a world at war, and at the end of the poem acknowledges the sheer impossibility of escaping from the horror of the contemporary world into the beauties of nature, of escaping, that is, from reflective consciousness into an immersion in raw sensation:

> I tread
> The white dust of a weed-bright lane; alone
> Upon Time-Present's tranquil outmost rim,
> Seeing the sunlight through a lens of dread,
> While anguish makes the English Landscape seem
> Inhuman as the jungle, and unreal
> Its peace. And meditating as I pace
> The afternoon away, upon the smile

25 Graham Sutherland, *Entrance to a Lane*, 1939, oil and canvas mounted on board, 61.5 × 50.8 cm, Tate, London.

26 RIGHT Graham Sutherland, front cover of David Gascoyne, *Poems 1937–42*, 1943, Private Collection.

(Like that worn by the dead) which Nature wears
In ignorance of our unnatural tears.
From time to time I think! How such a sun

Must glitter on their helmets! How bright-red
Against this sky's clear screen must ruins burn[43]

The passage offers a vivid parallel to the ambiguous bittersweet atmosphere of *Entrance to a Lane*. Sutherland's spatial compression and strident colour, combined with expanses of

opaque black, serve to inject sinister and fearful undertones into a scene that might otherwise evoke retreat from the cares of the world into the protective womb of nature.

Gascoyne's vision of a wasted landscape is elaborated in 'Gravel-Pit Field' of spring 1941, a poem which evidently made a particular impact on contemporary readers.[44] Gascoyne describes his vision of a 'scurfy pock-marked waste', which he had witnessed by the side of the Thames:

> Amidst this nondescript terrain
> Haphazardly the gravel-pits'
> Rough-hewn rust-coloured hollows yawn,
> Their steep declivities away
> From the field-surface dropping down
> Towards the depths below where rain-
> Water in turbid pools stagnates
> Like scraps of sky decaying in
> The sockets of a dead-man's stare.[45]

The resonance of such poems may be gauged from Derek Stanford's recollections: 'After Eliot, Gascoyne was the leading British poet to delineate the landscape of meaninglessness, to plumb the abyss of the emptiness of our time.'[46] Stanford described receiving *Poems 1937–1942* after his company had been billeted in Coleorton Hall, and discovering in both its visual and verbal imagery an imaginative counterpart to the actual environment in which he now found himself. Sutherland's cover 'suggested nothing so much as a sort of smouldering rubbish-tip in hell' (pl. 26), a landscape of the mind comparable to that evoked in Gascoyne's poetry:

> In full summer, the Leicestershire meadows stood basking in the sun, at first glance telling a peaceful pastoral story. This idyllic prospect, however, was no more than one of nature's well-meant lies. The land in wartime is a sad place, worked by women and foreign prisoners while its own tillers are away fighting. Moreover the fields about Coleorton lay on the borders of mining territory, and here disused or unwanted machinery, like satanic black engines of torture, troubled the eye when it strayed to the horizon. Time and place both combined to make my first serious reading of this poet, with the sultry, lowering landscape of his own verse, an unforgettable one.[47]

In the immediate wake of his collaboration with Gascoyne, Sutherland too sought out motifs that allowed him to project an imaginative terrain of arid, rocky, inhospitable formations, sparsely occupied by incongruous structures implying human labour or occupation. One thinks especially of his depictions of limestone quarries and opencast mines, made in summer 1943 for the WAAC from drawings made in Derbyshire and Wales (pl. 29). For all their documentary value, these scenes evidently possessed a strong emotional and imaginative significance for the artist.

Such concerns are generally remote of course from Bacon, whose paintings from the period focus on figures located in airless, claustrophobic interiors, redolent of the urban nightmare produced by persistent bomb and missile attacks. The single known exception is *Figure in a Landscape* of 1945 (pl. XII). Here the setting is grass, trees and bright blue sky. Yet 'joyous lyrical harmony' and an 'exhilarating sense of the openness of the open air' coexist uncannily, in Sylvester's words, 'with a suffocating menace'.[48] In the foreground of the picture a fragmentary figure is encountered whose posture emanates ease and relaxation, but who lacks a head and much else besides, and is juxtaposed against an obscure mechanical apparatus, a machine gun or perhaps a microphone. Like Sutherland's current work, with which certain stylistic parallels have already been noted, *Figure in a Landscape* subverts expectations of the natural landscape as a place of emotional solace.

AN INTENSE ONSLAUGHT

More direct references to wartime imagery are also encountered in the work of Sutherland and Bacon. As individuals, both shared the general concern to contribute in some way to the war effort. Sutherland was too old to serve in the armed forces, but after 1942 became involved in the activities of the local Home Guard.[49] More significantly, from 1940 to 1944 Sutherland worked for the WAAC, which was modelled on the scheme developed in the First World War, when artists were commissioned to depict the events and experiences of the war. The scheme had been inaugurated in late 1939, largely on the initiative of Kenneth Clark, and proceeded to offer work to artists who could be expected to 'record the war', effectively precluding artists committed to total abstraction.[50] The invitation reached Sutherland in June 1940, just as his part-time teaching at Chelsea was coming to an end, and he was about to embark on training as a 'munition gauge maker'.[51] He received a commission to make two drawings of the 'transport by rail of armaments and aeroplanes under net'.[52] A painting of *Camouflaged Bombers* was shown in June 1940 in the 'England in Wartime' exhibition at the Leicester Galleries. The juxtaposition here of work by Sutherland and Vivian Pitchforth prompted Raymond Mortimer to 'feel the difference between melodrama and tragedy':

> It will interest the connoisseur to notice how little difference a greatly increased realism makes to the general effect of a Sutherland. But the wider importance of the picture is that, while other works in the exhibition show the pathos, misery and courage produced by the war, this alone conveys the tragic sense – the perception, to which in England it has so far been mercifully difficult to attain, of war as a visitation sinister and calamitous beyond human intention or control.[53]

In August, he was given a brief 'to stand by to make pictures of debris and damage caused by air-raids'.[54] Such imagery was soon available in abundance, and Sutherland proceeded to produce paintings of devastated buildings in south Wales, and subsequently in London, especially the City and the East End, after the Blitz began in September 1940 (pls 27, 30, 31, and 89). He remarked at the time: 'Doing the scenes of devastation I have found most absorbing,

27 Graham Sutherland, *Devastation 1941: An East End Street*, 1941, ink and gouache on paper mounted on board, 64.5 × 114 cm, Tate, London.

though with the accompaniment of nightly raids, at all events during the earlier part of the work, not without its nerve wrecking element.'[55] The following spring, he declared that he found working in the East End 'profoundly interesting and moving', but wanted permission to take photographs as a supplement to drawing on the spot: 'it would be a great help as it is difficult to draw in some places without rousing a sense of resentment in the people'.[56]

From Sutherland's point of view, working for the WAAC provided him with a steady income for four and a half years, and prevented him from being called up for some other kind of war service. From late 1940 onwards, he was working under the terms of a series of six-month contracts issued by the Ministry of Information. In return for the actual works he produced on war subjects, which had to go through censorship, as well as for reproduction rights, he received a decent salary, starting at the equivalent of £650 a year and rising later on to £750.[57] In addition to bomb sites, he was commissioned to portray the fiery interiors of steel works in Wales (in 1941–42), and the tin mines of Cornwall, with their dark, mysterious tunnels (1942; pls 66 and 28). It was in some of the latter pictures that the human figure first assumed a dominant role in Sutherland's work, no doubt reflecting the impact of Henry Moore's studies of London Underground shelters of the previous year. Their shared focus in 1942 on images of miners working underground marked the closest point of convergence between the work of executed by Sutherland and Moore for the WAAC. The following year, Sutherland

28 Graham Sutherland, *Tin Mine: Miner Approaching*, 1942, gouache, chalk, wax crayon and ink on paper, mounted on board, 117.5 × 74.5 cm, British Council Collection.

was encouraged to depict limestone quarries in Derbyshire and open-cast mines in Wales, under the category of 'production subjects' (pl. 29). Finally, in late 1944, Sutherland was allowed to visit France, for the first time, in order to record the impact of Allied bombing on German flying-bomb sites. These campaigns of work generated some five hundred works in total, ranging from on-the-spot studies and sketches to larger, more resolved pictures suitable for public exhibition.

As with the other artists involved, the themes of Sutherland's works for the War Art scheme were proposed and chosen because of their suitability to his particular artistic idiom. Given his friendship with Clark, it is likely that Sutherland was able to exert some influence over the Committee's recommendations. He later acknowledged that he 'couldn't make much' of the kinds of subjects that he was initially asked to tackle, and that he was unable to treat his war art as completely separate from his existing body of work: 'not only did I feel that I had

29 Graham Sutherland, *Limestone Quarry: Working at the Cliff Face*, 1943, gouache and wax crayon on board, 61.6 × 54.6 cm, British Council.

to give value for money, but to contrive somehow to reflect in an immediate way the subjects set me. It was not until the advent of the air-raids that I could see any way to combine the aims of my work before the outbreak of war with the task then in front of me'.[58] Working with such imagery enabled Sutherland to find a new channel for his existing artistic commitments, in the same way that Moore's drawings of London underground stations presented a real life version of the reclining figures that had previously dominated his work as a sculptor. Sutherland remarked in February 1941: 'Nearly everyone says that the war has been a "good thing for me" as my war pictures a[re] "so much more understandable" than my landscapes. It's hard to convince people that the degree of abstraction – if you can call it that

– is identical!'.[59] His absorption of war imagery into the wider language of his work was partly accomplished by the use of a well-established creative process, transmuting first-hand sensations within the successive stages of the development of a composition. By his own account, Sutherland proceeded from notes and drawings on the spot, usually in pencil, to a 'work-out' stage, and these sketches in turn formed the basis for occasional finished pictures on a larger scale.[60] By submitting the raw materials of observation to a process of stylistic intensification and transformation, the artist believed he could evoke a deeper emotional and imaginative response in the viewer. In a 1941 radio discussion with Kenneth Clark and Henry Moore, Sutherland described his approach to working as a war artist:

> It's the force of the emotion in the presence of such a subject that determines and moulds the pictorial form one chooses . . . the sordidness and the anguish implied by some of the scenes of devastation will cause one to invent forms which are the pictorial essence of sordidness and anguish – dirty-looking forms, tormented forms, forms which take on an almost human aspect – forms, in fact, which are symbols of reality, and tragic reality at that . . . the point is, I think, that the forms which the artist creates, according to his inner capacity, will transcend natural appearances. To quote Maritain, such an art will recompose its peculiar world with that poetical reality, which resembles things in a far more profound and mysterious way than any direct evocation could possibly do.[61]

Such comments seem an appropriate commentary on the apocalyptic vision that informs Sutherland's work as a war artist. In the context of this study, it is also interesting to note how far his terminology and artistic outlook in 1941 prefigure Bacon's ambition, as articulated, for example, in the Sylvester interviews, to achieve a more profound realism through the interlocking of subject and form, than is attainable through more illustrative means.[62]

Several further aspects of the completed works manifest continuities with Sutherland's pre-war production. A preference for mysterious, nocturnal illumination, already present in etchings of the mid-1920s, found an extension in the menacing chiaroscuro of much of his landscape and war work between 1940 and 1942, as well as contemporary parallels in, for instance, Moore's shelter drawings and Piper's architectural studies. Moore may have pioneered the method of applying watercolour over waxy crayon to create a mysterious, blotchy effect. By May 1941, Sutherland's pictures too were 'rather mixtures technically, mostly being chalk, pen and gouache'.[63] His interest in narrow, enclosed spaces, with their rich metaphorical connotations, is carried over from a picture such as *Entrance to a Lane* (1939) to the depiction of long dark tunnels within the Cornish mines. Sutherland's tendency to focus in on specific natural forms, isolated from their wider context, was taken further in images of lift and ventilator shafts, dangling, broken machines, rolls of paper, and pieces of foundry equipment, extracted from the spectacle of destruction. Moreover, the writhing forms accentuated in, for example, *Gorse on Sea Wall* recur in images of horribly twisted lift shafts and girders created by bomb damage. Metamorphic suggestions of human and animal imagery emanate just as forcefully from certain war pictures. The forms of twisted girders and fallen lift shafts, with their warped metal frames, evoke the skeletons of human or animal life forms that have been subject to destructive violence (pl. 30). They thus read as surrogates for the human lives lost in the German bombing raids, which it would have been both crass and demoralising for Sutherland to show. In his memoir of his wartime activities, Sutherland recalled the effect of distorted lift-shafts that were all that remained of some buildings: 'in the way it had fallen it was like a wounded animal. It wasn't that these forms *looked* like animals, but their movements were animal movements. One shaft in particular, with a very strong lateral fall, suggested a wounded tiger in a painting by Delacroix' (pl. 31).[64] Comparable analogies came to mind in a steel works in Cardiff: 'As the hand feeds the mouth so did the long scoops which plunged into the furnace openings feed them, and the metal containers pouring molten iron into ladles had great encrusted mouths'.[65]

Sutherland's use of the generic title 'Devastation' for the bomb damage pictures, with its implications of a state of mind as well as a physical condition, epitomises his generalising concerns, although not giving away too many details might also have been a tacit requirement of the WAAC. Looking back at the end of the conflict, he provided Eric Newton with a revealing account of the more universal or mythic significance that different kinds of war imagery had held for him:

> At the beginning of the war the forms of destruction moved me tremendously. After that I began to feel drawn towards basic industries such as furnaces, mines and latterly quarries. These things seemed to symbolise a kind of eternal war; a constant of conflict between the forces of man and nature, intensified greatly during a war between nations, and in which man can only just emerge on top. The turning of iron ore into steel seemed so much a primitive combat (still, in spite of modern machinery, an elemental and almost crude process, with the floor of the teeming pit like some tremendous field). So too with the mines, quarries – perpetual conflict with intractable material. The sensation of conflict, therefore, was what I had to unload in pictorial terms. In each set of pictures I have expressed something perhaps of the same vision. But you will notice that the atmosphere is very different.[66]

Work by Sutherland featured regularly in the exhibitions of official war art that became a regular feature in the vacated galleries of the National Gallery. The critical responses the pictures elicited indicate that the artist's aims were closely in tune with the expectations of his audience. Piper's comments on a new display in May 1941 reveal that any hint of idealisation or propaganda would have been anathema: 'It is not camouflage nor uniforms, nor the clean lines of a gun, nor even heroic profiles, that make good subjects for war pictures; it is death and destruction, and the agony that stays about the rubbish pile and the grave.'[67] The 'tragic and submerged' figures in Moore's Shelter Drawings met this criterion, as did Nash's 'Dead Sea' of downed enemy planes. The remarks about Sutherland bring out the metamorphic undertones of his pictures of war scenes: 'If anyone still doubts the wisdom of employing artists who can make records of experience during war he should see these vivid

30 TOP Graham Sutherland, *Devastation in the City: Twisted Girders against a Background of Fire* (1941), 36.8 × 45.7 cm, Imperial War Museum, London.

31 Graham Sutherland, *Devastation: City, Fallen Lift-Shaft III*, 1941, ink, pencil and gouache, 12.5 × 14 cm, Wakefield City Art Gallery, Wakefield.

pictures and compare them with what the camera would say about the same subjects; twisted girders pouring over fired rubble-piles; a wall falling like a short man; the broken carcass of a lift-shaft; machinery dangling its severed limbs in the bare well of a mantle-factory'.[68] A series of popular books, *War Pictures by British Artists*, with reproductions of works created for the official scheme, provide further evidence for the powerful impact that Sutherland made. In the volume on production, comprising images of 'those Vulcan forges of the armament workshops and aircraft production factories', Cecil Beaton returned to the theme of the artist's advantages over photographers such as himself: 'In this world of molten metals, of glowing furnaces, soot and firework sparks, that only the painter can interpret, Graham Sutherland has reverently seized his opportunity to capture this fleeting phenomenon of sequined brilliance, of mystery, of glowing magic . . . Sutherland has also shown us the strange architecture that the necessity of war has built for us – an architecture that resembles something built in Babylon, or some other city of which no trace is now left.'[69] With reference to air raid imagery, Stephen Spender celebrated his ability to express the 'tragic and triumphant side of destruction': 'There is an unearthly glory about Graham Sutherland's study of *Devastation in an East End Street*; and his pictures of twisted girders have something in them of twisted humanity.'[70] In a similar vein, the young painter Keith Vaughan found a residue of consolation in the paintings of devastation he had contemplated in 1943 in another exhibition of war work at the National Gallery. He declared that, of all the war artists, Sutherland had 'most completely fulfilled the task allotted to him':

> Before any Sutherland picture one gets a powerful feeling of exuberance. And even when the material, as in some of the Blitz drawings, is nothing but the most complete desolation, one gets a feeling that the destruction is not final but that the organic principle of life remains; that the principles of growth and decay are almost inseparably inter-mixed . . . These pictures seem to me great for this reason; that no matter how far the artist's vision penetrates in its search for an aesthetic order, he never allows his imagination the wings of free fancy, but retains always a feeling for the original subject; never abandons the human scene for the realms of pure abstraction. Few painters maintain so surely this precarious balance.[71]

For such observers, Sutherland's pictures were powerful, and open to redemptive interpretations, precisely because they transcended banal illustration and captured the deeper emotional and even poetic resonance of their wartime subject-matter. Like the work of Moore or Nash, Sutherland's art matched up to Newton's recipe in 1945 for the 'three qualities' that the most successful war artists had to combine: 'First, to furnish a description of the "look" of the thing he is painting; second, to convince the spectator that the thing has been experienced as well as seen; and third, to convince to present his experience as an integrated whole. One could boil these three qualifications into the three words "accuracy", "intensity" and "beauty" . . . in the greatest art of all not only are they fused, but they are fused in approximately equal proportions'.[72]

*

If the war prompted Sutherland to adapt his existing artistic resources, it evidently caused Bacon, in more private and isolated circumstances, to acquire a renewed sense of artistic vocation. This at any rate was the impression he evidently conveyed both to John Russell, and to David Sylvester, who proceeded to claim that 'the necessary catalyst' for Bacon becoming a committed painter was the acute sense of mortality induced by living in London in 1944, 'the year of the V1s and V2s', which involved 'hearing at all times of the day and night the sound of isolated explosions each of which meant that a number of people not far away had suddenly been blown up'.[73] Whereas Sutherland's independent and commissioned pictures reflected a collective need to find some affirmative purpose and meaning within a 'tragic reality', Bacon's work seems to have created purely for himself and to have emanated from internal compulsions. However, stories like that of Sylvester suggest that Bacon resumed painting precisely in order to articulate some sense of what it felt like to be living through horrendous and traumatic times. He may even have been stimulated in part by an awareness of the interpretation of wartime imagery by artists like Sutherland, judging by the enthusiastic comments on seeing his pictures at the National Gallery in Bacon's note of February 1943.[74]

Notwithstanding the religious undertones indicated by its title, discussed below, *Three Studies for Figures at the Base of a Crucifixion* (1944) may also be read, on other levels, as a repository of legible references to distinctly contemporary forms of human experience. An overwhelming feature of the work is its direct allusion to physical suffering, absent from Sutherland's work on account of the dictates of the War Artists scheme as well perhaps as the artist's own inclinations. The sense of raw horror articulated by Bacon is matched, in the more direct idiom of journalism, by Cyril Connolly's editorial for the October 1943 issue of *Horizon*. For Connolly, current events confirmed that this was 'the Century of Fear':

> [Hitler] has contributed more pain to humanity than any other figure in the world's history . . . He has destroyed a Europe in which was apparent a steady, humanitarian trend . . . All this movement towards a better world one man has put into reverse by denying human dignity and restoring the torture chamber, the concentration camp, the secret police, the informer, the firing squad, on a scale which is in reality a cynical and diabolic act of defiance to humanity . . . It is very difficult in England to realise how intense is this onslaught across the Channel against the human body and the individual soul.[75]

By contrast, the hopes of the 1930s, whether for social reform, political progress at home and abroad, or merely the avoidance of military conflict, had been revealed to be an utter sham. The threat to civilised values came from men who embodied pure, unmitigated evil, and millions now found themselves vulnerable to deadly, arbitrary destruction.

The *Three Studies* might equally be said to convey the 'intense onslaught across the Channel against the human body and the individual soul', not to mention the experiences of the inhabitants of bombed British cities. Certainly to contemporary observers the pictures reflected all too directly the violence and aggression abroad in the wider world from which

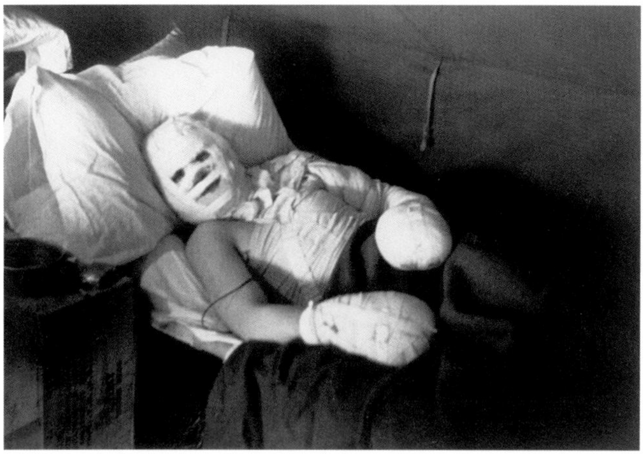

32 Lee Miller, *Bad Burns Case, 44th Evac Hospital, near La Cambe, Normandy*, 1944, photograph, Lee Miller Archives, England.

the paintings had emerged. Raymond Mortimer, for one, was clearly taken aback when he saw the triptych at the Lefevre Gallery, just as the end of hostilities suggested that rejoicing was finally in order: 'these pictures expressing his sense of the atrocious world into which we have survived seem to me symbols of outrage rather than works of art'.[76] With hindsight, Russell offered a vivid account of the work's impact on a more sympathetic observer:

> Immediately to the right of the door were images so unrelievedly awful that the mind shut snap at the sight of them. Their anatomy was half-human, half-animal, and they were confined in a low-ceilinged, windowless and oddly proportioned space. They could bite, probe, and suck, and they had very long eel-like necks, but their functioning in other respects was mysterious. Ears and mouths they had, but two of them at least were sightless. One was unpleasantly bandaged . . . Common to all three figures was a mindless voracity, an unregulated gluttony, a ravening undifferentiated capacity for hatred. Each was as if cornered, and only waiting for the chance to drag the observer down to its own level.[77]

Instead, they suggest a vision of man as degraded, debased and traumatised, the victim of some unspecified but clearly brutal process of torture, mental or physical, and even of dismemberment. The triptych had launched 'spectres at what we all hoped was going to be a feast'. They were the artistic correlative of all the other images of horrendous and inhuman violence that were blighting the general atmosphere of relief and celebration, such as photographs of the body of Mussolini hanging from a butcher's hook in Milan, and above all the images of piled-up splayed corpses which had been discovered when the Allied forces reached the Nazi concentration camps, beginning with Belsen and Dachau, at almost exactly the moment that the Lefevre Gallery group show opened in London.[78]

But what kind of imagery and experiences might actually have informed the conception of Bacon's triptych in 1943–44? It seems reasonable to discern a pictorial expression of the sense of fear induced by the Blitz, which again seemed to reduce man to animal instincts. A poetic parallel is provided by Cecil Day Lewis' *Ode in Fear*:

The bones, the stalwart spine,
The legs like bastions,
The nerves, the heart's natural combustions,
The head that hives our active thoughts – all pine,
Are quenched or paralysed
When fear puts unexpected questions
And makes the heroic body freeze like a beast surprised.[79]

In the Bacon, the emotional charge is conveyed with absolute immediacy through prominent details such as the bandaged head in the central panel, evoking the reality of pain and bodily disfigurement. A comparable sense of pathos and dehumanisation is conveyed in, for example, Lee Miller's 1944 photographs of wounded soldiers in a field hospital in France (pl. 32).[80] Bacon's deformations of the human body – the eyeless heads, gaping mouths, and the strong animal and bird overtones of the forms – provide the visual counterpart to another poetic description of the poignant condition to which the body had been reduced in wartime, as encountered in 'Soldiers Bathing' by Frank Prince, which appeared by chance in the same 1943 issue of *Poetry* (*London*) as Sutherland's Quarles illustrations:

. . . the body that was gross,
Rank, ravenous disgusting, in the act and in repose,
Its fever, filth and sweat, its bestial strength
And bestial decay . . .[81]

Equally, Bacon's screaming, semi-human creations, set within claustrophobic spaces, might be aligned with a strand in wartime literary imagery. One thinks, for example, of Elizabeth Bowen's contemporary story 'The Demon Lover', set in a desolate wartime London, in which a middle aged woman returns to her shut-up house, and becomes distraught by recollections of her fiancé promising to return just before he left to meet his end in the trenches of the First World War. She escapes into a taxi, but realises that her driver is in fact the ghost of her demon lover: 'Mrs Drover's mouth hung open for some seconds before she could issue her first scream. After that she continued to scream freely and to beat with her gloved hands on the glass all around, as the taxi, accelerating without mercy, made off with her into the hinterland of deserted streets.'[82] Turning to actualities, after the Blitz there came news of massive slaughter on the battlefields of Europe, and increasingly of the almost unimaginable horrors associated with the Nazis' persecution of the Jews. Some knowledge of the Holocaust gradually began to percolate through to the West. However, the stories were often dismissed as propaganda, and few took in the reality of the death camps until Allied troops witnessed them directly in April 1945, a discovery swiftly followed by the mass circulation of photographs and films. The previous year Arthur Koestler had expressed his fury that nobody wanted to know about 'the killing by hot steam, mass-electrocution and live burial of the total Jewish population in Europe. So far three million have died. It is the greatest mass-killing in recorded history; and it goes on daily, hourly, as regularly as the ticking of your watch.'[83] In autumn 1943, Koestler had even resorted to techniques of literary fiction to try to alert the British public to what was happening to the Jews in mainland Europe. A story appearing that October in *Horizon*, quite possibly known to Bacon, told of a train with windowless cattle-trucks full of Jews:

> Around midday the women in one of the carriages started to scream. First it was only one or two voices, then it was the whole carriage . . . That screaming tore right through one's brain and made one quiver and shake with the desire to join in the yelling with all the power of one's lungs and beat one's head against the iron wall of the carriage . . . Later we learned that one of the women in the truck, a nurse . . . had smuggled a razor with her. There were a number of girls in the truck who wanted to die instead of going to the brothels, but they didn't know how. So the nurse offered to help them open their veins, and she had already done it to about a dozen . . . But there was another party of women who were afraid that they would be punished for not reporting what was going on. They had quarrelled and argued all the time and then one woman had tried to take the razor away from the nurse; the suicide party had defended her and there was a fight in which one of the girls had her face slashed and started to scream; and then the others had joined in, screaming, shouting and dancing, and banging their heads against the walls.[84]

With Bacon's bestial creatures, we seem to be in comparable psychological and existential terrain. They embody fear and violence, but it is by no means clear whether we are confronted by aggressors or victims. The ambiguity is implicit in the image of the gaping mouth, which can convey a scream of fear and pain, and at the same time, the screaming out of threats and exhortations to inflict such pain. As Andrew Brighton remarks, the 'physiognomy of the mouth is such that rage, ecstasy and harangue are indistinguishable in appearance'.[85] Such contradictory readings apply to Sutherland's *Blasted Oak* (1941; pl. 33), where a human scream is transposed onto an uprooted tree root, as well as to the right-hand panel of Bacon's triptych, which carries the additional connotations of a yawning wild animal. It is above all the right-hand panel of the triptych that distills the 'capacity for hatred' that had come to the fore in recent years.

That this overtone was intended by Bacon is evident if the *Three Studies* are considered in the wider context of his work at the time. The received view is that his activity during the earlier part of the war is represented, albeit minimally, by a group of three paintings known as *Man in a Cap*, *Man Standing* (with a *Seated Man* on the back), and *Figure Getting out of a Car*.[86] None of these pictures were ever exhibited by Bacon, who probably meant, in fact, to destroy them. Several years later, they were discovered by his painter friend Robert Buhler, who took over Bacon's studio and eventually sold the paintings that had fortuitously come into his possession. They have rarely been seen since. Judging from the available reproductions, the pictures reveal little stylistic consistency. However, it has been established that they were all based on the documentary photographs of the Nazi leadership. That Bacon accumulated images of this particular type in his studio has been well-known ever since the

33 Graham Sutherland, *Blasted Oak* 1941, pen and wash, 30.5 × 38.1 cm, Private Collection.

34 Photographs in Bacon's studio in 1950 (as published by Sam Hunter in *Magazine of Art*, January 1952).

American critic Sam Hunter included a pair of images of Goebbels and Himmler extracted from *Picture Post* magazine amongst the two montages of found photographic material that accompanied his 1952 article on Bacon (pl. 34).[87] The shouting figure in *Man in a Cap* was largely synthesised from these images (pl. 35).[88] Equally, *Man Standing* was modelled on a photograph of Hitler looking out of the window, although this derivation is not betrayed in the sketchy picture as it stands (pl. 36). Bacon told Ronald Alley that an image of Hitler getting out of his car at one of the Nuremberg rallies had provided the starting point for *Figure Getting out of a Car* (pl. 38). The car survived relatively intact in the eventual picture, but Hitler himself was supplanted by a monstrous creature comparable to those inhabiting the *Three Studies*.

The pictures extended Bacon's habit of using photographs as the direct source for elements in his paintings. However, his turn to a more highly-charged imagery seems to mark a new departure. It also presupposes the currency from the late 1930s onwards of a new kind of journal, featuring numerous photographs integrated with the text. It is perhaps difficult now to recapture the novelty and excitement that, for instance, *Picture Post*, *Paris-Match* and *Life*

35 Francis Bacon, *Man in a Cap*, *c.*1941–42 oil on board, 94 × 73.5 cm, Private Collection.

36 Francis Bacon, *Man Standing*, *c.*1941– 42, oil on board, 99 × 71.5 cm, Private Collection.

37 John Heartfield, "*Goering: The Executioner of the Third Reich*", *Arbeieter-Illustreite-Zeitung* (AIZ, Prague), 14 September 1933, front page.

possessed for the generation of Bacon, who was clearly a keen consumer.[89] The documentary photographs they included depended upon the availability of the hand-held Leica camera, which could capture the most instantaneous events and images. In addition, there is an interesting precedent for Bacon in the highly political photomontages of an artist like John Heartfield. In particular, Heartfield's *Goering: The Executioner of the Third Reich* (1933) vividly foreshadows the grotesque violence and brutality that Bacon extricated from much the same raw material (pl. 37). Indeed, the juxtaposition raises the question of whether Bacon's adaptations from documentary photography might even, at some level, have been encouraged by the example of an artist working directly with fragments of mass-media imagery. Heartfield had moved to London in 1938, in flight from the growing German occupation of Europe, and his work was exhibited there in a one-man exhibition in 1939 and reproduced thereafter in magazines like *Picture Post* and *Lilliput*.[90] The common denominator between *Goering: The Executioner of the Third Reich* and Bacon's *Man in a Cap* is of course the focus on the mouth, distorted by rhetorical exertions into a distillation of hatred and violence. But whereas the Heartfield is a photomontage and an exercise in anti-fascist propaganda, created typically for

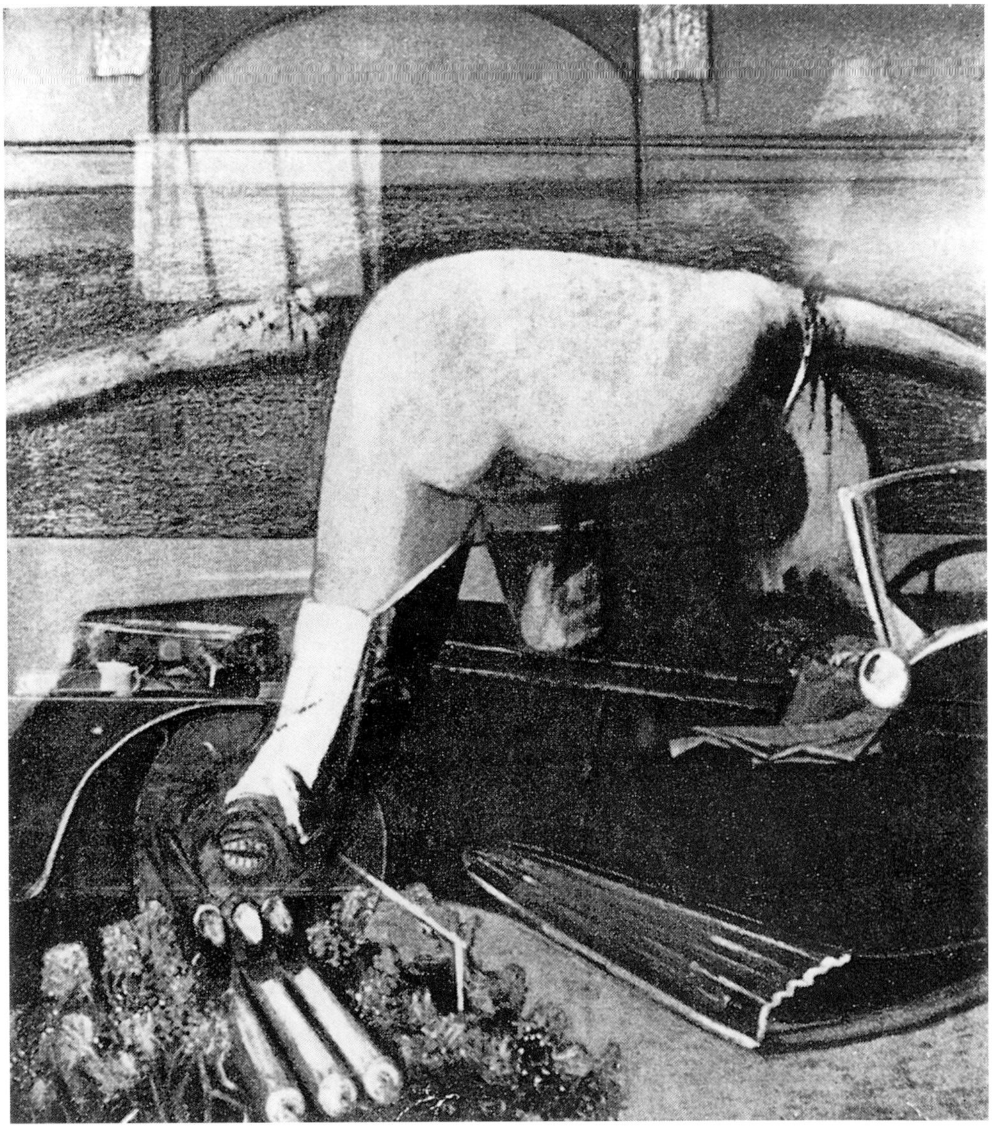

38 Francis Bacon, *Figure getting out of a Car*, *c.*1940–45, oil on canvas, 144.8 × 128.3 cm, subsequently modified by the artist, Private Collection.

dissemination in a mass circulation format, *Man in a Cap* is a painterly adaptation of photographic imagery, made for private imaginative purposes. We are presented in Bacon's painting with a puppet-like caricature of the type of the fascist demagogue, strutting and gesticulating on his podium. The editing out of the eyes, serving to dehumanise the figure, establishes a recurrent feature of Bacon's treatment of the human figure during the next few years. More specifically, *Man in a Cap prefigures* the overall orientation of the figure, as well as detailed treatment of the mouth, in the right-hand panel of the *Three Studies* triptych (pl. VIII). Here the reduction of the features to a gaping, shouting mouth, and the fusion of human attributes with those of some ferocious wild beast, reads as a yet more generalised evocation of the grotesque spectacle of the Nazi war leaders projecting their odious message to the masses. But there is more onus now on the spectator to excavate the meanings and contemporary allusions embedded within the image, which is also the case for the enigmatic suggestions of an open mouth screaming into a microphone, perhaps even belonging to a child-like figure holding, and therefore firing, a machine-gun placement, which might emerge from the very fluid, textural passage of paint to the right of *Figure in a Landscape* (1945; pl. XII).

Overall, such works tend to be understood as marking the moment at which Bacon moved away from relatively direct treatment of publicly available imagery towards a more hermetic, and thus typically modernist, means of expression. Hyman has evoked Bacon's efforts to 'veil his imagery, thereby preventing direct reference to contemporary politics in favour of allusions to the human condition'.[91] The first difficulty with this statement is that it presupposes a certain chronological development in Bacon's art. By implication, the three pictures overtly derived from current photographs precede the veiling of any such allusions in the triptych. However, it is problematic to draw such conclusions when the other three pictures, notably *Man in a Cap* and *Man Standing*, are plainly unfinished. Given the plentiful evidence that Bacon reworked his canvases extensively, treating these works as though they embodied his intentions for what he wanted finished pictures to look like is misleading. Moreover, it is difficult to date any of the abandoned works at all precisely. Alley noted that *Man in a Cap* bears an inscription referring to Petersfield, and presumably believed that *Man Standing* was comparable to *Man in a Cap* stylistically, which led him to assign both pictures to '1941–42 (?)'. The connections between *Man in a Cap* and the *Three Studies* include the supports, identically sized pieces of Sundeala board (also used for *Man Standing*), a dominant use of orange, and the inscriptions referring to Petersfield.[92] This evidence reinforces the idea that *Man in a Cap* was executed, and left unfinished, around 1942, when Bacon was experiencing a renewed motivation to paint, and found himself, in unfamiliar rural surroundings, with plenty of time on his hands. Indeed, we should presume that the fortuitous survivals stand for a significant phase of activity, the results of which were otherwise destroyed.

However, it is not so straightforward to align *Figure Getting out of a Car* with this body of work emanating from the middle of the war (pl. 38). The existing dates attributed to this picture range from 1939/40, as stated by Alley on the basis of Bacon's own recollection that it was painted 'well before' the *Three Studies*, to 1943, the year that Sylvester came to prefer, and to somewhere in the vicinity of 1945, in other words *after* the triptych, a possibility to which Bacon also gave credence when he was questioned on the matter many years after the event.[93] It is the final, later date that strikes me as preferable, given the work's clear parallels with other works from this time. For example, whereas the other two abandoned pictures as well as the triptych were executed on relatively small pieces of board, *Figure Getting out of a Car* is on a canvas of identical dimensions (around 145 × 128 cm) to *Figure in a Landscape* (1945), *Figure Study II* (1945–46) and the overpainted *Man with Microphones* (1946). In stylistic terms, the relatively complex spatial construction is also closer to these pictures than it is to the more schematic paintings from around 1941–44, in particular the *Three Studies*. The

39 Francis Bacon, *Man with Microphones*, 1946, oil on canvas, 145 × 127.8 cm, subsequently over-painted by the artist.

modelling of the 'figure' appears analogous to that in *Figure Study II*, while the textural band in the background recalls *Figure Study I*. It seems reasonable, therefore, to see the picture not as a step towards the *Three Studies*, including direct photographic allusions that Bacon would subsequently veil, but rather as a larger-scale and more complex reworking of the imagery of the central panel, restating the treatment of the mouth in particular, which Bacon probably executed at some point around 1945.

Given the difficulties outlined, it seems more profitable to view the Buhler pictures not as a stage preceding the *Three Studies*, which may or may not be factually correct in each case, but instead, taking a broader view, as contributions to a relatively coherent phase in Bacon's art which can be taken to run from around 1942, when he evidently resumed painting, to the moment of his departure for France in mid-1946. Such a phase would also embrace the *Three Studies*, the two pictures that are closely related to the triptych, *Figure in a Landscape* (1945), the two *Figure Study* compositions (1945–46), a further *Figure Study* that was photographed at the time but then evidently destroyed, and pictures from 1946 such as *Painting* and the overpainted *Man with Microphones* (pl. 39).[94] Together, this adds up to some twelve pictures, if the triptych is treated as a single work. The use of photographic source material, more or less overtly, is one shared feature. Otherwise, in looking across this body of work, doubtless no more than the fragmentary remnants of Bacon's production in this period, what can be discerned is not so much stylistic homogeneity as the elaboration of a repertoire of motifs. The basic format is imagery of single figures, more or less fragmented or distorted, and presented in the context of settings and a variety of fixtures or, one might say, attributes. Otherwise, recurrent elements, sometimes incongruously and bizarrely juxtaposed, include prominent mouths, microphones that take on the menacing aura of machine-gun placements, suits, metallic podiums or balconies, curtains, extravagant displays of flowers or plants, and opened-out black umbrellas. The cumulative impression of Bacon repeating and reworking ideas contradicts, or at any rate qualifies, the myth of a radically spontaneous, shaman-like creative process generating Bacon's pictures. *Painting* (1946) may indeed have started life as an image of a bird landing in a field, which was then completely reworked, as Bacon and Sylvester never tired of repeating. Nevertheless, it is perfectly possible that the imagery he eventually brought to realisation was not just the inspiration of the moment, but instead was something that had been rehearsed in previous canvases. For Bacon, developing ideas in this way may have served as a surrogate for the conventional procedure of using drawings to develop an image, which Sutherland continued to use, and which Bacon always claimed, albeit with some exaggeration, to have spurned.[95]

Identifying an iconographic vocabulary in Bacon's art at this time does not, however, facilitate the assignment of specific symbolic 'meanings' to, say, flowers or umbrellas. Resistance to such ready decoding seems a further constant in this entire body of work. The figures might be seen to fall into two broad categories. There appear, at one extreme, to be victims, figures imbued with manifest pathos, secluded within their own trauma and suffering – as in the left and central panels of the *Three Studies*, or the pair of *Figure Studies*. At the opposite extreme, there are those who inflict such suffering, sinister and menacing dictator figures with teeth bared as they at once snarl and harangue the mob. This strand of imagery, embracing *Man in a Cap*, *Painting* and *Man with Microphones*, was distilled, as have seen, from newspaper photographs of fascist leaders. It is interesting to note that the figure on the podium, speaking into the barrage of microphones, is often, in fact, framed by lavish bouquets of flowers, conferring a spurious aura of civilisation and moral dignity onto the proceedings. To adapt his own terminology about reading photographs, the viewer is perhaps invited to 'unlock' the 'reality' of modern life, the glimpse that such pictures provide, through the 'slight remove from fact' in a pictorial transformation, of the ferocious will to power and the sadistic violence that was barely concealed beneath the veneer of the state apparatus, political theatre and ritualistic behaviour that pervaded public life in Nazi Germany. But such readings can easily become too reductive. Moreover neither the victim or aggressor categories subsume the thoroughly ambiguous imagery of pictures like *Man Standing*, the right hand panel of the triptych, *Figure in a Landscape* and *Figure Getting out of a Car* – even though the first and last were at some level based on photographs of Hitler himself!

Collectively, Bacon's pictures from this period are best viewed as poetic generalisations of the feelings of fear and tragic despair prompted by current events, as projections of a state of mind. That mentality was dominated by a conviction that 'contemporary politics' and 'the human condition' were in fact two sides of the same coin, rather than the antitheses that we might wish, quite anachronistically, to read back onto the 1940s. On one occasion Bacon commented: 'I feel that people of my generation cannot really imagine human life without war'.[96] We might equally take the case of George Orwell, slightly older than Bacon but exactly the same age as Sutherland. In his review in 1940 of the current literary scene ('Inside the Whale'), Orwell noted that 'the war of 1914–18 was only a heightened moment in an almost continuous crisis'.[97] Likewise, the coming conflict 'will either last several years, or it will end the inconclusively and prepare the way for yet another war which will do the job once and for all . . . Almost certainly we are moving into an age of totalitarian dictatorships . . . The autonomous individual is going to be stamped out of existence . . . As for the writer he is sitting on a melting iceberg, a hangover from the bourgeois age, as surely doomed as the hippopotamus.'[98] Bacon undoubtedly shared this pessimistic, apocalyptic outlook. He was inclined, for instance, to describe how his earlier experiences in Ireland and Berlin had, so to speak, prepared him for the horrors of the Second World War: 'I could say, perhaps, I have been accustomed to always living through forms of violence – which may or may not have an effect upon one, but I think it probably does'.[99] For the last several decades, and for the foreseeable future, politics and war were inextricable, and to that extent the violence of war impinged on private life and imagination, his own included. The outlook informing Bacon's wartime paintings may be inferred, I suggest, from a fascinating passage in a letter to Sonia Orwell, widow of George, dating from December 1954. The context was an idea for an experimental, quasi-autobiographical book that Orwell was evidently encouraging, and which she and another woman friend had clearly discussed with Bacon. Nothing came of the idea, but Bacon's thoughts merit quotation at length, since they encapsulate his sense of the absolute interdependence of external events and inner life. The book would comprise:

> a kind of very personal history of what has happened since I can remember anything also the early blurred remembrance of childhood. On thinking about the book done from quotations it would be wonderful but I feel I should have to work with somebody for that. . . . I want to paint not hunt for newspaper cuttings . . . If I did the history I would like to do it with photographs and have already got through collecting them over years but I think a sort of life story which sees underneath of the events of the last 40 years so that you

> would not know whether it was imagination or fact is what I could do as the photographs themselves of events could be distorted into a personal private meaning or in fact it could be a book about the history of the past 40 years but so interlocked with what one imagines has happened and what one believes has happened from the records we know of but interlocked with history exerted through that time perhaps we could make something nearer to facts truer – and more exciting as though one was seeing the story of one's time for the first time . . . tell her there will be a lot of crime in it in fact I don't know how there will be much else.[100]

The photographs' density of suggestion was what Bacon wanted from his paintings, for himself and his audience. Indeed, this was presumably the quality that Bacon valued both in the *Three Studies*, to the extent that it was the first picture for eight years that he was willing to exhibit, and in the subsequent works that he chose to make public. Conversely, he may have regarded the pictures he abandoned or reworked as less successful because the association with familiar photographic imagery were too obvious or unassimilated, preventing a more radical ambiguity and open-endedness.

TRAGEDY RECURS

Bacon's artistic ambition was to tread a tightrope between conveying the texture of current wartime sensations and experiences, and suggesting deeper, more universal patterns of human behaviour that were once again making themselves manifest. Bacon's means to this end included not just the radical transformation of 'found' photographic imagery, but also the insertion into the *Three Studies* and its successors of references to more universal or mythic themes, relating in particular to classical Greek tragedy and the Passion of Jesus Christ. These were preoccupations that Bacon shared with Sutherland. Indeed, the two painters articulated an attitude that was widely diffused within contemporary British culture. For many, a key point of departure was a celebrated passage in T. S. Eliot's 1923 essay responding to the appearance of James Joyce's *Ulysses*:

> In using the myth, in manipulating a continuous parallel between contemporaneity and antiquity, Mr. Joyce is pursuing a method which others must pursue after him . . . It is simply a way of controlling, of ordering, of giving a shape and a significance to the immense panorama of futility and anarchy which is contemporary history. It is a method already adumbrated by Mr. Years, and of the need for which I believe Mr. Yeats to have been the first contemporary to be conscious . . . Psychology . . . , ethnology, and *The Golden Bough* have concurred to make possible what was impossible even a few years ago. Instead of narrative method, we may now use the mythical method. It is, I believe, a step towards making the modern world possible for art.[101]

As in *Ulysses* itself, one possible elaboration of Eliot's 'mythical method' was his recuperation of the classical inheritance. During the Second World War, one encounters several manifestations of this impulse, including *The Rescue. A Melodrama for Broadcasting based on Homer's Odyssey*, performed on BBC radio in November 1943. The writer was Edward Sackville-West, whose concurrent project was the Penguin Modern Masters volume on Sutherland, while the orchestral score was composed by Benjamin Britten. The subsequent book included a little-known series of illustrations by Henry Moore.[102] Another instance of British wartime classicism was *The Unquiet Grave*, published anonymously in 1944 by Cyril Connolly in the persona of Palinurus, the ill-fated pilot of Aeneas. As 'a war-book', preaching the redemption of a ghastly present through memory and immersion in great European, especially French literature, *The Unquiet Grave* provides rich insight into the strategies for mental and cultural survival that prevailed within the literary sub-culture around *Horizon*. In the context of the present study, it is worth noting Connolly's remark that Palinurus 'wished to proclaim his faith in the unity and continuity of Western culture in its moment of crisis. He chose his quotations to illustrate how we have gone on thinking the same things since the days of the ancient Greeks, how the present can always be illuminated by the past.'[103]

Sutherland's *Chimère* (1946; pl. 11) provides a visual parallel to such concerns. The sinister, composite creature in the picture refers to the classical chimera, a terrible monster with a dragon's tail, the body of a lion and a goat's head sprouting from its back, which was eventually fought and killed by the hero Bellepheron. However, Sutherland's use of the French term presumably establishes a reference to the poetry of the French romantic Gérard de Nerval, and his sonnet sequence 'Les Chimères'. Interestingly, de Nerval's imagery finds a direct echo in Gascoyne's poem 'The Fortress', included in *Poems 1937–42*, which foreshadows not just the brooding tone but also the title of Sutherland's subsequent painting:

> A heaving fortress built up like a breast
> Exposed like a huge breast high on its rock.
> Streaming with milky brightness, the domed top
> Wreathed in radiant rainbow cloud.
>
> The Shock
> Of vision stuns the hovering eye, which cannot see
> What caverns of deep blood those white walls hide,
> Concealing ever rampant underneath
> The dark chimera Death-in-Life
> Defending Life from death.[104]

During the war, there was in fact considerable interest in *Horizon* circles in the work of the early nineteenth-century French poet. As 'the champion of the anarchic life of impulse against the forces of order and restraint', Nerval seemed a strikingly relevant and contemporary figure, whose explorations of extreme states of mind, verging on insanity, were seen as foreshadowing symbolism and surrealism.[105] At any rate, one can imagine Sutherland responding enthusiastically to poetry described by Norman Cohn in a 1944 issue of *Horizon*: 'External objects are perceived as though for the first time, in a new and often strangely beautiful light. Nerval has described how it came to him, a subtle modification of the very texture of experience: ". . . tout dans la nature prenait les aspects nouveaux, et les voix secretes sortaient de la plante, de l'arbre, des animaux, des plus humbles insects, pour m'avertir et m'encourager." '[106] The same passage was cited at length in Connolly's *The Unquiet Grave*.[107] In *Les Chimères*, an affirmative, pantheistic outlook is presented in the third section, the 'Golden Verses'. The two preceding groups of poems explore a range of cultural references that echo preoccupations in wartime Britain that have already been discussed here. The first comprises apparitions in classical times and settings of the poet's lost beloved. The second describes Christ's despair and agony in anticipation of his crucifixion, and in response to his betrayal by God and man – it is out of pity for 'the madman' that Pilate decides to put him out of his misery. The conjunction of themes is especially interesting in relation to Sutherland's concurrent work in 1946 on *Chimère* and the Northampton *Crucifixion*.

Tragedy appeared to be the most potent literary tradition stemming from classical antiquity, given present circumstances. During the course of this discussion, the notion of the tragic has been encountered as deployed independently by, for instance, Sutherland, David Gascoyne, Eric Newton, John Piper and Stephen Spender. Their usage was in a sense firmly rooted; an interest in the possibility of reinventing this most ancient literary mode can be traced back at least as far as Nietzsche's *The Birth of Tragedy*, a widely read text by a philosopher who greatly appealed to Bacon.[108] All manner of subsequent writers had aspired to create their own versions of a tragic aesthetic in the media of drama or fiction.[109] In 1940 George Orwell described the 'pessimism of outlook' which had characterised the generation of Joyce, Eliot, Lawrence and so forth: 'If the keynote of the Georgian poets was "beauty of Nature", the keynote of the post-war writers would be "tragic sense of life" '.[110] Such an impulse understandably acquired momentum during the Second World War, when cultural discourse is strikingly replete with references to the tragic.

The ingredients for a profound sense of tragedy, such as widespread suffering, senseless violence and random destruction, were present in abundance during the war years. The pervasive and overwhelming sense that evil forces were in the ascendant ignited a sustained engagement with the form of artistic expression that speaks of 'the unalterable bias toward inhumanity and destruction in the drift of the world'.[111] Indeed, the literary historian Samuel Hynes has argued that a new mood is evident during the twelve months or so following autumn 1938: 'The sense of crisis, of powerful and active evil at work in the world, dominated consciousness in this, the last full year of peace, and appeared everywhere in the written record of those days – in poems and novels as well as in private letters and *Times* leaders.'[112] He cites as an example the critic Michael Robert's essay 'The Tragic Way', which epitomised how, during the last five years, 'the revolutionary view had come to seem, for most writers, untenable, and the tragic view one that history and observation confirmed.' Likewise, the ageing novelist E. M. Forster registered the current atmosphere of hope abandoned: 'there is nothing disgraceful in despair. In 1938–9 the more despair a man can take on board without sinking the more completely he is alive'.[113] During the years of actual military conflict, tragedy seemed all the more compelling as a means to encapsulate the contemporary condition of man. Commentators often remarked that wider circumstances were prompting writers and artists to manifest a 'tragic sense', a phrase coined in 1942 by John Lehmann, who as editor of *Penguin New Writing* played a key role in the wartime literary world.[114] The poet Roy Fuller articulated this sense the following November, having just returned to London from service as an RAF radar technician in East Africa:

> Beyond the word, the chosen images,
> Painful and moving as they are, I feel
> Unutterably the epoch's tragedies,
> Besides which this scene's cruelties are real
> But hopelessly inadequate[115]

Then in 1944 Kathleen Raine explains, for the benefit of a popular readership, why exactly it was that 'beautiful imagery' had disappeared from modern verse:

> To contemplate sensuous beauty in moods of mental stress and conflict and sorrow, is unbearably painful. In a tormented age, art has to transform the obsessive ugliness, not to offer the mirage of pleasure to suffering men . . . The necessity to heal the wounds of life by raising ugliness that has somehow to be endured, to the state of beauty, is as old as poetry . . . Tragedy recurs again and again as the theme of all art; the Christian art of Christ crucified; Greek tragedy, Shakespeare, Dostoyevski; Rilke's poetry of death, so terribly akin to the false mysticism with which the Nazi soldiers are driven in herds to the battlefields.[116]

This comment offers a precise distillation of the sensibility of the moment. In particular, Raine's synoptic concept of tragedy, embracing both Christian and ancient Greek narrative traditions, as well as more recent literary manifestations, offers a striking parallel to the thought processes of Bacon and Sutherland during the war years.

The period witnessed an international resurgence of interest in classical tragedy, especially in the creations of Aeschylus, the primal origin of the genre. The contemporary resonance of Aeschylus was asserted by Gilbert Murray, the celebrated Oxford classicist, in *Aeschylus: The Creator of Tragedy* (1940), a study that made a considerable impact on the New York avant-garde painter Mark Rothko.[117] An impulse to devise new variants on the great *Oresteia* dramas is apparent not only in T. S. Eliot's *The Family Reunion*, a play first performed in London in 1939, but also in *Les Mouches (The Flies)* by Jean-Paul Sartre, which was staged for the first time in Paris in 1943. Against this backdrop, it is not, therefore, surprising to find that a particular point of affinity between Bacon and Sutherland was their immersion in the work of Aeschylus. Doubtless, both men read the actual plays in translation, such as the new and more idiomatic versions produced between the wars by Murray, and they might perhaps have seen them performed. In each case, however, their assimilation of Aeschylean imagery was mediated by a specific critical commentary, namely W. B. Stanford's *Aeschylus in his Style*, a book whose appearance in 1942 could hardly have been more timely. Stanford's volume was not not one to be encountered casually, and the two artists' awareness of it provides striking evidence that they moved within sophisticated literary milieux.

Sutherland made frequent references to Aeschylus in statements about his work, but the evidence for the influence of Stanford's book comes from Robert Melville's account of a visit to the artist's Kent studio in 1952:

> A small book was lying on one of the work-tables. 'I wondered if you had read it,' Sutherland said. 'The commentary on personifying and synaesthetic images is absorbing. It's not unconnected with what I am attempting in my pictures.' It was *Aeschylus in his Style* by Professor W. B. Stanford of Dublin University.
>
> Several passages had been marked in red pencil. I started to read a verse quotation that was so marked, but was stopped by the phrase, *brightness from an ancient vine*, for it perfectly described the paintings of Vine Pergolas that were in Sutherland's last exhibition.
>
> . . . I found this passage marked in red: 'Aeschylus is outstanding in the boldness and vividness of his personifying metaphors. By them he creates a new kind of world in which grief can bite, fire and water are conspirators, the heart can wear a black robe . . .' In another passage he quotes an amazing line which is both personifying and synaesthetic image; a line which Sutherland had already pointed out to me: 'The reek of human blood smiles out at me' . . .
>
> Sutherland sometimes extends the range of an object by means of a pictorial parallel with a fully-developed Aeschylian metaphor, as when the Crown of Thorns, becoming a Thorn Head, assumes the attributes of a mocker, and its harmfulness laughs.[118]

It is unclear when Sutherland became aware of, or acquired, Stanford's book. Melville's account of the marked passages indicates that Sutherland made highly selective use of what is after all a specialist academic study, with extended technical analyses of Aeschylus' use of language which for the most part cite the classical texts only in the Greek original – a daunting prospect even if Sutherland had acquired 'an aptitude and liking for Latin and Greek' while at school.[119] It is clear that the marked passages that Melville quoted would have struck a chord with Sutherland. According to Stanford, 'Greek poetry in general abounds in personification, a sign partly of an animistic attitude to nature, and partly of an all-pervading anthropocentrism.'[120] In his monograph of 1944, Edward Sackville-West had discussed Sutherland's work in very similar terms, noting his rediscovery of the pantheistic vision underlying the religions 'of primitive people – of Homeric Greece in especial':

> Look at those stooks of corn: they are crouching soldiers. Look again, and they have turned back into quiet piles of folded stalks. Look at that gnarled oak, dead these hundred years:

> it is a tiger clawing the ground; at the *Metal Container pouring molten iron*: it is a mouth agape in rage. The double image is perfect, complete: these are the gods which surround us.[121]

From such a passage, and the evidence of a project like *The Rescue*, one might well gain a sense of Sackville-West's own engagement with classical literature, raising the possibility that he and Sutherland had talked about Stanford's book, and that it was through such contacts that Sutherland and perhaps Bacon too first became aware of *Aeschylus in his Style*.

It is well known that, for Bacon, Greek tragedy, and the work of Aeschlyus in particular, were powerful sources of inspiration. Towards the end of his life, he could still remark: 'I re-read Aeschylus all the time'.[122] That obsession was clearly in place by the 1940s. A copy of the 1946 edition of Gilbert Murray's translations of the *Oresteia* was unearthed in Bacon's studio after the artist's death.[123] Moreover, Bacon was already described as an avid reader of the ancient Greek tragedies in a review of his 1950 Hanover Gallery show. This text clearly reflects conversations with the artist, as well as Bacon's characteristic reflex reaction against the caricatured view of his work as mere melodramatic illustration of the human condition:

> The artist has told me that his motives are purely aesthetic. That is his obsession is with formal qualities, with forms at once concrete and dissolving, with the substance and texture of pigment, with the belief that every stroke of paint laid down ought to be a self-sufficient expression of the artist's idea. His reading, especially of Greek Tragedy, has influenced his attitude and inevitably shaped his patterns; but he would have us judge his paintings simply as works of art without seeking to read into them a symbolism never consciously premeditated.[124]

Several studies have noted the importance that Stanford's *Aeschylus in his Style* also possessed for Bacon, an inspiration that the artist readily acknowledged.[125] There is, once again, no evidence to indicate how or when Bacon first encountered the book, and whether it was he or Sutherland who conveyed their excitement to the other. There is no copy amongst the books found in Bacon's studio, but this does not mean he did not possess one at some point. It is known that Bacon too was especially taken with 'The reek of human blood smiles out at me', Stanford's new translation of a line from *The Eumenides*.[126] According to Sylvester, this single, haunting image formed the 'essential subject-matter' of the *Three Studies* triptych.[127] Stanford himself had commented upon the resonant ambiguity of the 'synaesthetic metaphor . . . The fact that the verb implies cheerfulness as well as brightness adds a peculiar grimness'.[128] Aside from particular verbal images, what inspiration might Bacon have derived from *Aeschylus in his Style*? Given Bacon's known fondness for medical illustrations, such as Clark's *Positioning in Radiography*, it is interesting to note that Stanford includes a long section on Aeschylus's use of medical terms and images: 'In medical science he found analogies and partial explanations for the physical foulness and destructiveness of sin, and in it he found help in trying to comprehend his own tangled and deeply felt emotions'.[129] But, for Bacon,

Aeschylus primarily suggested an artistic idiom fusing formal, elevated diction with an intense physicality and 'daring imagery sometimes bordering on the grotesque' that subverts our expectation of classical perfection, and contributes to the realisation of an unremittingly tragic tone.[130] Both Bacon and Sutherland would doubtless have identified with Stanford's description of the supreme gift of 'free imagination' on which Aeschylus could draw:

> In his work the world of appearances is constantly re-created in new perspectives and new relations by some unexpected, remote, but satisfying and true, interpretative image. Events are given new shades of colour, new depth or height, new affinities and relevance, in the jostling process of his imagination, where fact and fantasy, act and symbol, person and personification, freely associate.[131]

Indeed, Stanford's account was underpinned by a strong sense of the affinity of tone and method between the Oresteia and contemporary literature, and between Aeschylus and the contemporary conception of the artist. He argued that Aeschylus's 'obscurity' was 'chiefly the effect of his own intensely emotional spirit', and that 'one is more aware of the subconscious in Aeschylus than in most Greek poets': 'His presentation of the Eumenides, for example, is full of dark groans, maledictions and strange atavistic cruelties.'[132] Aeschylus, he writes, 'uses extraordinarily violent imagery to express the inner effects of emotion'.[133] For Stanford, the contemporaneity of the ancient tragedian's work was a product of parallel historical circumstances:

> the poets of the 1930s and 1940s are nearer Aeschylus in their obscurities and ambiguities . . . Political and social change made post-1918 Europe much more like Post-Peristratid Athens . . . The poets of today are obscure because they are trying to express . . . the outer chaos of twentieth-century civilisation and the inner spiritual chaos of their own minds.[134]

Aeschylus wished 'to emphasise the palpable, physical loathesomeness of sin', a 'sense of intense disgust and nausea' that Stanford thought T. S. Eliot had also captured in his *Family Reunion*.[135] One might argue that the work of Bacon and Sutherland was equally intended to convey a profound sense of revulsion in the face of the violence and 'spiritual chaos' that was now even more palpable.

One could hardly improve upon 'palpable, physical loathsomeness' as a description of Bacon's *Three Studies* triptych. Some commentators have focused on the possible impact that specific images, extracted from their wider narrative context in Stanford's book, may have had upon Bacon. Peppiatt compares another image that Bacon particularly cherished in Stanford's book, of 'Clytemnestra brooding like a hen over her sorrow', to the 'contained malevolence' of the left-hand figure of the *Three Studies*.[136] But the most telling sign of his interest in Aeschylus was Bacon's later comment that the components of the 1944 triptych, despite the Crucifixion reference in the title, were in fact 'sketches for the Eumenides (the Greek Furies)', as featured in Aeschylus's enactment of the tragedy of Orestes.[137] The repugnant and bestial aspects of Bacon's three painted creatures have encouraged comparisons with the priestess Pythia's vivid account, near the start of *The Eumenides*, of the terrifying vision of the Furies that had greeted her when she entered the Temple of Apollo, and encountered not merely a bloody Orestes praying at the altar:

> Around him, on the stone benches,
> Strange sleeping creatures.
> I would call them women but they are not women.
> Gorgon-faced – yet not Gorgons.
> Black, like the rags of soot that hang in a chimney,
> Like bats, yet wingless.
> Each of their faces a mess of weeping ulcers –
> The eyes, the mouth, ulcers.
> Their bodies exhale
> A stench like maggoty corpses.
> Their cloaks are saturated and stained
> With their own putrescence
> That oozes from them, into the stones.
> Who are they? What are they?
> Some other kind – inhuman.
> Monsters from a different world
> To be cursed by God and men.[138]

Equally, we might recall Apollo's own subsequent speech expelling the Furies from the temple:

> You do not belong here –
> These walls are defiled by your presence.
> You belong in the dungeon
> Furnished for torturers,
> The den of castration, mutilation,
> Flaying, dismemberment, impalement –
> That is your banqueting hall.
> Where eyes are extracted, windpipes drawn,
> Livers and bowels shaken onto the floor,
> Heads twisted from shoulders –
> That is your study.
> The chamber of screams is your resting place[139]

Such comparisons are certainly compelling, and suggest that, on one level, Bacon may have seen his three monstrous, semi-human beings as latter-day, pictorial equivalents to Aeschylus's repugnant brood, the agents of divine retribution.

Bacon's preoccupation with the theme of the Eumenides is very likely to have been triggered, or at any rate reinforced, by Eliot's adaptation of the Oresteia in *The Family Reunion*, which Bacon evidently saw several times and considered to be the best of Eliot's plays.[140] Eliot's inspiration is perhaps implicit in Bacon's use of Eumenides to describe the dark agents of fate and retribution; in the Aeschylus originals, the Furies are actually called the Erinyes until the last play in the Oresteia trilogy, when they are persuaded by Athena to become the more benign Eumenides.[141] The essential significance of *The Family Reunion* for Bacon was Eliot's demonstration that classical Greek tragedy could still be reinterpreted in a modern idiom, and in the light of current, post-Freudian preoccupations. The play was first conceived in 1936, and the following year Eliot reported that it would be a melancholy play, perhaps the most pessimistic thing he had ever written.[142] By March 1939, when *The Family Reunion* was first performed, the grounds for pessimism were far stronger. Critics were generally hostile to the Aeschylean undertone of the play, which is set in an English country house in the present day, and in particular to the inclusion of so arcane and undramatic a device as the Eumenides. Bacon, for his part, is likely to have sympathised with the reviewer who defended Eliot and asserted the contemporary resonance of this latest work: 'For us too, horror grows of overshadowing disaster . . . At a time like the present, in a world where . . . the air is dark with the wings of curses coming home to roost, surely the myth of the Eumenides – dread pursuers that avenge not private but communal crime – far from being academic has dreadful relevance'.[143] Conversely, the visual affinities with Aeschylus's descriptions do not extend to Eliot's play, where the Eumenides have no lines, and indeed are only visible to Harry, Lord Monchensey, the poignant Orestes figure in the drama, as well as to the audience. In the original production, starring Michael Redgrave as Harry, they made brief appearances, on the other side of the drawing room window, dressed in ordinary clothes. The fact that they were three is the only obvious point of contact with Bacon's pictorial imagery. In Eliot's play, it is clear that the horror of the Eumenides is essentially psychological. As 'the sleepless hunters', they symbolise the acute pain and guilt that Harry feels at having murdered his wife, by pushing her off an ocean liner in what everyone else believed was a terrible accident. He now confides in his family, only to learn in conversation with his Aunt Agatha that his own father, whom he had barely known, had planned to murder his mother. He comes to realise that it was, in fact, the inheritance of a family curse that had led him to imagine he had killed his wife. This insight allows Harry to confront his demons, and to reconcile himself to his destiny:

> Now I see
> I have been wounded in a war of phantoms,
> Not by human beings – they have no more power than I.
> The things I thought were real are shadows, and the real
> Are what I thought were private shadows. O that awful privacy
> Of the insane mind! Now I can live in public.
> Liberty is a different kind of pain from prison.[144]

The ultimately redemptive structure of Aeschylus's *The Eumenides* and Eliot's variation on the theme are countered not only by the horrifying impact of Bacon's figure style, but also by the potential narrative suggestions of the *Three Studies*. To use the term narrative may seem contentious in connection with a work by Bacon. The artist persistently asserted his strong aversion to any such interpretations as they tended to oversimplify and constrict meaning within paintings that he wanted to remain open to diverse readings.[145] During the period in which he was recording the interviews with Sylvester and working on his numerous later triptychs, Bacon in fact described this particular format as a solution to the problem of introducing more than one figure, while avoiding narrative: 'the moment there are several figures – at any rate several, figures on the same canvas – the story begins to be elaborated, the boredom sets in; the story talks louder than the paint'.[146] Yet Bacon also acknowledged that his interest in the triptych format related to his habit of visualizing images in series or sequences: 'I see every image all the time in a shifting way and almost in shifting sequences.'[147] He remarked: 'I suppose I could go on long beyond the triptych and do five or six together, but I find the triptych is a more balanced unit'.[148] From the perspective of the beholder, there is a strong temptation to look for narrative sequence even when one is faced by three distinct but interconnected images of single figures.

Contemplating the *Three Studies*, the viewer encounters continuities between the three component images, but also significant shifts of tone. The left-hand, most emphatically human, creature, with its exposed and downwardly inclined neck, seems to convey states of mind such as vulnerability, resignation, submission, and despair. The central image is plainly concerned with pain and raw suffering. As we have seen, the bestial hybrid to the right of the triptych emits a scream of anguish, which is also a bloodthirsty howl or roar. The visual logic of the arrangement is one of compositional symmetry, but this is counterpointed by contrasts of expressive effect between the two outer 'wings'. Such basic observations may then lead one to discern narrative implications. The viewer might take the view that he or she is confronted by an image in the centre of the triptych that presents unbearable human pain, flanked by two opposed responses to such a reality or prospect, either stoic resignation or violence. However, in looking at pictures, as in deciphering text, we automatically tend to read from left to right, a habit which Marius Maxwell exploited in his triptych of elephant photographs, a possible inspiration for Bacon, showing the unfolding of a dramatic and, so to speak, emotional narrative (pl. 40). In interpreting the Bacon we might plausibly construct a sequence progressing from weakness and submission, through to the pain inflicted upon the victim, and finally to the shedding of humanity and the blind thirst for revenge.[149] The repeated motif of the long tubular neck could even be taken to imply that we are witnessing successive manifestations, or metamorphoses, of a single life form. We may also notice that the simple perspectival constructions in the three panels do not add up to a single, continuous space, but rather appear to project the same interior space viewed, respectively, from closer to the left wall, dead centre, and then nearer to the right wall. Compositional symmetry, again, was doubtless a motivation, but the effect is also to imply a mobile observer, moving through space, from left to right, and therefore through time, a progression that tends to reinforce the emotional narrative described.

On the basis of such readings, the spectator is perhaps invited to consider the dynamics of human behaviour embodied allegorically in the figures of the furies and in the mechanics of divine retribution in Greek tragedy, but also informing actions much closer to home.

40 Marius Maxwell, plate from *Stalking Big Game with a Camera in Equatorial Africa* (1925).

In the Choephori, the second play in the Oresteia trilogy, the chorus of slave women of Argos offer the following reassurance to Electra, in the wake of the murders of Clytemnestra and Aegisthus:

Be brave. Blood of the murdered
Cries from the earth for blood.
The gods have fixed that law.
The Furies, screaming for blood,
Rise like miasma
From the fallen blood.
Pain creates pain, and ruin ruin.[150]

The same fundamental principle is applied to the contemporary wartime world in Auden's *September 1, 1939*, a poem that Bacon is likely to have known. Against a backdrop of collective despair – 'Waves of anger and fear/Circulate over the bright/And darkened lands of the earth/Obsessing our private lives' – Auden reflects on the roots of the present crisis in German history, both in the remote past and, by implication, in the wake of the First World War and the Treaty of Versailles:

Accurate scholarship can
Unearth the whole offence
From Luther until now
That has driven a culture mad,
Find what occurred at Linz,

What huge imago made
A psychopathic god:
I and the public know
What all children learn,
Those to whom evil is done
Do evil in return.[151]

These literary associations might suggest that when Bacon stated that the *Three Studies* were really a representation of the Eumenides, he did not simply mean that his monstrous imaginings were a latter-day depiction of the Furies, participants in Aeschylus's great drama of the same name. It is more likely, in the age of Freud and Jung, that Bacon conceived the furies as a symbol for an archetypal psychological mechanism, the process whereby suffering received is transmuted into aggression inflicted.

For Bacon and his contemporaries, then, Eliot's 'mythical method' came to provide not only a modernist artistic strategy but also a means of comprehending, and somehow dealing with, the descent into horror in the contemporary world. An example of this reflex outside artistic creativity is provided by Alan Moorehead's report on visiting Belsen, which appeared in *Horizon* in July 1945. Amidst a detailed account of the appalling scenes that he had witnessed in Germany, Moorehead articulated the same tendency as demonstrated by the work of Sutherland and Bacon to seek to understand the horrors of the present in relation to timeless or universal features of the human condition:

> It was all like a journey down to some Dantesque pit, leprous and frightening. And now that one emerged into the light again, one's first coherent reactions were not of disgust or anger or even, I think, of pity. Something else filled the mind, a frantic desire to ask: 'Why? Why? Why? Why had it happened?' With all one's soul one felt 'This is not war. Nor is it anything to do with here and now, with this one place and this one moment. This is timeless and the whole world and all mankind is involved in it. This touches me and I am responsible. Why has it happened? How did we let it happen?[152]

ON THE CROSS TREE NOW

Classical tragedy was not the only cultural resource that Sutherland and Bacon drew upon during the latter stages of the war. A more overt connection was their engagement with the imagery of Christ's Passion, and especially with the theme of the Crucifixion. It was, of course, under the title *Three Studies for Figures at the Base of a Crucifixion* that Bacon exhibited his seminal triptych in April 1945, even if the work's 'real subject' may have been, as he later asserted, the Eumenides. Sutherland's exactly parallel immersion in the theme of the Crucifixion resulted in his extensive *Thorn Tree* and *Thorn Head* series, with their metaphorical allusions to Christian imagery, and above all in his monumental altarpiece for St Matthew's church in Northampton (1946). Given their close contacts, one may infer that the two painters discussed the resonance of such subject matter in wartime circumstances. It is impossible of course to determine how far the one artist may have triggered the other's use of Crucifixion imagery at this stage, as opposed to their both responding to a preoccupation that was very much 'in the air'.

From early on in the Second World War, we encounter both in British culture and internationally a tendency to employ the theme as a commentary on the murderous oppressiveness of an ascendant fascism.[153] A celebrated poem by Edith Sitwell opened:

> Still falls the Rain –
> Dark as the world of man, black as our loss –
> Blind as the nineteen hundred and forty nails
> Upon the Cross.[154]

Equally, the impulse to paint 'the execution of Christ as a scene from contemporary life' is evident simultaneously in the work of the Italian leftist Renato Guttoso and the American Regionalist Thomas Hart Benton.[155] When the suggestion arose that he might work for the War Artists Advisory Committee, the English painter Stanley Spencer proposed painting a large allegorical Crucifixion, in which the sufferings of Christ would be accompanied by scenes drawn from the present conflict, such as the Nazi forces overrunning Poland.[156] The subject re-emerged in a more conventional form in the wartime work of Roy de Maistre, whom we have encountered as a friend of Sutherland and, especially, Bacon in the 1930s.[157] It is symptomatic of the prevalence of the theme that Crucifixion imagery should have come to the fore in the work of one artist, Bacon, who was a militant atheist, and of another, Sutherland, who was a committed Roman Catholic, but had not previously seen fit to channel his private spiritual beliefs into his art in so direct a fashion. Indeed, Stephen Spender later identified a 'religious mood' as one of the dominant characteristic of British culture during the war years, a mood 'compounded of seriousness through constant confrontation with death and destruction, of the sense of belonging to a community where all classes were drawn together in sympathy, of the phoenix-like rebirth of the English past from the ashes of burning cities, and of awe at the terror and grandeur of history endured'.[158] Yet the general emphasis in this wartime religiosity seems to have been less upon the possibility of future redemption than on the current horror and tragedy of the human condition. This sombre outlook was captured by the ageing Wyndham Lewis, who at the beginning of the war had fled from London to Canada, the setting in January 1943 for his lecture on 'Religious Experience and Contemporary Art'. Lewis sought to explain the current fascination in the art world with the gloomy strain of Catholic mysticism represented by the work of Georges Rouault:

> although I do not believe the period produces the outlook, in the case of the artist, necessarily, yet it may cause him to find favour with his contemporaries. Among the many sorts

41 Matthaus Grünewald, *Crucifixion*, from the Isenheim Altarpiece, *c.*1515, oil on wood, 269 × 307 cm, Musée d'Unterlinden, Colmar.

> of artists existing . . . we tend to select the one who corresponds to our mood.
>
> . . . the general complexion of the mundane landscape is, in these forties of the twentieth-century, uncommonly dark and uninviting. So much suffering, whichever way we turn our eyes, darkens – whatever the outcome – all our spirits.[159]

Within the framework of this desolate world-view, it became possible to see the inheritance of antiquity and the biblical narrative of Christ as fundamentally compatible rather than divergent.[160] The tragic mode in literature may have been rooted in classical drama, but no narrative seemed more inherently tragic in its human and spiritual connotations than Christ's Passion. At any rate, Kathleen Raine found no difficulty, as has been seen, in assimilating classical drama and Christ's Passion into a broad category of tragic expression. Sutherland himself recalled shortly afterwards that 'the 'dust drinks up the blood' and 'the reek of human blood smiles out at me' of Aeschylus' had been on his mind, as well as actual wartime atrocities, when he was developing his 1946 Crucifixion altarpiece.[161] Likewise, Robert Melville could readily describe Sutherland's treatment of the *Thorn Head* image, with its Christian connotations, as an Aeschylean metaphor. One might even argue that for visual artists, this poignant strand of Christian imagery formed a comparable resource to the tragic dramas of antiquity for successive generations of writers. Whereas the dramas of classical Athens were the archetypal tragic *narratives*, the Crucifixion was the quintessential tragic *image*.

By extension, one might find a certain parallel in the positions accorded to Aeschylus, as the original and most powerful of literary tragedians, and to the late medieval German painter Matthias Grünewald, whose pictures offered the most compelling prototype for an essentially tragic interpretation of the Crucifixion theme (pl. 41). Grünewald's harrowing renditions, above all in the *Isenheim Altarpiece* in Colmar, provided the inspiration for many later artists and writers who sought to reinterpret the Crucifixion in mythic or secular terms, as a symbol of man's tragic condition and capacity for violent cruelty to his fellows, in contrast to the more serene promise of salvation inherent in Italianate devotional imagery.[162] The beginnings of a latter-day Grünewaldian tradition have been traced from the late nineteenth-century through to expressionism and the work of artists active in the period of the Great War, such as Max Beckmann, who clearly projected the sufferings of Christ as the paradigm for the sufferings of the innocent multitude in the present.[163] The Isenheim altarpiece gained renewed currency in reproduction as a result of the publication in 1936 of a superbly illustrated folio devoted to the work under the imprint of *Cahiers d'Art*, featuring numerous details in black and white of the most telling manifestations of the artist's inventiveness and expressive power.[164] The introductory essay by Christian Zervos, who also edited the highly influential journal and had begun in 1932 to publish his great *catalogue raisonné* of the work of Picasso, emphasised how much the Isenheim altarpiece meant to contemporary artists and poets, and how strong a chord it struck with current anxieties.[165] Picasso's own immersion in Grünewald, as witnessed by his extensive series of drawn variants on the Isenheim altarpiece that were reproduced in 1933 in *Minotaure*, was doubtless a stimulus to Zervos, who dedicated his study to the most prestigious of living painters and to the poet Paul Eluard. The timely appearance of the folio assured the availability of Grünewald's imagery for artists and writers active during the period leading up to and including the Second World War. In October 1938, for example, at the time of the Munich crisis, Herbert Read interpreted Picasso's *Guernica* as a successor to the Isenheim altarpiece, a surrogate altarpiece for an age without communal religious faith: 'It is the modern Calvary, the agony in the bomb shattered ruins of human tenderness and frailty. It is a religious picture, painted, not with the same kind, but with the same degree of fervour that inspired Grünewald and the Master of the Avignon Pieta, Van Eyck and Bellini.'[166]

During the Second World War, works such as the Isenheim altarpiece provided the point of departure for a more direct revival of traditional religious imagery. That Grünewald was Sutherland's 'favourite painter' is perhaps all too apparent from the Northampton altarpiece. It was here that Sutherland most explicitly appropriated Grünewald's style and imagery, to the point of virtual pastiche in the view of some commentators at the time.[167] However, this enthusiasm can be traced back at least until the late 1930s, and perhaps to an encounter with the Zervos volume. At any rate, the impact of Grünewald seems already to be apparent in *Gorse on Sea Wall* (1939; pl. III), where the writhing finger-like shapes that Sutherland projected into the form of the root may be seen as a landscape variant on the extraordinarily expressive treatment of the hands of both Christ and Mary Magdalene in the altarpiece.[168]

42 Matthaus Grünewald, *Christ Bearing the Cross*, 1523/4, oil on wood, Kunsthalle, Karlsruhe (detail).

43 FAR RIGHT Matthaus Grünewald, *Mocking of Christ*, 1504/5, oil on panel, 109 × 73.5 cm, Alte Pinakothek, Munich.

Bacon clearly shared Sutherland's admiration for the work of Grünewald. We know from the Hunter montage that Bacon valued the photograph of Grünewald's Karlsruhe *Christ Bearing the Cross* that was in his studio.[169] Moreover, the 1944 triptych incorporates several echoes of Grünewald. The grotesque, kneeling figure to the right-hand side of the Karlsruhe painting, with his obscenely prominent ear, was perhaps one point of departure for the menacing, but also agonized, creature in the right-hand panel of the *Three Studies* triptych (pl. 42). The bandaged head in the central panel is almost certainly based on the image of Christ's head in the Munich *Mocking of Christ* by Grünewald, where the concealing of eyes likewise serves to heighten the pathos of the image (pl. 43).[170] At the same time, the raggedness of the contours of Bacon's drapery is rather more reminiscent of the torn drapery around Christ's abdomen in the Washington *Small Crucifixion*. The curious fragment of furniture, recalling the base of an antique circular table, which is positioned at the dead centre of the triptych, might also be read as echoing the projecting base of the cross to which Christ's feet are very visibly nailed in Grünewald's various versions of the image. Finally, the two figures of Mary, embodiments of searing grief, offer generalised precedents for the mournful draped figure in the left-hand panel of Bacon's triptych. One can surmise, then, that poring over a book of Grünewald reproductions played a comparable role in Bacon's creativity in the mid-1940s to his immersion in Marius Maxwell's rather different photographs of wild animals on the African plains, or press photographs of gangster-like dictators. The combining of such diverse images was a fundamental determinant of Bacon's pictures, which at their best seem suggestively equidistant from all their points of departure.

Not only painters took their cue from Grünewald. David Gascoyne was given a copy of the 1936 book by Zervos himself, and later acknowledged that his own poems addressing the events of the Passion had been crucially inspired by the reproductions it contained.[171] This inspiration seems particularly relevant for the anguished intensity and highly visual emphasis of Gascoyne's description of Christ on the cross in his poem 'Ecce Homo', which appeared in *Poems 1937–1942*, with its cover and illustrations by Sutherland. Nowhere in the culture of wartime Britain do we find a more vivid and powerful assertion of the contemporary resonance of the crucifixion than in Gascoyne's poem, which opens with the following stanzas:

Whose is this horrifying face,
This putrid flesh, discoloured, flayed,
Fed on by flies, scorched by the sun?
Whose are these hollow red-filmed eyes
And thorn-spiked head and spear-stuck side?
Behold the Man: He is Man's Son.

Forget the legend, tear the decent veil
That cowardice or interest devised
To make their mortal enemy a friend,
To hide the bitter truth all His wounds tell,
Lest the great scandal be no more disguised:
He is in agony till the world's end,

And we must never sleep during that Time!
He is suspended on the cross-tree now
And we are onlookers at the crime,
Callous contemporaries of the slow
Torture of God. Here is the hill
Made ghastly by His scattered blood

Whereon He hangs and suffers still:
See, the centurions wear riding-boots,
Black shirts and badges and peaked caps,
Greet one another with raised-arm salutes[172]

Beginning in 1939, religious imagery provided Gascoyne with the means to distil the sense of contemporary crisis. A key catalyst, in addition to Grünewald, was discovering the work of the French poet Pierre Jean Jouve. The two poets became friendly in 1938 when Gascoyne was living in Paris, in the throes of a prolonged spiritual crisis that led him into psychoanalysis with Jouve's wife. In January 1939, Gascoyne received a copy of Jouve's recently published *Kyrie* and recorded his response in his journal: 'Few writers could at first sight appear so remote from the world of politics, yet few poets have so profoundly suffered the events

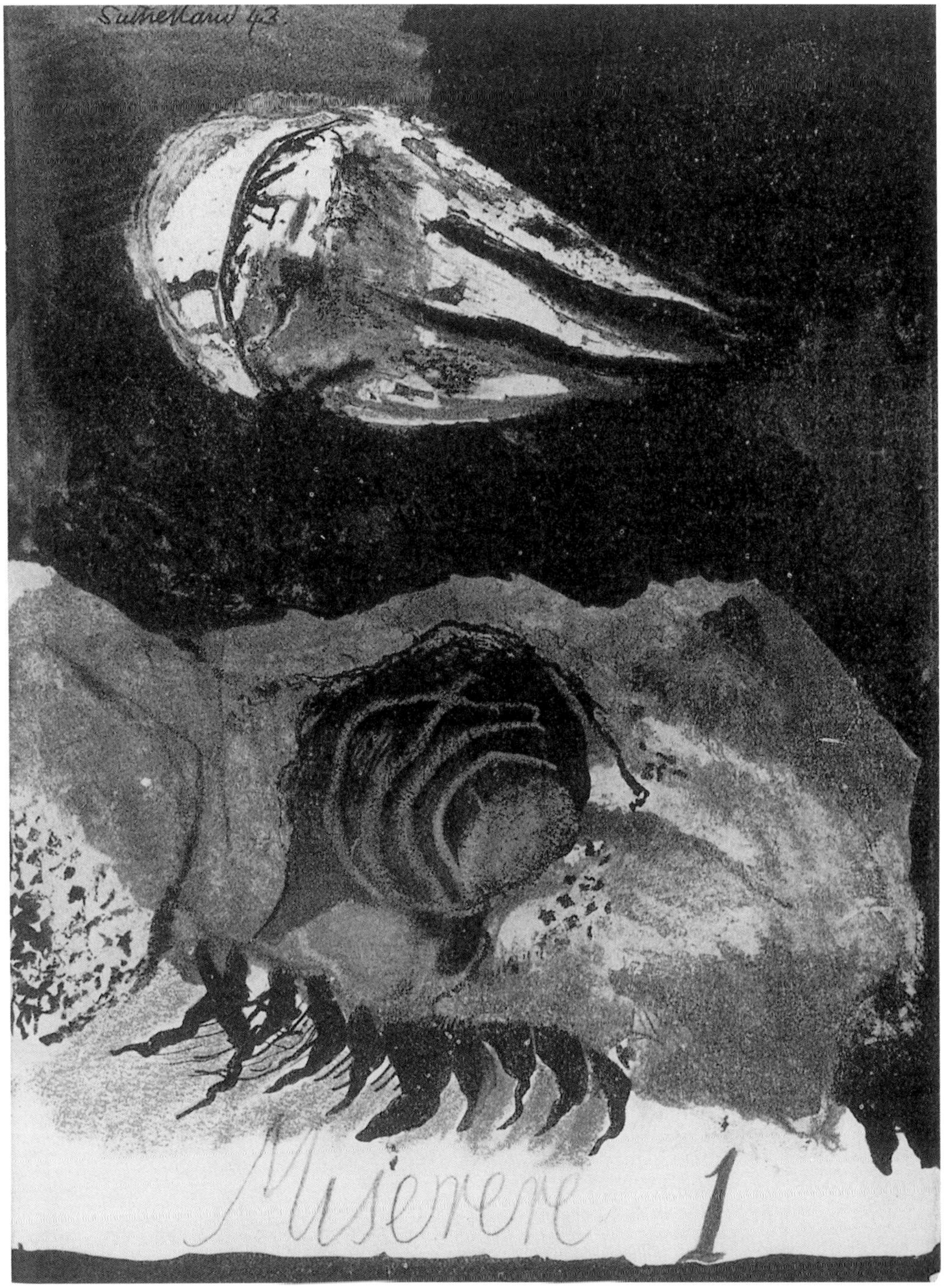

44 Graham Sutherland, frontispiece for ‘Miserere’ section in David Gascoyne, *Poems 1937–42* (1943), Private Collection.

of current history, Czechoslovakia, Austria, Spain; and I know of no one who has so fully expressed the *apocalyptic* atmosphere of our time or with so strong an accent of the “sublime”.’[173] It seems that Jouve’s *Kyrie* ‘triggered for Gascoyne the conception of a body of visionary poems with a traditional religious centre’.[174] Gascoyne’s religious perspective found an outlet in ‘Miserere’, the first of five sections into which Gascoyne grouped his recent poetry in *Poems 1937–42*. The section comprised a sequence of eight poems – 'Tenebrae', 'Pieta', 'De Profundis', 'Kyrie', 'Lachrymae', 'Ex Nihilo', 'Sanctus', and 'Ecce Homo' – that have been said to 'echo the Catholic liturgy and recreate the horror of the first Easter'.[175] In his frontispiece for this section, Sutherland juxtaposed a comet-like form moving ineffectively against the darkness of the sky, with a barren rock beneath, licked by flames, which opens onto a passageway leading down, it seems, to infernal regions (pl. 44). This bleak, apocalyptic image matches the imagery and despairing mood of several passages, including the opening poem 'Tenebrae':

> '*It is finished.*' The last nail
> Has consummated the inhuman pattern, and the veil
> Is torn. God's wounds are numbered.
> All is now withdrawn: void yawns
> The rock-hewn tomb. There is no more
> Regeneration in the stricken sun,
> The hope of faith no more,
> No height no depth no sign
> And no more history.
>
> Thus may it be: and worse.
> And may we know Thy perfect darkness
> And may we into Hell descend with Thee.[176]

This unremittingly sombre tone is sustained throughout the sequence of poems, notably in the vision of 'Ex Nihilo', which again seems to be echoed in Sutherland's illustration. We enter a consciousness 'cast down/Beneath the black glare of a netherworld's/Dead Suns, dust in my mouth':

> These latter years where I must learn
> The revelation of despair, and find
> Among the debris of all certainties
> The hardest stone on which to found
> Altar and shelter for Eternity.[177]

It is only in the last stanza of 'Ecce Homo' that we encounter any hope of deliverance, when we are encouraged to believe that 'the turning point of history/Must come':

> Not from a monstrance silver-wrought
> But from the tree of human pain
> Redeem our sterile misery
> Christ of Revolution and Poetry
> That man's long journey through the night
> May not have been in vain.[178]

As noted above, the Gascoyne volume made a significant impact in literary circles when it appeared in 1943.[179] Raine, for example, praised the particular beauty of the book, 'with its sombre illustrations by Graham Sutherland that so perfectly suited the poems'.[180] In *Horizon*, Spender declared that the appearance of *Poems 1937–1942* was 'the most important event in poetry in 1943'.[181] Although Gascoyne's poems suggested that 'tragedy through a veil of self-pity and drugs is the only tragedy we are able to write of today', Spender nevertheless commended Gascoyne's 'singleness of mind': 'The feeling of a poet writing each poem with his whole self today is . . . very rare.'[182] The background to this endorsement was Spender's perception of the acute problems faced by the literary artist in wartime, which exactly paralleled those confronted by visual artists like Sutherland: 'War poetry and the poetry of violence is particularly difficult to write because the images the poet uses mean either too much to the reader or too little . . . It is difficult to create experiences which are too close to us in the real world, within the ordered world of an imaginative use of language'.[183]

With the exception of a paraphrase of El Greco's *Agony in the Garden*, Sutherland's work to date had given no explicit indication of his private convictions, although it has been suggested that religious undertones emerged in some of his work as a war artist. In 1940, Eric Newton remarked that three pictures of bomb-damaged buildings showing at the National Gallery 'have a wild, crucified poignancy that gives the war a new meaning'.[184] Similar observations occur in a more recent commentary on a 1940 study of a fallen ventilator shaft: 'within the remains of a broken-down wall and shattered window-frame two pieces of debris intersect, forming the shape of a huge cross that takes up the whole of the foreground space, while tongues of livid, reddish flame begin to twist upward in the background. The cross is apparently a chance shape but it indicates the start of the city's martyrdom'.[185] Sutherland's depictions of wraith-like figures moving through the gloomy, mysterious tunnels of Cornish tin mines, or within the and fiery and fearsome interiors of Welsh steel works, brought to mind a Dantesque imagery: 'the man crawls up out of a narrow tunnel on his hands and knees or moves towards pushing a load like one of the damned in Dante's *Inferno*. The sense of fate, of being condemned, of perdition weighs on this sequence of drawings of the tin-mines . . . the analogy with Dante becomes even more acute in the group of drawings of the furnaces and steel foundries'.[186] It might be speculated, however, that Sutherland's move towards the use of explicitly Christian themes towards the end of the war was prompted in part, by his collaboration with Gascoyne. The poet later described their encounters whilst working on the book in 1942: 'I found Graham a quiet man, both warm and reserved, obviously possessed of a faith which found an affinity with something expressed in my poetry, though he seemed unwilling to discuss this explicitly.'[187] It may well have been Gascoyne's poems such as 'Ecce Homo' that demonstrated to Sutherland how religious themes, in particular the crucifixion, might be mobilised, given their potency in the contemporary, mainly secular world.

Another factor was the practical circumstance of the widespread destruction of churches and their contents in German bombing raids. John Rothenstein, director of the Tate gallery, took a particular interest in the future restoration of Catholic churches, and published appeals to the ecclesiastical authorities to prepare themselves to assume the role of patron of the arts. His article to this effect in *The Universe* produced a supportive and enthusiastic response from Sutherland (published in 20 March 1942), calling for the establishment of a committee of inquiry and planning.[188] As a Catholic, Sutherland doubtless saw a role for himself in reviving the moribund tradition of religious art, and he may have begun contemplating the idea of a Crucifixion picture around this time. At any rate, a preoccupation with the image of Christ Crucified seems to be reflected in *Tree Forms*, a highly anthropomorphic drawing of 1943, whose configuration closely foreshadows figure drawings he made three years later in connection with the altarpiece he made for St. Matthew's church, Northampton (pl. 45). However, in the latter case war damage was not a factor. The work was commissioned by Reverend Walter Hussey, who had seen war pictures by Sutherland at the National Gallery, and had also received a positive recommendation for the artist from Henry Moore, currently creating a *Madonna and Child* for the north transept of the church. Accordingly in February 1944 Kenneth Clark invited Sutherland to attend the unveiling of the work by Moore, when Hussey tentatively mooted the idea of a painted altarpiece to hang in the transept opposite. He suggested an *Agony in the Garden* 'because it could give some scope for landscape and there seemed to me to be a relationship between his work and El Greco'.[189] But the artist declared his ambition to do a Crucifixion instead, an idea to which Hussey readily consented as the pathos of the theme would complement Moore's more benign imagery.[190] The story again implies that Sutherland had the image in mind as a theme with present-day resonance.

It is interesting to note not only that Bacon and Sutherland were both drawn to creating images of the crucifixion around this time, but also that each artist also found the task more problematic in practice than in theory. As we shall see, in spring 1945 Bacon intended the *Three Studies* to accompany a big Crucifixion, but the latter failed to materialise. It eventually took Sutherland more than two and a half years to produce the picture for St Matthew's. This was plainly a challenging project for an artist who had previously specialised in small-scale pictures, and in landscape rather than figure-based imagery. But more specifically, the burden of historical precedent made it difficult to give the theme a fresh impact, and working for an ecclesiastical setting and an uninitiated audience posed problems as to how far Sutherland should modify, or depart from, his habitual pictorial idiom in favour of a greater legibility. His inhibitions are evident from Keith Vaughan's record of a conversation he had with Sutherland in April 1944:

> I asked him if it was still possible to paint the great myths; Prometheus, for instance, or a Crucifixion or an Agony in the Garden . . . He said there was no real reason why they should not be painted if one could feel strongly enough about them. The question of understanding the subject and not simply illustrating it was so important. It is essential that one believe in the reality of the subject. For example, it is possible to paint a picture of a man being attacked by a dog because such a situation, though not necessarily experience, is sufficiently near to experience for the imagination to be able to handle it truthfully . . . As for a Crucifixion he did not know whether there was anyone who could handle

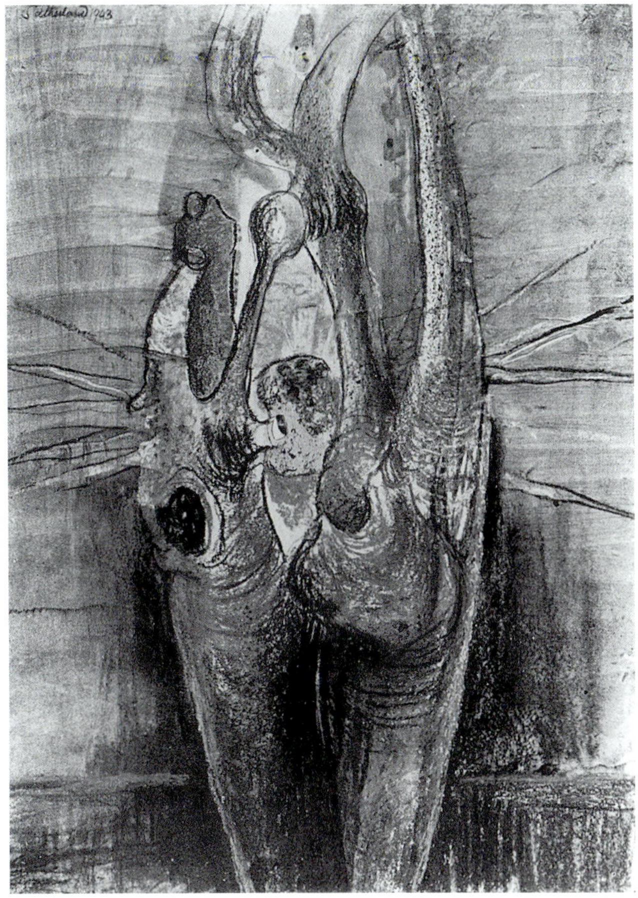

45 Graham Sutherland, *Tree Forms*, 1943, ink, chalk and gouache, 38.1 × 28 cm, Private Collection.

it. 'It is an embarrassing situation', he said, 'to say the least of it, to contemplate a man nailed to a piece of wood in the presence of his friends.'[191]

It might have seemed tactless to Sutherland to mention the possibility of the Northampton commission to Vaughan. However, Vaughan's account implies Sutherland's assent to the notion that the Crucifixion was a 'great myth', akin to those handed down in classical literature. Beneath the irony, one might detect Sutherland's uncertainty about how he might approach the task that had been broached with suitable personal and artistic conviction. This state of mind evidently caused Sutherland to procrastinate. Six months after their initial conversation, he explained to Hussey that all his energies had been channelled into war-related work:

> That is not to say that the problem of the 'Crucifixion' hasn't occupied me. I've thought of it a good deal while going about the trivial tasks of life, and in a way this enforced delay may not be a bad thing since I begin to feel rather more fitted for the task, and certainly a great deal more closely approaching the mood and feeling necessary, than I would have done six months ago.

> It does seem to me that there are only two ways of approaching the subject. On the one hand a treatment detached, formal hieratic (?) and impersonal. On the other, a (for want of better words) psychological or psychic and real (not necessarily naturalistic) treatment. I confess I incline towards the latter . . . In a way it's much more difficult. Symbolism in the sense that Gill used it in Westminster Cathedral is easier and to my mind inclined to be too soothing. That is not to say that the form of the composition shouldn't have great formality. It should, since emotions in art must be crystallised and the moment frozen. I think these ideas apply to other subjects, the 'Agony in the Garden' for instance which I haven't entirely abandoned as a subject.[192]

The following May he was still 'very absorbed by the idea of Crucifixion' but vacillating about whether he could carry it off, and whether he would have to fall back on the 'less difficult and less complex 'Way of the Cross' or Agony in the Garden'.[193]

At this stage he embarked upon new strands of landscape imagery, which dominated Sutherland's art during the second half of 1945. In a letter printed in the catalogue for his show at the Buchholz Gallery in New York, opening the following February, Sutherland acknowledged that the Crucifixion project was at the back of his mind, but also, characteristically, related the genesis of his latest pictures to a moment of epiphany whilst communing with nature:

> I had been thinking of the Crucifixion . . . my mind became preoccupied with the idea of thorns (the crown of thorns) and wounds made by thorns.
>
> Then on going into the country I began to notice thorn trees and bushes. Especially against the sky, the thorns on the branches established a limit of aerial space. They were like dividers pricking out points in space in all directions, encompassing the air, as it were solid and tangible. I'd never noticed this before: but all kinds of ideas for pictures started to come into my mind. Apart from the large 'Thorn Trees' I had several ideas for 'Thorn Head'. A sort of 'pricking' and demarcation of a hollow headshaped space enclosed by the points. All the paintings I have done started off with drawings and sketches direct from nature.[194]

As he elaborated the *Thorn Tree* idea, the composition increasingly suggested a head surmounted by a crown of thorns, a 'thorn-spiked head' in the idiom of Gascoyne's description of Christ.[195] In the more overtly anthropomorphic *Thorn Head* paintings, developed concurrently by focussing in on a detail to the left-hand side of the *Thorn Tree* design, the head of Christ and the crown of thorns seem to have become inextricably fused (pl. 46).

The new pictures can, to some degree, be seen to extend to Sutherland's recent artistic preoccupations. The head format followed on from the recent *Lane Opening* pictures (pl. XI), and the *Thorn Head* image looks back to the drawing Sutherland had used to introduce the 'Personal' section of Gascoyne's *Poems 1937–42* (pl. 47). Again, it is as though the sickle-like form, at once horn and thorn, and the human figure striding along it, distinct from one

46 Graham Sutherland, *Thorn Head*, 1947, oil on canvas, 112 × 79 cm, Private Collection.

47 Graham Sutherland, frontispiece for 'Personal' section in David Gascoyne, *Poems 1937–42* (1943), Private Collection.

48 Graham Sutherland, *Thistles*, 1945, oil and paper collage on card laid down on canvas, 61.5 × 71 cm, Private Collection.

another in the illustration, have now merged into a composite image. However, the thorn pictures are also symptomatic of Sutherland's general shift in 1945 from simpler horn-like forms to a more complex vocabulary of sharp, spiky, forms, which was also manifest in a series of images of thistles (pl. 48). For the artists, such forms carried a strong and immediate expressive charge, the visual equivalent to the Aeschylean metaphors, as evoked by W. B. Stanford, of the darkening mind gashed with fear or anxiety gashing the heart.[196] The configuration of spiky thorns suggests barbed wire and instruments of torture. At any rate, when the thorn pictures were first exhibited, in early 1946, they seemed to chime with the current mood. For example, Roger Marvell remarked:

> I do not know how far Graham Sutherland's thorns are deliberately symbolical.
>
> Oh, lift me as a wave, a leaf, a cloud!
> I fall upon the thorns of life! I bleed!
>
> Certainly these jagged forms are the flora appropriate to a crucified world in which atrocity has become endemic.[197]

If his preoccupation with the Crucifixion commission was one factor that informed Sutherland's new direction, another perhaps was the fact that his time as an official war artist was over. Moreover one senses a renewed impulse to channel feelings about the wider world into his art, as though he was picking up where he had left off in 1939–40 with the metamorphic *Gorse on Sea Wall* and tree root pictures. There is a certain symmetry in the appearance around the end of the conflict of the *Thorn Tree* and *Thorn Head* images, which most explicitly and powerfully articulated the sense of despair that accompanied and qualified any feelings of joy and relief that Allied victory was supposed to bring. Once again, we can helpfully consider the pictures in relation to the precise moment of their genesis. It appears that Sutherland's explorations of the theme go back to the spring of 1945. A date of 29 May 1945 is inscribed on two related drawings, which appear more closely based on direct observations from a motif.[198] Presumably, therefore, the idea ultimately originated during the trip that Sutherland and his wife had made to Pembrokeshire that April, on the proceeds perhaps of early sales from the Lefevre Gallery show in which he was exhibiting alongside Bacon.[199] For Sutherland, the pictures that eventually emerged were, in essence, 'about cruelty': 'thorns sprang from the idea of potential cruelty – to me they were the cruelty. I attempted to give the idea a double twist, as it were, by setting them in benign circumstances: a blue sky, green grass, Crucifixions under warmth – and blue skies are, in a sense, more powerfully horrifying'.[200] One might argue that this new vein of imagery constituted Sutherland's imaginative and emotional response to the particular circumstances of spring 1945. During April, Allied and Russian forces were advancing towards the heart of the crumbling Nazi empire. Russian troops finally entered Berlin, Hitler committed suicide on the 30th, and formal celebrations of victory, VE Day, were held in Britain on 8 May. But the good news of military successes was tempered by the traumatic discovery of the concentration camps. British tanks first entered Belsen, for example, on 15 April, and by the end of the month, photographs, films and verbal accounts of the unimaginable horrors encountered there were widely circulated in Britain.[201] This was, indeed, a 'double twist'. Sutherland's images seem precisely to register a confrontation with horrendous cruelty taking place in what might otherwise have seemed benign circumstances.

The thorn pictures functioned in some sense as a form of preparation and rehearsal for the big *Crucifixion*, for which he was presumably continuing to explore ideas. Nevertheless, it was not until summer 1946 that Hussey was able to put a concrete proposal about a Sutherland altarpiece to his church council. He showed sketches and, to bolster his case, cited a recent book that mentioned Sutherland as a suitable figure for the kind of church decoration that present times demanded: 'The men who come home from the war, and all the rest of us, have seen too much horror and evil; when we close our eyes terrible sights haunt us; the world is seething with bestiality; and it is all man's doing. Only the most profound, tragic, moving, sublime vision can redeem us.'[202] This was clearly the mood of the moment and Sutherland was given the go-ahead. However, progress was now held up by a shortage of materials. It transpired that nothing except paint, brushes and paper could be obtained without a 'priority permit', and canvas in particular was subject to rationing when it appeared every six months. Sutherland no longer had his WAAC permit, but through a contact at the Board of Trade he had managed to get hold of some Sundeala Board, on the pretext that he was doing some work for the 'Britain can make it' exhibition ('highly black market!'). But, to compound matters, his framemaker had neither the wood nor the space to make a stretcher and frame for the boards.[203] Early in September, Hussey showed his committee photographs of the final sketch and supportive letters from Kenneth Clark and from Eric Newton who declared: 'It is both a narrative painting and a religious symbol. It is more tragic than most of the Italian versions but it avoids the rather painful emphasis on purely physical suffering that one finds in German versions.'[204] In fact, Sutherland had progressively pared down the narrative dimensions of the image. He omitted any legible setting or the usual secondary figures, such as the two Marys and St John. In a large-scale study, Sutherland included a skull and bones at the foot of the cross, conventional indications of Golgotha, as well as plant forms flanking Christ's body, but these details were all edited out at a relatively late stage (pl. 49).

The finished work was finally unveiled on 16 November 1946 (pl. XV). The tragic aura of Sutherland's interpretation of the crucifixion was unmistakable. It is well known that, while contemplating the project, Sutherland looked at photographs of the camp at Belsen, just as Bacon evidently became obsessed by photographic traces of the hell that had been the death camps.[205] For Sutherland, the piles of splayed corpses provided a horrifying reincarnation of the image of Christ crucified and deposed: 'the whole idea of the depiction of Christ crucified became much more real to me . . . and it seemed to be possible to do this subject again'.[206] The contemplation of such ghastly images doubtless reinforced Sutherland's willingness to treat the figure of Christ as emaciated and distorted by agony. For some contemporary viewers, confronted by the altarpiece itself and then by the studies and variants which the artist exhibited at the Lefevre Gallery in the summer of 1947, this most hallowed of religious themes had retained none of its consoling force in Sutherland's hands. According to one critic, the picture 'mirrors the emotional time and place in which it was conceived; and it is as well to remember that Sutherland worked out his version of the subject in a bombed out island at the end of the cruelest war in history, when innocent men were undergoing mental and physical torments comparable in terror and intensity to Christ's death.'[207]

*

In early 1949, Robert Melville commented that Bacon was 'probably the only painter of our time to whom the Crucifixion comes as a natural subject'. However, his 1933 rendition, recently acquired by Sutherland's friend and supporter Colin Anderson, was, Melville believed, 'the only picture labelled as a Crucifixion that he has actually completed'.[208] The essay vividly evokes the pervasiveness of the theme in Bacon's art, implied even in a picture of a figure lying on a bed that is no longer extant, as well as its contemporary emotional resonance:

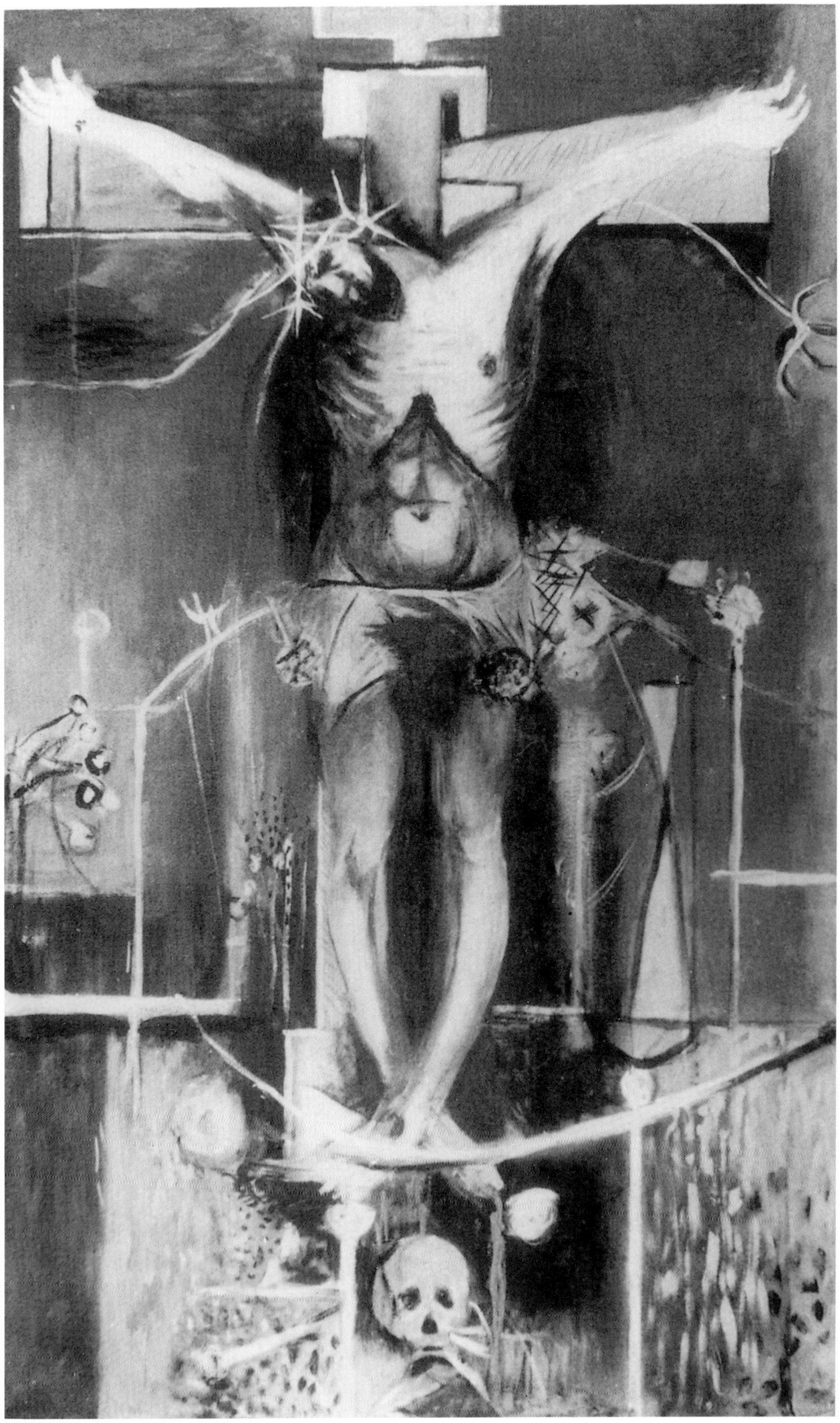

49 Graham Sutherland, large-scale preliminary study for *Crucifixion* altarpiece, 1946, present whereabouts unknown.

50 Gaetano Previati, *The Three Marys at the Foot of the Cross*, 1997, oil on canvas, 125 × 170 cm, Collection Calmarini, Milan.

> All the figures in the pictures I have seen are somehow related to the Crucifixion; either they are studies for figures at the foot of the cross, or secular studies for Christ Himself, sometimes stretched between the brass knobs of a bed, sometimes imitating the split-open carcass of a bullock. And in all the heads, pain and despair have partly eaten away the features. But always there is a phantasmal, mirage-like quality, as if these terrible forms were simply reflections of the uneasy, fear-haunted mind of modern man, to which the artist bears objective, but faintly sardonic, witness.[209]

It is well known that, by the time of his closer contacts with Sutherland, Bacon had been obsessed with this vein of imagery for a number of years. In the early 1930s he produced several paintings on the subject, including a lost *Wound for a Crucifixion* and the Anderson picture reproduced in 1933 in Herbert Read's *Art Now*.[210] The theme clearly had a constant and profound significance for Bacon as a symbol of man's essential mortality, vulnerability and bodily nature. It may also have possessed more private homosexual connotations for Bacon, given that the subject presents a naked male figure who is the innocent victim of extreme violence and persecution. Very little is known of Bacon's activities in the studio between 1933 and 1944, and it is conceivable that Crucifixion imagery continued to feature. Certainly, a rare recollection of his Glebe Place studio evoked 'a truly frightening room with dark blue walls and ceiling, with a vast mural of a crucified arm across the wall'.[211] Nevertheless, it seems reasonable to suppose that Bacon's allusions to the Crucifixion in his 1944 triptych and subsequent works were informed not just by longstanding impulses but also by his response to contemporary circumstances, when a private obsession could take on further, compelling layers of meaning, as well as by his close association with a fellow painter who was greatly preoccupied with the theme.

Confronted by Bacon's triptych, with its inherent connotations of an altarpiece format, and taking account of the work's title, *Three Studies for Figures at the Base of a Crucifixion*, the viewer may well feel inclined or required to seek out allusions to traditional religious iconography, such as, for example, the three crosses, Christ and the two thieves, on the hill of Gethsemane. The enigmatic fragment of furniture in the lower part of the central panel could evoke the ledge attached to the cross that commonly supports Christ's feet in traditional representations of the Crucifixion. A sophisticated observer may note echoes of Grünewald, and might also discern in Bacon's bestial hybrids a reference of sorts to the figures, such as the Virgin Mary, Mary Magdalene and St. John the Evangelist, who customarily functioned as the witnesses to Christ's agony and as the cues to our own emotional response. Thus Bacon's presentation seems to go one step further than an image such as *The Three Marys at the Foot of the Cross* by the late nineteenth-century Italian artist Gaetano Previati (1897; pl. 50). Here our attention is indeed focused on the grieving figures at the base of the Cross, and all we see of Christ is his nailed feet. With Bacon, the three figures are wholly detached from a historical narrative context, and the title refers to *a* rather than *the* Crucifixion, evoking, it has often been said, a general, less specifically Christian, sense of pathos.[212]

However, there may be other ways of interpreting Bacon's titling of the work. It is interesting to note that in April 1945 the triptych was actually listed as *Three Studies for Figures, at the Base of a Crucifixion*. The comma between 'figures' and 'at' was subsequently lost, but its presence changes the sense significantly. In place of an image of three figures who can be thought to be in some sense contemplating or witnessing a Crucifixion, we are confronted instead by three pictures of figures, with private connotations for Bacon, it subsequently transpired, of the Eumenides, which were to be hung, rather like a predella, beneath a Crucifixion painting. A Crucifixion, in this sense, does not imply the same downplaying of Christian overtones. The fact that other paintings from the 1940s are called, for instance, *Painting*, *Figure Study*, or *Head* reinforces Bacon's later indication that he had always disliked using titles to attach precise directives concerning the meaning of his pictures. He acknowledged that his gallery had a practical need for titles, and recounted how, in the case of one of the triptychs, they had made a title up on the basis of his remark that reading Eliot's 'Sweeney Agonistes' had informed his conception of the image: 'that is how those titles very often come about. But I really want to keep them as anonymous as possible, because I think that the titles lie within the images and people can read what they like into them'.[213] In the case of the 1944 triptych, a plausible sequence of events is that Bacon told someone at the gallery, who was responsible for the catalogue, what he had in mind – three studies for figures, with a Crucifixion above – and this was compressed into the title as printed. In the end, the Crucifixion did not materialise. Perhaps Bacon ran out of time, or worked on such a picture but decided that it was a failure artistically. At any rate, he settled, as it were, for the self-contained but nevertheless truncated version of his more ambitious idea. When the work was next exhibited, in late 1946, it was as *Studies for figures at the base of a crucifix*, which made his intentions clearer and more explicit.[214] By the time of his first one-man show three years later, he was presenting the pictures under the more neutral titles of *Study I–III*.[215] There was now nothing except a presumed triptych arrangement in the hang to suggest any overtones of religious imagery. It is possible that the work only acquired its definitive title at the point when Eric Hall presented it to the Tate in 1953. However, when Bacon stated in 1959 that the three studies were studies of the Furies, he also remarked that they were intended to be 'the base of a large Crucifixion which I may do still'.[216] His most detailed account appeared in an interview with Sylvester:

> I thought of them as the Eumenides, and at the time I saw the whole Crucifixion in which these would be there instead of the usual figures at the base of the cross. And I was going to put these on an armature around the cross, which itself was going to be raised, and the image on the cross was to be in the centre with these things arranged around it. But I never did that . . .[217]

Bacon was consistently willing to exhibit the *Three Studies* without the accompanying crucifix, though the title prompted the viewer to imagine its presence, and also without any indication in the title to the Eumenides, with whom the figures were, it appears, intimately associated in Bacon's own mind. These omissions served, it might be argued, to withhold from the viewer any private, autobiographical meanings that the work may have possessed for Bacon himself. Such alleged meanings are detected in the only sustained attempt to date to explain 'what the Eumenides are doing as witnesses to a Crucifixion scene', namely Ralf Lassøe's intricate psychoanalytical reading of Bacon's Crucifixions.[218] In summary, the author argues that it was Bacon's deeply traumatic relationship with his father that conditioned his readings of Aeschylus, Eliot, and, in all likelihood, Freud, as well as his particular clusterings of imagery. Concerning the Eumenides, Lassøe concludes that 'in so far as they stand for a repression of libidinal forces they are also bound up with the cause of that repression – i.e. the dictatorial influence of the 'dreaded father'. In the same way that the Crucifixion may be seen as a logical myth on which to project traumatic father/son dichotomy, so the Eumenides relate quite logically to the themes of guilt or persecution within the psychological structure of the family'.[219] This reading may indeed, on some level, correspond to the workings of Bacon's conscious or subconscious mind. The argument is impossible, in the end, to either prove or disprove. But, to the extent that it is plausible and coherent, Lassøe's interpretation is itself symptomatic of the fact that, once one relinquishes the possibility of a straightforward narrative connection between the lower and the projected, but unrealised, upper zones of Bacon's work, then reading, or making sense, of the work becomes a personal, open-ended, and essentially imaginative exercise for the spectator. For Lassøe, Bacon is fundamentally using his art to grapple with his private demons, rather than to comment in some way on the times in which he was living and working. As we have seen, however, Bacon himself tended to conflate private and public. The question that arises is whether Bacon's further conflation of classical and Christian imagery can be understood in relation to some accessible cultural context, rather than to ultimately inaccessible mental processes.

To explore this possibility I would like, once again, to juxtapose the *Three Studies* with Frank Prince's poem 'Soldiers Bathing'. Following its appearance in *Poetry London*, the poem was much admired in progressive literary circles in London; Spender, for example, quoted it in full and described it as 'magnificent' in his 1945 pamphlet *Poetry since 1939*.[220] It is quite possible that Bacon himself had encountered the work, given that he clearly took a keen interest in contemporary literature. However the affinities I shall propose may comprise parallel manifestations of a shared wartime sensibility, rather than any direct inspiration transmitted from poet to painter. Prince had seen active service in the Intelligence Corps, and took as the theme for his dramatic monologue the sense of 'pathos' that overwhelmed him when watching a group of fellow soldiers divesting and relaxing by the seashore. The poem unfolds as a meditation on the 'meaning' to be extracted from watching the soldiers temporarily escaping from the war. Analogies between the scene of bathing and certain celebrated works of art begin to insinuate themselves, just as the Bacon fuses an emphatic sense of the violence of the here and now with intimations of the imagery and formats of artistic tradition, such as the triptych and altarpieces by Grünewald. So when a naked soldier horses around – 'plays with death and animality' – the poet recalls Michelangelo's Cascina cartoon, where soldiers who have broken off from battle are now getting ready to rejoin the fray, 'forgetful of their bodies that are bare'. Prince continues with a further recollection of Renaissance art:

> And I think too of the theme another found
> When, shadowing lean bodies on a sinister red ground –
> Was it Antonio Pollaiuolo? –
> Painted a naked battle: warriors straddled, hacked the foe,
> Dug their bare toes into the soil and slew
> The brother naked-man who lay beneath their feet and drew
> His lips back from his teeth in a grimace.

There are obvious similarities with Bacon here, from the 'lean bodies on a sinister red ground' to the 'lips [drawn] back from the teeth in a grimace'. The reference is evidently to Pollaiuolo's engraving *The Battle of the Ten Nudes*. This does not actually possess a 'sinister red ground', and Prince seems to be conflating the print with related drawings with sepia backgrounds, such as a drawing in the British Museum. The poem seeks an explanation for the unremitting, sadistic violence of the fifteenth-century image:

> They were Italians who knew war's sorrow and disgrace
> And showed the things suspended, stripped, a theme
> Born out of the experience of war's horrible extreme

> Beneath a sky where even the air flows
> With *Lachrimae Christi*; and that rage, that bitterness, those blows,
> That hatred of the slain, what could it be
> But indirectly or brutally a commentary
> On the Crucifixion? For the picture burns
> With indignation and pity and despair and love by turns
> Because it is the obverse of the scene
> Where Christ hangs murdered, stripped, upon the Cross:
> I mean,
> That is the explanation of its rage.

The poem proceeds to develop the parallel with present times: 'And we too have our bitterness and pity that engage/ Thought, horror in this war. But night begins,/ Night of the mind'.

The ideas and imagery in Prince's poem may be transposed quite readily onto Bacon's triptych. For the three figures in the triptych, the Eumenides if you will, can likewise be read not so much as witnesses within a coherent narrative, but rather as a more oblique 'commentary on the Crucifixion'. For Bacon, the Crucifixion was a theme that he explored obsessively because it so vividly and poignantly encapsulated the fundamental reality, as he saw it, of human existence. It served him as 'a magnificent armature on which you can hang all sorts of feelings and sensations', to quote the phrase he later used in conversation with Sylvester, an armature permitting the exploration of 'all sorts of very private feelings about behaviour and about the way life is'.[221] The conjunction with the Eumenides would have made it plain that the message of the crucifixion had nothing to do with redemption and the fantasy of life after death, but rather with the more realistic sense, to Bacon's way of thinking, that we are all subject to mortal decay, at the mercy of human cruelty and unforeseen disaster, and that we are locked into a body and a set of instincts that we share with the animals. Bacon's experiences in Ireland during the Troubles, but above all in London during the war, when he witnessed the Blitz at first hand, instilled a profound awareness that 'death is like the shadow of life . . . while you're alive, the idea of death pursues you'.[222] Such a sense of the pathos of the human state would have emanated strongly from Bacon's Crucifixion, and its attendant commentary in the form of the three studies for figures.

As it stands, Bacon's *Three Studies* is about physical and mental pain, fear and dread, about confinement and the state of being reduced to the condition of a caged animal. In that sense, the triptych vividly projects indignation, pity and despair, to use Prince's terms. But the violent distortions and overt anguish coexist, surely deliberately, with suggestions of tenderness and beauty, or indeed love as the poem puts it. Witness the sensual, painterly treatment of areas of flesh, of anatomical details like the ear belonging to the right-hand creature, which implies a touching vulnerability, and of the very basic trappings such as grass and the bits of furniture. Above all, there is the bright, flat orange of the backgrounds, which in the end has a very different resonance from Prince's 'sinister red ground'. It is not at all suggestive of blood; indeed, it almost reads as decorative. We might recall in this context Bacon's remark to Michel Archimbauld many years later that orange is 'my favourite colour . . . I couldn't explain in any satisfactory way why I find it such a beautiful colour'.[223] The interplay of incongruous sensations and dissonant images is an arresting feature of the *Three Studies*, as it is of so much of Bacon's art. This dimension of his own work is compatible with his well-attested fascination with the remarkable verbal image from Aeschylus, 'The reek of human blood smiles out at me'.[224] In the *Three Studies*, horror and revulsion are likewise tinged with compassion, and brutal deformation with redeeming aesthetic gratification. The emotional fluidity of Bacon's picture is also paralleled by the concluding passages of 'Soldiers Bathing', where Prince characterises the contemporary 'night of the mind':

> Though every human deed concerns our blood,
> And even we must know what no one as yet has understood,
> That some great love is over what we do,
> And that is what has driven us to this fury, for so few
> Can suffer all the terror of that love:
> The terror of that love has set us spinning in this groove
> Greased with our blood.

At the end of the day, the soldiers dress and the presiding consciousness of the poem evokes his own state of mind:

> . . . as I drink the dusky air
> I feel a strange delight that fills me full,
> A gratitude, as if evil itself were beautiful;
> And kiss the wound in thought, while in the west
> I watch a streak of red that might have issued from Christ's breast.

Bacon's contradictory vision once again finds a striking counterpart in Prince's images of the beauty of evil, and of kissing the wound in thought. Of course, there are proper limits to the comparison. There are elements of stylistic conservatism and near-religiosity in Prince's poem that are remote from Bacon. But there is an underlying tone, an acute sense of the fragility of life, a mingling of pain and relish in the face of the human spectacle, that appear to straddle the two works. These themes are an overt expression of wartime experiences and feelings in Prince's poem. The juxtaposition may help us to gauge how far this was also the case with Bacon.

Oblique intimations of Christ's Passion can be found in subsequent paintings. Bacon's next two works were exhibited under the title *Figure Study*, but interestingly the second version was known for several years as 'Magdalene', though Bacon eventually disavowed the title and association (pl. XIV).[225] The picture can certainly be read as a distant echo of the despairing, grieving figures, of whom Mary Magdalene was one, that commonly feature in Crucifixions, as emotional prompts for the benefit of suitably devout spectators. Certainly, there seems a close correspondence between the imagery and tone of the Bacon and Sutherland's treatment of Mary Magdalene as a Christian version of a raving maenad in the small picture dating from 1946 (pl. 51). But the key work by Bacon in this context is *Painting* (1946; pl. XVI). Sutherland later characterised his thorn bush paintings as 'a kind of "stand-in" for a Crucifixion, and a crucified head'.[226] *Painting* might equally be described as a 'stand-in' for a Crucifixion. After his failure to realise the picture surmounting the *Three Studies* the previous spring, this picture became Bacon's vehicle for reworking the imagery and expressive resonance of the Crucifixion, with a great animal carcass standing in for Christ on the Cross. The connotations of the theme here are immediate and overwhelming. The upper part of the picture probably reads most directly, for the majority of viewers, as a splayed human torso, a handless and 'headless Crucifixion'.[227] However the alternative vein of imagery that insinuates itself is that of the meat seller; the torso reads as a splayed animal carcass, which would have been more explicit if the legs had not been extended to evoke human arms, and the garlands at the top evoke 'an old-fashioned butcher's shop with ceramic festoons on the walls',[228] just as the metallic framework with bones and chunks of meat attached suggest the metal bars and hooks on which butchers hung and displayed their wares. Even the blinds prompt an association with the sun blinds used to protect the meat. The work is clearly descended to some degree from the *Wound for a Crucifixion* that he had painted in the mid-1930s and subsequently, to his regret, destroyed. The earlier work apparently showed a 'very beautiful wound' in an abstract shape mounted on a sculptor's armature, a striking anticipation of the lower half of *Painting* (1946), where a metal armature is once again associated with Crucifixion imagery. Yet Bacon's new painting surely registers the very particular significance that meat assumed in wartime. On the one hand, it was a foodstuff much desired and in scant supply, subject necessarily to a stern regime of rationing. On the other hand, butchered meat was the condition to which men and women were themselves all too frequently being reduced, not just on some far away battlefield, but on the streets of London and other places that were subject to German bombing raids. The association is made in one of Sutherland's reminiscences of the period: 'From Butcher's shops which had been hit the meat spewed on the road, and I remember feeling quite sick when seeing this for the first time because I thought that here was a body which hadn't been picked up.'[229]

TYPES OF AMBIGUITY

To what extent do oppositions and ambiguities in the work of Sutherland and Bacon register an especially acute, wartime consciousness of the existential polarities of life and death, hope and fear? How far do such devices function as the pictorial equivalent to the unfolding of cathartic or redemptive meanings in other means of expression, as in Gascoyne's comments on the sacred music of Bach 'transfiguring grief and suffering into the radiance of a peaceful sky', which typified 'the operation of the greatest art: resolution of the most violent contradictions, creation of harmony out of opposites – elevation, consolation'? The notion

51 Graham Sutherland, *Weeping Magdalene*, 1946, oil on board, 61 × 51 cm, Private Collection.

that a picture could embrace contradictory associations and suggestions was clearly one that Sutherland and Bacon shared, but how might we discriminate between their realisations of this concern in practice?

Sutherland later remarked that he had been drawn to the Crucifixion because if its 'duality': 'It is the most tragic of themes and yet it contains an innate promise of salvation. It is the symbol of the precarious moment of balance, the infinitesimal space between black and white'. This emotional ambiguity was originally to have been reinforced by the use of 'warm blue sky' for the background, though the colour he finally chose, 'a violet-blue, traditionally the colour of death, was in part dictated by the need for harmony with the elements already present in the church'.[230] The possibility of a redemptive reading was inherent in the ecclesiastical setting, but the work was also seen at the time as epitomising the cruelty and violence of the present. The same ambivalence of mood was a feature, as we have seen, of the preceding thorn pictures. Indeed, it may be seen to extend a fundamental ambition informing Sutherland's mature art. The emotional tenor he sought in his paintings is encapsulated in his verbal description of the actual landscapes that provided many of his motifs. The places to which he was attracted induced a sense of impressive melancholy, 'an element of disquiet', and an 'emotional feeling of being on the brink of some drama'. They encompassed, in a remarkably small compass, such contrasting qualities as 'exultant strangeness', darkness and light, decay and life. The colours of the sunset, normally viewed as tranquil and benign, 'assume tones as of blood'.[231] Generally, the iconography of his paintings embodies a 'condensation of contrasts' in the words of J. T. Soby.[232] The living landscape incorporates symbols of death, such as animal skulls, uprooted trees, and sometimes forms that suggest both, as in *Tree Trunk Sprawling* of 1938.[233] In the 1936 *Red Tree* (pl. 11 and pl. 58), the suggestion of vital forces emerging fountain-like from within a dead tree recalls Dylan Thomas's celebrated meditation on the inextricability of creative and destructive energies in the celebrated 1933 poem that Sutherland could well have known: 'The force that through the green fuse drives the flower/ Drives my green age; that blasts the roots of trees/ Is my destroyer./ And I am dumb to tell the crooked rose/ My youth is bent by the same wintry fever'.[234] Elsewhere, dark prison-like enclosures are relieved by luminous pockets of space, suggesting potential escape. The forms of bombed buildings take on bodily connotations, and 'one gets a feeling that the destruction is not final but that the organic principle of life remains; that the principles of growth and decay are almost inseparably inter-mixed'.[235] The approach is summarised in Sutherland's comments in 1951 where he acknowledges that his work might reflect tragic times, but resists too simplistically bleak a reading:

> It has been said that my most typical images express a point of view dark and pessimistic. That is foreign to my mind. The precarious tension of opposites – happiness and unhappiness, beauty and ugliness – so near the point of equilibrium, can be interpreted, perhaps, according to the predilections and needs of the spectator – with delight or horror, as with the taste of bitter-sweet fruit. The painter is a kind of blotting paper; he soaks up impres-

> sions; he is very much part of the world. He cannot therefore avoid soaking up the implications of the apparent tragedy of 20th century civilisation. Subconsciously tragic pictures may be painted – and without, necessarily, having a tragic subject.[236]

Such an outlook doubtless took on a more powerful resonance in wartime circumstances, but it also reflects available cultural values. It is tempting, for example, to invoke the contemporary currency of the ideas of Sigmund Freud. By the mid-1930s, when Sutherland crystallised his art, Freud's writings were extensively available in English, and psychoanalytical thinking had become a pervasive influence. It is virtually inconceivable that Sutherland and, for that matter, Bacon would not have taken an enthusiastic interest in a body of ideas so rich and compelling in their portrayal of mental life, and so powerfully compatible with assumptions about the non-rational, now restyled unconscious, origins of artistic inspiration.[237] Bacon for his part remarked to an interviewer who had noted copies of Freud on his bookshelves, 'I like reading Freud very much because I like his way of explaining things'.[238] A basic familiarity with Freudian thinking is implicit in Sutherland's remark in 'A Trend in English Draughtsmanship' which describes elements in a scene becoming 'absorbed in the reservoir of the subconscious mind out of which emerge the reconstructed and re-created images'.[239] However, interpretation of Sutherland's art in psychoanalytical terms has never gone beyond Soby's suggestive comment in his 1948 essay: 'If the example of surrealism was a factor in Sutherland's decision to sharpen the psychological impact of his paintings, it is evident that in his art he has psychoanalysed not himself nor his fellow men, but nature.'[240]

Freud's own arrival in Britain in 1938, to live out his final fifteen months, was one more symptom of a dire and unfolding crisis in modern European life. That crisis was susceptible to comprehension, or at any rate rationalisation, in the light of the psychoanalyst's later, wide-ranging writings, such as *Civilization and its Discontents*. These involved an explicit projection onto the social fabric at large of ideas initially developed in the context of investigations of the individual psyche. Eventually, Freud came to believe that the interplay between two basic instincts, Eros (love) and the destructive 'death' instinct was fundamental to human society. Civilization comprised:

> A process in the service of Eros, whose purpose is to combine single human individuals, and after that families, then races, peoples and nations, into one great unity, the unity of mankind. But man's natural aggressive instinct, the hostility of each against all and all against each, oppose this programme of civilization. This aggressive instinct is the derivative . . . of the death instinct which we have found alongside of Eros and which shared world-dominion with it. And now, I think, the meaning of the evolution of civilization is no longer obscure to us. It must present the struggle between Eros and Death, between the instinct of life and the instinct of destruction as it works itself out in the human species.[241]

Freud argued that a healthy society entailed a certain repression of destructive urges, though this was not without its psychological consequences in the form of neurosis. But during the

1930s it became all too obvious that it was the forces of destruction that were ascendant. Armed with Freud, the rise of fascism and ethnic violence could be understood not just in narrowly geo-political terms, but also in deeper psychic and even mythic terms. As I have argued, such thinking informed Bacon's art. Likewise, in his encounters with landscape scenery and in his approach to religious themes, Sutherland brought to bear a commitment to Freudian patterns of thought. The 'precarious tension of opposites' explored in his paintings was visual, but also metaphorical, emblematic of the precarious equilibrium between conflicting instinctive forces that Freud had discerned within the psyche, and by extension within human society at large. In Sutherland's pictures, the viewer is invited to contemplate polarities: darkness and light, suffering and redemption, death and life. Equally, strident colours and loose brushwork are matched by careful linear draughtsmanship and even the visible evidence, frequently encountered in his work, of the meticulous squaring-up process by means of which conceptions were carried over from preparatory studies to finished paintings. Such multiple contrasts clearly encouraged readings of Sutherland's pictures as the visual counterpart to traditional redemptive narratives in, say, music or literature, where an immersion in pain and suffering gives way sequentially to an eventual harmony and consolation.

One might extrapolate from the example of the *Three Studies* that, to a degree, Bacon's pictures are susceptible to comparable analysis, but also that his imagery is, in the end, more open-ended and intangible, notwithstanding the extreme tangibility of physical presence that his pictures convey in terms of both depicted subject-matter and the paint surface itself. Associations are deliberately withheld – in the end, there is no Crucifixion hovering above the three figures, whose identity as Eumenides is not indicated – but the power and suggestivess of Bacon's imagery compels the viewer to project meanings and elaborate interpretations of their own. Moreover, Bacon's oppositions form part of a more radically fragmented pictorial idiom. Arguably, his bringing together of dissonant images is best viewed as an extension by other means of the aesthetic idiom of T. S. Eliot's poetry. I speculated earlier on Sutherland's interest in Eliot's anti-pastoral approach to landscape imagery. Bacon's admiration for the poet's work in general, over and above *The Family Reunion*, is well-documented. His friend Michael Wishart could only recall seeing Eliot, Pound and volumes of photographs by Muybridge on Bacon's bookshelves just after the war.[242] In 1962 David Sylvester noted that *The Waste Land* had 'long obsessed Bacon, who speaks of how it is "packed with memories" '.[243] In their subsequent interviews, the artist told Sylvester that he felt he had been influenced by Eliot: '*The Waste Land* especially and the poems before it have always affected me very much.'[244] Bacon added that 'they excite me and goad me to try and work much more', although he had hardly ever worked from particular lines or poems – 'it's the whole atmosphere that affects one'. The fusion in *The Waste Land* of imagery evoking the seedy banality of modern life with overt, but usually fragmentary, recollections of poetic tradition, and its loftier mode of diction, presages Bacon's insertion of contemporary squalor into old-masterly pictorial formats, as most obviously in *Painting* (1946). Indeed, Bacon's appropria-

52 Francis Bacon, *Figure Study 1*, 1945–6, oil on canvas, 123 × 105.5 cm, Scottish National Gallery of Modern Art, Edinburgh.

tions from the great masters might be aligned with an outlook which Edmund Wilson had identified in Eliot: 'Eliot, like Flaubert, feels that human life is now ignoble, sordid or tame, and he is haunted and tormented by intimations that it has once been otherwise'.[245]

Figure Study I provides an apt example of the rehearsal of such a sensibility in the work of Bacon (pl. 52). The human presence indicated by the title is merely implied in the picture itself by the external attributes of a herring-bone tweed coat, a trilby hat and a bunch of flowers. Close examination, however, reveals the shadow of what appears to be a hand and an arm, emerging from the jacket at an angle and evidently holding the flowers. The passage is just visible in the area of shadow cast by the hat, as evoked by a superimposed glaze of diluted black paint. Moreover, in the textured horizontal band at the top one can also make out a curved shape at the centre that may originally have been a head. The expanse of overcoat to the left has clearly been added to at the far left. In other words, the picture may have started off as a more straightforward, frontal presentation of a figure, but Bacon eventually chose to edit the image down to its final state, in which a slumped figure can be surmised from the placement of the various elements. In metaphorical terms, one might see the inner self, conventionally idealised as the repository of the soul and the higher emotions, as having been collapsed into a gaping void. Mellor notes that the 'dolorous, ashen overcoat' in both versions of *Figure Study* 'moulds profane dress into the attitudes of a classically draped, sculpted mourner'.[246] Equally, we might intuit that some profoundly melancholy or grieving state of mind is evoked by the outer trappings of someone visiting a hospital, for example, or attending a funeral. Whatever the precise connotations of the tragic aura given off by the picture, the suggestion of man's fall from grace is intensified by the unmistakable allusion in Bacon's treatment of the drapery to another Velásquez, the magnificent *Philip IV in Brown and Silver* in the National Gallery in London (pl. 53). The floating of a repeated pattern of white and grey marks over the brown underlay is uncannily reminiscent of the handling in the Velásquez. Moreover, the relationship of the vertical arm to the diagonal extension of the drapery to the left provides a further echo of the placement of the king's right arm and cloak. Bacon would have known the Velásquez from before the war, especially when it emerged in a much brighter and fresher state after a highly controversial cleaning.[247] It was one of fifty Old Master pictures that were shown in the National Gallery in summer 1945, heralding the subsequent return of the entire collection from its wartime sojourn in a Welsh hillside.[248] Bacon's allusion signifies one artist's emulation of a great predecessor, but at the same time it suggests the full arc of man's descent from confident composure into the current depths of tragedy and gloom. In sum, we would do well to attend to Lawrence Alloway, who wrote as effectively as anyone about Bacon's incorporation of 'numerous allusions to the Grand Manner' and his use of tradition as 'a shifting bundle of models and influences in a problematic relationship with recent experiences'.[249] Bacon's approach turns out to generate a different version of Sutherland's 'precarious tension of opposites'. According to Alloway:

53 Diego Velázquez, *Philip IV in Brown and Silver*, oil on canvas, 195 × 110 cm, National Gallery, London.

> even as the past is evoked by the structure of the paintings, it is questioned and undermined. A grand compositional display becomes a keyhole to intimacy . . . To Bacon, the

> Grand Manner is indispensable, as a frame against which to work, eroding and subverting it, but not removing it. He needs both the symbol of order, of which the Grand Manner provides an ample and long-lived example, and its opposite, intimate and unanticipated images. The two elements interlock, one giving body, one giving mystery, to the other.[250]

This analysis might be extended beyond Bacon's stylistic idiom to the physical presentation of his pictures. The illustrations to Melville's 1949 article in *Horizon* indicate not only that Bacon was committed to using old-masterly gilt frames, but also that he had already started mounting his pictures behind glass.[251] This was traditionally a means to protect pictures, but one senses that, for Bacon, it was intended at once to distance the spectator from an imaginary tactile response to the picture surface, and at the same time perhaps to incorporate his or her own reflection into the viewer's perceptions of the painted image. Moreover, both frame and glass served 'to reinforce the artificial nature of the painting', as Bacon commented in a particularly revealing account of the tension between contradictory qualities and associations that he valued in the experience yielded by great art, and that by implication he wanted his own work to arouse in the viewer:

> The more the artificiality of the painting is apparent, the better, and the more chance the painting has of working or of showing something. That might seem paradoxical, but it makes perfect sense in art: one achieves one's goal by using the maximum of artificial means, and one succeeds in doing something authentic when the artificiality is perfectly obvious. Take for example the Greek or classical poets; their language was very artificial and highly stylized. They all worked within strict constraints, and yet it's precisely in doing so that they produced their greatest works which give us, when we read them, that impression of freedom and spontaneity.[252]

Finally, Bacon's brand of indeterminacy is epitomised by *Painting* (1946; pl. xvi). How might this picture be interpreted, deploying points of reference that were significant to Bacon himself? Most immediately, the presiding fragmentary figure surrounded by bloody matter comes across as the butcher, literally the man behind the counter, but also the metaphorical butcher, as the carcass is his metaphorical victim. By reducing the features to a thick-set pale chin and tooth-laden lower lip, Bacon offers a distillation of inhuman brutality and bestial cruelty. The shadow cast by the umbrella, which can barely contain the implied head, completely conceals the eyes, which might offer windows onto, if not the soul, at least some accessible human core. The touches of red above the mouth suggest some wound that the figure desires to conceal, although the placement of the figure immediately beneath the carcass might also imply a fastidious concern to protect himself from further drips and splatters of blood. The sinister pool of blackness made by the shadow extends to the figure's garb, which is broken up only by the white collar and an utterly incongruous yellow flower. Cumulatively, such cues 'characterise' the figure as an embodiment of power and sadistic cruelty. He is simultaneously an executioner and a tyrant. We might recall the description of *Painting* by Sam Hunter, one of the most acute early commentators on Bacon:

> An orator-like figure . . . stands in a commanding public attitude on a raised dais. This creature of nightmare curiously suggests in its dark anonymity the modern European Everyman. Its visage dissolves into a lewd, simian grimace and gaping wound, while the platform fuses into some sort of barred contraption – does it suggest a cage, the subway turnstile or the medieval rack – and seems to have a machine-gun mount on it. The total effect is as if we had witnessed a conventional heroic pictorial representation disintegrate, first in a kind of unwholesome, poisonous 'real' atmosphere, and then in psychological space, under a hail of violent mental associations culled from headlines and illustrated catastrophic journalism.[253]

More specifically, Bacon's figure calls to mind wartime images of Nazi leaders like Goebbels, standing in all their finery before banks of microphones and surrounded by fabulous swathes of flowers, for which the bones and garlands are Bacon's equivalents. But, in the imagination of the viewer, he might well assume other identities, familiar from either life or literature. He is, perhaps, Pope IV, who had evidently colluded with the Nazi policy of extermination of the Jews. The collar reads as a variant on that worn by the cardinals depicted by, say, Velásquez, including of course the great *Innocent* X, to which this may be Bacon's first homage, especially given the overall affinity between the palette of reds, pinks, white and deep shadow and the colours of the Velásquez that he would have known from reproductions. The figure might evoke Pontius Pilate, Macbeth, or some enthroned figure in a Greek tragedy, perhaps Agamemnon brooding over the necessary sacrifice his own daughter Iphigenia, in order to secure favourable wind for his army sailing to war against Troy. Alternatively, one might think back to Joseph Conrad's novella *Heart of Darkness*. All Europe, we are told by Conrad's narrator, had contributed to the making of Kurtz, who compiled his eloquent, high-minded report for the International Society for the Suppression of Savage Customs, but ended up scrawling 'Exterminate all the Brutes' onto his manuscript. By this time, his nerves had gone wrong, and 'caused him to preside at certain midnight dances ending with unspeakable rites, which . . . were offered up to him'. The result of Marlow's identification of the ornamental posts in front of Kurtz's hut was 'to make me throw my head back as if before a blow'. They turned out to be dried skulls on posts, foreshadowing the bones and meat decorating the podium in Bacon's *Painting*.[254] The picture as a whole gives the spectator a sensation equivalent to Marlow's final sighting of Kurtz : 'I saw on that ivory face the expression of sombre pride, of ruthless power, of craven terror – of an intense and hopeless despair . . . He cried put in a whisper at some image, at some vision – he cried out twice, a cry that was no more than a breath – "The horror! The horror!" '[255]

The ambiguity of *Painting* operates on a number of levels. The image is both a crucifixion and a butcher's shop; the figure is equally Goebbels, Macbeth, or Kurtz. The setting is at once private and domestic (signified by the blinds and Persian carpet), and public (the umbrella, podium and microphones). The floor plane reads both as blood-spattered and as

54 Christopher Nevinson, *The Twentieth Century*, 1932–35, oil and canvas, 183.7 × 122.5 cm, The Laing Art Gallery, Newcastle upon Tyne, Tyne and Wear Museums Service.

a luxurious Persian carpet. Neither the blinds nor the metal railings construct a coherent spatial perspective. The montage construction of the picture as a whole suggests not just surrealist artistic imagery but also, perhaps, contemporary cinema posters. At the same time, *Painting* invites association with both the swagger portrait, as discussed earlier, with a crucifixion altarpiece and also with the tradition of monumental, allegorical imagery, with its lofty didactic objectives, as exemplified by Christopher Nevinson's *The Twentieth Century* (1932–35; pl. 54). The central brooding figures and montage construction are common to both pictures. The Nevinson was envisaged as the cartoon for a public mural, and offered an ambitious symbolic representation of 'the Clash between Thought, Mechanical Invention, Race Idolatry and the Regimentation of Youth'.[256] The Bacon looks as though it might mean something equally momentous, but in the end there is no finite message to decode, and 'the most violent contradictions' fail to resolve into any kind of consoling or elevating harmony. The reactions of the nervous system take priority over the rationalisations of the intellect. Adapting Eliot, one might well see such a picture as controlling, ordering, and giving shape and significance to the immense panorama of fear and violence that in 1946 was contemporary history.

CONTINUITIES

We return in this final section to the idea of the 'long Second World War', with its suggestion of fundamental continuities of outlook and mood superseding the apparent division of the 1940s into wartime and post-war halves. Certainly, an essential coherence to the period was projected in one of the first attempts to define the identity of the period, namely the exhibition *Ten Decades* that was mounted at the ICA in 1951. The section on the 1940s, which included a *Head* by Bacon and *Tapping a Steel Furnace* by Sutherland, was provided with the following gloss by the organiser of the show: 'Under the impact of the war, romanticism and expressionism become the prevailing styles. The realisation of the tragedy of the human situation, the sense of helplessness, and a certain nostalgic and desperate attempt to find roots in the English artistic tradition have grown more intense as the years have passed. The intellectual climate in the summer of 1951 is not so very different'.[257]

The critical discourse surrounding the work of Sutherland and Bacon in the late 1940s provides further evidence for the prolongation of a wartime sensibility. Thus the stylistic and thematic analogies between Sutherland's wartime production and the pictures he subsequently generated from motifs observed in the south of France seemed to be matched by continuities in tone and atmosphere. However delightful he may have found the Midi as an environment in which to live and work, as an imaginary terrain the place seemed far from straightforwardly arcadian in Sutherland's work. In this sense he was breaking with a long tradition of colourful, life-enhancing landscape imagery stemming from Monet's and Renoir's visit to the Midi in 1883, through to work by Signac, Matisse, Picasso and a great many others, including Sutherland's good friend Eardley Knollys with whom he and Kathleen had driven down through France on their first visit in 1947.[258] When Sutherland's south of France paintings were exhibited in 1948 at the Hanover Gallery, Raymond Mortimer noted that the artist 'remained fascinated by the fierce points he used in his pictures of thorns'. The affinity extended, he observed, to the gloom-laden emotional register of Sutherland's new work:

> Into the Mediterranean basin . . . into this gravely harmonious landscape, Mr Sutherland seems to have brought an obsessive, though unconscious, sense of tragedy . . . A world lacerated by wars, pustulent with concentration camps, is hardly calculated to produce idyllic painting . . . Mr. Sutherland, moreover, is a fervent Catholic and almost all the Catholic art of our time is tragic; the writings of Mauriac, Graham Greene . . . Their sense of what man might be fills them with disgust for what he is.

> Mr. Sutherland's earlier works seem infused with an almost pantheistic love of nature. He painted Welsh mountains as if they were animate beings with which he identified himself. But now more usually he seems to find in nature symbols of human suffering and cruelty. The Southern vegetation hardens into instruments of torture. The palm – traditional emblem of the martyr's victory – is degraded into a weapon for his executioner.[259]

If Mortimer's reading reflected the current mood, he nevertheless felt compelled to acknowledge its subjectivity. For the bright colours of the pictures allowed for a contrary, more optimistic reading, and he noted that the artist himself, presumably in conversation, 'goes so far as to consider them replete with gaiety'.[260] Like Bacon, Sutherland clearly liked to resist obvious and reductive responses to his pictures.

Mortimer's sense of Sutherland's fundamental disenchantment, if not his affirmative evaluation, was reinforced by the vituperative polemic launched by Geoffrey Grigson, whom we have encountered as a fervent admirer, like Sutherland himself, of the work of Samuel Palmer. The portentously titled 'Authentic and False' in the New 'Romanticism' had appeared in the March 1948 issue of *Horizon*.[261] For Grigson, an authentic, life-affirming possibility for art was represented by nineteenth-century predecessors such as Blake and Palmer, by contemporaries such as Henry Moore and by one or two unnamed younger artists – doubtless including John Craxton, the subject of another Grigson book – who had adapted the lessons of Piper and Sutherland to the expression of 'love and growth' rather than 'hate or death'.[262] Sutherland himself, however, is an object of special hostility. His pictures are admittedly 'sharply impressive in their sharp clattering of colour and darkness', but from nature, Grigson declared, Sutherland was only able to extract images of death, just as in his war pictures 'devastation and destruction . . . are accurately and powerfully horrible; are hell, which is his province . . . In St Matthew's Church at Northampton, Henry Moore's affirmative tenderness of the Madonna and Child faces the twists and cruelty of Sutherland's little-headed, crucified Christ who suggests no resurrection'.[263] In the painter's art, 'life sinks without tension into the black death of a denatured rock and a sapless claw'.[264] In sum, the art of Sutherland represents surrender rather than resistance to the spirit of the age: 'if this is an evil time and a time of the prevalent wish for death, that is no great reason for surrendering to a deathly admiration for its expression either in language or in paint'.[265]

Sutherland's own outlook seems to be echoed in the closing paragraphs of Kenneth Clark's *Landscape into Art* (1949), a hugely successful, synoptic account of the entire artistic genre, deriving from the Slade lectures Clark had given in Oxford.[266] Sutherland designed the jacket for the book and is one of the very few twentieth-century artists mentioned. Clark notes the disconcerting 'disappearance of a humanist scale – the way in which a thorn tree or a group of dead thistles suddenly assumes colossal proportions'.[267] As he draws to a conclusion, he ruminates upon the recent disruption by science of received ideas of 'nature': 'we have even lost faith in the stability of what we used hopefully to call 'the natural order'; and, what is worse, we know that we ourselves acquired the means of bringing that order to an end'.[268] In the present apocalyptic circumstances, escape into an ideal world is impossible. The best prospects for landscape painting reside in 'an extension of the pathetic fallacy, and the use of landscape as a focus for our own emotions'.[269] The hope he placed in expressionism, and in the coming of another Grünewald at a time of 'our new wars of religion', sounds with hindsight like a veiled manifesto for the work of Sutherland.[270]

Equally, the work of Bacon was taken by both his admirers and detractors to have captured the mood of the moment. For Melville, as noted, 'these terrible forms were simply reflections of the uneasy fear-haunted mind of modern man'.[271] Wyndham Lewis found Bacon, in his darkness, to be 'perfectly in tune with his time'.[272] Clark styled Bacon 'the interpreter of our contemporary nightmare', while, for a reviewer of his show in late 1950, 'this young painter has become accepted as a symbol of the unquiet mood of our time'.[273] One can also find a certain continuity between Bacon's paintings of the late 1940s and imagery more directly rooted in the experiences of wartime. The series of *Heads* tend to be viewed as concerned with 'what it feels like to be alone in a room', when one experiences a 'disintegration of the social being'.[274] This inner state is expressed by Bacon in painterly terms as a collapse of the outer form of the head into an image which reads both as 'the skull beneath the skin' and as a screaming mouth that is as much bestial as human. Whatever the wider resonance of the image, recollections of wartime dark nights of the soul may have been one layer of association that the pictures had for Bacon. An interesting point of reference is provided by David Gascoyne's poem 'A Wartime Dawn' of April 1940, where the sensations of going to bed in the unremitting darkness of the blackout render all the more vivid the sense of descent into an existential abyss:

> Dulled by the slow glare of the yellow bulb;
> As far from sleep still as at any hour
> Since distant midnight; with a hollow skull
> In which white vapours seem to reel
> Among limp muddles of old thought; till eyes
> Collapse into themselves like clams in mud . . .
> Hands paw the wall to reach the chilly switch;
> Then nerve-shot darkness gradually shakes
> Throughout the room

With gradual awakening comes the 'incommunicable desolation' associated with the prospect of another wartime day:

> Draw now with prickling hand the curtains back;
> Unpin the blackout cloth; let in
> Grim crack-of-dawn's first glimmer through the glass.[275]

It is the unpinning of the blackout cloth that especially brings to mind Bacon's *Head II* (pl. 102), where a curtain, with safety pin attached and opening onto blackness beyond, forms the backdrop to the disintegrating figure within. Whereas Sutherland's association with Gascoyne is well-established, there is no evidence that Gascoyne and Bacon knew one another, although both men were homosexual, or bisexual in Gascoyne's case, spent time in the legendary dives of 'Fitzrovia' and had friends in common such as Sutherland and Peter Watson. It is hard to believe, therefore, that they did not have some contact, although one can also imagine the often camp and deliberately outrageous Bacon finding Gascoyne an overly earnest figure.

The wartime photography of Lee Miller offers another set of parallels to Bacon's imagery. Again, it is not known if Bacon and Miller knew one another, though they moved in the same circles, shared a fascination with surrealism and Picasso, and had a mutual friend in Sutherland, whom Miller photographed.[276] The affinities between painter and photographer may arise from a shared response to, and willingness to confront, wartime revelations about man's infinite capacity for inhumanity. Miller's famous 1942 photograph of her fellow American photographer David Sherman, equipped with gas-mask, camera and umbrella in order to sally forth to record the war for *Life* magazine, provides a curious anticipation of the imagery of Bacon's *Figure Study II* (pl. 55 and pl. XIV). The umbrella is the initial common denominator, of course; in the Bacon, it serves to cast the face into shadow, except for the mouth, masking the figure's humanity as, in a more literal fashion, does Sherman's gas-mask. There is a shared dependence in the two works upon the surrealist device of the irrational, incongruous juxtaposition of banal everyday items, but of course the tone of the two images is utterly different. Miller and Bacon came into closer artistic alignment during the latter stages of the war, when she was accompanying the Allied invasion of Europe as a press photographer and was publishing accounts of her experiences, incongruously enough, in *Vogue* magazine. In 1944, for instance, both artist and photographer were drawn to the imagery of Christ's Passion, as presented in Sixteenth-Century North European art, when seeking to convey the pathos of their own violent times. In a field hospital in France, Miller witnessed a badly wounded soldier being bandaged up: 'In the chiaroscuro of khaki and white I was reminded of Hieronymus Bosch's painting "The Carrying of the Cross" '.[277] Moreover, Bacon and Sutherland were especially affected by the images emerging from the Nazi death camps, of which some of the most harrowing and most widely circulated were Miller's images of Buchenwald and Dachau. Miller's photograph of human remains in a cremation furnace at Buchenwald (pl. 56) provides a telling point of comparison with Bacon's *Painting* of the following year. In more metaphorical terms, the picture projects the same basic meaning that Miller's photos convey: to a degree that is almost beyond imagining, human bodies had come to be treated as animals in a slaughterhouse. The affinity between the two images extends from the frontality and symmetry of their spatial construction, at a formal level, to the sense of sheer horror they transmit through the juxtaposition of the dismemberment and butchering of the organic body and the hard metallic surfaces of modern technology, turned into an instrument of power and destruction.

Bacon's imagery is foreshadowed again in Miller's remarkable images of the SS guards at Buchenwald who had been identified out of uniform by the surviving inmates: 'If they catch

55 Lee Miller, *David E Sherman, dressed for war,* 1942, photograph, Lee Miller Archives, England.

56 Lee Miller, *Human remains in a cremation furnace, Buchenwald, Germany*, 1945, photograph, Lee Miller Archives, England.

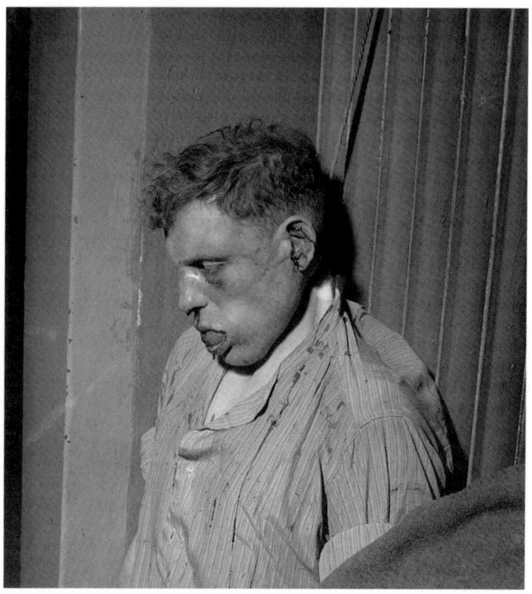

57 Lee Miller, *Suicided SS Guard, Buchenwald, Germany*, 1945, photograph, Lee Miller Archives, England.

them [Miller recorded] they give them a thorough working over and bring them back to the camp jail house. Their condition is terrible, but they are still alive and not as badly off as their new captors . . . one SS man had enough of everything and hanged himself sitting down by tying a string to the radiator. He was taken out on a stretcher, stripped and thrown on a heap of bony cadavers where he looked shockingly big, the well fed bastard'.[278] The image of the guard who killed himself looks ahead to Bacon's *Head I* of 1948 (pls 14 and 57). Similar ingredients are encountered in the two images – shallow, claustrophobic spaces, the backdrops of hard metal and geometry, the taut lengths of rope, and, at the centre of all this, the deformed and distorted features of a human head. At a deeper level, we encounter parallel visions of extreme human degradation. At Buchenwald, Miller encountered actual individuals, symbolising, she might have said, a whole nation, whose lust for destruction of their fellow humans could only culminate in self-destruction; individuals whose moral bestiality had, in death, found its true reflection in a grotesque outer aspect. The bleakness of her vision found an echo in the pictures Bacon created some three to four years after the appalling events to which she bore witness. In turn, Miller included a Bacon *Head* in the ICA exhibition *The Wonder and Horror of the Human Head*, which she and Penrose organised in 1953.[279]

Finally, Bacon's pictorial imagery manifests a more general compatibility with contemporary sensibilities. In the later issues of *Horizon* we encounter vivid expressions of the disposition to generalise from the very specific experiences of the Second World War to a more 'universal' account of the contemporary human condition. For instance, the 'extreme situation' is posited as the norm of everyday life in Albert Votav's essay from 1949, spanning literary criticism and sociology. We are informed that: 'With no possible comfort available outside his own tortured soul, the modern hero . . . is more lonely than man has ever been.' To describe the social environment that nurtured this state of affairs, Votav coined the phrase 'the concentration-camp universe', an explicitly metaphorical extension of the term commonly associated with the institutionalised extermination by the Nazis of Jews and other racial and political groupings. For Votav, however, this was not so much an aberration from civilised norms as a symptom of the general drift of contemporary life: 'in the concentration camp is realised nothing more than the logical extension of certain aspects of modern society'.[280] E. M. Forster's assertion that 'in 1938–9 the more despair a man can take on board without sinking the more completely he is alive' finds an echo in Cyril Connolly's editorial essay for what turned out to be the valedictory issue of *Horizon*, which appeared in the winter of 1949–50. In his 'Comment', Connolly took the opportunity to try to pull together the threads of contemporary culture and to define 'the inner trend of the Forties'.[281] For Connolly, the same fundamental message emanated from Paul Bowles's remarkable new novel *The Sheltering Sky*, in which the characters 'carry the loneliness and isolation of human beings, even those whose ties are closest, a stage further than any contemporary', and from Bacon's 'horror-fretted canvasses', discussed later in the issue by Robert Melville. Such works maintained a 'desperate struggle of the modern movement, between man, betrayed by science, bereft of religion, deserted by the pleasant imaginings of humanism against the blind fate of which he is now so expertly conscious'. The concluding sentiments with which Connolly signed off were well-turned, but bleak in the extreme: 'it is closing time in the Gardens of the West and from now on an artist will be judged only by the resonance of his solitude or the quality of his despair'.

3 INFLUENCES

Having looked at Sutherland and Bacon in the context of the Second World War, and the distinctive literary sensibility to which it gave rise in Britain, it is now worth considering how far their art was informed by aspects of the broader artistic and cultural climate of the period. Recent and contemporary literature will remain a significant point of reference, as will the immediate British milieu in which they operated. However, an international awareness was one of the distinctive characteristics of the period, not only before and after the actual war years, when artists and works of art could travel freely, but even during the long phase of wartime isolation, when patriotic instincts came to the fore and found strong expression in the realm of the arts. What, then, can be learnt from Bacon and Sutherland about the developing British reception of a European modernist culture that was itself multi-faceted rather than monolithic, and in a process of continual evolution in response to wider circumstances?

In what specific ways did each adapt to their own purposes the new creative possibilities that were emanating, for instance, from Paris?

Exploring such problems serves not only to illuminate the work of the two artists, and further aspects of their interchange, but also to qualify some pervasive assumptions in the literature about their supposedly divergent allegiances. For example, it is commonly maintained that Sutherland's art finds its essential moorings in 'neo-romanticism', a tendency in British art of the late 1930s and 1940s that is often presented, by defenders and detractors alike, as intrinsically hostile to the international modern movement. The perceived antidote was harking back to an older, native tradition of celebrating the natural landscape, epitomised by early nineteenth-century artists such as Turner, Constable and Palmer.[1] In contrast, the most influential discussions of Bacon's work emphasise the modernist and cosmopolitan character of his work. By opening his artfully constructed volume of interviews with an exchange about the Picasso derivations in *Three Studies for Figures at the Base of a Crucifixion*, David Sylvester implied a passing on of the torch.[2] The great master of the first half of the twentieth century had, we are encouraged to believe, found a worthy successor in one of the major figurative artists, on an international stage, during the decades after the Second World War. Other less partisan accounts have explored continuities between Bacon and the surrealist project, notably the challenging and dissident version of surrealism associated with Georges Bataille and the magazine *Documents*.[3]

Such readings of Sutherland and Bacon naturally offer an insight into their work, but they also produce reductive oversimplifications, especially in Sutherland's case, and they result in an exaggerated polarisation between the two artists' concerns and attitudes. By way of corrective, David Alan Mellor has suggestively argued that the art of Bacon possesses its own points of connection with the English artistic tradition, as embodied by figures such as Hogarth, Watts and Sickert.[4] Equally, the art of Sutherland seems, on more searching consideration, to be as strongly rooted in international and modernist interests as by a sense of national roots. Indeed, at the time of his closest personal and artistic interaction with Bacon, Sutherland was emphatically concerned with distinguishing his own art and outlook from the spirit of self-conscious parochialism, in tune with the emotional climate of wartime Britain, which was articulated by figures such as John Piper and Michael Ayrton. Indeed, in 1945 Sutherland took pains to rebut Ayrton's annexation of his work for a polemical crusade against the infiltration of European avant-garde approaches, in particular the 'evil influence' of Picasso.[5] In a letter that he published in response to Ayrton's pronouncement, Sutherland asserted that Picasso had been an important inspiration for his work, and he proceeded to describe the various ways in which a painter might be 'influenced', including the creative development of possibilities that an older artist had opened up, constituting 'the method of tradition'. In January 1947, Sutherland published a further corrective in *The New Statesman*, stating his objections to Benedict Nicolson's observation that English painting had 'gained from the enforced insularity of the war', and that he, Sutherland, and several others had 'turned their backs on Paris to seek inspiration in the English romantic movement of the early nineteenth century'. For Sutherland, this represented 'yet another example of the habit of art historians to oversimplify – to label and pigeonhole':

> I do not deny that I received great adolescent stimulus from Palmer and Blake; but that does not mean I turn my back on Paris. The question of influences is not as easy as that, and is surely a more complex and subtle matter . . .
>
> Painters are affected by things which come to them from all over the place; from many kinds of painting and many things.
>
> One absorbs what one needs at a given time.[6]

These sentiments give a revealing insight into their author's attitudes, but they also provide an appropriate starting point for a discussion of, amongst other things, Bacon's and Sutherland's artistic 'influences'. This now outmoded usage, with its implication of passivity, is of course wholly inadequate to the complex and selective processes of transformation and adaptation by which artists derive stimulation for their own work by looking at other art, whether past or present.[7] Such adaptations are bound to be purposeful, and conditioned by the accidents of what they had encountered of another culture, as well as by existing concerns and values that predispose them to respond to certain aspects rather than others in the work under scrutiny. Moreover, I shall argue that Sutherland and Bacon, and perhaps many other artists besides, were excited at some level by large-scale ideas or programmes that were generally 'in the air', such as surrealism or existentialism, but that what really provoked and challenged them were specific works by particular artists or writers that they happened to know about and that struck an imaginative chord. Such movements were diverse and incoherent in their artistic manifestations, and must have seemed even more so at the time than they do with the clarifying benefit of hindsight. In sum, I want to avoid measuring these two artists' creative assimilations against some essentialist definition of what, say, surrealism or existentialism stood for.

Before embarking on a detailed discussion of this theme, it seems appropriate to indicate certain general aspects of the organisation of the material that may seem incongruous. First, whereas the discussion so far has contained highly integrated accounts of Sutherland and Bacon, and their diverse layers of affinity, this chapter includes extended sections devoted exclusively to Sutherland, at the beginning, and predominantly to Bacon, towards the end. In between there comes a lengthy passage in which they are, once again, viewed in conjunction with one another. The relative separation of the two artists is symptomatic of the fact that this chapter focuses rather more on divergences between Bacon and Sutherland, in part reflecting a generational gulf, within the general theme of their shared interest in the currents of contemporary art, while its predecessors, by contrast, sought to establish similarities. Secondly, in order to place Sutherland's work and attitudes in relevant contexts, we need to step outside the chronological limits that otherwise govern this study, and to start by looking back to the 1930s. The work of this period reveals that his artistic roots are indeed a complex and subtle matter, with his responses to particular manifestations of modern

European art mediated by a larger framework of attitudes, newly crystallised in Britain and clearly assimilated by Sutherland, which valued the potential for an interplay between native and international stimuli, and between modernism and tradition, as opposed to the more familiar sense that these represented alternative possibilities. It is necessary, in consequence, to look in some detail at indigenous points of departure for Sutherland's work and thinking, before directly considering his international affinities.

SUTHERLAND'S ROOTS

Sutherland's signature artistic idiom was first properly manifest in a group of paintings dating from 1936, in particular *Welsh Landscape with Roads* and the two versions of *Red Tree* (pl. 11 and 58). The experimental and transitional character of such pictures is reflected in the stylistic inconsistencies and the lack of technical assurance that certainly afflict both *Welsh Landscape with Roads* and what is usually presumed to be the initial version of *Red Tree*, which is quite freely worked, in contrast to its more precise and schematic successor.[8] The fact that these images were not exhibited in the International Surrealist Exhibition, which opened in the summer of 1936, implies that they were executed, or completed, during the second half of the year. Both versions of *Red Tree* were exhibited, separately, in commercial group shows in early 1937, from one of which Kenneth Clark presumably acquired the more painterly variant.[9] *Welsh Landscape with Roads* almost certainly corresponds to the *Welsh Landscape* of similar dimensions shown in an exhibition of *British Contemporary Art* at the Rosenberg and Helft Gallery.[10] All three paintings were executed in oil on canvas, whereas much of his surviving work from the first half of the 1930s comprised smaller-scale work on paper. This suggests either that Sutherland was raising his sights, or, more likely, that at some point he destroyed a previous body of oils.[11]

Sutherland's creation of a distinctive idiom was one component in a wider reinvention of his artistic identity in the mid-1930s. He identified a personal field of subject-matter, the landscape of Pembrokeshire. He acquired a new set of friends and supporters, Kenneth Clark especially, but also Colin Anderson, Robert Wellington, John Piper and Myfanwy Evans, and Oliver Simon of the Curwen Press. Their enthusiasm for his work, combined no doubt with Sutherland's own ambition to make a mark as he moved into his early thirties, prompted his publication of three essays that together serve to illuminate the attitudes that shaped his current work. It is worth noting that Sutherland was being taken seriously for his sensibility, so to speak, well before he had provided much evidence that his actual work was going to make a significant contribution. 'A Trend in English Draughtsmanship' (1936) and 'Graven Images: Line Engraving and the Illustrated Book' (1937) both appeared in *Signature*, a new, beautifully designed and illustrated magazine, edited by Oliver Simon, which focussed on both historical and contemporary approaches to typography, the graphic arts and fine book

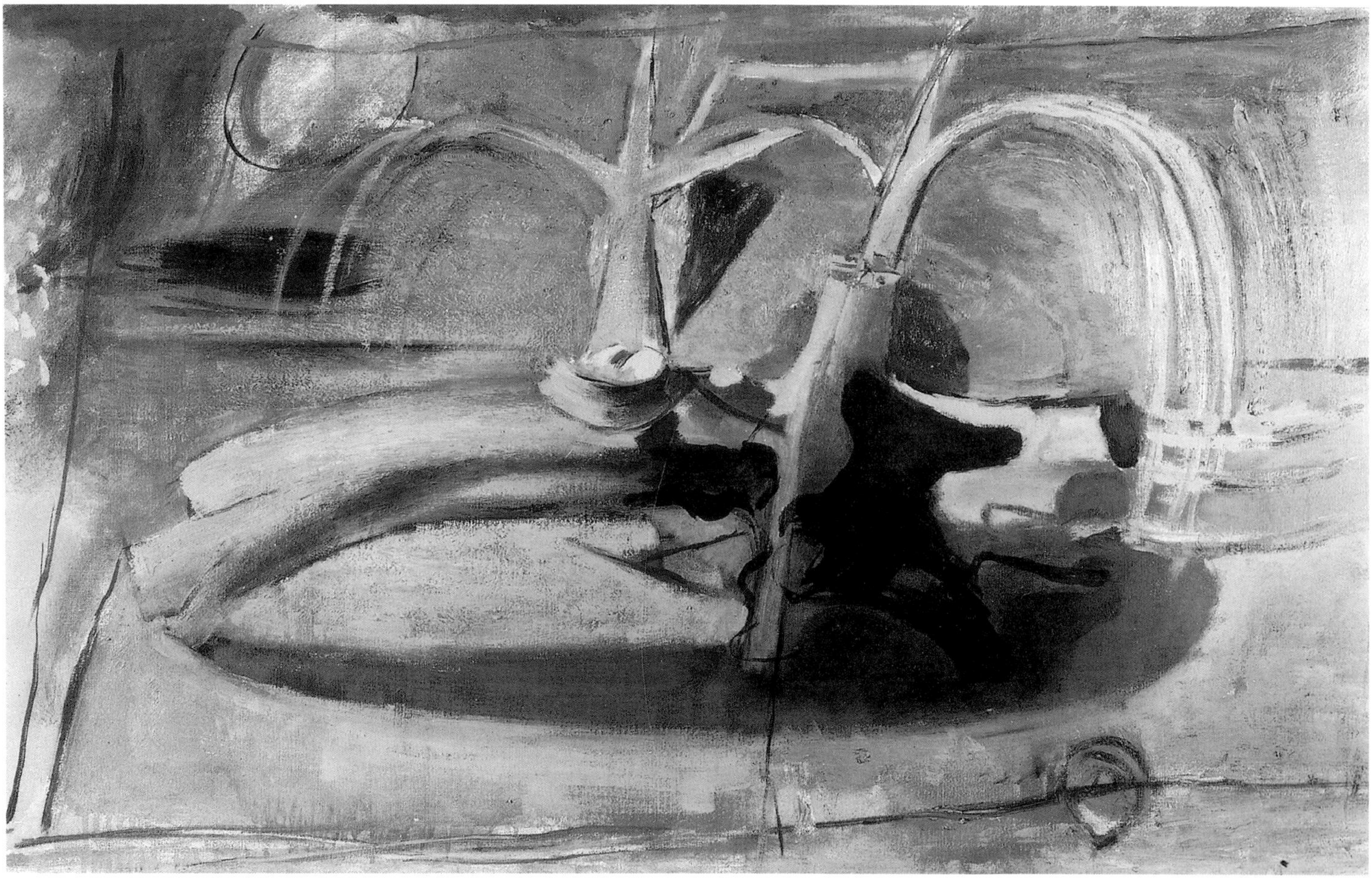

58 Graham Sutherland, *Red Tree*, 1936, oil on canvas, 55.8 × 91.5 cm, Private Collection.

production.[12] Other artists featured in *Signature*, who shared Sutherland's combined interests in fine art and these more applied areas of activity, included Paul Nash, Edward Bawden, Eric Ravilious and John Piper. The critic Geoffrey Grigson contributed articles on George Stubbs and Samuel Palmer. The significance of *Signature* has tended to be overlooked, although, according to Andrew Causey, no journal 'can make a greater claim to have stimulated the taste that became Neo-Romanticism'.[13] Finally, Sutherland's 'An English Stone Landmark' was published in *The Painter's Object* (1937), the anthology of texts on contemporary art devised by Myfanwy Evans, also editor of the avant-garde magazine *Axis* (1935–37).[14] The book comprised a mixture of new essays by English artists, such as Nash, Julian Trevelyan, Moore, Piper and Sutherland, and translated texts by prominent European artists including de Chirico, Hélion, Ernst, Kandinsky, Léger, Ozenfant, Moholy-Nagy and the celebrated Zervos interview with Picasso. The appearance of these essays suggests that Sutherland identified with, and was valued by, a specific faction within the London avant-garde, distinct from the groupings associated with social realism, surrealism and abstraction. It was a faction that combined a wide-ranging curiosity about European modernism with an unashamed interest in distinctively English artistic and vernacular traditions, and also in the native scene, as represented in *The Painter's Object* by Nash ('Swanage, or Seaside Surrealism') and Sutherland's meditations on Brimham Rock in 'An English Stone Landmark'.

In the most general terms, Sutherland's new works from 1936 can be seen as rehearsing a symbiotic association between 'primitive' landscape imagery and stylistic simplification or abstraction, whose previous history had extended from post-impressionism in the 1880s, via fauvism, expressionism and so forth, through to the *faux-naïve* landscapes that Ben Nicholson and others had painted in Cumberland in the late 1920s. The country landscape had always been Sutherland's stock in trade. When he turned from etching to painting in the early 1930s, he began working with motifs encountered on trips to Kent, Dorset, Cornwall and elsewhere. However, following his first visit in 1934, it was the landscape of west Pembrokeshire that became his favoured and personal vehicle for exploring the primitivist landscape genre. He had apparently been urged to visit the area by Robert Wellington, who ran the art gallery connected to Zwemmer's art bookshop between 1929 and 1935.[15] Wellington himself had evidently visited Pembrokeshire for the first time in 1933, a year in which he arranged one-man shows of work by Bawden and Ravilious, alongside more international exhibitions devoted, for example, to 'Modern French Masters'.[16] Such English artists took their bearings from Paul Nash, and the same was true, as will become apparent, of Sutherland. They also exemplified a relatively conventional treatment of landscape imagery, modest in scale and degree of formalisation, that is widely encountered in the 1930s. This type of art correlates with a larger cultural phenomenon, namely the tendency to project an idealised fantasy of rural, traditional and ancient England, as an antidote to the dreariness, shallowness and uniformity that were perceived to characterise modern life not just in the town and the city, but also in that hinterland between city and country that the motor car had transformed into a site of suburbia, ribbon development and mass middle-class escapism.[17] On the surface, Sutherland's paintings from the latter part of 1936 bear a family resemblance to a picture like Bawden's *Essex Landscape* from the same year (pl. 59), although the comparison highlights Sutherland's departures from this less ambitious idiom.

The greater remoteness of Pembrokeshire went hand in hand with Sutherland's pursuit of a more psychologically resonant and less obviously picturesque interpretation of landscape imagery. At the time, the place was extremely difficult to reach, except by means of slow country roads, and it retained a certain wild and 'unspoilt' character, not so much rural as primordial. Here, at least, it seemed possible to extend the long tradition, going back to Richard Wilson in the eighteenth century, of discerning a certain sublime power in the Welsh landscape. A book about Wales, published in 1937 and aimed at a popular readership, observed that 'a man wandering among the cromlechs and stone circles of the windy Pembrokeshire hills may warm his imagination with many glowing visions' of ancient civilisations and religious rituals.[18] Another passage evoked the Western coastal area that was to become Sutherland country: 'these are the oldest lands of Wales, the ancient ribs and earliest rocks of geologic time, cut only by little streams which drain these plateaux. These streams have worn steep watercourses down to the creeks of the coast, so that you will find in Pembrokeshire

59 Edward Bawden, *Essex Landscape*, 1936, watercolour, 45.7 × 57.9 cm, Private Collection.

the roads full of sudden descents, the hills turning sharply downward from the plain, sloping to a bridge, and mounting the other side again'.[19] Moreover, Pembrokeshire is in Britain but not in England, neither geographically or culturally. In 'Welsh Sketch Book', Sutherland recalled his first impressions: 'I was visiting a country, a part of which, at least, spoke a foreign tongue, and it certainly seemed very foreign to me, though sufficiently accessible for me to feel that I could claim it as my own'.[20] In this respect, Sutherland's imaginative appropriation of Pembrokeshire might even be connected to that veritable obsession with the concept of being 'abroad' that Paul Fussell has identified in current British literary culture.[21] During the mid-1930s, the manifestations of this impulse in fiction and travel books encompassed publications by Isherwood, Orwell, Greene, Byron, Waugh, Auden and many others. Though less far-flung than Africa or Iceland, Sutherland's Pembrokeshire was nevertheless one more variation on the cult of the unfamiliar, the unspoilt and the remote. His paintings projected an 'internal Tahiti', to use Robert Hughes' felicitous phrase describing the contemporary vogue in current American art for motifs extracted from the remarkable landscape of the Southwestern United States.[22] Indeed Raymond Mortimer's review of Sutherland's one-man show in 1938 stated that 'the artist's vision has extracted from Welsh landscapes oranges and pinks as sumptuous as those that forced themselves upon Gauguin in tropical Tahiti'.[23]

The preconceptions that shaped his observations of nature can be understood from Sutherland's public account of his approach in a closely related pair of essays, 'An English Stone

Landmark' (1937) and the celebrated 'Welsh Sketch Book', which he agreed to write for publication in *Horizon* magazine in 1942. Each comprises a detailed account of visiting, and submitting to the spirit of, certain actual places, rather than giving a direct account of Sutherland's own work in response to such experiences. The 1937 essay gives a first-person narrative of his encounter with an extraordinary natural sight, a 'primitive environment' dominated by bizarre and ancient rock formations. Sutherland describes crossing a plain 'redeemed from emptiness by the road which curves across it', and catching a first sight of 'innumerable sharp forms' seen against 'the effulgent figure of the sun'. When approached, the 'real vastness of the assemblage' is revealed, and the spatial distribution of the rocks, can be more readily grasped: 'each intricate grouping unfolds the limit of another'.[24] The 'strangeness of the scene' is enhanced by the contrast between the 'dismal privacy' of these natural forms, and the presence of a single house, a patch of corn, and cattle who appear 'restless, as if disturbed by the foreboding atmosphere of the place'. The bare facts of the scene are transmuted and made all the more uncanny by the play of natural light and by the viewer's imaginative projection of analogies. Thus the setting sun turns the monoliths 'yellow, pink and vermilion': 'The coloured patches which streak the surfaces give emphasis to the form and variety to the eye'. They 'assume tones as of blood', while the lichens 'evoke the texture and form that we associate with the uncontrolled blots on French marbled paper'. With some stones, the 'corrosion of their surfaces . . . gives them the appearance of bound bundles of wood'. But the dominant impressions are anthropomorphic. The large stones near the house 'rise, like unmentionable bathers, from pools of water'; they 'bend forward' and support 'on their backs small rocks like little slothful heads'. One 'huge conglomerate mass of stone' is 'shaped like a growth which one sometimes sees attached to the nose of a peasant', although because it is stone 'it is divested of the horror that such an affliction inspires'. The priority accorded to subjective sensations, as opposed to factual description, is indicated by the fact that no geographical details are supplied in the text. It is only the inclusion of a picture postcard as an illustration to the essay that tells us that Sutherland is evoking Brimham Rock in Yorkshire. Nor of course do we learn that his visit had been suggested initially by Jack Beddington, in connection with a commission to design a Shell Poster which also appeared in 1937, though it did not feature in *The Painter's Object* (pl. 60). Appropriately given its purpose of encouraging motor trips to natural sights, Sutherland's poster seems relatively descriptive in style and picturesque in conception. In the essay, by contrast, he seeks to convey the awesome mystery of the scene and the powerful emotional and imaginative impact it exerted upon him, especially when seen in fading light at the end of the day, rather than in the clear daylight presented in the poster. One senses that it is the essay rather than the image that Sutherland felt most free to convey the essential spirit, as he saw it, of the strange landscape around Brimham Rock.

In 'Welsh Sketch Book', Sutherland described those features and aspects of the remote Pembrokeshire landscape that had so 'delighted' him on his first visit and during his subse-

60 Graham Sutherland, *Brimham Rock*, 1937, gouache, 53.3 × 97.5 cm, courtesy Shell Art Collection.

quent regular stays, and which had formed the starting point for so much of his work as a painter. This was preferable to characterising his art directly: 'I would rather write to you about such places than about the paintings themselves: for how can a painter explain his paintings?'[25] Describing 'the country that one likes . . . and its peculiarities' might serve to 'give some hint as to the genesis of the paintings', though the mysteries of the creative process defied rationalisation: 'It is quite impossible to follow with any exactitude the path taken by the brain in the fixing of images seen by the eye, stored in the mind, and drawn out of the subconscious.'[26] The essay proceeds to give a detailed topographic and visual account of two coastal areas to the north and south of St Bride's Bay, the most westerly tip of Pembrokeshire jutting out into the Irish Sea. At times, Sutherland is clearly evoking sensations that had also found visual expression. *Welsh Landscape with Roads* is the artistic counterpart to one passage:

> The astonishing fertility of these valleys and the complexity of the roads running through them is a delight to the eye. The roads form strong and mysterious arabesques as they rise in terraces, in sight, hidden, turning and splitting as they finally disappear into the sky. To see a solitary human figure descending such a road at the solemn moment of sunset is to realise the enveloping quality of the earth, which can create . . . a mysterious space limit –

> a womb-like enclosure – which gives the human form an extraordinary focus and significance.[27]

Equally, there is an unmistakeable reference to pictures such as *Entrance to a Lane* (1939; pl. 25) in the account of a different area of countryside, the descent to an estuary through damp woodland, which is 'all dark, save where the mossy lanes . . . which dive down to the opening, admit the sun, hinged, as it were, to the top of the trees'.[28] As in the pictures, Sutherland's verbal description of physical sensations is constantly mutating into more imaginative responses. He emphasises the 'exultant strangeness of the place, for strange it certainly is, many people whom I know hate it, and I cannot but admit that it possesses an element of disquiet'.[29] Elsewhere he describes the 'whole setting' in terms of 'exuberance – of darkness and light, of decay and life. Rarely have I been so conscious of the contrasting of those elements in so small a compass'.[30] The place had given him an 'emotional feeling of being on the brink of some drama'.[31] Sutherland indicates that conveying the essential resonance of observed motifs had required a process of stylistic transformation, or paraphrase in his own terminology:

> It was in this country that I began to learn painting. It seemed impossible here for me to sit down and make finished paintings 'from nature'. Indeed, there were no 'ready-made' subjects for me to paint. The spaces and concentrations of this clearly constructed land were stuff for storing in the mind. Their essence was intellectual and emotional . . . I found that I could express what I felt only by paraphrasing what I saw . . . I felt as much part of the earth as my features were part of me. I did not feel that my imagination was in conflict with the real, but that reality was a dispersed and disintegrated form of imagination.[32]

He had soon given up 'painting on the spot'.[33] Instead, he immersed himself in the landscape and was able to use sketchbook drawings to make paintings at a remove in time and space, in his Kent studio, which sought to recreate and distil the original heightened sensation, rather than to describe the mere topographical data. The title of *Welsh Landscape with Roads* is deliberately unspecific, as was the case for most of Sutherland's landscapes. Moreover, the composition seems to have been constructed from ideas present in several different drawings and sketchbook studies, though it primarily derives from an ink and wash study, presumably made on the spot, depicting the valley above Porthclais.[34] The inclusion of the animal skull and of the running figure, which was much larger in sketches and probably at an earlier stage of what is clearly a heavily reworked painting, are especially important in creating a mysterious and highly charged atmosphere. As Sutherland remarked in 'Welsh Sketch Book', 'The mind wanders from contemplation of living cattle to their ghosts. It is no uncommon sight to see a horse's skull or horse's skull or horns of cattle lying bleached in the sun. Neither do we feel that the black-green ribs of half-buried wrecks and the phantom tree roots, bleached and washed by the waves, exist but to emphasise the extraordinary completeness of the scene.'[35]

61 Henry Moore, *Reclining Figure*, Elmwood, length 93.3 cm, Albright-Knox Art Gallery, Buffalo, New York.

It was in the two versions of *Red Tree* that Sutherland began to focus on such phantom tree roots as a subject. In the more painterly version, the dominant root form is set against a summary landscape backdrop, suggesting an encounter in the natural world. But in its companion picture, the background is reduced to a rhythmic arrangement of flat planes, evoking light and space in only the most generalised terms. Whilst downplaying the landscape context, Sutherland also heightened the suggestion of bodily associations in the root by means of both the smooth biomorphic forms that he extracted from his more irregular starting point and the use of a pinkish brown colouring. This was an interest he had evidently hit upon in Wales: 'it was in this area that I learned that landscape was not necessarily scenic, but that its parts have an individual figurative detachment'.[36] It is interesting that Sutherland should have chosen to accompany 'An English Stone Landmark' with a reproduction of *Red Tree*, along with *Mobile Mask*. The anthropomorphism of this new picture complemented his account of Brimham Rock. Moreover, the very evident fusion of natural and human suggestions brings to mind Henry Moore's current drawings and reclining figure carvings (pl. 61). In 'A Trend in English Draughtsmanship' (1936) Sutherland illustrated a drawing by his friend, and fellow teacher at Chelsea, and commented that in Moore's drawings he found the artist 'discovering one thing with the help of another, and by their resemblance making the unknown known'.[37] Moore was of course an inveterate collector of natural found objects, and had been using bones, pebbles and the like as the starting point for 'transformation' drawings since the early 1930s, an inspiration he acknowledged in his own essay in *The Painter's Object*.[38] The sculptor was doubtless one inspiration for the habit that Sutherland himself acquired of lighting upon natural elements and taking them back to his studio, for purposes of artistic transmutation. In 1941, the two artists articulated the common bases of their work in the contributions they made to a BBC radio discussion, also featuring Kenneth Clark. According to Sutherland, the painter must 'learn to recognise himself . . . both materially and spiritually in the landscape and the landscape in himself'. He expressed agreement with Moore's way of thinking, which corresponded, according to Clark, with a 'Wordsworthian relationship to nature'. Sutherland elaborated: 'Personally I find that practically all the figurative elements are contained in landscape. In a sense the landscape painter must look at the landscape as if it were himself . . . he will tend to find that the forms and qualities which start him off, excite his ideas and stimulate his emotions, are the more rare and hidden forms.'[39]

In 1942 Sutherland acknowledged that he had been working with a necessary 'singleness of purpose', and that for the last few years he had been 'preoccupied with a particular aspect of landscape' as well as 'a particular area of country'. The aspect that engaged him is implicit in the striking continuities between 'An English Stone Landmark' and 'Welsh Sketch Book', despite the differences in date and geographical point of reference. In the latter essay, he once again focuses on sunset as the ideal time of day for gleaning the most vivid and intense experiences that Pembrokeshire can offer: 'The quality of light here is magical and transforming . . . Watching from the gloom as the sun's rays strike the further bank, one has the sensation of the after tranquillity of an *explosion* of light.'[40] In both places, Sutherland relishes the evidence of a very basic human use and occupation of the landscape. Another feature that is 'complete' in the spectacle of Pembrokeshire is 'the life of the few inhabitants – almost biblical in its sober dignity'.[41] In fact 'Welsh Sketch Book' contains not only broad analogies with his account of a scene he had encountered in Yorkshire, but also specific echoes and repetitions from his earlier text. Both essays describe traversing a 'wide plain', becoming aware of 'an irregular contour on the horizon' and encountering a 'vast congregation' of rocks as well as houses that, subsuming very minor verbal variations, give scale and quicken by their implications our apprehension of the strangeness of the scene.[42] Overall, such evidence from Sutherland's writings suggests the extent to which it was a preconceived ideal of landscape that preoccupied him, and took priority over topographical particulars.

Finally, 'An English Stone Landmark' suggests a significant point of departure for Sutherland's vision of the natural landscape. Following the elaborate description of Brimham Moor, the 'significance' of the scene is intimated by means of an unidentified quotation from D. H. Lawrence: 'Is it the natural beauty of proportion . . . contrasted with the more studied or ecstatic proportion of mental or spiritual consciousness we are accustomed to?' The final sentence seems to nod obliquely towards the work of Moore, also an enthusiastic reader of Lawrence, and to imply perhaps that one might discern the roots of Moore's art in his native Yorkshire environment: 'Melancholy, impressive and integral such as this, is the basis of sculpture.'[43] In order to understand Sutherland, it is relevant to note John Russell's comment about John Piper, which could equally have applied to Moore: 'his was the generation that read every word of Lawrence as and when it came out'.[44] Certainly, considered as texts, Sutherland's set-piece descriptions of his encounters with places in Yorkshire and Pembrokeshire seem to echo D. H. Lawrence's remarkable, intensely visual accounts of his visits to remote places in Sardinia, Sicily or New Mexico, the kind of writing that clearly provided the source for the question that Sutherland quoted. His use of the term 'complete' is very Lawrentian. Sutherland's Pembrokeshire at times sounds very like the 'scrubby' landscape of Sardinia, with occasional glimpses of cattle and cultivation, and all the 'strange magic' of the island encapsulated in a sight such as this: 'Among the low, moor-like hills, away in a hollow of the wide landscape, one solitary figure . . . working alone, as if eternally'.[45] We might also see, in Sutherland's response to landscape scenery infused with the glow and colours of sunset, a recollection of, for example, Lawrence's ecstatic and more overtly metaphysical response to sensations at the end of the day during his visit to a little village in Italy: 'Where, then, is the meeting-point: where in mankind is the ecstasy of light and dark together, the supreme transcendence of the afterglow, day hovering in the embrace of the coming night like two angels embracing in the heavens . . . Where is the transcendent knowledge in our hearts, uniting sun and darkness, day and night, spirit and senses?'[46] I would argue that, at a deeper level, Sutherland drew sustenance from Lawrence's underlying, highly primitivist outlook: 'The spirit of place is a strange thing. Our mechanical age tries to override it. But it does not succeed. In the end, the strange, sinister spirit of the place, so diverse and adverse in differing places, will smash our mechanical oneness into smithereens.'[47] For Lawrence, places untouched by modernity were distinguished by their singularity. Paradoxically, what Sutherland absorbed from Lawrence was not merely a somewhat over-heated prose style but also a fascination with a particular *kind* of landscape, ancient, rugged, luminous and generally remote from English scenery. It may be that Sutherland's essential sensibility as a landscape artist was triggered by reading D. H. Lawrence at least as much as it was by anything he encountered in contemporary visual art.

'A Trend in English Draughtsmanship' (1936) constituted Sutherland's attempt to construct a pedigree for his own concerns. This essay raises the question of how far his responses to the natural landscape were also underpinned by an engagement with the aesthetic values and pictorial precedents of nineteenth-century romanticism. In later describing the impact of Palmer and Blake as merely an 'adolescent stimulus', Sutherland implied that their influence was confined to the etchings he had produced during the late 1920s, reflecting a renewed interest in Palmer's work epitomised by the major exhibition at the Victoria and Albert Museum in 1926 (pl. 62).[48] In a later interview with Andrew Forge, Sutherland amplified this account of a progression in his work from national to international allegiances: 'Between the years 1927 and 1930 I was very conscious of the English tradition, and rather aggressive about it. I used to think, for instance, of Samuel Palmer as the English Van Gogh. . . . Afterwards, between, say, 1935 and the war, I was not really conscious at all of being specifically English in tradition.'[49] This statement plainly contradicts the evidence of Sutherland's work and pronouncements during the decade or so following his crystallisation of an independent artistic identity. In 'A Trend in English Draughtsmanship' he conceded that the impulse towards

62 Graham Sutherland, *Village*, 1925, etching, 17.5 × 22.5 cm, Cecil Higgins Art Gallery, Bedford.

a subjective vision 'has derived an immense stimulus from abroad', but he also maintained that 'the best English work, whilst retaining its essential universality, shows definite native characteristics'.[50] His positive sense of English roots was explicit when he quoted approvingly Jean Cocteau's remark that the more a poet sings in his genealogical tree, the more his singing is in tune.[51] Sutherland expressed his admiration for the work of Turner and Blake, who were both 'born out of due time, but today we have reached a stage at which we can appreciate their genius and, at least, their influence has made it possible for us to understand work of contemporary artists whose method of approach is comparable.'[52] The latter category included Nash, Moore and, by implication, himself. This sense of a continuous artistic tradition found one of its most elaborate expressions in John Piper's book *British Romantic Artists*, published in 1942, a manifesto for the burgeoning neo-romanticism that concluded with several enthusiastic sentences about Sutherland and was supported by a reproduction of one of the steel works pictures executed for the war artists scheme.[53]

From the late 1930s onwards, Sutherland's work was widely perceived and celebrated by others as a reincarnation of the subjective, pantheistic vision of poets like Wordsworth, and of Turner, Palmer and Blake amongst visual artists. Sutherland was evidently quite happy for his early supporters, such as Kenneth Clark and Edward Sackville-West, both close friends of the artist, to emphasise the English, and specifically romantic, dimension of his art. In the catalogue for his first one-man show, Clark celebrated Sutherland as an individualist who

63 John Constable, *The Cornfield*, 1826, oil on canvas, 143 × 122 cm, National Gallery, London.

was hard to categorise, and as a 'poetical' painter in the tradition of Blake and Palmer: 'his colour and design are a joy to the eye, but they exist and acquire their force through his magical vision of nature'. Furthermore, his work was ultimately rooted in observation: 'Nearly all the pictures . . . have been painted from small, careful drawings done on the spot, and followed most accurately'. They are no more surrealist than abstract, since 'he never consciously introduces images on account of their psychological associations'.[54] It is interesting to note that, in another more extended essay from 1938, Clark projected an identical set of aesthetic values onto John Constable, 'still an object of veneration to young painters with very different ideals'.[55] Constable was at once the 'most universal' and the 'most English' of painters, whose general creative principles 'still hold good today', even if his particular vein of effects and imagery was exhausted. Landscape painting should involve a 'profound intimacy with the countryside portrayed'; the temptation to use the picture-making formulas of continental schools is as strong today . . . and any young painter who would resist it must have something of Constable's courage and determination'.[56] Clark summarised thus the fundamental lesson of Constable's art: 'We can no longer accept a doctrine of naïve imitation, but we can, and must, accept nature as the material means through which pictorial emotion can be expressed. Indeed, it is only by studying nature with humility that we can discover our own emotions and learn to re-create them as shape and colour.'[57] It sounds very much as though he had contemporaries like Sutherland in mind.

Sutherland's own identification with this native tradition is suggested by the visual continuities between *Entrance to a Lane* (1939), for instance, and the receding funnel of space and strong oppositions of light and dark that inform a Constable such as *The Cornfield* (pl. 63). Likewise, in his private correspondence with Clark, Sutherland laid stress on the role of direct observation in the genesis of his paintings. During a trip to Pembrokeshire in September 1936, he remarked that it was 'very lovely unspoiled country and I am getting material for a good deal of work'.[58] By 1938–39, as will become apparent, his work revealed a growing assurance and a willingness to transform and subordinate his natural source material. Yet his running commentary indicates not just the continuing importance for his work of specific places and motifs, but also perhaps his sensitivity to the preconceptions that Clark brought to his work, which may be indicative of the general relationship that developed between an insecure artist and his confident and worldly patron, even though they were very close in age. From one letter it can be inferred that Clark had been to see the paintings intended for Sutherland's forthcoming show at Rosenberg and Helft, and had been forthright in expressing both aesthetic criticisms and reservations about the commercial wisdom of the direction in which the work was heading. In defending himself, Sutherland emphasised how much he relied on Clark's interest and help:

> And this, of course, does make me regret any development in my work of the kind we discussed; for I do value immensely your criticism and I act on it where possible; when I say this, I mean that lately my work has been a matter of instinct rather than intellect and it has been a question, so to say, of giving myself my head.
>
> As to the sketches, I do feel that any loss is, on the whole, more due to the increase in scale than any conscious extra stiffening; for most of the paintings were done within ten days or so of the execution of the actual sketch. I don't *know* about this, and should welcome an opportunity to discuss it further with you. I *do* feel that the geography of these places is vitally important to me even at the risk of turning into G Pembrokeshire Sutherland & I do feel that if some of the people who at present find difficulty with my work saw the actual country and places from which the work was done, much of the difficulty would disappear.
>
> At all events I hope intensely for my sake – & for yours (since all your evangelising would otherwise be pointless) that my 'muse' leads me into easier works – or that there is a change in those people you were telling me about![59]

In summer 1939, Sutherland returned to extolling the Pembrokeshire landscape: 'everything here is very quiet and primitive and full of unexpected material which I hope I can grasp'.[60] That November, he was under pressure to produce new work for the Leicester Gallery show in 1940, and was planning a further visit: 'With small, fairly complete pen & wash drawings, done out of doors, by my side, I can work fairly quickly. Rain curtailed the acquisition of as large a summer stock as last year, and without notes, the memory of that which I want to express is insufficiently quickened. I depend more and more on the letter of an actual series of forms as a starting point and then I feel free'.[61] Next time he remarked:

64 Graham Sutherland, *Western Hills*, 1938/ 1941, oil on canvas, 55.5 × 90.5 cm, Scottish National Gallery of Modern Art, Edinburgh.

> The country here is tremendously impressive: for variety, size, poetry and colour I had no idea that these islands contained anything like it. I believe one could do really great work with such a stimulus. I have been working every day & have found some electrifying motifs. It is not easy country, and perhaps needs a closer familiarity than most. I believe that I may have enough material for 8 new pictures. Yesterday we were spellbound at sunset by the effect of the sun coming though holes in the clouds and making orange red patches in the blue black mountains.[62]

Sutherland's visual work suggests that his selection and interpretation of landscape motifs was conditioned in part by a wide-ranging interest in English romantic art. In the final realisation of *Western Hills*, for example, which he began around 1938 and reworked in the early part of the war, one might well discern recollections of Turner's exploration of the poetic possibilities of light and atmosphere (pl. 64). But according to Sackville-West, who wrote the first monograph on Sutherland for the Penguin Modern Masters series, Blake and Palmer constituted 'most obviously perhaps the focus of Sutherland's deepest admiration', and 'the pointers to the emotion behind Sutherland's painting'.[63] Sutherland's fundamental ambition for his own work is implicit in the admiration he expressed in 1936 for the late work of Blake

65 William Blake, *The Blighted Corn: Illustration to Thornton's Pastorals of Virgil*, 1821, wood-engraving, 3.4 × 7.3 cm, Tate, London.

(pl. 65) in 'A Trend in English Draughtsmanship', and the criticisms he directed at the artist's previous reliance on 'a conceived mental image':

> Had he nourished his conceptual ideas by familiarising himself with the ways of nature, his art might have reached the perfection of its maturity at an earlier period. But be this as it may, it is almost solely in the Dante drawings and the wood-engravings executed for Ambrose Philip's imitation of Virgil's Ist Eclogue – works executed towards the end of his life – that we see Blake at the height of his powers, and achieving complete unity of expression. In these works, too, the pictorial life is so little adulterated with literary associations that nothing matters except the self-contained vitality which they manifest . . .
>
> In them we see a mysterious grandeur and a flaring ecstasy. What strange and exciting vistas they open up for us! This tree, so like yet so unlike the trees of our visual knowledge, so universal yet so intimate, obeys no laws except those of its creators. These stark forms clothed in rich lambent colours, blithe or grave, are strangely familiar yet disturbingly unprecedented. What power they have to move us![64]

He seems to have been particularly engaged with Blake during the war years. In April 1942, for instance, Sutherland wrote to Sackville-West: 'Don't you think the new Tate Gallery Blake's are the most exciting artistic event for years?'[65] This was a response to the exhibition at the National Gallery of the Tate's wartime acquisitions, which included his own *Green Tree Form,* shown alongside the group of Blake colour prints presented by W. Graham Robertson, featuring such major masterpieces as *Elohim Creating Adam, Nebuchadnezzar* and *Newton.*[66] During the same month the 'Welsh Sketchbook' appeared, in which Sutherland noted that the 'form and scale of the rocks here [Pembrokeshire], and the minutiae on them' bore a striking similarity to Blake's treatment of the background in the Newton drawing.[67] Blake's imagery of Inferno in the Dante illustrations, which had been in the Tate collection since 1919, seems a significant point of reference for Sutherland's gloomy, hellish vision of the

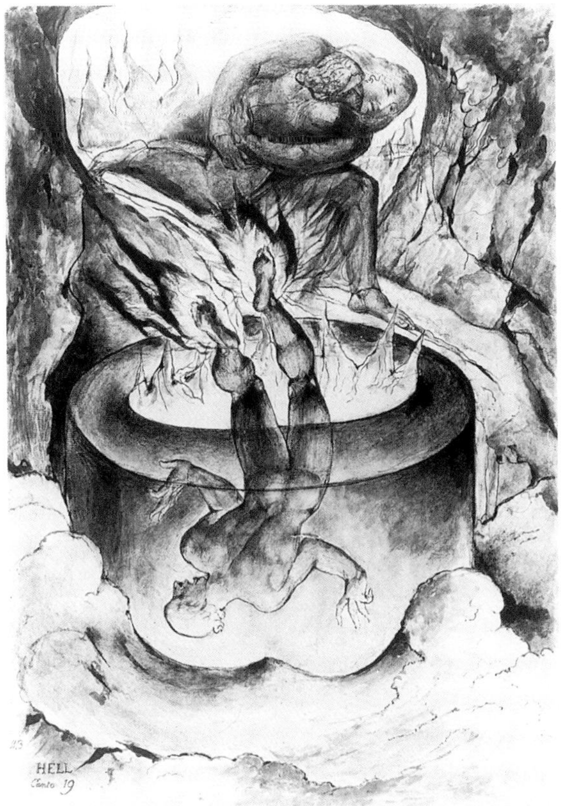

66 William Blake, *The Simoniac Pope*, 1824–27, pen and watercolour, 52.7 × 36.8 cm, Tate, London.

67 FAR RIGHT Graham Sutherland, *Slag Ladles*, 1942, gouache, pastel and ink on paper, 51.5 × 37.8 cm, Imperial War Museum, London.

looming interiors of Welsh steel works (pls 66–67). Equally, as has often been noted, his illustrations to Gascoyne's *Poems 1937–42* reveal an immersion in Blake's illustrated books such as *Jerusalem*. The impression of spontaneity in graphic style, and the mixture of image and hand-written text, strongly evokes the precedent of Blake. Sutherland remarked that he had conceived the volume 'as something to be read and carried about in the pocket . . . slightly reminiscent of the 'knockabout' quality of the original editions of Blake's *Songs of Innocence*'.[68]

Similarly, the art of Samuel Palmer continued to inform Sutherland's work. His renewed attention should be seen in the context of a wider climate of appreciation for Palmer's early work, as opposed to the artist's more conventional later production. This seems to have emerged in response to the group of pictures shown in 1934 at the *Royal Academy Exhibition of British Art*.[69] Palmer's youthful paintings appeared to pick up from where Blake's illustrations to Virgil's *Eclogues* had left off. As with Blake's work, their visionary intensity and their emphatic stylisation of natural forms made them more accessible to contemporary sensibilities than the naturalistic strands in romanticism. This compatibility was apparent from the sustained and fervent advocacy of early Palmer works in the writings of Geoffrey Grigson, the editor of *New Verse* and a committed promoter of artistic and literary modernism in general, and the work of Wyndham Lewis and Henry Moore in particular. The first fruit of Grigson's admiration was the essay he published in 1937 in *Signature* magazine, with which

Sutherland was closely associated. Grigson's book *Samuel Palmer: The Visionary Years* of 1947 provides further evidence for the context in which Sutherland resumed his interest in the nineteenth-century artist. Grigson acknowledged, for example, that it was Herbert Read who had 'first stirred me to an interest in Palmer', and it will become clear that Read was also a key figure in shaping Sutherland's outlook.[70]

Grigson also paid tribute to the role of Kenneth Clark, who had acquired several important works by Palmer for the Ashmolean Museum in Oxford before he took over at the National Gallery.[71] Clark's private collection included several works by Palmer, and he doubtless delighted in showing them to someone like Sutherland, and promoting Palmer as a model for contemporary practice. Indeed, Clark seems to have regarded Sutherland as a latter-day Palmer figure, who even, like his romantic predecessor, lived and worked in rural Kent. One might read a symbolic passing of the torch into Clark's gesture of giving Sutherland a small drawing by Palmer of *The Valley Farm* (pl. 68).[72] Although not a very typical Palmer, this closely foreshadows the composition and spatial organisation of Sutherland's *Welsh Landscape with Roads*. It is unclear whether a direct knowledge of this Palmer entered into the conception of the 1936 picture, or whether instead Clark acquired the picture subsequently and gave it to Sutherland because it reminded him so forcibly of Sutherland's own work. Clark also owned a Palmer pencil drawing of gnarled trees, one of them dead and suggestive of an upturned writhing hand, which foreshadows a strand in Sutherland's landscape imagery that emerged during the late 1930s (pl. 69).[73] But, for Sutherland, one suspects that the most significant of Clark's own Palmer works was *A Cornfield by Moonlight, with the Evening Star* (1826–32; pl. 70). This picture had been lent by Clark to the 1934 show and was subsequently illustrated in colour in Piper's *British Romantic Artists*.[74] More than any other picture, it clearly served as a talisman for Sutherland, informing not just his approach to imagery and style, but also his technique of combining pen drawing with body colour. In paintings such as *Welsh Landscape* (1936), *Welsh Mountains* (1938; pl. 80), and *Black Landscape* (1939–40; pl. 24), Sutherland was rehearsing his own variant of the way in which Palmer constructed enclosed spaces, using pathways, mounds, trees and the contours of distant hills to create a rhythmical articulation of the design and to generate strongly defined shapes that could contain a dense accumulation of descriptive detail. Works by Palmer such as *A Cornfield by Moonlight* remained the main model for Sutherland's interest in the effects of sunset and nocturnal light, endowing the natural landscape with a mysterious emotional charge.[75] But whereas the overtly derivative etchings of a decade earlier also inherited a mood of benign tranquillity from Palmer, the later paintings subvert Palmer's pastoral vision, projecting instead a darkness that is emotional as well as visual.

68 Samuel Palmer, *The Valley Farm*, pen and ink, 21 × 33 cm, British Museum, London.

Even from this relatively cursory account, it is evident that Sutherland's later remarks, about a shift from adolescent enthusiasm for Palmer to full-blown engagement with Picasso and European modernism, present a wholly misleading impression of his development. One suspects that he became irked and defensive about being set up as a key point of inspiration for a narrowly parochial impulse in British art that he disliked, and which, for him, represented the stultification of an artistic outlook that had originally seemed highly creative and

69 FAR LEFT Samuel Palmer, *Ancient Trees, Lullingstone Park*, 1828, pencil on paper, Private Collection.

70 Samuel Palmer, *Cornfield by Moonlight with the Evening Star*, *c.*1830, watercolour, gouache and pen, 19.7 × 25.8 cm, British Museum, London.

progressive. For Sutherland, looking back to English romanticism was not in conflict but rather perfectly compatible with deriving inspiration from the contemporary experimental art that he knew from exhibitions and art magazines. There was no inherent contradiction between these two points of reference; indeed the tension and interplay between them seemed highly productive for the generation of new and original work. The idea that European modernism could serve to reinforce and extend, as opposed to hindering, an English artist's capacity to extend the native landscape tradition, is likewise encountered in the thinking of artist friends who took their cue from Sutherland. John Craxton recalled of the period around 1941: 'Sutherland had been, and was, a breakthrough for English painting . . . Picasso, Miró, Ernst and Masson were more accessible . . . but Sutherland was close . . . Sutherland taught me how to look at landscape.'[76] Keith Vaughan had travelled a parallel trajectory and remarked in 1947: 'What Picasso did to the human figure, Graham Sutherland is doing to the landscape. I think he is the first painter to relate the full discoveries of the twentieth century in France to the English romantic tradition.'[77] The artist in his circle to whom such an outlook was anathema was Francis Bacon. Indeed, one factor in Sutherland's impulse to distance himself around the end of the war from native allegiances may have been his friendship with Bacon, whose dismissive comments about the Nash brothers in one of his letters to Sutherland certainly suggest that he saw little merit in a type of work that had been crucial for Sutherland throughout the 1930s and early 1940s.[78] To a degree, perhaps, Bacon's appeal for Sutherland was precisely his complete freedom from a sense of English identity that had now become vulgarised and trivialised under the pressure of wartime patriotism.

A concern to relate 'the full discoveries of the twentieth century in France to the English Romantic tradition' can be viewed not as an idiosyncratic impulse, but rather as the trace in Sutherland's work of the wider artistic climate in which he crystallised his approach. We have seen that some two years elapsed between Sutherland's discovery of Pembrokeshire in 1934 and his forging of a suitable language to convey its essential qualities and mood. This coincided with a key period of transition in the history of English modernism. As an artist consciously striving to modernise his art in the mid-1930s, Sutherland would undoubtedly have been conscious of the emergence of a new progressive grouping in Britain under the banner of *Unit One*, launched in 1933.[79] The artists involved, such as Barbara Hepworth, Henry Moore, Paul Nash, Ben Nicholson and Edward Wadsworth, were relatively disparate in many of their artistic concerns, but since the late 1920s they had shared an enthusiastic immersion in European modernism, in either or both of its abstract and surrealist manifestations. Nash was the prime mover behind *Unit One*, while the critic Herbert Read edited and introduced the book that served to promote the artists and their exhibition. I would maintain that Sutherland's art and outlook were influenced more directly and decisively by these two figures than by anybody else in his immediate environment, with the possible exception of Kenneth Clark, and that one of the principal attitudes they shared and transmitted to Sutherland was precisely a sense of the compatibility of European modernism and English romanticism.[80] A consciously inclusive outlook began to gather momentum from 1933/4 onwards, and became an increasingly visible feature of the British art world during the second half of the decade, promoted in magazines such as *Axis*, *Architectural Review* and *Signature*.[81]

Herbert Read's advocacy of modern art to an English audience entailed promoting both the latest European achievements, and also the work of home-grown modernists such as Moore. Read's initial phase of activity as propagandist for the cause culminated in the publication in 1933 of *Art Now: An Introduction to the Theory of Modern Painting and Sculpture*, and in the following year of *Unit One*, *Art and Industry*, a book-length primer in a functionalist approach to design inspired by the Bauhaus, and the first monograph on Moore.[82] It is clear that encountering *Art Now* was extremely important for Sutherland. In 1936 he described the book as 'an exhaustive and masterly analysis of the whole field of art'.[83] He retained his copy of the book throughout his life.[84] The fact that it is a first edition suggests that he acquired the book before 1936, when a second, updated version appeared. It seems likely that *Art Now* was a major factor in Sutherland's 'conversion' to modernism in a broad sense. Read offered an enthusiastic, though typically schematic, high-flown, and non-partisan account of several key currents in the art of recent decades, from cubism and expressionism to *neue sachlichkeit*, abstract art and surrealism, as well as major figures who transcended narrow movement divisions, such as Matisse and Picasso. The book is divided into separate blocks of text and full-page illustrations (128 in all, with British artists featured alongside figures from continental Europe). For Sutherland, *Art Now* functioned as both a conceptual and a visual stimulus. For much of the time, his copy clearly lived in the studio. The cover is spattered with paint, and several of the double-page pairings of images accumulated quantities of dust and flecks of paint and pencil, suggesting that Sutherland would sometimes leave the book open beside him while working on his own compositions. The pages that are most heavily distressed in this way contain reproductions of Picasso's *Baigneuse* (1929) and Francis Bacon's *Crucifixion* (1933); a pair of Miró 'automatist' *Paintings* from 1927; Miró's *Baigneuse* (1932) and Picasso's *Abstraction* (1930); two more Picasso so-called *Abstrac-*

tions from 1926 and 1929; André Masson's *Battle of the Fishes* (1928) and Jean Lurçat's *New York* (1930); and two successive spreads featuring work by Klee (pl. 71).[85] It is not in fact the case, despite repeated assertions to this effect, that the page with the Bacon illustration is 'the most heavily thumbed'.[86]

Sutherland also read the text with diligence and interest. His marginal annotations most frequently indicate his identification with Read's essentially Bergsonian emphasis on the role of the imagination and subjective interpretation in modern art, as opposed, respectively, to the intellect and objective observation, as a means to attain a deeper penetration into reality. In broad terms, it was Read's framework of ideas and distinctions in *Art Now* that subsequently underpinned Sutherland's own 'A Trend in English Draughtsmanship'. The artist sought here 'to describe and distinguish a type of art', to lay out an approach to art that is, in essence, 'subjective, and depends on the disposition of the artist to design from his inner consciousness'. The artists he chose to discuss were united across time in their bias towards an essentially subjective mode of artistic apprehension, whereby the objects of experience are absorbed and reinvented by the artist to convey his imaginative vision, rather than being subjected to either a descriptive rendition or a purely formal interpretation. The subjective versus objective polarity comes straight from *Art Now*.[87] In 'A Trend in English Draughtsmanship', and again in the radio interview to which he contributed in 1941, Sutherland quoted Jacques Maritain's characterisation of art as 'recomposing its peculiar world with that poetic reality which resembles things in a far more profound and mysterious way than any direct evocation could possibly do'. He could have encountered Maritain's ideas and terminology directly, since *Art and Scholasticism* was translated in 1930, but, one again, he may instead have been familiar with the enthusiastic summary in Read's *In Defence of Shelley*, a book of essays that also appeared in 1936.[88]

One sentence that Sutherland savoured in *Art Now* indicates a combination of enthusiasms that he presumably shared with Read: 'After a century or so we have arrived at the point of accepting the genius of Blake; in the same mood we shall one day accept the comparable genius of Max Ernst'.[89] Sutherland doubtless appreciated the fact that, alongside his radical modernism, at least in an English context, Read retained and promoted a positive attachment to what seemed most valuable within a distinctively English cultural tradition, an aspect of his thinking that has received renewed attention in recent years.[90] Read had published an important monograph on Staffordshire pottery figures in 1929, and continued to extol the values of simple, hand-crafted functional items from the vernacular tradition in *Art and Industry* (1934). A preoccupation with English romantic literature, and its values of self-exploration and immersion in the natural world as a means to spiritual revelation, underlay Read's autobiography of his Yorkshire childhood, *The Innocent Eye* (1933), and his visionary novel *The Green Child* (1935). Such concerns also found a critical outlet in his study of Wordsworth (1930), and his book on *Form in Modern Poetry* (1932), a critique of T. S. Eliot's doctrine of impersonality. Read's engagement with the native artistic tradition was emphatically conveyed in two publications from 1933, the year in which the internationalist *Art Now*

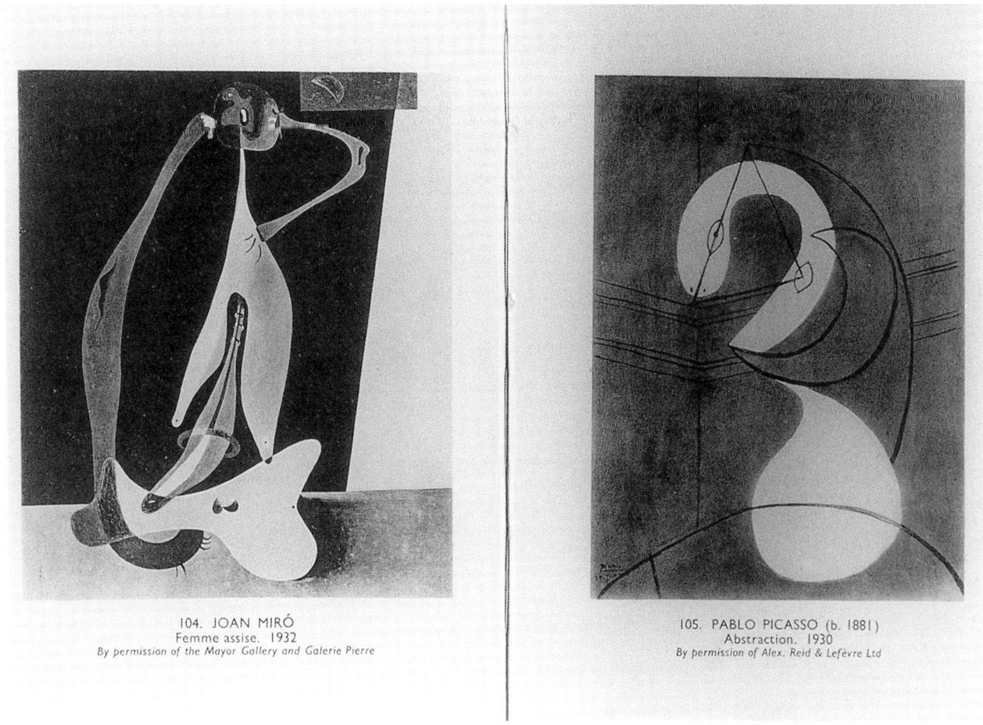

71 Double-page spread from Herbert Read, *Art Now* (1933).

appeared. In an article on 'English Art', he emphasised that English art had tended to be linear, 'predominantly romantic' and claimed that Blake 'embodied consciously and consistently the original characteristics of our art'.[91] More wide-ranging is the anthology of writings that Read edited under the title *The English Vision*.[92] His introduction offers a revealing insight into the resonance that the topic held, for himself and doubtless much of his readership, at this particular historical moment. He was writing in the year that Hitler became German Chancellor, and it was in direct opposition to a fascist ideal of race that his very positive conception of enduring English values was formulated. Read was at pains to emphasise that he was not presenting 'the English ideal' from the nostalgic perspective of 'conservatism or reaction'.[93] Rather, it had always been an 'active and dynamic' force, and therefore retained the potential for future expansion beyond its native shores, since 'alone of national ideals, the English ideal transcends nationality', and even possesses 'universal validity'.[94] For Read, a reminder of 'those traditions of liberty, justice and toleration which have always guided our destinies' had a particular value given 'the uncertain and catastrophic times which lie before us', and the imperative 'to offer to the distracted world one ideal which is above the intolerant extremes which now tyrannise over millions of unhappy people.'[95] In the final section of the anthology, 'The Ultimate Ideal', three of the five texts are by William Blake, who clearly embodied, for Read, the most powerful literary expression of progressive national feeling allied to innovative poetic vision.

The same general sensibility is encountered in Paul Nash, whose work and personal encouragement also played a crucial role in Sutherland's development.[96] The two men were evidently friends, though the exact character and extent of their relationship is not documented. They were certainly in contact by the late 1920s. The inspiration from Nash's work begins to become apparent in Sutherland's *Pastoral* (1930), one of the last of the etchings in which he had specialised during the 1920s (pl. 72). Here the trees already take on anthropomorphic suggestions, as though the gnarled male and slender female personifications were gesturing to one another across the space, implying some obscure narrative. One senses the impact of Nash's recent landscapes, such as *Landscape at Iden* and *February* (both 1929), and also perhaps the direct example of Giorgio de Chirico, whose work Nash had recently discovered in a one-man exhibition at the Tooth Gallery in London.[97] In 1935, Nash wrote admiringly about Sutherland in an article for *Signature* on the subject of new draughtsmen.[98] In 'A Trend in English Draughtsmanship', which looked at a closely related theme and appeared of course in the same magazine, Sutherland was able to reciprocate. He expressed great admiration for Nash's 'series of paintings of extraordinary significance and power', and described the illustrations to Thomas Browne's *Urne Buriall and the Garden of Cyrus* as 'a poetic and imaginative achievement without equal to-day in this country'.[99]

Nash's commitment to a psychologically-charged mode of landscape painting was sustained by the examples of European metaphysical art and surrealism, especially the interpretation of the so-called 'hand-painted dream picture'.[100] Equally, the pool of ideas and artistic possibilities inherent in surrealism formed a recurrent theme in Nash's concurrent body of critical writings. Yet, as with Read, another strand was the role of nationality in art, and the components of Englishness in particular, topics upon which Nash was reflecting with some regularity from late 1931 onwards.[101] Above all, Nash used his personal essay in *Unit One* to reflect upon the way in which a creative engagement with imported modernist idioms could serve to facilitate the renewed expression of native inclinations, in contrast to the mere rehearsal of predictable cultural clichés: 'The international character of modern art, by destroying the false values of nationalism, opens the way to a purely academic approach to the question of national idiosyncrasy, and in proportion as art becomes more abstract, so the nuances of national or racial distinction become more subtle and, consequently, more interesting to trace.'[102] Nash proceeded to define, or at any rate evoke with due subtlety, what a distinctively English approach might comprise, beneath the manifest diversity of style and genre within the history of English art. To articulate this he resorted to the somewhat vague formulations of '*genius loci*', or the spirit of place, and 'a subjective art', ideas that converge on the search for imaginative revelation and encompass such varied figures as Turner and Blake.[103]

It was after *Unit One* that surrealism assumed its most decisive importance for English writers, artists and critics. Means of transmission included the great *International Surrealist Exhibition*, held at the New Burlington Galleries in London in summer 1936, with its accompanying book-length exposition of the movement edited by Read. There were also the many one-man shows throughout the 1930s devoted to the leading surrealist artists at venues such as the Mayor and London Galleries, as well as the acquisition of many important surrealist works by British collectors such as Roland Penrose, and the availability in England of the

72 Graham Sutherland *Pastoral*, 1930, etching, 13 × 19.5 cm, Private Collection.

several beautifully-produced illustrated magazines, such as *Minotaure* and *Cahiers d'Art*, that conveyed the full range of the movement's visual and literary output.[104] Nash and Read were predisposed to identify continuities between surrealism, to date a primarily European movement, and the aesthetic priorities of nineteenth-century romanticism, to which British writers and artists had made an especially rich contribution. The general outlook to which they both subscribed might be summed up in a remark made by Nash in 1937: 'The appeal of Surrealism . . . is exceedingly powerful, and its power comes from the sense of its message, which says release yourselves, live your dreams, open your minds, enter your poetic heritage.'[105] It became a commonplace to assert that surrealism was not so much a revolutionary departure as a latter-day variation upon a disposition to celebrate imagination and fantasy that had longstanding roots in English culture. David Gascoyne's pioneering account of surrealism, published in 1935, and the English contributions to the 1936 catalogue, all served to reinforce the idea that surrealism was the latest reworking of an older romantic conception of art, which meant that contemporary English adherents, the descendants of William Blake, were, in Herbert Read's phrase, 'to the manner born'.[106]

Sutherland was represented in the *International Surrealist Exhibition* by two works, *Thunder Sounding* and *Mobile Mask*. It is not known whether he or the organisers were responsible for the selection of these rather weak and atypical paintings, which represent a

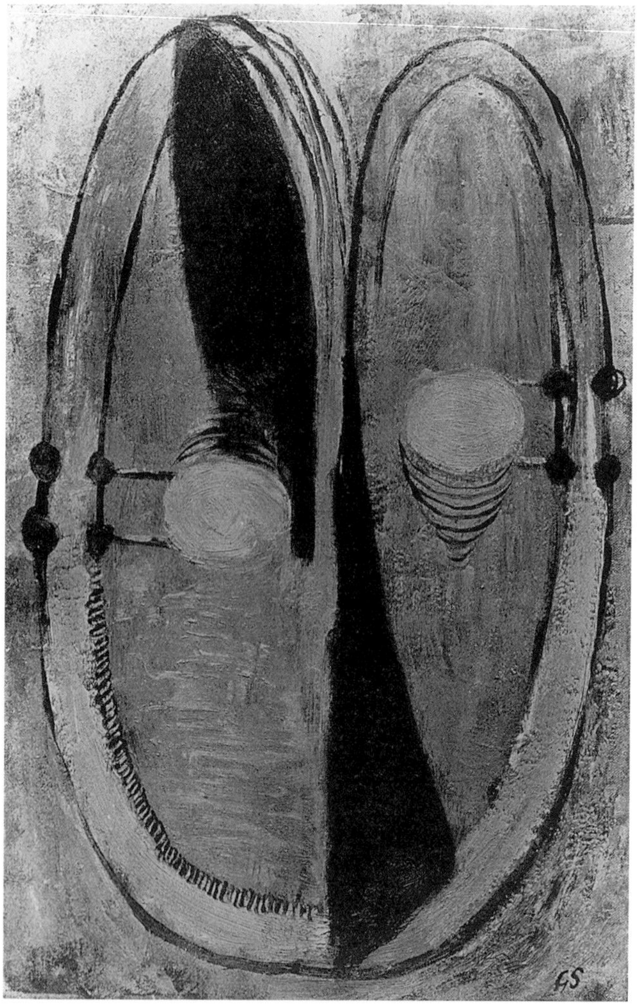

73 Graham Sutherland *Mobile Mask*, 1936, oil on canvas, Private Collection.

somewhat whimsical attempt to ape the latest artistic language (pl. 73).[107] *Mobile Mask* implies an interest in the heads that Picasso had produced in the late 1920s, although the configuration also suggests an awareness of the curvilinear, symmetrical structure that Picasso devised for *Girl in Front of a Mirror* (1932). By chance, the two pictures were reproduced a few pages apart in *The Painter's Object*.[108] Perhaps because of the half-hearted surrealism of these works, and the fact that Sutherland took no part otherwise in any of the organisational or promotional activities of the movement, he is not generally associated with the burgeoning of British surrealism, and he barely features, for instance, in Michel Remy's detailed chronicle.[109] Nevertheless, 'A Trend in English Draughtsmanship' expressed Sutherland's sympathy with the widespread notion that the indigenous cultural inheritance and the 'immense stimulus from abroad', doubtless an oblique reference to surrealism, could only reinforce one another in nurturing a new, subjective art. It was presumably no accident that the appearance of 'A Trend in English Draughtsmanship' in the Summer 1936 issue of *Signature* coincided with the surrealist show, although it is hard to see much connection between the ideas he expounded and the pictures he exhibited.

In the wake of the exhibition, Sutherland reverted to landscape imagery, but in a more innovatory spirit, which enabled him to create the group of pictures in which he established a more personal artistic identity. It was in the two versions of *Red Tree* of 1936 that Sutherland first explored the idea of focusing on a particular 'found object' encountered in the landscape. He later acknowledged, with particular reference to this image: 'The one field in which the surrealists helped me to widen my range was in their propagation of the idea that there was worthy subject matter for painting, in objects the painter would never have looked at before . . . Surrealism helped me to realise that forms which interested me existed already in nature'.[110] The surrealist preoccupation during the 1930s with the found object culminated around 1936, and many examples were included in the London exhibition. The natural object was one of the ten categories of object that the surrealists themselves itemised.[111] But focusing on things found in the natural landscape, which might take on fantastic and anthropomorphic associations, became an especially strong feature of British surrealism. Hence Read's choice of example in the 1936 book of essays on surrealism: 'If I am walking along the beach and my eye catches a sea-worn and sun-bleached knot of wood whose shape and colour strongly appeal to me (which may in any case have a psychological explanation) the act of identification makes that object as expressive of my personality as if I had actually carved the wood into that shape. Selection is also creation.'[112] Read was doubtless responding to the work of artist friends such as Nash and Moore. Nash had elaborated this approach not only in paintings such as *Event on the Downs* and *Druid Landscape*, both dating from 1934, but also in photographs that he began to show in the mid-1930s, and in object-sculptures, such as *Marsh Personage*, which he displayed at the 1936 exhibition and elsewhere (pl. 74). In spring 1937 Nash commented on the recent direction of his work: 'I began to discover the significance of the so-called inanimate object. Henceforth Nature became endowed for me with new life. The landscape, too, seemed now possessed of different animation. To contemplate the personal beauty of stone and leaf, bark and shell, and to exalt them to be principles of imaginary happenings, became a new interest'.[113]

Nash also provided telling models for Sutherland's more panoramic renditions of the landscape ideal that he had located in Pembrokeshire. The surrealist preoccupation with sensations of the marvellous and mysterious, conveyed by means of bizarre juxtapositions, had encouraged Nash to take his bearings from the romantic interest in remote landscape imagery in general, and from the particular theme of landscape scenery bearing the traces of ancient human occupancy and use, through features such as megaliths and burial mounds.[114] His rehearsal of this idea was epitomised by abstracted interpretations of the prehistoric megaliths at Avebury, which he had first visited in 1933, and their verbal corollary in his descriptive texts for the *Shell Guide to Dorset*, which appeared in 1936 (pl. 75). In stylistic terms, Nash demonstrated how the artist might transform the natural scene, by means of an elaboration and abstraction of its visual features, in order to evoke for the spectator the sense of metaphysical drama that he had experienced in front of the scene. In this respect, Sutherland's *Welsh Landscape with Roads* might be compared with Nash's *Landscape of the Megaliths* (1934) or *Equivalents for the Megaliths* (1935) as an image of a 'mysterious', primordial landscape,

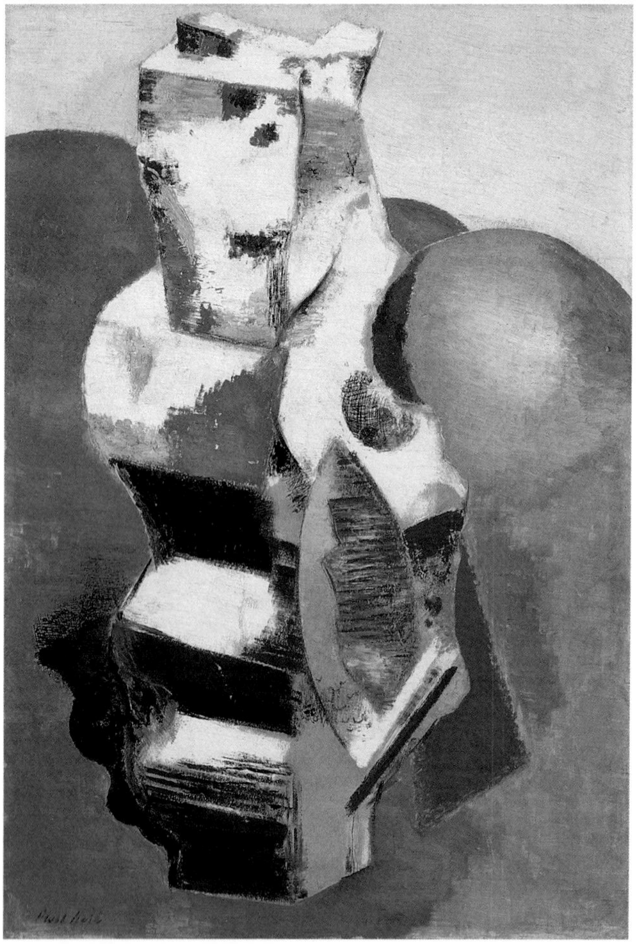

74 Paul Nash, *Druid Landscape*, 1934, oil on board, 58.5 × 40.5 cm, British Council Collection.

remote from urban civilisation, which metaphorically evokes regions of the mind existing at a deeper level than the surface clutter of consciousness. The pictures feature the stylised simplification of natural features, the use of a high horizon to articulate space, and a dramatic juxtaposition between the distant panorama and incongruous foreground elements, respectively the abstracted megaliths and the cow's skull. Sutherland's apparent inclusion of a group of megalithic stones, on the plateau beneath the setting sun, came in the wake of several more descriptive studies of such features, and marked an obvious point of continuity with Nash's imagery. Indeed, part of the attraction of Pembrokeshire was precisely the fact that the landscape was not just unspoilt but that it also contained prehistoric remains. It exuded, one might say, something of the same 'genius loci' that Avebury had given off so affectingly for Nash. The imagery of Sutherland's work continued to echo themes previously or simultaneously explored by Nash, especially in his photographs. The title and imagery of *Red Monolith* (1938) recall Nash's preoccupation with the theme of megaliths, prehistoric stones rising mysteriously out of the organic forms of the landscape, though Sutherland's actual starting point was another tree form. In its simplicity, the painting is particularly close to Nash's

75 Paul Nash *Landscape of the Megaliths*, 1934, oil on canvas, 49.5 × 73.2 cm, British Council Collection.

current photographs such as *Monolith in a Wood*. Equally, Nash's images of stone walls by the sea shore and close-up plant studies foreshadow Sutherland's *Gorse on Sea Wall* (pls III and 76). The anthropomorphic vertical tree forms are predecessors for an image such as *Association of Oaks* (1940). Moreover, Nash's studies of monstrous uprooted trees in a series of photographs, which lead to various watercolours and the oil painting *Monster Field* (1939), can be seen to anticipate Sutherland's tree form pictures from 1940.

It was not only Sutherland, of course, who believed that Nash offered a powerful and inspirational example in the latter part of the 1930s, in terms of the ideal of the artist that he embodied as well as particular features of his style and imagery. Sutherland's response can be aligned with the veneration of Nash in the latter issues of the magazine *Axis*, where Nash stood for a distinctively English artistic identity in the best and most sophisticated sense, given the circumstances at the time. In her essay 'Paul Nash, 1937' in the last issue, Myfanwy Evans emphasised that the artist's work had 'absorbed the English climate'.[115] His art conveyed a remarkable sense of time not as clearly and prosaically divisible into 'now' and 'then', but rather as 'an indefinable sense of scarcely-shifting permanence': 'He has no interest in the past as *past*, but the accumulated intenseness of the past as *present* is his special concern and joy. The contour of things past is given the aura of things present, so the reality *and* the romanticism of both is intensified.'[116] Nash's 'unique inclusiveness . . . makes him able in these sectarian days to hold an apparently middle course without suffering for it'. Different kinds of natural scenery, and different forms of artistic expression, might be fused together within an imaginative continuum, an opposite mentality to that which constructs rigid barriers between past and present, national and international, traditional and experimental. This outlook extended to an unwillingness to separate fine art from those areas of applied art in which both Nash and Sutherland consistently operated, in part of course for economic reasons, such as book illustration, posters, and the design of fabrics and other everyday, functional items.[117] Finally, in Evans' opinion, Nash also stood for an emphatic individualism, as opposed to the pervasive contemporary tendency to fit the individual into 'a school, a move-

76 Paul Nash, *Stones and Seaweed, Study 2*, mid 1930s, photograph, Tate Archive, London.

ment, a mass, a class'.[118] In all these respects, the characterisation of Nash would surely have struck a chord with Sutherland, who likewise was at pains to resist classifications and pigeonholing.

Yet, there are also clear differences between the approaches and sensibilities of the two artists. The implicit reference to English romantic artists, and to Samuel Palmer in particular, is a much more overt feature of Sutherland's work. Sutherland's version of a primeval landscape was far less closely aligned with contemporary preservationist and archaeological concerns than was the case with Nash, whose landscapes consistently project, I would maintain, a certain intellectuality and emotional detachment. A major aspect of this is the quality of incongruous juxtaposition that he clearly relished between the natural elements in a landscape and the emphatic geometry of the structures men have always seen fit to impose on nature, whether these be the serried ranks of trees in orchards, the flood defences on the coast at Dymchurch, or the monumental prehistoric remains encountered at places like Avebury. It is the sheer oddity of such scenery to which Nash, sometimes with a certain irony, seems to be drawing our attention. Moreover, the frequent inclusion of details with an apparent symbolic resonance indicates that the roots of his art lie in intellectual and literary interests, and permits his pictures to become springboards for elaborate allegorical readings. In visual terms, Nash's pictures are distinguished by their clarity of organisation and compositional rigour. Typically, this structural emphasis is reinforced by his preference for a limpid daylight illumination that produces geometric patterns of shadow, and also by an undemonstrative dryness and lack of fluency, verging on positive awkwardness, in the actual application of paint. Together, such aspects of content and form signify a stance of detached, cerebrally informed interrogation before the spectacle of the natural world, an attitude equally apparent, it is worth noting, in his work as a photographer. It is entirely symptomatic of such a sensibility that he should have found powerful inspiration in the work of de Chirico, and also that he and Magritte should have found much to admire in one another's work. The tenor of Sutherland's work stands in opposition to many characteristics of Nash's art. The obscurity of many of his pictures, the mysterious, theatrical effects of light and colour, and the nervous fluidity of touch that Nash himself responded to in 1935, all contribute to an effect of extreme emotionality. If Nash's pictures project and invite a controlled act of interpretation, Sutherland's convey a sense of revelation and of submission to overwhelming sensations. It is to the viewer's feelings, rather than his or her intellect, that Sutherland's pictures seem to make their primary address.

Equally, the two artists' respective attitudes at this time towards contemporary European art provide a telling point of distinction. As has been shown, Sutherland's artistic idiom was powerfully shaped by figures such as Read, Nash and Moore, who demonstrated how ideas and values originating in surrealism might be mediated through self-consciously British sensibilities. Yet the work of modern European artists was also a direct and significant point of departure for Sutherland, more so than it was at this stage for Nash, who had been at his most responsive to external stimuli in the early 1930s and who was now pursuing a relatively self-contained evolution. Although Sutherland is not known to have actually travelled abroad until 1944, he had ample opportunity in London to look at contemporary, especially surrealist, painting not least in the great 1936 exhibition to which he had, in a minor way, contributed. Reproductions were available in books such as Read's *Art Now*, but Sutherland later emphasised the crucial role played by illustrated magazines, especially the lavishly produced *Cahiers d'Art*:

> I became aware of certain foreign artists; the 1936 exhibition had been held, with that big Miro painting of 'The Reaper'. And I became aware, after I had started work in Pembrokeshire, that unconsciously some of my forms – to me at least – started to look a little bit like the kind of things I had been seeing at the time as reproductions in *Cahiers d'Art*. My feelings then were, not that I was trying to be un-English, but that for the first time in my life I was aware that there was something going on beyond the English tradition.[119]

Amongst other leading journals, *Cahiers d'Art* was available in Zwemmer's book shop. Moreover Peter Watson's flat contained a wonderful repository of back issues of *Minotaure*, *Verve*, *Cahiers d'Art* and other avant-garde magazines, to which the artists and writers in Watson's circle, which included Sutherland, had virtually open access.[120] During the war, such volumes remained a crucial resource for artists, when European modern art was much less easy to view in the original. The visual echoes, conscious or otherwise, which Sutherland himself began to recognise, are apparent in the paintings. Thus Sutherland's second, more stylised second version of *Red Tree* recalls not just Moore but also the biomorphic idiom of recent work by Miró, such as the 1932 *Baigneuse* included in Read's *Art Now*, as well as Picasso's stylised imagery of Marie-Therese Walter. Indeed, Sutherland's work in 1936 and over the next couple of years indicates a general and profound admiration for the particular combination of economical and apparently spontaneous drawing with expansive shapes, enclosing flat vibrant colour, that was so distinctive to the paintings of Miró.

Sutherland's concurrent interest in the work of André Masson has, likewise, failed to gain the attention it deserves. The romantic topos of the natural landscape as a site of visionary and ecstatic revelation certainly informed the pictures that Masson produced in the wake of a traumatic experience in the mountains of Monserrat near Barcelona, which took place on I January 1935. The June 1936 issue of *Minotaure* featured reproductions of two of the pictures, accompanied by a poem by Masson and a text by Georges Bataille.[121] Masson's highly charged images of an arid and barren Spanish landscape may, to a significant degree, have shaped Sutherland's decisions about the motifs that he would extract from the very different landscape of Pembrokeshire, and about the artistic language that would convey the subjective nature of his responses. He could well have seen the Masson exhibition that was showing at the Wildenstein Gallery in London from 12 February to 6 March 1936. This included twenty-three oil paintings, along with watercolours, drawings and prints, focussing on the artist's work since his move to Spain in 1934.[122] The characterisation of Masson, who was temporarily estranged from the surrealist group, in the preface to the catalogue might also have struck a chord with Sutherland: 'The Surrealists claimed him [Masson] for a time, but again he escaped from the restrictions of an organised school of painting. He turned to Nature and his own imagination for his inspiration.' We may infer Sutherland's interest in Masson, and the likelihood of his having seen the London show, from the documented enthusiasm of his friend Kenneth Clark. It is known that Clark acquired *Cortège Printanier*, one of Masson's series of insect paintings, from the Wildenstein Gallery show.[123] Clark and Masson even met when the artist visited London for twelve days in connection with his exhibition, and Masson retained fond memories of the encounter.[124] It is possible that Clark and Sutherland may have visited the London show together. They would almost certainly have talked about Masson's work and its innovatory, distinctively contemporary reinvention of the traditional genre of landscape painting.

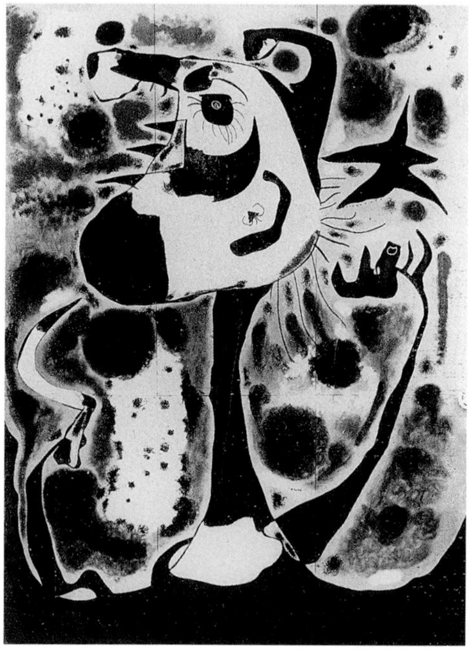

77 Joan Miro, *The Reaper*, 1937, lost (as illustrated in *Cahiers d'Art*, no. 12, 1937).

Sutherland's *Welsh Landscape with Roads* bears remarkably close comparison to works by Masson such as *Ibdes in Aragon* (1935; pl. 78). This is apparent in the fluid handling of paint, the vivid use of colour, the rhythmical organisation of the design and the juxtaposition of sharply defined foreground elements – the skull in the Sutherland and the cock in the Masson – against a deep landscape backdrop. This painting was in fact the second Masson to be acquired by Clark, who evidently bought *Ibdes in Aragon* in February 1937 directly from the Galerie Simon, during a visit to Paris. The picture had recently been included in Masson's one-man show at the gallery.[125] There is no evidence that it was included in the earlier Wildenstein show, which would have substantiated the argument that it was a specific source

78 André Masson, *Ibdes in Aragon*, 1935, oil on canvas, 60 × 92 cm, Tate, London.

of inspiration for Sutherland's *Welsh Landscape with Roads*. It may that Clark responded to this Masson, consciously or otherwise, because it struck a chord with the work of his favourite modern English painter. Although the images are much more diverse in spirit, and indeed function, it is interesting to note a further affinity between Sutherland's *Brimham Rock* of 1937 and Masson's *Dawn at Monserrat* from 1935 (pls 60 and 79). In the Masson, a group of blocky, vertical forms in the foreground, ambiguously figurative and stone-like, appear as witnesses, gazing across a rocky plane at a spectacular, effulgent display in the sky, involving an exploding volcano, rotating sun and general swirl of planetary and cloud activity. It is an image that seems poised between an ecstatic awareness of life-giving natural energies and a sense of almost apocalyptic destruction. Although Sutherland's approach in *Brimham Rock* is far more descriptive in style, and more whimsical in mood, one might nevertheless discern an echo of Masson in the stylised shapes of the clouds, in the colours of the sunset and in the emphasis upon the anthropomorphic properties of the great stones.

Sutherland's affinities with Miró and Masson suggest that the divisions between mainstream and English Surrealism are sometimes exaggerated. Andrew Causey echoes a widespread assumption when he states that 'outside England Surrealist art was not much concerned with nature in the sense of landscape . . . though they may be judged the most interesting British artists of the movement, Nash and Sutherland, at least, were out of step as landscape artists with international Surrealism'.[126] Is such a clear distinction entirely valid? Landscape imagery and settings surely play a prominent role, albeit in very diverse ways, not only in the work of Miró and Masson, but also in that of Dali, Tanguy and Ernst, especially in the period during which surrealism was being discovered in England. As a general phenomenon, this tendency seems to have received little consideration in the literature on sur-

79 André Masson *Dawn at Montserrat*, 1935, oil on canvas, 51 × 65 cm, Private Collection.

realist art. It raises of course the issue of continuities and connections between surrealism and romanticism, addressed as part of a wider thesis in Robert Rosenblum's *Modern Painting and the Northern Romantic Tradition.*[127] The discussion of Sutherland fits squarely into Rosenblum's model, and immediately precedes an analysis of the romantic dimensions of the art of Max Ernst.[128] For several commentators, Ernst's immersion in his own heritage of German romantic art and literature has provided an illuminating context for discussing both the jungle landscapes of the mid-1930s, metaphorical images of 'the human subconscious, of suppressed drives, of dream and nightmare', and also his essay 'The Forest' of 1934, published in *Minotaure.*[129] In turn, Ernst's interests find an echo in André Breton's article for *Le Surréalisme au Service de la Révolution* regarding the writer Achim von Arnim as a visionary and precursor of surrealism.[130] In the visual sphere, one might note parallels between the British rediscovery of Blake and Palmer and the fact that the first major study of the art of Caspar David Friedrich appeared in *Minotaure.*[131] In fact Blake himself was an object of keen interest in surrealist circles. Masson and Bataille shared a passionate enthusiasm and even planned to publish a monograph on Blake's work, though this idea never came to fruition.[132] As late as 1947, works by Blake were exhibited in Paris at the impeccably avant-garde Galerie René Drouin, accompanied by essays and illustrations in the current *Cahiers d'Art.*[133] On the basis of such evidence, the British reading of surrealism as a latter-day form of visionary romanticism can be regarded as less of an idiosyncratic, and by implication cautious and conservative, adaptation, and more as a manifestation of one particular strand within the unfolding of surrealism itself, especially in its later stages.

Before moving on from the pictures of 1936, it is worth pointing, finally, to the striking analogy provided by current American art, produced at a time when the nature and distinctiveness of American artistic identity was an even stronger preoccupation than in Britain. Sutherland's inclusion of an animal skull in *Welsh Landscape with Roads* recalls a rich vein of subject-matter in the work of Georgia O'Keeffe, inaugurated in 1929. Equally, the barren aridity of Sutherland's landscape imagery, and the use of heightened colour, loosely recalls O'Keefe's New Mexico landscapes. The parallel may well be entirely coincidental, though it may be noted that Paul Nash had visited the United States in 1931, and subsequently produced an article on current American art.[134] Another article on American landscape painting was promised, indicating Nash's sense of the interest of the topic, although this never appeared.[135] It is quite possible, then, that through Nash, Sutherland had at least some familiarity with artists such as O'Keefe. The 'romance' of the American Southwest in English cultural life was undoubtedly enhanced by D. H. Lawrence's enraptured accounts of the region and of Indian culture in Taos. In fact, Sutherland's cluster of affinities suggests the need for a wide-ranging examination and iconology of landscape art in the interwar period, especially in the 1930s, that would embrace international and British contributions.[136] It may, for example, prove helpful to draw a broad distinction between a more neutral sense of landscape as a repository for effects of densely organised formal structure, in the wake of Cézanne, and the subsequent emergence of more highly charged, metamorphic and theatrical approaches. The latter engaged not just Masson, Ernst and others in France, but also Marsden Hartley and Ansel Adams in America, and Diego Rivera in Mexico. The projection of bodily associations and suggestions onto landscape imagery is a theme that embraced, for instance, O'Keefe and the photography of Edward Weston in America, and Sutherland, Moore and the Scottish painter William Johnstone in Britain. An investigation of such phenomena might build on Rosenblum's assertion of the romantic inheritance in modern art, but also take into account more specific cultural and ideological factors, at a time of economic and political crisis and during a general waning of machine-age utopianism. Such factors seem to have predisposed many artists, quite independently from one another, to revisit the natural landscape as a locus of primitive energies and elemental sensations.

THE TRUE IDEA OF METAMORPHOSIS

The pictures of late 1936 established the broad concerns and themes of Sutherland's art. His increasingly assured work from the latter part of the decade reveals a continuing and wide-ranging assimilation of modern European art. The monumental *Welsh Mountains* (1938; pl. 80) is clearly derived from watercolours such as *Black Landscape* and *Sun Setting Between*

Hills, but, in the final canvas, an emphatic symmetry and linear precision are imposed onto the picturesque irregularity of the studies. The clarity of the design, the playing off of positive colour against large expanses of flat black, and the mixing here and elsewhere of sand with thick paint, cumulatively suggests that Sutherland had been paying attention to the current work of Georges Braque. There were in fact several Braque shows in London during the 1930s, which Sutherland could easily have seen. The analogy was made in exhibition reviews by Raymond Mortimer.[137] A certain affinity with Cézanne's images of Mont Sainte-Victoire – an artist who acted as a talisman of course for Braque – can be related to Sutherland's ownership of a copy of the big Fritz Novotny monograph on Cézanne, published by Phaidon in 1937, and also of the catalogue of the centenary show that Sutherland saw at the Rosenberg and Helft Gallery in 1939, a few months after his own one-man show, in which *Welsh Mountains* was probably exhibited.[138] Sutherland's increased structural concerns are also apparent in the print *Clegyr-Boia II*, which was published in *Signature* in July 1938. The motif is an outcrop of rock near St. David's, which is transformed into a highly abstract slab-like formation, with little sense of spatial coherence or recession. The configuration in the print is further pared down in *Red Monolith* (1938; pl. 82), which was first shown in the Rosenberg and Helft show, and which acted, in turn, as a point of departure for *Gorse on Sea Wall*, painted a year or so later. In *Red Monolith* the indication of a wider landscape setting is minimal, and the design is, again, symmetrical and iconic. Although the design was based on studies of a tree form, Sutherland's simplified treatment results in an image that might equally be read as a stone slab, as implied by the title, or even as a vestigial human presence. The extensive use of sand on the picture's surface may again relate to Braque, but it is also worth noting that a Masson one-man show at the Mayor Gallery in March 1938 included several examples of a series of works by Masson in which the underlying, unmodulated ground is emphatically textured with sand.[139] Another possible point of reference was Max Ernst's petrified forest pictures from the late 1920s, which possess both a primordial, apocalyptic quality and, in visual terms, a combined frontality, compositional simplicity and richness of surface texture that Sutherland could well have found stimulating (pl. 81). Sutherland had ready access to Ernst's latest work through one-man exhibitions in London at the Mayor Gallery in 1937, at the Redfern and London galleries the following year.[140] Like the 1936 Masson works discussed above, such pictures by Ernst illustrated the potential compatibility between surrealism and the landscape genre.

80 Graham Sutherland, *Welsh Mountains*, 1937/8, oil on canvas, 56 × 91.6 cm, Art Gallery of New South Wales, Sydney.

The Leeds *Sunrise between Hedges* (1939) reveals the extent to which Sutherland had emerged from Nash's shadow, in part by means of his assimilation of ideas from European modernism (pl. 84). The starting point was an observed sensation of the sun rising directly above a road at the brow of a hill, turning the flanking hedges into dramatic *contre-jour* shapes. Flower-like forms at either side suggest the close-up foreground from which the scene is registered. Over and above the continued landscape reference, one can find residual echoes of a Nash such as *Landscape of the Megaliths* in the general organisation, the floating of repeated lines articulating the space over patches of flat colour, and the preference for a palette

81 Max Ernst, *Forest and Sun*, 1927, oil on canvas, 81 × 101 cm, Private Collection.

dominated by ochres and notes of red. The overall impression of the Sutherland, however, is considerably more abstract. There are fewer descriptive indications of detail and texture to facilitate one's reading of the natural scene. The several elements are more integrated into a balanced and rhythmical design. Compared with Nash, the fluid, loose application of the paint creates an effect of transparency and spatial interpenetration. The stronger contrasts of colour and light reinforce the emphasis on optical effect at the expense of material solidity. The resultant ecstatic, revelatory quality aligns the picture not so much with Nash as with Turner, Palmer and Masson's Spanish landscapes. Its painterly freedom, on the other hand, with thinly applied paint producing visible drips and random configurations, has prompted apt comparisons with the more automatist work of Miró.[141] Such sources of inspiration are familiar from the preceding discussion, but the boldness and immateriality of the Sutherland raises the possibility that the early work of Wassily Kandinsky was a further source of inspiration. In particular, he could have seen Kandinsky's *Cossacks* (1910–11) in the important *Twentieth Century German Art* exhibition mounted at the New Burlington Galleries in Summer 1938 (pl. 83). The picture was bought from the exhibition and immediately presented to the Tate Gallery, where it was presumably put on show.[142] One may imagine Sutherland responding to the degree of abstraction in the Kandinsky, particularly its freedom from received forms of spatial coherence, and its apocalyptic aura. A specific stylistic feature that

82 Graham Sutherland *Red Monolith*, 1938, oil on canvas, 99.7 × 61.5 cm, Hirshhorn Museum and Sculpture Garden, Smithsonian Institution, Washington DC. Gift of Joseph H. Hirshhorn, 1996.

G. Sutherland 38

83 Wassily Kandinsky, *Cossacks*, 1910–11, oil on canvas, 64.9 × 130.2 cm, Tate, London.

Sutherland seems to have developed is Kandinsky's separating out of strong black lines, defining the structural organisation, and amorphous patches of colour. In the Sutherland, the tall verticals of the flowers, juxtaposed with the repeated curved horizontals towards the centre, recall the equivalent passage in *Cossacks* comprising the more upright spears and the three curved lines in front of the castle. The smudgy passage in the Kandinsky, describing the sun-like element beneath the rainbow, may equally have encouraged Sutherland to conceive the description of bright red light falling on the hedge, situated near the centre of *Sunrise Between Hedges*, where strong colour likewise bleeds into surrounding greys.

Sutherland's art was acquiring a boldness and independence, rooted to some degree in his scrutiny of the modern European art that was being extensively promoted by London galleries, as the axis of the art market shifted westwards in response to the growing political crisis. By the end of the decade, it was the art of Picasso that had come to provide the most compelling point of departure for Sutherland. His admiration for Picasso is evident from his objections in 1945 to Michael Ayrton's simple-minded advice to artists to look at nature and at painters concerned with nature, a category from which Picasso was excluded. For Sutherland, Ayrton's view was mistaken: 'Surely Picasso is, at his best, deeply concerned with nature. He had admitted this concern (conversation with Zervos . . .), and it is just this fact which opens such a vast gulf between him and his imitators'. Christian Zervos' report of a conversation with Picasso, first published in *Cahiers d'Art* in 1935, had appeared in translation in *The Painter's Object*, followed immediately by Sutherland's 'An English Stone Landmark'.[143]

84 RIGHT Graham Sutherland, *Sunrise between Hedges*, 1939, oil on canvas, 54.6 × 90.2 cm, Leeds City Art Galleries.

Picasso was reported to have stated: 'There is no abstract art. You must always begin with something. Afterwards you can remove all traces of reality: there's no danger then, anyway, because the idea of the object will have left an indelible mark . . . Whether he likes it or not, Man is the instrument of nature, it forces on him its character and appearance.'[144] Such thinking evidently informed Sutherland's ideal of a creative process starting with the observation of a natural scene or found object, which would then be subjected to a process of heightening and transformation, with a view to conveying its essential expressive charge. Picasso offered a corrective to the more inward-looking versions of surrealist art, although in other respects his work clearly seemed in close alignment with surrealism. Before the war, a considerable quantity of works by Picasso had entered British private collections, especially that built up by Roland Penrose, an artist and collector also steeped in surrealism.[145] Works by Picasso could also be contemplated at leisure and length through the medium of illustrated books, such as the 1938 monograph by Gertrude Stein, a copy of which Kenneth Clark seems to have given Sutherland, and especially in the pages of *Cahiers d'Art,* where Picasso featured more extensively than ever during the second half of the 1930s.[146] At any rate, Sutherland clearly came to share the perception, by now internationally widespread, that Picasso stood head and shoulders above all other modern artists. Such a judgement was no longer rooted in mere admiration for Picasso's artistic virtuosity. It was the example of Picasso, especially in *Guernica* and related works, that now prompted and permitted other artists, Sutherland and Bacon included, to conceive an ambition to convey in suitably modernist terms the violence and tragic tenor of contemporary life.

Picasso's great mural had been shown at the *International Exhibition* in Paris in the summer of 1937. The following October, after an international tour, the painting, preparatory drawings and related works such as *The Dream and Lie of Franco* were exhibited at the New Burlington Galleries in central London, and then in several other British venues, before ending up in New York (pl. 85).[147] The comments of Herbert Read, in his review of the London show, show how an image prompted by outrage at a specific event during the Spanish Civil War had by the latter part of 1938 come to assume a far wider significance in the present age of 'disillusion, despair and destruction': 'Not only Guernica, but Spain; not only Spain, but Europe, is symbolised in this allegory.'[148] Picasso now seemed to have become a different kind of artist, who had turned away from self-engrossment and who was seemingly impelled to capture the historical moment, to express in artistic terms what it felt like to be living through the gathering European crisis, which was inexorably leading to a war to stop fascism. The picture could be assimilated to the more 'archetypal' ways of comprehending the horrors of the present that were considered here earlier. Michel Leiris interpreted *Guernica* as a 'black and white canvas that depicts ancient tragedy'.[149] As noted, Read also described the picture as a 'religious picture' and a 'modern Calvary'. The fundamental compatibility of Greek and Christian traditions at this point are further implicit in Cyril Connolly's choice of exemplary artists: 'The masterpieces appropriate to our time are in the style of the early de Chirico, the later Rouault and Picasso's Guernica; sombre, magnificent yet personal statements of our tragedy; work of strong and noble architecture austerely coloured by loneliness and despair'.[150] For his part, Sutherland described the profound and visceral impact that *Guernica*, and especially its preliminary studies, exerted upon his own work:

> Picasso's Guernica drawings seemed to open up a philosophy and to point a way whereby – by a kind of paraphrase of appearances – things could be made to look more vital and real. The forms I saw in this series pointed to a passionate involvement in the character of the subject, whereby the feeling for it was trapped and made concrete. Like the subject and yet unlike . . . Everything I saw at this time exhorted me to a greater freedom. Only Picasso however seemed to have the true idea of metamorphosis, whereby things found a new form through feeling.[151]

No doubt memories of viewing *Guernica* and its studies in the original doubtless had a lasting significance. However, Picasso's imagery continued to be readily accessible in the form of large, high-quality reproductions in the special issue of *Cahiers d'Art* that illustrated the

85 Pablo Picasso, *Guernica* and related studies, 1937 (installation photographs of 1938 exhibition at New Burlington Galleries, London, as illustrated in *Cahiers d'Art*, no. 14, 1939).

painting, photographs recording its process of creation, and the preparatory drawings, with accompanying texts by Zervos, Leiris and so forth.[152] Sutherland obviously knew the issue because it also contained the reproduction of Miró's *Reaper* that he specifically recalled encountering in the publication.

The inspiration of this body of work by Picasso is everywhere apparent in Sutherland's work during the period of the descent into war, beginning with *Gorse on Sea Wall* (1939). In this key transitional picture, the spiral unwinding of the root was elaborated not just from the agonised hands of Christ in Grünewald's *Isenheim Altarpiece*, as noted, but also from details such as the twisting, screaming head of the dying horse in *Guernica*. The prickly forms just to the left seem the equivalent, as emotive cues, to the 'exploding' light fixture that Picasso inserted, as a surrogate for the bombs, directly above the poignant image of the horse. The absence of modelling and emphatic outlines marks a stylistic response to *Guernica*. Indeed impressions of the Picasso may have merged with Sutherland's recollections of the closely related idiom of Miró's *The Reaper*, which foreshadows the general symmetrical format of *Gorse on Sea Wall*, and the spiky, star-like forms played off against softer and more fluid pas-

sages (pl. 77). In Sutherland's subsequent work, *Guernica* remained a vital point of departure. The writhing form of a tree root in Sutherland's *Midsummer Landscape* (1940) reads as a further descendant of Picasso's horse, especially as it is portrayed in some of the early preliminary studies, subsiding to the ground, mortally wounded, rather than rearing and screaming in agony (pls 86 and 87). *Blasted Oak* (1941) recalls the downward twist of the horse's head in Picasso's studies (pl. 33). The curving, hollowed out form, suggesting the screaming mouth at the top of a neck-like trunk, seems strikingly close to a group of pencil sketches, leading to an oil painting with comparably dark background, that came early on in the gestation of *Guernica*. Picasso focussed here on the image of an upturned horse's head, with a spike for a tongue that encapsulates the raw violence of the image, a solution to which he returned in the final painting, with modifications to the angle at which the head is set. The lumbering, monstrous form in *Green Tree Form: Interior of Woods* (1940) might be seen as transmuted from Picasso's preparatory studies of the distraught mother clutching her dead infant (pls VII and 88). The 'leg' of the uprooted tree trunk matches the arm with which the mother supports her convulsed body, just as the strong diagonal line defining its upper edge recalls the angled leg with which Picasso's figure seeks to propel herself forward. *Guernica* equally left its mark on Sutherland's purpose-made work as a war artist. In his first images of devastated buildings, it is not just the jagged forms and flattened shapes, but also the imagery of flames and explosion and the nocturnal ambience, producing strong contrasts of light and shadow, that suggest that he had discovered in nature an objective correlative to Picasso's imaginative inventions (pl. 89). The twisted lift-shafts and girders that featured in subsequent works

86 Pablo Picasso, *Study for Guernica*, 1937, pencil, 24.1 × 45.6 cm, Museo National Centro de Arte Reina Sofia, Madrid (as illustrated in *Cahiers d'Art*, no. 12, 1937).

87 RIGHT Graham Sutherland, *Midsummer Landscape*, 1940, pencil, ink and gouache on paper, 68.6 × 48.3 cm, Birmingham Museums and Art Gallery, Birmingham.

88 Pablo Picasso, *Study for Guernica*, 1937, pencil and ink, 24 × 45.3 cm, Museo National Centro de Arte Reina Sofia, Madrid (as illustrated in *Cahiers d'Art*, no. 12, 1937).

prompted by visits to London appear likewise to be descended from the head of Picasso's horse, contorted in pain and anguish. In a large drawing of 1942 in which Sutherland synthesised several motifs of bombed structures, with a view to creating a large painting, the entire compositional structure in terms of the patterns of lights and darks and the interplay of shapes seems to be a virtual pastiche of Picasso's monumental design.[153] The artist recalled how important Picasso's mural was for this phase of his work:

> The conception of the idea of stress, both physical and mental, and how forms could be modified by emotion had been even before the war, much in my mind. It was crystallised and strengthened by my understanding of Picasso's studies for *Guernica*. Faces become distorted by tears and mouths open in fear . . . I had seen aspects of this idea in certain kinds of destruction. So did I, too, in the steel works.[154]

It is not surprising that *Guernica* affected wider perceptions of Picasso's work and artistic evolution. A Picasso exhibition in London in Spring 1939, which was dominated by relatively decorative still life paintings, prompted Kenneth Clark to reflect upon the bewildering diversity of Picasso's art.[155] In the course of what Sutherland, for one, found 'a very just assessment of these new paintings & indeed of the whole position of Picasso', Clark declared: 'I believe that Picasso is most himself when he is violent . . . In the studies for Guernica he was fighting with the gloves off . . . and the result was the most powerful creation in all his work'.[156] If *Guernica* made some aspects of Picasso's work look less compelling, it brought others into prominence. The lavishly illustrated issue of *Cahiers d'Art*, which appeared in December 1938, was mainly given over again to Picasso, but this time with a particular focus on several series of little known works produced between 1927 and 1930.[157] These included small canvases of the human head, subjected to savage distortions and reductions, a selec-

89 Graham Sutherland, *Devastation: Farmhouse in Wales*, 1940, oil on canvas, 64.5 × 113.4 cm, Cheltenham Art Gallery and Museum.

tion of the studies that led up to the *Crucifixion* painting of 1930, and a large selection of sheets from a sketchbook of spring 1927 in which Picasso explored highly sculptural and sexually charged images of a female bather on the seashore, frequently holding a key in the lock of a beach hut. Together, this body of imagery highlighted Picasso's most expressionistic deformations of the human body, establishing the broad current in his work that would eventually culminate in *Guernica*.[158]

Visual comparisons suggest that Sutherland again paid close attention to this 1938 issue of *Cahiers d'Art*. In *Gorse on Sea Wall*, Sutherland seems also to have learnt from the organisation of shapes in the small head paintings. Equally, the thin, scrubby paint application that is conveyed by such Picasso reproductions may have encouraged Sutherland likewise to simplify his own means of application, and to edit out the kinds of graphic flourish that might have detracted from the stark expressive charge of the picture. Moreover, his anthropomorphic treatment of tree forms in works such as *Green Tree Form: Interior of Woods* and, especially, the vertical *Association of Oaks* suggest that Sutherland had looked with admiration at Picasso's bulbous reinventions of human anatomy in the 1927 sketchbook. Sutherland seems to have adapted not just particular, somewhat bony forms, but also details such as the repeated curving lines that serve to define their three-dimensionality (pls v, 90 and 91). Such

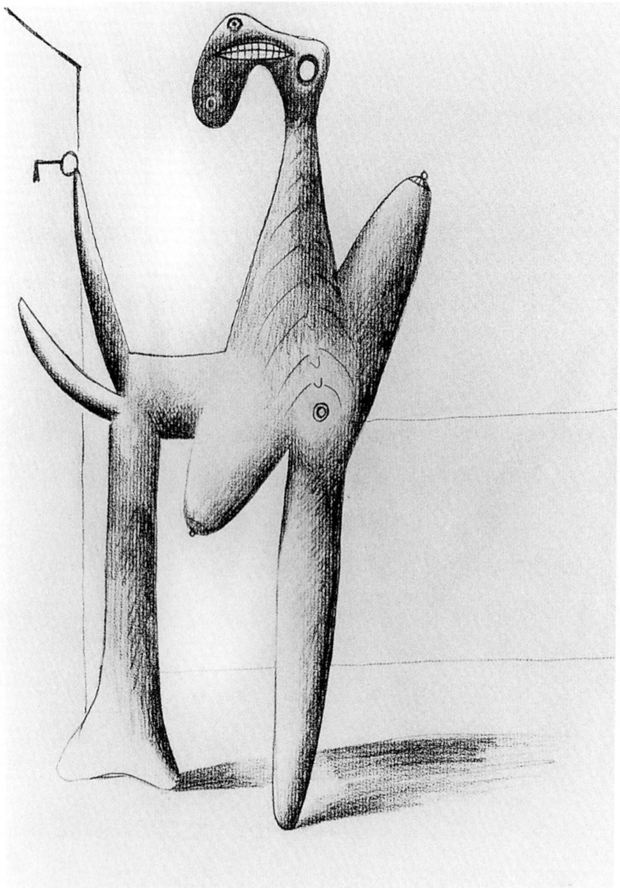

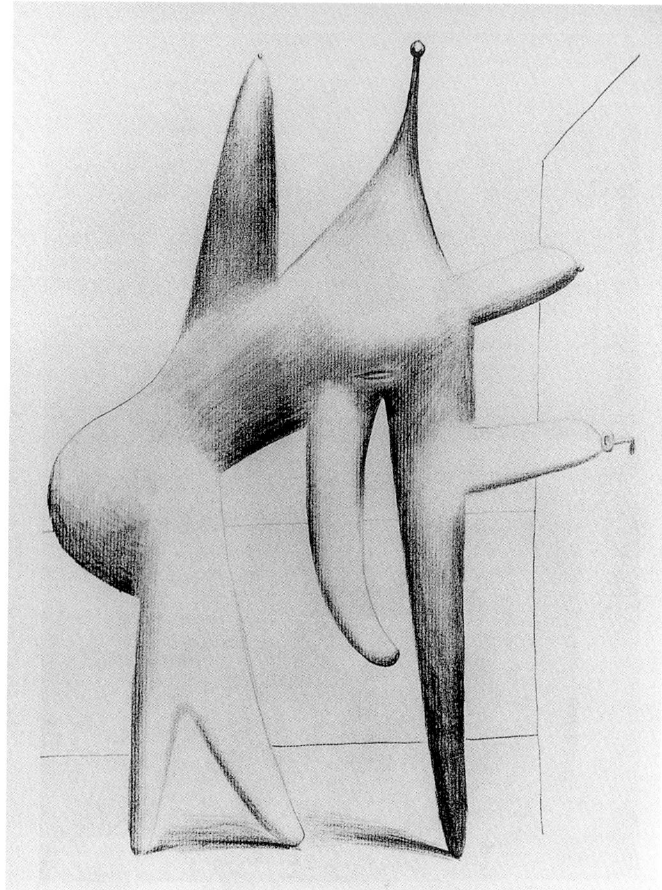

Picasso works prompted a shift of emphasis in Sutherland's work around 1940. Raymond Mortimer chose to criticise the overtly anthropomorphic aspect of the two works noted; *Green Tree Form* was 'too breasted for my taste', while *Association of Oaks* 'makes a caricature of the human couple'. An occasional surrealist undertone – 'the disquieting suggestion of animal or genital shapes intrudes on aesthetic contemplation' – was, for Mortimer, the only qualification to an 'effect of certainty and power which I have never had from an English contemporary'.[159] The most obvious derivation from the 1927 sketchbook is a small work on paper from 1945, *Horned Form*, which amounts to a virtual pastiche of Picasso's imagery of bulbous figures and huts on the seashore.[160]

Finally, the contents of *Cahiers d'Art*, before the wartime cessation of publication, suggest that reproductions of work by Picasso and André Masson played complementary roles in stimulating Sutherland's direction at the end of the decade. Masson was probably the most conspicuous of the surrealist artists in late 1930s issues of the magazine, in part no doubt because the extreme thematic and stylistic violence of his work at this time, since his reconciliation with the surrealist movement, made him appear to be a close ally to Picasso. In the

90 FAR LEFT Pablo Picasso, *Bather*, graphite pencil on paper, 30 × 23 cm, Musée Picasso, Paris (page from 1927 Sketchbook, as illustrated in *Cahiers d'Art*, no. 13, 1938).

91 Pablo Picasso, *Bather*, graphite pencil on paper, 30 × 23 cm, Musée Picasso, Paris (page from 1927 Sketchbook, as illustrated in *Cahiers d'Art*, no. 13, 1938).

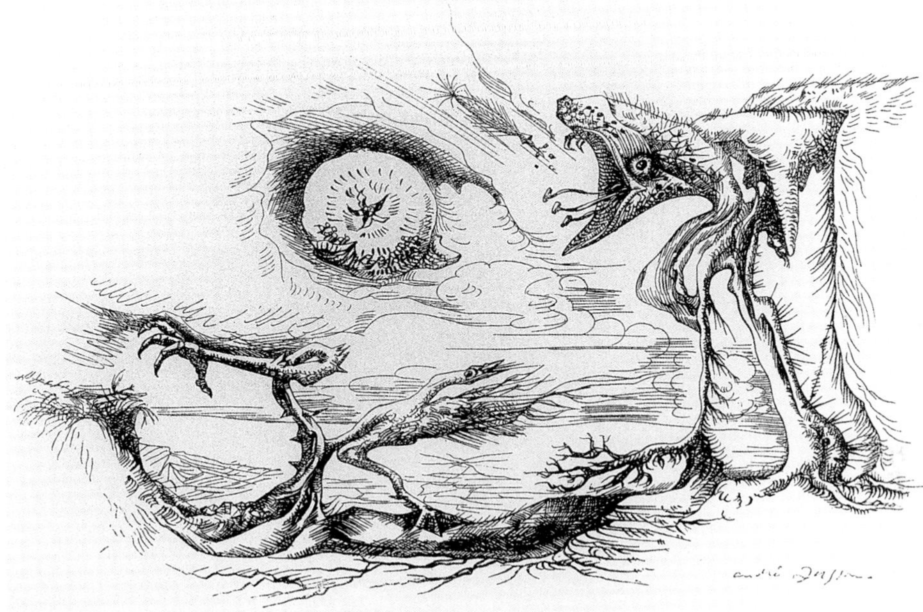

92 André Masson, *At the same time the trap and the prey*, 1939, etching (from illustrations of *Mythologie de la Nature* in *Cahiers d'Art*, no. 14, 1939).

final pre-war issue of *Minotaure*, Breton contrasted Masson with other distinguished artists of the time whose work nevertheless 'utterly fail[ed] to reflect this epoch's tragic sense of dread'.[161] The second of the 1939 issues of *Cahiers d'Art* featured a group of the extraordinary, metamorphic etchings that Masson created under the heading *Mythologie de la Nature* (pl. 92).[162] Metamorphic images such as *At the Same time the Trap and the Prey* are strikingly analogous to Sutherlands such as *Green Tree Form* (1940), reflecting either Sutherland's direct awareness of Masson, or else a shared derivation from the expressionistic idiom of Picasso's *Guernica*.

Compared to Picasso or Masson, this entire group of found object paintings by Sutherland, in the wake of *Gorse on Sea Wall*, seem ultimately more muted, in both pictorial and expressive terms. They proclaim their origins in a process of observation and abstraction from nature, whereas the artists he was looking at relied, one senses, on purely imaginative impulses. Yet the natural root forms in Sutherland's paintings seem to be not only extracted from their wider landscape context, but also stripped of their familiar and easily legible identities. This is especially true of *Tree Form* (1941), one of the last and most descriptive in the series and arguably one of the most mysterious and affecting of Sutherland's creations (pl. 93). It is a gloomy picture in every sense, which might well prompt analogies with an artist such as Max Ernst. At the same time, one wonders whether Sutherland could conceivably have encountered one of the most remarkable products of contemporary French literature, namely Jean-Paul Sartre's novel *La Nausée* (*Nausea*), published in France in 1938. We shall return to this book in more detail in the context of Bacon and existentialism, but for present purposes it is worth recalling a crucial episode where the narrator is sitting in the park:

> The root of the chestnut tree plunged into the ground just underneath my bench. I no longer remembered that it was a root . . . Words had disappeared, and with them the meaning of things, the methods of using them, the feeble landmarks which men have traced on their surface. I was sitting, slightly bent, my head bowed, alone in front of that black, knotty mass, which was utterly crude and frightened me. And then I had this revelation.[163]

This was a metaphysical sense of the absolute absurdity or contingency of things, which provided 'the key to Existence, the key to my Nausea, to my own life'.[164] His experience of the root epitomised the gulf between physical existence in the raw, and the conceptualisations that we seek to project or impose:

> Faced with that big, rugged paw, neither ignorance nor knowledge had any importance; the world of explanations and reasons is not that of existence. A circle is not absurd, it is clearly explicable by the rotation of a segment of a straight line around one of its extremities. But a circle doesn't exist either. That root, on the other hand, existed in so far that I could not explain it. Knotty, inert, nameless, it fascinated me, filled my eyes, repeatedly brought me back to my own existence . . . I saw clearly that you could not pass from its function as a root, as a suction-pump, *to that*, to that hard, compact sea-lion skin, to that oily, horny, stubborn look.[165]

*

While certain aspects of Sutherland's work appeared compatible with the nostalgic agenda of neo-romanticism, from another perspective his art was aligned with resistance to this tendency. It must be recalled that, during the Second World War, an engagement with European modernism continued to prevail in progressive cultural circles in England. *Horizon* magazine epitomised the impulse to keep the flame burning, to maintain at least a residual internationalism during the long years of isolation. In 1943, Peter Watson stated this position emphatically in a letter to John Craxton: 'Nostalgia for the past is not a valid vehicle for art now, I am sure of that.'[166] Although providing a forum for artists in Britain was a major priority, *Horizon* succeeded to a lesser degree in covering the work of significant figures who were still based in Europe. Critical accounts of individual artists included Ruthven Todd and Jankel Adler on Paul Klee, who died in 1940 (published in 1940 and 1942), Watson himself on Miró (1941), and Robert Melville on the evolution of the 'double head' in the work of Picasso (1942).[167] Magritte's *The Black Flag* was illustrated in an issue in 1943.[168] As noted, a group of recent works by Picasso were illustrated in 1944.[169] There were also occasional translations of

93 Graham Sutherland, *Tree Form* (1941), oil on canvas mounted on board, 40.5 × 30.5 cm, Leeds City Art Galleries.

artists' texts, notably Giorgio de Chirico's 'Sensitiveness'.[170] The clear preference for the surrealist wing of modern art, shared by Connolly and Watson, was reflected in the reprinting from *The Nation* of Clement Greenberg's essay on surrealist painting.[171] Reproductions in a magazine such as *Horizon*, as well as the pre-war art journals, were an obvious stimulus in the straitened circumstances of wartime. Yet, surprisingly enough, several of London's commercial galleries remained in business during the war years, and even managed to devote the occasional exhibition to important European artists. The Redfern Gallery seems to have been the most active in showing such work, perhaps because they were in the fortunate position of possessing stocks of paintings and works on paper accumulated before the war.

Against this backdrop, Bacon's *Three Studies for Figures at the Base of a Crucifixion* (1944) shows that a strong interest in European modernism, above all the art of Picasso and Masson, comprised a further area of common ground when he and Sutherland became close during the latter part of the war. The affinities noted between the triptych and Sutherland's paintings from around 1940, such as the two versions of *Green Tree Form*, can be seen as a consequence not just of the two artists' mutual interchange, but also of their shared points of departure. Bacon certainly embraced the enthusiasm for surrealism and Picasso that was current within Sutherland's milieu. His particular fascination with Picasso was, of course, longstanding. Bacon's continuing preoccupation with Crucifixion imagery reflected in part the example of the Picassos reproduced in *Minotaure* and *Cahiers d'Art*. The highly schematised figure style characteristic of Picasso's paintings of the late 1920s provided the dominant inspiration for several pictures, including the pair of lost Bacons from around 1936, which in certain respects anticipate the imagery and stylistic idiom of the central panel, in particular, of the *Three Studies*.[172] It has also been maintained that recollections of *Guernica* informed the triptych, even though Bacon later dismissed the work as not one of Picasso's best – as indeed, with hindsight, did Picasso himself.[173] The cloaked figure of the mother clutching her dead infant, explored in Picasso's preliminary sketches, may at some level have shaped Bacon's conception of the left-hand image (pl. iv). More tellingly perhaps, the right-hand panel of the triptych can be read as a synthesis of elements deriving from Picasso's dying horse and mother and baby studies for *Guernica* (pl. viii). The former contributed the screaming mouth with its prominent rows of teeth, emanating from an extended tubular neck whose downward inclination in some Picasso studies was noted in relation to Sutherland's *Green Tree Form*. The Picasso precedents for *Green Tree Form* are again relevant for elements of Bacon's image, such as the vertical support of the front arm, the overall diagonal configuration of the form, and the upturned screaming head. In broader terms, Bacon may have been affected by the way in which *Guernica* itself falls into three sections, rather like a triptych, as Peppiat observes. The Picasso foreshadows the simple, linear construction of pictorial space in the *Three Studies*.

In broader terms, an awareness of *Guernica* seems relevant to aspects of Bacon's conception of the triptych that have already arisen in the course of this study. Thus Picasso's highly expressive use of animal imagery, including the bull and especially the horse, as surrogates for human feelings and sensations of physical agony, must surely have complemented and reinforced Bacon's fascination with the work of wildlife photographers such as Marius Maxwell, and at some level informed the bestial suggestions that he incorporated into his own triptych. Likewise, Bacon's engagement with Greek tragedy and the theme of the Eumenides is inconceivable without the general precedent of the deployment of classical imagery in Picasso's art of the 1930s, itself stimulated by the usage of classical myth in the writings of Sigmund Freud (as in the Oedipus Complex) and in turn within the iconography of the surrealist movement that owed so much to Freud (as in the journal *Minotaure*, published between 1933 and 1939). In relation to the triptych's religious dimension, one might note that Picasso's preoccupation with the image of the Crucifixion, and in particular its treatment in the hands of Grünewald, remained one a residual reference in *Guernica* and related works from 1937 such as the *Weeping Woman* series.[174] The photographs in *Cahiers d'Art* showing the several stages of the making of *Guernica* perhaps played some part in shaping Bacon's commitment to an improvisatory picture-making process. Bacon's grisaille rendition of his three hybrid creatures, with its implicit allusion to black and white photography, echoed the more comprehensive use of this method in *Guernica*. Above all, however, Bacon, like Sutherland, was galvanised, by the example that Picasso offered of an avant-garde artist turned witness to his times. The *Three Studies* represented Bacon's own attempt to go beyond illustrative references to contemporary imagery, and instead to give pictorial embodiment to the essential 'disillusion, despair and destruction' of contemporary life, to borrow Read's phrase about *Guernica*.

At the same time, we may note significant divergences between Bacon's triptych and the monumental Picasso mural. Notably, Bacon employed a more sculptural approach to form, a departure from his own Picasso-derived work a few years previously. In this context, he readily acknowledged the stimulus he derived from the same Picasso sketchbook drawings of 1927, with their emphatic modelling and bizarre deformations of the human body, that we encountered as possible prompts to Sutherland's more anthropomorphic direction around 1940. Bacon famously described to David Sylvester his excitement at Picasso's idea 'of organic forms that relate to the human image; but is a complete distortion of it'.[175] As an example of this approach, it is worth choosing one of the series where the bony forms, as well as details such as the prominent teeth and linear striations, may have provided Bacon with one of his starting points for the creatures in the triptych (pl. 94). It tends to be assumed that Bacon had been familiar with these works by Picasso, amongst others, from the time of his visit to Paris in the late 1920s. In fact, the sketchbook in question was little known until it was reproduced in the 1938 issue of *Cahiers d'Art*, dedicated to Picasso. We may, then, imagine Bacon and Sutherland together poring over the illustrations in this remarkable issue of the magazine, and perhaps discussing Picasso as the blueprint for a deformed, dehumanised vision of the body, which could serve to articulate the tragic condition of contemporary man.[176] Bacon's images, like Sutherland's, explore a sustained ambiguity of human and animal imagery, whereas Picasso's are essentially abstractions from the human figure. Their hybrids

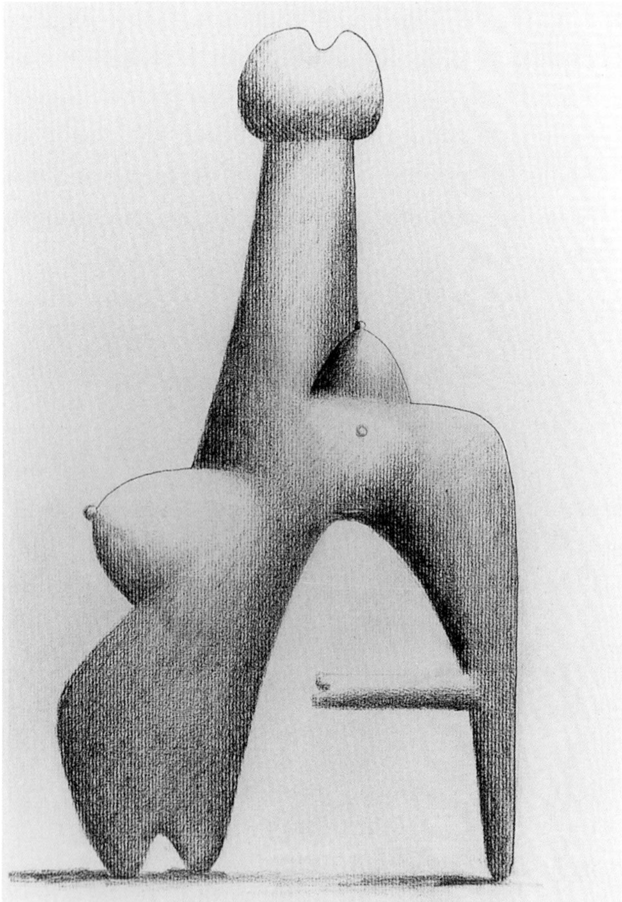

94 Pablo Picasso, *Bather*, graphite pencil on paper, 30 × 23 cm, Musée Picasso, Paris (page from 1927 Sketchbook, as illustrated in *Cahiers d'Art*, no. 13, 1938).

are also without any indication of gender, while the Picassos are self-evidently a highly sexualised male fantasy of the female body. Picasso's imagery in the sketchbook of 1927 is disquieting, but ultimately playful and witty, whereas that of Bacon and Sutherland strikes a decidedly sombre note. Bacon's substitution of airless interiors for Picasso's beaches and huts reinforces this shift of emphasis. Overall, it would appear that during the war period Bacon and Sutherland shared a strong and highly productive admiration for particular strands in Picasso's art, but they also manifest certain common divergences from Picasso's example, reinforcing the view that an interchange between the two British artists was highly significant for the progress of their work.

The argument that the experience of living through the Second World War crucially informed the work of Bacon and Sutherland is reinforced by noting parallels between Bacon's triptych and the remarkable body of work that Picasso himself produced during the war years, in the wake of *Guernica*, a phase that has only of late started to receive the detailed scrutiny it deserves.[177] In stylistic terms, Bacon's approach recalls the sculptural emphasis and shallow, minimal space of recent Picasso paintings such as *Woman Dressing her Hair* (1940), a comparison that also, it has to be said, highlights Bacon's relative lack of pictorial sophistication in the *Three Studies*. Another dimension of the Bacon is foreshadowed by *Bust of a Woman* (1941), where Picasso fused the features of a figure with those of his Afghan hound Kazbek, creating a more explicit synthesis of human and animal imagery than had been customary in his pre-war work.[178] Generally, a powerful mood of fear and terror, projected through iconography and deformations of the body, runs through much of Picasso's work from the late 1930s onwards. It is difficult, however, to see how Bacon could have known Picasso's recent and current work during the war, when communications were virtually non-existent. Several illustrated publications appeared at the time, but they are unlikely to have crossed the English Channel.[179] Presumably, the situation started to ease after the Liberation of Paris in August 1944. Certainly Jack Bilbo of the Modern Art Gallery was able to publish a volume illustrating a group of recent Picassos, four of which were also illustrated in the October 1944 issue of *Horizon*.[180] A new issue of *Cahiers d'Art*, the first since the fall of Paris, appeared in late 1944, and may have become available in Britain quite soon thereafter.[181] Normal service was, as it were, gradually being resumed.

NEWS OUT OF FRANCE

The focus so far has been on the continuing importance for Sutherland and Bacon of aspects of pre-war European art, available as a resource during the relatively isolated war years in the form of illustrated books and magazines such as *Cahiers d'Art*, as well as occasional exhibitions in commercial galleries. After 1945, of course, a fuller range of contacts became possible once again. How far, then can the work of these two artists be aligned with artistic and cultural developments associated more particularly with the post-war period? It is undoubtedly true that a renewed interest in modern European art was characteristic of the milieu in which they moved. As soon as hostilities were over, there was clearly an immense surge of interest in developments in French cultural life during the course of the last six years, and a strong desire to restore the lines of international communication. In Paris, once again the capital of modern art, one might visit all manner of major exhibitions featuring the great names who had dominated art before the war. Equally, at the commercial gallery run by René Drouin, one could see work by young abstract artists, but also the representatives of a new and challenging figuration, such as Jean Dubuffet, Fautrier and Wols.[182] Important exhibitions were organised in London – *Matisse and Picasso* (1945–46) and *Braque and Rouault* (1947) at the Victoria and Albert Museum, *40,000 Years of Modern Art* (1948) and *Forty Years of Modern Art* (1948–49) at the new Institute of Contemporary Art, presided over by Penrose, Watson, Read and so forth. Once again, the pages of *Horizon*, house journal of the London intelligentsia, vividly encapsulate the renewed commitment to French culture. A special issue devoted to 'News out of France' appeared in May 1945, featuring several translations (Jean-Paul Sartre, Paul Valéry and an illustrated essay on Braque by Jean Paulhan, translated by

Peter Watson); a prose poem by Francis Ponge; and reviews of recent French literature by John Russell ('The Existential Theatre'), Stephen Spender on wartime poetry, and Philip Toynbee.[183] Cyril Connolly described how his trip to Paris in January had made him 'indescribably happy. London seemed utterly remote – a grey, sick wilderness on another planet, for in Paris the civilian virtues triumph – personal relations, adult-minded seriousness, aliveness, love of the arts. Literature is immensely important there'.[184] Subsequently, a wider international coverage was pursued in the magazine, but in June 1947, Connolly remained in no doubt that a small area of central Paris 'still contains what is most alive in the arts of Europe'.[185]

In the sphere of the visual arts, the renewed climate of internationalism was reflected in *Horizon* in a spate of articles either by or about significant French artists, with increasing attention also given to other European centres and to America. The magazine covered, in chronological sequence, Braque, Masson, Jacques Villon, Duchamp, Klee and 'The State of Painting in Paris' by D. H. Kahnweiler (1945); Delvaux, Matisse, Lam, Gris, Arp, surrealism and Lipschitz (1946); Laurens, European Painters in Mexico (for example Carrington, Paalen, Onslow-Ford), contemporary American art, Ben Shahn and Morris Graves, and Herbert Read on 'The Fate of Modern Painting' (1947); Artaud, Balthus, Bauchant, Marino Marini, contemporary German art, and 'Negro Art and Cubism' (1948); and, finally, expressionism, Brancusi, Giacometti, Morandi, Matta, the challenge of American Art, and Léonid (1949).[186] Only the occasional contribution now gave consideration to younger British figures such as Louis Le Broquy (1946), Eduardo Paolozzi (1947), as well, of course, as Bacon, who featured in the very final issue of *Horizon*.[187] It is quite evident where Peter Watson's real attachments lay from a remark to Connolly about the inclusion of the first of these: 'It's time for another Horizon British (Eire) art discovery. This is the only way to reconcile undue interest in Continental artists.'[188]

During this period, Sutherland continued to take his primary bearings from artists of the pre-war generation. The strongly linear idiom, combined with bold, flatly applied colours, which Sutherland employed in the *Thorn Head* series (1945/6) might suggest an engagement with the latest work of Picasso, including the wartime still-life paintings exhibited at the Victoria and Albert Museum in December 1945 (pl. 46).[189] However, a more direct precedent for the head-and-shoulders format, the agonised tone and disquieting sharpness of the forms is provided by Picasso's *Weeping Woman* of 1937, a major masterpiece that Sutherland could have viewed in the collection of Roland Penrose. This picture, like certain metaphors in Aeschylus, epitomised for Sutherland a 'poetry which enlightens the significance and nature of things': 'by a deliberate method . . . [Picasso] underlines and embodies the very essence of grief . . . It may be interesting . . . when one regards Picasso's gnashing woman to recall that Aeschylus tells us that "grief bites" '.[190] There is also a distant recollection in these pictures of the passage in *Guernica* describing the horse's screaming head, with its spiked tongue echoing the jagged contour of the light above. In the Northampton *Crucifixion* (1946) and related works on the theme, the simplified configurations of the cross and of Christ's anatomy are

95 Julio Gonzalez, *Head with Mirror* (as illustrated in *Cahiers d'Art*, nos 1–4, 1935, p. 33).

ultimately less reminiscent of the Grünewald original than they are of Picasso's variations on the Isenheim altarpiece, which Sutherland could have studied in *Minotaure*. The treatment of Mary Magdalene in a subsequent depiction of *The Deposition* (1946) seems to echo the left-hand figure in Picasso's *Three Dancers* of 1925.[191]

Once Sutherland started spending considerable periods of time in the South of France, he soon got to know artists such as Matisse and Picasso personally, since they were all living in close proximity, and had friends in common such as Douglas Cooper.[192] But Sutherland's attitude was not one of blind admiration. Soon after his first visit to the Riviera, he informed Clark: 'The Picassos at Antibes are a poor lot – except for one which is *magnificent* and new'.[193] Critics have frequently remarked on Sutherland's 'increasing indebtedness to Picasso and Matisse at this date [1948]'.[194] This factor may account for the increasing stridency of palette and simplification of design that his work manifests, though this was the direction in which his painting was already heading in 1944–45. Yet Sutherland's imagery was very different, and comparison with such figures highlights the relatively literal character of his response to the strange and exotic visual environment in which he now found himself. The same might be said of his colourful depictions of cicadas from 1948, which contain a distant echo of Masson's many insect paintings from the early 1930s. Telling analogies have also been proposed between the *Thorn Head* and *Palm Tree* pictures and the drawings and welded sculpture of Picasso's friend Julio Gonzalez, which Sutherland once again could have seen reproduced in *Cahiers d'Art* in 1935, 1936 and 1947 (pl. 95).[195] Otherwise, Sutherland's art at this time finds its closest affinities in the work of artists who had also taken their inspiration from the examples of Picasso and surrealism. There is an interesting family resemblance with the spiky linearity of the emphatically 'primitivist' work of Wilfredo Lam, whose burgeoning reputation around the end of the war was reflected in articles in *Cahiers d'Art* and *Horizon*, and in the purchase of pictures by Lee Miller and Peter Watson.[196] Equally, the late work of Arshile Gorky in America, which Sutherland almost certainly did not know about, provides a further parallel instance of metamorphic imagery given a sharply pointed and disquieting cast, as well as a creative process rooted in the transformation of small-scale motifs extracted from the natural landscape. Gorky, like Lam, was much admired in New York surrealist circles during the war.

In its mythic imagery and enigmatic, hybrid forms, a Sutherland such as *Chimère* I (1946; pl. 11) also recalls the current work of Mark Rothko. Indeed, the loose affinities between Bacon's 1944 triptych and Willem de Kooning's biomorphic and equally Picassoesque *Pink Angels* (1945) seem to reinforce the argument that artists on either side of the Atlantic had arrived at comparable positions, prompted by surrealism and an impulse to convey the 'tragic' atmosphere of the war.[197] The key distinction of course lies in the Americans' concerted moves into highly original abstract idioms from around 1947 onwards.

*

Even more than is the case with Sutherland, Bacon's work after the *Three Studies* demands consideration within an international frame of reference. The triptych came to mark the symbolic beginning of Bacon's artistic career, but it also marked the culmination of his overt apprenticeship to Picasso. For Bacon, as for a figure like Jackson Pollock in the United States, escaping from the shadow of Picasso was clearly an important motor to artistic innovation. To what degree, then, did his work in the years 1945–46 embody his responses to alternative stimuli in contemporary art? An obvious candidate for consideration is surrealism. Later in life, Bacon tended to dismiss the association; he informed Michel Archimbaud that he had 'never liked Surrealist painting' and stated clearly that 'my pictures were not at all Surrealist!'[198] He proceeded to give a somewhat more nuanced account. He acknowledged, for instance, that he had admired the work of the surrealist writers, and observed:

> My relationship with Surrealism is a little complicated. I think I've been influenced by what the movement represented in terms of revolt against the establishment, in politics, religion and the arts, but my pictures haven't really shown any direct influence. Well, perhaps a little in my early work. Even in *Painting* of 1946. But in the end, my painting has nothing to do with Surrealist painting.[199]

Bacon had doubtless been looking at surrealist art since the 1930s, though his own work was deemed by Roland Penrose, reasonably enough, to be insufficiently surrealist for inclusion in the great 1936 show in London.[200] There is indeed a superficial analogy between a work like *Painting* (1946) and the method of irrational and disconcerting juxtaposition employed by Surrealist painters such as Ernst or Magritte, although one might doubt whether this arose from identical concerns. The leading surrealism specialist Dawn Ades has argued that Bacon's acceptance of subconscious impulses and chance suggest a general association with the movement, but this does not indicate 'a commitment to the Surrealists' ideas and beliefs in any systematic way'. In essence, he never shared their programmatic interest in 'quarrying the unconscious' by means of either 'automatist' techniques that circumvented conscious control, or using pictorial symbolism to evoke the irrational mechanisms of the dream.[201] In pictorial terms, it is unlikely that Bacon would have derived much benefit from, at one extreme, the more purely abstract manifestations of surrealism, associated with the work of artists like

Miró, or, at the opposite extreme, from the deliberately conventional, representational styles cultivated by such figures as Magritte and Dali. Instead, one may imagine him responding to artists such as Picasso in whose work strong and legible imagery is combined with an overt process of artistic transformation. This raises the possibility Bacon may have derived inspiration from the same figures who had provided significant pointers for Sutherland in the late 1930s, namely Ernst and Masson. In general, Ernst does not seem especially relevant, although Sylvester for one found it 'difficult to believe' that Bacon could have painted *Figure Study 1* (1945–46) without having seen the comparable positioning and treatment of the tweed jacket and hat in Ernst's *The Couple* of 1924.[202] The affinities with Masson, however, seem far more revealing, especially given the discussion earlier of the likely influence of Masson's work in the mid-1930s upon the landscapes of Sutherland.

Throughout the 1940s too, one can observe a particular pattern of British interest in Masson's work. In 1942, for instance, the critic Robert Melville published an essay in *Arson*, a one-off surrealist journal, which expressed strong admiration for the artist's work of the late 1930s.[203] The following spring, a show of paintings and graphic work by Masson was mounted at the Redfern Gallery.[204] The artist's essay 'Painting is a Wager' appeared in translation in *Horizon* to coincide with the show.[205] This was also the moment at which Bacon and Sutherland re-established contact. It seems reasonable to speculate that they both visited the show, possibly even together, and that it would have formed a topic of conversation. The Redfern Gallery, after all, regularly included work by Sutherland in its summer exhibitions. Then, in 1945, a pair of wartime pictures by Masson was illustrated in the July issue of *Horizon*.[206] These were accompanied by a further text, 'A Crisis of the Imaginary'.[207] In 1947 the *Horizon* imprint even produced a special edition of *André Masson and His Universe*. This was a modified version of the newly published French anthology of texts by Masson and his supporters, edited by Michel Leiris and Georges Limbour, but with Douglas Cooper's translations of four of the texts interpolated into the front of the volume.[208] As late as 1950, David Sylvester could assert that Masson and Giacometti, aged fifty-four and forty-eight respectively, constituted 'the real avant-garde of contemporary art'.[209] Alongside this critical enthusiasm, it was Masson's highly distinctive work of the late 1930s that provided, one might argue, the most compelling pictorial inspiration for the body of work that Bacon created in the wake of the *Three Studies*. Masson, above all, foreshadowed Bacon's ambition to convey visceral, profoundly disturbing imagery in an idiom that relied not only on illustration but also on manipulations of colour, space and painterly touch in order to engage the viewer's emotional and imaginative responses to a picture's imagery. The terms in which Breton characterised Masson's 'tragic sense of dread' in 1939 are, if anything, even more resonant in relation to Bacon: 'the problem is no longer . . . to know if a painting "stands-up" in a wheat field for instance, but if it stands up alongside the daily newspaper. Very few works are strong enough to submit to such a test, and applying it entails a radical upheaval of values'.[210] To elaborate more specific parallels, one might note a certain continuity between Masson's nightmarish *Louis XVI Armchair* (1938–39; pl. 96), reproduced in *Minotaure* in 1939, and the seated, cen-

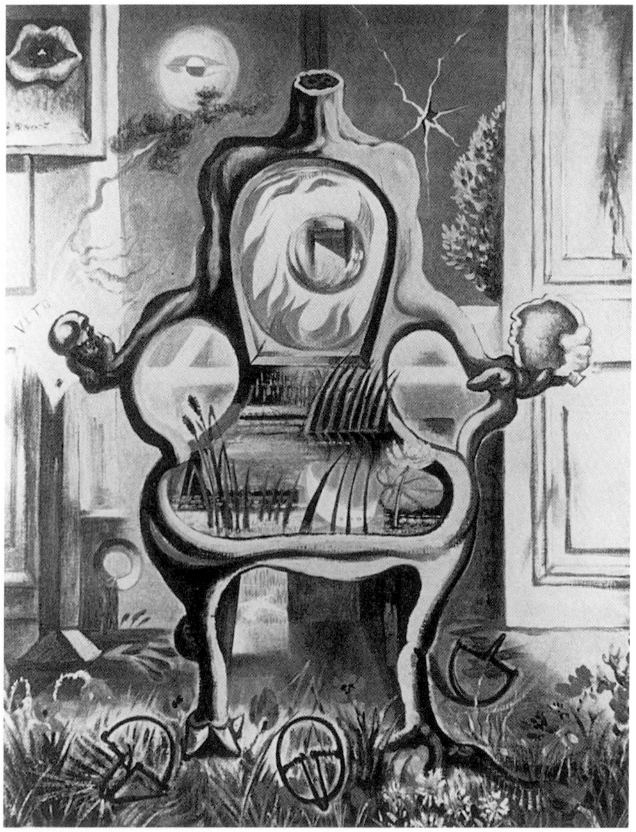

96 André Masson, *Louis XVI Armchair*, 1938–39, oil on canvas, 71.2 × 57.8 cm, Private CoLlection, U.S.A.

97 André Masson, *Gradiva*, 1939, oil on canvas, 97 × 130 cm, Private Collection.

trally placed, and of course equally decapitated figure in Bacon's *Figure in a Landscape* (1945; pl. XII).[211] In this work by Masson, as in the better-known *Gradiva* (1939; pl. 97), the suggestion of a domestic space incongruously invaded by attributes of the natural landscape anticipates Bacon's insertion of a grassy patch into an interior in the right-hand panel of the *Three Studies*, and especially of flower and plant elements (not to mention an opened umbrella) into the shallow enclosed spaces of the two versions of *Figure Study*. One could also compare several aspects of *Figure Study II* (pl. XIV) with their more elaborate, not to say Baroque, equivalents in *Gradiva*, noting Bacon's placing of the figure, emphatically modelled, within a frontal interior endowed with geometric panelling, linear indicators of a perspectival space, and a lurid orange coloration. It is also worth noting, of course, the air of consuming, inward distress that afflicts both figures, with Masson's gaping vagina reading as a surrogate for the scream that Bacon describes more literally. Equally, the shocking confrontation of rib of beef and vagina in *Gradiva* looks forward to Bacon's juxtaposition of cuts of meat and open mouth in *Painting* (1946; pl. XVI).[212] The connection between Bacon and Masson is reinforced by the two artists' shared sense of affinity with the thought processes of Georges Bataille, discussed below. Masson may well have been the single most important European influence on Bacon's work in the mid-1940s. Given what has already been discussed such an interest may have been reinforced by Bacon's current friendship with Sutherland.

A very different, and more personal, dimension to Bacon's engagement with surrealism emerges from his relationship with Peter Rose Pulham, now a neglected figure who was also in contact with Watson and the *Horizon* circle.[213] Pulham had started off as a society and fashion photographer. His interest in surrealism, and Man Ray in particular, led him to give up commercial photography and to move to Paris, where he lived between about 1937 and summer 1940. In her recollections of the period, Pulham's then girlfriend described him as 'a passionate surrealist, as were most of his friends and the painters he admired'. Those she recalled meeting through Pulham add up to a litany of the leading surrealist and neo-romantic figures; Meret Oppenheim, Leonor Fini, Eugene Berman, Ernst, Dali, Balthus, Picasso, Giacometti, André Derain, Christian Bérard, as well as several surrealist writers.[214] With the onset of war, Pulham eventually had no choice but to return to England. He settled in Chelsea, and joined the Auxiliary Fire Service. By now he was mostly committed to painting and had his first one-man show at the Redfern Gallery in 1943, shortly after the Masson exhibition and in conjunction, in fact, with a display of Masson drawings.[215] His work subsequently became increasingly experimental, judging from a Bill Brandt photograph of Pulham in his studio.[216] It was around this time that Pulham and Bacon got to know one another. They were certainly close friends by the time David Sylvester got to know Bacon.[217] Bacon and Pulham both became fixtures of the bohemian pubs and clubs of Soho. Alcohol, which evidently contributed to Pulham's early death in 1956, was only one of their mutual interests. They shared an admiration for the more avant-garde types of cinema that had emanated from Russian and France.[218] No doubt surrealism and the Paris art scene before the war were regularly discussed. In relation to Bacon's later imagery, it is suggestive to note Pulham's recollections of seeing Artaud's adaptation of Shelley's *Cenci*, with décor by Balthus, and 'all the traditional symbols of horror. . . . Assassins, daggers, the shadows of a greedy Pope, guards with black featureless faces'.[219] After 1946, both men spent much of their time in France. Isabel Rawsthorne was a great mutual friend.[220] In 1950, Pulham had a further one-man show at the Hanover Gallery, where Sutherland and, more recently, Bacon had also exhibited.[221] Pulham's own work as a painter has lapsed into obscurity, but at a certain point he seems to have come very much under Bacon's sway, judging from a surviving picture from the period.[222]

Bacon, for his part, may conceivably have been affected by Pulham's highly distinctive approach to photography. In his book *British Photographers* of 1944, Cecil Beaton noted that Pulham's photographs 'appear to be developed in a particularly virulent poison, probably violet or viridian coloured; his prints have a mysterious, pernicious and enigmatic quality; but his extremely interesting work has received little encouragement, and . . . he has now switched to painting'.[223] In fact, Pulham continued, sporadically, to work with photography as a creative medium, alongside his painting. It was presumably in the later 1930s that he started to create highly unconventional and experimental prints. These could involve manipulating dark and light in certain areas of a print, during the development process. He also 'began staining prints with ink and dirtying them with rubbish'.[224] Effectively, as Mellor remarks, the prints became paintings, conjured into being by procedures akin to the automatist techniques used by surrealist painters. The photographic image was treated as a kind of ready-made, a starting point for a process of improvisation, analogous to Ernst's rubbings from a floor board or Masson's scatterings of glue and sand upon bare canvas. Such departures no doubt reflected the wider climate of photographic innovation that was current within the surrealist movement in Paris during the second half of the 1930s. For Pulham, a key motivation behind his technical experiments was 'to kill the slickness which modern materials seemed to force upon one'.[225] The same aesthetic was manifest in less extreme form in his negative comments on contemporary, especially, one surmises, German new objectivity photography: 'both the curiously precise detailed flatness of early photographs, and the vagueness of press photographs reproduced through a coarse screen on bad paper, seem to me more convincing, more realistic, than those which show every pore of your skin'.[226]

There are obvious affinities here not only with Bacon's fascination with newspaper imagery but also with his fundamental approach to painting, in which any semblance of decorative facility was suppressed in favour of the visceral impact of the image itself and the medium in which it was embedded. The phrase 'mysterious, pernicious and enigmatic', which Beaton applied to Pulham's prints, could hardly be bettered as an evocation of Bacon's paintings. Pulham's darkroom procedures find an echo, albeit at a much less sophisticated level of technique, in Bacon's own propensity for manipulating and working into photographic images. The recent excavation and cataloguing of the contents of Bacon's studio have revealed how, throughout his career, he would extract photographs from books and magazines, and sometimes cut into them, or construct montages, or superimpose painted or drawn marks. Such appropriations and transformations are clearly a kind of graphic equivalent to the process that he relied on in making his paintings, whereby he would start, it appears, by copying a photographic image onto the canvas, doubtless rather broadly, and then proceed to modify or even entirely to obliterate this initial point of departure through successive improvisations. Manipulating photographic imagery in these several ways can be seen as the form that 'drawing' took within Bacon's distinctive creative processes. There is evidence that Bacon embarked upon this way of working during the early part of the war, with the pictures loosely based on photographs of Nazi leaders such as *Man in a Cap* and *Man Standing*. It is not clear whether he had operated in this fashion previously, or whether his friendship with Pulham was a significant filter through which subversive, quintessentially surrealist approaches to the photographic image came to find a remote echo in Bacon's studio practices.

Recapitulating an earlier argument about Sutherland, it might be said of Bacon that an engagement with surrealism did not preclude the assimilation of other aspects of European art from between the wars. One such indication may be provided by Robert Melville's reference to Pavel Tchelitchev in his 1949 essay for *Horizon*, as mentioned earlier (pl. 23). Sylvester recalled that Bonnard and Soutine were the two modern artists 'for whose handling of paint Bacon constantly expressed enormous admiration' during the 1950s.[227] Such preferences may have become established somewhat earlier. Bonnard's work was widely exhibited in Paris and London after the war, and in the wake of the artist's death in January 1947. Aside from encouraging a looser touch and a more direct representation of the human figure, his pictures may have had some effect on Bacon's choices of imagery when his work was at most tender in mood. There is, for example, a certain affinity between the poignant *Head III* (1949), depicting a bespectacled figure looking back over his shoulder in the direction of the viewer, and some of Bonnard's later self-portraits. Equally, *Study from the Human Body* (1949; pl. XIX) may contain a distant echo of the naked figures seen from behind in Bonnard's pictures of bathroom interiors (pl. 98). The more extreme painterly methods of Chaim Soutine were clearly a decisive point of reference for Bacon's work from the mid 1950s onwards, but the abattoir imagery of *Painting* (1946) already provides an obvious point of comparison. To some degree, Bacon's concerns are foreshadowed by Picasso's still-life images of butchered animal parts from late 1939, themselves prompted, it has been suggested, by the example of Goyas such as *Pieces of Rib, Loin and a Head of Mutton*, on show in Paris during the 1930s, as well as by the atmosphere of foreboding at the start of the war.[228] Notwithstanding the precedents for Bacon's specific imagery of the suspended carcass in the work of Rembrandt and several romantic artists, there was a more recent model in the series of paintings on this theme by Soutine from the mid-1920s, one strand in an entire iconography of dead animals in the latter's output. Bacon's direct familiarity with such work probably can be assumed. For a couple of years before the war, Soutine's painting had been extensively exhibited in commercial galleries in London.[229] In 1943, one of the beef carcass pictures was shown in a mixed twentieth-century French painting show at the Lefevre gallery.[230] The owner was Eardley Knollys, proprietor of the Storran Gallery, where one of the Soutine shows had taken place in 1938 and where, the following year, Sutherland had exhibited his 'paraphrase' of El Greco's

Agony in the Garden. It was Knollys, a close friend, who evidently introduced Sutherland to the South of France after the war.[231] At some point, Bacon would almost certainly have met Knollys through Sutherland, and may therefore have had further opportunity to look at Soutine's work in the original. It would be interesting, in fact, to explore the wider importance that the art of Soutine may have held around this time for British 'neo-romantic' artists such as Craxton, Clough, and especially Lucian Freud, whose work likewise reveals an obsessive preoccupation with dead animals. Soutine's death in 1944 prompted a flood of publications and exhibitions. Indeed, the artist's soaring reputation amongst artists, in America as well as Europe, is very much a post-war phenomenon, during which period Soutine came to seem not so much an idiosyncratic and marginal artist, but rather the archetype of the alienated 'existentialist' artist. Raymond Cogniat's representative account in 1945 of Soutine's proclivity for destroying his pictures in despair would have struck a chord with Bacon, as would the evocation of his improvised creative procedures: 'he reinvents his technique at every second, each brushstroke is unforeseen and without repetition'. The tragic resonance of Soutine's work, constantly reiterated, could hardly have been more pertinent in the aftermath of the Second World War: 'Soutine makes us hesitate between the horror of decomposed flesh and the splendour of gems, for the world he offers us, the world he creates or dreams up, resembles just as much the gleaming of stones as a charnel-house in putrefaction . . . He is in our time an open and magnificent wound, the scream that no other has uttered'.[232]

98 Pierre Bonnard, *Nude in front of a Mirror*, oil on canvas, 154 × 104.5 cm, Galleria Internazionale d'Arte Moderna di Ca' Pesaro, Venice.

*

By comparison with- Sutherland, it appears that Bacon was more open to fresh stimuli, visual and intellectual, during the late 1940s, reflecting perhaps a distinction in age, as well as in temperament, between the two artists. Bacon's work, in the years after the war, was characterised by a restless experimentation, as far as one can gauge from the available evidence. His several remarks to Sutherland about the work he was doing during the second half of 1946 indicate that he was continuing to paint, and there is no reason to think that this was not the case at other times. The body of work included in the Hanover Gallery exhibition of late 1949 was preceded by a period of more than three years from which next to nothing survives, with the exception of one painting exhibited in 1948.[233] During this period, Bacon too was in France for extended periods of time. Much less is known about his movements – whether, for instance he travelled much between France and Britain, and whether he spent time anywhere other than Monte Carlo – and it is not known whether there were periods in which Bacon worked more or less intensively. He described to Sutherland how he found that the absence of culture in Monte Carlo could actually be conducive to creativity. Bacon's letters also reveal how much he relished visiting Paris, and keeping up with artistic events. He spent two or three weeks there in November 1946, and clearly took a keen interest in current art.

Another theme of Bacon's initial letters was the vast exhibition of contemporary art that was mounted in Paris in late 1946 under the aegis of UNESCO.[234] The British Council was responsible for organising the British section. Looking ahead to this event, Bacon revealed himself to be rather less fastidious and anxious than Sutherland about showing his work in such survey exhibitions: 'About what you say of the show in Paris, as I have sold the picture to the Redfern, they can do what they like with it and I do not really mind. I do hope you will decide to show. I know exactly what you say about these sort of exhibitions but what happens apart from trying to paint somewhere near to what one wants seems to matter less and less'.[235] However, Bacon's dismissive instincts were aroused by the actual spectacle:

> The Unesco show was awful. I have not seen a single notice but all that is just as meaningless here as in England. I think the English section was a little better than the others, mostly because it was the best room and because the Picassos were very bad and the Braque awful in the French section and when it comes down to the present stuff, Pignon, Esteve, Tal-Coat and all that it is a new low in clever ideas and bright colour. I know there is a lesson for us to take to heart in that, or at any rate for me.[236]

Even their own work seemed to contribute to the dispiriting effect: 'The thing I was very shocked by when I saw our things at Unesco, your three and mine, was the boring lack of reality, the lack of immediacy which we have so often talked about. I think it is also why so many Picassos are beginning to look so jaded now. It is the terrible decoration we are all contaminated by'. Bacon looked forward enthusiastically to one forthcoming exhibition: 'I hear Balthus is having a big show at Wildenstein at that time. I hear they are marvellous . . . They are so disturbing I hear'.[237] In the event, Bacon found himself deflated:

> I saw Balthus' things in Paris but they are no good. He is trying to get the tenderness which we would all love to get for a change, but it can't be done that way, it can only come as a technical thing and not as illustration or at least I feel that. I feel more and more that nothing matters or will happen until someone makes a new technical synthesis that can carry over from the sensation to our nervous system.[238]

Such terminology directly foreshadows the outlook that Bacon articulated in later statements and interviews. During the next couple of years, he may well have continued to visit Paris, either travelling up from the south or stopping off en route to or from England. If so, however, there is no evidence concerning what exhibitions he saw, in Paris, London or elsewhere, or indeed which artists he may have encountered, other than known friends such as Sutherland. Nor, unfortunately, is there any documentation of Bacon's reading at the time.

What evidence, then, can be extracted from the paintings themselves about Bacon's affinities with current art in Europe? Two of the most striking characteristics of the pictures in his one-man show in 1949 were a preoccupation with the image of the single human figure, presented with relative naturalism in several works, and a distinctive technique in which an emphatically textural build-up of marks was combined with a predominantly grisaille palette. Bacon's impastoed surfaces and tonal emphasis may be associated in general terms with Balthus's post-war work, in which he was clearly interested. Later, Bacon remarked that he admired 'some aspects' of Balthus's work, and indicated that his favourite picture was the pre-war composition *La Rue*.[239] A figure like Balthus doubtless intrigued Bacon because he epitomised a continuing commitment to the human image at a time when this approach was generally unfashionable. As much as anything, it is the emphasis on the material, textural presence of paint as a principal bearer of the meanings and emotional resonances of the image that differentiates Bacon in the late 1940s from the more linear and illustrative art of Sutherland. In this context, the concurrent emergence in France of a highly textural, painterly idiom may be noted, with Jean Fautrier the decisive innovator. Fautrier's *Otages* (*Hostages*), crudely applied, impastoed slabs of thick paste overlaid with rough marks and layers of colour, were exhibited in Paris in autumn 1945.[240] Like Bacon's more conventionally drawn images, shown a few months earlier in London, they evoked an imagery of dismembered, tortured bodies and disfigured, sometimes skull-like heads, rooted in Fautrier's direct experiences and knowledge of German atrocities in occupied France. The reception of the *Otages* evokes a sensibility reminiscent of contemporary Britain. In his preface to the catalogue, André Malraux talked about 'the first attempt to dissect contemporary pain, down to its tragic ideograms'.[241] Francis Ponge discerned in the paintings an echo of images of Crucifixion: 'But in these 'religious paintings' the 'shot person replaces the crucified. An anonymous man replaces the Christ of paintings'.[242] Such critics also brought out a recurrent ambiguity in Fautrier's work that we have, once again, encountered in Bacon – what Yve-Alain Bois refers to as the 'pairing of rapture and horror'.[243] Suggestions of violence and the visceral presence of raw matter, implicit in the rough slabs of paste, coexist with beauty and an almost vulgar sensuality in the superimposed layers of colour. More generally, the unfolding of an '*informe*' aesthetic in French art of the second half of the 1940s and into the 1950s, in the wake of Fautrier's *Otages*, provides a valuable context for considering Bacon's pursuit of 'a new technical synthesis'.

Equally open to existential and tragic readings, the work produced by Alberto Giacometti in the late 1940s provides a further point of reference for Bacon. Giacometti had initially turned his back on surrealism, and embarked upon more descriptive figurative work, in the

99 Alberto Giacometti, *Head on a Rod*, 1947, plaster, painted reddish in spots, 50 × 12.5 × 17 cm, Alberto Giacometti-Stiftung, Zürich, on permanent loan to the Kunstmuseum, Basel.

second half of the 1930s. But it was only after the Second World War that he acquired the confidence to extend this approach into large-scale modelled sculptures, which he began to exhibit alongside their parallel manifestation in painting. The resulting body of work has been closely aligned with Bacon by several commentators, notably their mutual friend and critical supporter David Sylvester.[244] The most obvious links are thematic. The moving figure occurs both in Bacon's *Study from the Human Body* (1949) and in Giacometti's *Walking Man* (1947) and other sculptures. Both artists were strongly attracted to the motif of the upturned, screaming head, with its powerful expressive charge and its connotations of a death mask. Giacometti's *Head on a Rod* of 1947 (pl. 99), in crudely painted plaster, has been interpreted in conjunction with a passage from the artist's 1946 essay 'The Dream, the Sphinx and the Death of T': 'I began to see heads in empty space, in the space that surrounds them . . . It was no longer a living head but an object that I saw like any other object, no, not like any other object, like something simultaneously alive and dead.'[245] Such thinking could apply equally well to images by Bacon such as the *Heads* series. These paintings may be read on one level as representations of a metaphorical disintegration of the solitary inner self, the human social façade giving way to a raw, animalistic sense of existential pain. But Bacon's images, too, suggest the decomposition before our eyes of flesh and blood, revealing the underlying bone. In Bacon's paintings, psychological isolation is further suggested by spatial devices, such as curtains that create shallow enclosed settings (as in *Head II* and *Head III* and *Study from the Human Body*), and skeletal frames or cages that appear to imprison the figures (in *Head I* and *Head VI* and *Study for Portrait*). Such framing of figures finds another echo in Giacometti's sculpture. Adapted from his earlier surrealist works such as *Suspended Ball* (1930), the format featured in several of the post-war figure pieces, for instance *The Nose* of 1947 and *The Cage (Woman and Head)* and *Imprisoned Statuette* from 1950. For both artists, the frame served to focus and concentrate the image around the figure, but also to establish connotations of confinement and claustrophobia, and to imply a distance between image and viewer. A comparable notion of 'the visceral life that rumbles on beneath the rigid framework of every rational structure' is articulated in an essay of 1947 on Masson by Giacometti's old friend Michel Leiris.[246] The work of Bacon and Giacometti further converges on an assertion of the making process in their finished works, so that the improvised working of clay or paint results in a palpable sense of the medium. The paintings of the two artists share a monochromatic palette, with contrasting extremes of light and shadow, and a fluid application, at any rate in some of Giacometti's works, that suggests the activity of smearing and a sensation of solid form dissolving into the surrounding space. Yet Giacometti's more characteristic building up of the surface with graphic linear marks is quite different from Bacon's more textural painterly methods. Equally distinct is the open spatial quality of the bulk of Giacometti's pictures from the late 1940s. It is interesting that Bacon always said that he much preferred Giacometti's drawings to his sculpture.[247] One drawing in which Giacometti took soundings from the Velásquez's *Innocent X* exemplifies not just a specific shared admiration, but also a common interest in the resources of artistic tradition.[248]

Are such affinities anything more than coincidental? The two artists had no direct contact at this stage, though when they met in the mid-1950s, or even later, they became great friends. Bacon could, however, have got to know about Giacometti's post-war work in various ways. An illustrated article appeared in 1946 in *Cahiers d'Art*.[249] Miniscule works were evidently exhibited in commercial galleries in Paris in 1946 and again in June 1947.[250] Bacon doubtless also encountered the famous catalogue of Giacometti's one-man show in 1948 at the Pierre Matisse gallery in New York, which featured reproductions of the more recent large-scale pieces as well as an extended meditation on Giacometti's work by Sartre. Since this modest publication evidently came to assume a talismanic status amongst avant-garde British artists, we can at lease speculate that it was known to Bacon.[251] A more direct link to Giacometti was provided by the circle of friends in which Bacon was beginning to move in London. An acquaintance between Peter Watson and Giacometti went back to the period before the war, and was resumed in September 1945 judging from Watson's account to Cyril Connolly of his time in Switzerland:

> I went and saw Giacometti at Maloja. His war work consists of 4 almost identical statues 3″ high 1/8″ wide [marginal sketch]. However I have asked for photographs. They must surely be key works in his production. His mother thinks he has gone mad and wishes he would make lamps and consoles for Nelson Rockefeller, just as he used to do.[252]

It is recorded that Watson, Freud and Giacometti met together in the Café Flore in the summer of 1946.[253] Watson's contacts are further attested by a Giacometti portrait drawing dated 1947, subsequently owned by Roland Penrose.[254] Watson also commissioned Giacometti and his brother Diego to make a chandelier, sadly lost, for the new *Horizon* offices in Bedford Square.[255] His admiration lay behind the appearance of Michel Leiris's evocative illustrated article on Giacometti in the June 1949 issue of *Horizon* (pl. 100).[256] For Leiris, Giacometti aspired 'to set up votive stones, to materialise experiences, to give a lasting consistency to whatever is fugitive or impossible, to fix realities by borrowing, if necessary', from naturalism only what is necessary to carry conviction.'[257] A passage on the creative process generating the works might equally have had a resonance for Bacon:

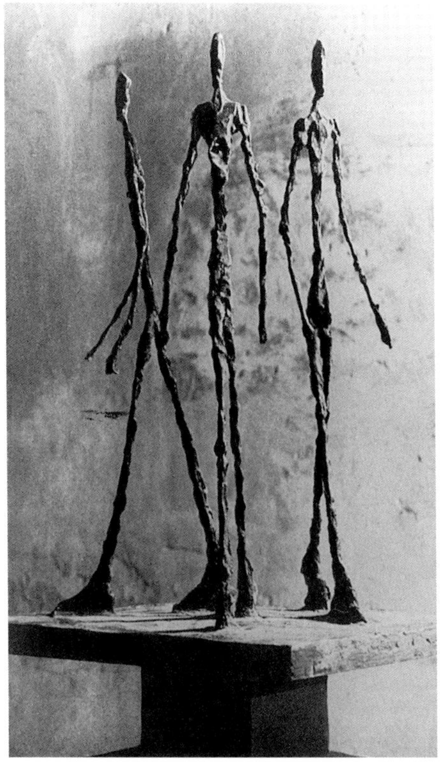

100 Alberto Giacometti, *Three Men Walking*, 1948/9 (as illustrated in *Horizon* (London), no. 114, June 1949).

> Accent on speed, without which creation could not happen. Instead of the patently elaborated work of art we now have something which rises up suddenly and which is all the more evident for looking as though it had suddenly arrived, without either roots or history: instantaneous and outside time. Given this view it is better to destroy completely than to try and correct. Watching the sort of mass sacrifices in which Giacometti indulges I have sometimes wondered whether sculpture is not for him simply a way of making something that can at once be destroyed.[258]

That same year, a pair of Giacometti paintings (*Interior* and *Seated Man*), as well as an important sculpture *(Man Pointing)*, were acquired by the Tate Gallery.[259] Such purchasing indicates a strong level of interest and appreciation, given the general feebleness of the Tate's modern collection at this stage. Evidently Sutherland, a newly appointed trustee, was a 'particularly fervent advocate' of acquiring the Giacomettis.[260] Since Bacon and Sutherland were great friends at this time, it seems likely that they would have discussed Giacometti. By this time, Bacon was also in contact with figures such as Sylvester and Edouardo Paolozzi, who had both spent the last couple of years in Paris and had befriended Giacometti. From 1950 onwards, actual works by Giacometti became available for study at first hand in London, for example in the Hanover Gallery, Sutherland and Bacon's dealer, where a *Portrait* was included in a mixed show which also featured Bacon's *Head*, along with two works by Sutherland and Freud.[261]

The engagement on the part of Sutherland and Bacon with the portrait format may also reflect an awareness of the general re-emergence of the genre in the art of the late 1940s amongst artists based in both London and Paris, a phenomenon that has gone largely unremarked.[262] From a French perspective, special significance may be attached to the exhibition of recent work by Picasso, including a group of portraits, at the 1944 *Salon d'Automne*. In his review, Georges Limbour noted that 'Artists are giving up portraiture, which has become an unpopular genre . . . Picasso, however, has restored its expressive importance and at the same time given it a new meaning.'[263] Further research is needed to gauge the impact of Picasso on a wider revaluation and reinvention of the genre that encompassed Giacometti and Masson, the two former surrealist artists who were most generally admired after the war.

Portrait imagery was a significant strand in Giacometti's postwar work, notably in his paintings and drawings. Aside from the familiar images of his brother Diego and his wife Annette, Giacometti produced many drawings of literary figures from the Left Bank circles in which he moved, some of which were printed as book illustrations.[264] Bacon stated that he had 'always loved Giacometti's portraits, particularly those done in pencil or charcoal'.[265] Given Sutherland's support as a trustee for buying works for the Tate, and the apparent interest of friends such as Bacon and Watson, one might speculate whether Sutherland too might, on one level, have been inspired by the example of Giacometti to take up portraiture with the making of *Somerset Maugham* in 1949 (pl. xvii). For all the obvious differences, there are actually quite striking parallels between the Sutherland, and, in particular, Giacometti's 1948 *Diego Seated* (pl. 101), an earlier version of the portrait of Diego acquired by the Tate. It is worth noting the two sitter's poses, the folded arms, the red neck scarves, even the narrow, somewhat claustrophobic vertical format which is affected in the Giacometti by the inclusion of an internal painted frame. Sutherland could have encountered *Diego Seated*, since Giacometti released it from the studio into the hands of the Pierre Loeb Gallery, and the picture was acquired in 1949 by the English collectors Robert and Lisa Sainsbury.[266] Even if these specific affinities are fortuitous, an awareness of this type of work by an admired French contemporary may have been a factor in precipitating the relatively abrupt shift in Sutherland's direction that the *Somerset Maugham* portrait represents. Portraiture also became a significant strand in Masson's work of the late 1940s. Limbour's review of Masson's 1946 show in Paris, translated for *André Masson and His Universe*, noted that: 'An unusual number of portraits gives the impression that Masson is today? pursuing man's image in a less symbolic, less mythical way than before . . . today, influenced perhaps by the ordeals experienced by humanity, he goes directly to man, without passing through legend or philosophy'.[267] Likewise, Michel Leiris' 'Portraits', accompanied by several illustrations, explored 'a form of art which has a most particular appeal' for Masson: 'Whether analogical, imaginary or based on experience . . . all these portraits are evidence of the artist's will to conjure up on canvas the palpable presence of some human being, pervaded to the utmost with a destiny which is particularly his.'[268]

As a means to understand Bacon's motivations, it is worth considering why portraiture came to the fore at this particular moment. The reassertion of the value, but also the pathos and fragility, inhering within the individual, can be interpreted as a reaction to the extreme dehumanisation associated with the war, and above all with post-war revelations about the Holocaust, which Limbour understatedly referred to, in connection with Masson's portraits, as the 'ordeals experienced by humanity'. Against this backdrop, it could be noted that innovative portraiture also dominated two of the most remarkable one-man shows in Paris in 1947. Dubuffet's caricatural, brutalist images of many of the new artists and writers dominated his show at the Galerie René Drouin that October. Three months earlier, Antonin Artaud's recent, intense portrait drawings had been exhibited at the Galerie Pierre, a year or so after the artist's release from psychiatric hospital.[269] The disembodied heads and visceral

101 Alberto Giacometti *Diego Seated*, 1948, oil on canvas, 80.6 × 50.2 cm, Robert and Lisa Sainsbury Collection, University of East Anglia, Norwich.

use of the medium in these drawings possess a certain affinity with, for instance, Bacon's *Head III*. In 'The Human Face', an essay he wrote for the catalogue, Artaud asserted the possibility of a reanimated portraiture, in terms that Bacon might well have found compelling:

> The human face bears in fact a kind of perpetual death on its face from which it's up to the painter precisely to save it
>
> In giving its own features back to it.
>
> For the thousands and thousands of years in fact that the human face has been speaking and breathing
>
> One somehow has the impression that it has not yet started to say what it is and what it knows.
>
> And I don't know of any painter in the history of art from Holbein to Ingres who succeeded in making this face of man speak . . .
>
> Only Van Gogh was able to draw out of a human head a portrait which was the explosive rocket of the beating of a buried heart.
>
> His own.[270]

Once again, Bacon probably knew at least something of Artaud given the keen interest in his work shown by Peter Watson. A proposal to publish one of Artaud's poems in *Horizon*, with an introduction, resulted in the revelatory text 'Letter to Peter Watson', dated 27 July 1946.[271] For some reason this did not appear, but Artaud's 'Van Gogh: The Suicide provoked by Society' featured in the June 1948 issue.[272] This essay on the position of extreme alienation forced upon the artist by modern society is also likely to have struck a chord with Bacon, who shared a profound interest in Van Gogh's paintings and letters.

The notion that art, perhaps portraiture in particular, could encapsulate fundamentally tragic aspects of the human condition raises the complex problem of the significance for Bacon of the intellectual and cultural climate associated with existentialism.[273] Crudely speaking, the term registered a preoccupation with the fundamental nature of human subjectivity and experience that had underpinned a rich, not to say arcane, philosophical tradition stemming from Kierkegaard and Nietzsche in the nineteenth century, through to subsequent German thinkers such as Husserl, Jaspers and Heidegger. In the 1940s, and to an extent in the late 1930s, these philosophical concerns were elaborated by French thinkers such as Jean-Paul Sartre and Maurice Merleau-Ponty. However, after the war the idea of existentialism also migrated, so to speak, to a more popular level of culture. A somewhat metaphysical and theoretical notion of anguish, in response to the open-endedness of human freedom, struck a chord in the context of the mood of acute pessimism and despair that flowed, understandably enough, from the war years into the succeeding period. The realities of the present gave extraordinary vividness and resonance to a philosophy that confronted 'Being and Nothingness', in the title of Sartre's famous 1943 tract – what kind of authentic existence was possible in the face of the collapse of human values and the all too evident reality of death? This was the very broad issue that 'existentialism' seemed to crystallise. In a 1946 lecture, Sartre noted that the term 'is now so loosely applied to so many things that it no longer means anything at all'.[274] Likewise an admission that 'in fact there are as many existentialisms as there are existentialist philosophers' featured in Paul Foulquié's philosophical study of the new movement, which appeared in France in 1947 and again in the following year in an English translation by the poet and critic Kathleen Raine.[275]

Bacon was responsive not so much to codified theoretical programmes as to a range of texts, images and ideas, emanating from post-war Paris, that seemed to echo his own imaginative predispositions. The contemporary French literature that seems to provide revealing commentary on Bacon's art embraces both figures who had been associated with surrealism in its heyday, such as Artaud, Bataille and Eluard, and also writers such as Sartre who were more obviously identified with post-war existentialism. Timothy Hyman has drawn a striking and suggestive analogy between many aspects of Bacon's pictures exhibited at the Hanover Gallery in late 1949 and the imagery of a poem by Paul Eluard, 'Song of the Last Delay', which had appeared in translation in an English literary magazine earlier that same year.[276] Georges Bataille was another figure with a complex relationship to surrealism, who remained a singular and influential figure on the post-war Parisian scene. In 1985, during Bacon's lifetime, Dawn Ades pointed to his affinities with the alternative or dissident Surrealism promoted by

Bataille and the magazine *Documents* (1929/30), copies of which, she noted, Bacon possessed.[277] Revealing points of comparison include the Boiffard photograph of an open screaming mouth, accompanying Bataille's 'critical dictionary' entry on the mouth: 'On great occasions human life is concentrated bestially in the mouth, anger makes one clench one's teeth, terror and atrocious suffering make the mouth the organ of tearing cries'. It seems a short step from such manifestations of Bataille's anti-idealist conflation of man and beast to Bacon's *Three Studies* triptych, *Figure Study II* and the late 1940s *Head* paintings. In addition, *Painting* (1946), with its fusion of Crucifixion and butcher's shop imagery, is vividly foreshadowed by the photographs of the slaughterhouse at La Villette by Eli Lotar, and Bataille's entry on the abattoir, asserting the association of slaughter and sacrifice: 'The slaughter house rises out of religion in the sense that the temple of distant epochs served a dual function, being used at the same time for supplication and killings. From this resulted a disturbing coincidence between mythological mysteries and the lugubrious grandeur of places where blood flows.'[278]

Yet there may be more to be said about the affinity. Ades' argument presents a limited view of Bataille as a figure of the inter-war period, and as a dissident surrealist. Yet, by the time of Bacon's pictures, Bataille himself was in transit 'from a renegade surrealism to an alliance with a more Existentialist ethos', and he has been aligned, for example, with Fautrier.[279] In Foulquié's 1947 survey, Bataille features as an existentalist alongside such figures as Sartre, Simone de Beauvoir and Gabriel Marcel.[280] It is known that Bacon for his part followed Bataille's post-war writings from the remark by their mutual friend Sonia Orwell, after the writer's death in 1962, that she and Bacon were the only people in England who admired his books.[281] The connection between Bataille's and Bacon's circles can be traced back, as ever, to the late 1940s and *Horizon*. A letter to Orwell from Spring 1948 indicates that Bataille was planning to publish a text on the Marquis de Sade in the magazine, and also that he was expecting to come to London the following month.[282] Aside from Orwell, other mutual friends again included Isabel Rawsthorne, whom Bacon evidently referred to as Bataille's girlfriend,[283] and of course Michel Leiris, Bataille's close collaborator since 1924 who later came to know Bacon well, and produced essays on his work that Bacon regarded as an especially authoritative distillation of his concerns. Bataille too came to regard Bacon as one of the most important painters of his generation.[284]

Although it is impossible to determine what Bacon read, and when, nonetheless numerous parallels can be identified with Bataille that invite detailed investigation.[285] For present purposes, the indication of some broad areas of compatibility will suffice.[286] Bataille remained very close to Masson, arguably the surrealist artist to whom Bacon felt the closest affinity. The two men shared obsessive interests in, for instance, gambling, the suggestive power of photographs, and the interplay between the violent and the erotic. Both were militant atheists, with a strong inclination towards the blasphemous and a perverse, subversive use of religious imagery. They each took their bearings from the iconoclastic and atheistic outlook of Nietzsche. Bataille's wartime book *On Nietzsche* (1944) uses the philosopher Nietzsche's own writings as the springboard for expounding a world-view appropriate to times of violence and tragedy, and in the wake of the death of God. In the same year in which Bacon completed his *Three Studies for Figures at the Base of a Crucifixion*, Bataille quoted Nietzsche to the effect that 'The Crucified Christ is the most sublime of symbols – even at present.'[287] Again following the lead of Nietzsche, the two men had a strong feeling for Greek tragedy. They had in common a profoundly transgressive and anti-idealist sensibility – it was images such as slaughtered carcasses, excrement and base animal existence that provided the most suitable metaphors for describing the human condition. Moreover, Bacon's entire ethos of 'exhilarated despair' could apply equally well to Bataille. Something of the writer's sensibility comes across from a passage in a wartime text, on the theme of 'The Torment' arising from consciousness of the absurdity of existence. Bataille's recollections of an experience that occured fifteen years earlier, walking late at night through the streets of Paris, have strongly Baconian resonances:

> I was extremely young then, chaotic and full of empty intoxications: a round of unseemly vertiginous ideas, but ideas already full of anxieties, rigorous and crucifying, ran though my mind . . . What is certain is that this freedom, at the same time as the 'impossible' which I had run up against, burst in my head. A space constellated with laughter opened its dark abyss before me . . . I laughed divinely: the umbrella, having descended upon my head, covered me (I expressly covered myself with this black shroud). I laughed as perhaps one had never laughed; the extreme depth of each thing opened itself up – laid bare, as if I were dead.[288]

For all the obvious differences, it is difficult to think of a more precise equivalent to the anguished interiority distilled in a picture such as Bacon's *Figure Study II*, or other figures from around 1946 with wide-open mouths, shrouded within their black umbrellas.

Bataille was a rather specialised taste. Sartre, on the other hand, and the general style of thought with which he was closely identified, became astonishingly influential after the war, a phenomenon that emerged almost as quickly in London as in Paris. In the circles surrounding *Horizon*, as in Sartre's own polemical writings, surrealism was now seen to have had its day. In his survey of the Parisian literary world for the 'News out of France' issue of May 1945, Connolly insisted that Sartre 'occupies a dominant position in the world of French literature today. He is to its prose what Eluard is to its poetry . . . Taken as a philosopher, a novelist, a dramatist and a critic, his bulk is enormous, and tends to obscure perhaps the equally gifted Camus.'[289] Although Connolly had not met Sartre, who was in America during his trip to Paris, it was something of a coup to be able to include a translation of Sartre's 'The Case for Responsible Literature', a manifesto for 'committed' writing that would only appear a few months later in its author's own magazine *Les Temps Modernes*.[290] John Russell's account in the same issue of the *Existential Theatre* provided a wide-ranging and enthusiastic assessment of Sartre's work, and to a lesser extent of Camus.'[291] Subsequent issues of *Horizon* included the philosopher A. J. Ayer's extended, albeit sceptical essays about Sartre and Camus, and Sonia Orwell's review of *The Roads to Freedom* and the fictional work of de Beauvoir.[292]

In his valedictory editorial of 1949, Connolly conceded that after the war 'we became a display window for Sartre and Camus'.[293] By now, Sartre's major writings were available in English translation, including philosophical writings such as *Sketch for a Theory of the Emotions*, *The Psychology of Imagination*, and the brief and accessible *Existentialism and Humanism* (1948), not to mention the plays (*The Flies* and *In Camera*), short stories (*Intimacy*) and novels (the first two parts of *Roads to Freedom* trilogy).[294] It would be difficult to exaggerate the guru status that Sartre acquired during these years, on both sides of the Channel and the Atlantic.

The fact that Bacon's art struck many observers, from the time of his one-man show onwards, as a visual counterpart to the existentialist view of the world was clearly crucial in establishing his reputation in artistic and intellectual circles. Numerous subsequent readings were foreshadowed in Neville Wallis's description of the Hanover Gallery exhibition as 'the most profoundly disquieting manifestation I have yet seen of that malaise which, since the last war, has inspired the philosophy of Sartre and the drama of frustration of Tennessee Williams'.[295] Bacon and Sartre had only the most fleeting personal connection. Bacon used to tell the story of meeting Sartre, in the company of Simone de Beauvoir, Sonia Orwell and Lucian Freud, at the Gargoyle Club in London, and that Sartre was 'very charming' and told him to make contact when he was in Paris, which he never did.[296] The encounter probably occurred in 1951.[297] The presence of Bacon's friend Sonia Orwell is telling. For very few people in Britain were more immersed than Orwell in contemporary French literature and ideas, as we glean for example from her reviews in *Horizon*. She had the advantage of being able to read such material more fluently than Bacon, who readily acknowledged that his own French was 'patchy and inadequate'.[298] Orwell was a regular visitor to Paris and, through Peter Watson initially, came to know many of the leading Left Bank intellectuals and writers, such as Leiris, Jacques Lacan, and Georges Bataille. By 1947, in fact, she had become involved in a relationship with the philosopher Maurice Merleau-Ponty.[299] Through conversations with Sonia Orwell, then, not to mention Peter Watson himself, Bacon would have been well placed to acquire a grasp of existentialist thinking. The ideas were generally in the air, but they were also being closely and enthusiastically followed in the circles in which he moved in post-war London.

As with Bataille it is possible to discern several specific affinities between Bacon and Sartre. The latter, for example, shared Bacon's enthusiasm for the art of Grünewald.[300] The Aeschylus Oresteia tragedies were the explicit point of departure for Sartre's tragic drama *Les Mouches* (The Flies), which was first performed in Paris in 1943, the year before Bacon produced his own variant on the Eumenides in his *Three Studies* triptych. In Sartre's play, the Eumenides are the 'bloated flies' of the title; Russell's essay for *Horizon* evoked the vigorous treatment of their 'ritual dances and bestial hymns', and described the culminating moment at which Orestes takes upon himself his crimes of those of his people, and departs from the sanctuary accompanied by 'the screaming company of the Furies'.[301] It can only be speculated whether an awareness of Sartre's drama informed Bacon's sense that a grouping together of three of his figure studies might, on one level, read as images of the Eumenides. It can be inferred, however, that a strong interest took hold of Bacon at some point from Isabel Rawsthorne's comment in early 1951: 'Francis abandoned the idea of doing a décor for 'Les Mouches' in English translation which is a pity as that would have been interesting'.[302]

It would have soon become apparent that Sartre was a close friend of Giacometti's and the most influential spokesman for the sculptor's post-war work, which has often tended to be perceived as an expression of 'the drama of the human condition and those feelings of anxiety, vulnerability and alienation expressed in the writings of Jean-Paul Sartre'.[303] Sartre also wrote about Masson, and the two men collaborated in 1946 on the sets for a Sartre play. Moreover, a broad affinity between Bacon and existentialism can readily be identified in the outlook on art and life articulated in the interviews with Sylvester. Germane passages include Bacon's declaration: 'I think of life as meaningless; but we give it meaning during our own existence. We create certain attitudes which give it a meaning while we exist, though they in themselves are meaningless, really.'[304] Elsewhere he talked about 'the will to make oneself absolutely free. Will is the wrong word, because in the end you could call it despair. Because it comes out of an absolute feeling that it's impossible to do these things, so I might as well just do anything. And out of anything one sees what happens'.[305] Such attitudes distil the Sartrean conviction that received structures of belief were inauthentic and bankrupt, leaving the individual with the necessity, and therefore the responsibility, of reinventing a set of values, whether moral, ideological or aesthetic.

Can we go beyond generic affinities of outlook to extract a specifically Sartrean or existentialist dimension from Bacon's imagery of the human figure in his paintings? The possibility was implicit in a well-known passage in the 1964 monograph on Bacon by the same John Russell who had provided the enthusiastic account of recent plays by Sartre and others for *Horizon*. Russell remarked of the late 1940s *Head* pictures:

> Looking at them, we realise that although European painting includes a great many portraits of individuals in rooms, they are never about what it feels like to be alone in a room: the painter always makes two . . . The garbage of the psyche has been put out at the back door; all buttons are done up . . . What painting had never shown before is the disintegration of the social being which takes place when one is alone in a room which has no looking glass. We may feel at such times that the accepted hierarchy of our features is collapsing, and that we are by turns all teeth, all eye, all ear, all nose.[306]

There are also suggestive parallels to Bacon's pictorial conception in one of the key texts that served to foster an existentialist sensibility, namely Sartre's philosophical novel *La Nausée* (*Nausea*). This had been published in France in 1938, but due to the war it only appeared in English translation in early 1949, initially bearing the title *The Diary of Antoine Roquentin*.[307] In a passage quite early on in Sartre's novel, the narrator undergoes an experience of nausea, the term he uses to describe the alarming sensation of things breaking loose from their comforting names and categories, and assuming instead a viscous presence as raw, oppressive matter. Roquentin is sitting at his desk, overwhelmed by the meaninglessness of his work as a historian, when he catches sight of his own features:

102 Francis Bacon *Head II*, 1949, oil on canvas, 80.5 × 65 cm, Ulster Museum Collection, Belfast.

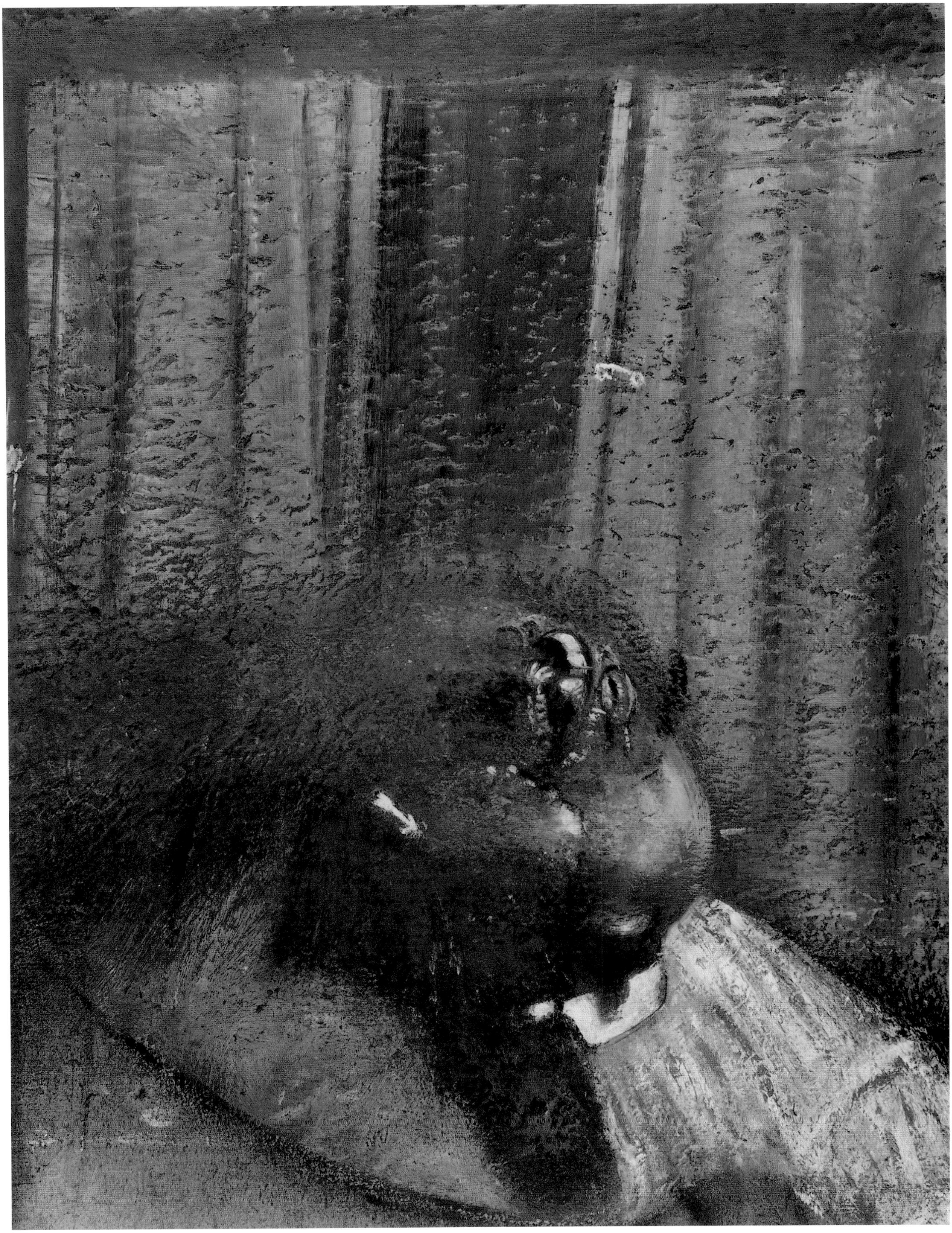

> It is a trap. I know I am going to let myself be caught in it. I have. The grey thing appears in the mirror. I go over and look at it, I can no longer get away . . . My glance slowly and wearily travels over my forehead, my cheeks. It finds nothing firm . . . When I was little, my Aunt Bigeois told me 'If you look at yourself too long in the mirror, you'll see a monkey.' I must have looked at myself even longer than that: what I see is well below the monkey, on the fringe of the vegetable world, at the level of jellyfish . . . I see a slight tremor, I see the insipid flesh blossoming and palpitating with abandon. The eyes especially are horrible seen so close. They are glassy, soft, blind, red-rimmed, they look like fish scales . . . I would like to take hold of myself: an acute, vivid sensation would deliver me. I plaster my left hand against my cheek, I pull the skin; I grimace at myself. An entire half of my face yields, the left half of the mouth twists and swells, uncovering a tooth, the eye opens on a white globe, on pink, bleeding flesh. That is not what I was looking for: nothing strong, nothing new; soft, flaccid, stale![308]

There is an uncanny affinity between this account and the sense of physical and psychic dissolution conveyed by *Head II* (pl. 102). Both text and image seem very like the inversion of portraiture evoked by Russell, where we confront not the social façade but rather 'the disintegration of the social being which takes place when one is alone in a room'. Interestingly, the portrait format was in fact a major concern of Sartre's writings on the eve of the Second World War. *The Psychology of Imagination*, another pre-war text translated in 1949, contains extensive philosophical discussions of portraiture, and how artistic and mental images differ from one another.[309] In the work of both Sartre and Bacon, formulaic 'official' portraiture to a heightened sense of the private self. Sartre contributed an essay on this very topic to an issue of the magazine *Verve* in 1939.[310] The official or court portraitist is chastised for being a servile flatterer, a creator of icons that serve the cause of oppression and utterly negate human actualities. Such attitudes correspond to another passage in *Nausea*, where Roquentin describes at length his experience of visiting Bouville museum. The serried ranks of local worthies, meticulously described in all their finery, and with all their attributes of status, induce a growing mood of alienation and self-denigration. In the eyes of a merchant, he reads a 'calm, implacable judgement' which

> pierced me like a sword and called in question my very right to exist. And it was true, I had already realised that: I hadn't any right to exist. I had appeared by chance, I existed like a stone, a plant, a microbe. My life grew in a haphazard way and in all directions.[311]

Subsequently, he begins to see through the idealising conventions, especially when he becomes locked into an encounter with Jean Parrotin:

> I knew, as a result of contemplating for a long time a certain portrait of Philip II in the library of the Escurial, that, when you look straight at a face ablaze with a sense of privilege, this fire dies out after a moment, and only an ashy residue remain: it was this residue which interested me.

> Parrotin put up a good fight. But all of a sudden, the light in his eyes went out, the picture grew dim.
>
> What was left? Blind eyes, a mouth as thin as a dead snake, and cheeks. The pale round cheeks of a child: they spread out over the canvas . . . How long had it taken his wife to notice them? . . . One day, I imagine, as her husband was sleeping beside her . . . she had ventured to look him in the face: all this flesh had appeared to her without any defence, bloated, slavering, vaguely obscene.[312]

Without wishing to push the comparison too far, since there is clearly more of an ideological dimension in Sartre, it seems to me that Bacon's *Head VI* (pl. XVIII) communicates a similar dismantling of a pictorial embodiment of power and privilege. It is as though the *Innocent X* we know, and are duly overawed by, has dissolved before our eyes – the picture has grown dim, and the light in his eyes has assuredly gone out, veiled by streaks of dry black paint, dragged across the coarse canvas, which constitute an exact visual equivalent to Sartre's 'ashy residue'. From close to, the paint actually looks like a deposit of soot. We are vouchsafed a glimpse of the horror beneath the façade, comparable to Mme Parrotin's moment of revelation in Roquentin's fantasy standing before her husband's portrait.

Both in *Head VI* and in *Study for a Portrait* the white paint, summarily modelling the face and hands and defining the space frame, evokes rather different associations when one stands close up to the painting. Were we to fantasise less a brush wielded by human hand than a snail leaving its deposit on the surface, we would be fully in tune with Bacon's thought processes. In November 1950, William Townsend recorded the following observations in his diary, following a lunch with Bacon and William Coldstream: 'Francis gave us some wonderful illustrations of the things that interest him, "a trap set out and a smear across it, a kind of slime, showing that a human being had passed through" '.[313] Five years later, Bacon used similar terminology in the text for an exhibition catalogue: 'I would like my pictures to look as if a human being had passed through them, like a snail, leaving a trail of the human presence and memory trace of past events, as the snail leaves its slime'.[314] The terminology is very distinctive. It is interesting, then, to note the long section in Sartre's *Being and Nothingness* that is centred on the image of the 'slimy', from *le visqueux*.[315] Commentators frequently noted the particular vividness of the section towards the end of *Being and Nothingness*, where Sartre broaches the psychological associations of sliminess, which are clearly related to the sense of nausea explored in his earlier novel.[316] The slimy is 'essentially ambiguous because its fluidity exists in slow motion; there is a sticky thickness in its liquidity'. Slime is 'the agony of water. It presents itself as a phenomenon in process of becoming'. Sartre talks about 'the snare of the slimy: it is fluidity which holds me and which compromises me; I cannot *slide* on this slime, all its suction cups hold me back; it can not slide over me, it clings to me like a leech.'[317] It is a 'trap', a 'horrible image' because a 'consciousness which became slimy would be transformed by the thick stickiness of its ideas'.[318] At the same time, from childhood onwards, the slimy has more positive connotations: it 'transcends all distinctions between psychic and physical, between the brute existent and the meanings of the world; it is a possible meaning of being'.[319] Whether or not Bacon knew this passage, in his paintings as well as his verbal commentary he manifested a sensibility for the slimy that corresponds vividly to Sartre's description.

The remarks that Townsend attributed to Bacon offer a revealing commentary on *Study from the Human Body*, which was exhibited as *Study for Figure* in late 1949 (pl. XIX).[320] The picture embodies his solution to the problem of how feeling might be not so much illustrated as embodied within a 'new technical synthesis'. Both figure and curtains are merely suggested by brushmarks that register as traces of the painter's own creative activity. The viewer is drawn into empathising imaginatively with the physical process of dragging a loaded brush across the rough texture of canvas. The action of 'smearing' very much comes to mind. The marks themselves evoke the texture of an elephant or hippopotamus hide, or indeed 'slime', the glistening trail left by a snail. The consistency of Bacon's technique means that the human body and the curtains seem to be relatively homogeneous in material terms, rather than differentiated from one another. It is as though man and his physical environment partake of a common, or universal, substance, which is somewhat viscous or slimy. This effect is reinforced by the consistent presence of the colour grey, and by Bacon's withholding of definition in the painting of the body, so that the left arm fades into the surrounding curtain. To the left of the figure's left leg, a dragged mark ambiguously suggests the contour of the body and a fold of curtain. Likewise, the spinal column is absorbed into the vertical rhythm of the folds. Generally, the paint itself seems both a manifestation of primordial slime-like matter, and also the ideal means to represent a human being 'passing through'. In more illustrative terms, all that is encountered in the picture is a naked figure seen from the rear, in the process of traversing the gap between two large curtains. Fairly literal associations may be made with a stage or a shower. Comparisons with Bonnard's treatment of the latter vein of imagery may be relevant for Bacon and his move towards a more descriptive figure style, but they also highlight how the simplicity and avoidance of naturalistic detail in Bacon's image work against such circumstantial connotations, and encourage more metaphorical readings. It might be noted that it is not merely the hand that has pulled open the right-hand curtain; instead, the figure seems to have employed his entire body, along the length of his arm and leg, to push his way through. This might confer a certain sense of physical strain and slowness onto the figure, or a material weightiness and resistance onto the expanse of curtain. The only other element in the picture is the safety pin, a sharp counterpoint to the surrounding softness of fabric and flesh, and a further indication of the challenge posed by the task of crossing the barrier created by the curtain. By extension, several commentators have noted the general sense of tenderness that the picture conveys, and one might recall Bacon's remark to Sutherland about Balthus failing to achieve 'the tenderness which we would all love to get for a change'. There is perhaps a suggestion of vulnerability in the nakedness of the body and the slightly bowed head, suggesting a self-absorbed, melancholy state of mind. Alternatively, the direction of the head could imply a gaze in the direction of a sexual partner behind the curtain, if we infer a possible reference to the kinds of private club that doubtless provided a means at this period for homosexual encounters. The orthogonal lines might suggest a bed behind the curtain. The picture may, then, evoke a lover, an object of bodily desire and possession recalled in memory. The loving attention to the painting of the buttocks seems to heighten the association. As we have seen, this figure seems to be the first surviving work in which Bacon lifts from the photography of Eadweard Muybridge, in particular from the images of paired wrestlers that clearly had strongly sexual connotations for the artist. His decision to make a painting that, on one level, so directly expressed his gay identity might conceivably be connected to current French culture, especially Jean Genet's emergence on the literary scene, with the strong admiration and support of figures like Sartre. Genet's books such as *Our Lady of the Flowers*, *Miracle of the Rose* and *The Thief's Journal* describe homosexual experience with an astonishing openness for their time, and a degree of familiarity with such work may have been liberating for Bacon. In short, *Study from the Human Body* is a highly resonant image, inviting imaginative engagement on the part of the viewer. It can indeed be seen to capture, or trap, an image of a human being passing through – passing though a curtain, but also, we might feel, passing though life, or moving in and out of one's own life. Sylvester speaks aptly about the 'elegiac poignancy of its sense of farewell'.[321]

In conclusion, the pictures that Bacon exhibited at the Hanover Gallery in November 1949 were created just as British engagement with what one might loosely term French existentialist culture was crystallising. The appearance of, for instance, translations of Sartre's *Nausea* and Leiris's Giacometti essay in *Horizon* encapsulate this moment of discovery and assimilation, the prelude to a more broadly based flourishing of existentialist concerns and attitudes in Britain during the early 1950s. Given the visual and literary parallels noted above, it is easy to see why Bacon's paintings seemed to observers to distil the mood of the moment. I would want to maintain that their existentialist aura was not entirely coincidental. The evidence is fragmentary and inconclusive, but to some degree the pictures seem to have been the product of a conscious and informed awareness on Bacon's part of new ideas and images emanating from Paris, filtered through a very singular sensibility.[322]

This book began by seeking to establish a continuing pattern of dialogue and visual affinity between Sutherland and Bacon from around 1943/44 to the turn of the decade and beyond. In this final chapter, the argument has been reinforced from yet another perspective by the evidence of their shared engagement with certain contemporary European artists such as Masson, Picasso and Giacometti. The evolution of both artists confirms the cogency of Sutherland's observations, made in response to the corraling of his work for a parochial neo-romanticism, to the effect that influence, or the adaptation of available resources, is a complex and subtle matter, and that painters are affected by all manner of stimuli, absorbing what they need at a given time. They respond above all, I believe, to strongly realised and suggestive images, whether visual or verbal, rather than to programmatic systems of thought. Certain asymmetries have also come more to the fore as this study has unfolded. Sutherland's combined interests in European modernism and the indigenous landscape tradition are remote from Bacon, and they reflect the distinctive sensibility of the mid- to late 1930s, the key moment of his artistic formation. Equally, Bacon's interests in Sartre and Bataille are not matched by Sutherland, and can be seen as symptomatic of the period some ten years later, when Bacon in turn consolidated his artistic identity. Overall, this has been an exercise in exploring connections, affinities and differences, which are intended cumulatively to clarify and sharpen our understanding of Francis Bacon and Graham Sutherland. The underlying approach is entirely in line with sentiments expressed by Bacon himself, in the course of reflections about the impossibility of making absolute judgements of value and knowing what will pass the test of time: 'what seems more interesting to me is the history of painting or of the arts in general – in order to understand what's made a certain painter, look at where he's come from, see who and what has inspired his work, see if he has managed to add something . . . I'm sure that every artist is influenced by his particular heritage and is placed at a certain point in time'.[323]

APPENDIX

BACON'S LETTERS TO SUTHERLAND

LETTER ONE

Bedales Lodge
Steep
Petersfield
8\2\43
Dear Graham
I have been meaning to write to you for ages to know how you and Kathleen are. If you are ever in London now will you both come and have some dinner with me one night. I would love to see you again or if Kathleen can't manage it perhaps you will come. I am more often in London than here now so will you write to me at 1 Glebe Place and make your own date. I still know one or two places where the food is not too bad. I hope you are working a lot. I must tell you how much I like some of your paintings in the National Gallery. I do hope I shall see you both. My best wishes.
Francis Bacon

LETTER TWO[1]

7 Cromwell Place
SW7
Wednesday [1944?]
Dear Graham
Here is the gin at last. I am so sorry not to have sent it but I could not get a box to put it in and I thought it would get broken if I sent it in paper. I do hope you are both well and have not been too much molested by the bombing. I do hope I shall see you both soon. Do come in when you can. I have to go away for a week next Wednesday but after that and before I shall be here I hope. Please do not send a cheque for the gin or anything foolish like that, it is a present and in any case I owe you such a lot for colours. My very best love to you and Kathleen
Yours,
Francis

LETTER THREE

7 Cromwell Place,
SW7
Tuesday
My dear Graham,
It was so terribly nice of you and Kathleen to have offered me the house while you were away and if I was not going to Cornwall I would have loved to accept it but thank you so much for thinking of it. I hope you have good weather while you are away and you will be able to do what you want to. I would love to come down for the day to see you both and the pictures. I will telephone you when you come back. Thank you again for your terribly kind thought. My love to you both,
Francis

LETTER FOUR[2]

. . . the centre of a group of 3 (the old story) as I have not been able to get the stretcher made yet as the people who make them are closed for a holiday. I am just hanging the piece of canvas on the wall and it seems quite pleasant to not to have the tyranny of the stretcher and be able to alter the dimensions as one wants. I don't know if you would like this place or not. I like the light and going to the casino in the evening after working and it is really quite pleasant to feel so isolated here but if I get the pictures finished I should like to go to Paris in October. Just before I left London M[3] gave me a lovely book on Rembrandt with some superb drawings especially one of a crying man. I expect you know it. I didn't and it was a wonderful shock to come across it for the first time. Nobody here is at all interested in ART which is perhaps a comfort and when they try to paint this landscape it is quite unbelievable, especially when they try to use the flowering bouganvillea and all that it turns into a wonderful lesbian postcard. I do hope it won't be long before I see you both. I think you might really love working here. I do want to thank you Graham for all you have done for me. I know I should not have been able to sell anything if you had not been good enough to mention my work to other people. All my love to you both.
Francis.

Hotel Ré
Monte Carlo
Aug 20 [1946]
My dear Graham
I was glad to hear from you and thank you so much for spraying the picture. I believe all the magenta except the blinds wants doing. I am so glad to hear about your work. I feel from the way you write you are not too dissatisfied with it. I would love to see some photographs. I hope you will have some by the time you come out. The strung man sounds very exciting. I feel it is very much your subject. About what you say of the show in Paris as I have sold the picture to the Redfern they can do what they like with it and I do not really mind. I do hope you will decide to show. I know exactly what you say about these sort of exhibitions but what happens apart from trying to paint somewhere near to what one wants seems to matter less and less. I am sure Douglas[4] will make an attack on you if he can but really as a champion of decorators as he is rapidly becoming I think from the point of view of sorting things out it is all to the good to be attacked by that prissy old voluptuary. His phobias are rapidly getting the better of his judgements.

About the weather here if you decide to stay on there should be lovely sun until the end of October and very often during the winter up to Christmas there is strong sun up to about 4 o'clock. I saw Rory in the casino a week or two ago but it was all a very smart party and I was very unlucky. I did not like to go and speak to him as there were lots of jewels and white shirts and ties and Lady K in a crinoline. It will really be lovely to see you and Kathleen. I don't know how much you will like this place. I don't know whether I want to stay after the winter here or not. I feel I don't want to go back to England at all for a long time if I go to Paris in the autumn. I thought I would look around for a large room or studio that I could go to from here for some weeks at a time perhaps. If you still think of part of the year in Paris perhaps we could find something we could use alternatively.
All my love to you both and do let me know when you're coming.
Love,
Francis

Hotel Ré
Monte Carlo
Oct 19th [1946]
My dear Graham,
I got Kathleen's postcard yesterday. I am so disappointed you will not be coming down here. I am going to Paris on the 1st of November for 2 or 3 weeks. I have heard of a room there only 2000 francs a month and if it is possible to work in I shall take it. I will be at the Hotel
St. Romain
Rue St. Roch
1ere
Is there any chance of you and Kathy being over at that time? I should so like to see you both. I do hope the work is going well but I am sure it is.

I am working on 3 sketches of the Velasquez portrait of Pope Innocent II [sic]. I have practically finished one. I find them very exciting to do but don't know yet if they are going to come off or not. Eric is over in London and I am sure he would like to see you. I do hope you may be in Paris when I am there. I hear Balthus is having a big show at Wildenstein at that time. I hear they are marvellous will that attract you they are so disturbing I hear All my love to you both and do come over if you can. Love,
Francis

Hotel Ré
Monte Carlo
Dec 30 [1946]
Dearest Graham,
It was lovely to hear from you but Eric and I were so disappointed you both could not come here it would have been so lovely to have see you. It is lovely weather here and I am sure it would do you both good. You must have been working very hard on the crucifixion. I am so glad it has been a success and well received it is good from the financial point of view. I know you feel as I do about the other part of it and the boredom of being liked by well-meaning fools. The Unesco show was awful. I have not seen a single notice but all that is just as meaningless here as in England. I think the English section was a little better than the others mostly because it was the best room and because the Picassos were very bad and the Braque awful in the French section and when it comes down to the present stuff, Pignon, Esteve, Tal-Coat and all that, it is a new low in clever ideas and bright colour. I know there is a lesson for us to take to heart in that, or at any rate for me. Since starting this letter Lance Sieveking has just drifted in from intellectual shadowland with Picture Post. He doesn't understand you but is *thrilled* and after all this I still haven't seen your picture as he tore the two pages out to keep and forgot to bring them and only had the part with Mervyn Peake. He is very well meaning but my dear really to be avoided. We had a two hour discussion on the aesthetics of Paul and John Nash the other day. All that need be said could be said in one word but we went on and on and on because they were such lovely chaps. I saw Balthus' things in Paris but they are no good. He is trying to get the tenderness which we would all love to get for a change but it can't be done that way it can only come as a technical thing and not as illustration or at least I feel that. I feel more and more that nothing matters or will happen until someone makes a new technical synthesis that can carry over from the sensation to our nervous system [insert: .That sounds too grandiloquent . . . I don't think our Kathy will able to get hold of that one now]. The thing I was very shocked by when I saw our things at Unesco, your 3 and mine, was the boring lack of reality, the lack of immediacy which we have so often talked about. I think it is also why so many Picassos are beginning to look so jaded now. It is the terrible decoration we are all contaminated by.

On rereading this letter it sounds like a cross between a discarded parlourmaid and darling Douglas but you'll know what I mean. You and Eric are the only two people I have had the luck to know who feel these things. I don't know how the copy of the Velasquez will turn out. I have practically finished one I think and am going to start on a portrait I want to do, but it is thrilling to paint from a picture which really excites you. I am sick to death of everything I've ever done in the past but continue to think like a child or a fool that I'm on the edge of doing a good painting. I think you might like this place to work in. At first I found it too distracting but now I love it and find it very good for pictures falling ready made into the mind. I paint dozens every week there. It is completely insulated against modern art and interesting people which is really very pleasant. Its too artificial for me to live in I couldn't. [insert: You know my dear I couldn't live such an artificial life.] I feel you would like it too as it is beginning to get people of all nationalities passing through and as it is very small it seems concentrated in that way. It would be so lovely if you and Kathy felt like working here and I always feel with a little clever manipulation the Casino would buy our pictures.

Sir K and Lady J and John Piper, Ruby M, A[6] and Julian Trevelian[7], Peter Watson I can't think of them all now. You know my dear all these tremendously real people. I know Kathy could make out a much better list of Reel Geniuses more than this. The weather is so lovely and sometimes the colour is wonderful with a gorgeous pink haze over things that Renoir tried to catch – this is just to let you both know I'm not so superficial as you think.

My love and all best wishes to you both and do come down soon. I am longing to see you. I would love to see the details of the crucifixion and hope to get a Picture Post. Reel love to you both not nasty insincere Love
Francis

LETTER EIGHT

22 Jan[uary] [19]47
Dearest Kathy
Thank you so much for your letter. it is really exciting to think I may see you and Graham before too long. About Paris, I would have simply loved to have met you there but there are two things – for the first time for ages I feel like doing lots of work and secondly at the moment until another allowance I am rather short of money to go to Paris. I think you would love being down here the weather should be lovely then it is like spring here now. About expenses, I could find you a very good room in a hotel here very reasonably and you must come and have meals with us in the flat. There is even a possibility that you could have the flat to stay in as we have got it until the end of March and we are looking for another as I do not want to stay in this one and we have heard of another and may have to take it before the end of this lease as they as they are so hard to get. But in any case come as soon as you can. One can live quite cheaply and also fabulously. If you could get it could you possibly bring me some white (zinc white) paint and 3 tubes of marble medium, Holland nearly always has it, and some *lamp* black if it is not too much of a bother. Do ask Graham if he can bring the details of the crucifixion. I got a picture post and thought it looked most awfully good and the colour sounded very exciting. Do come soon and stay as long as you can. If you want any information about anything here let me know.
All my love to you both
Francis.
If I make some money in the Casino which is always possible, I will wire you and come to Paris for a few days, but make your arrangements as though I not going to be there. In any case do come as soon as possible. I will try and make the money to come to Paris. I can always get a room at the last minute. Love. F

LETTER NINE[8]

[1954][9]
My dear Graham
Just to wish you and Kathy all the best for the New Year. Have just been down to Naples for a few days. Much more exciting and beautiful for me than here. The weather has been lovely.
All best wishes
Francis

ACKNOWLEDGEMENTS

In compiling this study, over a period of several years, I have accumulated many debts of gratitude. The staff of several institutions have been extremely helpful in allowing me access to collections and archival and library materials: the Tate Gallery and the Imperial War Museum, London; the Scottish National Gallery of Modern Art, and the National, University, and College of Art Libraries, Edinburgh; the National Museum and Gallery of Wales, Cardiff; and the Hugh Lane Gallery, Dublin. At the Tate, Matthew Gale and Chris Stephens were kind enough to show me their unpublished catalogue entries on the gallery's Sutherland and Bacon holdings. The footnotes to this study demonstrate my awareness that many other scholars in the field have produced valuable work in this general field over the last twenty years or so, work that has informed my own by a process of either assimilation of or reaction against the arguments I have encountered. I have also benefited from comments in response to the lectures and papers on this project presented to several conferences and research seminars. At Yale, it has been a great pleasure working with Gillian Malpass and Paul Sloman. I am grateful to the Paul Mellon Foundation for supporting the publication and to the Carnegie Trust and the Research Committee of the School of Arts, Culture and Environment at Edinburgh University for help with illustration costs. Closest to hand, my colleagues, especially Professor Richard Thomson, and students in the History of Art (formerly Fine Art) department at the University of Edinburgh, have been a constant source of stimulation and encouragement. Finally, two people have read and commented helpfully and constructively on the manuscript for this book, thereby earning my most profound gratitude. The first is my friend and colleague Elizabeth Cowling, Picasso specialist *sans pareil.* It has been a privilege to work all these years alongside someone who shares my own interests in looking hard at works of art, and in seeing them as the residue of a creative process that, for all its complexity, might be imaginatively reconstructed. The second is Christina Lodder, Professor of Art History at the University of St Andrews and also my wife. I have learnt an enormous amount about the processes and disciplines of scholarship from Christina, not least from the experience of collaborating with her on a big book on Naum Gabo (*Constructing Modernity: the Art and Career of Naum Gabo*, Yale University Press, 2000). I am also grateful to her, and to our daughter Lucy, for tolerating my appalling self-absorption and neurotic insecurities, which writing books seems only to make worse.

NOTES

ABBREVIATIONS

Bacon letter nos 1–9	originals in Cardiff (see below), reprinted here as Appendix.
Cardiff	Graham Sutherland Papers, National Museum and Gallery of Wales, Cardiff.
Dublin	Francis Bacon Archive, Hugh Lane Gallery, Dublin.
IWM	Archives of Imperial War Museum, London.
Tate	Tate Gallery Archive, London
UCL	University College Library, London

INTRODUCTION

1 The biographies in question are Roger Berthoud, *Graham Sutherland* (Faber & Faber, London 1982) and Michael Peppiatt, *Francis Bacon: Anatomy of an Enigma* (Weidenfeld and Nicholson, London 1996).

2 Most recently by James Beechey in 'Graham Sutherland. London and Chichester', *Burlington Magazine*, CXLV, September 2003, p. 666.

3 On Sylvester's promotion of Bacon at the expense of Sutherland, see James Hyman, *The Battle for Realism* (Yale University Press, London and New Haven, 2001) pp. 98–99; the reverse position was asserted in Peter Fuller, 'Nature and Raw Flesh: Sutherland and Bacon', in Boris Ford, ed., *The Cambridge Guide to the Arts in Britain IX Since the Second World War*, (Cambridge University Press, Cambridge 1988) pp. 119–30.

4 Cardiff.

5 This remark is based upon a study of the contents of the

Bacon studio in Dublin.

6 The sketchbooks are mainly in Tate, as are Sutherland's revealing letters to Kenneth Clark and Edward Sackville-West. The artist's correspondence with the War Artists Committee is held by IWM.

7 Bacon's correspondence with the Hanover Gallery begins at this point (Tate). One letter to Sonia Orwell from the South of France probably dates from the late 1940s (Orwell Papers, UCL).

INTERACTIONS

1 Bacon letter no. 1.

2 Bacon's phrase from David Sylvester, *Interviews with Francis Bacon* (Thames and Hudson, London, 1993) p. 189.

3 Peppiatt, *Francis Bacon*, pp. 83–84.

4 Ibid.

5 Bacon letter no. 1.

6 John Russell, *Francis Bacon* (Thames and Hudson, London, 1979) p. 20.

7 Peppiatt, *Francis Bacon*, p. 84.

8 Bacon got to know Cooper through Roy de Maistre (Peppiatt, *Francis Bacon*, p. 49). The Bacon *Crucifixion* reproduced in Herbert Read's *Art Now* (Faber & Faber, London, 1933) was presented as 'By permission of the Mayor Gallery' (plate 61), and the gallery sold the picture to Sir Michael Sadler from the exhibition that accompanied the book. Berthoud notes that Cooper and Sutherland met around 1936–37 and that the Mayor Gallery sold several small works; Berthoud, *Graham Sutherland*, p. 85. Five pictures by Sutherland were evidently sold by the gallery in 1938–39, Heather Johnson, *Roy de Maistre: The English Years, 1930–1968* (Craftsman House, Sydney, 1995) p. 72.

9 The fullest account of this unrealised plan is provided by Johnson (*Roy de Maistre*, pp. 64–67); further background on the show is given in Berthoud, *Graham Sutherland*, p. 86, drawing on the author's interviews with Robert Wellington.

10 See Johnson, *Roy de Maistre*, pp. 18–29; Peppiatt, *Francis Bacon*, chapter 3; Andrew Brighton, *Francis Bacon* (Tate Publishing, London, 2001) pp. 22–28.

11 *An exhibition of paintings in connection with a scheme to provide a permanent Gallery for the constant display of works by contemporary Painters and Sculptors at the Galleries of 43 Old Bond Street kindly lent by Thomas Agnew and Sons Ltd*, London (January 1937). Sutherland exhibited *Thunder Sounding, Butterfly Catcher, Tree no. 2* and *Mask*; Bacon showed *Figures in Garden, Seated Figure, Abstraction* and *Abstraction from the Human Form*.

12 See Agnew Gallery file of press cuttings, to which I was kindly given access by the gallery archivist Jane Hamilton.

13 See Johnson, *Roy de Maistre*, pp. 97–100, where de Maistre's lost portrait of Eric Hall is reproduced (p. 99); Daniel Farson, *The Gilded Gutter Life of Francis Bacon* (Vintage, London, 1994) pp. 31–32; Peppiatt, *Francis Bacon*, pp. 75–76.

14 Peppiatt, *Francis Bacon*, p. 66–68.

15 Eric Hall, ' "A New Idiom" in Painting', *Sunday Times*, 24 January 1937.

16 Farson, *The Gilded Gutter Life*, p. 32, citing the testimony of Victor Pasmore.

17 Peppiatt, *Francis Bacon* is generally the most informative source on Hall.

18 *Francis Bacon in Conversation with Michel Archimbaud* (Phaidon, London, 1993) pp. 24–25.

19 Peppiatt, *Francis Bacon*, p. 101. Peppiatt discovered that Hall was listed on the electoral register as living at 7 Cromwell Place from 1947 onwards.

20 Bacon letter no. 2.

21 Bacon letter no. 3.

22 Bacon letters nos 3 and 2.

23 *Francis Bacon in Conversation with Michel Archimbaud*, p. 25.

24 Information on Clark from Meryle Secrest, *Kenneth Clark. A Biography* (Weidenfeld and Nicholson, London, 1984) chapters 8–9.

25 The exchange is summarised in Emma Barker, "English abstraction: Nicholson, Hepworth and Moore in the 1930s", Steve Edwards and Paul Wood, eds, *Art of the Avant-Gardes* (Yale University Press, New Haven and London, 2004) p. 296.

26 Kenneth Clark, *Another Part of the Wood* (John Murray, London, 1974) pp. 254–55. The first of Sutherland's letters to Clark dates form 3 September 1936, and expresses gratitude for the latter's purchase of pictures (Kenneth Clark Papers, Tate).

27 *Recent Works of Graham Sutherland*, Rosenberg and Helft Gallery, London, 20 September to 8 October, 1938. The quotation comes from Robert Melville, 'A Panorama of Modern Art', *World Review* (London), March 1949, p. 44.

28 Ibid., p. 44.

29 Sutherland, letter to Clark, 28 February 1938, Tate.

30 Anon., *Recent Works of Graham Sutherland*, (n. p.). Clark's authorship is claimed by Berthoud, *Graham Sutherland*, p. 90. In the catalogue, Clark is given as the owner of *Red Tree* and *Black Landscape* (nos 2 and 18).

31 Raymond Mortimer, 'An Arrival', *The New Statesman and Nation*, XVI, 1 October 1938, p. 490.

32 See the Sutherland portraits in the Lee Miller Archive, and as reproduced and discussed in Val Williams and David Mellor, *Too Short a Summer: The Photographs of Peter Rose Pulham* (Impressions Gallery of Photography, York, 1979), pp. 21 and 23.

33 Berthoud, *Graham Sutherland*, p. 97. Sutherland's popularity with collectors is evident from the listing of his work in the catalogue of the joint retrospective *Henry Moore, John Piper, Graham Sutherland*, Temple Newsam, Leeds, 1941. A high proportion were borrowed from by

private and public collections, including nine works belonging to Kenneth Clark and three to Colin Anderson.

34 Raymond Mortimer, 'Notes on Shows', *The New Statesman and Nation*, XIX, 11 May 1940, p. 613.

35 'Art and Life. Part of a discussion between V. S. Pritchett, Graham Sutherland, Sir Kenneth Clark, and Henry Moore', *The Listener*, London, 13 November 1941, pp. 657–59.

36 *Tate Gallery Wartime Acquisitions*, National Gallery, London, April–May 1942. A version of this show toured Britain for the next eighteen months. The first Sutherland to enter a public collection was probably *Sunrise between Hedges* (1939), acquired by Leeds City Art Gallery.

37 Sutherland, letter to Edward Sackville-West, 24 May [1941], Tate. Sutherland thanked Sackville-West for mentioning his work to Russell.

38 Edward Sackville-West, *Graham Sutherland*, The Penguin Modern Painters, ed. K. Clark (Penguin, Harmondsworth, 1944).

39 Sutherland, letter to Edward Sackville-West, 6 September [1942], Tate.

40 Michael Luke, *David Tennant and the Gargoyle Years* (Weidenfeld and Nicholson, London, 1991) p. 182. For a general account, see Michael Shelden, *Friends of Promise. Cyril Connolly and the World of Horizon* (Hamish Hamilton, London, 1989).

41 Peter Watson is often acknowledged to be a key figure in this period, and there is considerable biographical information in, for example, Shelden's *Friends of Promise*. However, his collecting, patronage and general role within the British art and literary worlds have not been subject to detailed investigation. Three caches of Watson letters could fruitfully be used for such a study, those to Cyril Connolly (Connolly Papers, University of Tulsa, Oklahoma), to Sonia Orwell (Orwell Papers, University College Library, London), and to John Craxton. Lucian Freud's superb portrait of Watson from the mid-1940s is in the collection of the Victoria and Albert Museum, London.

42 Clement Greenberg, 'Avant-Garde and Kitsch', *Horizon*, no. 4, April 1940, pp. 255–73; Ben Nicholson, 'Notes on Abstract Art, no. 22, October 1941, pp. 272–76; Herbert Read, 'Art in an Electric Atmosphere', no. 17, May 1941, pp. 308–13; 'Vulgarity and Impotence. Speculations on the Present State of the Arts', no. 28, April 1942, pp. 267–76; 'Art and Crisis', no. 53, May 1944, pp. 336–50.

43 The intention was present from the start. According to Connolly's 'Comment' in the third issue, 'owing to his duties at the Ministry of Information, Kenneth Clark is unable to edit a special art number, but we hope to spread the articles on or by young English painters through future numbers, together with the sixteen illustrations which subscribers were promised' (*Horizon*, no. 3, March 1940, p. 150).

44 S. Brownwell 'The Euston Road Group', *Horizon*, no. 17, May 1941, pp. 348–50; P. Hendy 'Henry Moore', no. 21, September 1941, pp. 200–207; J. Piper 'Frances Hodgkins', no. 24, December 1941, pp. 413–16; J. Tonge, 'Scottish Paintings', no. 29, May 1942, pp. 331–35; R. Wyndham 'Matthew Smith', no. 32, August 1942, pp. 108–13; S. Berlin and B. Nicholson 'Alfred Wallis I and II', no. 37, January 1943, pp. 41–53; P. Hendy 'Paul Nash' and E. H. Ramsden 'Barbara Hepworth', no. 42, June 1943, pp. 413–17 and 418–21; H. S. Ede 'David Jones', no. 44, August 1943, pp. 125–36; B. Jonzen 'A Visit to Mr Sickert at Broadstairs', no. 45, September 1943, pp. 194–203; reproductions of paintings by Julian Trevelyan, no. 47, November 1943, between pages 297 and 298; Stephen Spender 'The Work and Opinions of Cecil Collins', no. 50, February 1944, pp. 115–19; H. S. Williamson 'Ceri Richards', no. 52, April 1944, pp. 277–82; 'Constructive Art: An Exchange of Letters between Naum Gabo and Herbert Read', no. 55, July 1944, pp. 57–64; Robert Ironside 'Victor Pasmore', no. 63, March 1945, pp. 163–69.

45 Reproductions of Paintings by John Craxton, no. 27, March 1942 and no. 53, May 1944; by Robert Colquhoun, no. 56, August 1944; by Lucian Freud, no. 4, April 1940, no. 41, May 1943.

46 Reproduced in *Horizon*, no. 3, March 1940, between pages 68 and 69.

47 See annotated copy of catalogue for the Rosenberg and Helft Gallery exhibition, Tate (no. 23).

48 Graham Sutherland, 'Welsh Sketch Book', *Horizon*, no. 28, April 1942, pp. 225–35; draft manuscript, Cardiff.

49 *La Litterature Anglaise depuis La Guerre* (Editions Horizon, London, 1945). I am grateful to I. D. Edrich, dealer in Modern First Editions and Literary Periodicals, for allowing me access to a copy of this exceedingly rare item.

50 Peter Watson, 'Note sur Deux Peintres Anglais', *La Litterature Anglaise depuis La Guerre*, pp. 24–27.

51 *The Intruding Bull* (1944) and *Horned Tree Form* (1944, in the collection of W. A. Evill), *Horizon*, no. 67, July 1945, between pp. 24–25.

52 See *Graham Sutherland, a Retrospective Selection, 1938–51*, Institute of Contemporary Art, London, 20 June–5 August 1951, no. 31 (*Man Walking*); Douglas Cooper, *The Work of Graham Sutherland* (Lund Humphries, London, 1961) gives Watson as the previous owner of a *Thorn Tree* drawing by then owned by his lover Norman Fowler (p. 75, no. 78b).

53 Melville, 'A Panorama of Modern Art', p. 44.

54 The best general account of the movement unfortunately remains unpublished, namely Virginia Button, *The Aesthetic of Decline: English Neo-Romanticism c.1935–56*, PhD thesis, Courtauld Institute of Art, University of London, 1992.

55 Berthoud, *Graham Sutherland*, p. 110. One of the most striking instance of Sutherland's inspiration is Craxton's *Welsh Estuary Foreshore* (1943), Scottish National Gallery of Modern Art, Edinburgh.

56 Robert Ironside, *Painting since 1939* (Longman, Green

and Co., London, 1947) p. 37.

57 Berthoud, *Graham Sutherland*, p. 111. No reference is given for the dating of the meeting to 1943. It is dated to early 1945 in William Feaver, 'Lucian Freud: Life into Art', *Lucian Freud* (Tate, London, 2002) p. 26.

58 Craig Hartley, 'Beyond Description. Freud as an Etcher', *Lucian Freud. Etchings 1946–2004*, National Galleries of Scotland, Edinburgh, p. 10.

59 *Recent Paintings by Francis Bacon, Frances Hodgkins, Henry Moore, Matthew Smith, Graham Sutherland*, Lefevre Galleries, London, 1–30 April, 1945.

60 Berthoud, *Graham Sutherland*, p. 114.

61 Ibid., p. 119.

62 It was probably several years later that the two works in the 1945 show were either sold or given to loyal Bacon supporters, the *Three Studies* to Eric Hall and *Figure in a Landscape* to his cousin Diana Watson; R. Alley and J. Rothenstein, *Francis Bacon* (Thames and Hudson, London, 1964) nos 15 and 16. Isabel Rawsthorne describes seeing both works in Bacon's studio in 1949 (Isabel Rawsthorne, letter to Peter Rose Pulham, 21 March [1949], Rawsthorne Papers, Tate).

63 *Recent Paintings by Francis Bacon, Frances Hodgkins, Henry Moore, Matthew Smith, Graham Sutherland*, Lefevre Galleries, London, 1–30 April, 1945.

64 Sutherland, letter to Kenneth Clark, 18 September 1944 (Tate). The Impington project refers to a projected collaboration with Henry Moore to produce a related mural and sculpture for the interior of Gropius and Fry's Impington Village College. Sutherland envisaged an arcadian landscape backdrop to Moore's Family Group. See the many studies in one of Sutherland's sketchbook (no. 10) in the Tate Archive. The project eventually fell through.

65 Tate (no. 12).

66 Andrew Durham, 'Notes on Technique', in Dawn Ades, Andrew Forge *et al.*, *Francis Bacon* (Tate Gallery, London 1985) p. 231. The board had been in production by the Sundeala company since the late nineteenth century, and still is at the time of writing.

67 See letters to Chelsea Art Stores, 6 October 1944; to Chelsea Art Stores, 24 October, denying permission; from Secretary of Paper Control, Reading, 26 October, 1944, explaining suitability and authorising supply, Graham Sutherland file, War Artists Archive, IWM.

68 An affinity between the *Three Studies* and *Horned Forms* has previously been remarked in Rolf Lassøe 'Francis Bacon's Crucifixions and Related Themes', *Hafnia* (Copenhagen), no. 11, 1987, p. 36 (n. 20), and by David Cohen in 'Antibes: Graham Sutherland', *Burlington Magazine*, October 1998, p. 709.

69 Illustrated in colour in *Sutherland: Une Rétrospective*, Musée Picasso, Antibes, 1998, p. 34.

70 John Russell, *Francis Bacon* (Thames and Hudson, London, 1964) p. 24.

71 Marius Maxwell, *Stalking Big Game with a Camera in Equatorial Africa* (Medici Society, London, 1924; 113 plates).

72 Sam Hunter, 'Francis Bacon: the Anatomy of Horror', *Magazine of Art*, New York, January 1952, p. 12; several plates removed from book at Dublin. One plate from this source was reproduced by Sylvester in *Interviews with Francis Bacon*, p. 33.

73 Maxwell, *Stalking Big Game*, plate between pp. 96–97.

74 Ibid., plate between pp. 112–13.

75 Ibid., plate between pp. 120–21.

76 Ibid., plate between pp. 54–55

77 See *Sutherland: Une Rétrospective*, p. 34.

78 For the suggestion that Bacon adapted the mouth on the central panel from an illustration in *La Maladie de la Bouche*, which he had acquired by 1935, see Matthew Gale, draft catalogue entry for Tate Gallery on *Three Studies for Figures at the Base of a Crucifixion* (NO6171). I am very grateful to Dr. Gale for showing me his illuminating and suggestive text. For a reproduction of a plate from *La Maladie de la Bouche* found in Bacon's studio (Dublin), see Wilfried Seipel, Barbara Steffen and Christoph Vitali, eds, *Francis Bacon and the Tradition of Art* (Skira, Milan, 2003) p. 160.

79 The terms were used in the Sutherland interview 'Modern Art Explained by Modern Artists' (1944), reprinted in *Graham Sutherland. Correspondences. Selected Writings on Art*, ed. Julian Andrews (The Graham and Kathleen Sutherland Foundation, 1982) p. 56.

80 See Margarita Cappock, 'Works on paper by Francis Bacon in the Hugh Lane Gallery, Dublin', *Burlington Magazine* CXLX, February 2003, p. 75 and fig. 5.

81 Gale, draft catalogue entry on *Three Studies for Figures at the Base of a Crucifixion.*

82 Alley and Rothenstein, *Francis Bacon*, D1–2.

83 Alley and Rothenstein, *Francis Bacon*, A3.

84 Reproduced in colour in David Sylvester, *Francis Bacon. The Human Body* (South Bank Centre, London, 1998) catalogue 1. This picture is not recorded in Alley and Rothenstein. It may have been an earlier trial-run since there is much more evidence of overpainting and alterations than in the final work. See Stephen Hackney 'Francis Bacon (1909–1992): *Three Studies for Figures at the Base of a Crucifixion*', in *Paint and Purpose. A Study of Technique in British Art* (Tate Gallery Publishing, London) p. 179.

85 *Horizon*, no. 67, July 1945, between pp. 24–25.

86 Gale, draft catalogue entry on *Three Studies for Figures at the Base of a Crucifixion.*

87 Ibid.

88 Ibid.

89 Gianfranco Bruno, ed., *Graham Sutherland: Storia Segreta 1922–1979* (Edizioni Colombo, Genova, 1991) fig. 107 (p. 90).

90 Ronald Alley, *Graham Sutherland*, Tate Gallery, London, 1982, pp. 82–83, catalogue entry no. 65.

91 Maxwell, *Stalking Big Game*, plate between pp. 98–99.

92 *Recent Paintings by Francis Bacon, Frances Hodgkins, Henry Moore, Matthew Smith, Graham Sutherland*, Lefevre Galleries, London, nos 38 and 41. The pictures are reproduced in Cooper, *The Work of Graham Sutherland*, plates 61a–b.

93 Maxwell, *Stalking Big Game*, plate opposite p. 82. Having noticed this derivation, I discovered that, according to Gale (draft catalogue entry on *Figure in a Landscape*), the comparison was also made in an unpublished PhD dissertation by David Boxer, *The Early Work of Francis Bacon* (John Hopkins University, Baltimore, Maryland, 1975) p. 165. I have not had the opportunity to consult Boxer's work.

94 *Quelques contemporains anglais*, shown at 28 Ave. des Champs Elysées, Paris, 1945–46.

95 British Council, *Tableaux Britanniques modernes appartenant à la Tate Gallery*, Paris 1946 (circulated to Athens, Berne, Brussels, Rome, Stockholm, Vienna), nos. 108–12 by Sutherland.

96 *Graham Sutherland*, Buchholz Gallery, Curt Valentin, New York, 26 February to 23 March, 1946. See also Berthoud, *Graham Sutherland*, pp. 124–25.

97 *Recent Paintings by Ben Nicholson, Graham Sutherland and Francis Bacon, Robert Colquhoun, John Craxton, Lucian Freud, Robert MacBryde, Julian Trvelyan*, Lefevre Gallery, London, February 1946.

98 Roger Marvell, 'New Pictures', *The New Statesman and Nation*, XXXI, 16 February 1946, p. 119.

99 Ibid.

100 Alley and Rothenstein, *Francis Bacon*, A5, record that *Man with Microphones* was shown at the Lefevre Gallery (*British Painters Past and Present*, July–August 1946), and then reproduced both in the catalogue of *Seventh Exhibition*, Anglo-French Centre, London, November –December 1946, though on this occasion it was not exhibited, and in James Thrall Soby, *Contemporary Painters*, Museum of Modern Art, New York, 1948, p. 151. Bacon seems however to have lost faith in the picture, and to have reworked the canvas completely around 1948–49, judging by the use of a grisaille palette and the direct derivation from a photographic source, features that align the picture, as shown later in this chapter, with Bacon's work towards the end of the decade. This version in turn had two large sections violently excised, but all three elements survived in the artist's studio and now form part of the Bacon Studio in Dublin. The work is reproduced in its present state in *Francis Bacon's Studio at the Hugh Lane*, Hugh Lane Gallery, Dublin, 1998; fig. 34. The two states tend to be presented in the wrong chronological sequence in Bacon literature, a confusion stemming from the fact that the photographs of the first and revised states seem to have been accidentally transposed in Alley's catalogue. The brief commentary makes it clear, however, that Alley knew which version came first. Elements such as the umbrella are clearly visible as pentimenti in the mutilated Dublin picture.

101 Cooper, *The Work of Graham Sutherland*, plate 69a.

102 *Sutherland: Une Rétrospective*, plate 59.

103 Cooper, *The Work of Graham Sutherland*, plates 70–71.

104 Apparently, Sutherland later 'restored' the fading background of *Chimère I* (Berthoud, *Graham Sutherland*, p. 264).

105 Hunter, 'Francis Bacon: the Anatomy of Horror', p. 13.

106 Garlake also notes connections between these 1946 pictures, and proposes that Sutherland was appropriating ideas from Bacon; Margaret Garlake, *New Art New World: British Art in Postwar Society* (Yale University Press, New Haven and London 1998). p. 191.

107 Tate.

108 *Summer Exhibition*, Redfern Gallery, London, July–September 1946, no. 11; UNESCO, *Exposition d'Art Moderne*, November–December 1946, Musée d'Art Moderne, Paris, 'Grande-Bretagne' section, nos 1 and 55–57. The Bacon is given as Redfern Gallery Collection. Two years later, Brausen sold the painting on to the Museum of Modern Art, New York (Peppiatt, *Francis Bacon*, pp. 117–18).

109 Reproduced in colour in Alley, *Graham Sutherland*, p. 35.

110 *Paul Nash, Henry Moore, John Piper, Graham Sutherland*, Redfern Gallery, London, 6–29 January 1944; *Sutherland . . . Adler . . . Mayersohn . . . Bachmann*, 31 October–23 November 1946.

111 *Summer Exhibition*, Redfern Gallery, London, July–September 1946 (11).

112 Bacon letter no. 5.

113 Bacon letter no. 4.

114 Berthoud, *Graham Sutherland*, p. 130.

115 Berthoud, *Graham Sutherland*, p. 130.

116 Feaver, 'Lucian Freud: Life into Art', *Lucian Freud*, p. 26. The story also appears in Berthoud, *Graham Sutherland*, p. 128.

117 Herbert Read, letters to Ben Nicholson, Herbert Read Archive, University of Victoria, British Columbia.

118 Cooper, *The Work of Graham Sutherland*, p. 34.

119 For a colour reproduction of *Christ Carrying the Cross*, see Bruno, *Graham Sutherland: Storia Segreta*, p. 23.

120 Fitzwilliam Museum, Cambridge, reproduced in Alley, *Graham Sutherland*, p. 112.

121 David Sylvester, *Looking Back at Francis Bacon* (Thames and Hudson, London, 2000) p. 33.

122 Cooper, *The Work of Graham Sutherland*, catalogue no. 87. Related studies are sometimes dated to 1944, but this is surely incorrect.

123 See David Alan Mellor, ed., *A Paradise Lost: The Neo-Romantic Imagination in Britain 1935–55* (Barbican Art Gallery, London, 1987) p. 13.

124 Cyril Connolly, 'The Coming of the Crisis – I', reprinted in *Ideas and Places* (Weidenfeld and Nicholson, London, 1953) p. 142.

125 Cited in Peter Conradi, *Iris Murdoch: A Life* (W. W. Norton, New York and London, 2001) p. 214. Murdoch herself epitomised this outlook.

126 See correspondence with WAAC, IWM, indicating that he was in France 9–24 December 1924, and including the remark 'the trip to Paris as far as I was concerned was well worth it and I was very moved by France generally' (Sutherland letter, 7 February 1945).
127 Graham Sutherland, 'Images Wrought from Destruction', 1971 essay reprinted in *Sutherland: The War Drawings* (Imperial War Museum, London, 1982) p. 8.
128 Berthoud, *Graham Sutherland*, pp. 125–26.
129 Bacon letter no. 4.
130 Bacon letter no. 5.
131 Bacon letter no. 7.
132 Ibid.
133 Bacon letter no. 8.
134 Bacon letter no. 5
135 Bacon letter no. 7.
136 Bacon letter no. 8.
137 Bacon letter no. 5.
138 Ibid.
139 Bacon letter no. 4.
140 Ibid.
141 Bacon letter no. 6.
142 Bacon letter no. 7.
143 15 February–11 March 1939 (catalogue introduction by Raymond Mortimer). The show also included Matthew Smith, Rodrigo Moynihan, Sickert and several of the Euston Road School painters.
144 Bacon letter no. 7.
145 Entry of 13 February 1947, cited in Richard Shone, 'Benedict Nicolson: A Portrait', *The Burlington Magazine*, February 2004, no. 1211, CXLVI, p. 93.
146 Berthoud, *Graham Sutherland*, p. 131. No source is given for this information.
147 Bacon letter no. 9.
148 Berthoud, *Graham Sutherland*, p. 132.
149 Berthoud, *Graham Sutherland*, p. 133.
150 The details of Sutherland's travels are provided in Ibid, pp. 135–37, and 139ff. A handwritten list by the artist indicates that Sutherland was in the South of France 15 April–18 May 1946, 9 October–9 December 1946, 7 August–7 September, 1947, 23 October–5 December 1947, 13 March–22 June 1949, 13 November 1949–January 1950 and 7 August–10 September 1950 (Cardiff).
151 Berthoud, *Graham Sutherland*, p. 144.
152 Berthoud, *Graham Sutherland*, p. 133, describes the Sutherlands as having been 'mildly addicted' to roulette for five years or so.
153 Ibid., p. 129.
154 See list of works in Cooper, *The Work of Graham Sutherland*, pp. 75–76, nos 70 and 81; see collections catalogue on the British Council web-site.
155 *Preliminary Paintings for 'The Northampton Crucifixion' by Graham Sutherland*, Lefevre Gallery, London 1–31 July, 1947.
156 *Paintings by Graham Sutherland*, Hanover Gallery, London, 2 June–11 July 1948; *Graham Sutherland*, Buchholz Gallery, Curt Valentin, New York, 16 November–4 December 1948.
157 Bernard Denvir, 'Exhibitions: Graham Sutherland', *Tribune*, 11 June 1948.
158 'The Midas Touch', *Daily Graphic*, 3 June 1948; 'Success Stories', *What's On in London*, 11 June 1948.
159 *Lilliput*, August 1944, p. 139 (in a series of artist portraits); Berthoud, *Graham Sutherland*, p. 139; Soby, *Contemporary Painters*, pp. 134–39.
160 Isabel Rawsthorne, letter to Peter Rose Pulham, 14 December [1948], Rawsthorne Papers, Tate. Pulham was a mutual friend of Bacon and Rawsthorne, who seems at this stage not to have known Bacon for long. On Rawsthorne, virtually the only source is *Isabel Rawsthorne 1912–1992* (Mercer Art Gallery, Harrogate, 1997–98).
161 Alley, *Graham Sutherland*, p. 14.
162 Graham Sutherland, 'Thoughts on Painting', *The Listener* (London), XLVI, 6 September 1951, reprinted in *Graham Sutherland. Correspondences*, p. 74.
163 Sutherland, letter to Kenneth Clark, 12 November [1947], Tate.
164 M. H. Middleton, 'Art', *Spectator* (London), 18 June 1948, p. 734.
165 *La Jeune Peinture en Grande-Bretagne*, Galerie René Drouin, 23 Jan–21 February, subsequently shown in Brussels (organised by the British Council).
166 Sutherland, letter to the Melvilles, 20 November 1948, Robert Melville Papers, Tate.
167 *Summer Exhibition*, Redfern Gallery, London, July to September 1948 (no. 161).
168 Walter Michel and C. J. Fox, eds, *Wyndham Lewis on Art* (Thames and Hudson, London, 1969) p. 393 (reprinted section from exhibition review of 12 May 1949).
169 *Francis Bacon: Paintings; Robin Ironside: Coloured Drawings*, Hanover Gallery, London, 8 November–10 December 1949.
170 'Art for the Few', *Observer*, 13 November 1949; annotated copy of the catalogue in the Hanover Gallery archive (Tate), which indicates that eventually all but one of the twelve works listed were sold.
171 Michel and Fox, *Wyndham Lewis on Art*, p. 394.
172 Isabel Rawsthorne, letter to Peter Rose Pulham, 25 November [1949], Rawsthorne Papers, Tate.
173 'Good but Ghoulish', *Daily Herald*, 10 November 1949.
174 Sutherland, 'Thoughts on Painting', p. 72.
175 The present whereabouts of the Sutherland are unknown. The archival photograph reproduced (Cardiff) is signed and dated 1950. This picture was the basis of Sutherland's 1950 lithograph *Standing Form against Curtain*, 1949 (reproduced in Roberto Tassi, *Graham Sutherland: Complete Graphic Work* [Thames and Hudson, London, 1978] plate 52), listed as no. 1 in the catalogue of *Recent Paintings – Graham Sutherland*, Hanover Gallery, London, 20 June–4 August 1951 was sold as *Standing Form, Red Background (against Curtain)*,

1949, Christie's, London, 26 October 1994, lot 112.

176 *Standing Form against a Hedge* was also first exhibited in *Recent Paintings – Graham Sutherland*, Hanover Gallery, London, 20 June – 4 August 1951.

177 Martin Harrison, Francis Bacon in Camera (Thames and Hudson, London, 2005) appeared too late for me to consult it.

178 David Marr notes, without giving any source for the information, the 'odd passion of de Maistre and Bacon for newspaper photographs', which was subsequently shared by their mutual friend Patrick White; see *Patrick White: A Life* (Jonathon Cape, London, 1991) p. 169.

179 Sylvester (*Looking Back at Francis Bacon*, p. 25) argued that Sickert's *The Miner* (1935–36) was a specific source for Bacon's treatment of drapery in *Figure in a Landscape* (1945). Bacon's early development coincided with numerous Sickert exhibitions in London (see list in Wendy Baron and Richard Shone, eds, *Sickert Paintings* (Yale University Press, New Haven and London, 1992) pp. 356–57.

180 Reproduced in Alley, *Graham Sutherland*, p. 110.

181 Hunter, 'Francis Bacon: the Anatomy of Horror', p. 12.

182 Sylvester, *Interviews with Francis Bacon*, p. 30.

183 'Francis Bacon: I painted to be loved', *The Art Newspaper*, no. 137, June 2003, p. 28.

184 Hugh Davies, *Francis Bacon: The Early and Middle Years, 1928–58* (Garland Publishing, London and New York) pp. 127–29. The image seems to derive from the nearmost figure in one of Muybridge's plates of wrestlers (Eadweard Muybridge, *Muybridge's Complete Human and Animal Locomotion* (Dover Publications, New York) I, plate 346, farthest left of the third row of images).

185 The relevant Sutherland is reproduced in Tassi, *Graham Sutherland*, plate 40. Compare the third image in the wrestling sequence of which the final image later formed the springboard for Bacon's 1953 *Two Figures* (see Muybridge, *Human and Animal Locomotion*, plate 347). Sutherland's images of fencing and jumping figures (Ibid., plates 41 and 43) seem to derive more loosely from the photographs of men boxing and jumping assembled in the second volume of this great Muybridge compilation. Needless to say, ever since their first publication in the 1880s Muybridge's photographs had served as a regular point of reference for painters.

186 Alley and Rothenstein, A5 (wrongly given as first version). Compare for example K. C. Clark, *Positioning in Radiography* (Heinemann, London 1939) p. 41.

187 Barbara Steffen, 'Chance and the Tradition of Art in Francis Bacon's Work', in Seipel, *Francis Bacon and the Tradition of Art*, pp. 32–5.

188 Bacon's well-known derivations from this section of *Battleship Potemkin* raises an interesting parallel with the film critic Roger Manvell, an exact contemporary of Bacon's, and in the 1940s the most prominent British writer on cinema as an art form. The current prestige of the Odessa steps sequence is evident from the text and illustrations of Manvell's survey book *Film* (Penguin, Harmondsworth, editions in 1944 and 1946), and 'The Poetry of the Film', in Fred Murnau, ed., *New Road. Directions in European Art and Letters*, IV (Grey Walls Press, London, 1946) p. 157. The possible significance of *Film* for Bacon is also touched on by Hyman (*The Battle for Realism*, pp. 147–48). One of the plates in Sam Hunter's 1950 montage of photographs from Bacon's studio had been extracted from Rachel Low and Roger Manvell, *The History of the British Film 1896–1906*, London, 1948. Wider consideration of his writings indicates that, like Bacon, Manvell combined strong interests in cinema and Nazi propaganda. No contacts between the two men are documented.

189 Reproduced in Sylvester, *Looking Back at Francis Bacon*, pp. 57 and 41.

190 Isabel Rawsthorne, letter to Peter Rose Pulham, 3 July [1949], Rawsthorne Papers, Tate.

191 The connection between Bacon and Paolozzi comes across from Isabel Rawsthorne's correspondence with Peter Rose Pulham, as in the reference to 'several nights of drink and conversation with Francis and Eduardo' (letter to Pulham, 3 March [1950], Tate) See also Robin Spencer, ed., *Eduardo Paolozzi: Writings and Interviews* (Oxford University Press Oxford, 2000). Admiration for Bacon is discussed on pp. 16–17 and 277–78; Victoria Walsh, *Nigel Henderson: Parallel of Life and Art* (Thames and Hudson, London, 2001); and Martin Harrison, *Transition. The London Art Scene in the Fifties* (Merrell, London, 2002) pp. 48–59.

192 For a detailed account of the project see Berthoud, *Graham Sutherland*, pp. 133–43.

193 Sutherland, 'Thoughts on Painting', p. 73.

194 Museum of Modern Art, New York.

195 Sylvester, *Looking Back at Francis Bacon*, p. 68.

196 See Andrew Wilton, *The Swagger Portrait: Grand Manner Portraiture In Britain from Van Dyck to Augustus John 1630–1930* (Tate Gallery, London, 1992).

197 Such Van Dyckian devices feature in, for instance, Cecil Beaton's portrait of the Queen Mother, 1948.

198 'What a curious figure he [Bacon] is! He now wants to paint portraits of living people. Is going to do one of Lucian for the Festival competition. 'They are bound to look at it if its Lucian – even K Clark"', Isabel Rawsthorne, letter to Peter Rose Pulham, 30 December [1950], Rawsthorne Papers, Tate. The reference here is to the exhibition *60 Paintings for '51*, a Festival of Britain event staged in 1951, which included, for example, Freud's *Interior in Paddington*. Bacon was indeed one of the artists invited to contribute in February 1950, but the Freud portrait was not in the end the work shown. See *25 from 51*, Sheffield City Art Galleries, 1978, pp. 11 and 32.

199 See *Portraits by Graham Sutherland*, National Portrait Gallery, London, 1977. Criticism of Sutherland's rather academic approach to portraiture is already evident in Denys Sutton's response to the first exhibition of the

Somerset Maugham portrait; 'Living Art for Britain's Festival: Retrospective at the Institute of Contemporary Art', *Artnews*, no. 4, Summer 1951, p. 54.

200 Sylvester, *Interviews with Francis Bacon*, p. 63.

201 See ICA brochures and flyers in Roland Penrose Archive, Scottish National Gallery of Modern Art, Edinburgh.

202 *40,000 years of Modern Art*, Institute of Contemporary Art, London, 1948.

203 A lecture by Melville on Sutherland was scheduled for 15 December 1949, according to an ICA flyer (ICA archive, Tate).

204 *Graham Sutherland, a retrospective selection, 1938–51*, Institute of Contemporary Art, London, 20 June–5 August 1951. The Dover Street galleries had opened in December 1950.

205 *Forty Years of Modern Art*, ICA (Academy Hall, London), February–March 1948; *Figure in a Landscape* (1945) was shown in *London-Paris: New Trends in Painting and Sculpture*, ICA, March–April 1950.

206 Sutherland's photograph of *Green and Orange Landscape* (1947) is inscribed Peter Watson Collection (Cardiff).

207 David Sylvester, letter to the author, 23 June 1999.

208 'In two days we are leaving here . . . & going to Villefranche as I want to see Francis Bacon and see the Picassos in the Antibes Museum', Peter Watson, letter to Sonia Orwell, Sunday July 6 [late 1940s], Orwell papers, UCL. In a letter to Orwell from Monaco dated December 8, possibly also from the late 1940s, and encouraging her to visit, Bacon himself asked her to 'give my love to Peter if he is still in London'.

209 See the essays by Alan Pryce-Jones, Roland Penrose, Priaulx Rainier, Michel Wishart and David Mellor in the special Cyril Connolly memorial issue of *Adam* (nos 385–90, 1974–75).

210 Priaulx Rainier, 'Personal Recollections', *Adam*, p. 95.

211 Andrew Sinclair, *Francis Bacon: His Life and Violent Times* (Sinclair-Stevenson, London, 1993) p. 90.

212 See Hilary Spurling, *The Girl from the Fiction Department* (Hamish Hamilton, London, 2002). Sonia Brownwell became Sonia Orwell in 1949, when she married the writer shortly before his death.

213 Ibid., p. 59.

214 'Art for the Few', *Observer*, 13 November 1949.

215 Cyril Connolly, 'Comment', *Horizon*, nos 120–21, December 1949–January 1950, p. 360. See chapter 2 for further discussion of this issue of *Horizon*.

216 Robert Melville, *Picasso: Master of the Phantom* (Oxford University Press, Oxford, 1939); see also *Surrealism in Birmingham 1935–1954*, Birmingham Museums and Art Gallery, 2001, including a chronology of Melville's career (pp. 62–64).

217 Melville, 'A Panorama of Modern Art', pp. 40–45.

218 Ibid., p. 41.

219 Ibid., p. 43.

220 Ibid., p. 45.

221 *Graham Sutherland* (Ambassador Editions, London, 1950), with essay 'The Imagery of Graham Sutherland' by Robert Melville (not paginated).

222 Robert Melville, 'Francis Bacon', *Horizon*, nos. 120–21, December 1949–January 1950, pp. 419–23. Melville subsequently wrote two further important early texts on the artist, 'The Iconoclasm of Francis Bacon', *World Review*, January 1951, pp. 63–64; 'A Note on the Recent Paintings of Francis Bacon', *World Review*, February 1952, pp. 31–32.

223 Ibid., pp. 420–21.

224 Ibid., p. 422.

225 Ibid., p. 420.

226 Ibid.

227 Melville, 'Francis Bacon', p. 421.

228 These comprise the *Three Studies* triptych, *Painting*, a *Head* (Collection Wright Ludington), *Study for a Portrait* and *Study for a Figure. Figure with Monkey* and *Head VI* were reproduced in a more conventional manner.

229 'The Midas Touch', *Daily Graphic*, 3 June 1948.

230 Isabel Rawsthorne mentions that Bacon arranged for her to meet with 'Graham's framer' (letter to Peter Rose Pulham, 31 December [?1948], Tate). Sutherland's dealings with the Chelsea Art Stores around 1944/45 are discussed earlier in this chapter.

231 Raymond Mortimer, 'Graham Sutherland's New Paintings', *Harper's Bazaar*, July 1948, p. 44.

232 Clark's interpretation of Sutherland in *The Art of Landscape* is discussed further in chapter 2.

233 See Luke, *David Tennant and the Gargoyle Years*, pp. 183 and 49. The names that follow are taken from the roll-call included amongst the book's illustrations. See also Peppiatt, *Francis Bacon*, pp. 106–7.

234 Luke, *David Tennant and the Gargoyle Years*, p. 182.

235 See chapter 3 for further discussion of Pulham and Bacon.

236 Berthoud, *Graham Sutherland*, pp. 145–46.

237 Alley, *Graham Sutherland*, p. 20.

238 Stephen Spender 'English Painting in the Fifties', Robert Richman, ed., *The Arts at Mid-Century* (Horizon Press, New York, 1954) p. 221.

239 Ibid., p. 225.

240 Bacon letter no. 9.

241 Berthoud, *Graham Sutherland*, p. 168.

242 Rothenstein, *Brave Day Hideous Night*, p. 219.

243 Alley and Rothenstein, *Francis Bacon*.

244 For example *Head II* (1952, Private Collection) and *Head III* (1953, Tate Gallery).

245 Hyman, *The Battle for Realism*, p. 99. See also Berthoud, *Graham Sutherland*, pp. 159–60.

246 Farson, *The Gilded Gutter Life*, p. 198.

247 Berthoud, *Graham Sutherland*, pp. 159–60.

248 Stephen Spender, *Journal 1939–1983* (Faber & Faber, London, 1985) p. 235. See also Farson, *The Gilded Gutter Life*, p. 100.

249 Hyman, *The Battle for Realism*, pp. 99–100.

250 Farson, *The Gilded Gutter Life*, p. 197.

251 Southampton City Art Gallery.
252 John Richardson, *The Sorcerer's Apprentice* (Alfred A Knopf, New York, 2000), p. 166.
253 Ibid., pp. 193–99.
254 1976 interview with Paul Nicholls, reprinted in Sutherland, *Correspondences*, p. 115.
255 William Boyd, 'The Primacy of the Line', *Graham Sutherland* (Bernard Jacobson Ltd, London, 1993), n.p.
256 Hyman, *The Battle for Realism*, p. 99.

DEVASTATION

1 Sutherland, 'Images Wrought from Destruction', p. 9.
2 David Gascoyne, *Collected Journals 1936–42* (Skoob Books, London, 1991), p. 148.
3 A. J. P. Taylor, *The Second World War* (Penguin, Harmondsworth, 1976) p. 31.
4 For a helpful overview, see M. Sissons and P. French, eds, *The Age of Austerity* (Hodder and Stoughton, London, 1963).
5 P. H. Newby, *The Novel 1945–1950* (London, 1951), cited in Randall Stevenson, *The British Novel since the Thirties* (B. T. Batsford, London, 1986) p. 116.
6 Cited in Garlake, *New Art New World*, p. 3.
7 Kathleen Raine, 'English Poetry at Mid-Century', in Richman, ed., *The Arts at Mid-Century*, p. 214.
8 The phrase is adapted from Eric Hobsbawn, *Age of Extremes. The Short Twentieth Century 1914–1991* (Abacus, London, 1995).
9 *The Complete Poems and Plays of T. S. Eliot*, (Faber & Faber, London) p. 202.
10 Gascoyne, *Collected Journals*, p. 200.
11 Gascoyne, 'Farewell Chorus', *Poems 1937–1942*, pp. 53–54.
12 Ibid., p. 54.
13 David Mellor, 'John Craxton: the Pastoral', Mellor, ed., *A Paradise Lost*, p. 40.
14 Geoffrey Grigson, 'Samuel Palmer: The Politics of an Artist', *Horizon*, no. 23, November 1941, pp. 314–28 (with reproductions of two 1825 drawings from the collection of the Ashmolean Museum).
15 Sutherland, postcard to Paul Nash, 16 September 1938, Paul Nash Papers, Tate.
16 Berthoud, *Graham Sutherland*, p. 90. A selection of the drawings that formed the basis for *Gorse on Sea Wall* was reproduced, with a date of 1938, amongst the illustrations accompanying 'Welsh Sketch Book' (p. 232).
17 See the five small sketchbook studies grouped together for the illustration in Sutherland, 'Welsh Sketch Book', p. 232.
18 Sutherland, 'Welsh Sketch Book', p. 235.
19 'Landscape and Figures: Graham Sutherland, O. M., discusses his art with Andrew Forge', *The Listener*, 26 July 1962, p. 133.
20 Melville, *Graham Sutherland*, n. p.
21 The list of exhibits includes, for example, a watercolour entitled 'Blasted Tree' (no. 17).
22 The importance of Picasso for Sutherland and Bacon is discussed in detail in chapter 3.
23 October 1938 text reprinted in Eric Newton, *In My View* (Longman, Green & Co., London, 1950) p. 85.
24 Sutherland, 'Images Wrought from Destruction', p. 4.
25 Sutherland, letter to Edward Sackville-West, 8 February 1941, Tate.
26 John Piper, 'Three Painters', *The Spectator*, 5 May 1940, p. 626. Piper was reviewing a show of Sutherland, Walter Sickert and Walter Goetz at the Leicester Galleries.
27 A. C. Sewter, 'Round the Art Exhibitions', *The Listener*, 16 May 1940, p. 980.
28 Eric Newton, 'Graham Sutherland', *Sunday Times*, 2 May 1940.
29 Cited in Herbert Read, *Wordsworth* (Jonathan Cape, London and Toronto, 1930) p. 55. Sutherland may well have known this book, given the admiration for Read's writings on art considered in chapter 3.
30 Ibid., p. 61.
31 *The Complete Poems and Plays of T. S. Eliot*, p. 24.
32 Kathleen Raine, 'The Poet of our Time', Richard March and Tambimuttu, eds, *T. S. Eliot* (Editions Poetry London, London, 1948) p. 78.
33 Edmund Wilson, *Axel's Castle* (William Collins, Glasgow, 1961, originally published in 1931) p. 96
34 Ibid., p. 90.
35 David Gascoyne, *Poems 1937–1942* (Nicholson and Watson, PL Editions, London, 1943).
36 For detailed factual information, see Alan Smith, 'Poetry London 1939–1951', reprinted in Jane Williams, ed, *Tambimuttu: Bridge Between Two Worlds* (Peter Owen, London, 1989) pp. 275–290. The books also included Kathleen Raine's first volume of verse *Stone and Flower* (1945), with illustrations from Barbara Hepworth, and Nicholas Moore's *The Glass Tower* (1945), for which Lucian Freud provided a set of drawings. They were beautifully printed by Oliver Simon, another Sutherland admirer, at the Curwen Press; see Kathleen Raine, *Autobiographies* (Skoob Books, London, 1991) p. 224.
37 David Gascoyne 'PL Editions and Graham Sutherland', reprinted in *David Gascoyne: Selected Prose 1934–1996* (Enitharmon, London, 1998) p. 263. Peter Watson had acquired the Sutherland from the one-man show at the Leicester Galleries in May 1940. According to Berthoud, Herbert Read had first suggested to Tambimuttu that Sutherland would be an appropriate artist to illustrate Gascoyne (Berthoud, *Graham Sutherland*, p. 108). Watson and Gascoyne had been close friends for some time, and met regularly in both London and Paris, where Gascoyne lived for long periods before the war. Gascoyne would stay for several weeks at a time in Watson's London flat (see Gascoyne, *Collected Journals*, e.g. pp. 233 and 277). Watson duly sent the manuscripts to Sutherland, who responded positively. He did eighteen drawings in all, and eight were eventually used, two separate images for the

front and back covers, a title page and frontispieces for the five sections into which Gascoyne had divided his poems (Cardiff). Sutherland presumably worked on the project during the latter part of 1942, given that the volume was advertised in the November/December 1942 issue of *Poetry London* (*Poetry London*, II: viii November and December 1942, recto of front cover). Publication problems meant it did not appear until January 1944 (Stephen Spender 'Lessons of Poetry 1943', *Horizon*, no. 51, March 1944, p. 212).

38 Gascoyne, 'PL Editions and Graham Sutherland', p. 263.

39 Ibid., p. 267.

40 *Poetry (London)* II: ix May 1943.

41 A. T. Tolley, *The Poetry of the Forties* (Manchester University Press, Manchesterm, 1985) p. 144. On Gascoyne's interest in Palmer see Gascoyne, *Collected Journals*, pp. 329–30.

42 Gascoyne, *Collected Journals*, p. 254 (entry for 16 August 1939).

43 Ibid., p 58.

44 It is, for instance, the poem by Gascoyne quoted at length in Stephen Spender, *Poetry since 1939*, pp. 148–49.

45 Ibid., p. 59.

46 Derek Stanford, *Inside the Forties: Literary Memoirs 1937–1957* (Sidgwick and Jackson, London, 1977), p. 110.

47 Ibid., p. 106.

48 Sylvester, *Looking back at Francis Bacon*, p. 22.

49 Berthoud, *Graham Sutherland*, p. 106.

50 Meirion and Susie Harries, *The War Artists* (Michael Joseph, London, 1983) p. 161.

51 See E. M. O'R. Dickey, Secretary to Artists' Advisory Committee, letter of invitation to Sutherland, 6 June 1940; Sutherland, letter to Dickey, 7 August 1940, IWM. For a useful account of Sutherland's war work, based on the documentary file at the IWM, see the chronology (pp. 62–64), and Julian Andrews, 'Graham Sutherland and the War Artists' Advisory Committee' (pp. 11–19) in *Sutherland: The War Drawings* (Imperial War Museum, London, 1982).

52 Harries, *The War Artists*, p. 186.

53 Raymond Mortimer, 'War Pictures. Exhibition at the Leicester Gallery', *New Statesman*, 1 June 1940.

54 Harries, *The War Artists*, p. 187.

55 Sutherland, letter to Dickey, 1 October 1940, IWM.

56 Sutherland, letter to Dickey, 16 May 1941, IWM. Several such photographs survive amongst the Sutherland archive in Cardiff.

57 Contracts, IWM.

58 Sutherland, 'Images Wrought from Destruction', p. 4.

59 Sutherland, letter to Edward Sackville-West, 8 February 1941, Tate.

60 Ibid., p. 154.

61 'Art and Life', *The Listener*, p. 657.

62 The terminological affinity between the two artists is also noted in Garlake, *New Art New World*, p. 191.

63 Sutherland, letter to Dickey, 16 May 1941, IWM.

64 Sutherland, 'Images Wrought from Destruction', p. 1.

65 Ibid., p. 8.

66 Sutherland, draft letter to Eric Newton at the time of the making of 'Out of Chaos', Cardiff.

67 John Piper, 'New War Pictures', *The Spectator*, 23 May 1941, reprinted David Fraser Jenkins, *John Piper. The Forties* (Philip Wilson, London, 2000) p. 50.

68 Ibid.

69 Cecil Beaton, 'Introduction', *Production. War Pictures by British Artists (Second Series, No. 2*, Oxford University Press, London, 1943) p. 6.

70 Stephen Spender, 'Introduction', *Air Raids. War Pictures by British Artists (Second Series No. 4*, Oxford University Press, London, 1943) p. 7.

71 Art Critic [Keith Vaughan], 'War Artists and the War', *The Penguin New Writing* no. 16 (Penguin Books, Harmondsworth, March, 1943) pp. 115–16.

72 Eric Newton, *War Through Artists' Eyes* (John Murray, London, 1945), p. 8. Five pictures by Sutherland featured in Newton's survey of the most effective products of the War Art project.

73 David Sylvester, 'Bacon's Course', *Figurabile: Francis Bacon*, pp. 19–20.

74 Bacon letter no. 1.

75 [Cyril Connolly], 'Comment', *Horizon*, No. 46, October 1943, pp. 221–22.

76 Cited in Peppiatt, *Francis Bacon*, p. 109.

77 Russell, *Francis Bacon*, p. 10.

78 Russell, *Francis Bacon*, p. 11.

79 R. Blythe, ed., *Components of the Scene* (Penguin, Harmondsworth, 1966) p. 117.

80 Anthony Penrose, ed., *Lee Miller's War* (Condé Nast, London, 1992).

81 Frank Prince, 'Soldiers Bathing', published in *Poetry (London)*, II: ix May 1943, pp. 31–32. The poem is quoted in full in S. Spender 'Poetry', R. Speaight, H. Reed, S. Spender and J. Hayward, *Since 1939* (Phoenix House, London, 1949), pp. 152–53. It appeared thereafter in several variants.

82 Quoted in Hermione Lee, *Elizabeth Bowen* (Vintage, London, 1999) p. 155.

83 Reprinted in Arthur Koestler, *The Yogi and the Commissar* (Collier Books, New York, 1961) p. 86. Koestler's 'The Mixed Transport', a fictionalized account of the Nazi's barbaric treatment of the Jews, had appeared in the October 1943 issue of *Horizon* (no. 46, pp. 242–52).

84 Arthur Koestler, 'The Mixed Transport', pp. 247–48.

85 Brighton, *Francis Bacon*, pp. 45–46.

86 See Alley and Rothenstein, *Francis Bacon*, Appendix A (abandoned pictures) for reproductions and information concerning *Man in a Cap* (A1), *Man Standing* (A2 verso) and *Landscape with Car* (A4).

87 Hunter, 'Francis Bacon: the Anatomy of Horror', p. 12.

88 Bacon's appropriation of photographic images of Nazi leaders is discussed in Davies, *Francis Bacon: The Early and Middle Years*, pp. 39–42.

89 Dublin, indicating the mass of such material that remained in the studio.

90 See Peter Pachnicke and Klaus Honnef, eds, *John Heartfield* (Harry Abrams, New York, 1993), pp. 26–27 and 310–12.

91 Hyman, *The Battle for Realism*, p. 100.

92 Gale, *Three Studies* draft catalogue entry, p. 18.

93 Sylvester, however, suggests that *Figure getting out of a Car* was probably executed around 1943 (Sylvester, *Looking Back at Francis* Bacon, p. 18). Gale summarises the available, contradictory evidence, including that of an unpublished Ph.D dissertation by David Boxer who cites Bacon's own statement that the picture postdated the *Three Studies*, justifying its dating to 1945 (*Three Studies* draft catalogue entry, pp. 17–18). *Figure getting out of a Car* was reworked around 1946 as *Landscape with Car*.

94 For the destroyed *Figure* Study, see Alley and Rothenstein, *Francis Bacon*, D1.

95 See Matthew Gale, *Francis Bacon: Working on Paper* (Tate Gallery, London, 1999).

96 *Francis Bacon in Conversation with Michel Archimbaud*, p. 150.

97 Orwell, 'Inside the Whale', reprinted in *Collected Essays, Journalism and Letters* I, ed. Sonia Orwell and Ian Angus (Penguin Books, Harmondsworth, 1970) p. 575.

98 ibid., p. 576.

99 Sylvester, *Interviews with Francis Bacon*, p. 81.

100 Bacon, letter to Sonia Orwell, 13 December 1954, Orwell papers, UCL. The letter was composed in a hotel in Rome.

101 T. S. Eliot, 'Ulysses, Order, and Myth' (1923), reprinted in Frank Kermode, ed., *Selected Prose of T. S. Eliot*, (Faber & Faber, London, 1975) pp. 177–78.

102 Edward Sackville-West, *The Rescue. A Melodrama for Broadcasting based on Homer's Odyssey* (Secker and Warburg, London, 1945). Moore and Sutherland were evidently considered as possible designers for Britten's *Peter Grimes*, first staged in June 1945 and arguably the most powerful musical expression of the current tragic aesthetic (see Peter Stansky and William Abrahams, *London's Burning*, Constable, London, 1994, p. 160). The eventual designer was Britten's old friend Kenneth Green. We know that Sutherland and Canon Hussey went together to see one of the early performances; Walter Hussey, *Patron of Art* (Weidenfield and Nicholson, London, 1985) pp. 52–53.

103 Cyril Connolly, *Palinurus. The Unquiet Grave* (Penguin, Harmondsworth, 1967) p. 12.

104 Gascoyne, *Poems 1937–42*, p. 12. See 'Gérard de Nerval's 'Chimeras', translated and with an introduction by Daniel Mark Epstein, *The New Criterion*, December 2000, pp. 31–43. Gascoyne's poem seems to be based on Sonnet II in the 'Christ on the Mount of Olives' sequence.

105 Norman Cohn, 'Gérard de Nerval', *Horizon*, IX, no. 50, 1944, p. 132 and 137. Cohn is best known as the author of *The Pursuit of the Millenium* (1957).

106 Ibid., p. 136.

107 Connolly, *Palinurus. The Unquiet Grave*, p. 90.

108 Along with more recent editions, Bacon's library included a 1924 edition of *The Complete Works of Nietzsche* (Dublin).

109 For a recent analytical survey of the survival and elaboration of tragedy, see Terry Eagleton, *Sweet Violence. The Idea of the Tragic* (Blackwell, Oxford, 2003).

110 George Orwell, 'Inside the Whale' (1940), p. 555.

111 George Steiner, *The Death of Tragedy* (Faber & Faber, London, 1963) p. 291.

112 Samuel Hynes, *The Auden Generation: Literature and Politics in England in the 1930s* (Faber & Faber, London), pp. 296–97.

113 Ibid., p. 339.

114 Cited in Robert Hewison's lively account of the period, *Under Seige: Literary Life in London 1939–45* (Weidenfield and Nicholson, London, 1977) p. 115.

115 Ibid., p. 137.

116 Kathleen Raine, 'Literature in the Modern World', in J. R. M. Brumwell, ed., *This Changing World* (George Routledge and Sons, London, 1945) p. 207.

117 Gilbert Murray, *Aeschylus: The Creator of Tragedy* (Oxford University Press, Oxford, 1940); David Anfam, *Mark Rothko: The Works on Canvas* (Yale University Press, New Haven and London, 1999) pp. 47 and 50.

118 Robert Melville, 'Graham Sutherland', *World Review*, February 1952, pp. 61–62 and 64. The reference is to W. B. Stanford, *Aeschylus in his Style* (Dublin University Press, Dublin, 1942).

119 Sackville-West, *Graham Sutherland*, p. 5.

120 Stanford, *Aeschylus in his Style*, p. 91.

121 Sackville-West, *Graham Sutherland*, pp. 11–12.

122 *Francis Bacon in Conversation with Michel Archimbaud*, p. 112.

123 Dublin.

124 Neville Wallis, 'Francis Bacon', *The Observer*, 29 September 1950 p. 6, a review of *Francis Bacon: Recent Paintings*, Hanover Gallery, London, 14 September–21 October 1950. The invitations to the show made reference to 'Three Studies from the Painting of Innocent X by Velasquez' (Hanover Gallery archive, Tate). However these were withdrawn by the artist at the last minute, and other works substituted.

125 See Davies, *Francis Bacon: the Early and Middle Years*, pp. 51–56; Ades, 'Web of Images', pp. 19–21; Peppiatt, *Francis Bacon*, pp. 89–92.

126 The line occurs in Stanford, *Aeschylus in his Style*, p. 109.

127 Sylvester, *Looking Back at Francis Bacon*, p. 21.

128 Ibid.

129 Stanford, *Aeschylus in his Style*, p. 57.

130 A phrase from Stanford's characterisation of the 'voice of antiquity on Aeschylus's style' (Ibid., pp. 12–13).

131 Ibid., p. 86.

132 Ibid., p. 130.

133 Ibid., p. 129.

134 Ibid., p. 128.

135 Ibid., p. 55.
136 Peppiatt, *Francis Bacon*, p. 92.
137 Alley and Rothenstein, *Francis Bacon,* citing a letter from Bacon dated 9 January 1959 (p. 35).
138 Aeschylus, *The Oresteia. A New Translation by Ted Hughes* (Faber & Faber, London, 1999) pp. 152–53. Some of this passage, in Robert Fagles' 1970s translation, is compared to the *Three Studies* in Ades, 'Web of Images', p. 13.
139 Ibid., p. 159.
140 This connection is discussed in Peppiatt, *Francis Bacon*, pp. 89–90.
141 Ibid., p. 328, n. 9.
142 Peter Ackroyd, *T. S. Eliot* (London, Abacus, 1985), p. 245.
143 Maud Bodkin, 'The Eumenides and Present-Day Consciousness', *Adelphi*, May 1939, pp. 411–13, reprinted in Michael Grant, ed., *T. S. Eliot: The Critical Heritage* II (Routledge and Kegan Paul, London, 1982) p. 386. Bodkin's view was elaborated in her 1941 book *The Quest for Salvation in an Ancient and Modern Play*.
144 *The Complete Plays and Poems of T. S. Eliot*, p. 335.
145 For example, see Sylvester, *Interviews with Francis Bacon*, p. 22 and 65.
146 Ibid., p. 22.
147 Ibid., p. 21.
148 Ibid., p. 84.
149 My own reading is in accord with the 'transition' described in Ziva Amishai-Maisels, *Depiction and Interpretation. The Influence of the Holocaust on the Visual Arts* (Pergamon Press, Oxford, New York, Seoul, Tokyo, 1993) p. 190.
150 Aeschylus, *The Oresteia: A New Translation*, pp. 111–12.
151 Edward Mendelson, ed., *W. H. Auden. Selected Poems* (Faber & Faber, London, 1979) p. 86.
152 Alan Moorehead, 'Glimpses of Germany II – Belsen', *Horizon*, no. 67, July 1945, p. 31.
153 See Amishai-Maisels, *Depiction and Interpretation*, pp. 178–97.
154 Blythe, *Components of the Scene*, p. 62.
155 Guttoso is quoted in Enrico Crispolti, 'Guttoso, Crucifixion', *The Body on the Cross*, (Musée Picasso, Paris, 1993) p. 107; Benton's *Again* is reproduced in Stephen Polcari, *Abstract Expressionism and the Modern Experience* (Cambridge University Press, Cambridge, 1991) p. 21.
156 Keith Bell, *Stanley Spencer: A Complete Catalogue of the Paintings* (Phaidon, London, 1992) p. 476
157 See, for example, de Maistre's *Crucifixion* (1942–44), Leicester City Art Gallery.
158 Stephen Spender, *The Thirties and After* (Collins, Glasgow, 1978) p. 96.
159 Michel and Fox, *Wyndham Lewis on Art*, p. 373.
160 George Steiner has asserted that Christianity is inherently 'an anti-tragic vision of the world', since the sorrow experienced by believers in the contemplation of Christ's death on the cross serves, ultimately, as the bridge to redemption and eternal salvation; see Steiner, *The Death of Tragedy*, pp. 331–32. This position is disputed in Eagleton, *Sweet Violence*, pp. 37–39.
161 Robert Melville Papers, Tate.
162 See Christian Heck, 'Between Myth and Model: Grünewald's *Crucifixions* and Twentieth-Century Art', *The Body on the Cross*, pp. 84–106. This very useful outline locates the beginning of avant-garde appropriations in Huysman's novel *Là-Bas* (1891), with its description of the Grünewald *Crucifixion* now in Karlsruhe. A complementary study by Frances Carey has emphasised the pervasiveness of a secularised apocalyptic imagery of the end of the world and Last Judgment in the modernist imagination. She traces its unfolding through figures such as Baudelaire and Nietzche, the symbolist and expressionist movements, and onwards through to more recent manifestations. See Frances Carey, 'The Apocalyptic Imagination: between Tradition and Modernity', *The Apocalypse and the Shape of Things to Come* (British Museum, London, 1999) pp. 270–96. Characteristically, such themes served to articulate an attitude of profound despair in the face of the cataclysms and upheavals of the modern era. It is the world of the here and now which is heading for disintegration; redemption, if envisaged at all, will eventually take the form of socialism, a new spirituality, or some other earthly occurrence that will restore order.
163 Cork, *A Bitter Truth*, pp. 181–82.
164 Christian Zervos, *Matthias Grünewald – Le Retable d'Issenheim* (Cahiers d'Art, Paris, 1936). The publication is set into a wider context in Andrée Hayum, *The Isenheim Altarpiece: God's Medicine and the Painter's Vision* (Princeton University Press, Princeton, 1989) chapter IV ('Afterlife of a Monument').
165 Zervos, 'Actualité de Grünewald', Ibid., p. 1.
166 Herbert Read, 'Picasso's *Guernica*', *London Bulletin*, no. 6, October 1938, p. 6.
167 Marcus Whiffen, 'Graham Sutherland's "Crucifixion"', *Architectural Review,* London, no. 603, March 1947, pp. 105–7.
168 This point is also made by Melville in the introduction to his 1950 monograph (n. p.).
169 A reproduction featured in the montage accompanying Hunter, 'Francis Bacon: the Anatomy of Horror', p. 12.
170 Peppiatt, *Francis Bacon*, p. 87. The two passages are juxtaposed in *The Body on the Cross*, p. 96.
171 Michel Remy, *David Gascoyne, ou l'urgence de l'exprimé* (Presses Universitaires de Nancy, Nancy, 1984) p. 124.
172 Gascoyne, *Poems 1937–42*, p. 5.
173 Gascoyne, *Collected Journals 1936–42*, p. 243.
174 Tolley, *The Poetry of the Forties*, p. 143.
175 Ibid., p. 141.
176 Gascoyne *Poems 1937–42*, p. 1.
177 Ibid., pp. 3–4. Gascoyne himself connected Sutherland's illustration to these two poems ('PL Editions and Graham Sutherland', p. 264).
178 *Poems 1937–42*, p. 7.

179 It enjoyed the distinction of going into three editions by 1948.
180 Raine, *Autobiographies*, p. 224.
181 Spender, 'Lessons of Poetry 1943', p. 212.
182 Ibid., p. 212.
183 Ibid., p. 209.
184 Newton, *In My View*, p. 117.
185 Roberto Tassi, 'A Descent into the Inferno', in Tassi, *Sutherland: the Wartime Drawings*, p. 15.
186 Ibid., p. 16.
187 Gascoyne, 'PL Editions and Graham Sutherland', pp. 263–64.
188 John Rothenstein, *Brave Day Hideous Night* (Hamish Hamilton, London, 1966) pp. 135–36.
189 Walter Hussey, *Patron of Art* (Weidenfield and Nicholson, London, 1985) p. 50.
190 Ibid., p. 50. The story of the genesis of the commission is also recounted in Berthoud, *Graham Sutherland*, pp. 113–14.
191 Keith Vaughan, *Journal and Drawings* (Alan Ross, London, 1966) pp. 82–83.
192 Sutherland, letter to Hussey, 3 October 1944, cited in Hussey, *Patron of Art*, pp. 51–52.
193 Sutherland, letter to Hussey, 30 May 1945, cited in Hussey, *Patron of Art* p. 52.
194 Graham Sutherland, letter to Curt Valentin dated 1–24–1946, in *Graham Sutherland*, Buchholz Gallery, New York, 26 February–23 March 1946, n. p.
195 This development is discernible in the progression between the versions acquired by Kenneth Clark and the British Council (see Alley, *Graham Sutherland,* nos. 124–25).
196 Stanford, *Aeschylus in his Style*, p. 129.
197 Marvell, 'New Pictures', p. 119. The quotation is from Shelley's 'Ode to the West Wind'.
198 Cooper, *The Work of Graham Sutherland*, plate 78a.
199 Berthoud, *Graham* Sutherland, pp. 120–21.
200 See also the comments to Robert Melville cited in Garlake, *New Art New World*, p. 266, n. 57.
201 Martin Gilbert, *The Holocaust: The Jewish Tragedy* (Fontana, London, 1987) pp. 793–96.
202 Hussey, *Patron of Art*, pp. 54–55, quoting from Hans Feibusch's *Mural Painting*.
203 Sutherland, letter to Hussey, 19 August 1946, Hussey, *Patron of Art,* pp. 55–56.
204 Ibid., p. 58.
205 Andrew Sinclair records, presumably on the basis of information from the artist, that Bacon saw cinema newsreels about the Nazi death camps (*Francis Bacon: His Life and Violent Times*, p. 99).
206 Sutherland, 'Images Wrought from Destruction', p. 153.
207 Benedict Nicholson, 'Graham Sutherland's "Crucifixion"', *Magazine of Art* XL, November 1947, p. 29.
208 Melville, 'A Panorama of Modern Art', p. 45.
209 Ibid.
210 For a general discussion of this group of works, see Peppiatt, *Francis Bacon*, chapter 4.
211 Farson, *The Gilded Gutter Life*, p. 37.
212 Reproduced in *1900* (Royal Academy, London, 2000) p. 305.
213 Sylvester, *Interviews with Francis Bacon,* p. 197.
214 *Seventh Exhibition: Adler, Bacon, Colquhoun, Hubert, MacBryde, Trevelyan*, Anglo-French Art Centre, London, November–December 1946 (6–8).
215 *Francis Bacon, Paintings*, Hanover Gallery, November–December 1949 (1–3).
216 Alley and Rothenstein, *Francis Bacon*, p. 35.
217 Sylvester, *Interviews with Francis Bacon,* p. 112.
218 Ralf Lassøe, 'Francis Bacon's Crucifixions and Related Themes', *Hafnia* (Copenhagen), no. 11, 1987, pp. 7–38.
219 Ibid., pp. 28–29.
220 Spender, 'Poetry', in *Since 1939*. p. 152.
221 Sylvester, *Interviews*, p. 44 and 46.
222 *Francis Bacon in Conversation with Michel Archimbaud*, p. 153.
223 Ibid., p. 170.
224 Stanford, *Aeschylus in his Style*, p. 109.
225 Alley and Rothenstein, *Francis Bacon*, p. 39.
226 Sutherland, 'Thoughts on Painting', p. 71.
227 The phrase is Sylvester's (*Looking Back at Francis Bacon*, p. 30).
228 Ibid., p. 30.
229 Sutherland, 'Images Wrought from Destruction', p. 2.
230 Sutherland, 'Thoughts on Painting', p. 73.
231 Graham Sutherland, 'An English Stone Landmark', in Myfanwy Evans, ed., *The Painter's Object* (Gerald Howe, London, 1937) pp. 36–37.
232 Soby, *Contemporary Painters,* p. 136.
233 Sackville-West, *Graham Sutherland*, plate 6.
234 First published in 1933. The same passage is juxtaposed with Sutherland's work in Yorke, *The Spirit of Place*, p. 119.
235 Art Critic [Keith Vaughan], 'War Artists and the War', *The Penguin New Writing* XVI (Penguin, Harmondsworth, March 1943) pp. 115–16.
236 Sutherland, 'Thoughts on Painting', pp. 74–75.
237 On the wider context, see Stephen Frosh, 'Psychoanalysis in Britain: "The Rituals of Destruction"', David Bradshaw, ed., *A Concise Companion to Modernism* (Blackwell, Oxford, 2003) pp. 116–137.
238 *Francis Bacon in Conversation with Michel Archimbaud*, p. 84.
239 Sutherland, 'An English Stone Landmark', p. 8.
240 Soby, *Contemporary Painters,* p. 136.
241 Cited in Anthony Storr, *Freud* (Oxford University Press, Oxford, 1989) p. 53.
242 Wishart's autobiography is quoted in Peppiatt *Francis Bacon*, p. 105. See R. Lassøe, 'Francis Bacon and T. S. Eliot', *Hafnia*, 1983, pp. 113–30.
243 David Sylvester, *About Modern Art: Critical Essays 1948–97* (Pimlico, London, 1997) p. 174.
244 Sylvester, *Interviews*, p. 152.
245 Wilson, *Axel's Castle*, p. 86.

246 David Mellor, 'Francis Bacon: Affinities, Contexts', p. 97. Lassøe draws an illuminating analogy with Marlow's account of his first confrontation with Kurtz in *Heart of Darkness* ('Francis Bacon's Crucifixions and Related Themes', pp. 36–37, n. 40).
247 See Frank Rutter, 'The Galleries: Velasquez', *The Sunday Times,* 3 January 1937; A. D. B. (David) Sylvester, 'A Chapter of Revelations', *The Penguin New Writing* XIII (Penguin Books, London, 1948) p. 101.
248 Eric Newton's review from June 1945 was reprinted in *In My View.*
249 Lawrence Alloway, 'Introduction', *Francis Bacon*, Solomon R. Guggenheim Museum, New York, 1963, p. 14.
250 Ibid., p. 17.
251 Sylvester notes that this was the case with the photograph of *Figure getting out of a Car* (*Looking Back at Francis Bacon*, pp. 22–4). In the *Horizon* plates there is a clear reflection of the head of the photographer in the reproduction of *Study for a Portrait.*
252 *Francis Bacon in Conversation with Michel Archimbaud,* p. 167.
253 Hunter, 'Francis Bacon: the Anatomy of Horror', p. 12.
254 Joseph Conrad, *Heart of Darkness* (1902; Penguin Books, Harmondsworth, 1973) pp. 71–72 and 82.
255 Ibid., p. 100.
256 Richard Ingleby, Jonathon Black, David Cohen, Gordon Cooke, *C. R. W. Nevinson. The Twentieth Century* (Merrell Holberton, London, 1999) p. 51.
257 Benedict Nicolson, *Ten Decades,* ICA, London, 1951.
258 See Richard Thomson, *Monet to Matisse: Landscape Painting in France 1874–1914,* National Galleries of Scotland, Edinburgh, chapters 5 and 6; and Kenneth Silver, *Making Paradise: Art, Modernity and the Myth of the French Riviera* (MIT Press, Cambridge, Mass., and London, 2001). On Knollys, see Berthoud, *Graham Sutherland*, p. 132.
259 Raymond Mortimer, 'Graham Sutherland's New Paintings', *Harper's Bazaar*, July 1948, p. 71. As if in confirmation of Mortimer's interpretation, Robert Melville subsequently noted the presence on Sutherland's bookshelves of Catholic authors such as Maritain, Mauriac, Greene, Waugh and Claudel. In their reported conversation, the artist acknowledged his religious faith, though he refused to speculate about its direct effect on his work (Melville, 'Graham Sutherland', p. 63).
260 Mortimer, 'Graham Sutherland's New Paintings', p. 71.
261 Geoffrey Grigson, 'Authentic and False in the New "Romanticism"', *Horizon*, no. 99, March 1948, pp. 203–13.
262 Ibid., p. 213. In the same year, Grigson published an admiring monograph on Craxton (Geoffrey Grigson, *John Craxton: Paintings and Drawings* [Horizon, London, 1948]).
263 Ibid., p. 205 and 206–7.
264 Ibid., p. 209.
265 Ibid., p. 208.
266 I have used the Penguin edition of 1956. Clark remarked (p. 15) that the relevant lectures had been given during the first year of his Slade Professorship (1946–50).
267 Ibid., p. 150
268 Ibid., p. 151.
269 Ibid., p. 152.
270 Ibid.
271 Ibid.
272 Michel and Fox, *Wyndham Lewis on Art*, p. 394.
273 Wallis, 'Francis Bacon', p. 6.
274 Russell, *Francis Bacon*, p. 38.
275 Gascoyne, *Poems 1937–42*, p. 55.
276 Both were members of the Gargoyle Club, and Bacon was a regular visitor after the war to Farley Farm. Miller's husband Roland Penrose acquired a painting, and wrote the catalogue preface for Bacon's 1957 show at the Rive Droite Gallery in Paris; see Roland Penrose, *Scrap Book 1900–1981* (Thames and Hudson, London, 1981) pp. 234–5.
277 Penrose *Lee Miller's War*, p. 17.
278 Ibid., p. 165.
279 I am grateful to Richard Calvocoressi for this observation.
280 Albert Votav, 'The Literature of Extreme Situations', *Horizon*, no. 117, 1949, p. 153 and 157.
281 [Cyril Connolly], 'Comment', *Horizon*, nos 120–21, December 1949–January 1950, pp. 359–62.

INFLUENCES

1 The obvious examples include Harrison, *English Art and Modernism 1900–1939* (Allen Lane, London, 1981), pp. 319–24; Yorke, *The Spirit of Place*, Chapter Three; Mellor, *A Paradise Lost*; Garlake, *New Art New World*, chapter 4.
2 Sylvester, *Interviews with Francis Bacon*, p. 9.
3 Ades, 'Web of Images', pp. 12–15 and 18–19.
4 David Mellor, 'Francis Bacon: Affinities, Contexts and the British Visual Tradition', in Achille Bonito Oliva, ed., *Francis Bacon: Figurabile* (Museo Correr, Venice, 1993) pp. 95–104.
5 See Edward Sackville-West, 'Radio Notes', Michael Ayrton, 'The Influence of Picasso', and Graham Sutherland, 'Influence of Picasso', *The New Statesman and Nation*, XXIX, 1945, pp. 207 (31 March), 242 (14 April) and 274 (28 April) respectively. There is also a description of the heated exchange in Sutherland, letter to Edward Sackville-West, 10 April 1945, Tate.
6 Graham Sutherland, 'English Painting', *The New Statesman and Nation*, XXXIII, no. 831, 25 January 1947, p. 74.
7 The wisest account of 'influence' remains Michael Baxandall, *Patterns of Intention* (Yale University Press, New Haven and London, 1985), especially pp. 58–62.
8 Alley, *Graham Sutherland*, p. 77.
9 Ibid. *Red Tree* is listed as belonging to Kenneth Clark in the Rosenberg and Helft catalogue no. 2.
10 *British Contemporary Art*, Rosenberg and Helft, London,

January–February 1937, no. 29. This identification is made by Chris Stephens, unpublished Tate Gallery catalogue entry on *Welsh Landscape with Roads* (no. 5666). I am very grateful to Dr. Stephens for showing me his draft entries on the Tate's important collection of Sutherlands. The argument is reinforced by Sutherland's letter to Kenneth Clark seeking advice about whether to include the picture, now finished but seen by Clark at an incomplete stage, which is identified by a marginal sketch of *Welsh Landscape with Roads* (n.d. [December 1936], Tate).

11 Sutherland's archive contains a rather battered reproduction of what looks like an elaboration in paint of the idiom of the later etchings from around 1930 (Cardiff).

12 Graham Sutherland, 'A Trend in English Draughtsmanship' and 'Graven Images: Line Engraving and the Illustrated Book', *Signature*, respectively nos 3, pp. 7–13, and 6, pp. 28–34. Sutherland's relations with Simon and his presence in *Signature* are covered in Pat Gilmour, *Artists at Curwen* (Tate Gallery, London, 1977) pp. 35–37 and 80–84.

13 Andrew Causey, 'Introduction', *Paul Nash. Writings on Art* (Oxford University Press, Oxford, 2000) p. 26.

14 Sutherland, 'An English Stone Landmark', pp. 89–93.

15 Berthoud, *Graham Sutherland*, p. 76.

16 Nigel Vaux Halliday, *More than a Bookshop. Zwemmer's and Art in the Twentieth century* (Oxford University Press, Oxford, 1991) p. 304.

17 See *Landscape in Britain 1850–1950*, Arts Council of Great Britain, 1983; Valentine Cunningham, *British Writers of the Thirties* (Oxford University Press, Oxford 1988), p. 228ff.

18 Eiluned and Peter Lewis, *The Land of Wales* (Batsford, London, 1937) p. 3.

19 Ibid., p. 34.

20 Sutherland, 'Welsh Sketchbook', p. 225.

21 Paul Fussell, *Abroad* (Oxford University Press, Oxford, 1980).

22 Robert Hughes, *American Visions* (Harvill, London, 1997) p. 388.

23 Raymond Mortimer, 'An Arrival', *New Statesman and Nation*, XVI, 1 October 1938, p. 490.

24 Sutherland, 'An English Stone Landmark', p. 91.

25 Sutherland, 'Welsh Sketchbook', p. 225.

26 Ibid., p. 225.

27 Ibid., p. 226.

28 Ibid., p. 230.

29 Ibid., p. 230.

30 Ibid., p. 230.

31 Ibid., p. 235.

32 Ibid., p. 234.

33 Ibid., p. 234.

34 See Stephens, unpublished Tate Gallery catalogue entry on *Welsh Landscape with Roads*.

35 Sutherland, 'Welsh Sketchbook', p. 230.

36 Ibid., p. 235.

37 Sutherland, 'A Trend in English Draughtsmanship', p. 12.

38 Henry Moore, 'Notes on Sculpture', in Evans, *The Painter's Object*, pp. 21–29.

39 'Art and Life'.

40 Ibid., p. 234.

41 Ibid., p. 230.

42 Berthoud, *Graham Sutherland*, p. 82.

43 Sutherland, 'An English Stone Landmark', p. 92.

44 John Russell, 'Introduction', *John Piper* (Tate Gallery, London, 1983), p. 13.

45 D. H. Lawrence, *Sea and Sardinia* (Penguin, Harmondsworth, 1944) p. 78 (originally published in 1923).

46 D. H. Lawrence, 'The Spinner and the Monks' (1916), *Selected Essays* (Penguin, Harmondsworth, 1950) p. 138.

47 Ibid., p. 62.

48 *An Exhibition of Drawings, Etchings and Woodcuts, by Samuel Palmer & Other Disciples of William Blake*, Victoria and Albert Museum, London, 1926.

49 'Landscape and Figures', p. 132.

50 Sutherland, 'A Trend in English Draughtsmanship', pp. 7 and 11.

51 Ibid., p. 11.

52 Ibid., p. 11.

53 John Piper, *British Romantic Artists* (Collins, London), p. 48 and facing p. 41.

54 Anon. [Kenneth Clark], 'Graham Sutherland', Rosenberg and Helft Gallery, *Graham Sutherland*, 1938, n. p.

55 Kenneth Clark, 'Constable, Prophet of Impressionism', R. S. Lambert, ed., *Art in England*, (Penguin, Harmondsworth, 1938) p. 35.

56 Ibid., p. 41.

57 Ibid., pp. 42–43.

58 Sutherland, letter to Kenneth Clark, 14 September 1'936, Tate.

59 Sutherland, letter to Kenneth Clark, 7 September 1938, Tate.

60 Sutherland, letter to Kenneth Clark, 13 July 1939, Tate.

61 Sutherland, letter to Kenneth Clark, 26 November 1939, Tate.

62 Sutherland, letter to Kenneth Clark, 27 December 1939?, Tate.

63 Sackville-West, *Graham Sutherland*, 1944, pp. 9 and 10.

64 Ibid., p. 10.

65 Sutherland, letter to Sackville-West, 20 April 1942, Tate.

66 *The Tate Gallery's Wartime Acquisitions*, National Gallery, London, April–May 1942, nos 135 (Sutherland) and 8, 10 and 11 (Blake).

67 Sutherland, 'Welsh Sketchbook', p. 230.

68 Sutherland, letter to Keith Vaughan, 7 February 1943, cited in Berthoud, *Graham Sutherland*, p. 108.

69 See Alan Powers, 'The Reluctant Romantics: *Axis* Magazine 1935–37', in David Corbett, Ysanne Holt and Fiona Russell, eds, *The Geographies of Englishness: Landscape and the National Past 1880–1940* (Yale University Press, New Haven and London, 2002) pp.

264–65.

70 Geoffrey Grigson, *Samuel Palmer. The Visionary Years* (Kegan Paul, London, 1947) p. xi.

71 Ibid., pp. ix and 176–77. The catalogue entry indicates that *Cornfield by Moonlight, with the Evening Star* had been acquired by Clark in 1929.

72 Ibid., pp. 171–72 (No. 67). Clark is given as the previous owner, and it seems likely that he would have given the drawing to Sutherland. The work was subsequently donated by Kathleen Sutherland to the British Museum, along with two late Palmer prints that Sutherland owned.

73 Ibid., p. 170 (No. 61).

74 Piper, *British Romantic Artists*, facing p. 32 (as *Harvest Moon*).

75 For a valuable account of the early etchings and the elements of continuity with Sutherland's mature art, see *Graham Sutherland: The Early Years 1921–40* (Goldsmiths' Gallery, London, 1986; text by Nanette Aldred).

76 'Dialogue with the Artist', *John Craxton: Paintings and Drawings 1941–1966* (Whitechapel Art Gallery, London, 1967) p. 9.

77 Keith Vaughan, 'A View of English Painting', *The Penguin New Writing*, no. 31, 1947, p. 144.

78 Bacon letter no. 7.

79 Harrison, *English Art and Modernism*, chapter 9.

80 The recent sympathetic rediscovery of this outlook is evident from several revisionist accounts in Corbett, Holt and Russell, *The Geographies of Englishness*.

81 See Andrew Causey, 'English Art and "The National Character", 1933–34', in ibid., pp. 275–302.

82 There is a useful chronology of Read's activities and publications in Benedict Read and David Thistlewood, eds, *Herbert Read: A British Vision of World Art* (Leeds City Art Gallery, Leeds, 1993) pp. 146–166.

83 Sutherland, 'A Trend in English Draughtsmanship', p. 7.

84 Tate.

85 Read, *Art Now*, plates 60–61, 98–99, 102–107, 116–19. The Picasso/Bacon pages are illustrated in Brighton, *Francis Bacon*, p. 28.

86 Berthoud, *Graham Sutherland*, p. 87.

87 See Read, *Art Now*, p. 99, with pencil annotations. On the origins of the subjective/objective dichotomy, see W. H. Abrams *The Mirror and the Lamp: Romantic Theory and the Critical Tradition* (Oxford University Press, Oxford, 1953).

88 Herbert Read, *In Defence of Shelley & Other Essays* (William Heinemann, London and Toronto, 1936) pp. 160–61.

89 Read, *Art Now*, p. 140.

90 My discussion of Read in connection with Sutherland has been stimulated by Chris Stephen's alignment of Read and Ben Nicholson, and his subtle realisation of a concern to 'see an English cultural identity informing and shaping the development and reception of modernism in Britain in the inter-war period' (Chris Stephens, 'Ben Nicholson: Modernism, Craft and the English Vernacular', in Corbett, Holt and Russell, *The Geographies of Englishness*, pp. 225–47).

91 Herbert Read, 'English Art', in *The Philosophy of Modern Art* (Faber & Faber, London 1952) pp. 250 and 260 (reprinted from *The Burlington Magazine* LXIII, December 1933). The essay was also reprinted in *In Defence of Shelley*.

92 Herbert Read, *The English Vision: an Anthology* (Eyre and Spottiswoode, London, 1933).

93 Ibid., pp. vi–vii.

94 Ibid., p. vii.

95 Ibid., pp. vi–vii.

96 On Nash's commitment to nature, see Andrew Causey, *Paul Nash* (Clarendon Press, Oxford 1980) p. 112.

97 The two Nashes are reproduced in Causey, *Paul Nash*, pp. 152 and 171.'

98 Paul Nash, 'New Draughtsmanship', *Signature*, no. 1, November 1935, pp. 28–29.

99 Sutherland, 'A Trend in English Draughtsmanship', p. 12.

100 Nash's dialogue with European art is illuminated by Causey, *Paul Nash*, *passim*.

101 Causey, 'Introduction', *Paul Nash: Writings on Art*, p. 12.

102 Reprinted in Ibid., p. 108.

103 Ibid.

104 See Michel Remy, *Surrealism in Britain*, (Ashgate, Aldershot, 1999); *Roland Penrose. Lee Miller. The Surrealist and the Photographer* (Scottish National Gallery of Modern Art, Edinburgh, 2001).

105 Ibid., p. 131, and also *Paul Nash*, pp. 262–63.

106 Herbert Read, 'Introduction', *The International Surrealist Exhibition*, New Burlington Galleries, London, 11 June–4 July 1936, p. 13.

107 Alley, *Graham Sutherland*, nos 45–46.

108 Evans, *The Painter's Object*, pp. 83 and 89.

109 Remy, *Surrealism in Britain*.

110 'Graham Sutherland Explains his Art', *Illustrated London News*, CCXVIII, 19 February 1966, p. 30.

111 See Jennifer Mundy, ed., *Surrealism: Desire Unbound* (Tate, London, 2001) p. 96.

112 Herbert Read 'Introduction', in H. Read, ed., *Surrealism*, p. 64.

113 Paul Nash, 'Foreword', *Watercolours, Drawings, Collages and Objects by Paul Nash*, Redfern Gallery, London, April 29–May 29 1937, n.p. Nash's use of the natural found object is discussed in Causey, *Paul Nash*, p. 253ff.

114 For a wide-ranging discussion of this phenomenon in British culture, see Sam Smiles, 'Equivalents for the Megaliths', in Corbett, Holt and Russell, *The Geographies of Englishness*, pp. 199–224.

115 Myfanwy Evans, 'Paul Nash, 1937', *Axis*, no. 8, Early Winter 1937, pp. 12–13.

116 Ibid., p. 12.

117 For a useful account of Sutherland's design work, see Alley, *Graham Sutherland*.

118 Evans, 'Paul Nash, 1937', p. 12.

119 'Landscape and Figures', p. 132.

120 Yorke, *The Spirit of Place*, p. 307.

121 For a recent discussion of these works, see David Lomas, *The Haunted Self: Surrealism, Psychoanalysis, Subjectivity* (Yale University Press, New Haven and London) pp. 42–44.

122 *Exhibition of Works by André Masson*, Wildenstein Gallery, London, 12 February to 6 March 1936.

123 No. 19 in catalogue. See Francoise Levaillant, ed., *André Masson. Les Années Surréalistes. Correspondence 1916–1942* (La Manufacture, Paris, 1990), p. 241, n. 4.

124 Ibid., p. 361, reprinting Masson's letter to D. H. Kahnweiler [February 1937], recalling the favourable impression Clark had made on him in London. See also William Rubin and Carolyn Lanchner, *André Masson* (The Museum of Modern Art, New York, 1976), p. 215.

125 Ibid., p. 362, n. 7. See the entry on *Ibdes in Aragon* in Ronald Alley, *Catalogue of the Tate Gallery's Collection of Modern Art other than works by British Artists* (Tate Gallery and Sotheby Parke Bernet, London), pp. 489–90.

126 Causey, *Paul Nash: Writings on Art*, pp. 28–29.

127 Robert Rosenblum, *Modern Painting and the Northern Romantic Tradition* (Thames and Hudson, London, 1975).

128 Ibid., pp. 162–72.

129 Karin von Maur, 'Max Ernst and Romanticism', Werner Spies, ed., *Max Ernst: A Retrospective* (Tate Gallery, London 1991) p. 346.

130 Ibid., p. 342.

131 Madeleine Landsberg, 'Caspar David Friedrich. Peintre de l'Angoisse Romantique', *Minotaure*, Nos 12–13, May 1939, pp. 25–28.

132 Lomas, *The Haunted Self*, p. 195.

133 Pierre Mabille, 'William Blake' and Katherine Raine, 'Notes sur Blake créatur de mythes', *Cahiers d'Art*, 1947, pp. 117–34.

134 Causey, *Paul Nash: Writings on Art*, pp. 61–63.

135 Ibid., p. 62.

136 One of the few studies even to broach this terrain is Charles Harrison, 'The Effects of Landscape', in W. J. T. Mitchell, ed., *Landscape and Power* (University of Chicago Press, Chicago, 1994) pp. 203–40. He aptly remarks that 'an international show of landscape painting from 1920 to 1945 would be very intriguing' (p. 237, n. 23).

137 In 1938 Mortimer noted 'greys and browns reminiscent of Braque in their severe refinement' ('An Arrival', p. 450).

138 Catalogue and letter from Rosenberg and Helft Gallery to Sutherland, 22 May 1939, thanking him for visiting the show, and indicating the possibility of a joint show with Moore in September (Cardiff). The argument that *Welsh Mountains* was shown in the Rosenberg and Helft Gallery show is presented in Alley, *Graham Sutherland*, p. 80.

139 *André Masson, Recent Works*, Mayor Gallery, London, 8–26 March 1938.

140 A common derivation from the work of Ernst probably underlies the interesting affinities between *Red Monolith* and paintings by the future abstract expressionist Clyfford Still from the early 1940s.

141 *100 Years of Art in Britain*, Leeds City Art Gallery, Leeds, p. 97.

142 See Alley, *Catalogue of the Tate Gallery's Collection of Modern Art*, pp. 380–81.

143 'Conversation with Picasso', in Evans, *The Painter's Object*, pp. 81–88. The interview had originally been published in the special 1935 issue of *Cahiers d'Art* devoted to Picasso 1930–35.

144 Ibid., p. 84.

145 See *Picasso in British Collections*, London Gallery, London, May 1939; Roland Penrose, *Lee Miller: The Surrealist and the Photographer*.

146 Gertrude Stein, *Picasso*, 1938, with inscription by Clark (Cardiff).

147 For the work's exhibition history, see Hershel B. Chipp, *Picasso's Guernica* (Thames and Hudson, London, 1989) pp. 156–59.

148 Read, 'Picasso's *Guernica*', p. 6.

149 Leiris' comments from *Cahiers d' Art*, nos 4–5, 1937.

150 Connolly, *Palinurus. The Unquiet Grave*, p. 121.

151 Berthoud, *Graham Sutherland*, p. 92.

152 *Cahiers d'Art*, nos 4–5, 1937.

153 Ibid., plate 53.

154 Sutherland, *Images Wrought from Destraction*, p. 8.

155 Kenneth Clark, 'Recent Paintings by Picasso', *The Listener*, 9 March 1939, pp. 517–18.

156 Sutherland, letter to Clark, 'Sunday' [March 1939], Clark papers, Tate.

157 *Cahiers d'Art*, nos 3–10, 1938, illustrations pp. 81–136.

158 Ibid. The numerous illustrations are accompanied by Christian Zervos, 'Tableaux Magiques de Picasso' (pp. 73–80) and Paul Eluard's poem 'A Pablo Picasso' (pp. 137–40).

159 Raymond Mortimer, 'Notes on Shows', *The New Statesman and Nation*, CXIX, no. 481, 11 May 1940, p. 613. Nanette Aldred goes further in suggesting that in these works 'the landscape is transformed into violent images of fetishized female bodies, fragmented and grotesque they are like the manipulated and mutilated forms of Hans Bellmer's poupées which were shown alongside Henry Morre's work at the International Surrealist exhibition', *Graham Sutherland: The Early Years 1921–40*, p. 13.

160 Reproduced in *Sutherland: Une Rétrospecive*, p. 8.

161 Dawn Ades, *Andre Masson* (Academy Editions, London, 1994) p. 19.

162 *Cahiers d'Art*, nos 5–10, 1939.

163 Jean-Paul Sartre, *The Diary of Antoine Roquentin* (John Lehmann, London, 1949), translated by Lloyd Alexander (hereafter *Nausea*), p. 182. First published 1938.

164 Ibid., p. 185.

165 Ibid., pp. 185–86.

166 Cited in David Alan Mellor, 'A taste for tragic excellence', *Adam. An International Review*, 1974–75, p. 101.

167 Ruthven Todd, 'Paul Klee 1879–1940', no. 12, December

1940, pp. 340–44; Peter Watson, 'Joan Miro', no. 20, August 1941, pp. 131–33; J. Adler, 'Memories of Paul Klee', no. 34, October 1942, pp. 264–67; Robert Melville, 'The Evolution of the Double Head in the Art of Picasso', no. 35, November 1942, pp. 343–51.

168 *Horizon*, no. 48, December 1943, between pp. 282–83; now Scottish National Gallery of Modern Art.

169 *Horizon*, no. 58, October 1944, between pages 250 and 251.

170 G. de Chirico, 'Sensitiveness', *Horizon*, no. 55, July 1944, pp. 65–68.

171 Clement Greenberg, 'Surrealist Painting', *Horizon*, no. 61, January 1945, pp. 49–56.

172 Alley and Rotherstein, *Francis Bacon*, D 1–2. See Davies, *Francis Bacon: The Early and Middle Years*, pp. 46–47.

173 Peppiatt, *Francis Bacon*, p. 88; *Francis Bacon in Conversation with Michel Archimbaud*, p. 34. Elizabeth Cowling notes that Picasso came 'to feel that as a work of art it was compromised by its political massage', *Picasso: Style and Meaning* (Phaidon, London, 2002) p. 589.

174 Ibid., pp. 580 and 592–98.

175 Sylvester, *Interviews with Francis Bacon*, p. 8.

176 One might also speculate that Bacon's interest in the great Poussin *Massacre of the Innocents* might have been triggered not just by a visit to Chantilly on his first trip to Europe but also by the appearance of a reproduction in *Minotaure* (no. 9, October 1936, p. 16).

177 Steven A. Nash, ed., *Picasso and the War Years 1937–1945* (Thames and Hudson, London, 1999).

178 Nash, 'Introduction: Picasso, Art and War', Ibid., pp. 33–34.

179 Ibid., p. 26.

180 *Horizon*, no. 58, October 1944, between pages 250 and 251.

181 *Cahiers d'Art* 1940–44; Nash, *Picasso and the War Years* p. 29.

182 On the role of the Drouin Gallery see Frances Morris, 'Introduction', *Paris Post War. Art and Existentialism 1945–55* (Tate Gallery, London, 1993) p. 21.

183 *Horizon*, no. 65, May 1945.

184 Cyril Connolly, 'Comment', Ibid., p. 296. See Shelden, *Friends of Promise*, chapter 6 ('The Spoils of Victory').

185 Cyril Connolly, 'Comment', *Horizon*, no. 90, June 1947, p. 304.

186 Excluding the Masson material cited above, see Jean Paulhan, 'Braque le Patron', *Horizon*, no. 65, May 1945, pp. 329–39; Raymond Mortimer, 'Jacques Villon', no. 68, August 1945 pp. 99–100; Harriet and Sidney Janis, 'Marcel Duchamp Anti-Artist', no. 70, October 1945, pp. 257–68; D. H. Kahnweiler, 'The State of Painting in Paris', no. 71, November 1945, pp. 333–41; Robert Ironside, 'Paul Klee', no. 72, December 1945, pp. 413–17; C. Goemans, 'Paul Delvaux', no. 73, January 1946, pp. 32–36; Henri Matisse, 'Observations on Painting', No. 75, March 1946, 185–87; P. Loeb, 'Wilfredo Lam', no. 76, April 1946, pp. 265–68; J. Gris, 'On the Possibilities of Painting', no. 80, August 1946, pp. 113–22; C. Giedion-Welcker, 'Jean Arp', no. 82, October 1946, pp. 232–39; N. Calas, 'Magic Icons', no. 83, November 1946, pp. 304–15 (on surrealism); J. Cassou, 'Lipschitz', no. 84, December, 1946, pp. 373–80; L. Kochnitsky, 'Henri Laurens', no. 85, January 1947, pp. 15–24; Miró reproductions, no. 88, April 1947, between pp. 262–63; G. Regler, 'Five European Painters in Mexico', no. 91, August 1947, pp. 96–101; Clement Greenberg, 'The present Prospects of American Painting and Sculpture' and J. T. Soby, 'Ben Shahn and M Graves', nos 93–94, October 1947, pp. 20–30 and 48–58; Herbert Read, 'The Fate of Modern Painting', no. 95, November 1947, pp. 242–54; Picasso lithographs, no. 96, December 1947, between pp. 340–41; Antonin Artaud, 'Van Gogh: The Suicide provoked by Society', no. 97, January 1948, pp. 46–50; Benedict Nicolson, 'Cubism and Juan Gris', no. 99, March 1948, pp. 225–27; Robert Ironside, 'Balthus', no. 100, April 1948, pp. 263–67; Bernard Denvir, 'André Bauchant', no. 102, June 1948, pp. 31–43; L. Vitali, 'Contemporary Sculptors VII – Marino Marini', no. 105, September 1948, pp. 203–7; plates of contemporary German artists, no. 107, November 1948, between pp. 328–29; D. H. Kahnweiler, 'Negro Art and Cubism', no. 108, December 1948, pp. 412–20; J. P. Hodin, 'Expressionism', no. 109, January 1949, pp. 38–53; C. Giedion-Welcker, 'Constantin Brancusi', No. 111, March 1949, pp. 193–202; Michel Leiris, 'Contemporary Sculptors VIII – Thoughts around Alberto Giacometti', No. 114, June 1949, pp. 411–17; U. Apollonio, 'The Painting of Giorgio Morandi', no. 115, July 1949, pp. 31–42; plates of Matisse tapestries, no. 116, August 1949, between pp. 121–22; Pierre Mabille, 'Matta and the New Reality', no. 117, September 1949, pp. 184–90; Denys Sutton, 'The Challenge of American Art', no. 118, October 1949, pp. 268–84; J. T. Soby, 'Léonid', no. 119, November 1949, pp. 330–38. The translators tended to be either Douglas Cooper or Peter Watson.

187 E. O. O'Malley, 'Louis Le Broquy', *Horizon*, no. 79, July 1946; Robert Melville, 'Eduardo Paolozzi', no. 92, September 1947, pp. 212–13; Freud and Craxton illustrations accompanying Read's 'The Fate of Modern painting' essay in the November 1947 issue.

188 Peter Watson, letter to Cyril Connolly, 17 July [1946], Cyril Connolly Papers, University of Tulsa, Oklahoma.

189 *Picasso and Matisse*, Victoria and Albert Museum, London, December 1945.

190 Sutherland, 'Thoughts on Painting', p. 70.

191 Alley, *Graham Sutherland*, 1982, p. 130.

192 Berthoud, *Graham Sutherland*, pp. 135–36.

193 Sutherland, letter to Kenneth Clark, 12 November [1947], Tate. His interest in Picasso at this time is also apparent from, for example, Sketchbook 15, Tate.

194 Alley, *Graham Sutherland*, p. 116.

195 See Garlake, *New Art New World*, pp. 188–89. Gonzalez sculptures were reproduced in *Cahiers d'Art*, nos 1–4, 1935, pp. 32–34; nos 6–7, 1936, pp. 201–2; and 1947, pp. 135–41 (also drawings).

196 The catalogue of the ICA show *Forty Years of Modern Art*, 1948, gives Watson as the owner of Lam's *Annunciation*

(144) and Lipschitz's *Pegasus* (46). Lam's *The Rite* (1945) is ascribed to the collection of Lee Miller in the ICA catalogue *40 Years of Modern Art*, 1948.

197 The affinity is noted briefly by Polcari, *Abstract Expressionism and the Modern Experience*, pp. 343–45. De Kooning's *Pink Angels* is reproduced as plate 23. The idea of the tragic loomed large in the thinking of Newman, Rothko, Still, Gottlieb etc. in the early to mid-1940s.

198 *Francis Bacon in Conversation with Michel Archimbaud*, pp. 127–28.

199 Ibid., p. 128.

200 Peppiat, *Francis Bacon*, p. 71.

201 Ades, 'Web of Images', p. 12.

202 Sylvester, *Looking Back at Francis Bacon*, p. 25.

203 Robert Melville, 'André Masson', *Arson*, no. 1, 1942, pp. 25–26 (copy of this rare item at Tate).

204 *A. Masson: Paintings, Drawings, Etchings*, Redfern Gallery, London, 11 March – 3 April 1943.

205 André Masson, 'Painting is a Wager', *Horizon*, no. 39, pp. 178–93. The essay was reprinted from *Cahiers du Sud*.

206 Masson's *Meditation on an Oak Leaf* (1942) and *Le Pain* (1944) were reproduced in *Horizon*, no. 67, July 1945, between pp. 40–41.

207 André Masson, 'A Crisis of the Imaginary', *Horizon*, no. 67, July 1945, pp. 42–45.

208 Michel Leiris and Georges Limbour, eds, *André Masson and His Universe*, (Horizon, London, 1947).

209 Cited in Ibid., p. 16.

210 Rubin and Lanchner, *André Masson*, p. 148.

211 A full-page illustration of the picture accompanied Breton's essay 'Prestige d'André Masson', *Minotaure*, nos. 12–13, May 1939, p. 14.

212 Hyman also compares Masson's *Gradiva* with Bacon's *Three Studies*, though the point he makes is somewhat obscure (Hyman, *The Battle for Realism*, p. 15).

213 See *Too Short a Summer* for basic information, illustrations, and two essays by Pulham himself, 'The Camera and the Artist', published in 1952 in *The Listener* magazine, and the unpublished 'My Photography', written shortly before his death in 1956.

214 Theodora Fitzgibbon, *With Love: An Autobiography 1938–46* (Pan, London, 1983) p. 16.

215 *Peter Rose Pulham. Also French and English Paintings. Drawings by André Masson*, Redfern Gallery, London, n.d. [1943]. The Pulham show included landscapes and cityscapes such as the Tate's *l'Hotel Sully, Courtyard with Figures* (no. 14; 1943).

216 *Lilliput*, August 1944, p. 139, as part of a feature on wartime Chelsea. The studio contains what lool like abstract pictures with strongly defined forms floating in space.

217 David Sylvester, letter to the author, 25 June 1999; their meeting is dated to 1943 in Martin Harrison, *Transition*, p. 54, with a footnote acknowledging Sylvester.

218 Fitzgibbon, *With Love*, p. 116.

219 David Mellor, 'The Photography of Peter Rose Pulham in the Nineteen-Thirties', *Too Short a Summer*, p. 10.

220 Both sides of correspondence in Isabel Rawsthorne papers, Tate.

221 *Exhibition of work by P. Rose Pulham, E. Q. Nicholson and Keith Vaughan*, Hanover Gallery, London, 21 March–15 April 1950. Pulam had shown 17 pictures from 1943 to 1947 in *Gouaches and Drawings by John Banting. The Work of Edith Rimmington. Oil Paintings and Gouaches by Peter Rose Pulham.* The London Gallery, London, 23 June–24 July 1948.

222 Pulham's *Grisaille Figure* (1947) is illustrated in Harrison, *Transition*, p. 85.

223 Cecil Beaton, *British Photographers* (William Collins, London, 1944) p. 44. A montaged portrait of Christian Berard is illustrated on p. 43.

224 Mellor, 'The Photography of Peter Rose Pulham in the Nineteen-Thirties', p. 10. For an example of Pulham's experimental techniques, see the late 1930s portrait of Leonora Fini, reproduced in *Too Short a Summer* (p. 3).

225 Pulham 'My Photography', in *Too Short a Summer*, p. 15.

226 Pulham, 'The Camera and the Artist', (1952), reprinted in *Too Short a Summer*, p. 17.

227 Sylvester recalled that Bonnard and Soutine were the two modern artists 'for whose handling of paint Bacon constantly expressed enormous admiration' (Sylvester, *Looking Back at Francis Bacon*, p. 87).

228 Cowling, *Picasso*, pp. 619–20.

229 Maurice Tuchman, Esti Dunow and Klaus Perls, *Chaim Soutine (1893–1943). Catalogue Raisonné* (Taschen, Cologne, 2001) p. 88.

230 Tuchman, *Soutine*, p. 470, No. 99.

231 Berthoud, *Graham Sutherland*, pp. 92, 123 and 132–33.

232 Cited in Romy Golan, 'Blind Alley: Soutine's Reception after World War II', Norman Kleebat and Kenneth Silver, eds, *An Expressionist in Paris. The Paintings of Chaim Soutine* (Prestel, Munich/The Jewish Museum, New York, 1998) p. 71.

233 *Head I* was shown in *Summer Exhibition*, Redfern Gallery, London, July to September 1948 (161).

234 UNESCO, *Exposition Internationale d'Art Moderne*, Musée d'Art Moderne, Paris, November–December 1946.

235 Bacon letter no. 5.

236 Bacon letter no. 7.

237 Bacon letter no. 6.

238 Bacon letter no. 7.

239 *Francis Bacon in Conversation with Michel Archimbaud*, p. 68.

240 *Les Otages, peintures et sculptures de Jean Fautrier*, Galerie René Drouin, Paris, 26 October–17 November, 1945.

241 *Paris Post War*, Tate Gallery, p. 89.

242 Ibid.

243 Yve-Alain Bois, 'The Falling Trapeze', in *Jean Fautrier 1898–1964*, Curtis Carter and Karen Butler, eds, (Yale University Press, New Haven and London, 2002) p. 59.

244 Sylvester, *Looking Back at Francis Bacon*, pp. 194–204. The parallel is also touched on in Hyman, *The Battle for*

Realism, pp. 16 and 212 (n. 11).
245 Cited in *Alberto Giacometti 1901-1966* (Scottish National Gallery of Modern Art, Edinburgh, 1996), p. 160 (catalogue entry by Patrick Elliot).
246 Cited in Hyman, *The Battle for Realism*, p. 138.
247 *Francis Bacon. In Conversation with Michel Archimbaud*, p. 71.
248 Reproduced in *Alberto Giacometti* (Museum of Modern Art, New York, 2001) p. 126.
249 'Alberto Giacometti, sculptures et dessins recents', *Cahiers d'Art*, 1945–46, pp. 253–68.
250 Reinhold Hohl, *Alberto Giacometti* (Thames and Hudson, London 1972) p. 318.
251 David Sylvester's term as cited in David Mellor, 'Existentialism and Post-War British Art', in *Paris Post-War*, p. 53.
252 Peter Watson, letter to Cyril Connolly, '2 September' [1945], Cyril Connolly Papers, University of Tulsa, Oklahoma.
253 Halliday, *More than a Bookshop*, p. 278.
254 Penrose, *Scrapbook 1900–81*, p. 144.
255 Spalding, *The Girl from the Fiction Department*, p. 81.
256 Michel Leiris, 'Contemporary Sculptors VIII – Thoughts around Alberto Giacometti', *Horizon*, no. 114, June 1949, pp. 411–17 (translated by Douglas Cooper).
257 Ibid., p. 413.
258 Ibid., p. 416.
259 Alley, *Catalogue of the Tate Gallery's Collection*, pp. 278–80.
260 Berthoud, *Graham Sutherland*, p. 168, citing information from William Coldstream and Roland Alley.
261 *Oeuvres Choisis*, Hanover Gallery, London, 4 July–11 August 1950, nos 21–26.
262 Hyman discerns affinities between the portraiture of Lucian Freud and figures such as Balthus and Gruber (Hyman, *The Battle for Realism*, p. 106).
263 Reprinted in Marilyn McCully, ed., *A Picasso Anthology: Documents, Criticism, Reminiscences* (Thames and Hudson, London, 1981) p. 223.
264 See *Histoire de Rats* (Editions de Minuit, Paris 1947).
265 *Francis Bacon in Conversation with Michel Archimbaud*, p. 70.
266 Steven Hooper, ed., *Robert and Lisa Sainsbury Collection* I (Yale University Press, New Haven and London, 1997) pp. liii and 47–49.
267 Georges Limbour, 'About an Exhibition', Leiris and Limbour, eds, *André Masson and His Universe*, p. IV.
268 Michel Leiris, 'Portraits', ibid., p. XI.
269 *Portraits et dessins par Antoine Artaud*, Galerie Pierre, Paris, 4–20 July, 1947.
270 C. Eshleman, ed., *Watchfiends and Rack Screams. Works from the Final Period by Antonin Artaud* (Exact Change, Boston, 1995) pp. 277–78.
271 Antonin Artaud, 'To Peter Watson', in C. Schumacher, ed., *Artaud on Theatre* (Methuen, London, 1989) pp. 173–79.
272 Antonin Artaud, 'Van Gogh: The Suicide provoked by Society', *Horizon*, no. 97, January 1948, pp. 46–50.
273 *Paris Post War*, Tate Gallery, 1993, provides the most searching examination to date of the complex interplay between art, literature and ideas within the existentialist framework. For a useful recent account of the movement see the introductory essay in Paul MacDonald (ed.), *The Existentialist Reader: An Anthology of Key Texts* (Edinburgh University Press, Edinburgh, 2000).
274 Jean-Paul Sartre, *Existentialism and Humanism* (Methuen, London, 1948) pp. 25–26.
275 Paul Foulquié, *Existentialism*, translated from the French by Kathleen Raine (Dennis Dobson, London, 1948) p. 41.
276 Hyman, *The Battle for Realism*, pp. 135–36.
277 Ibid., p. 12. The past tense is interesting given that Bacon was still alive. Certainly no issues of *Documents* were found in the studio after his death (judging from the database of the Bacon archive). The suggestion that Bacon had been affected by *Documents* came from Ades, and Bacon accepted the idea in an interview (Dawn Ades, correspondence with the author).
278 Ibid., p. 18.
279 Sarah Wilson, 'Fêting the Wound: Georges Bataille and Jean Fautrier in the 1940s', *Bataille. Writing the Sacred*, Carolyn Gill, ed., (Routledge, London and New York, 1995) p. 172.
280 Foulquié, *Existentialism* makes scattered references to Bataille in the text and refers to *L'Expérience Intérieure* (1943) and *Le Coupable* (1944).
281 Spurling, *The Girl from the Fiction Department*, p. 130. This was surely overstating the case.
282 Georges Bataille, letter to Sonia Orwell, 19 April 1948, Orwell Papers, UCL. An undated postcard from Cyril Connolly, from the same period, reports that he had dined with the Batailles in Paris, en route for Avignon. Peter Watson clearly moved in the same circles.
283 Farson, *The Gilded Gutter Life*, p. 167.
284 George Bataille, *The Tears of Eros* (City Light Books, San Francisco, 1989) p. 187.
285 In the wake of Dawn Ades's initial conjectures, the topic has been addressed in an essay on the internet by Peter Jones, 'Bacon and Bataille' (http://www.creview.com/artcrit/acjone.htm), and Rina Arya is working on a PhD at the University of Glasgow on 'Recovering the Sacred in Bacon and Bataille'.
286 The following remarks draw upon Michael Surya, *Georges Bataille. An Intellectual Biography* (Verso, London and New York 2002).
287 Georges Bataille, *On Nietzsche* (Athlone, London, 1992) p. 17.
288 From *L'Experience Intérieure* (1943), reprinted in Fred Botting and Scott Wilson, eds, *The Bataille Reader* (Blackwell, Oxford, 1997) p. 65.
289 Cyril Connolly, 'Comment', *Horizon*, no. 65, May 1945, p. 302.
290 Jean-Paul Sartre, 'The Case for Responsible Literature', *Horizon*, no. 65, May 1945, pp. 307–12.
291 John Russell, 'The Existential Theatre', Ibid., pp. 319–29.
292 Coverage of existentialism in the magazine includes

Reyner Heppenstall, 'L'Existentialismo', *Horizon*, no. 63, March 1945, pp. 211–25; Nancy Cunard, 'Letter from Paris', no. 66, June 1945, p. 396; Stephen Spender, 'Comment' no. 67, July 1945, pp. 5–10; A. J. Ayer, 'Novelist-Philosophers – Jean-Paul Sartre' (part one), Ibid., pp. 12–26 (part two, no. 68, pp. 101–10); Sonia Brownwell, review of first two volumes of Sartre's *Roads to Freedom* trilogy and Simone de Beauvoir's *Le Sang des Autres*, no. 73, January 1946, pp. 66–71; A. J. Ayer, 'Novelist-Philosophers VIII – Albert Camus', no. 75, March 1946, pp. 155–68; Olivier Todd, review of Sartre's *Existentialism and Humanism*, no. 105, September 1948, pp. 221–24.

293 Cyril Connolly, 'Comment', *Horizon*, nos 120–1, December–January 1949–50.

294 The publication of Sartre in translation is usefully indicated in the bibliography to Iris Murdoch, *Sartre*, (Fontana, Glasgow, 1967 edition) pp. 125–26.

295 N. Wallis, 'Nightmare', *The Observer*, 20 November 1949. The existentialist climate of the early 1950s is addressed in Hyman, *The Battle for Realism*, p. 360.

296 Luke, *David Tennant and the Gargoyle Years*. See also Sinclair, *Francis Bacon* p. 115.

297 The same event is mentioned in Simone de Beauvoir, *Force of Circumstance* (Penguin, Harmondsworth, 1968) p. 260. She notes Orwell's and Freud's presence, although not Bacon's.

298 *Francis Bacon in Conversation with Michel Archimbaud*, p. 124.

299 See Spalding, *The Girl from the Fiction Department*, chapter 3.

300 George Howard Bauer, *Sartre and the Artist* (University of Chicago Press, Chicago, 1969) p. 112.

301 Russell, 'The Existential Theatre', p. 325.

302 Isabel Rawsthorne, letter to Peter Rose Pulham, 10 January 1951, Rawsthorne papers, Tate.

303 Patrick Elliot, 'Alberto Giacometti: an Introduction', *Alberto Giacometti 1901–1966*, p. 22.

304 Sylvester, *Interviews with Francis Bacon*, p. 133.

305 Ibid., 13.

306 Russell, *Francis Bacon*, p. 38.

307 Sartre, *Nausea*. The copy in the National Library of Scotland is stamped 27 March 1949.

308 Ibid., pp. 27–28.

309 Jean-Paul Sartre, *The Psychology of Imagination*, London 1949.

310 Jean-Paul Sartre, 'Portraits Officials', *Verve* (Paris), nos 5–6, July–October 1939, pp. 9–12.

311 Sartre, *Nausea* p. 124.

312 Ibid., pp. 130–1.

313 *The Townsend Journals: An Artist's Record of his Times 1928–51*, ed. Andrew Forge (Tate Gallery, London, 1976) p. 92.

314 Cited in Peppiat, *Francis Bacon*, pp. 163–54.

315 Jean-Paul Sartre, *Being and Nothingness*, translated and with an introduction by Hazel E. Barnes (Methuen, London, 1957) pp. 602–15.

316 For example, Murdoch, *Sartre*, p. 21; John Pasmore, *A Hundred Years of Philosophyy* (Penguin, Harmondsworth, 1968), pp. 493–94.

317 Sartre, *Being and Nothingness*, p. 607.

318 Ibid., p. 610.

319 Ibid., pp. 611–12.

320 Bacon insisted on the new title when the painting was exhibited at the Venice Biennale in 1954. See Alley and Rothenstein, *Francis Bacon*, No. 26, p. 46.

321 Sylvester, *Looking Back at Francis Bacon*, p. 54.

322 By implication I am taking issue here with Ades's arguments, fuelled by her own, extremely valuable, impulse to relate Bacon to Bataillean Surrealism, that Bacon's outlook differs from the stoic and moralistic tendencies in Sartre's thinking, as projected in the published lecture *Existentialism and Humanism*, and that connections with existentialism are 'necessarily of a tenuous kind, given that it was primarily a theoretical and literary movement' ('Web of Images', pp. 11–12). Bataillean surrealism and existentialism feed into one another, and Bacon was in some ways a very literary artist who could certainly have taken inspiration from, say, Sartre's imaginative or even philosophical writings, without necessarily subscribing to all aspects of Sartre's doctrine.

323 *Francis Bacon in Conversation with Michel Archimbaud*, pp. 76–77.

APPENDIX

The correspondence has been transcribed from the originals preserved among Graham Sutherland's papers. These form part of the Graham and Kathleen Sutherland Foundation, currently in the custodianship of the National Galleries and Museums of Wales, Cardiff. Bacon's handwriting is very difficult to decipher, since he wrote at speed and used very thin paper. His punctuation and spelling are also fairly erratic. Therefore, in the interests of clarity, I have taken the liberty of inserting some minor corrections and minimal punctuation.

1 The second sheet of this letter was clearly taken from a book, with the printed title 'ALBRECHT ALTDORFER UND SEIN KREIS, MÜNCHEN 1938' appearing upside-down at the bottom.

2 This letter is incomplete.

3 The name is indecipherable.

4 Presumably Douglas Cooper.

5 Drama producer with BBC and close friend of Paul Nash.

6 Illegible, possibly Angus.

7 The artist Julian Trevelyan.

8 This short note is written on a postcard of the plaza of the Plaza del Popolo, Rome.

9 The postmark is illegible but the stamp is printed with the caption 'Interpol Roma 1954'.

PHOTO CREDITS

INDEX

Figure numbers are italicised; plate numbers are given in roman numerals